HERMANN BROCH

THE

SLEEP-
WALKERS

Translated by
WILLA and EDWIN MUIR

NORTH POINT PRESS : SAN FRANCISCO
1985

North Point Press
850 Talbot Avenue
Berkeley, California
94706

CONTENTS

PAGE

PART ONE: THE ROMANTIC (1888)   7

PART TWO: THE ANARCHIST (1903)   159

PART THREE: THE REALIST (1918)   341

PART ONE

THE ROMANTIC
(1888)

I

In the year 1888 Herr von Pasenow was seventy, and there were people who felt an extraordinary and inexplicable repulsion when they saw him coming towards them in the streets of Berlin, indeed, who in their dislike of him actually maintained that he must be an evil old man. Small, but well made, neither a shrivelled ancient nor a pot-belly, he was extraordinarily well proportioned, and the top-hat which he always sported in Berlin did not look in the least ridiculous on him. He wore Kaiser Wilhelm I. whiskers, but cut somewhat shorter, and on his cheeks there was none of that white fluff which gave the Emperor his affable appearance; even his hair, which had scarcely thinned yet, showed no more than a few white strands; in spite of his seventy years it had kept its youthful fairness, a reddish blond that reminded one of rotting straw and really did not suit an old man, for whom one would have liked to imagine a more venerable covering. But Herr von Pasenow was accustomed to the colour of his hair, nor in his judgment did his monocle look in the least too youthful. When he gazed in the mirror he recognized there the face that had returned his gaze fifty years before. Yet though Herr von Pasenow was not displeased with himself, there were people whom the looks of this old man filled with discomfort, and who could not comprehend how any woman could ever have looked upon him or embraced him with desire in her eyes; and at most they would allow him only the Polish maids on his estate, and held that even these he must have got round by that slightly hysterical and yet arrogant aggressiveness which is often characteristic of small men. Whether this was true or not, it was the belief of his two sons, and it goes without saying that he did not share it. For, after all, sons' thoughts are often coloured by prejudice, and it would have been easy to accuse his sons of injustice and bias in spite of the uncomfortable feeling which the sight of Herr von Pasenow aroused, a really remarkable feeling of discomfort that actually increased when he had passed by and one chanced to look after him. Perhaps that was due to the fact that his back view made one doubtful of his age, for his movements were neither like those of an old man, nor like those of a youth, nor like those of a man in the prime of life. And as doubt gives rise to discomfort, it is possible that some chance stroller might have resented as undignified the man's style of progression, and if he should have gone on to characterize it as overweening and vulgar, as feebly rakish and swaggering, one would not have been surprised. Such things, of course, are a matter of temperament: yet one can quite well imagine some young man, blinded with hatred, hurrying back to thrust his cane between the legs of any man who walked in that way, so as to bring him down by hook or by crook and break his legs and put an end for ever to such a style of walking. Herr von Pasenow, however, went straight on with very quick steps; he held his head erect as small men generally do; and as he held himself very erect too, his little belly was stuck slightly forward, one might almost have said that he carried it in front of him; yes, that he was carrying his whole person somewhere or other, belly and all, a hateful gift which nobody wanted. Yet as a simile really accounts for nothing, those ill opinions would have remained without solid foundation, and perhaps one might even have grown ashamed of them until one noticed the walking-stick accompanying his legs. The stick moved to a regular rhythm, rose almost to the height of his knees, returned with a little sharp impact to the ground and rose again, and the feet went on beside it. And these too rose higher than feet should do, the toes shot out a little too far as if they were presenting his shoe-soles in contempt to approaching pedestrians, and the heels were deposited again with a little sharp impact on the pavement. So the two legs and the walking-stick went on together, suggesting the involuntary fancy that this man, had he come to the world as a horse, would have been a pacer; but the horrible and disgusting thing was that he was a three-legged pacer, a tripod that had set itself in motion. And it was horrible, too, to realize that the three-legged purposiveness of the man's walk must be as deceptive as its undeviating rapidity: that it was directed towards nothing at all! For nobody who had a serious end in view could walk like that, and if for a moment one involuntarily thought of a profiteer inexorably conveying himself to some poor man's house to collect a debt, one saw at once how inadequate and prosaic was such a notion, and one was terrified by the intuition that it was a devil's walk, like a dog hobbling on three legs—a rectilinear zigzag . . . enough: for anyone who analysed Herr von Pasenow's walk with loving hate might have discovered all this and more. Most people, after all, lend themselves to such experiments. There is always something that will fit. And if Herr von Pasenow did not really lead a busy life, but on the contrary expended ample time in fulfilling the decorative and other obligations which a quietly secure income brings with it, yet—and that too expressed his character—he was always bustling, and mere sauntering was far from his nature. Besides, visiting Berlin but twice a year, he had abundance to do when he was there. Just now he was on his way to his younger son, Lieutenant Joachim von Pasenow.

Whenever Joachim von Pasenow met his father, memories of his boyhood thronged up in him as was natural enough: but the most vivid of these were always the events preceding his entrance to the cadet school in Culm. True, it was only fragments of the past that fleetingly emerged, and important and trivial things flowed chaotically through one another. So perhaps it may seem idle and superfluous to mention Jan, the steward, whose image, though he was a quite secondary figure, obtruded itself in front of all the others. But this may have been because Jan was not really a man, but a beard. For hours one could gaze at him and meditate whether, behind that dishevelled landscape covered with impenetrable yet soft undergrowth, a human creature was concealed. Even when Jan spoke—but he did not speak much—one could not be certain of this, for his words took form behind his beard as behind a curtain, and it might as easily have been another who uttered them. But most exciting of all was when Jan yawned; for then the hairy superficies gaped at a pre-ordained point, substantiating the fact that this was also the place where Jan conveyed food into himself. When Joachim had run to him to tell him of his approaching entrance into the cadet school, Jan was having his dinner; and he sat there cutting bread into chunks and silently listening. At last he said: " Well, is the young master glad? " And then Joachim became aware that he was not in the least glad; he actually felt he wanted to cry; but as there was no immediate pretext for that, he only nodded and said that he was glad.

Then there was the Iron Cross that hung in a glass-covered frame in the big drawing-room. It had belonged to a Pasenow who, in the year 1813, had held a high position in the army. Seeing that it always hung on the wall, the great fuss that was made when Uncle Bernhard received one too was somewhat puzzling. Joachim was still ashamed, now in 1888, that he had ever been so stupid. But perhaps he had been embittered merely because they had tried to make the cadet school more palatable to him by dangling the Iron Cross before him. In any case his brother Helmuth would have been a more suitable subject for the cadet school, and in spite of the years that had passed Joachim still considered it a ridiculous arrangement that the elder son had to take to the land and the younger to the army. The Iron Cross had left him quite indifferent, but Helmuth had been filled with wild enthusiasm when Uncle Bernhard had taken part in the storming of Kissingen with his division, the Goeben. In any case he wasn't even a real uncle, but only a cousin of their father's.

His mother was taller than his father, and everything on the home farm was managed by her. Strange how little attention Helmuth and he had paid to her; they had been like their father in that. They had ignored her stubborn and lackadaisical: " Don't do that," and were only annoyed when she added: " Look out, or your father will catch you." And they weren't in the least daunted when she employed her final threat: " Well, I'm really going to tell your father this time," and scarcely minded even when she fulfilled the threat; for then their father only threw them an angry look and went on his way with his stiff, purposive stride. It was a just punishment on their mother for trying to side with the common enemy.

At that time the predecessor of the present pastor was still in office. He had yellowish white side-whiskers which were hardly distinguishable from the hue of his skin, and when he came to dinner on festival days he used to compare their mother with Empress Luise in the midst of her brood of children. That had been a little ludicrous, but it had made one proud all the same. Then the pastor had acquired yet another habit, that of laying his hand on Joachim's head and calling him " young warrior "; for all of them, even the Polish maids in the kitchen, were already talking about the cadet school in Culm. Nevertheless Joachim was still waiting at that time for the final decision. At table one day his mother had said that she didn't see the necessity of sending Joachim away; he could quite well enter later as an ensign; that was how it had invariably been done, and the custom had always been kept. But Uncle Bernhard replied that the new army required capable men and that in Culm a proper lad would soon find his place. Joachim's father had remained disagreeably silent—as always when his wife said anything, for he never listened to her. Except, indeed, on her birthday, when he clinked glasses with her, and then he borrowed the pastor's comparison and called her his Empress Luise. Perhaps his mother was really against his being sent to Culm, but one could put no dependence on her: she always finished by taking sides with his father.

His mother was very punctual. In the byre at milking time, and in the hen-house when the eggs were being collected she was never absent; in the morning one could always find her in the kitchen, and in the afternoon in the laundry, where she counted the stiff starched linen along with the maids. It was on one of these occasions that he had first heard the news. He had been with his mother in the byre, his nostrils were full of the heavy odour of the stalls, then they stepped out into the cold wintry air and saw Uncle Bernhard coming towards them across the yard. Uncle Bernhard still carried a stick; for after being wounded one was allowed to carry a stick, all convalescents carried sticks even when they had ceased to limp badly. His mother had remained standing, and Joachim had gripped Uncle Bernhard's stick and held it fast. Even to-day he still clearly remembered the ivory crook carved with a coat of arms. Uncle Bernhard said: " Congratulate me, cousin; I've just been made a major." Joachim glanced up at the Major: he was even taller than Joachim's mother and had drawn himself up with a little jerk, proudly yet as if at the word of command, and looked still more warrior-like and straight than usual; and perhaps he had actually grown taller; in any case he was a better match for her than Joachim's father. He had a short beard, but one could see his mouth. Joachim wondered whether it was a great honour to hold a major's stick, and then decided to be slightly proud of it. " Yes," Uncle Bernhard went on, " but now it will mean an end of these lovely days at Stolpin." Joachim's mother replied that it was both good news and bad news, and this was a complicated response which he could not quite understand. They were standing in the snow; his mother had on her brown fur coat which was as soft as herself, and under her fur cap her fair hair escaped. Joachim was always glad when he remembered that he had the same fair hair as his mother, for it meant that he too would become taller than his father, perhaps as tall as Uncle Bernhard; and when Uncle Bernhard nodded to him now, saying, " We'll soon be comrades in the King's uniform," for a moment he felt pleased at the thought. But as his mother only sighed and made no objection, submitting herself just as if she were standing before his father, he let go the stick and ran away to Jan.

He could not discuss the matter with Helmuth; for Helmuth envied him and talked like the grown-ups, who all said that a future soldier should be proud and happy. Jan was the only one who was neither a hypocrite nor a deceiver; he had only asked if the young master was glad, and had not behaved as if he believed it. Of course Helmuth and the others probably meant well and perhaps only wanted to comfort him. Joachim had never got over the fact that at that time he had been secretly convinced of Helmuth's treachery and hypocrisy; for though he had tried to make it good immediately by presenting all his toys to Helmuth, yet he could not have taken them with him into the cadet school, and so it was not a real expiation. He had given Helmuth also his half of the pony which the two boys shared in common, so that Helmuth possessed a whole horse to himself. These weeks had been pregnant with trouble, and yet good; never, before or afterwards, had he been so intimate with his brother. Then, it is true, came the accident with the pony. For the time being Helmuth had renounced his new rights, and Joachim was given full control of it. But of course that did not mean very much, for in these weeks the ground had been soft and heavy, and there was a standing prohibition against riding in the fields when the ground was in that state. But Joachim felt the superior right of one who would soon be going away, and as Helmuth was agreeable, rode out into the fields on the pretext of giving the pony exercise. He had only started on a quite short canter when the accident happened; the front leg of the pony was caught in a deep hole; it fell and could not get up again. Helmuth came running, and after him the coachman. The pony lay with its dishevelled head in the mire, its tongue hanging sideways out of its mouth. Joachim could still see Helmuth and himself kneeling there and stroking the pony's head, but he could not remember any longer how they had got home and only knew that he had found himself in the kitchen, which had suddenly become very still, and that everybody was staring at him as if he had committed a crime. Then he had heard his mother's voice: " Your father must be told." And then he was suddenly in his father's study, and it seemed to him that the punishment which his mother had menaced him with so often in that hateful sentence, was now, after being stored up and accumulated, about to fall on his head. But nothing happened. His father only kept on walking up and down the room in silence, and Joachim tried to stand straight, gazing at the antlers on the wall. Still nothing happened, and his eyes began to wander and remained fixed on the bluish sand in the frilled paper that covered the polished brown hexagonal spittoon beside the stove. He had almost forgotten why he was there; but the room seemed vaster than ever and there was an icy weight on his chest. Finally his father stuck the monocle into his eye: " It's high time that you were out of the house "; and then Joachim knew that they had all been duping him, even Helmuth himself, and at that moment he was glad that the pony had broken its leg; for his mother, too, had been telling tales on him so as to get him out of the house. Then he could see that his father was taking his pistol out of its case. And then he vomited. Next day he learned from the doctor that he was suffering from concussion, and that made him proud. Helmuth sat on his bed, and although Joachim knew that the pony had been shot by his father, neither of them said a word about it, and these were very happy days, strangely secure and remote from the lives of all the grown-ups. Nevertheless they came to an end, and after a delay of a few weeks he was deposited at the cadet school in Culm. Yet when he stood there before his narrow bed, so distant and remote from his sick-bed at Stolpin, it almost seemed to him that he had brought the remoteness with him, and at the beginning that made his new surroundings endurable.

Naturally there were a great number of things belonging to this time that he had forgotten, yet a disturbing residue remained, and in his dreams he sometimes imagined that he was speaking Polish. When he was made lieutenant he presented Helmuth with a horse which he had himself ridden for a long time. Yet he could not free himself from the feeling that he was still slightly in his brother's debt, and sometimes even thought of Helmuth as an importunate creditor. But that was all nonsense, and he very seldom thought of it. It was only when his father came to Berlin that those ideas awakened again, and when he asked after his mother and Helmuth he never forgot to inquire after the health of the nag as well.

Now that Joachim von Pasenow had put on his civilian frock-coat and between the two corners of his peaked stiff collar his chin was enjoying unaccustomed freedom, now that he had fixed on his curly-brimmed top-hat and picked up a walking-stick with a pointed ivory crook handle, now that he was on the way to the hotel to take out his father for the obligatory evening's entertainment, suddenly Eduard von Bertrand's image rose up before him, and he felt glad his civilian clothes did not sit on him with by any means the same inevitability as on that gentleman, whom in secret he sometimes thought of as a traitor. Unfortunately it was only to be expected and feared that he would meet Bertrand in the fashionable resorts he would have to visit with his father that evening, and already during the performance in the Winter Garden he was keeping an eye open for him and seriously considering the question whether he could introduce such a man to his father.

The problem still occupied him as they were being driven in a droshky through Friedrichstrasse to the Jäger Casino. They sat stiffly and silently, with their sticks between their knees, on the tattered black-leather seats, and when a chance girl on her beat shouted something to them Joachim stared straight in front, while his father, his monocle rigidly fixed, muttered: " Idiotic." Yes, since Herr von Pasenow had first come to Berlin many things had changed, and even if one accepted it, yet one could not close one's eyes to the fact that the innovating policy of the founder of the Reich had produced some very curious fruits. Herr von Pasenow said, as he was accustomed to say every year: " Paris itself isn't any worse than this," and when they stopped in front of the Jäger Casino the row of flaring gas-lamps before it, drawing the attention of passers-by to the entrance, excited his disapproval.

A narrow wooden stair led up to the first floor where the dancing-halls were, and Herr von Pasenow climbed it with the bustling, undeviating air which was characteristic of him. A black-haired girl was descending. She squeezed herself into a corner of the landing to let the visitors pass; and as she could not help smiling, it seemed, at the old gentleman's fussiness, Joachim made a somewhat embarrassed and deprecatory gesture. And once more he felt a compulsion to picture Bertrand either as this girl's lover, or as her bully, or as something else equally fantastic; and no sooner was he in the dancing-hall than he looked searchingly around for him. But of course Bertrand was not there: on the contrary Joachim found two officers from his own regiment, and now he remembered for the first time that it had been himself who had incited them to come to the casino, so that he might not be left alone with his father, or with his father and Bertrand.

In acknowledgment of his age and position Herr von Pasenow was greeted with a slight, stiff bow and a click of the heels, as if he were a military superior, and it was indeed with the air of a commanding general that he inquired if the gentlemen were enjoying themselves: he would

feel honoured if they would drink a glass of champagne with him; whereupon the gentlemen made known their agreement by clicking their heels
again. A new bottle of champagne was brought. They all sat stiffly and
dumbly in their chairs, drank to each other in silence, and regarded the
hall, the white-and-gilt decorations, the gas flames that hissed, surrounded
by tobacco smoke, on the branches of the great circular chandelier, and
stared at the dancers who were revolving in the middle of the floor. At
last Herr von Pasenow said: " Well, gentlemen, I hope that you aren't
refraining from the company of the fair sex on my account." Bows and
smiles. " Some pretty girls here too. As I was coming upstairs I met
a very promising piece, black hair, and with eyes that you young fellows
couldn't remain indifferent to." Joachim was so ashamed that he could
have throttled the old man to suppress such unseemly words, but already
one of his comrades was replying that it must have been Ruzena, really
an unusually pretty girl, and one couldn't deny her a certain elegance
either; anyhow, most of the ladies here were better than might be expected, for the management were very strict in selecting their girls and
laid a great deal of importance on the maintenance of a refined tone.
Meanwhile Ruzena had returned to the dancing-hall; she had taken the
arm of a fair girl, and as they sauntered past the tables and boxes with
their high coiffures and tight-laced figures they actually produced an
elegant impression. As they were passing Herr von Pasenow's table they
were asked jestingly whether Ruzena's ears had not been tingling, and
Herr von Pasenow added that, to judge from her name, he must be
addressing a fair Pole, consequently almost a countrywoman of his. No,
she was not Polish, said Ruzena, but Bohemian, or as people said in this
country, Czech; but Bohemian was more correct, for the proper name of
her country was Bohemia. " All the better," said Herr von Pasenow,
" the Poles are no good . . . unreliable. . . . Well, it doesn't matter."
    Meanwhile the two girls had sat down, and Ruzena began to talk in
a deep voice, laughing at herself, for she had not yet learned to speak
German correctly. Joachim was annoyed at his father for conjuring up
the memory of the Polish maids, but was forced himself to think of one
of the harvest workers who, when he was a little boy, had lifted him up
on to the wagon with the sheaves. Yet though in her hard, staccato pro-
nunciation she made hay of the German language, still she was a young
lady, stiffly corseted, who lifted her champagne-glass to her lips with a
proper air, and so was not in the least like a Polish harvest worker; whether

the talk about his father and the maids were true or not. Joachim had
nothing to do with that, but this gentle girl wasn't to be treated by the old
man in the way he was probably accustomed to. All the same Joachim was
unable to envisage the life of a Bohemian girl as any different from that
of a Polish one—indeed even among German civilians it was difficult to
divine the individual behind the puppet—and when he tried to imagine
Ruzena as coming out of a good home, with a good matronly mother and
a decent suitor with gloves on, it did not fit her; and he could not get
rid of the feeling that in Bohemia life must be wild and low, as among
the Tartars. He was sorry for Ruzena, although she reminded him
somewhat of a humble little beast of prey in whose throat a dark cry is
strangled, dark as the Bohemian forests, and he longed to know whether
one could talk to her as one talked to a lady; for all this was so terrifying
and yet seductive, and in a way justified his father and his father's lewd
intentions. He was afraid that Ruzena, too, would see through these, and
he sought for an answer in her face; she noticed it and smiled to him;
yet she let the old man fondle her hand which was hanging languidly
over the edge of the table, and the old man did it quite openly, and tried
at the same time to summon up his scraps of Polish to erect a lingual
hedge round the girl and himself. Of course it was wrong of her to allow
him such liberties, and when at Stolpin they maintained that Polish
maids were quite unreliable perhaps they were right. Yet perhaps she
was only weak, and one's honour demanded that she should be protected
from the old man's advances. But that would be the duty of her lover;
if Bertrand possessed the slightest vestige of chivalry he was in duty
bound to appear now to put everything in order with a word. And
suddenly Joachim began to talk about Bertrand to his fellow-officers:
hadn't they heard any word of Bertrand lately and of what he was
doing; yes, a curiously reserved fellow, Eduard von Bertrand. But his
comrades, who had already drunk a good deal of champagne, gave him
confused answers and were beyond being surprised at anything, even at
the pertinacity with which Joachim harped on the theme of Bertrand; and
cunningly and persistently as he brought out the name in a loud and
distinct voice, not even the girls twitched an eyelash, and the suspicion
mounted within him that Bertrand might have sunk so low as to come
here under an assumed name; and so he turned directly to Ruzena and
asked whether she didn't know von Bertrand—until the old man,
keen of hearing, and officious as ever in spite of the champagne, asked

why Joachim was so hot on the track of this von Bertrand: " You're as eager about him as if he were hidden somewhere in the place." Joachim reddened and denied it, but the old man had been set going: yes, he had known the father well, old Colonel von Bertrand. He had departed this life, very likely it was this Eduard who had brought him to his grave. When his waster of a son had chucked the army he had taken it, people said, very much to heart; nobody knew why, or whether there mightn't have been something shady behind it. Joachim became indignant. " Pardon me, but that's only empty gossip—and the last thing that Bertrand can be called is a waster! " " Gently, gently," replied the old man, turning again to Ruzena's hand, on which he now pressed a long kiss; Ruzena calmly permitted it and regarded Joachim, whose soft fair hair reminded her of the children at the village school in Bohemia. " I not will flatter you," she said in her staccato voice to the old man, " but nice hair has your son." Then she seized the head of her friend, held it pressed to Joachim's, and was delighted to see that the colour of the hair was the same. " Would be beautiful pair," she declared to the two heads, and ran her hands through their hair. The other girl shrieked, because her coiffure was being disarranged; Joachim felt a soft hand touching the back of his head, he had a slight sensation of dizziness and threw his head back as if he wished to catch the hand between his neck and his collar and force it to remain there; but then the hand slipped of its own accord down to the back of his neck, and stroked it quickly and timorously, and was gone. " Gently, gently! " he heard his father's dry voice again, and then he noticed that the old man had taken out his pocket-book, had drawn out two large notes, and was on the point of pressing them on the two girls. Yes, that was just how he used to throw marks to the harvest girls when he was in a good mood, and though Joachim wanted to intervene now he could not prevent the fifty-mark note from being pressed into Ruzena's hand, nor her from sticking it gaily into her pocket. " Thanks, papa," she said, then she bettered her words, " papa-in-law," and winked at Joachim. Joachim was pale with rage: the old man would buy a girl for him for fifty marks, would he? Quick of hearing, the old man caught Ruzena's quip and seized on it: " So! It seems to me that my young rascal has caught your fancy. . . . Well, you have my blessing. . . ." Swine, thought Joachim. But now the old man was in full sail: " Ruzena, my sweet child, to-morrow I'll call on you and fix up the match in proper style, all tip-top. What shall I bring you as a wedding gift? . . . But you must tell me the address of your castle. . . ." Joachim looked away like one who at an execution does not wish to see the axe falling, but Ruzena suddenly stiffened, her eyes went blind, her lips quivered, she pushed away a hand that was stretched out in help or concern, and ran away to cry herself out beside the woman who attended to the lavatory.

"Well, well," said Herr von Pasenow, "but it must be quite late! I'm afraid we must be going, gentlemen." In the droshky father and son sat side by side, stiff and hostile, their sticks between their knees. At last the old man said: "Well, she accepted the fifty marks, all the same. And then she took to her heels." What a wretch, thought Joachim.

On the theme of the military uniform Bertrand could have supplied some such theory as this:

Once upon a time it was the Church alone that was exalted as judge over mankind, and every layman knew that he was a sinner. Nowadays it is the layman who has to judge his fellow-sinner if all values are not to fall into anarchy, and instead of weeping with him, brother must say to brother: "You have done wrong." And as once it was only the garments of the priest that marked a man off from his fellows as something higher, some hint of the layman peeping through even the uniform and the robe of office, so, when the great intolerance of faith was lost, the secular robe of office had to supplant the sacred one, and society had to separate itself into secular hierarchies with secular uniforms and invest these with the absolute authority of a creed. And because, when the secular exalts itself as the absolute, the result is always romanticism, so the real and characteristic romanticism of that age was the cult of the uniform, which implied, as it were, a superterrestrial and supertemporal idea of uniform, an idea which did not really exist and yet was so powerful that it took hold of men far more completely than any secular vocation could, a non-existent and yet so potent idea that it transformed the man in uniform into a property of his uniform, and never into a professional man in the civilian sense; and this perhaps simply because the man who wears the uniform is content to feel that he is fulfilling the most essential function of his age and therefore guaranteeing the security of his own life.

This is what Bertrand might have said; but though it is certain that not every wearer of uniform is conscious of such things, yet it may be maintained that everyone who has worn a uniform for many years finds in it a better organization of life than the man who merely exchanges one civilian suit in the evening for another civilian suit during the day. True, the soldier has no real need to think deeply of these things, for a generic uniform provides its wearer with a definitive line of demarcation between his person and the world; it is like a hard casing against which one's personality and the world beat sharply and distinctly and are differentiated from each other; for it is the uniform's true function to manifest and ordain order in the world, to arrest the confusion and flux of life, just as it conceals whatever in the human body is soft and flowing, covering up the soldier's underclothes and skin, and decreeing that sentries on guard should wear white gloves. So when in the morning a man has fastened up his uniform to the last button, he acquires a second and thicker hide, and feels that he has returned to his more essential and steadfast being. Closed up in his hard casing, braced in with straps and belts, he begins to forget his own undergarments, and the uncertainty of life, yes, life itself, recedes to a distance. Then, after he has finished by pulling down his tunic so that it stretches smooth and without a crease over chest and back,—then even the child whom he sincerely loves, and the woman in whose embrace he begot that child, recede into such a civilian remoteness that the mouths which they present to him in fare-well are almost strange to him, and his home becomes something foreign, which in his uniform he dare not enter. Should he next proceed in his uniform to the barracks or to his office, it must not be thought pride that makes him ignore men otherwise clothed; it is simply that he can no longer comprehend that such alien and barbarous raiment can clothe anything even faintly resembling actual humanity as he feels it in himself. Yet this does not mean that the man in uniform has become blind, nor that he is filled with blind prejudices, as is commonly assumed; he remains all the time a man like you and me, dreams of food and love, even reads his newspaper at breakfast; but he is no longer tied to things, and as they scarcely concern him any longer he is able to divide them into the good and the bad, for on intolerance and lack of understanding the security of life is based.

Whenever Joachim von Pasenow was compelled to put on civilian clothes Eduard von Bertrand came into his mind, and he was always glad that mufti did not sit on him with the same assurance as on that man; yet he was very eager to know what Bertrand's views were on the question of uniform. For Eduard von Bertrand had of course every reason to reflect on the problem, seeing that he had laid aside the uniform once for all and decided for the clothing of a civilian. That had been astonishing enough. He had been passed out of the cadet school in Culm two years before Pasenow, and while there had acted exactly like the others; had like the others worn white trousers in summer, had eaten at the same table, had passed his examinations like the others; and yet when he became a second lieutenant the incomprehensible thing happened: without ostensible cause he quitted the service and vanished into a kind of life quite foreign to him—vanished into the labyrinth of the city, as people called it, into a labyrinth from which he emerged only now and then. If one met him in the street one was always a little uncertain whether to greet him or not, feeling that he was a traitor who had carried over to another world and there offered up something which had been a common possession, and that in confronting him one was exposed and naked, while he himself gave away nothing about his motives and his life, and maintained always the same equable friendly reserve. But perhaps the disturbing factor lay simply in Bertrand's civilian clothes, in the fact that his white stiff shirt-front was so exposed that one really had to feel ashamed for him. Besides, Bertrand himself had once declared in Culm that no genuine soldier would ever allow his shirt-cuffs to appear below his sleeves, because everything connected with being born, sleeping, loving and dying—in short, everything civilian— was a matter of underclothing; and even if such paradoxes had always been characteristic of Bertrand, no less than the airy gesture with which he was accustomed, lazily and disdainfully, to disavow them afterwards, yet obviously he must have been troubled at that time by the problem of the uniform. And about the underclothing and the shirt-cuffs he may have been partly right: for instance when one reflected—and Bertrand always awakened such unpleasant reflections—that all men, civilians and Joachim's father not excepted, wore their shirts stuck into their trousers. For that reason Joachim actually did not like to encounter anyone in the men's barracks with his tunic open; there was something indecent about it, which gave one a vague inkling of the justification for the regulation that when visiting certain resorts and for other erotic purposes mufti must be worn; and more, which made it appear almost like an offence against the regulations that such beings as married officers and married non-commissioned officers should exist. When the married sergeant-

major reported for morning service and opened two buttons of his tunic
so as to draw out of the opening, which laid bare his checked shirt, his
huge red-leather book, Joachim generally ran his fingers over his own
tunic buttons, and felt secure only when he had certified that they were
all in order. He could almost have wished that the uniform was a direct
emanation of his skin, and often he thought to himself that that was the
real function of a uniform, and wished at least that his underclothes
could by a distinctive pattern be made a component part of the uniform.
For it was uncanny to think that every soldier carried about with him
under his tunic the anarchical passions common to all men. Perhaps the
world would have gone off the rails altogether had not someone at the last
moment invented stiff shirt-fronts for the civilians, thus transforming
the shirt into a white board and making it quite unrecognizable as underclothing. Joachim recalled his astonishment as a child, when, looking at
the portrait of his grandfather, he had recognized that that gentleman
did not wear a stiff shirt, but a lace jabot. But then in his time men
had had a deeper and more intimate faith, and did not need to seek any
further bulwark against anarchy. Of course all these notions were rather
silly and obviously only an overflow from the kind of things Bertrand
said, which had neither rhyme nor reason; Pasenow was almost ashamed
of thinking of them in front of the sergeant-major, and when they surged
up he thrust them aside and with a jerk resumed his stiff, official bearing.

But even if he thrust aside those thoughts as foolish, and accepted the
uniform as a decree of nature, there was more in all this than a mere
question of attire, more than a something which gave his life style at
least, if not content. Often he fancied that by saying " Comrades in the
King's uniform " he could put an end to the whole question, and to
Bertrand too, although in doing so he was far from desiring to express
any extraordinary reverence for the King's uniform or to indulge an
overweening vanity; he was rather concerned that his elegance of figure
should neither exceed nor fall short of a definitely demarcated and prescribed correctness, and he had actually been a little flattered when once
some ladies expressed the opinion, which was well grounded, that the
straight, wooden cut of the uniform and the glaring colours of the bright
cloth went but indifferently with his face, and that the brown-velvet
jacket and flowing necktie of an artist would suit him far better. The
fact that in spite of this the uniform meant much more to him may be
explained by the obstinacy which he inherited from his mother, who

always stuck immovably to a custom once formed. And sometimes it seemed that for him there could never be any other attire, although he was still full of resentment at his mother for submitting herself without a struggle to Uncle Bernhard's opinions. And now, of course, it had all been decided, and if one has been accustomed to wear a uniform from one's tenth year, sooner or later it grows into one's flesh like the shirt of Nessus, and no one, and least of all Joachim von Pasenow, will be able to specify then where the frontier between his self and his uniform lies. For even if his military vocation had not grown into him, as he into it, his uniform would still have been the symbol for many things; in the course of years he had fattened and rounded it with so many ideas that, securely enclosed in it, he could no longer live without it; enclosed and cut off from the world and the house of his father in such security and peace that he could scarce distinguish, scarce notice, that his uniform left him only a thin strip of personal and human freedom no broader than the narrow strip of starched cuff which was all that an officer was allowed to show. He did not like to put on mufti, and he was glad that his uniform protected him from visits to questionable resorts, where he pictured the civilian Bertrand in the company of loose women. For often he was overcome with the uncanny fear that he too might slip into the same inexplicable rut as Bertrand. And that also was why he bore a grudge against his father for his having to accompany him, and in mufti at that, on the obligatory round of the Berlin night haunts with which ended, in accordance with tradition, the old man's visits to the capital of the Empire.

When next day Joachim escorted his father to the train the latter said: " Well, as soon as you're a captain, and that won't be long now, we'll have to think of finding a wife for you. How about Elisabeth? The Baddensens have a nice little property over there at Lestow, and it will all go to the girl some day." Joachim said nothing. Yesterday he almost bought me a girl for fifty marks, he thought, and to-day he is trying to arrange a legitimate engagement. Or had the old man himself some hankerings after Elisabeth, as after the other girl, whose fingers Joachim could still feel on the back of his neck? But it was incredible to him that anyone at all should dare to think of Elisabeth with sensual desire, and still more incredible that any man should want to incite his son to violate a saint because he was unable to do it himself. Joachim almost felt like asking his father's pardon for the monstrous suspicion; but really the old man was capable of anything. Yes, it was one s duty to protect all the women in the world from this old man, Joachim thought as they were walking along the platform, and while he saluted the departing train he was still thinking it. But when the train had disappeared his thoughts returned to Ruzena.

And in the evening he was still thinking of Ruzena. There are evenings in spring when the twilight lasts far longer than the astronomically prescribed period. Then a thin smoky mist sinks over the city and gives it the subdued suspense of evenings preceding a holiday. And at the same time it is as if this subdued, pale grey mist had netted so much light that brighter strands remain in it even when it has become quite black and velvety. So these twilights last very long, so long that the proprietors of shops forget to close them; they stand gossiping with their acquaintances before the doors, until a passing policeman smilingly draws their attention to the fact that they are exceeding the regulation closing-time. And even then a beam of light shines from many a shop, for in the back room the family are sitting at their supper; they have not put up the shutters as usual in front of the door, but only placed a chair there to show that customers cannot be served; and when they have finished their supper they will come out, bringing their chairs with them, and take their ease before the shop-door. They are enviable, the small shopkeepers and tradespeople who live behind their shops, enviable in winter when they put up the heavy shutters so as to enjoy doubly the warmth and security of the lighted room, through whose glass door at Christmas-time the glittering Christmas-tree can be seen from the shop; enviable in the mild spring and autumn evenings when, holding a cat, or stroking the soft head of a dog, they sit before their doors as on a terraced garden.

Returning from the barracks Joachim walked through the streets of the suburb. It was not fitting for one of his rank to do this, and the officers always drove home in the regimental carriages. Nobody ever went walking here—even Bertrand would not have thought of it—and the fact that he himself was doing so now was as disturbing to Joachim as if he had made a false step. Was it not almost as if in doing so he were humiliating himself for Ruzena's sake? Or was it an indirect humiliation of Ruzena? For in his fantasy she now occupied quite definitely a suburban flat, perhaps that very cellar-like little shop before whose dark entry greens and vegetables were spread for purchase; and perhaps it was Ruzena's mother who squatted in front of it, knitting and talking in her dark foreign speech. He smelt the smoky odour of paraffin lamps. In the low vaulted cellar a light shone out. It came from a lamp fixed into the dingy wall at the back. He felt he could almost sit there himself with Ruzena before the cellar, her hand ruffling his hair. But he was startled when he became conscious of this thought, and to drive it away he tried to imagine that over Lestow the same light grey dusk was settling. And in the park, silent under the mist and already fragrant with dewy herbs, he saw Elisabeth; she was walking slowly towards the house, from whose windows the soft light of the paraffin lamps shone out into the falling dusk, and her little dog was there too, and it, too, seemed to be tired after the day. But as he thought more intently and intimately it was Ruzena and himself that he saw on the terrace in front of the house, and Ruzena's caressing hand was resting on the back of his head.

It went without saying that in those beautiful spring days one was in good spirits, and that business was flourishing. Bertrand, who had been in Berlin for a few days, felt this too. Yet in his heart he knew his good spirits came simply from the success which, for years now, had followed all his transactions, and conversely that his good spirits were needed to bring about further success. It was like a propitious gliding with the current, and instead of himself making towards the things he wanted he saw them come floating towards him. Perhaps this had been one of the reasons why he had left the regiment: there were so many things which invited him and from which at that time he was excluded. What did the brass plates of banks, solicitors and export firms mean to him then? They were only empty words at which one did not look, or which disturbed one. Now he knew a great number of things about banks, knew what took place behind the counter, yes, understood not only all that was connoted by the inscriptions discount, foreign exchange, deposits, and so on, but knew also what went on in the directors' offices, could size up a bank by its deposits and its reserves, and draw lively conclusions from a fluctuation in shares. He understood such export terms as transit and bonded warehouse, and all this had come very natural to him, had become as matter of course as the brass plate in the Steinweg in Hamburg: Eduard von Bertrand, Cotton Importer." And the fact that now a similar plate could be seen in the Rolandstrasse in Bremen and the Cotton Exchange in Liverpool actually gave him a feeling of pride.

When in Unter den Linden he met Pasenow, angular in his long military coat with the epaulets, his very shoulders angular, while he himself was comfortably clad in a suit of English cloth, he felt quite elated, greeted Pasenow airily and familiarly as he always greeted his old comrades, and asked him without further ado if he had lunched yet and if he would come with him to Dressel's.

Taken aback by the sudden encounter and the quick cordiality, Pasenow forgot how much he had been thinking of Bertrand these last few days; once more he felt ashamed to be talking in his spick-and-span uniform to a man who stood before him naked, as it were, in mufti, and he would have been glad to evade the invitation. But all that he found himself saying was that it was a terribly long time since he had seen Bertrand. Oh, considering the monotonous and settled life he led that wasn't surprising, replied Bertrand. To himself, on the contrary, always harried and on the move as he was, it seemed only yesterday that they had worn their swords for the first time in Unter den Linden and had their first supper at Dressel's—by this time they had entered—and yet they had grown older meanwhile. Pasenow thought: " He talks too much," but because it pleased him to think that Bertrand possessed obnoxious qualities, or because he vaguely felt that his friend's previous taciturnity had always mortified him—in spite of his horror of being indiscreet he asked where Bertrand had been all this time. Bertrand made a slight deprecatory gesture with his hand as if he were dismissing something quite unimportant: " Oh, lots of places. I'm just back from America." Hm, America—for Joachim America was still the country where unruly or disinherited or degenerate sons were sent, and old von Bertrand must have died of grief after all! But again this thought did not seem to fit the assured and obviously prosperous man who sat opposite him. Of course Pasenow had heard often of such ne'er-do-wells working their way up over there as farmers and then returning to Germany to look for a German bride, and perhaps this fellow had come to fetch Ruzena; but no, she wasn't German but Czech, or rather, for that was the proper term, Bohemian. Yet, as the idea still stuck in his mind, he asked: " And you're going back again? " " No, not immediately, I must go to India first." A mere adventurer, in fact! And Pasenow cast a glance round the restaurant, feeling embarrassed to be sitting there with an adventurer; yet there was nothing else for it but to see it through: " So you're always travelling, then? " " Oh, it's only on business that I travel—but I like travelling about. Of course a man should always do what his demon drives him to." And with that the cat was out of the bag; now he knew; Bertrand had quitted the service simply to go into business, from mere greed, mere avarice. But, thick-skinned as these profiteers always were, Bertrand did not feel his contempt and went on without embarrassment: " Look here, Pasenow! It's more and more incomprehensible to me how you can stick it out here. Why don't you at least report for colonial service, seeing that the country has provided that amusement for you? " Pasenow and his comrades had never bothered themselves about the colonial problem: that was the preserve of the navy; all the same he felt indignant: " Amusement? " Bertrand had once more that ironical curl to his lips: " Well, what else is there in it? A little private amusement and glory for the soldiers immediately concerned. All honour, of course, to Dr Peters, and if he had appeared earlier I should certainly have been with him, but what other elements are there except pure romanticism? It's romantic from every point of view— except for the activities of the Catholic and Protestant missions, of course, who are doing sober and useful work. But as for the rest—a joke, nothing but a joke." He spoke so disdainfully that Pasenow was honestly in- dignant, but what he said sounded merely as if he were offended: " Why should we Germans fall behind the other countries? " " I'll tell you something, Pasenow: first, England is England; second, even in England every day isn't a holiday; third, I shall always invest my spare capital in English colonies rather than in German; so, you see, even from a business point of view it's romantic for us to have colonies; and fourthly, as I said before, it's only the Church that ever has a real palpable interest in colonial expansion." Joachim von Pasenow's mortified admiration grew, and along with it the suspicion that this Bertrand fellow was trying to blind him and dupe him and lead him into a trap by his enigmatic and conceited generalizations. In some way all this went with Bertrand's hair, which was quite unmilitary, indeed almost curly. It was theatrical in some way. The words, " the pit," " the bottomless pit," came into Joachim's mind: why did this man keep on talking of religion and the Church? But before he could gather himself together to reply Bertrand had already noticed his astonishment: " Yes, you see, Europe has already become a pretty dubious field for the Church. But Africa, on the other hand! Hundreds of millions of souls as raw material for the Faith. And you can rest assured that a baptized negro is a better Christian than twenty Europeans. If the Catholics and the Protestants want to steal a

march on each other for the winning of these fanatics it's very understandable; for there's where the future of their religion lies; there will
be found the future warriors of the faith who will march out one day,
burning and slaying in Christ's name, against a heathen Europe sunk in
corruption, to set at last, amid the smoking ruins of Rome, a black Pope
on the throne of Peter." That's like Revelation, thought Pasenow; he's
blaspheming now. And what did the souls of negroes matter to him?
Slave-dealing had surely been abolished, although a man obsessed by
greed for filthy lucre might even be capable of that. And Bertrand had
just been talking of his demon. But perhaps he had only been joking;
even in the cadet school one had never known when Bertrand was serious.
" You're joking! And as for the Spahis and Turcos, we've settled with
them for good." Bertrand could not but smile, and he smiled so winningly
and frankly that Joachim too could not keep himself from smiling. So
they smiled frankly at each other and their souls nodded to each other
through the windows of their eyes, just for an instant, like two neighbours who have never greeted each other and now happen to lean out of
their windows at the same moment, pleased and embarrassed by this
unforeseen and simultaneous greeting. Convention rescued them out
of their embarrassment, and lifting his glass Bertrand said: " Prosit,
Pasenow! " and Pasenow replied: " Prosit, Bertrand! " whereupon they
had both to smile again.

When they left the restaurant and were standing in Unter den Linden
under the somewhat parched, motionless trees in the hot light of the
afternoon sun, Pasenow remembered the reply which he had been too
shy to utter when they were having lunch: " I really can't understand
what quarrel you have with the faith of us Europeans. It seems to me
that you people who live in cities don't have the proper understanding
for that. When one has grown up in the country, like myself, one has
quite a different attitude to these things. And our peasants out there are
far more closely bound to religion than you seem to think." In saying
this to Bertrand's face he felt somehow daring, like a subaltern trying
to explain what strategy was to a Staff officer, and he was a little afraid
lest Bertrand should take it badly. But Bertrand only replied cheerfully:
" Well, then, probably everything will turn out splendidly after all."
And then they exchanged addresses and promised that they would
remain in touch with each other.

Pasenow took a droshky and drove out to the west end to the races.

The Rhine wine, the afternoon heat, and perhaps also the strangeness of his encounter, had left behind his forehead and at the back of his temples —he would have dearly liked to take off his stiff cap—a dark, flawed feeling, reminding him of the leather seat he was sitting on, which he was prodding with his gloved finger-tips; it was actually a little sticky, so hotly did the sun burn upon it. He was sorry he had not invited Bertrand to go with him, but he was glad at least that his father was no longer in Berlin, for he would certainly have been sitting there beside him. Yet on the other hand he was sincerely glad not to have Bertrand accompanying him in his civilian clothes. But perhaps Bertrand wanted to give him a surprise and had called for Ruzena now, and they would all meet at the races again. Like a family. But of course that was all nonsense. Not even Bertrand would show himself at the races with a girl like that.

When a few days later Leindorff, one of Joachim's fellow-officers, received a visit from his father, to Pasenow it was like a sign from heaven bidding him go to the Jäger Casino and be there before old Leindorff, whom he already saw mounting the narrow stairs with an undeviating, bustling air. He drove to his flat in the regimental carriage and put on his civilian clothes. Then he set out. At the corner he met two soldiers; he was about to bring up his hand perfunctorily to his cap in reply to their salute, when he noticed that they had not saluted him at all, and realised that instead of his cap he was wearing his top-hat. All this was somehow comic and he could not help smiling, because it was so absurd to think that old Count Leindorff, half paralysed as he was, thinking of nothing but his consultations with his doctors, should visit the Jäger Casino that evening. Probably the wisest thing would be simply to turn back, but as he could do that at any time he liked, he enjoyed the slight feeling of freedom this gave him and went on. Yet he would rather have gone for a stroll in the suburbs to see again the little cellar-like greengrocery-shop and the smoking paraffin lamp; but of course he really could not parade in the northern suburbs in his frock-coat and top-hat. Out there the twilight would probably be again as magical as on that other evening, but here in the actual centre of the city everything seemed hostile to Nature: above the noisy light and the innumerable shop-windows and the animated life of the streets, even the sky and the air seemed so urban and unfamiliar that it was like a fortunate and reassuring, yet disconcerting, rediscovery of familiar things when he found a little linen-shop, in whose narrow window lace, ruches and half-finished hand-worked embroideries picked out in blue were lying, and saw a glass door at the back which obviously led to a living-room. Behind the counter a white-haired woman—she seemed almost a lady—was sitting, and beside her was a young girl whose face he could not see; both of them were busied with hand-work. He examined the wares in the window and wondered whether it might not please Ruzena to present her with a few of those lace handkerchiefs. But this too seemed to him absurd, so he walked on, but at the first corner turned and went back again, driven by his desire to see the averted face of the girl. He bought three flimsy handkerchiefs without really deciding to give them to Ruzena, quite haphazardly, simply to please the old lady by buying something. The girl's looks, however, were indifferent; indeed she actually looked cross. Then he went home.

In winter during the Court festivities, to which without admitting it the Baroness looked forward, and in spring during the races and the summer shopping, the Baddensen family occupied a trim house in the west end, and one Sunday morning Joachim von Pasenow paid the ladies his duty call. It was seldom that he visited this outlying villa suburb, an imitation of the English model which was spreading rapidly, although only rich families accustomed to a permanent equipage could live here without being keenly aware of the disadvantage of its distance from the city. But for those privileged persons who could afford to qualify this spatial disadvantage the place was a little rustic paradise, and walking through the trim streets between the villas Pasenow was pleasantly and delight-fully penetrated by a sense of the superiority of the neighbourhood. During the last few days he had become uncertain about many things, and this in some inexplicable way was connected with Bertrand; some pillar or other of life had become shaky, and though everything still remained in its old place, because the parts reciprocally supported each other, yet along with a vague wish that the vaulted arch of this equilibrium might cave in and entomb beneath it all that was tottering and uncertain, a fear had arisen at the same time that the wish might really be fulfilled, and there had grown within him a longing for per-manence, security and peace. Well, this comfortable neighbourhood with its castellar edifices in the most excellent Renaissance, Baroque and Swiss styles, surrounded by carefully tended gardens in which one could hear the scrape of gardeners' rakes, the hiss of garden hoses and the splashing of fountains; all this breathed out a great and insular security, so that one could not really believe in Bertrand's dictum that even in England every day was not a holiday. From open windows rang out *études* by Stephen Heller and Clementi: the daughters of these families could devote themselves to their pianos in complete security: theirs was a safe and gentle existence, filled with friendship until friendship should give place to love and love once more die away into friendship. Far off, but not too far off, a cock crowed as if he too wished to indicate the rusticity of this well-planned suburb: yes, if Bertrand had grown up on the land he would not be spreading insecurity, and had they allowed Joachim himself to stay at home he wouldn't have been so susceptible to this feeling of insecurity. It would be lovely to walk with Elisabeth through the fields, and take the ears of the ripening corn between one's expert fingers, and in the evenings, when the heavy odour of the byre was carried on the wind, to cross the neatly swept yard and look on while the cows were being milked. Elisabeth would stand there among the great rustical beasts, far too slight for the ponderousness of her surroundings, and what in his mother had seemed merely natural and homely would be in her both homely and touching. But for him it was much too late for all that, for him whom they had made an outcast, and he was—now the thought struck him—as homeless as Bertrand.

And now the fold of the garden, whose railings were concealed by hedges, enclosed him. The security of nature here was still further enhanced by the fact that the Baroness had had one of the plush sofas from the drawing-room brought out into the garden: it stood there like something exotic reared in a hot-house, with its turned legs and swivelled feet resting on the gravel, lauding the friendliness of a climate and a civilized nature which permitted it such a station; its hue was a fading damask rose. Elisabeth and Joachim sat on iron garden-chairs, whose metal seats were pierced with stars like frozen Brussels lace.

After they had exhausted the excellences of the neighbourhood, which were bound to appeal particularly to one accustomed to and fond of country ways, Joachim was asked about his life in the town, and he could not help expressing his longing for the country and trying to justify it. He found that the ladies completely agreed with him; the Baroness in particular assured him again and again that—he mustn't be surprised—but often for days, yes, even for weeks, she never went into the centre of the town, so terrified, yes, terrified, was she of the hubbub, the noise and the tremendous traffic. Well, replied Pasenow, here she had a real haven, and the conversation flowed again for some time round the theme of the superior neighbourhood, until the Baroness, as if she had a delightful surprise in store, informed him almost with an air of secrecy that they had been offered the chance of buying the little house which they had come to love so much. And in the anticipatory joy of possession she invited him to look through the house, to make a *tour du propriétaire*, she added ironically and with a slight touch of embarrassment.

As usual the reception-rooms lay on the ground floor and the bed-rooms upstairs. Yes, in the dining-room, which with its carved old German furniture breathed out an oppressive comfort, they were going to make a winter-garden with a fountain, and perhaps transform the drawing-room too. Then they climbed the stairs, at the top and the bottom of which were velvet hangings, and the Baroness went on opening door after door, passing over only the more intimate ones. Hesitatingly and with a slight blush Elisabeth's room was revealed to the masculine eye, but even the cloud of white lace with which her bed, window, washing-table and mirror were hung did not fill Joachim with such a painful and ashamed feeling as the bedroom of her parents; indeed he could almost have reproached the Baroness for making him free of the household and compelling him to be a co-witness of her shame. For now, before his eyes, before everybody's eyes, plainly dis-played even before Elisabeth, whom he felt such knowledge confounded and violated, the two beds stood side by side, ready for the sexual uses of the Baroness, whom he now suddenly saw before him, not indeed naked, but unladylike and brazen: here was the double bedchamber, and now in a flash it seemed to him the central point of the house, its hidden and yet obviously visible altar, round which all the other rooms were built. And in the same flash he saw clearly that every house in the long row of villas which he had passed had as its central point a similar bedroom, and that the sonatinas and the *études* sent out through the open windows, behind which the spring breeze softly waved the lace curtains, were only intended to veil the actual facts. So everywhere towards evening the beds of the master and mistress were decked with the sheets that were folded with such hypocritical glossiness in the linen-room, and the servants and the children knew why this was done;

everywhere the maids and the children slept, chaste and unpaired, round the coupled central point of the house, they chaste and pure, yet at the service and command of the unchaste and the shameless. How had the Baroness dared, when she was lauding the advantages of the neighbourhood, to include among these the nearness of the church? Should not she enter it with humility, and as it were barefoot? Perhaps this was what Bertrand had meant when he spoke of the unchristian age, and it became intelligible to Joachim that the black warriors of God must fall on this abomination with fire and sword, so as again to restore true chastity and Christlikeness. He looked across at Elisabeth and thought he read from her glance that she shared his indignation. And that she should be fated to the same desecration, that indeed he himself should be the man chosen to perform that act of desecration, filled him with such compassion that he longed to steal her away, simply that he might watch before her door, so that undisturbed and unviolated she might dream for ever in a dream of white lace.

Affably conducted back to the ground floor by the ladies, he parted from them with the promise to return soon. In the street he became aware of the emptiness of his visit; he thought how dismayed the ladies would be if they heard Bertrand talking, and he actually wished that they could hear him for once.

When a man has adopted the habit of not noticing his fellow-creatures —in consequence perhaps of the caste-like seclusion of his life, and of a certain slowness in emotional reaction—he is bound to be surprised at himself if his eye should be attracted and held by two strange young men standing talking together near him. This is what happened to Joachim one evening in the foyer of the Opera House. The two gentlemen were obviously foreigners and not much over twenty; he was inclined to take them for Italians, not merely because of the cut of their clothes which was a little unusual, but because one of them, a black-eyed and black-haired fellow, wore an upward-curling Italian moustache. And although it went against Joachim's grain to listen to the conversation of strangers, he perceived that they were employing a foreign language which was not Italian, and he felt constrained to listen more carefully, until with a slight sensation of alarm he thought he could tell that they were speaking Czech, or more correctly, Bohemian. His alarm was quite unfounded, and still more unfounded seemed to him the feeling of infidelity to Elisabeth which supervened on it. Of course it was possible, if also unlikely, that Ruzena might be in the audience and that these two young men might presently visit her in her box, as he himself had often visited Elisabeth in hers; and perhaps there was really a resemblance between Ruzena and the young man with the little black moustache and the far too curly black head, and not merely in the colour of their hair; probably it was the slightly too small mouth and the lips which stood out too vividly from the olive face, the nose, too short and delicately chiselled, and the smile which was in some way challenging—yes, challenging was the right word—and nevertheless seemed to be asking for forgiveness.

Yet all this seemed preposterous, and it might well be that the resemblance was only a fancy of his; for when he thought of Ruzena now he had to admit to himself that her image had completely faded, indeed that he would not recognize her if he met her again in the street, and that he could see her only through the medium and in the mask of this young man. That reassured him and made the incident in some way safe, but without giving him any feeling of satisfaction, for at the same time and in some other layer of his mind he felt that it was somehow dreadful and unspeakable for the girl to be concealed behind the mask of a man, and even after the interval he could not rid himself of this feeling. They were presenting Gounod's *Faust*, and even the sugary harmonies seemed to him not so fatuous as the operatic convention on the stage, where no one, not even Faust himself, noticed that in the beloved lineaments of Margaret those of Valentine lay concealed, and that it was for this, and this alone, that Margaret had to suffer. Perhaps Mephistopheles knew it, and Joachim was glad that Elisabeth had no brothers. When after the performance he again ran into Ruzena's brother, he was thankful that now the sister too was set beyond his reach, and he felt so sure of himself that, in spite of his uniform, he turned in the direction of Jägerstrasse. And the feeling of infidelity, too, was gone.

It was only when he turned into Friedrichstrasse that he became conscious that he could not visit the casino in his uniform. He was disappointed and continued to walk along Jägerstrasse. What should he do? He turned round the next corner, came back to Jägerstrasse again, and caught himself peeping under the hats of passing girls, often half expecting to hear a few words of Italian. But when he was again approaching the Jäger Casino the voice he heard was not Italian, but hard and staccato. " But you not know me any more? " " Ruzena," Pasenow said reluctantly and thought at the same time: How painful! There he was standing in the open street in his uniform with this girl, he who only a few days ago had been ashamed of being seen with Bertrand in his civilian clothes, and instead of going away he was, forgetting all convention, almost happy, yes, completely happy, simply because the girl was going on talking: " Where is papa to-night? He comes not to-night? " She shouldn't have reminded him of his father: " No, nothing doing to-night, little Ruzena: the "—what had she called him?—" the old gentleman isn't coming to-night either." . . . Yes, and now he must hurry away. Ruzena gazed at him in dismay: " So long keep me waiting and now not . . ." But, and her face cleared, he must pay her a visit. He gazed into her apprehensively questioning face as if he wished to print it finally on his mind, but seeking at the same time to discover if her southern brother with the curled moustache was hidden in it. There was some resemblance; but while he was wondering whether a girl who bore her brother in her face could be anything to him, he remembered his own brother, fair-haired and masculine with his short beard, and that brought him back to actuality. Of course that was different; Helmuth was a country gentleman, a huntsman, and had nothing in common with those soft southern people; and yet it was a reassurance. His eyes still searched her face, but his aversion faded and he felt a need to do her a kindness, to say something comforting to her, so that she might cherish a happy memory of him; he still hesitated; no, he would not visit her, but . . . " But? " the word sounded anxious and expectant. Joachim himself did not know at first what was to follow the " but," and then he suddenly knew: " We could meet somewhere and have lunch together." Yes, yes, yes, yes; she knew a little place: to-morrow! No, it couldn't be to-morrow, but on Wednesday he had leave, and they arranged to meet on Wednesday. Then she stood on the tips of her toes and whispered into his ear: " You're good, nice man," and ran away, and vanished through the door over which the gas-jets were burning. Pasenow saw his father bustling up the stairs with his quick and purposive tread, and his heart contracted perceptibly and very painfully.

Ruzena was enchanted by the conventionally stiff courtesy with which Joachim had treated her in the restaurant, and in her delight she even forgot her disappointment that he had appeared in mufti. It was a cool, rainy day; yet she did not want to give up her programme, and so after lunch they had driven out through Charlottenburg to the Havel. Already in the droshky Ruzena had pulled off one of Joachim's gloves, and now, as they went along the river-path, she took his arm and pushed it under hers. They went slowly, walking through a landscape expectant in its stillness, and yet which had nothing to expect save the rain and the evening. The sky hung softly over it, sometimes united indissolubly to the earth by a veil of rain, and for them too, wandering through the stillness, there seemed to be nothing left but expectation, and it was as though all the life in them had flowed to their fingers, which, clasped and folded in upon each other, slept like the petals of an unopened bud. Shoulder leaning against shoulder, from the distance resembling the two sides of a triangle, they walked along the river-path in silence, for neither knew what it was that drew them together. But quite unexpectedly while they were walking along Ruzena bent over his hand, which lay in hers, and kissed it before he could draw it away. He looked into eyes that were swimming with tears, and at lips that twitched with sobs, yet managed to say: " When you meet me on stairs I say, Ruzena, I say, he not for you, never for you. And now you here. . . ." But she did not reach up her mouth for the expected kiss, but fell again, almost greedily, on his hand, and when he tried to free it, bit into it with her teeth, not sharply, but as gently and cautiously as a little dog playing: then looking at the mark contentedly she said: " Now let us walk on again. Rain matters not." The rain sank quietly into the river, and rustled softly on the leaves of the willows. A boat lay half-sunk near the bank; under a little wooden bridge a runnel poured more rapidly into the placid flow of the river, and Joachim too felt himself being floated away, as though the longing which filled him were a soft, light out-flowing of his heart, a breathing flood longing to be merged in the breath of his beloved, and to be lost as in an ocean of immeasurable peace. It was as though the summer were dissolving, so that the very water seemed light, rustling from the leaves, and hanging on the grasses in clear drops. A soft misty veil rose in the distance, and when they turned round it had closed them in behind, so that in walking they seemed to be standing still. When the rain came on more violently they sought the protection of the trees, beneath which the ground was still dry, a patch of unreleased summer dust almost pitiable in the release of everything

around. Ruzena pulled out her hat-pins, not only because their constraint
irked her, but also to protect Joachim from their sharp points, took off
her hat, and leant her back against him as if he were a protective tree.
She had bent back her head, and when he sank his, his lips touched her
brow and the dark curls that framed it. He did not see the faint and
slightly stupid furrows on her forehead, perhaps because he was too
near to distinguish them, perhaps because seeing had melted completely
into feeling. But she felt his arms round her, his hands in hers, felt as
if she were among the branches of a tree, and his breath on her brow
was like the rustling of the rain on the leaves; so motionless did they
stand, and so at one was the grey sky with the level waters, that the
willows on the little island seemed to float as in a grey insubstantial sea,
hanging or resting there, one did not know which. But then she looked
at the wet sleeve of her coat and whispered softly that they must turn
back.

Yet though now the rain beat on their faces, they dared not hasten,
for that would have dispelled the charm, and they only became sure of
themselves again when they were drinking coffee in the little inn. Now
the rain ran faster and faster down the panes of the rustic veranda, and
splashed thinly from the gutters. Whenever the landlady left the room
Ruzena set down her cup, took his out of his hand, and seizing his head
drew it quite close to hers, so close—and they had not yet kissed—that
their glances melted together, and the tension was quite unendurable in
its sweetness. But when, as in a dark cave, they sat in the droshky under
the covered roof with the rain-flaps let down, the faint soft drumming
of the raindrops on the stretched leather above them, seeing nothing
of the world save the coachman's cape and two wet grey strips of roadway through the opening on either side, and soon not even seeing that,
then their faces bowed towards each other, met, and melted together,
dreaming and flowing like the river, lost irrecoverably, and ever found
again, and again sunk timelessly. It was a kiss that lasted for an hour
and fourteen minutes. Then the droshky stopped before Ruzena's door.
Yet when he made to enter with her she shook her head, and he turned
to go; but the pain of parting from her was so great that after a few
steps he turned back, and driven by his own dread and drawn by hers,
seized her hand, which was still motionlessly outstretched in longing; and
as if already dreaming they ascended like sleepwalkers the dark stairs,
which creaked under their feet, crossed the dark entrance-room, and in

her bedroom, which lay in the gloom of the early rainy twilight, sank on
the dark rug that covered the bed, seeking once more the kiss from
which they had been torn, their faces wet with rain or with tears, they
did not know which. But then Ruzena freed herself and guided his
hands to the fastenings that held her dress at the back, and her singing
voice was dark. " Open that," she whispered, tearing at the same time
at his necktie and the buttons of his vest. And as if in sudden, precipitate humility, whether towards him or towards God, who can say,
she fell on her knees, her head against the foot of the bed, and quickly
unfastened his shoes. Oh, how terrible that was—for why should they
not sink down together, forgetting the casings in which they were held?
—and yet how grateful he was to her that she made it easier, and so
touchingly; oh, the deliverance of the smile with which she threw open
the bed into which they flung themselves. But the sharp-cornered
starched plastron of his shirt, cutting against her chin, still irked her,
and opening it and squeezing her face between the sharp angles she
ordered: " Put that off "; and now they felt release and freedom, felt
the softness of their bodies, felt their breathing stifled by the urgency
of emotion, and their delight rising up out of their dread. Oh, dread of
life streaming from the living flesh with which the bones are clothed,
softness of the skin spread and stretched over it, dreadful warning of
the skeleton and the many-ribbed breast frame which he can now
embrace, and which, breathing, now presses against him, its heart beating against his. Oh, sweet fragrance of the flesh, humid exhalation, soft
runnels beneath the breasts, darkness of the armpits. But still Joachim
was too confused, still they were both too confused, to know the delight
they felt; they knew only that they were together and yet that they
must still seek each other. In the darkness he saw Ruzena's face, but it
seemed to be flowing away, flowing between the dark banks of her hair,
and he had to put out his hand to touch it and assure himself that it
was there; he found her brow and her eyelids beneath which the hard
eyeballs rested, found the satisfying curve of her cheeks and the line of
her mouth opened for his kiss. Wave beat against wave of longing;
drawn by the flood his kiss found hers; and while the willows of the
river grew up and up, stretching from bank to bank, enclosing them as
in a sacred grotto in whose profound peace the security of the eternal
sea slumbers, it was—so faintly did he say it, stifled and no longer
breathing, but only seeking for her breath—it was like a cry that she

heard: " I love you "; and she opened, like a shell in the sea she opened, and he sank drowning into her.

Without warning the news reached him that his brother was dead. He had fallen in a duel with a Polish land proprietor. Had it happened a few weeks before Joachim might not have been so shaken. In the twenty years which he had spent away from home the image of his brother had faded more and more, and when he thought of him he saw only the fair-haired lad in his boy's suit—they had always been dressed alike until Joachim had been sent into the cadet school—and even now the first thing that came into his mind was a child's coffin. Yet immediately, side by side with it, rose Helmuth's masculine blond-bearded form, the same form which had come to him that evening in the Jägerstrasse when he had been afraid that he saw something more in a girl's face than was there: oh, then the clear eyes of the huntsman had rescued him from the nightmare into which another had wished to draw and entangle him, and those eyes which had been lent him then Helmuth had closed now for ever, perhaps in order that he himself might have them always. Had he required this of Helmuth? He had no feeling of guilt, yet it was as if his brother's death had come about for his sake; yes, as if he had been the cause of it. Strange that Helmuth had worn Uncle Bernhard's beard, the same short beard which left the mouth free; and now it seemed to Joachim that he had always held Helmuth respon-sible for the cadet school and his military career, and not Uncle Bernhard who was really to blame. Still, Helmuth had been allowed to stay at home, and besides he had played the hypocrite—that was probably the explanation; yet all this was very confusing, and the more so because Joachim had known for a long time now that his brother's life was not enviable. He saw the child's coffin before him again, and a feeling of bitterness against his father rose up in him. So the old man had succeeded at last in driving his other son out of the house too. It gave him an acrid feeling of relief to throw the responsibility for his brother's death on his father.

He returned to Stolpin for the funeral. When he arrived a letter from Helmuth was awaiting him: " I don't know whether I shall come alive out of this rather unnecessary affair. Naturally I hope so; still it is almost a matter of indifference to me. I recognize that there is something called a code of honour which in this shoddy life gives a hint of some higher idea to which one may submit oneself. I hope that you have found more value in your life than I have found in mine. I have often envied you your military career; in the army one serves at least something greater than oneself. I don't know, of course, how you think about it, but I'm writing you to warn you (in case I should fall) not to give up your career for the sake of taking over the estate. You'll have to do that sooner or later of course, but as long as father is alive it would be better, all things considered, for you to stay away, unless mother should need you. I send you lots of good wishes." Here followed a varied list of instructions for Joachim to carry out, and at the end, somewhat unexpectedly, the wish that he might be less lonely than Helmuth had been.

His parents were remarkably collected, his mother no less than his father. His father gripped his hand and said: " He died for honour, for the honour of his name," and with his sharp, purposive stride walked in silence from end to end of the room. Soon he repeated again: " He died for honour," and went out through the door.

They had laid the coffin in the big drawing-room. In the antechamber Joachim already could smell the heavy perfume of the flowers and wreaths: too heavy for a child's coffin—a stubborn and meaningless thought—and yet he remained hesitating within the heavily curtained door, and did not dare to look across, but stared at the floor. The floor he knew well, knew the triangular parquet which bordered the threshold, knew the recurring pattern that ran across the room, and when he followed it with his eyes, as he had often done as a child picking his steps along the geometrical figures, his glance reached the black cloth spread under the bier. A few leaves, fallen from the wreaths, were lying there. He had a longing to walk along the pattern again, took a few steps, and looked at the coffin. It was not a child's coffin, and that was good; but he still shrank from looking with his own seeing eyes into those dead ones, into eyes which must be so completely quenched that the face of the boy would be drowned in them, perhaps drawing himself after it, the brother to whom those eyes had now been given; and the fancy that he himself was lying there grew so strong that it was like a release and piece of good fortune when, stepping nearer, he saw that the coffin was covered. Someone said that the dead man's face had been mutilated by the bullet. He hardly listened to this, but remained standing beside the coffin, his hand resting on the lid. And seized by the impotence that overcomes human beings in the presence of the dead and the silence of death, where all accepted things recede and fall away, where the long familiar breaks and falls and is frozen in its fall, where the air becomes thin and incapable of supporting one, it seemed to him that he would never be able to move from his station beside the bier, and it caused him a great effort to remember that this was the big drawing-room, and that the coffin was standing in the place usually occupied by the piano, and that behind it there must be a strip of parquet never yet walked on; he went slowly over and touched the black-draped wall, felt under the gloomy hangings the picture-frames and the frame of the case where the Iron Cross hung, and this refound fragment of actuality transformed death in a novel and almost exciting way into a matter of drapery, accommodating almost cheerfully the fact that Helmuth in his coffin, decked with all his flowers, had been introduced into this room like a new piece of furniture, thus once more reducing the incomprehensible so radically to the comprehensible, the certain and assured, that the experience of those few minutes—or had it been only seconds? —passed over into a soothing feeling of quiet confidence. His father appeared accompanied by several gentlemen, and Joachim heard him once more saying repeatedly: " He died for honour." But when the gentlemen had left and Joachim thought he was alone, suddenly he heard again: " He died for honour," and saw his father, small and forlorn, standing beside the bier. He felt it his duty to go up to him. " Come, father," he said, leading him away. At the door his father looked into his face and said: " He died for honour," as if he wished to learn the words by heart, and wished Joachim also to do so.

Then a great number of people arrived. The village fire brigade were standing in the yard. The neighbouring military associations also put in an appearance, making an orderly show of top-hats and frock-coats on which not infrequently an Iron Cross was to be seen. Carriages from the houses in the vicinity drove up, and while the vehicles were being directed to a place where they could remain in the shade, Joachim had to greet the visitors and do the honours beside his brother's coffin. Baron von Baddensen arrived alone, for his wife and daughter were still in Berlin, and as Joachim greeted him he was seized by the thought, angrily dismissed at once, that this gentleman might well now regard the only remaining son at Stolpin as a desirable son-in-law, and he felt ashamed for Elisabeth. From the gable of the house a black flag hung motionlessly, almost reaching down to the terrace.

His mother descended the stairs on his father's arm. The visitors were astonished at her calmness, indeed admired her. But her calmness was probably due simply to the slowness of feeling that characterized her. The funeral procession formed up, and as the carriages turned into the village street, and the house of God lay before them, everyone was heartily glad that they could now step out of the dust and heat of the afternoon sun, which had burned fiercely on their thick mourning-suits and uniforms, into the cool white church. The pastor gave an address in which the quality of honour was much stressed and by adroit turns linked with the honour that is due to God: to the pealing of the organ their voices rose, acknowledging that from our loved ones we must part . . . with pain and smart, and Joachim kept waiting for the rhyme to see that it came. Then on foot they proceeded to the cemetery, over whose portal glittered in golden letters: " Rest in Peace," and the equipages followed slowly in a long-stretching cloud of dust. The sunny sky arched, a violet-blue, over the dry, crumbling earth that was waiting for them to give Helmuth's body into its keeping; though indeed it was not the earth, but only the family vault, a little open cellar, that was yawning as if in boredom for the newcomer. When Joachim had three times emptied the little spade into the hole he looked down, saw the ends of his grandfather's and his uncle's coffins, and thought that it was because they had to keep a place for his father that they had not buried Uncle Bernhard here. But then as the shovelled earth fell on the lid of Helmuth's coffin and the stony sides of the tomb, standing there with the toy shovel in his hand he could not help thinking of days spent as a child in the soft river-sand, and he saw his brother again as a boy, saw himself lying on the bier, and it seemed to him that the dryness of this summer day was cheating Helmuth not only out of his parents, but out of death itself. For Joachim thought of a soft rainy day for his own death, a day in which the heavens themselves would sink to receive his soul, so that it might flow away as in Ruzena's arms. Unchaste thoughts, out of place here, but it was not he alone who was responsible for them, but all the others to whom now he gave place at the graveside, yes, even his father shared in the blame for them: for all their religion was a sham, was brittle and dusty and at the mercy of the sun and the rain. Could one not almost wish for the negro host, so that they might sweep all this away, and the Saviour might arise in new glory and lead men back to His kingdom? A Christ hung on the marble cross over the tomb, clothed only with the rag that covered His loins and the crown of thorns from which the bronze blood-drops fell, and Joachim too felt drops on his cheeks; perhaps they were tears that he had not noticed, perhaps however it was only the oppressive heat; he did not know, and went on shaking the hands that were held out to him.

The military associations and the fire brigade had accorded the dead man the last honour of a march past and a sharp leftward turn of their heads; their boots rang sharply on the gravel of the path, and four abreast they marched stiffly out through the cemetery gates to the curt, military commands of their officer. Standing on the steps of the family vault, Herr von Pasenow with his hat in his hand, Joachim with his hand to his cap, Frau von Pasenow between them, they acknowledged the march past. The other soldiers present stood at attention with their hands raised in salute. Thereupon the equipages advanced, and Joachim and his parents stepped into their carriage, whose doorhandle and other silver furnishings, no less than the silver of the harness, had been carefully covered with *crêpe* by the coachman; Joachim assured himself that the very whip had been decorated with a *crêpe* rosette. Now his mother was crying, and Joachim, who could think of nothing to say to comfort her, once more could not comprehend why it should have been Helmuth, and not himself, who had been hit by the fatal bullet. But his father sat stiffly on the black-leather seat, which was not hard and tattered like the seats of the Berlin droshkies, but flexible and well quilted with leather buttons. Several times his father seemed on the point of saying something, something to sum up the line of thought that obviously occupied and completely absorbed him, for he made as if to speak, but then fell into blank silence again, only moving his lips soundlessly; at last he said sharply: " They have accorded him the last honours," lifted one finger as if he were waiting for something more, or wished to add something, then laid his hand back palm downwards on his knee again. Between the end of his black glove and his cuff with its great black cuff-link a strip of reddish-haired skin was visible.

The next few days passed in silence. Frau von Pasenow went about her business; she was in the byre at milking time, in the hen-house when the eggs were collected, in the laundry. Joachim rode out a few times into the fields; it was the horse that he had given to Helmuth, and to take it out now was like a service of love to the dead. At evening the yard was swept and the servants sat on the benches before their wing enjoying the soft, cool breeze. Once during the night there was a thunderstorm, and Joachim realized with alarm that he had almost forgotten Ruzena. He had seen little of his father, who sat for the most part in his study reading the letters of condolence or registering them in a book. The pastor, who now arrived every day, often staying for dinner, was the only one who spoke of the dead, but as he brought out only a sort of professional platitudes they were but little regarded, and his only listener seemed to be Herr von Pasenow, for he now and then nodded his head and seemed on the point of saying something that lay very urgently on his mind; but he always finished merely by repeating the pastor's last few words with a nod to emphasize them, as for instance: " Ay, ay, Herr Pastor, sorely tried parents."

Then Joachim had to leave for Berlin. When he went to say good-bye to his father the old man began again to march up and down. Joachim remembered countless similar good-byes in this room which he disliked so much, well as he knew it, with the hunt trophies on the walls, the spittoon in the corner beside the stove, the writing equipment on the desk, which probably had stood as it was now since his grandfather's time, the pile of sport journals on the table, most of them uncut. He waited for his father to stick his monocle in his eye as usual and dismiss him with a curt: " Well, a pleasant journey, Joachim." But this time his father said nothing, but only continued to walk up and down, his hands behind his back, so that Joachim got up a second time. " Really, father, I must be going now, or I'll miss my train." " Well, a pleasant journey, Joachim," the accustomed reply came at last, " but there's something I want to say to you. I'm afraid you'll have to come here for good soon. The place has become empty, yes, empty . . ." he looked round him . . . " but some people don't see that . . . of course one must maintain one's honour . . ." he had begun his walk again, then, confidentially: " And what about Elisabeth? We spoke about it before. . . ." " Father, it's high time I was away," said Joachim, " else I'll lose my train." The old man held out his hand, and Joachim took it unwillingly.

As he drove through the village he saw from the church clock that he was still in ample time for the train; indeed he had known that before. The church door chancing to be open, he ordered the coachman to stop. He had an offence to wipe off, an offence against the church which had been merely a pleasantly cool place to him, against the pastor to whose well-meaning words he had not listened, against Helmuth whose burial he had dishonoured with profane thoughts; in a word, an offence against God. He entered and tried to recapture the feelings which as a child had been his when every Sunday he had stood here as before the face of God. At that time he had known a great number of hymns, and had sung them with ardour. But it would hardly do for him to begin singing now quite by himself, in the church. He must confine himself to assembling his thoughts and concentrating them on God and his own sinfulness, his littleness and wretchedness before God. But his thoughts refused to seek God. The only thing that came into his mind was a sentence from Isaiah which he had once heard in this place: "The ox knoweth his owner, and the ass his master's crib: but Israel doth not know, my people doth not consider." Yes, Bertrand was right, they had lost their faith; and now he tried to say the Lord's Prayer with closed eyes, being careful not to utter a single word emptily, but to grasp the meaning of each; and when he came to the words, " as we forgive our debtors," the tender, apprehensive and yet trustful feelings of his childhood rose in him again; he remembered that he had always applied this passage to his father and from it had drawn the confidence that he would be able to forgive his father, yes, to feel all the love towards him which it was the duty of a child to feel; and now he remembered again that the old man had spoken of his loneliness, of which he was visibly afraid, and which one must make lighter for him. As Joachim left the church the words " uplifted and strengthened " came into his mind, and they did not seem empty to him, but full of new and encouraging meaning. He resolved to visit Elisabeth.

In the carriage the phrase arose in his mind again, again he thought " uplifted and strengthened," but now it was associated with the image of a starched [1] shirt-front and the joyful expectation of seeing Ruzena again.

II

A pedestrian was coming from the direction of Königstrasse. He was corpulent and square-built, indeed actually squat, and everything about him was so extraordinarily soft that one might have fancied that he was

[1] In German the same word serves for " strengthened " and " starched."

poured into his clothes every morning. He was a serious pedestrian, he wore a grey-lustre coat over his trousers of black cloth, and his chest was covered with a brown beard. He was obviously in a hurry, yet his walk was not rapid and undeviating, but a sort of purposive waddle such as suited a soft-bodied purposive man who was in a hurry. But it was not only the beard that concealed his face; he wore eyeglasses as well, through which he shot severe glances at the passers-by; and it was literally impossible to picture to oneself that a man like this, waddling with such haste in pursuit of some urgent business and shooting out such sharp and severe glances in spite of his soft appearance, was probably a kind and affectionate fellow in some other sphere of his existence, and that there must be women to whom he unbent in love, women and children to whom the beard uncovered a kindly smile, women who might dare to seek in a kiss the rosy lips in their dark-bearded cave.

When Joachim caught sight of this man he had mechanically followed him. It did not matter to him in any case where he went. Since he had learned that Bertrand had a Berlin agent for his firm, and that the office was in one of the streets between the Alexanderplatz and the Stock Exchange, he had sometimes felt drawn to this neighbourhood as formerly he had felt drawn to the working-class suburb—and the fact that he no longer had any need to look for Ruzena out there was almost like a promotion for her. But he did not come here, all the same, on the chance of meeting Bertrand: on the contrary he avoided the place whenever he knew Bertrand was in Berlin, nor indeed had he any interest in Bertrand's agent. It was simply so strange to him that these should be the surroundings in which one had to picture Bertrand's real life; and when he walked through those streets it sometimes happened that he not only scrutinized the fronts of the houses, as if to discover what offices were concealed behind them, but even peeped under the hats of the civilians as if they were women. Sometimes he wondered at this himself, for he was unaware that he searched these faces to discover whether their existence was so totally different from his own, and whether they could give him a clue to any qualities that Bertrand might have adopted from them, but still kept concealed. Yes, the secrecy of this life of theirs was so complete that they did not even need beards to hide themselves behind. Indeed they would have looked a little more confidential and less hypocritical to him if they had worn beards, and this may have been one of the reasons why he sauntered in the wake of the fat, hurrying man. Suddenly it seemed to him that the man in front of him fitted very strangely the picture he had always had of Bertrand's agent. It was silly, perhaps, but when several passers-by greeted the man Joachim was quite delighted that Bertrand's agent should enjoy so much respect. He would not have been excessively surprised if Bertrand himself, melodramatically transformed, small and corpulent and full-bearded, had waddled up to him: for why should Bertrand have preserved his former external appearance, seeing that he had slipped into a different world? And even though Joachim knew that what he thought was without sense or sequence, yet it was as though the apparently confused skein concealed a sequence: one had only to disentangle the threads which bound Ruzena to these people and find this deeper and very secret knot—and perhaps an end of one thread had lain in his hand that time when he had divined Bertrand as Ruzena's real lover; but now his hand was empty, and all that he had to go on was that Bertrand had once excused himself on the plea that he had to spend the evening with a business friend, and Joachim could not rid himself of the idea that this man had been the business friend. Probably they had both gone to the Jäger Casino, and the man had stuck a fifty-mark note into Ruzena's hand.

When a man follows another in the street, even if it is only mechanically and with ostensible indifference, he will soon find himself attaching all sorts of wishes, benevolent and malevolent, to the man he is following. Probably he will want at least to see the man's face and wish that he should turn round, even though since his brother's death he has thought himself invulnerable against the temptation to seek in every half-feared face the face of his mistress. In any case there is nothing to explain why the sudden thought should have come to Joachim that the erect bearing of all the people here in this street was quite unjustified, that it was incompatible with their better knowledge, or due merely to an abysmal unawareness that some time all their bodies would have to stretch themselves out in death. And yet the walk of the man in front was not in the least sharp, rapid or headlong, nor was there any fear that he might fall and break one of his legs, for he was far too soft for that to happen.

Now the man had stopped at the corner of Rochstrasse as if he were waiting for something; it was possible that he was waiting to get the fifty marks back from Joachim. And Joachim was really in honour bound to give them back, and suddenly he felt a hot rush of shame at the thought that, for fear lest people might think he kept a paid woman, or because if he stopped to reflect on it he might begin to doubt Ruzena's love, he had left her in her old hateful employment; and it was as if the scales had fallen from his eyes: he, a Prussian officer, was the secret lover of a woman who accepted money from other men. An offence against honour could be wiped out only by a pistol bullet, yet before he could think this out, with all its dreadful consequences, the know-ledge swam up, swam up like an image of Bertrand, that the man was crossing Rochstrasse and that Joachim must not let him out of sight until he . . . yes, until he . . . that was not so easy to get right. Bertrand had it easy; he belonged to this world and the other as well, and Ruzena too had a foot in each world. Was that the reason why they by rights belonged to each other? But now his thoughts jostled each other like the people in the crowd round about him, and even though he saw a goal in front of him which he wanted them to reach, it swam and wavered and was lost to view like the back of the fat man before him. If he had stolen Ruzena from her legitimate possessor, then it was perhaps fitting that he should keep her hidden now as his stolen property. He tried to maintain a stiff and erect bearing, and no longer to look at the civilians. The dense crowd around him, the hubbub, as the Baroness called it, all this commercial turmoil full of faces and backs, seemed to him a soft, gliding, dissolving mass which one could not lay hold on. What did it all lead to? And with a jerk regaining his prescribed military bearing, he suddenly thought with relief that one could love only some-one who belonged to an alien world. That was why he would never dare to love Elisabeth, and also why Ruzena had to be a Bohemian. Love meant to take refuge from one's own world in another's, and so in spite of his jealousy and shame he had left Ruzena in her world, so that her flight to him should be ever sweet and new. The garrison band was playing a little in front of him, and he held himself still more stiffly, as stiffly as when he attended church parade on Sundays. At the corner of Spandauerstrasse the man slowed down and hesitated at the edge of the thoroughfare; evidently a business man like this was afraid of the horses in the roadway. It was of course silly, the idea that he must refund money to this man; but Ruzena must be taken out of the casino, that was definite. In any case she would always remain a Bohemian, a being out of another world. But where did he fit in himself? Whither was he sliding? And Bertrand? Again Bertrand rose before him, astonishingly soft and small, glancing severely through his eyeglasses, strange to Joachim, strange to Ruzena who was a Bohemian, strange to Elisabeth who walked in a still park, strange to them all, and yet familiar when he turned round and the beard parted in a friendly smile, inciting women to kiss the dark cave where his mouth was concealed. His hand on his sword-hilt, Joachim remained standing as if the nearness of the garrison band provided him with protection and new strength against the Evil One. Bertrand's image arose, iridescent, uncanny. It emerged and vanished again: " vanished in the labyrinth of the city," the words came back to Joachim, and " labyrinth " had a diabolically underworld ring. Bertrand was concealed in all those shapes, and he had betrayed everybody: Joachim, his fellow-officers, the women, everybody. But now he noticed that Bertrand's representative had crossed Spandauerstrasse in good style at a sharp trot. Joachim thought with relief that henceforth he would keep Ruzena out of reach of them both. No, he could not be accused of stealing Ruzena; on the contrary it was his duty to protect Elisabeth as well from Bertrand. Oh, he knew, the Devil was full of wiles. But a soldier must never fly. If he fled he would deliver Elisabeth defencelessly to that man, he would himself be one of those who hid in the labyrinth of the city and were afraid of the horses' hoofs; and it would be not only an avowal of his guilt as a thief, it would mean also the renunciation for ever of his attempt to tear from that man the secret of his treachery. He must follow him farther, yet not surreptitiously like a spy, but openly as was fitting; and he would not keep Ruzena concealed either. So in the middle of the Stock Exchange quarter, though admittedly in the vicinity of the garrison band too, everything suddenly grew quiet round Joachim von Pasenow, as quiet and transparent as the clear blue sky which looked down between the two rows of buildings.

He had now a somewhat vague, yet urgent, wish to catch up the man and tell him that he was going to take Ruzena out of the casino and from now on make no secret about her; but he had taken only a few steps when he saw the other waddling hastily into the Stock Exchange. For a moment Joachim remained staring at the entrance: was this the place of metamorphosis? Would Bertrand himself come out now? He considered whether he should take Bertrand at once to meet Ruzena, and decided no: for Bertrand belonged to the world of the night clubs, and it was from that very world that he must now rescue Ruzena. But that would come all right; and how lovely it would be to forget all about it and wander with Ruzena in a still park beside a still lake. He stood still in front of the Stock Exchange. He longed for the country. The traffic roared round him; above him thundered the trains. He no longer stared at the passers-by, even though he felt that they were foreign and strange. He would avoid this neighbourhood in future. In the midst of the hubbub round the Stock Exchange Joachim von Pasenow held himself stiff and erect. He would be very good to Ruzena.

Bertrand paid him a visit of condolence, and Joachim was again not quite clear whether to regard this as considerate or presumptuous: one could take it as the one or the other. Bertrand remembered Helmuth, who had visited Culm occasionally, though seldom enough, and his memory was extraordinarily exact: "Yes, a fair, quiet youth, very reserved . . . I fancy he envied us . . . he couldn't have changed much later either . . . and he resembled you." That, now, was just a little too familiar again, almost as if Bertrand wished to exploit Helmuth's death for his own advantage; however, it was no wonder if Bertrand remembered all that had to do with his former military career with such astonishing exactitude: one liked to recall happy times that one had lost. Yet Bertrand did not speak at all in a sentimental way, but quietly and soberly, so that Helmuth's death assumed a more human and natural aspect, and in some way, under Bertrand's touch, became objective, timeless and endurable. To his brother's duel Joachim had not really devoted much thought; all the opinions that had been pronounced on it and the comments recurring again and again in the letters of condolence pointed in the same direction: that Helmuth had been tragically caught by the unalterable fatality of his sense of honour, from which there was no escape. Bertrand however began:
" The most extraordinary thing is that we live in a world of machinery and railways, and that at the same time as the railways are running and the factories working two people can stand opposite each other and shoot at each other."
Bertrand had no sense of honour left, Joachim told himself, and yet his remarks seemed natural and illuminating. But Bertrand went on:

" That may be, of course, because it's a question of sentiment."

" The sentiment of honour," said Joachim.

" Yes, honour and so forth."

Joachim looked up—was Bertrand laughing at him again? He would have liked to reply that one must not judge such things merely from the standpoint of the city man; out there in the country people's feelings were less artificial and meant more. Really Bertrand did not know anything about it. But of course one could not say such things to one's guest, and Joachim silently held out his cigar-case. But Bertrand drew his English pipe and leather tobacco-pouch from his pocket:

" It's extraordinary that it should be the most superficial and perishable things that are actually the most persistent. Physically a human being can adapt himself with incredible quickness to new conditions of life. But even his skin and the colour of his hair are more persistent than his bony structure."

Joachim regarded Bertrand's fair skin and far too wavy hair and waited to see where all this was going to lead.

Bertrand noticed at once that he had not made himself clear enough:

" Well, the most persistent things in us are, let us say, our so-called feelings. We carry an indestructible fund of conservatism about with us. I mean our feelings, or rather conventions of feeling, for actually they aren't living feelings, but atavisms."

" So you consider that conservative principles are atavistic? "

" Oh, sometimes, but not always. However, I wasn't really thinking of them. What I meant was that our feelings always lag half-a-century or a full century behind our actual lives. One's feelings are always less human than the society one lives in. Just consider that a Lessing or a Voltaire accepted without question the fact that in their time men were still broken on the wheel—a thing that to us with our feelings is unimaginable. And do you imagine that we are in a different case? "

Well, Joachim had never bothered his head over such things. Perhaps Bertrand was right. But why was he saying all this to him? He was talking like a writer for the newspapers.

Bertrand went on:

" We take it quite as a matter of course that two men, both of them honourable—for your brother would not have fought with a man who was not honourable—should of a morning stand and shoot at each other.

And the fact that we put up with such a thing, and that they do it, shows
how completely imprisoned we all are in conventional feeling. But
feelings are inert, and that's why they're so cruel. The world is ruled
by the inertia of feeling."

The inertia of feeling! Joachim was struck by the phrase: was he not
himself full of inertia, was it not a criminal inertia that had prevented
him from summoning enough imagination to provide Ruzena with
money in spite of her objections, and to take her out of the casino?
He asked in alarm:

" Do you actually describe honour as inertia of feeling? "

" Oh, Pasenow, you ask too embarrassing questions." Bertrand had
assumed again the winning smile with which he always bridged over
differences of opinion. " It seems to me that honour is a very living
feeling, but none the less all obsolete forms are full of inertia, and one
has to be very tired oneself to give oneself over to a dead and romantic
convention of feeling. One has to be in despair and see no way out
before one can do that. . . ."

Yes, Helmuth had been tired. But what did Bertrand want? How
was one to rid oneself of convention? With dismay Joachim saw the
danger that like Bertrand one might begin to let everything slide if one
began to transgress convention. Certainly in his connection with Ruzena
he had already slipped through convention in the strict sense, but now he
must not go any further, and honour itself demanded that he should
be true to Ruzena! Perhaps Helmuth had vaguely surmised this when
he warned him against returning to the estate. For then Ruzena would be
lost. So he asked abruptly: " What do you think of the state of German
agriculture? " almost hoping that Bertrand, who always had practical
reasons for what he said, would also warn him against taking over the
estate.

" Hard to say, Pasenow, especially for anyone who knows so little
about agriculture as myself. . . . Of course we still have the feudal
prejudice that, as we all live on God's earth, those who cultivate it have
the most stable existence." Bertrand made a slightly disdainful gesture,
and Joachim von Pasenow felt disappointed, yet relieved as well, at the
thought that he belonged to this favoured caste, while Bertrand's insecure
business existence was only, as it were, a preliminary step to a more
stable life. Apparently he regretted after all that he had quitted the
regiment; as an officer in the Guards he could easily have married an

estate. But that was a reflection worthy of his father himself, and Joachim
dismissed it and merely asked whether Bertrand intended to adopt a
settled life later on. No, Bertrand thought he would hardly be able to
do that now: he wasn't a man who could endure living in one place for
very long. And then they talked about Stolpin and the shooting there,
and Joachim invited Bertrand to come down for the shooting in autumn.
And suddenly the door-bell rang: Ruzena! Joachim thought, and he
looked at Bertrand almost with hostility. Bertrand had been sitting there
now for two hours, drinking tea and smoking, and his visit could no
longer, by any stretch, be called a mere visit of condolence. Yet at the
same time Joachim had to admit that it had been himself who had
pointed to the armchair and produced the cigars and induced Bertrand
to stay, although he should have known that Ruzena would be certain to
come. Of course now that the thing had happened there was no turning
back: naturally it would have been more in order if he had consulted
Ruzena first. She would probably feel put out, probably she herself
desired the secrecy which he was now preparing to infringe, perhaps in
her simple goodness she wished to avoid any chance of her disgracing
him—perhaps, indeed, she wasn't quite equal to social occasions; but
he was no longer capable of judging that, for when he tried to call up
her image all that he saw was her face and her loosened hair on the
pillow beside him. He remembered the fragrance of her body, but could
hardly tell any longer how she looked when she was dressed. Well,
after all Bertrand was a civilian, and himself wore his hair too long,
and so it could not matter very much to him. So Joachim said: " Look
here, Bertrand, I'm just having a visit from a nice girl; may I invite
you to have supper with us? " " How romantic! " replied Bertrand; of
course he would be delighted if he was not in the way.

Joachim went out to greet Ruzena and prepare her for the news.
She was visibly disconcerted to find a stranger present. But she was
amiable to Bertrand, and Bertrand was amiable to her. Joachim indeed
was displeased by the assumption of friendliness with which they treated
each other. It was decided that they should dine at home; the valet was
sent out for ham and wine, and Ruzena ran after him; he was to bring
apple-tarts and cream too. She was delighted to be allowed to preside
in the kitchen and make potato-puffs. A little later she called Joachim
out to the kitchen; he thought at first that she only wanted to show
herself in her huge white apron, the cooking-spoon in her hand, and

was preparing to appreciate this touching picture of housewifely loveli-
ness; but she was leaning against the kitchen door sobbing; it was almost
like another occasion when as a little boy he had gone to the great
kitchen to seek his mother, and one of the maids—probably she had just
been given notice—was sobbing so bitterly that he longed to cry with
her, but was restrained by a feeling of shame. " Now you not love me
no more," Ruzena sobbed on his shoulder, and although they kissed
each other more passionately than ever, she would not be comforted.
" Is finished, I know, is finished . . ." she kept on repeating, " but go
back now, must cook." She dried her tears and smiled. But he went
back unwillingly, and it was unwillingly that he thought of Bertrand in
the other room; of course it was childish of her, childish to think that
their love was finished simply because of Bertrand, yet nevertheless it
was real feminine instinct, yes, real feminine instinct, one couldn't call
it anything else, and Joachim felt suddenly dejected. For even though
Bertrand in his cynical way received him with the words, " She's
charming," and awakened in him the grateful pride of King Candaules,
the menacing thought remained unshaken: if he went back to Stolpin
Ruzena would be lost to him, and then it would all be over. If
Bertrand had only dissuaded him at least from having anything to
do with agriculture! Or did Bertrand want—and perhaps even against
his own convictions—to force him into a country life simply to get
him out of Berlin and then win Ruzena, whom in spite of everything
he probably regarded as his legitimate property? But that was
unthinkable.

Ruzena, followed by the valet, entered with the big tray. She had
taken off her apron, and sitting between the two men at the little round
table played the grand lady, and in her sing-song, staccato voice made
conversation with Bertrand, whom she encouraged to talk of his travels.
The two windows were standing open, but in spite of the dark summer
night outside, the soft paraffin lamp over the table reminded Joachim
of winter and Christmas and the security of the little living-rooms
behind the shops. How strange that he should have forgotten all about
the lace handkerchiefs which, in a fit of vague longing, he had bought
for Ruzena that evening! They were still lying in the chest of drawers,
and he would give them to her now if Bertrand were not here and if
she were not listening so intently to those stories about the cotton
plantations and the poor negroes whose fathers were still slaves—yes,

really, actual slaves whom one could sell. What? Were the girls sold
too? Ruzena shuddered and Bertrand laughed, laughed easily and
pleasantly: " Oh, you mustn't be afraid, little slave-girl, nothing will
happen to you." Why did Bertrand say that? Was he hinting at buying
Ruzena or getting her as a gift? Joachim could not but think of the
resemblance between slave and Slav and reflected that all negroes were
alike, so that one could hardly tell one from another, and it seemed to
him again that Bertrand was trying to entangle him in a maze and to
remind him that Ruzena could not be distinguished from her Italian-
Slav brother. Was that why Bertrand had conjured up the picture of
the black hordes? But Bertrand was only smiling at him, and he was
fair, almost as fair as Helmuth, though without the beard, and his hair
was wavy, far too wavy, instead of being brushed stiffly back; and for
a moment everything was confused again and one did not know to whom
Ruzena belonged by rights. If the bullet had found him instead of
his brother, then Helmuth would have been sitting here in his place,
and Helmuth would also have had the strength to protect Elisabeth.
Perhaps Ruzena would have been a little beneath Helmuth; all the
same he himself was nothing more than his brother's deputy. Joachim
was dismayed when this became clear to him, dismayed at the thought
that one individual could deputize for another, that Bertrand should
have a soft little bearded deputy, and that from this standpoint even
his father's ideas were excusable: for why Ruzena in particular, why
himself in particular? why not Elisabeth when it came to that? it was
all indifferent in some way or other, and he understood the feeling of
weariness that had driven Helmuth to his death. Even if Ruzena was
right and their love was nearing its end, yet now suddenly everything
had receded to a great distance in which Ruzena's face and Bertrand's
could scarcely be told from each other. The convention of feeling,
Bertrand had called it.

Ruzena, on the other hand, seemed to have forgotten her gloomy
prophecies. She had felt for Joachim's hand under the table, and when
in panic good breeding, and with a side-glance at Bertrand, he had
found safety for it on the open publicity of the brightly lit tablecloth,
Ruzena seized it again and fondled it; and Joachim, once more happy
in that possessive caress, overcame his shame with a slight effort and
held her hand in his, so that it could be seen quite publicly that they
belonged by right to each other. And besides they were not doing any-

thing wrong; for in the Bible it said that when a brother died without leaving children his wife must not marry a stranger, but must take the brother of her dead husband. Yes, it had been something like that anyway, and it was absurd to think that he could betray Helmuth with a woman. But then Bertrand tapped on his glass and proposed a little toast, and once more one did not know whether he intended it seriously or whether he was joking or whether the few glasses of champagne had been already too much for him, so extraordinarily difficult to understand was his speech; in which he spoke of the German housewife, who was most charming when she was an imitation housewife, for play was the true reality of this life, for which reason art was always more beautiful than nature, peasant costume better at a ball than in a village, and the home of a German soldier complete only when, escaping from its accustomed austerity, although violated, no doubt, by the presence of a traditionless man of business, it was at the same time consecrated by the presence of the loveliest of Bohemian ladies; and so he asked the company to drink to the health of their beautiful hostess. Yes, that was all somewhat obscure and insidious, and one could not rightly tell whether all this play on the idea of *imitation* might not mean much the same as he himself had meant by deputizing; but as Bertrand continued to gaze at Ruzena very kindly in spite of the somewhat ironical expression round his lips, one knew that it was intended as a compliment to her and that one could dismiss all those puzzling thoughts; and the supper finished in a mood of general and pleasant gaiety.

Later they insisted on accompanying Bertrand to his lodgings, partly perhaps because they did not wish it to be too obvious that Ruzena was spending the night with Joachim. Ruzena in the middle, they walked through the quiet streets, all three separately, for Joachim did not dare to offer his arm to her. When Bertrand had disappeared behind the door of his lodgings they looked at each other, and Ruzena asked very seriously and humbly: " Will you see me to the casino? " He noticed the sadness and seriousness in her voice, but he felt in response only a weary indifference, and almost found himself replying as seriously in the affirmative, and could at that moment have said good-bye for ever to her; and if Bertrand had come back to lead her away Joachim could even have borne that. Nevertheless the thought of the casino was unendurable. And ashamed that he needed such a spur, yet almost glad of it too, he took her arm in silence. That night they loved each other more passionately than ever. Nevertheless Joachim forgot this time also to give Ruzena her lace handkerchiefs.

Every day when the little one-horse mail-van returned from the train and drew up at the village post office, a messenger from the estate was already leaning against the counter; true, he was only a private messenger, yet he belonged to the post office and had himself become an official in a sense, perhaps indeed with a superior status to the two actual officials there, not however because of any personal qualifications, even though he might have grown grey in service, but simply because he came from the big house and his dignity was a prescriptive fact which had already existed for many decades, and certainly reached back to the time when there was not yet any State postal service, nothing but a post-chaise that drove infrequently through the village and left the letters at the inn. The great black post-bag whose straps had worn a diagonal stripe across the shoulders of the servant's coat had survived many messengers, and certainly it too must have dated from that long-dead and perhaps happier time; for even the oldest man in the village could remember since his earliest childhood the post-bag hanging on its hook and the messenger leaning against the counter; and by interrogating their memory the old people could count up all the estate messengers who had gaily taken the road with the diagonal stripe on their jackets and were now all resting in the churchyard. So the post-bag was older and more venerable than the new-fashioned post office which had been opened after 1848, that stormy year, older than the hook which, as a mark of respect for the post-bag, or as a final act of official homage to the people at the big house, had been hammered in there when the post office was opened, fixed there also, perhaps, as a reminder that in spite of the violence of progress old customs were not to be forgotten. For in the new post office the old custom of giving preference to the letters for the big house was still maintained, and is probably maintained to this day. So when the coachman came in with the greyish brown mail-bag, and with that disdainful gesture which expresses an ordinary coachman's attitude to mail-bags threw it on the worn counter, the postmaster, who knew better the respect due to human and official customs, unloosed with scarcely concealed solemnity the seal and the fastenings, and arranged the confusion of packets in little piles according to their size, so as to look through them and separate them more expeditiously: then, all this having been accomplished in good order, the first thing that he did was always to put on one side the letters for the big house, and, before attending to anything else, to take a key from his desk and walk over to the post-bag hanging on its hook with its metal-plated mouth silently contemplating this procedure; then, inserting the key in the middle of the metal plate, he threw open the bag, which gaped at him, shamelessly showing its grey-canvas lining, and hurriedly, as if he could no longer endure the sight of that gaping canvas maw, he slipped in the letters and newspapers and also the smaller packets, gave the lower jaw of the bag a little push so that it snapped shut, turned the key again, and put it back in his desk. But now the messenger, who till then had remained a mere spectator, lifted up the heavy post-bag, slung it by its hard, worn strap over his shoulders, took the bigger parcels in his hand, and in this way brought the mail one or two hours sooner to the big house than the postman, who had to traverse the whole village first, could have done; a remarkably expeditious method which ensured that, by means of the messenger and the post-bag, an old tradition was continued, and also the practical needs of the gentry and the servants on the estate well looked after.

Joachim now received news from his home oftener than before; for the most part his father sent him curt accounts of what was happening in a sloping, running hand which reminded one so strongly of his walk that it, too, might actually be called three-legged. Joachim was informed of the visits that his parents had received, the shooting and harvest prospects, also a few particulars about the state of the crops; and generally the letters ended with the sentence: " It would be advisable for you to make preparations as soon as possible for returning here, for it is preferable that you should work yourself in sooner rather than later, and everything takes time.—Your loving Father." Joachim still felt his old dislike for this handwriting, and he read these letters with a more exacerbated inattention than usual, for each admonition that he should quit the service and return to his home was like an attempt to drag him down into a civilian and insecure existence, pretty much, indeed, as if one were to rob him of his uniform and fling him naked into the Alexanderplatz, so that all those strange and busy people could rub shoulders with him. Well, let them call it inertia of feeling;

all the same he wasn't a coward, and he would face calmly the revolver of an opponent, or march out gladly against the traditional enemy, France; but the dangers of a civilian life were of a more obscure and incomprehensible kind. Chaos and disorder everywhere, without a hierarchy, without discipline, and, yes, even without punctuality. When on his way from his flat to the barracks he passed Borsig's machine factory at the start or the finish of the day's work, and saw the workers standing before the factory gates like an exotic, dun-coloured race, much the same as the people of Bohemia, he was aware of their sinister looks, and when one or the other tugged at a black-leather cap in greeting, he never dared to respond, for he was afraid of branding the friendly workmen as turncoats, as men who had come over to his side. For he felt that those who hated him were justified, perhaps partly because he divined that they would hate Bertrand, in spite of his civilian clothes, no less than himself. There was something of that too lurking in Ruzena's aversion to Bertrand. All this was disturbing and confusing, and to Joachim it was as though his ship had sprung a leak which people were urging him to widen. But what seemed completely absurd to him was his father's demand that he should quit the service for Elisabeth's sake; for if there was one thing that could make a man worthy of her it was the distinction of being superior, in outward attire at least, to all the impurity and disorder of life; to rob him of his uniform, therefore, was to degrade Elisabeth. So he pushed aside as an importunate and dangerous exaction all thought of a civilian life or a life at home, yet to avoid flat disobedience to his father he appeared at the station with a bouquet of flowers when Elisabeth and her mother left for their summer stay at Lestow.

The conductor in front of the waiting train stood at attention when he caught sight of Joachim, and there was a silent understanding between the two men, an understanding in the eye of the trusty subordinate that he was to look after the ladies of his superior. And although it was a slight violation of good manners to leave the Baroness alone in her carriage, where she was installed with her maid and her luggage, yet when Elisabeth expressed a wish to walk along the train until the bell rang Joachim felt that it was a friendly mark of distinction. They walked up and down on the firmly trampled soil between the lines, and when they passed the open door of the carriage Joachim did not omit to glance up with a slight bow, while the Baroness smiled down at him.

Elisabeth said how much she was looking forward to being home again, and that she absolutely counted on seeing him often at Lestow during his furlough, which of course he would spend as usual—and this sad year especially—with his parents. She was wearing a short English travelling suit of light grey cloth, and the blue travelling veil which covered her little hat went well with the colour of her costume. It was almost a matter of surprise to him that a creature who always seemed so thoughtful should be able to summon the trifling interest, the frivolous taste, necessary to choose advantageous clothes, particularly as he guessed that the grey of the costume and the blue of the veil had probably been selected to suit the colour of her eyes, which alternated between a serious grey and a merry blue. But it was difficult to put this thought into words, and so Joachim was glad when the bell signalled and the conductor asked the passengers to take their places. Elisabeth put her foot on the foot-board, and by adroitly half-turning her body to continue her conversation with Joachim avoided providing the horrid spectacle of a lady bent forward clambering into her compartment; yet when she reached the top step it could no longer be helped, and she stooped resolutely through the low door. Now Joachim was standing beside the train with his face raised towards her, and the thought of his father whom he had looked up to in the same place not so long ago got entangled so strangely with his glimpse of the tails of Elisabeth's grey jacket and the marriage project which his father had hinted at in such unsavoury terms, that the very name of this girl with the grey-blue eyes and the grey jacket, though he saw her physically above him in the carriage-door, suddenly seemed irrelevant and, as it were, effaced from his memory, submerged horribly and surprisingly in his amazed indignation that there should be men like his father who in their depravity had the brazenness to apportion a pure creature like this for her lifetime to some man who would both humiliate and desecrate her. But clearly as he had recognized her as a woman at the moment of her resolute entry into the carriage, he painfully recognized at the same moment that he could not expect from her the sweetness of his nights with Ruzena, neither their glowing passion, nor their twilight dreaminess, but a serious, perhaps religious submission, unimaginable to him not only because it had to happen without either travelling costume or uniform, but also because the comparison with Ruzena, whom he had rescued from men's degrading lusts, seemed almost a blasphemy. But already the bell had rung a third time, and while he stood on the platform saluting them the ladies fluttered their lace handkerchiefs, until at last only two white dots could be seen, and a thread of tender longing detached itself from Joachim's heart and stretched and span its way to the white dots at the very last moment, before they vanished in the distance.

Saluted stiffly by the porter and the staff, he left the station and stepped out into the Küstrinerplatz. The square looked empty and a little unkempt, gloomy too, although it was still penetrated by the sun, a kind of borrowed sun, while the real one was shining outside on the golden fields. And if this reminded him, in a way very difficult to understand, of Ruzena, yet it was true that Ruzena, full as she was of the sun, yet dark and a little unkempt, was as closely akin to Berlin as Elisabeth was to the fields through which she was travelling now, and to her father's house standing in its park. There was an orderly satisfaction in coming to this conclusion. Nevertheless he was glad that he had rescued Ruzena from her obscure occupation with its false glitter, glad that he was about to free her from the tangle of threads which stretched over this whole city, from this net which he felt everywhere, in the Alexanderplatz and in the dingy machine factory and in the suburb with the little greengrocer's shop, an impenetrable, incomprehensible net of civilian values which was invisible and yet darkened everything. He must deliver Ruzena from these entanglements, for here too he had to prove himself worthy of Elisabeth. But this was only a very vague thought, a thought which moreover he had no wish to make clear, probably because it would have seemed absurd even to himself.

Eduard von Bertrand, who found himself in a position to extend his industrial commitments in Bohemia, suddenly remembered Ruzena in Prague, felt a sort of homesickness for her, and wished he could say something kind to comfort her. And as he did not know her address he wrote to Pasenow, saying that in grateful recollection of their last meeting he hoped to meet him again when he stopped at Berlin on his way back to Hamburg, and added his kindest regards to Ruzena, praising up her beautiful country. Then he took a stroll through the town.

After the evening when Bertrand and Ruzena had met, Pasenow had expected something unexpected and solemn, something perhaps even dreadful, to happen; for example that Bertrand might repay in the same coin the privilege and confidence into which he had been admitted that evening, though an abduction of Ruzena also did not lie beyond the sphere of possibility; for business men were conscienceless. But when neither the one thing nor the other happened, and Bertrand simply departed according to programme, not even sending a line, Joachim actually felt hurt. Then quite unexpectedly came the letter from Prague; he showed it to Ruzena and said hesitatingly: " You seem to have made an impression on Bertrand." Ruzena made a grimace: " Not care. Not like your friend; he's ugly man." Joachim defended Bertrand, saying that he wasn't ugly. " Not know: not like him: says such things," Ruzena decided, " mustn't come again." Joachim was very well pleased by her words, though he felt urgently in need of Bertrand's help, especially when she added: " To-morrow I go to dramatic school." He knew that she would not go unless he conducted her, for of course she couldn't very well, but how could he conduct her there? How did one set about such a thing? Ruzena was quite resolved to " work," and the planning of an occupation for her provided a new subject of conversation with the unusual charm of seriousness, although Joachim felt quite helpless in front of all the questions it threw up. Perhaps he felt that an ordinary vocation would rob her of the exotic grace with which she hovered between two worlds, and cast her back into her native barbarism; and it was indeed for this reason that his imagination stopped at the idea of a part as an actress, an idea with which Ruzena concurred enthusiastically: " You see how famous will I be! You love me then." But the prospect was a distant one, and nothing happened. Bertrand had once spoken of the vegetative indolence in which most people lived; probably it was much the same as that inertia of feeling he had talked about. Yes, if Bertrand were only here: with his knowledge of the world and his practical experience, perhaps he might be of some help. And so when Bertrand reached Berlin he found an urgent invitation from Pasenow awaiting him in reply to his friendly note.

It could be managed, Bertrand said, to the great astonishment of both of them, it could be managed, though they mustn't imagine that the stage provided either an easy career or one with a particularly brilliant future. Of course he had better connections in Hamburg, but he would be glad to do what he could here. And then things developed far more quickly than they had hoped for; in a few days Ruzena was summoned to a voice test which she stood not too badly, and shortly after that she was engaged as a chorus girl. Joachim's suspicion that his friend's sudden readiness to oblige sprang from his designs on Ruzena could not hold out against Bertrand's benevolently indifferent, one might almost say clinical, attitude. It would all have been much clearer if Bertrand had made his efforts on Ruzena's behalf a pretext for openly declaring his love for her. In his heart Joachim was now seriously offended with Bertrand, who had indeed spent three evenings in his and Ruzena's company talking in his usual irrepressible way, but had showed nothing except the old friendly reserve of which Joachim was already sick, and still remained a stranger though he had done more for Ruzena than Joachim himself with his mooning, romantic fancies. All this was very painful. What was this fellow Bertrand after? Now that he was going away, and, as was only fitting, declined all thanks from or on behalf of Ruzena, he was expressing once more the hope that he would soon see Joachim again. Wasn't it hypocritical? And Joachim, astonished at himself, replied: " I'm afraid, Bertrand, that you won't find me in Berlin when you come next, for I'll have to go to Stolpin for a few weeks after the manœuvres. But if you would really like to visit me there I should be awfully glad to see you." And Bertrand accepted.

It had always been a custom of Herr von Pasenow to await the arrival of the post in his study. From time immemorial a place had been kept free on the table beside the pile of sports journals, and on this place the messenger had duly to deposit his bag. And although on most days the contents of the bag were disappointing, often consisting of nothing but two or three journals, yet Herr von Pasenow always took down the key from the antler-rack, where he used to hang it, and opened the lock in the yellow brass plate with the same avid eagerness. And while the messenger, cap in hand, waited in silence, gazing at the floor, Herr von Pasenow took out the letters and packets, sat down with them at his desk, set aside first those for himself and his family, and after carefully scrutinizing the addresses on the others handed them to the messenger to take to the servants they were destined for. Sometimes he had to put a curb upon himself to refrain from opening this or the other letter addressed to one of the maids, for this seemed to him an obvious right, a variation of the *jus primæ noctis* of the master; and the fact that the secrecy of the post should protect menials was a new-fangled notion that went against the grain. Nevertheless there were a few among the servants who actually complained about his external scrutiny of their envelopes, especially as the master did not scruple to inquire afterwards into the contents of the letters and to quiz the maids. This had led already to violent scenes, which had ended however with dismissals, and the rebels no longer objected openly, but either fetched their letters from the post office themselves, or gave secret instructions to the post-master to have them delivered by the postman. Yes, for some time even the deceased young master had been seen daily dismounting from his horse at the post office so as to collect his correspondence; it may have been that he was expecting letters from some lady which he did not want the old man to see, or that he was engaged on business which must remain secret; but the postmaster, who usually was free enough with his information, could not confirm either of those suppositions, as the few letters which Helmuth von Pasenow received gave no clue. Nevertheless the obstinate rumour persisted that, through some machina-tions or other with the post office, the old man had ruined a project of marriage and the happiness of his son. The women on the estate and in the village stuck to this with particular obstinacy, and perhaps they were not so very far wrong, for Helmuth had become more and more indifferent and melancholy, had soon discontinued his rides to the village, and had let his letters be brought again in the great post-bag to the estate and his father's writing-table.

Herr von Pasenow had always had this passion for the post, and so it was not a matter for surprise that as time went on it should become more intense. Now he often so arranged his morning ride or walk as to meet the messenger, and then it was seen that, instead of leaving the key hanging on the antler-rack, he now carried it in his pocket so that he might unlock the bag under the open sky. There he would busily look through the letters but then put them back in the bag again so as not to disturb the household ritual, which was still gone through in the usual way. One morning, however, he actually got as far as the post office where the messenger was still leaning against the counter, and waited until the mail-bag was emptied on the worn table, and then, together with the postmaster, arranged and sorted the letters. When the messenger related this extraordinary incident at the big house the house-maid Agnes, known everywhere for her sharp tongue, remarked: " Now he's beginning to suspect himself." That was of course a saying without any sense in it, and the unshakable obstinacy with which she, more than any of the others, maintained that the master was responsible for his son's death may perhaps be put down as a belated outcome of the resentment which she had nursed for years at being quizzed by the old man about her correspondence while she was still young and buxom.

Yes, Herr von Pasenow had always been queer about the post, and so his behaviour now was nothing to be surprised at. Nor was it a surprising thing that the pastor was invited to supper more often, nor that in his walks Herr von Pasenow now and then actually presented himself at the parsonage. No, there was nothing strange in that, and the pastor regarded it as the fruit of the spiritual comfort he had expended. Only Herr von Pasenow himself knew that it was an inexplicable and mysterious impulse which drove him to the pastor although he could not endure the man, an undefined hope that the voice which was uplifted in the church must needs reveal to him something for which he was waiting, something which, in spite of his fear that it would never be vouchsafed, he was not able even to name to himself. When the pastor brought the conversation round to Helmuth, often Herr von Pasenow would say: " It doesn't matter," and to his own astonishment would change the subject as if he were afraid of the Unknown he was yet longing for. But sometimes there were days when he suffered the Unknown to draw near, and then it was like a game which he had played as a child: someone hid a ring where it could be seen, hanging it perhaps on a chandelier or a key, and when the seeker moved away from it the others shouted " Cold," and when he drew near they said " Warm," or " Hot." And so it was quite natural that once when the pastor began to speak of Helmuth, Herr von Pasenow should say, suddenly and clearly, " Hot, hot! " and almost clap his hands. The pastor agreed politely that it had indeed been very warm that day, and Herr von Pasenow found himself back in his surroundings again. Yet it was strange how close things were to each other: one thought one was in the middle of a childish game, and yet death was already taking a hand. So " Yes, yes, it's warm," said Herr von Pasenow, though he looked as if he were freezing, " yes, in these hot nights the barns easily take fire."

The thought of the heat did not leave him even at supper: " In Berlin it must be terribly hot these days. Joachim hasn't said anything about it, though . . . but then he says so little in his letters in any case." The pastor touched on the strenuous duties of the service. " Service! What service? " asked Herr von Pasenow so sharply that in his confusion the pastor could not think of an answer. The pastor meant of course, Frau von Pasenow put in, that the service did not give Joachim much leisure for writing, especially now when the manœuvres were on. " Well then, he should leave the service," growled Herr von Pasenow. Then he drank several glasses of wine rapidly one after another and declared that he felt better. He filled the pastor's glass: " Drink up, Pastor, drinking warms you, and when you see double you feel less lonely." " The man who has God with him is never lonely, Herr von Pasenow," replied the pastor, and Herr von Pasenow found the reproof tactless. Hadn't he always rendered to God what was God's and to the Emperor, or more correctly the King, what was his due? One son was serving the King and did not write, and the other God had taken to Himself, and the world was empty and cold. Yes, it was easy for the pastor to talk so loftily; his house was full, too full for his circumstances, and now there was another on the way again. It wasn't so difficult to have God with one in these circumstances: he would have liked to tell the pastor that, but he dared not fall out with him, for who would be left then, when nobody wanted to visit him now except . . . then, just when It was becoming visible, the thought broke off and hid itself, and Herr von Pasenow said softly and dreamily: " It must be warm in the byre." Frau von Pasenow looked in dismay at her husband: had he been drinking his wine too fast? But Herr von Pasenow had got up and stood listening near the window; the lamp lighted up only the table, else she must have seen the expression of terrified expectation on his face, which vanished however when the crunching tread of the night watchman became audible on the gravel outside. Herr von Pasenow went to the window, leant out and called: " Jürgen." And when Jürgen's heavy footsteps halted before the window Herr von Pasenow ordered him to keep an eye on the barns. " It's just twelve years since the big barn on the home farm was burned down on a warm night like this." And when Jürgen dutifully remembered and said: " No fear, sir," for Frau von Pasenow too the incident passed again into the accustomed and the ordinary, so that she thought no more of it when Herr von Pasenow said good-night, adding that he had still a letter to write which must go by the morning post. At the door he turned round again: " Tell me, Herr Pastor, why do we have children? You should know: you've had plenty of practice." And he scuttled away tittering, but a little like a dog hobbling on three legs.

Alone with the pastor, Frau von Pasenow said: " I'm glad to see him in better spirits again. Since the departure of our poor Helmuth he's been very downcast."

As August drew towards its end the doors of the theatre opened again. Ruzena now had visiting-cards on which she was designated as an actress, and Joachim would soon have to depart to Upper Franconia for the manœuvres. He was annoyed at Bertrand for having established Ruzena in a profession which in reality was no less disreputable than her work in the Jäger Casino. Of course one could not but put some of the blame on Ruzena herself for allowing herself to be implicated in such a profession, though perhaps still more on her mother for not having brought up her daughter better. But all that he had intended to do to remedy that had been ruined now through Bertrand. Perhaps indeed things were actually worse than before. For in the casino you knew where you were, and everything was plain sailing: the stage, on the other hand, had its own peculiar atmosphere, an atmosphere of homage and bouquets; and nowhere else was it so difficult for a young girl to remain respectable. That was generally admitted. Yes, it only meant a deeper and deeper descent, and Ruzena refused to see this, but instead was actually proud of her new profession and her visiting-cards. With an air of great consequence she recounted green-room gossip and all the scandal of the boards which he had no wish to listen to, and into the twilight of their life together reflections from the glare of the footlights were now perpetually breaking. How could he have ever imagined that he would find his way to her or that she had really belonged to him, she who had been lost from the beginning? He still sought her, but the stage had arisen before him like a menace, and when she eagerly recounted the love affairs of her colleagues, he saw in this a challenge and the firm intention of her awakened ambition to do what they did, saw too that this would mean a return to her former life, which had probably been spent not so very differently: for human beings were always drawn back inevitably to their starting-point. He regretted the shattered bliss of his twilit passion, the lost sweetness of longing which still filled his heart, it was true, and brought tears to his eyes, yet bore within it the presage of an eternal parting.

And now too emerged once more a fancy of which he had thought himself rid for good, and if he felt no compulsion now to seek in Ruzena's face for that of her Italian brother, yet it was engraved there in a perhaps more baffling form, engraved as the indelible countenance of that life from which he had not been able to deliver her. And again his suspicions awoke that it was Bertrand who had suggested this fancy to him, who had engineered it all, and who like Mephistopheles wished to destroy everything, not even sparing Ruzena. And on the top of this the manœuvres were approaching: how would he find Ruzena on his return? Would he ever, indeed, find her again? They promised each other that they would write often, daily; but Ruzena had all sorts of difficulties with her German, and as moreover she was proud of her visiting-cards, and he was unwilling to destroy her childish pleasure, the post often brought him nothing but one of those cards with the hateful inscription "Actress" and the words "Send lots of luv," a word which seemed to desecrate the sweetness of her kisses. Nevertheless he was greatly disturbed when for a few days he received no word from her, although he had to tell himself that his rapid movements during the manœuvres made a delay of the post quite explicable; and he was delighted when presently one of the horrid little cards arrived. And suddenly and without warning, like a memory, there came the thought that Bertrand too was a sort of actor.

Ruzena really longed for Joachim. His letters contained descriptions of his camp life and the evenings in the little villages, where he would feel really happy only "if you, dear, sweet little Ruzena, were beside me." And when he requested her to look at the moon at nine o'clock in the evening precisely, so that their glances might meet up there, she ran to the stage door during the interval, and though the interval did not come until half-past nine she gazed up dutifully at the sky. To her it seemed that that early spring afternoon in the rain still held her fast and paralysed something in her; the flood-tide which had submerged her then was only gradually receding, and although the girl's will was not strong enough and she had besides no resources out of which to erect dams to hold the waters, yet the air which she breathed in and out was still permeated with a soft humidity. True, she envied those colleagues who received bouquets at their dressing-room doors, but she envied them simply for Joachim's sake, since he ought to have had a celebrated diva as a lover. And although a woman in love often carries about with her that suggestion of the erotic which to many men is so delicately attractive, the men who laid their homage before the actresses were of a different type, and not likely to recognize such gentle indications.

So it happened that Ruzena was more inviolate than ever when she received Joachim on his return to Berlin after the manœuvres, and she looked on this as a victory, a victory on which, she nevertheless knew, defeat would follow; but she did not want to acknowledge this and stifled the knowledge under embraces.

Ever since the train had left the station and she had waved good-bye with her lace handkerchief, Elisabeth had been trying to make clear to herself whether she loved Joachim. It was an almost joyful ground for reassurance that the feeling which she hopefully designated as love should have such a very unassuming and civilized appearance; one had actually to search one's mind to discern it, for it was so faint and thin that only against a background of silvery ennui did it become visible. But now that she drew nearer and nearer to her home, and her ennui was changed into mounting impatience, the soft contours of the image faded; and when the Baron met them at the station with the new pair of horses, and also when they reached Lestow, and the green tree-tops of the peaceful park appeared, enclosed by the quiet massiveness of the gate—the first surprise, for to right and left two new lodges had been erected, so that the ladies uttered cries of lively astonishment, which were but the prelude, however, to the many they would utter in the next few days—it was only too comprehensible that Elisabeth should no longer think of love at all. For the Baron had once more employed the absence of his two ladies, or as he sometimes called them to Elisabeth's gratified pride, his two wives, to carry out countless improvements and embellishments to the house, alterations which delighted them and gained for him many words of praise and tender gratitude. They had indeed every cause to be proud of their artistic papa; although he had no exaggerated respect for the existing order and had already adorned the old manor-house with all sorts of additions, he yet had an eye for more than mere architecture; for he never forgot that there was always a free space on a wall where a new picture would look well, a corner which could be set off by a massive vase, or a sideboard which could be furnished with a gold-embroidered velvet cloth: and he was the man to carry out his ideas. Since their marriage the Baron and the Baroness had become collectors, and the continual further perfecting of their home had grown for them into a sort of perpetuation of their first engagement, and had remained so even after the arrival of their daughter. As time went on Elisabeth indeed became conscious that her parents' passion for emphasizing the various family festivals of the year, for celebrating the birthdays and continually thinking out new surprises, had a deeper significance and was connected in a profound way, difficult to fathom, with their delight, indeed one might almost call it their greed, in surrounding themselves continuously with new things. Certainly Elisabeth did not know that every collector hopes with the never-attained, never-attainable and yet inexorably striven-for absolute completeness of his collection to pass beyond the assembled things themselves, to pass over into infinity, and, entirely subsumed in his collection, to attain his own consummation and the suspension of death. Elisabeth did not know this, but surrounded by all those beautiful dead things gathered together and piled up around her, surrounded by all those beautiful pictures, she divined nevertheless that the pictures were hung up as though to strengthen the walls, and that all those dead things were put there to cover, perhaps also to conceal and guard, something intensely living; something with which she herself was so intimately bound that she could not but feel at times when a new picture was brought in that it was a little brother or sister; something which begged to be cherished and was cherished by her parents as though their common life together depended upon it. She divined the fear behind all this, fear that sought to drown in festivals the monotony of every day which is the outward sign of growing old, fear that was always reassuring itself—by perpetual fresh surprises—that they were all alive and in the flesh and definitively together, and that their circle was closed for ever. And just as the Baron was always adding new stretches of his property to the park, whose dark and thickly grown copses were now surrounded on almost every side by wide borders of tender light-green young wood, so it seemed to Elisabeth that with almost feminine solicitude he wished to turn all their life into an ever more spacious enclosed park full of pleasant resting-places, and that he would reach his goal and be free of all apprehension only when the park had spread over the whole earth, attaining its object of becoming a park in which Elisabeth might walk about for ever. It is true that occasionally something in her rebelled against this gentle and inescapable compulsion, but as her resistance was hardly ever very definite, it dissolved into the sunny contours of the hills that lay in the distance beyond the seclusion of the park.

" Oh! " cried the Baroness as they stood admiring the new pergola in

the rosarium. " Oh, how pretty! It might have been set up for a bride."
She smiled at Elisabeth, and the Baron smiled too, but in their eyes
could be read their fear of the ineluctable menace, their helplessness,
their fore-knowledge of a coming infidelity and treachery which nevertheless they forgave in advance, for they too had sinned. How terrible
it was that the mere thought of her future marriage should seem already
to oppress her parents. And Elisabeth put all thoughts of marriage
completely out of her mind, so completely indeed that it almost seemed
to her that she could listen without compunction to her parents when,
as a sort of concession to her presumable destiny to fall in love and at
the same time as a sort of act of recognition which raised her to their
own level, giving her almost the status of a sister, they talked of a possible
match. Perhaps that was why, when her mother pressed a tender kiss
on her cheek, Elisabeth could not help thinking of her Aunt Brigitte's
wedding day, could not help feeling that this kiss too was a kiss of
farewell: for just so had her mother kissed Aunt Brigitte, kissed her with
tears, with tears although she had declared that she was very happy
and was delighted with her new young brother-in-law. But of course
that was all long past now; it was childish to muse on it, and going
between her parents Elisabeth put her arms round their shoulders and
walked with them to the pergola, where they sat down. The rose-beds,
threaded with narrow, symmetrically winding paths, blazed with all their
hues and were full of fragrance, yet all the shadows were not yet dispersed, and the Baron said, pointing sadly towards one bed: " I've tried
to set some Manettis there, but I'm afraid our climate is too rough for
them," and as if he wished to bribe his daughter with the promise, he
added: " but if it succeeds and they grow all right, then they'll belong
to Elisabeth." Elisabeth felt the pressure of his hand, and it was almost
like an intimation that there was something that could never be clutched
firmly enough, something that might almost be time itself, something
compressed and twisted like a watch-spring and that was threatening
to uncoil, to wind out between their fingers, becoming longer and longer,
an alarming, long, thin white band which presently would begin to
creep, seeking to twine round her like an evil snake, until she became
fat and old and hideous. Perhaps her mother too was feeling this, for
she said: " When the child leaves us one day we'll sit out here by ourselves." And, conscious of her guilt, Elisabeth said: " But I'm going to
stay with you always," said it with a feeling of shame, for she did not

believe it herself, and yet it sounded like the renewal of an old vow.
" In any case, I can't see why she shouldn't stay here with her husband
when that happens," the Baroness went on. But her father warded the
subject off: " It's a long time still before that can happen." And Elisabeth
could not help once more thinking of Aunt Brigitte, who passed her days
in Würbendorf, and had grown fat, and squabbled with her children,
and had now so little in common with the beloved figure of former days
that one could not imagine she had ever existed and was almost ashamed
of the happiness that she had once given one. And yet Würbendorf
was a gayer and friendlier place than Stolpin, and everybody had been
delighted to get a new young relation in Uncle Albert. It may have been
that it was not really Aunt Brigitte whom she had loved so much, and
that it was simply the admission of a new relation into the circle that
had roused such exciting and dear emotions. For if one were related to
everybody the world would be like a well-kept park, and to acquire a
new relation would be like planting a new variety of rose in the garden.
Infidelity and treachery would then turn to lighter offences; she had
surely divined that already at the time when she had been so glad about
Uncle Albert; and in the ocean of injustice surrounding them it was
perhaps on this little islet of forgiveness that her parents now sought
refuge when they spoke of her possible marriage as of an auspicious fate.
But the Baroness had not yet given up her idea; and as life consists of
compromises she said: " Besides, our little house in the west end will
always be ready for them." But Elisabeth's hand still lay in her father's
and felt its pressure, and Elisabeth would not hear of compromise.
"No; I'll stay with you," she repeated almost defiantly, and she remembered how bitterly she had resented as a child being banished from her
parents' bedroom and not being allowed to watch over their breathing;
still, though the Baroness had always had a weakness for talking about
death, which she said often came upon people in their sleep, and though
she had alarmed Elisabeth and her husband with such sayings, yet there
had been the morning's joyful surprise that the night had not parted
them for ever, a surprise which grew into a daily renewed wild longing
that they should take one another by the hand and hold on so fast that
they could never be torn asunder. So they sat now in the pergola, which
was filled with the roses' scent; Elisabeth's little dog came scampering
up and greeted her as though he had found her for eternity, and put
his paws on her knees. The stems of the rose-trees stood up stiff and

hard against the green wall of the garden and the clear blue sky. Never would she be able to greet a stranger, no matter how nearly related he was to her, with the same intense joy in the morning; never would she think of his birthday with such passionate and almost pious devotion as of that of her father; never would she surround him with that incomprehensible and yet sublime anxiety which was love. And having recognized this she now smiled affectionately at her parents and stroked the head of her little dog Bello, which with apprehensively loving eyes gazed up devotedly at her.

Later she began to feel bored, and the faint feeling of resistance too returned once more. Then it was not unpleasant to think of Joachim, and she remembered his slim figure as he had stood bowing slightly, in his long angular officer's coat, on the platform. But his image got strangely and inextricably entangled with that of her young Aunt Brigitte, and by this time she could not make out whether it was Joachim who was going to marry Brigitte, or she herself who was going to wed the young Uncle Albert of her childhood. And although she knew that love was not what it was represented to be in operas and romances, yet this much was certain, that she could think of Joachim without apprehension; indeed, even when she tried to picture to herself that the departing train might have caught his sword and flung him under the wheels, the picture filled her with horror certainly, but not with that sweet sorrow and dread, that trembling anxiety, which bound her to the lives of her parents. When she recognized this it was as though she had renounced something, and yet there was a sort of melancholy relief in it. Nevertheless she resolved to ask Joachim some time what was his birthday.

Joachim had returned to Stolpin. While he was still on his way from the station, just after he had passed through the village and reached the first fields on the estate, a new feeling had unexpectedly risen in him: he tried to find words for it and found them: my property. When he got down at the manor-house he was furnished with a new sentiment of home.

Now he was with his father and mother, and if their company had been restricted to the breakfast-hour it would have been very tolerable; it was a pleasure to sit out under the great lime-trees, the cool sunny garden stretching before him; and the rich yellow butter, the honey and

the big basket of fruit, were all in pleasing contrast to his hurried break-
fasts in the army. But already the midday and evening meals were an
affliction; the more the day advanced the more their companionship
weighed on all three, and if in the mornings the old people felt happy
at the reappearance of their absent son, and, it may be, daily expected
something beautiful and life-giving from him, yet the day—punctuated
by the meals—turned stage by stage into a disappointment, and towards
late afternoon Joachim's presence had grown almost into an intensification of their mutual unendurable loneliness; indeed even the prospect
of the post, the one ray of light in the monotony of the day, was made
poorer by their son's presence, and if the old man in spite of this still
went out every morning to meet the messenger, it was almost an act
of despair, was almost like a veiled appeal to Joachim to go away for
heaven's sake and send a few letters. And yet Herr von Pasenow himself
seemed to know he was awaiting something quite different from Joachim's
letters, and that the messenger for whom he was looking was not the
messenger with the letter-bag.

Joachim made a few faint attempts to become more intimate with
his parents. He went to see his father in the room decorated with the
antlers, and inquired about the harvest and the shooting, and hoped
perhaps that the old man might be gratified by this indirect attempt to
follow his request to " work himself in." But either his father had forgotten his request, or did not himself know very much about what was
happening on the estate; for he gave only reluctant or evasive responses
and once actually said: " You needn't trouble yourself about that so
early in the day," and Joachim, though relieved from a burdensome
obligation, could not help thinking again of the time when he had been
sent to the cadet school and robbed for the first time of his home. But
now he had returned and was awaiting a guest of his own. It was a
pleasant sensation, and though it hid within it a good deal of hostility
towards his father, Joachim was not aware of this; indeed he hoped
that his parents would be delighted with this interruption of their growing
boredom and look forward with the same impatience as himself to
Bertrand's arrival. He submitted to his father's going through his correspondence, and when finally the old man handed it over to him with the
words: " Unfortunately there still seems to be no news of your friend,
that is, if he's coming at all," Joachim refused to read anything but
regret into the sentence, although it had a malicious ring. His irritation

did not come to a head until once he saw a letter from Ruzena in his
father's hands. Yet the old man made no comment, but only stuck his
monocle in his eye and observed: " Really, you must pay the Baddensens
a visit soon; it's high time you did." Well, that might be taken as sarcasm,
or it might not: but in any case it was sufficient to spoil so completely
Joachim's pleasure at the prospect of seeing Elisabeth that he kept
putting off the visit again and again; and though her image and her
fluttering handkerchief had faithfully accompanied him till now, he felt
himself filled more and more urgently with the wish, which he pictured
in his imagination, that Eduard von Bertrand should be sitting beside
him on the seat of the carriage when he drew up before the front door
at Lestow.

But that did not happen, at least to begin with, for one day Elisabeth
and her mother paid a belated visit of condolence to Herr and Frau
von Pasenow. Elisabeth felt disappointed, and yet in some way relieved,
that Joachim was not there when they arrived; she felt also a little
offended. They sat in the smaller drawing-room, and the ladies learned
from Herr von Pasenow that Helmuth had died for the honour of his
name. Elisabeth involuntarily remembered that perhaps in no very long
time she too would bear this name for which someone had fallen, and
with an access of pride and pleased astonishment she realized that Herr
and Frau von Pasenow would then become new relations. They talked
about the melancholy occurrence, and Herr von Pasenow said: " That's
how it is when one has sons; they die for honour or for their king and
country—it's stupid having sons," he added sharply and challengingly.
" Oh, but daughters get married, and before you know they're away,"
responded the Baroness with an almost meaning smile, " and we old
people are always left behind alone." Herr von Pasenow did not reply,
as would have been polite, that the Baroness could not by any means
be regarded as old, but became quite still, staring fixedly in front of
him, and after a short silence said: " Yes, we're left behind alone, left
behind alone," and after he had reflected a little longer with obvious
concentration, " and we die alone." " But, Herr von Pasenow, we have
no need to think of dying yet! " the Baroness brought out in a dutifully
cheerful voice. " Oh, we needn't think of that for a long time yet: the
rain brings sunshine, my dear Herr von Pasenow; you must always try
to remember that." Herr von Pasenow found his way back to reality
and became again the cavalier: " Provided that the sunshine comes

to us in your person, Baroness," he said, and without waiting for the Baroness's flattered response he went on: " yet how strange things are now . . . the house is empty, and even the post brings nothing. I've written Joachim, but I don't hear much from him; he's at the manœuvres." Frau von Pasenow turned in dismay to her husband: " But . . . but, you know Joachim is here." A venomous glance was her punishment for this correction. " Well, did he write, yes or no? And where is he now? " and there would have been a mild squabble if the canary in its cage had not released its quiver of golden notes. They gathered round it as round a fountain and for a few moments forgot everything else: it was as though this slender golden thread of sound, rising and falling, were winding itself round them and linking them in that unity on which the comfort of their living and dying was established; it was as though this thread which wavered up and filled their being, and yet curved and wound back again to its source, suspended their speech, perhaps because it was a thin, golden ornament in space, perhaps because it brought to their minds for a few moments that they belonged to each other, and lifted them out of the dreadful stillness whose re-verberations rise like an impenetrable wall of deafening silence between human being and human being, a wall through which the human voice cannot penetrate, so that it has to falter and die. But now that the canary was singing not even Herr von Pasenow himself could hear that dreadful stillness, and they all had a feeling of warmth when Frau von Pasenow said: " But now we must have some coffee." And when they went through the big drawing-room, whose curtains were drawn to keep out the afternoon sun, none of them remembered that Helmuth had lain there on his bier.

Then Joachim arrived and Elisabeth had a second disappointment, for her memory held an image in uniform, and now he was dressed in hunting kit. They were distant and embarrassed towards each other, and even when with the others they had returned to the drawing-room, and Elisabeth was standing before the canary's cage amusing herself by pushing a finger through the wires and seeing the little creature pecking wrathfully at it, even while she was deciding that in her own drawing-room—if she ever should marry—she would always have a little yellow bird such as this one, even then she could no longer associate Joachim with the idea of marriage. Yet that was actually rather pleasant and reassuring and made it easier for her as she said good-bye to arrange that they should at an early date go out riding together. Before that, of course, he must pay them a call.

Bertrand had at last found time to comply with Pasenow's invitation, and on the way down stepped out of the evening train for a two days' stay in Berlin. Naturally enough he wanted to have news of Ruzena; so he made straight for the theatre and sent his name, along with a bouquet of flowers, to her dressing-room. Ruzena was delighted when she got his card, delighted too with the flowers, and it flattered her that Bertrand should be waiting for her at the stage door at the end of the performance: " Well, little Ruzena, how are you getting on? " And Ruzena replied in one breath that she was getting on splendidly, splendidly, oh, really very badly, because she longed so much for Joachim; but now of course she felt all right because she was so delighted that Bertrand had called for her, for he was such an intimate friend of Joachim's. But when they were sitting opposite each other in the restaurant, having talked a great deal about Joachim, Ruzena, as often happened with her, became suddenly sad: " Now you go to Joachim and I have stay here: world is unjust." " Of course world is unjust, and far worse than you have any conception of, little Ruzena "—it seemed to both of them natural that he should address her as " du "—" and it was partly my anxiety about you that brought me here." " What you mean by that? " " Well, I don't like your being in this stage business." " Why? It very nice." " I was too hasty in giving in to you both . . . just because you were romantic and had formed God knows what picture of the stage." " I not understand what you mean." " Well, never mind, but it's out of the question for you to stay in it. What can it lead to finally? What is to become of you, child? Someone must look after you, and that can't be done with romantic notions." Ruzena replied stiffly and on her dignity that she could quite well look after herself, and Joachim could just go if he wanted to be rid of her, he could just go, " and you bad man, to come here just to speak ill of friend "; then she cried and gave Bertrand hostile looks through her tears. He found it difficult to reassure her, for she persisted that he was a bad man and a bad friend who wanted to spoil her happy evening. And all at once she grew very pale and fixed terrified eyes upon him: " He sent you to say he finish with me: all over! " " But, Ruzena! " " No, you can say ten time no, I know it; oh, you bad, both two of you. You brought me here, so to shame me."

Bertrand saw that by rational means nothing could be done; yet in her untutored suspicions there was perhaps a divination of the real state of affairs and its hopelessness. She looked as desperate as a little animal that does not know where to turn. And yet perhaps it would be good for her to regard the future more soberly. So he merely shook his head and replied: " Tell me, child, couldn't you go back to your own home and stay there while Joachim is away? " All that she could draw from this was that she was going to be sent away. " But, Ruzena, who wants to send you away? Only it would be much better for you to be with your people than alone here in Berlin in this silly stage life. . . ." She would not let him finish: " I have nobody, all bad to me . . . I have nobody, and you want send me away." " But be reasonable, Ruzena: when Pasenow is in Berlin again you can come back too." Ruzena would not listen any more to him and said she was going. But he did not want to let her go like that, and considered how he could turn her thoughts in a happier direction; at last he hit upon the idea that they should write Joachim a letter between them. Ruzena agreed at once; so he had notepaper brought and wrote: " In warm remembrance of a happy evening with you, kindest greetings from Bertrand," and she added: " And lots of luv from Ruzena." She pressed a kiss on the letter, but she could not restrain her tears. " All over," she repeated again and asked him to take her home. Bertrand gave in. But so that he might not have to leave her too soon to her melancholy fancies he suggested that they should go on foot. To calm her—for words were useless —he took her hand like a kind and skilful doctor; she snuggled close to him gratefully and as if seeking support and with a faint pressure left her hand in his. She's just a little animal, thought Bertrand, and hoping to cheer her he said: " Yes, Ruzena, am I not a bad friend and an enemy of yours? " But she did not reply. A slight but tender irritation at her confused thinking arose in him and extended to take in Joachim too, whom he held responsible for Ruzena and her fate, and who yet seemed no less confused than the girl herself. It may have been because he could feel the warmth of her body that, at any rate for the space of a moment, he had the malicious thought that Joachim deserved to be betrayed with Ruzena: but he did not entertain this seriously and soon found again the affectionate good will which he had always cherished for Joachim. To him Joachim and Ruzena seemed creatures who lived only with a small fraction of their being in the time to which they

belonged, the age to which their years entitled them; and the greater
part of them was somewhere else, perhaps on another star or in another
century, or perhaps simply in their childhood. Bertrand was struck by
the fact that the world was full of people belonging to different centuries,
who had to live together, and were even contemporaries; that accounted
perhaps for their instability and their difficulty in understanding one
another rationally; the extraordinary thing was that, nevertheless, there
was a kind of human solidarity and an understanding that bridged the
years. Probably Joachim, too, only needed to have his hand stroked.
What should and what could he talk to him about? What object was
there really in this visit to Stolpin? Bertrand felt irritated, but then he
remembered that he would have to talk to Joachim of Ruzena's future;
that gave a rational meaning to the journey and the waste of time,
and once more restored to good spirits he squeezed Ruzena's hand.

They said good-night before her door; then they stood facing each
other dumbly for a few moments, and it looked as though Ruzena were
still expecting something. Bertrand smiled and before she could give him
her mouth kissed her somewhat avuncularly on the cheek. She touched
his hand lightly and was about to slip away, but he kept her for a moment
in the doorway: " Well, Ruzena, I'm leaving to-morrow morning. What
message am I to give to Joachim? " " Nothing," she replied quickly
and crossly, but then she reflected: " You bad, but I come to station."
" Good-night, Ruzena," said Bertrand, and again the slight feeling of
exasperation rose in him, but as he could still feel on his lips the downy
softness of her cheek he continued walking to and fro in the dark street,
gazing up at the block and waiting for a light to appear behind one
of the windows. But either her light had been burning before or her room
looked out on the back yard—Joachim might surely have got her better
lodgings—at any rate Bertrand waited in vain, and after he had regarded
the block for some time, he decided that he had done quite enough for
the cause of romanticism, lit a cigar and went home.

While the reception-rooms were provided with parquet-flooring, the
guest-rooms on the first floor had merely polished boards, huge planks
of soft white wood separated from each other by somewhat darker
connecting boards. The trunks from which those planks were once cut
must have been gigantic ones, and although the wood was rather soft,
yet their size and uniformity witnessed to the opulence of the man who

had had them laid here. The joinings between the planks and the boards were closely fitted, and where they had widened on account of the shrinking of the wood they were so neatly plugged with chips that one scarcely noticed it. The furniture had obviously been made by the village carpenter and probably dated from the time when Napoleon's armies had passed through the vicinity; at least it forced one to think of that time, remotely reminding one of that style which is usually called Empire; however, it may have belonged to a slightly earlier or later period, for it diverged with all sorts of bulging lines from the severity of that norm. Here, for instance, was a wardrobe whose mirrored front was violently divided in two by a vertical strip of wood, and there were chests of drawers which, by possessing too many or too few shelves, offended against the laws of pure symmetry. Yet even although these furnishings were ranged against the walls almost without plan, even although the bed was stationed in the most inconvenient way between two doors, and the great white-tiled stove in the corner was squeezed between two cupboards, yet the spacious room had a comfortable and easy look, very pleasant when the sun shone through the white curtains, and the window, with its cross-bars, was mirrored on the glittering polish of the furniture. At such moments, indeed, it could actually happen that the great crucifix which hung on the wall over the bed no longer seemed a mere ornament or a customary article of furniture, but became once more what it had originally been when it was brought here: an admonition and reminder to the guest, warning him that he was in a Christian household, in a house which, it was true, provided in hosts of ways for his bodily comfort and from which he could ride out to the hunt in a merry company and return to devote himself to a hearty supper with abundance of strong wines, a house too where the roughest of practical jokes was permitted him, and where, at the time when the furniture in this room was joinered, an eye was closed if he should take a fancy to one of the maids; but a house nevertheless where it was considered inevitable that the guest, no matter how heavy he might feel after his wine, would have on retiring a desire to remember his soul and to repent of his sins. And it was in accordance with this essentially austere way of thought that over the sofa covered with green repp should be hung a sober and austere steel-engraving which in many of the guests' minds awakened thoughts of Queen Luise, for it represented a stately lady in antique robes—*La Mère des Gracches* was the title of the picture

—and not only did this costume remind them of the Queen, but the altar towards which she was lifting her arms also suggested the altar of the Fatherland. Certainly the majority of the huntsmen who had slept in this room had led a worldly life, seizing advantage and enjoyment wherever they offered, not scrupling to screw from the dealers the most they could for their grain and their pigs, devoted to a savage pastime in which God's creatures were shot down barbarously in heaps, many of them, too, filled with lust for women; but insolently as they claimed the arrogant and sinful life they led as an obvious right and privilege granted by Heaven, they were prepared to sacrifice it at any moment for the honour of the Fatherland or the glory of God, and even if the opportunity should never arise, yet this readiness to regard life as something secondary and scarcely worth considering was so potent that its sinfulness hardly counted for anything in the balance. And they did not feel that they were sinful when in the morning mist they strode through the faintly crackling undergrowth, or when at evening they climbed a steep, narrow ladder to a look-out perch, and gazed across bush and clearing, where the midges still wove their dances, to the edge of the wood. Then when the moist fragrance of grass and tree rose up to them and along the dry bulwark of the perch an ant came running and vanished in the bark, then sometimes in their souls, though they were pragmatic fellows with their feet firmly planted on the earth, something awoke that rang like music, and the lives they had lived and had still to live were concentrated so intensely into one moment that they could still feel the touch of their mother's hand on their hair as if for eternity, while another shape already stood before them, separated from them no longer by any span of time, any span of space, the shape which they did not fear: Death. Then all the woods around might turn for them into the wood of the Cross, for nowhere do the magical and the earthly lie closer together than in the heart of the hunter, and when the buck appears on the border of the clearing, then the illumination is bodily present and life seems to be timeless, evanescent and eternal, held in one's closed hand, so that the shot which kills a strange life is like a symbol of the need to save one's own life in the arms of grace. Always the hunter goes out to find the Cross in the antlers of the deer, and for that illumination the price even of death seems to him not too high. And so, too, when after his abundant supper, he returns to his room, he can presume to lift his eyes again to the crucifix, and, though from afar off, to think of the eternity in which his life is embedded. And perhaps in front of that eternity even the cleanliness of his body weighs no more in the balance than the sinfulness of his earthly life: on the wash-table stands a basin whose smallness is in ludicrous contrast to the size of the hunter and the customary dimensions of his life, and the jug, too, holds far less water than the wine he is accustomed to drink. Even the small commode beside the bed, which in the guise of a cupboard gives hospitality to a night-vessel, merely ratifies the inadequate proportions of the rest. The hunter employs it and flings himself on the groaning bed.

In this chamber, admirably suited to the needs of hunters for generations past, Bertrand was installed during his stay at Stolpin.

Among the remarkable memories which Bertrand brought back with him from his stay at Stolpin his picture of old Herr von Pasenow was not the least strange. On his very first day, immediately after breakfast, he was invited by the old gentleman to accompany him on his walk and be shown over the estate. It was a dull, thundery morning; the air was motionless, but the stillness was broken by the muffled thud of the flails coming from the direction of the two threshing-floors. Herr von Pasenow seemed to find pleasure in the rhythm; several times he remained standing and kept time with his stick. Then he asked: " Would you like to see the byres? " and set off towards the long, low sheds; but in the middle of the yard he stopped, shaking his head: " No use, the cows are out grazing." Bertrand inquired politely what breeds they were; Herr von Pasenow first gazed at him as though he did not understand the question, then said with a shrug of the shoulders " It doesn't matter," and led his guest out through the gate: all round the little hollow in which lay the farm hills broadened in field after field, and everywhere the harvest work was in progress. " It all belongs to the estate," said Herr von Pasenow, making a proud circular sweep with his stick; then his uplifted arm with the stick remained motionlessly fixed in one direction; Bertrand followed it with his eyes and saw the village church tower rising behind a hill. " That's where the post office is," Herr von Pasenow confided to him, making straight for the village. The heat was oppressive; the dull thudding of the flails fell gradually into silence behind them, and only the hissing of the scythes, the sound of blades being sharpened, and the rustling of the falling grain still hung in the air. Herr von Pasenow came to a stop: "Are you sometimes afraid too?" Bertrand was startled, but felt sympathetically touched by this very human question: "Me? Oh, often!" Herr von Pasenow grew interested and came nearer: "When are you afraid? When everything is still?" Bertrand saw that there was something wrong here: "No, stillness is sometimes wonderful: I simply love this stillness over the fields." Herr von Pasenow seemed put out and annoyed: "You don't understand. . . ." After a pause he began again: "Have you any children?" "To the best of my knowledge, no, Herr von Pasenow." "Well, then." Herr von Pasenow looked at his watch and peered into the distance; he shook his head: "Incomprehensible," he said to himself, then to Bertrand: "Well, then *when* are you afraid?"— yet he did not wait for an answer, but looked again at his watch: "But he should have been here by now." Then he looked Bertrand full in the face: "Will you write to me sometimes when you're on your travels?" Bertrand said yes; he would be glad to do so, and Herr von Pasenow seemed greatly pleased. "Yes, do write to me, I'm interested, I'm interested in lots of things . . . write and tell me too when you're afraid . . . but he isn't here yet; you see nobody writes to me, not even my sons. . . ." Then far away a man with a black bag became visible. "There he is!" Herr von Pasenow set off at a brisk pace, stick and legs going together, and as soon as the man was within hearing distance he screamed at him: "Where have you been idling all this time? This is the last time that you'll go for the post . . . you're dismissed, do you hear? you're dismissed!" He had grown red and waved his stick in the man's face; while the latter, obviously used to such encounters, calmly took the bag from his shoulder and handed it to his master, who almost docilely drew the key from his waistcoat-pocket and with trembling fingers turned it in the lock. With a trembling hand he dived into the post-bag, but when he drew out only a few journals it looked as if his fit of rage were about to repeat itself, for he held his mail speechlessly under the messenger's nose. But thereupon he evidently recollected the presence of his guest, for he showed the journals to Bertrand: "Here, you can see for yourself," he grumbled and put them back in the bag, locked it, and said as they walked on again: "I'll have to go and live in the town this year, I'm afraid: it's too quiet for me here."

They had just reached the village when the first drops of the thunder shower fell, and Herr von Pasenow proposed that they should seek refuge in the pastor's house until it passed over. " You'll have to meet him in any case," he added. He was furious on learning that the pastor was not at home, and when the lady of the house said that her husband was at the school he broke out: " You seem to think too that you can tell an old man any story you like, but I'm not so old as not to know that this is the school holidays." Yes, but she hadn't meant that the pastor was teaching in the school, and besides he would be back in a minute. " Taradiddles," grumbled Herr von Pasenow, but the lady refused to be daunted and asked the gentlemen to sit down and she would get them a glass of wine. When she had left the room Herr von Pasenow leant over to Bertrand: " He always tries to avoid me, for he knows that I see through him." " See through what, Herr von Pasenow?" " Why, that he's a thoroughly ignorant and incapable pastor, of course. But unfortunately I must keep on good terms with him all the same. Here in the country you're thrown on the mercy of everyone and . . ." he hesitated, and added more softly: " and besides, he's in charge of the graves." The pastor came in and Bertrand was introduced to him as a friend of Joachim's. " Yes, one comes and the other goes," said Herr von Pasenow dreamily, and they did not know whether this indirect reference to poor Helmuth was intended as a compliment or an insult to Bertrand. " Yes, and this is our theologian," he went on with his introduction, while the theologian smiled awkwardly. The Frau Pastor brought in the wine and a few slices of cold ham, and Herr von Pasenow emptied his glass hastily. While the others were still sitting round the table he went and stood at the window, tapped on the panes the rhythm of the threshing flails, and stared at the clouds as though he were impatient to get away. Into the halting phrases of the conversation he threw from the window: " Tell me, Herr von Bertrand, have you ever in your life met a learned theologian who knew nothing about the next world? " " Herr von Pasenow is pleased to have his joke with me," said the abashed pastor. " Be so good then as to tell me yourself in what respect the priest of God is distinguished from us ordinary people if he has no connection with the next world? " Herr von Pasenow had turned round and now stared angrily and sharply through his monocle at the pastor. " And if he has learned anything about it, which I permit myself to doubt, what right has he to conceal it from us? . . . to conceal it from me? " He became somewhat more placable, " from me . . . on his own admission a sorely tried father." The pastor replied softly:

" God alone can send you a message, Herr von Pasenow; please believe me when I say that." Herr von Pasenow shrugged his shoulders: " Oh, I believe it . . . I believe it, take my word for that." After a pause, turning to the window with another shrug he said: " It doesn't matter," and glanced, once more drumming on the panes, along the street. The rain was falling more slowly, and Herr von Pasenow gave the word: " Now we can go." As he left he shook the pastor's hand: " And don't forget to call on us . . . for supper to-night, what? Our young friend will be there too." Then they went. There were pools in the village street, but on the fields the soil was almost dry again, the rain had hardly served to efface the cracks in the ground. The sky was still covered by a faint white veil, but the scorching sun, which would soon break through, could already be felt. Herr von Pasenow was silent and did not make any response to Bertrand's conversation. But once he stopped and said solemnly with his stick uplifted: " You must be very much on your guard with these learned divines. Keep that in mind."

On the following days these morning walks were repeated, and occasionally Joachim joined in them. But when Joachim was there the old man was morose and silent and even gave up his attempts to discover what Bertrand's fears were. Indirectly and tentatively as he usually framed his questions, he now remained completely silent about them. But Joachim too was silent. For he too did not dare to ask Bertrand the questions he wished to have answered, and Bertrand remained obstinately in possession of his revelations. In this way the three of them wandered over the fields, and both father and son took it ill of Bertrand that he should disappoint their eager expectations. But Bertrand had the greatest difficulty in keeping a conversation going.

If at first Joachim had postponed his visit to Lestow because he had a fixed picture of arriving there with Bertrand, so now the slight annoyance which he felt against Bertrand was perhaps to blame for the fact that he postponed it still further: a vague hope had risen in him that if Bertrand would only speak out now, everything would fall into its place so smoothly and easily that without further ado he would be able straightway to take him to Lestow. But as in spite of this inducement, of which besides he knew nothing, Bertrand in the most disappointing manner persevered in his silence, Joachim was finally driven to make a decision and went alone. One afternoon he drove over to Lestow in the gig, his legs smoothly and decorously wrapped in the carriage rug, the whip held at the correct angle before him, and the reins running easily in his brown-gloved hand. When he left his father had said: " At last," and now Joachim was filled with distaste for this fantastic marriage project.

In front arose the church spire of the neighbouring village; a Catholic church, and it reminded him of Ruzena's Roman Catholic creed: Bertrand had told him about Ruzena. Wouldn't the most honest thing be to break off his silly stay here, and simply go back to her? Everything here was beginning to disgust him: the dust on the road, the dusty, wilting leaves of the trees beside it announcing the approach of autumn; he loathed it all. Since Bertrand's arrival he had been longing again for his uniform; two men in the same uniform, that was something impersonal, the King's badge; two men in the same kind of civilian clothes, that was shameless, it was like two brothers; and he felt that the short civilian jacket which left visible one's legs and the opening of one's trousers was in some way shameless. Elisabeth, who was condemned to seeing men in short jackets and unconcealed trousers, was to be pitied—strange that he had never had such regrets where Ruzena was concerned—but at least for this visit he should have put on his uniform. The broad white cravat with the horseshoe tie-pin concealed the opening of his waistcoat; that was good. He put up his hand and made certain that it was properly in place. It was not for nothing that they laid a cloth over the lower parts of the dead lying on their biers. Helmuth too had driven along this road to Lestow, had called on Elisabeth and her mother, and dust like this had been poured on him in his grave. Had his brother really left Elisabeth to him as a legacy? Or Ruzena? Or perhaps even Bertrand? They should have given Bertrand Helmuth's room, instead of putting him in the solitary guest-chamber; but that would not have been right either. It was all like a sort of inevitable clockwork which yet in some way depended on his own will and simply for that reason seemed inevitable and self-evident, certainly more inevitable than the clockwork routine of the service. But he could not follow out any further these thoughts, behind which lay probably something terrible, for now he was driving into the village and must keep a look-out for the children playing on the road; just beyond the village he turned into the park through the gate flanked right and left by the two lodges.

" I'm delighted to see you here again at last, Herr von Pasenow,"
said the Baron, meeting him in the hall, and when Joachim mentioned
the guest because of whom his visit had been postponed the Baron
reproached him for not having brought Bertrand along with him.
Joachim himself could not understand now why he had not done so;
certainly it would have given no offence; but when Elisabeth entered
he thought after all that it was better that he should have come alone.
He found her very beautiful, even Bertrand would not be able to resist
the charm of such beauty, that was certain, and as certainly he would
never dare in her presence to maintain that far too unconstrained tone
which was customary with him. Nevertheless Joachim could almost
have wished to see him doing so, somewhat as one wishes to hear
a coarse word spoken in a church or even to be present at an
execution.

They had tea on the terrace, and Joachim, who sat beside Elisabeth,
had the sensation that he had been in the same position not so very
long ago. But when could it have been? Almost three years had passed
since his last visit to Lestow, and then it had been late autumn and it
would not have been possible to sit out on the terrace. But while he
was still brooding over this, and it seemed to him that during that visit
they had had to light the lights in the house, a fantastic association led
his thoughts quite into the absurd, and the confusion became almost
inextricable, for his accomplice Bertrand—it repelled him a little that the
word accomplice should occur to him—for the accomplice and witness
of his intimacy with Ruzena was evidently expected to keep him company
beside Elisabeth too! How on earth could he have ever thought of
introducing him to his parents? The fatalistic feeling that through
Bertrand's agency he had slipped from the straight path came back
again, and suddenly the idea that after his tea he would have to stand
up in his civilian clothes became painful to him; he would have liked
to leave his serviette lying on his knees, but already they were proposing
a walk through the park. When the farm buildings came in sight the
Baron observed that now of course his guest would soon be coming
back to live in the country; at least his father had hinted at it. Joachim,
filled with renewed antagonism to his father's attempt to determine his
life, would have liked to reply that he had no intention of returning to
his parents' house; of course one could not say such things, it would
not be quite in accordance with the truth nor with his newly found

attachment to his home and his property; and so he merely said that it wasn't an easy matter to leave the service, all the more as he would soon be given a captaincy. And one could not give up a profession one had grown fond of so easily as all that, even on grounds of sentiment; he had seen that most clearly in the case of his friend, Herr von Bertrand, who in spite of his many striking successes in business still probably longed in secret to be back with his regiment. And as though against his will he began to speak of Bertrand's world-wide business dealings and long journeys, and he surrounded him, almost with a boy's fantasy, with the nimbus of the explorer, until the ladies could not help express-ing their delight over their approaching acquaintance with such an interesting man. All the same Pasenow had the impression that they were all afraid, if not of Bertrand, yet of the life which he led, for Elisabeth became almost subdued and remarked that she was quite incapable of thinking of a brother, say, or some other near relation, being so far away that one could never tell with certainty what part of the world he was in. And the Baron agreed that only a man without a family could lead such a life. A sailor's life, he added. But Joachim, not wishing to be outshone too much by his friend, and feeling, indeed, that here he was nothing less than his friend's deputy, now related that Bertrand had encouraged him to report for the colonial service, and the Baroness said with severity: " You can't do that and leave your parents alone." " No," said the Baron, " your place is in your father's fields," and Joachim was rather pleased to hear it. Then they turned back and, led by Elisabeth's dog, reached again the wide clearing in front of the house. The moist and dewy fragrance of the grass was already rising, and the lights in the house were being lit, for the evenings were beginning to draw in.

When Joachim drove away darkness was falling. The last he saw of Elisabeth was her silhouette on the terrace; she had taken off her garden hat and in the twilight of the fading day she stood against the clear sky which was ribbed with reddish bars of cloud. Joachim could see distinctly the heavy knot of hair at the nape of her neck, and he asked himself why it was that he thought this girl so beautiful, so beautiful that Ruzena's sweetness seemed to vanish from his memory when he saw her. And yet it was for Ruzena that he longed, and not for Elisabeth's purity. Why was Elisabeth beautiful? The trees beside the road rose darkly and the dust smelt cool, as it would smell probably in a cave or a cellar. But in the west a reddish strip still hung in the darkening sky over the rolling landscape.

On the same afternoon that Joachim paid his visit to Lestow, and just after he had driven away, Herr von Pasenow climbed the stairs to the first floor and knocked at Bertrand's door: " I must pay you a visit too . . ." and then as if in secret understanding " I've got rid of him, . . . it wasn't an easy business! " Bertrand murmured a few polite words: he would have been delighted to come down. " No," said Herr von Pasenow, " good form must be preserved. But after tea we'll go for a little walk. I've some things I want to talk to you about." He sat down for a little to preserve the form of his visit, but with his accustomed restlessness presently left the room, to return before the door was closed after him and say: " I only want to see that you have everything you need. In this house you can't depend on anybody." He walked round the room, regarded *La Mère des Gracches*, examined the floor, and then said genially: " Well then, till tea-time."—

Having lighted their cigars they strolled through the park, crossed the kitchen gardens, on whose trees the fruit was already ripening, and at last reached the fields. Herr von Pasenow was obviously in a good humour. A group of women harvest workers came towards them. So as to make place for the gentlemen they formed up in single file at the side of the path, and one after another curtsied as they passed. Herr von Pasenow peered at each one under her head-cloth, and when the single file had passed he said: " Stalwart wenches." " Poles? " asked Bertrand. " Of course, that is, the most of them . . . well, they're an unreliable pack." It was lovely here, Bertrand went on, and he sincerely envied the life of a country gentleman. Herr von Pasenow clapped him on the shoulder: " You could lead it if you liked." Bertrand shook his head: that wasn't such a simple matter, and besides one had to be brought up to it. " I'll see to that," Herr von Pasenow replied with a confidential smile. Then he became silent and Bertrand waited. But Herr von Pasenow seemed to have forgotten what he had wanted to say, for after a long pause he gave utterance to the outcome of his thoughts: " Of course you must write me . . . often, yes." Then: " If you'll come and live here we need have no more fears: both of us need have no more fears . . . what? " He had put his hand on Bertrand's arm, and gazed at him anxiously. " But, Herr von Pasenow, why should we have any fears?" Herr von Pasenow seemed astonished: "But you said . . ." he stared in front of him. "Well, it doesn't matter . . ." He remained standing, then turned round, and it looked as though he were about to turn back again. But he recollected himself and went on. After a while he asked: "Have you been to see him yet?" "Him?" "Well, to see the grave." Bertrand felt a little ashamed; but in the atmosphere of this house there had really been no fitting opportunity to express a wish to visit the grave. As he was preparing to answer the question as diplomatically as possible in the negative, Herr von Pasenow laughed and said with satisfaction: "Well, then we have still something to do," and as another pleasant surprise for his guest pointed with his stick at the wall of the cemetery, which lay before them. "You go in, I'll wait for you here," he commanded, and when Bertrand hesitated for a little he added impatiently and sharply: "No, I'm not coming with you," and he led Bertrand as far as the gate, over which in golden letters glittered the inscription: "Rest in Peace." Bertrand entered and after he had remained for a due period by the grave returned again. Herr von Pasenow was marching backwards and forwards along the wall with visible impatience: "Were you with him? . . . well . . .?" Bertrand pressed his hand, but Herr von Pasenow apparently desired no sympathy and was waiting for him to say something; he even made a gesture as of encouragement, and when in spite of this nothing followed, he sighed: "He died for the honour of his name . . . yes, and meanwhile Joachim pays visits." Once more he pointed with his stick, this time in the direction of Lestow. Later with a titter he supplemented his thought: "I've sent him a-courting," and as though this reminded him that he had something he wished to discuss with Bertrand: "Right! I'm told you're good at business matters." Well, yes, but only in his special branch, replied Bertrand. "Well, for our business that will do well enough. You see, my dear fellow, I'm naturally in need of advice now that he's dead." He paused for a little and then said importantly: "Question of inheritance." Bertrand replied that Herr von Pasenow must surely have a confidential legal adviser who would guide him, but Herr von Pasenow paid no attention: "Joachim will be provided for through his marriage; he could be disinherited "; and he laughed again. Bertrand tried to turn the conversation and pointed to a hare: "They'll soon be out with the guns again, Herr von Pasenow." "Yes, yes, he can come to the shooting if he likes; he's all right for things like that. . . .

we'll invite him, what? and of course he must write to us; we'll soon bring him up to the scratch there, what?" As Herr von Pasenow laughed, Bertrand smiled too, though he felt very uncomfortable. He was a little annoyed at Joachim for delivering him up to this man; but how incapable the fellow showed himself even here to have allowed this old dotard to get into such a mood! Had the clumsy creature invited him here too, to straighten out his affairs? So he said: "Yes, yes, Herr von Pasenow, we'll soon lick him into shape." And this appeared to be the tone that the old man wished him to adopt. He leant on Bertrand's arm, carefully suiting his step to that of his companion, and did not remove his arm again even when they reached the house. Though darkness had fallen they walked up and down the yard until Joachim drove up. When Joachim jumped down from the gig Herr von Pasenow said: "Let me introduce my friend, Herr von Bertrand," and with a somewhat casual wave of the hand: " and this is my son . . . just back from his courting," he added facetiously. The smell of the byres came across on the wind, and Herr von Pasenow felt in good spirits.

"She isn't really beautiful," Bertrand told himself as he regarded Elisabeth sitting at the piano; "her mouth is too large and her lips are of a curiously soft and almost evil sensuality. But when she smiles she's charming."

It was to a "musical tea" that Joachim and Bertrand had been invited. Elisabeth's accompanists in Spohr's trio were an old friend from a neighbouring estate and the indigent local teacher, and when the silvery crystalline drops of the piano fell into the brown stream of the two stringed instruments it seemed to Joachim that it was all due to Elisabeth. He loved music, although he did not understand much about it, but now he thought he had caught its meaning; it was pure and clear and hovered high above everything as on a silvery cloud, and from its celestial height let fall its cold and pure drops on the earth. And perhaps only to Elisabeth did it manifest itself, even though Bertrand, as he remembered from the days in Culm, could play a little on the violin. No, it did not look as if Bertrand would try to conquer Elisabeth from the musical side. When asked about his violin-playing he had replied evasively, with a deprecatory wave of the hand; and it may have been pure hypocrisy—for it had sounded cynical enough—when on the way back he had found nothing better to say than: " If she would only play something else than that horribly boring Spohr! "—

They had arranged to go riding: Joachim and Bertrand called for Elisabeth. Joachim rode Helmuth's horse, which had now once more become his property. They galloped over the stubble-fields where the shocks were still standing, and then at a sharp trot turned into a narrow forest-path. Joachim let his friend ride in front with Elisabeth, and while he followed it seemed to him that in her long black riding-habit she looked still taller and slenderer than usual. He would have liked to turn away his eyes, but she did not sit quite faultlessly on her horse and it disturbed him; she bent a little too far forward as she sat, and as she rose and sank, touching the saddle and then rebounding again, up and down, he could not but recall the day when he had said good-bye to her in the station, and the despicable wish that he could desire her as a woman rose up again, doubly despicable since his father, and before Bertrand too, had spoken of his courting. But almost more loathsome was the thought that Elisabeth's parents too, yes, her very mother, might regard him as an object of desire for their daughter, hold him up to her as an attraction, both of them persuaded that they might reckon upon this desire, that it would appear and that it would not fail their expectations. Yet something more essential, more profound, remained still concealed behind all this, an indefinite idea of which Joachim desired to remain ignorant, although he felt his mouth becoming dry and his face hot; it was indefinite, and yet it made him angry that they should dare to consider Elisabeth capable of such things; he felt ashamed before her and ashamed for her. Let Bertrand have her if he wanted to, he thought, forgetting that in doing so he was committing the self-same offence which he had just rejected with such indignation. But suddenly that did not matter, suddenly it seemed to him that Bertrand did not come into the question: with his wavy hair he was so feminine, in some way sisterly, with a sisterly solicitude to which perhaps Elisabeth could be safely confided. That was not quite true, of course, yet for a moment it was reassuring. Besides, what was it really that made her beautiful? And he contemplated her body bobbing up and down and her hips returning to the saddle again and again. And doing this he discovered that it was not beauty, but far more truly the opposite of beauty, that awakened desire; but he pushed the thought aside, and the picture of Elisabeth clambering into her carriage still in his mind,

his thoughts flew to Ruzena, whose countless imperfections made her
so charming. He let his horse fall into a walk to increase the distance
between him and the couple in front, and drew Ruzena's last letter from
his breast-pocket. The notepaper smelt of the perfume which he had
given her, and he breathed again the air of their illicit intimacy. Yes,
that was where he belonged, that was where he wanted to be, and he
felt he was a voluntary exile from society, and yet an outcast; he felt
unworthy of Elisabeth. Bertrand was his accomplice, true, but Bertrand
had the cleaner hands, and when Joachim recognized this he saw too
why Bertrand had always treated him and Ruzena with a touch of
superiority, of the avuncular, as a doctor might treat one, and had kept
his own secrets hidden. A father's secrets should never be uncovered;
that was as it should be, and yet because of it that fellow in front of
him was in a position, was at liberty, to ride by Elisabeth's side, though
he too was unworthy, yet better than Joachim himself. He thought of
Helmuth. And as though he wanted Helmuth's horse at least to be
beside them, he set it to a trot. Its hoofs thudded softly on the leafy
ground, and when they encountered a twig he could hear the sharp
cracking of the wood. The leather of the saddle creaked pleasantly, and
from the darkness of the leafage came a cool wind.

He overtook them at the border of a long clearing which rose gently.
The coolness of the woods was as if cut off here, and one could smell
the sun's heat rising from the grass. With the lash of her riding-whip
Elisabeth flicked at the horse-flies that had fixed themselves to her
mount, and the horse, which knew the way, was impatient, awaiting its
usual gallop over the clearing. Joachim felt superior to Bertrand; no
matter how wide his business interests might be, at a desk one did not
acquire the practice necessary to leap over obstacles. Elisabeth pointed
out the hurdles, a hedge which she was accustomed to take, a fallen
tree-trunk, and a ditch. They were not difficult. The groom was left
behind at the edge of the clearing: Elisabeth took the lead, and Joachim
again came last, not merely out of politeness, but because he wanted
to see how Bertrand would take the jumps. The grass had not yet been
mown, and it rustled lightly and sharply against the legs of the horses.
Elisabeth rode first towards the ditch; it was a mere trifle, and it was
only to be expected that Bertrand would take it. But when the hedge
too was taken by Bertrand in good style Joachim felt really annoyed;
the tree-trunk was far too easy, his last hope was gone. Joachim's horse,

which was trying to overhaul the others, was pulling hard at the curb, and Joachim had to hold it back to preserve his distance. Now came the tree-trunk; Elisabeth and Bertrand had negotiated it easily, almost elegantly; and Joachim gave his horse a free head for the leap. But when it was gathering itself for the jump he checked it suddenly, why he was never able to tell; the horse stumbled on the trunk, came down sideways and rolled over him on the grass. This of course happened very quickly, and when the other two turned round he and the horse were quietly standing together in front of the trunk, the bridle still in his hands. " What's happened? " Happened? He didn't know himself: he examined his horse's legs, it was lame in one forefoot; it would have to be taken home. The finger of God, thought Joachim; it was not Bertrand but himself who had fallen, and now it was only right and just that he must go away and leave Elisabeth with that fellow. When Elisabeth suggested that he should take her groom's mount and send him back with the lame horse, he declined morosely, for he still saw in the incident a judgment from God. And after all it was Helmuth's horse and it could not be entrusted to anyone. He started for home at a walking pace and resolved to return to Berlin as soon as possible.

They rode side by side along the forest-path. Although the groom followed at a short distance Elisabeth had the feeling that she was deserted by Joachim, a feeling which acutely depressed her. Perhaps she felt Bertrand's glance hovering round her face. " Her mouth is strange," Bertrand told himself, " and her eyes have that clearness which I love so much. She would be an easily wounded and provoking and really difficult mistress. Her hands are too big for a woman, thin and slender. She's a sensual boy, that's what she is. But she's charming." To escape from her depression Elisabeth tried to start a conversation, although a little time before she had already made the remark with which she began:

" Herr von Pasenow has told us a lot about you and your great travels."

" Yes? He has told me a lot about your great beauty."

Elisabeth did not reply.

" Doesn't that please you? "

" I have no wish to hear anything about my alleged beauty."

" You are very beautiful."

Elisabeth said a little uncertainly: " I didn't think that you were one of the lady-killers."

She's cleverer than I imagined, thought Bertrand, and he replied: " I couldn't bring myself even to utter that awful term, not even if I wanted to be insulting. But I'm not being a lady-killer; you know well enough how beautiful you are."

" Then why do you tell me? "

" Because I'll never see you again."

Elisabeth looked at him in surprise.

" Of course you don't like anyone to talk to you of your beauty, for behind the compliment you suspect the wooer. But if I go away and never see you again, then logically I can't be trying to court you and am justified in telling you the nicest things I can."

Elisabeth had to laugh.

" Dreadful that one can listen to nice things only from a complete stranger."

" At least one can believe them only from a complete stranger. Intimacy contains necessarily the seeds of dishonesty and falsehood."

" If that were true it would be really frightful."

" Of course it is true, but that doesn't make it at all frightful. Intimacy is the slyest and really meanest kind of courting. Instead of simply saying that one desires a woman because she's beautiful, one insinuates oneself into her confidence, so as to catch her off her guard."

Elisabeth reflected for a little, then she said: " Isn't there something outrageous behind your words? "

" No, for I'm going away . . . a stranger can afford to speak the truth."

" I'm afraid of everything strange."

" Because you're attracted by it. You're beautiful, Elisabeth. May I call you that for this one day? "

They rode in silence side by side. Then she said, finding the right words: " What do you really want? "

" Nothing."

" But then there's no meaning in all this."

" I want the same thing as everybody else who courts you and tells you for that reason that you're beautiful; but I'm more honest."

" I don't want anyone to court me."

" Perhaps what you hate is simply the dishonest form it takes."

" Aren't you really more dishonest than the others? "

" I'm going away."

" What does that prove? "

" Among other things, well, my modesty."

" How? "

" To court a woman means to offer oneself to her as the living biped that one is, and that's indecent. And it's quite possible, indeed quite probable, that that's why you hate any kind of courting."

" I cannot say."

" Love is an absolute thing, Elisabeth, and when the absolute tries to express itself in earthly terms, then it always turns into pathos, simply because it can't be demonstrated. And as the whole thing then becomes so horribly earthly, the pathos is always very funny, represented by the gentleman who goes down on his knees to get you to accede to all his wishes; and if one loves you one must avoid that."

Was his intention in saying this to intimate that he loved her? As he became silent she looked at him questioningly. He appeared to understand:

" There is a true pathos, and we call it eternity. And as there is no positive eternity for human beings it must be a negative one and can be put in the words ' never-to-meet-again.' If I go away now, eternity is here; then you will be eternally remote from me and I can say that I love you."

" Don't say such dreadful things."

" Perhaps it's the absolute clearness of my feelings that makes me talk like this to you. But perhaps there's a little hate and resentment too in my forcing you to listen to my monologue, jealousy perhaps, because you'll stay here and live on."

" Real jealousy? "

" Yes, jealousy, and a little pride as well. For there's the wish in it to let a stone fall into the well of your soul, so that it may rest there for ever."

" So you want to intrude yourself into my intimacy too? "

" It may be. But still stronger is the wish that the stone may turn into a talisman for you."

" When? "

" When the man will kneel before you whom I'm jealous of at this moment, the man who will offer you with that antiquated gesture his physical proximity: then the memory of, let us say, an aseptic form of love may help to remind you that behind every pseudo-æsthetic gesture in love there is hidden a still grosser reality."

" Do you say that to all the women you run away from? "

" One should say it to them all, but I generally run away before it comes to that."

Elisabeth stared reflectively at her horse's mane. Then she said: " I don't know, but all this sounds strangely unnatural and beside the point to me."

" If you're thinking of the propagation of the human race, then of course it's unnatural. But do you find it more natural that some man or other, who lives somewhere at present, eating and drinking and looking after his affairs, will meet you some time by a stupid chance, and take a suitable opportunity of telling you how beautiful you are, getting down on one knee before you, so that afterwards, having gone through certain formalities, the two of you might produce children. Do you find that quite natural? "

" Be silent! That's dreadful! . . . That's horrible! "

" Yes, it is dreadful, but not because I speak of it as it is; for it's a still more dreadful thing to think that you're certainly destined, and very soon, to experience it and not merely to hear about it."

Elisabeth fought down her tears; she said with an effort: " But why, in Heaven's name, should I hear about it? . . . please, please, be silent."

" What are you afraid of, Elisabeth? "

She replied softly: " I'm afraid enough as it is."

" Of what? "

" Of everything unknown, of others, of what's to come . . . I can't express it. I have a desperate hope that what is still to come will be as familiar to me as everything that's familiar now. My father and mother belong to each other after all. But you want to take away my hope from me."

" And you refuse to see the danger because you're afraid of it. Isn't it one's duty to shake you awake so that you mightn't let your life run away, or dry to dust, or shrink to nothing, or something like that, out of mere indifference, or conventional notions, or ignorance? . . . Elisabeth, I mean very well by you."

Once more Elisabeth found the right words when she said softly, hesitatingly, against her will: " Then why don't you stay? "

" I've only been flung in your way by mere chance. And if I remained it would be as much an assault on your feelings as those I've been trying to warn you against; a somewhat aseptic assault, but still an assault."

" What should I do? "

" That can be answered only negatively: nothing that isn't approved by every fibre of you. No one can come to fulfilment except by submitting freely and absolutely to the law of his feelings and his nature —forgive the pathos."

" Nobody ever helps me."

" No, you are alone, as alone as you will be on your deathbed."

" It isn't true. It isn't true, what you say. I've never been alone, nor are my father and mother alone. You talk like that because you want to be alone . . . or perhaps because it gives you pleasure to torment me? "

" Elisabeth, you are so beautiful that perhaps your fulfilment and completion lie simply in your beauty. Why should I torment you? But all I've said is true, and I've not said the worst either."

" Don't torment me."

" Somewhere in everybody there's an insane hope that the little scrap of love that is given us will fling that bridge over the void. Be on your guard against the pathos of love."

" What are you warning me against now? "

" All pathos comes to this, that it promises us a mystery and tries to redeem its promise by a cliché. I should like to see you safeguarded against that kind of love."

" You're a poor creature."

" Because I show my empty pockets? Be on your guard against anyone who doesn't show them."

" No, not that. I feel that you're more to be pitied than the others, even than those others you talked about. . . ."

" I must warn you again. Never pity anyone in this business. A love born of pity is no better than a love that's bought."

" Oh! "

" Yes, you won't admit that, Elisabeth. Well, put it this way then: the woman who sins out of pity presents afterwards the most pitiless reckoning."

Elisabeth looked at him almost with hostility: " I have no pity for you."

" But you shouldn't look at me so angrily, all the same, although it's almost honester that you should."

" Why honester? "

Bertrand was silent. Then after a while he said: " Listen, Elisabeth, one must carry even honesty to the bitter end. I don't like to say such things. But I love you. I state that with all the seriousness and all the honesty that one can be capable of in these matters of feeling. And I know, too, that you could come to love me——"

" For Heaven's sake, be silent . . ."

" Why? I don't overestimate these vague emotional states in the least, and I won't try to be pathetic. Yet no man can quench the insane hope that some time he'll find that mystical bridge of love. But just because of that I must go away. There is only one real kind of pathos, the pathos of separation, of pain . . . if one wants to make the bridge capable of holding, then one must stretch it so far that no weight can be put on it. If after that——"

" Oh, be silent."

" If after that necessity is still stronger than all that one has voluntarily set against it, if the tension of an indescribable longing becomes so sharp that it threatens to cut the world in two, then the proven hope may arise that the weak individual destiny of two human beings is lifted above the chaos of chance, above a stale and sentimental melancholy, above a mechanical and fortuitous intimacy."

And as though he were talking to himself and no longer to Elisabeth, he continued: " I believe, and this is my deepest belief, that only by a dreadful intensification of itself, only when in a sense it becomes infinite, can the strangeness parting two human beings be transformed into its opposite, into absolute recognition, and let that thing come to life which hovers in front of love as its unattainable goal, and yet is its condition: the mystery of oneness. The gradual accustoming of oneself to another, the gradual deepening of intimacy, evokes no mystery whatever."

Elisabeth was crying.

He went on softly: " I should like you never to know and suffer from love except in that final and unattainable form. And even if I should not be the one, I would not be jealous of anybody then. But I suffer and feel jealous and impotent when I think that you will put up with something cheaper. Are you crying because perfection is unattainable? Then you are right to cry. Oh, I love you, I long to sink in your strangeness, I long that you might be the final and predestined woman for me. . . ."

Now once more they rode on in silence side by side; they emerged from the forest and came to a field-path leading down to the main road which they had to take to get back. When he caught sight of the dusty road, which lay white under the sunlight and the pale sky, he drew up his horse so that in the shadow of the trees he might say again; very softly, and as in farewell: " I love you . . . love you, it's fantastic." But that they should ride together after this on the dry, sunny road seemed to both of them impossible, and she felt grateful to him when he stopped and said: " I'll try to overtake our unlucky friend, I think," and then, very softly: " Farewell." She gave him her hand. He bowed over it and she heard once more: " Farewell." She said nothing, but when he had turned to go she cried: " Herr von Bertrand! " He came back; she hesitated for a little, then she said: " Till we meet again." She would have liked to say " Farewell," but it seemed out of place and theatrical. When after a little he looked round, he could hardly distinguish any longer which of the two figures was Elisabeth and which the groom; they were already too far away and the sun blinded his eyes.

Peter the serving-man stood on the terrace at Lestow and struck the gong. The Baroness had initiated this manner of announcing meals after a visit to England with her husband, and it had since become a custom. And although Peter the serving-man had been striking the gong for several years, he still remained a little ashamed of causing such a childish din, especially as the sound carried as far as the village street and had once gained him the nickname of " The Drummer." Consequently he struck the gong discreetly, eliciting from it only a few deep tones that reverberated roundly in the silence of the park, and the rest of his performance was a flat, unmusical, brazen something that thinly died away.

Riding at a slow footpace through the noonday village street, Elisabeth heard the serving-man softly beating the gong and admonishing her that the time had come to change her dress. Nevertheless she did not hasten her horse's pace, and if she had not been so lost in thought it might have struck her that to-day, perhaps for the first time in her life, she felt a sort of repugnance for the family gathering at the lunch-table, indeed that her return to the beautiful, quiet park, her entry through the gate with the two lodges, weighed on her with a feeling of heavy oppression. A disturbing longing for distant things had risen up in her and along with this longing an absurd idea, doubly absurd in this midday heat, that Bertrand could not thrive in this cold climate, and that consequently he had always to flee and always to be saying good-bye. The echoes of the gong had died away. She dismounted in the yard, the groom holding her horse by the bridle; she hurried into the house, the tail of her riding-habit over her arm; she went up the steps, went the familiar way, yet as if in a waking dream. A mild fit of courage came over her, a somewhat melancholy pleasure at the thought of going wherever she pleased, of taking her destiny in her own hands and directing it; but her thoughts did not go very far and remained held up by the question what her parents would say if she appeared at the lunch-table in her riding-habit. Joachim von Pasenow too was one of those who could be shocked by such offences. Her little dog Bello tumbled down the stairs barking, mechanically she gave him her riding-whip; but she did not smile at the pride with which he carried it to her boudoir, and artfully as he laid himself at her feet, devoutly gazing up at her as though he found in her beauty fulfilment and consummation, Elisabeth did not stroke his head, but went up to the mirror and gazed into it for a long time without recognizing herself, seeing only the slender black silhouette; and it was as though the figure in the mirror and she herself were receding from each other in an immobility which slowly dissolved only when the maid entered, according to the daily custom, to help her to take off her riding-habit. But while the girl knelt before her to pull off her riding-boots, while her outstretched feet slipped with a light, cool sensation from the long boots and lay, small now in their black silken stockings, on the maid's knee, she sought anew in the mirror that receding image, receding, as it were, in flight to someone or other who lived somewhere or other and perhaps would some day go on his knees before her. Her riding-whip was still lying on the carpet. Elisabeth tried to recall Bertrand at the railway station in his long, angular service coat, his sword by his side, and imagined that the departing train had caught him and was dragging him with it. There was a certain malicious pleasure in the fancy, but also a stifling fear such as she had never felt before. She sat with her head bent back, her hands at her temples, as though in this posture she could free herself from the power of an unexpected compulsion. " Still, nothing has happened,"

something said within her, and she could not understand her vague
feeling of excitement, which yet seemed so strangely definite that it
could almost be expressed in words: cut the world in two. It was not
quite definite, certainly, yet a frontier line had been drawn, and what
had once been indivisible, this closed world of hers, now fell asunder,
and her parents stood at the other side of the frontier line. Behind all
this was fear, the fear from which her parents wished to guard her as
though their very life depended upon it; but the thing they feared had
now broken in, strangely moving and exciting, and yet not in the least
fearful. One could say " Du " to a stranger: that was all. And it was
so little that Elisabeth became almost sad. She got up resolutely; no,
she would not resign herself to a stale and sentimental melancholy.
She went up to the mirror and patted her hair straight.

At the foot of the great staircase on an ebony frame hung the dull,
yellow, bronze gong, decorated with flat Chinese designs. A genuine
piece which the Baron had purchased in London. Peter the serving-
man held the baton with the soft, grey leather head in one hand, while
he gazed at his watch and waited. Fourteen minutes had elapsed since
his first announcement, and when the watch-hand reached the fifteenth
Peter would deliver three discreet taps on the bronze plate.

III

On the following day Bertrand excused himself from breakfasting
with the family, then waylaid Joachim and told him that to his sincere
regret he had been called away on business, and must leave the very
next morning. Joachim's first feeling was one of relief. " I'll come with
you," he said, looking gratefully at Bertrand, who had, it was obvious,
given Elisabeth up. And to show him that he too would renounce her
he added kindly: " I don't know of anything to keep me here."

Joachim went to impart this decision to his father. But when Herr
von Pasenow started in surprise and asked suspiciously, with his usual
indiscretion: " How is that possible? He hasn't had any letters since the
day before yesterday," Joachim too was startled: how, indeed, was that
possible? What could have moved Bertrand to the renunciation? And
along with a feeling of shame at becoming his father's accomplice in
indiscretion by posing these questions, the vision arose of a friendly
triumph: it was because Elisabeth loved him, Joachim von Pasenow,

that she had rebuffed Bertrand. Of course it was quite incredible that anyone should have had the face to propose to a lady so hastily, almost in the twinkling of an eye. But anything was possible to a business man who thought he had the chance of a rich heiress. Joachim was not able to pursue these reflections, for he was startled by the sudden change in his father's appearance; he was huddled up in the chair by the writing-table and with a vacant stare was muttering: " The scoundrel, the scoundrel . . . he has broken his promise." Then he looked at Joachim and screamed: " Out you get, you and your fine friend . . . you're in the plot too! " " But, Father! " " Out you go, both of you; get out! " He had sprung to his feet, and advanced upon his retreating son, driving him in short rushes towards the door. And at every pause he thrust forward his head and spat at him: " Get out! " When Joachim was in the corridor the old man slammed the door, but opened it again immediately and stuck his head out: " And tell him not to dare to write to me. Tell him I've no further interest in him." The door crashed to and Joachim heard the key being turned.

He found his mother in the garden; she showed no great consternation: " He's not one to say much, but for some days he has seemed angry with you. I think he can't forgive you for not giving up the army. Still, it is queer." When they turned towards the house she added: " Perhaps he was offended, too, because you brought your friend down here so soon; I think it might be better for me to see him first alone." Joachim escorted her upstairs; the door giving on the corridor was locked, and there was no answer to her knocking. It was a little uncanny, and so they went round to the large drawing-room, since it was just possible that he might have left his study by the other door. Through the chain of empty rooms they reached the study and found it unlocked. Frau von Pasenow opened the door and Joachim saw his father sitting motionless at the writing-table, a quill in his hand. He did not move even when Frau von Pasenow advanced and bent over him. He had pressed so heavily on the quill-point that it was splintered; and on the paper stood the words: " I disinherit for dishonourable conduct my . . ." and then came the splutter of ink made by the broken quill. " In the name of God, what has happened? " But he made no answer. Helplessly his wife regarded him; when she noticed that the inkpot too had been upset she hastily seized the blotting-pad and tried to mop up the mess. He thrust her away with his elbow and then caught sight of Joachim in the doorway, grinned malignantly, and attempted to go on writing with the broken quill. When it caught again in the paper and tore a hole in it he groaned aloud, pointed his forefinger at his son and cried: " Out with him! " At the same time he tried to rise, but apparently found it impossible, for he collapsed again in a huddle, disregarding the flowing ink, and sank forward over the writing-table with his face on his arms like a crying child. Joachim whispered to his mother: " I'll call the doctor," and ran downstairs to send a messenger to the village.

The doctor came and sent Herr von Pasenow to bed. He administered bromide and spoke of a cold-water cure; it was simply a nervous breakdown following on the death of his son. Yes, yes, that was the doctor's banal explanation. But it was no explanation. There was more in it than that, and it could not be mere coincidence; the accident to Helmuth's horse had been a kind of preliminary warning, and now when, in spite of everything, Joachim was about to triumph over Bertrand, now when Elisabeth for his sake had rebuffed Bertrand and he was making ready to play Bertrand false and to play Ruzena false, ostensibly in obedience to his father, now was the hour for fate to strike. An accomplice who betrayed his fellow-accomplices; accused, and rightly accused, by his father of plotting with Bertrand! Must not the whole web now fall to pieces, and treachery cancel treachery? And Bertrand must appropriate Ruzena again to convince the father that he was no longer the son's accomplice and to avenge himself for Elisabeth's refusal! In all the foul and hateful suspicion with which Joachim now regarded Bertrand's departure to Berlin, he saw only his own departure postponed indefinitely, and that tormented him more than his anxiety about his afflicted father. The tangled web unravelled itself only to be knotted in fresh tangles. Was this what his father had in mind when he had pressed him to visit Lestow? And besides, it was impossible to discover what had happened between his father and Bertrand. Perhaps it might have been cleared up if he could have mentioned to Bertrand the old man's dark insinuations, but he had to confine himself to announcing his sudden illness. He begged Bertrand to explain the situation to Ruzena; in any case he would himself come to Berlin soon for a few days, to get his leave extended and see to other things. Well, said Bertrand, as Joachim escorted him to the station, well, and what was to become of Ruzena now? Of course it was to be hoped that Herr von Pasenow would soon recover, but Joachim's presence in Stolpin would none the less become more and more indispensable. " She ought to be provided with some regular occupation," he observed; " something she enjoys doing; that would help her over the difficult times ahead." Joachim was offended, for after all that was his own affair; he said hesitatingly: " But the theatre you got her into, she enjoys herself there." Bertrand dismissed this statement with a wave of the hand, and Joachim stared at him uncomprehendingly. " But don't you worry, Pasenow, we'll find something or other." And although it was a worry that had not previously occurred to Joachim, he was now sincerely glad to have it so lightly taken off his shoulders by Bertrand.

Since the old man's illness, which still kept him in bed the greater part of the day, life had become curiously simplified. Joachim could now reflect more quietly on many things, and some of the riddles appeared less obscure, or at least more approachable. But now an almost insoluble problem confronted him, and it was no use trying to decipher it in Elisabeth's face, for her face itself constituted the problem. Lying back in her chair she was gazing at the autumn landscape, and her up-tilted face, thrown back almost at a right angle to the taut line of the throat, was like an irregular roof set upon the pillar of her neck. One could perhaps say just as well that it rested like a leaf on the calyx of the throat, or that it was a lid covering the throat, for it was really no longer a face, merely a continuation of the throat, an extension from the throat, with a far-off resemblance to the head of a serpent. Joachim followed the line of her throat; the chin jutted out like a hill, behind which lay the landscape of her face. Softly rounded the rim of the crater which was her mouth, dark the cavern of the nose, divided by a white pillar. Like a miniature beard sprouted the hedge of the eyebrows, and beyond the clearing of the forehead, cut by finely ploughed furrows, was the edge of the forest. Joachim was again forced to ask the question why a woman can be desirable, but nothing gave him an answer; it remained insoluble and perplexing. He shut his eyelids a little and peered through the slits at the landscape of that extended face. It blended at once with the real landscape, the woodland verge of the hair bordered the yellowing leaves of the forest, and the glass balls that decorated the rose-beds in the garden glittered with the same light as the jewel that in the shadow of the cheek—ah, was it still a cheek?—shone as an ear-ring.

This was both startling and comforting, and when the eye combined these separate things into a unity so strange, past all disjoining, one was curiously reminded of something, transposed into some mode that lay beyond convention far back in childhood, and the unsolved riddle was like a sign that had emerged from the sea of memory.

They were sitting in the shady front garden of the little inn; their horses were in the yard behind with the groom. From the rustling of the leaves above them one could tell that it was September. For it was no longer the clear, soft purling of spring leafage, nor yet the full note of summer: in summer the trees simply rustle without much variation, but in the early days of autumn a sharper, silvery metallic tone is already perceptible, as if the broad harmony in the flowing sap were breaking up. When autumn begins the midday hours are quite motionless; the sun still shines with summer warmth, and when a lighter, cooler breeze comes wandering through the branches there is, as it were, a streak of spring in the air. The leaves that drop from the trees on to the rough inn table are not yet yellowed, but dry and brittle for all their greenness, and the summer-like sunshine seems then doubly precious. With its bow pointing upstream the fisherman's boat lies in the channel; the water glides past smoothly, as if moving in broad planes. These autumn days have none of the drowsiness of summer noons; a soft and watchful serenity lies over everything.

Elisabeth said: " Why do we live here? In the south there would be days like this all the year round." Joachim recalled the southern face of the Italian with the black moustache. But in Elisabeth's features it was impossible now to descry those of an Italian, or even of a brother, so removed were they from humanity, so akin to the landscape. He tried to find in them again their ordinary shape, and when it suddenly reappeared, when the nose became a nose again, the mouth a mouth, the eye an eye, the transformation was once more startling, and he was comforted only by the smoothness of her hair, which was not too insistently waved. " Why? Don't you like the winter? " " Your friend's right; one ought to travel," was her answer. " He wants to go to India," said Joachim, and thought of its olive-skinned races and of Ruzena. Why had he never once thought of travelling abroad with Ruzena? He was aware of Elisabeth's eyes on his face, felt caught and turned aside. But if anyone was to blame for this fever for travel it was Bertrand. His need to compensate himself for the lack of an ordered life and to deaden his regrets by business deals and exotic journeys was infectious, and if Elisabeth was yearning for the south it was perhaps because she regretted—even though she had refused Bertrand—that she was not travelling by his side. He heard Elisabeth's voice: " How long have we known each other? " He cast it up; it wasn't so easy to determine; when he was a twelve-year-old boy home for the holidays he had often visited Lestow with his parents. And at that time Elisabeth was only a few weeks old. " So I've known you always, all my life," decided Elisabeth, " and yet I've never really been aware of you; I've always counted you among the grown-ups." Joachim said nothing. " And I suppose you've never been aware of me either," she went on. Oh yes, he said, he had, one day when she suddenly blossomed out as a young lady, all at once and most surprisingly. Elisabeth said: " But now we're almost contemporaries. . . . When is your birthday, by the way? " And without waiting for an answer she added: " Can you still remember what I looked like as a child? " Joachim had to think back; in the Baroness's drawing-room there hung a portrait of Elisabeth as a child that obstinately displaced the actual memory. " It's queer," he said; " I know very well what you looked like, and yet . . ." He wanted to say that he could not find the child's face in hers, although of course it must be there, but as he looked at her once more her face ceased to be a face at all, and was simply hill and valley again, covered with something called skin. As if she wanted to challenge his thoughts she said: " With a little effort I can see what you looked like as a boy, in spite of the moustache." She laughed. " That's really funny; I must try to do it with my father too." " Can you see me as an old man as well? " Elisabeth eyed him keenly: " That's queer; no, I can't . . . but wait a minute, yes, I can: you'll be still more like your mother, with a nice, round face, and your moustache will be white and bushy. . . . But what about me as an old woman? Shall I create a very dignified impression? " Joachim declared himself incapable of imagining it. " Oh, don't be gallant, do tell me." " Excuse me, I'd rather not. There's something unpleasant in suddenly looking like one's parents or one's brother or anything else than oneself . . . it makes so many things meaningless." " Is that your friend Bertrand's opinion too? " " No, not so far as I know: why should you think so? " " Oh, only that it would be like him." " I don't know, but Bertrand seems to me so much concerned with the external details of his busy life that he simply never thinks of things like that. He is never fully himself."

Elisabeth smiled. " You mean that he always sees things from a great distance? Through the eyes of a stranger, as it were? " What was she thinking of? What was she hinting at? He despised himself for his curiosity, he felt that he was unchivalrous, and at the same time realized anew that it was an unchivalrous proceeding to let a woman fall into another man's hands instead of shielding her, shielding her from everybody. Yet he was really pledged to marry Elisabeth. But Elisabeth looked far from unhappy as she said: " It has been lovely; but now we must go home for lunch, they're expecting us."

They rode homewards, and the tower of Lestow was already in sight when she said, as if she had been reflecting on their conversation: " It's queer, all the same, how closely intimacy and strangeness are knit together. Perhaps you are right in not wanting to think of growing old." Joachim, preoccupied with thoughts of Ruzena, did not understand her in the least, but this time he did not concern himself about it.

If there was one thing that contributed to Herr von Pasenow's recovery it was the mail-bag. One morning while he was still in bed the thought struck him: " Who's looking after the post-bag? Joachim, I suppose." No, Joachim wasn't bothering about it. He grumbled that Joachim never bothered about anything, but seemed relieved, insisted on getting up, and slowly went to his study. When the messenger appeared the usual ritual was gone through, and it was rehearsed as usual from that day on. And if Frau von Pasenow happened to be in the room she had to listen to the usual complaint that nobody wrote to him. He asked often enough if Joachim was about the place, but he refused to see him. And when he heard that Joachim had to go for a few days to Berlin he said: " Inform him that I forbid it." Sometimes he forgot this, and complained that not even his own children wrote to him; and this put the idea into his wife's head of getting Joachim to write a letter of reconciliation to his father. Joachim remembered the congratulations that he and his brother had had to inscribe on rose-bordered paper whenever his parents had a birthday; it had been a frightful torment to him. He declined to submit to it again and announced that he was going away. They could conceal it from his father if they liked.

He set off without enthusiasm; if he had once objected to having a marriage prescribed for him, he now rebelled in the same way against the fact that his three days' sojourn in Berlin plighted him to three nights with Ruzena. He found it degrading for Ruzena too. He would have preferred to put off their meeting as long as possible, and to prevent her at least from coming to the station he had omitted to mention the time of his arrival. In the train it occurred to him that he ought to bring her a present of some kind; but since neither partridges nor other game would have been suitable, the only thing he could do was to buy her something in Berlin; so it was a good thing she would not be at the station. He tried to think of a suitable gift for her, but his imagination lagged; he could not hit upon anything and wavered back and forward between perfume and gloves; oh, well, in Berlin he would find something or other.

When he reached his flat the first thing he did was to write a note to Bertrand, who would certainly be glad to have at last an opportunity of discussing with him the weird events of his last day at Stolpin. He wrote to Ruzena also, and sent both notes by a messenger with instructions to wait for an answer. He felt pleasantly at home in his flat. The warmth of summer still brooded captive behind the shuttered windows. Joachim opened a shutter and basked in the stillness of the street; it was late afternoon, rain might fall before night, there was a grey wall of cloud in the western sky. The vines on the fences of the front gardens were red, yellow chestnut leaves lay on the pavement, and the horses in the shafts of the four cabs at the corner of the street stood with their forelegs bent in peaceful resignation. Joachim leaned out of the window and watched his valet open the others; if the man had leaned out too Joachim would have smiled and nodded to him along the house-front. And while his bags were being unpacked he stayed there at the window, gazing at the quiet, darkening street. Then he drew his head in; the rooms had become cooler, only here and there a stray patch of summer still lingered in the air, filling him with a sweet melancholy. But it did him good to feel his uniform on him again; he walked about among his private belongings, surveying them and his books. Yes, he would do more reading this winter. Then he winced; in three days' time he was due to leave all this again. He sat down as if to show that he was a settled occupant, ordered the windows to be shut, and asked for tea. Some time later the messenger, whom he had forgotten, came back: Herr von Bertrand was not in Berlin, but was expected in the next few days, and the lady had given no answer except simply that she was coming at once. To Joachim it was as if some slight hope had finally

vanished; he could almost have wished that the messages were reversed
and that it was Bertrand who was to come at once. Besides, he had
intended to go out and buy a present. In a few minutes, however, the
door-bell rang; Ruzena was there.

When he was a cadet and learning to swim he had balked at jumping
in, until one day he was summarily thrown into the water by the swimming
instructor; and after all it was simply pleasant in the water, and he
had laughed. Ruzena came in like a whirlwind and flew to embrace him.
It was pleasant in the water, and they sat hand in hand, exchanging
kisses, and Ruzena babbled on about things that seemed irrelevant.
None of his uneasiness remained, and his happiness would have been
almost cloudless had not his vexation at forgetting Ruzena's present
suddenly obtruded itself with renewed force. But since God had arranged
everything for good, if not for the best, He led Joachim to the cupboard
in which the lace handkerchiefs had been lying unremembered for
months. And while Ruzena, as usual, made ready their supper, Joachim
found tissue-paper and a light blue ribbon and slipped the package
under Ruzena's plate. And before they knew where they were they had
gone to bed.

It was not until next day that Joachim recollected how soon he must
depart again. Hesitatingly he broke the news to Ruzena. But the outbreak of misery or anger that he had expected did not follow. Ruzena
merely made the simple statement: " Can't go; stay here." Joachim was
struck; she was right after all, why shouldn't he stay? What spell could
it have been that made him stray aimlessly about the yard at home and
keep out of his father's way? Moreover, it seemed imperatively necessary
to wait in Berlin for Bertrand. Perhaps this was a breach of good form,
a kind of civilian irregularity, into which Ruzena was enticing him, but
it gave him a slight sense of freedom. He decided to sleep on the matter,
and since he did so in Ruzena's company he wrote next day to his mother
saying that his military duties would keep him longer in Berlin than he
had anticipated; a duplicate of the letter, which he enclosed, was for her
to give to his father should she think it expedient. Later he reflected
that there wasn't much sense in doing that, since his father opened all the
letters anyhow; but by that time it was too late; the letter was posted .

He had reported himself for duty, and was standing in the riding-
school. The riding-masters were a sergeant-major and a corporal, each

with a long whip, and along the walls was ranged a restive chain of horses mounted by recruits in coarse linen tunics. The place smelt like a vault, and the soft sand in which one's feet sank reminded him with a faint nostalgia of Helmuth and the dust he had strewn upon him. The sergeant-major cracked his whip and ordered a trot. Rhythmically the linen-clad figures by the wall began to bob up and down. Elisabeth would soon be coming to Berlin for the autumn season. But that was not quite true: they never came until October, nor could the house possibly be ready for them yet. And indeed it wasn't really Elisabeth he was waiting for, but Bertrand; of course it was Bertrand he meant. He saw Bertrand and Elisabeth riding before him at a trot, both rising and sinking in their stirrups. It was amazing how Elisabeth's face had melted into the landscape and how he had strained to recapture it again. He wondered if the same could have happened to Bertrand's face; he tried to imagine that one of the figures along the wall was Bertrand rising and sinking in his stirrups, but he abandoned the attempt; it was some-how blasphemous, and he was glad that Helmuth's face had been hidden from him. Now the sergeant-major ordered a walking pace, and the white jumping-posts and hurdles were brought out. He was involun-tarily reminded of clowns, and suddenly he understood a saying of Bertrand's, that the Fatherland was defended by a set of circus clowns. It was still incomprehensible to him how he had managed to come a cropper over that tree.

He drove once more past Borsig's engineering works. Once more there were workmen standing about. He had really had enough of that kind of thing. It wasn't his world, and he had no need to barricade himself from it behind a gay uniform. True, Bertrand belonged to it, perhaps reluctantly, but still he was acclimatized; well, he had had enough of Bertrand too: the best thing after all would be to return to Stolpin. In spite of that, however, he stopped his carriage at Bertrand's door, and was delighted to hear that Herr von Bertrand was expected that evening. Good; he would look in anyhow for a few minutes, and he left a note to that effect.

They went together to the theatre, where Ruzena displayed her mechanical gestures as a chorus girl. During the interval Bertrand said: " That's no job for her; we'll have to find her something else," and Joachim once more had a feeling of security. When they were at supper Bertrand turned to Ruzena: " Tell me, Ruzena, you're going to become a famous and marvellous actress now, aren't you?" Of course she was, wasn't that just what she was going to do! "Ah, but what if you should think better of it and change your mind? We've gone to a lot of trouble to give you the chance of becoming famous, and what if you should suddenly leave us in the lurch and make us look silly? What shall we do with you then?" Ruzena became reflective and suggested: "Well, there's the Jäger Casino." "No, no, Ruzena, one should never turn back when one has begun to climb. It must be something better than the theatre." Ruzena began to cry: "There's nothing at all for poor girl like me. He is bad friend, Joachim." Joachim said: "Bertrand's only joking, Ruzena." But he himself was uncomfortable and thought that Bertrand was overstepping the limits of tact. Bertrand, however, laughed: "There's no need to cry just because we're considering how to make you rich and famous, Ruzena. You'll have to keep all of us then." Joachim was shocked; one could see how commercial life vulgarized a man.

Later he said to Bertrand: "Why do you torment her?" Bertrand answered: "Well, we have to prepare her, and one can operate only on a healthy body. Now's the time." He spoke like a surgeon.

What Joachim had half feared had now happened. His letter had fallen into his father's hands, and the old man had obviously begun to rave again, for his mother wrote that there had been a fresh stroke. Joachim was amazed by his own indifference. He felt no obligation to go home, there was still plenty of time for that. Helmuth had charged him to stand by his mother, but it was little that one could do to help her; she would have to bear alone the fate she had taken upon herself. He wrote that he would come as soon as he could and stayed where he was, leaving things to take their own course, performing his duties, taking no steps whatever to make a change, and with an inexplicable fear thrusting aside every thought that suggested change. For it often required an actual effort to hold things firmly in their proper shapes, an effort so difficult that many a time all those people who bustled about as if all was in order seemed to him limited, blind and almost crazy. At first he had not thought much about it, but when for a second time he saw the military spectacle in terms of a circus he decided that Bertrand was to blame for everything. Why, even his uniform refused to sit upon him as well as formerly: the epaulets on his shoulders suddenly worried

him, and the cuffs of his shirt, and one morning before the glass he
asked himself why it should be on the left side that he had to wear his
sword. He took refuge in thoughts of Ruzena, telling himself that his
love for her, her love for him, was something exempt from all ambiguous
conventions. And then, when he gazed long into her eyes and stroked
her eyelids with a gently caressing finger, and she took it to be love, he
was often merely losing himself in an agonizing game, letting her face
grow dimmer and more indefinite, until it touched the boundary at
which it threatened to lose its human character, and the face became
no face at all. Things were elusive as a melody that one thinks one
cannot forget and yet loses the thread of, only to be compelled to seek
it again and again in anguish. It was an uncanny and hopeless game to
play, and with angry irritation he wished that Bertrand could be saddled
with the blame for that queer state of mind as well. Had he not, indeed,
spoken of his demon? Ruzena divined Joachim's irritation, and her
suspicion of Bertrand, which had rankled in her since that last evening,
flared out after a long, sullen silence with clumsy abruptness: " You
not love me any more . . . or have to ask friend's permission . . . or
has Bertrand already forbidden? " And although they were angry and
wounding words, Joachim was glad of them, for they came as a relief,
confirming his own suspicion that the demonic root of all his afflictions
was in Bertrand. And it even seemed to him like the final emanation of
such an evil, Mephistophelian and treacherous influence that the aversion
Ruzena shared with him should bring her no nearer, but rather, by
provoking rude and uncontrolled outbursts, should put her more on a
level with Bertrand and his equally offensive jokes; between his mistress
and his friend, both unstable, between these two civilians, he felt as if
caught and helplessly ground between two millstones of tactlessness.
He felt the smell of bad company, and often could not tell whether
Bertrand had led him to Ruzena, or Ruzena had been the means
of bringing him to Bertrand, until in alarm he realized that he
was no longer capable of grasping the evanescent, dissolving mass
of life, and that he was slipping more and more quickly, more and
more profoundly, into brain-sick confusion, and that everything had
become unsure. But when he thought of finding in religion some
way out of this chaos, the abyss opened afresh that parted him from
the civilians, for it was on the other side of the abyss that there
stood the civilian Bertrand, a Freethinker, and the Catholic Ruzena,

both beyond his reach, and it almost looked as if they exulted in his isolation.

He was glad that he was due for church parade on Sunday. But even into this military rite he was dogged by civilian values. For the faces of the rank and file who had marched, as enjoined, in two parallel columns into the House of God, were the everyday faces of the drill-ground and the riding-school; not one of them was devout, not one was solemn. The men must have been recruited from Borsig's engineering works; real peasants' sons from the country would not have stood there so indifferently. Except for the non-commissioned officers, standing piously at attention, not one of them was listening to the sermon. The temptation to label this ritual, too, a circus came affrightingly near. Joachim shut his eyes and tried to pray, as he had tried to pray in the village church. Perhaps he was not praying, but when the soldiers joined in the anthem, his voice raised itself among the others, although he did not know it, for with the hymn that he had sung as a child there rose also the memory of a picture, the memory of a small, brightly coloured holy picture, and once the picture was clearly imaged he remembered, too, that it was the black-haired Polish cook who had brought it to him: he heard her deep, sing-song voice and saw her seamed finger, with its chapped tip, tracing its way over all that brightness, pointing out that here was the earth on which men lived, and up above it, not too remotely above it, the Holy Family sat peacefully together on a silvery rain-cloud portrayed in the brightest of colours, and the gold that adorned their garments rivalled in splendour their golden haloes. Even now he did not dare to recall how blissful it had been to imagine oneself as a member of that Catholic Holy Family, reposing on that silver cloud in the arms of the virgin Mother of God or in the lap of the black-haired Pole . . . that was a point he could not now decide, but he was sure that the rapture was permeated by fear at its blasphemous presumption and at the heresy in a born Protestant's yielding to such a wish and such imagined bliss, and that he had not dared to make room for the wrathful Father in that picture; he did not want Him there at all. And while he strained his attention and bent his will to realize the picture more closely, it was as if the silver cloud floated up a little higher, as if it even began to evaporate upwards, and with it the figures that rested upon it; they seemed lightly to dissolve and float away on the melody of the anthem, a soft effluence that in no way effaced the remembered imagery, but rather illumined and defined it, so that for a moment he was even inclined to believe that it was the needful resolution into evangelical truth of a Catholic holy picture: the Virgin's hair, too, seemed no longer dusky, and she was less like the Polish woman, nor was she Ruzena, but her locks brightened and became more golden, and might almost have been the maiden tresses of Elisabeth. All that was a little peculiar and yet a deliverance, a ray of light and the promise of coming grace in the midst of obscurity; for was it not an act of grace that permitted a Catholic picture to resolve itself into evangelical truth? And the fluidity of the figures, a fluidity as gracious as the murmuring of rain or the mist on a drizzling spring evening, made him aware that the dissolution he so feared of the human face into a blankness of mobile heights and hollows might be the first step towards its new and more radiant integration within the blissful company in the cloud, no mere rough copy of earthly features but an initiation into the pure image, the crystalline drop that falls singing from the cloud. And even if this more exalted countenance wore no earthly beauty or familiarity, but was at first alien and alarming, perhaps still more alarming than the blending of a face with a landscape, yet it was the first step upwards, the presentiment of an awful divinity, but also the surety for that divine life in which all earthly life is resolved, dissolving like the face of Ruzena and the face of Elisabeth, perhaps even dissolving like the shape of Bertrand. So it was no longer the childish picture of old, with an actual father and mother, that now displayed itself: true, it hovered still on the same spot, floating in the midst of the same silver cloud, and he himself still sat in the same way at the feet of the figures as once he had sat at his mother's feet, himself a boyish Jesus; but the picture had grown in meaning, no longer the imagined wish of a boy, but the assurance of an attainable end, and he knew that he had taken the first painful step towards that end, that he had entered upon his probation, although only on the threshold of what was to come. His feeling was one almost of pride. But then the blissful picture faded; it vanished like an imperceptibly ceasing rain, and that Elisabeth was part of it came as a final drop of realization from the veiling mist. Perhaps that was a sign from God. He opened his eyes; the anthem was closing, and Joachim thought that he saw many of the young men gazing up to heaven with the same trust and resolute ardour as himself.

In the afternoon he met Ruzena. He said: " Bertrand is right; the theatre is no fit place for you. Would you not like to have a shop and sell pretty things, lace, for instance, and fine embroidery?" And in his mind's eye he saw a glass door with a homely lamp burning behind it. But Ruzena looked at him quietly, and, as now often occurred, tears rose into her dark eyes. " Bad men you are," she said, and held his hand.

In view of his patient's fresh relapse the doctor had asked for a consultation, and it fell to Joachim, as a matter of course, to escort the nerve specialist to Stolpin. He regarded it as a part of the penance he was to undergo, and was more strongly confirmed in this belief when the doctor, with an amiable detachment, set to questioning him about the nature of the illness, the course it had previously run, and the general family situation. For these questions appeared to Joachim an inquisition, courteous enough, but none the less a keen and probing inquisition, and he expected the inquisitor suddenly to give him a severe look through his eyeglasses and to point an outstretched finger at him; already he heard the accusing damning sound of the frightful word: murderer. Yet the amiable old gentleman with the spectacles showed no disposition to utter that frightful but emancipating word, remarking merely that the shock of his son's death had certainly occasioned the deplorable symptoms that were now afflicting Herr von Pasenow, although the original roots of the malady might lie deeper. Joachim began to regard the specialist with mistrust and yet with a certain satisfaction, being convinced that a man who expressed such opinions was incapable of helping the sufferer.

Then conversation died away, and Joachim saw the familiar fields and trees gliding past. The rhythm of the train had set the specialist nodding drowsily, his chin between the points of his stiff collar, and his white beard spread over his shirt-front. It was unimaginable to Joachim that he also might be as old as that one day, unimaginable too that the other had once been young and that a woman might have looked for kisses in his beard; surely some trace of that would still have been perceptible in the beard, like a feather or a straw. He drew his hand over his own face; it was an imposture on Elisabeth that of the kisses which Ruzena had given him in farewell not a trace remained: God was merciful to mankind in drawing a veil over the future, but pitiless in that He removed all traces of the past; would it not be merciful to brand a man's deeds on him? But God seared the brand only on a man's conscience, and not even a nerve specialist could discover it. Helmuth had been branded, and that was why he could not be looked at in his coffin. But his father too was branded; anyone who behaved as he did could not but look furtive.

Herr von Pasenow was out of bed, but in a state of complete apathy; nevertheless Joachim's presence was concealed from him in case he should have a fresh outbreak of rage. He met the strange doctor with indifference, but presently took him for a notary and broached the subject of making a new will. Joachim was to be disinherited for dishonourable conduct, yes, but he wasn't a hard father, he only wanted Joachim to beget him a grandson on Elisabeth. The child must thereupon be brought into the house and become the heir. After some reflection he added that Joachim must not be permitted to see the child, or it would be disinherited too. His mother hesitatingly informed Joachim of this, and, contrary to her custom, fell into lamentation: where was all this going to lead to! Joachim shrugged his shoulders; he merely felt again what a disgrace it was to have a parent who dared to mention the possibility of children by himself and Elisabeth.

The nerve specialist too had shrugged his shoulders; there was no need to give up hope, he said; Herr von Pasenow was still extraordinarily vigorous, but for the present there was nothing to do but await developments; only the patient should not be allowed to stay too much in bed, for that might lower his vitality, considering his years. Frau von Pasenow objected that her husband was very desirous of staying in bed, for he always felt cold, and it seemed, too, that he was tormented by some secret fear that abated only when he was in his bedroom. Well, of course, one must act according to the patient's condition, observed the nerve specialist; all he could say was that in the care of his colleague—here the local doctor bowed his thanks—Herr von Pasenow was in the very best of hands.

It had grown late, the pastor had turned up, and the evening meal was served. Suddenly Herr von Pasenow appeared in the doorway: " So, there are supper-parties here without my knowledge; apparently because the new master of the house has arrived." Joachim made to leave the room. " Stay where you are and keep your seat," commanded Herr von Pasenow, setting himself down at the head of the table in the big chair that was left vacant for him even in his absence; obviously he

was somewhat conciliated by this discovery. He insisted on having the
courses served to him again: " Things need setting in order here. Herr
Notary, have you been properly looked after? Have you been offered
your choice of red or white wine? I see nothing but red wine. Why is
there no champagne? A will should have a bottle of champagne cracked
upon it." He laughed to himself. " Well, what about that champagne? "
he hectored the parlourmaid. " Must I go foraging myself? " The nerve
specialist was the first to regain his composure, and to save the situation
said he would gladly accept a glass of champagne. Triumphantly Herr
von Pasenow surveyed the table: " Yes, things need setting in order
again. Nobody has any sense of honour . . ." then in a low voice to
the specialist, " Helmuth, you know, died for honour. But he never
writes to me. Perhaps he's still resentful . . ." he thought it over, " or
this pastor here intercepts the letters. Wants to keep his own secrets,
doesn't want laymen to get a peep behind the scenes. But as soon as
there's any disorder in the churchyard he'll take to his heels, the man
of God. That I'll go bail for." " But, Herr von Pasenow, the churchyard is in the best of order." " Apparently, Herr Notary, apparently,
but it's nothing but eyewash, only it's not so easy for us to discover it
because we don't understand their language; they're quite obviously
hiding from us. We others only hear how silent they are, and yet they're
complaining to us all the time. That's why everybody's so afraid, and
when a guest comes I have to take him out myself, old as I am," he,
darted a hostile look at Joachim, " a man without honour of course
can't screw up his courage to it and sneaks out of sight in the byre."
" Well, Herr von Pasenow, you must yourself have to see often enough
that everything's all right and inspect the fields; you must in any case
go out." " I like doing it, Herr Notary, and I do it too. But as soon
as one sets foot outside the door they often block the road completely,
the air's so full of them, so full that not a sound can find its way past
them." He shuddered, seized the physician's glass, and before anyone
could hinder him emptied it at a gulp. " You must visit me often,
Herr Notary, we'll make wills together. And meanwhile won't you
write to me? " he implored. " Or will you disappoint me too," he
looked suspiciously at him, " and perhaps conspire with the others? . . .
he has tricked me already with someone, that creature there. . . ." He
had sprung to his feet, and his finger pointed at Joachim. Then he
seized a plate, and, shutting one eye as if he were taking aim, screamed:

" I've ordered him to get married. . . ." But the specialist was already beside him and laid a hand on his arm: " Come with me, Herr von Pasenow; we'll go to your room and talk there for a little longer." Herr von Pasenow gazed at him blankly; the other met his eye steadily: " Come along, we'll have a little talk all by ourselves." " All by ourselves, really? And I shan't be afraid any more. . . ." He smiled helplessly and patted the doctor's cheek. " Yes, we'll let them see." He made a contemptuous gesture towards the company and suffered himself to be led away.

Joachim had buried his face in his hands. Yes, his father had branded him; the blow had fallen now, and yet he rebelled against it. The pastor came up to him, and as if from afar he heard the banal words of comfort; his father was right in that, too: this minister of the Church was a poor makeshift, or else he would have known that the curse of a father lies irremediably upon his children; he would have known that it is the voice of God Himself that speaks through one's father's mouth and proclaims the hour of trial. Oh, that was why his father's wits were clouded now, for no man could be God's mouthpiece and not suffer for it. And of course the pastor must be a commonplace creature; for if he were really an instrument of God on earth he too would mouth strange sayings. Yet God had pointed the way to His grace without the mediation of priests; there was no getting away from that, one must win that grace alone and in suffering. Joachim said: " I thank you for your kindly words, Pastor; we shall certainly be often in need of your consolation." Then the doctor returned; Herr von Pasenow had been given an injection and was now asleep.

The nerve specialist stayed in the house for two more days. And when shortly afterwards a profoundly disquieting telegram of Bertrand's arrived from Berlin, and the invalid's condition remained obviously unchanged, Joachim too was enabled to depart.

Bertrand had come back to Berlin. In the afternoon he went to visit Joachim, but found only Ruzena in the flat. She was tidying up the bedroom, and when Bertrand appeared she said: " I not speak to you." " Hallo, Ruzena, you're very amiable." " I not speak to you, know what you are." " Am I a bad friend again, my little Ruzena? " " Not your little Ruzena." " Very well, then, what's the matter? " " What's matter! . . . know it all, you send him away. I spit on your lace-shop." " All right, a lace-shop I may have, I don't mind, but that's no reason for not speaking to me. What's the matter with my lace-shop? " In silence Ruzena went on putting underlinen into the chest of drawers; Bertrand drew up a chair and waited with amusement for what was to come. " If it was my flat, throw you out, not let you sit." " Look here, Ruzena, in all seriousness what's gone wrong? Has the old man been taken bad again, so that Pasenow had to go off? " " Not pretend you not know; I not so stupid." " I'm afraid you are, little one." She turned her back on him and went on with her task. " Not let you laugh over me . . . not let anybody laugh over me." Bertrand went up to her and took her head between his hands to look into her face. She tore herself away. " Not touch me. First you send him away and then laugh over me." Bertrand understood it all, except for the reference to the lace-shop. " Well, Ruzena, so you don't believe that old Herr von Pasenow is ill? " " Believe nothing, you all against me." Bertrand grew a little impatient. " Apparently if the old man dies it will be just to spite the little Ruzena." " If you kill him he die." Bertrand would have liked to help her, but it was not easy; he knew that there was not much to be done with her in that mood, and he rose to go. " You should be killed," said Ruzena in conclusion. Bertrand was amused. " All right," he remarked, " I have no objection, but will that make things any better? " " So you have no objection, no objection? " Ruzena hunted excitedly in a drawer, " but make mock at me, yes? " . . . she went on hunting, " . . . no objection . . ." and found what she was looking for. Bristling with hostility, Joachim's army revolver in her hand, she faced up to Bertrand. This is too silly, thought Bertrand. " Ruzena, put that down at once." " You have no objection." A touch of anger and even of shame prevented Bertrand from simply quitting the room; he took a step towards Ruzena with the idea of seizing the weapon, and all at once a shot rang out, followed by a second when the revolver that she had let fall hit the floor. " That's really too stupid," said Bertrand, and bent down to pick it up. The valet came rushing in, but Bertrand explained that the thing had fallen on the floor and gone off. " Tell the Lieutenant that he shouldn't keep pistols lying about loaded." The valet went out again. " Well, Ruzena, are you a silly goose or not? " Ruzena stood white and petrified, pointed to Bertrand and said: " There! " Blood was dripping from his sleeve. " Let me locked up," she stammered. Bertrand took off his coat and undid the shirt-sleeve; he had felt nothing; his arm seemed only grazed, but it would be necessary to see a doctor about it. He ordered the valet to call a cab. With some linen of Joachim's he made a provisional bandage and bade Ruzena wash away the blood, but she was so upset and confused that he had to help her. " So, Ruzena; and you'd better come with me, for now I can't let you stay here alone. You won't be locked up if you'll admit that you are a silly goose." She followed him mechanically. At his doctor's door he enjoined her to wait for him in the cab.

He told the doctor that by a clumsy accident he had had his arm grazed by a bullet. " Well, you've been lucky, but don't treat the matter too lightly; you'd better lie up for a day or two in hospital." Bertrand thought that this was exaggerated caution, but as he went down the steps he became aware that he felt dizzy. To his amazement he found no trace of Ruzena in the cab. Not very nice of her, he thought.

He drove home first and collected everything that a practical man of some standing needs for a sojourn in hospital, and after being admitted to a ward he sent a note to Ruzena with the request that she should come and visit him. The messenger returned with the news that the lady hadn't come home yet. That was strange and almost disquieting; but he was not in the mood to take any fresh step that day. Next morning he sent another message; she had still not come home, nor had she been seen in Joachim's flat. That decided him to send a wire to Stolpin, and two days later Joachim arrived.

Bertrand felt no call to give Joachim a truthful account of what had happened; the tale of an accident caused by Ruzena's clumsiness sounded plausible enough. He ended up: " Since then she's vanished completely. That might mean nothing at all, but a girl in such an excited state might easily do something foolish." Joachim thought: what has he been doing to her? But he was suddenly horrified to remember that often enough, sometimes in jest, but sometimes in deadly earnest, Ruzena had threatened to throw herself into the water. He saw the grey willows on the banks of the Havel, the tree under which they had once sheltered; yes, she must be lying there in the river. For the space of a heart-beat he felt flattered by this romantic situation. But then the horror of it flooded over him again. Inevitable fate, inescapable discipline of God! And if he had prayed in the church, while still full of hope before his visit to Stolpin, that his father's illness might not be a penance laid upon him, the son, but merely one of the chances of life, the finger of God now showed him that even that prayer had been sinful. One dared not question God's discipline; there was no such thing as chance; for Bertrand, although he had parted in apparent enmity from Herr von Pasenow and was now depreciating the revolver incident as a stupid accident, was only trying to disguise the fact that he was an emissary of evil, deliberately chosen by God and by Herr von Pasenow to discipline the penitent, to lure him into temptation, to lead him into snares, so that in his extremity he might learn that the tempted is as much to blame as the tempter, and with the same fatality, now and always, brings ruin on those nearest him, and that no effort of his can avail to cheat the Tempter of his victims. When a man has come to such knowledge, is it not better for him to destroy himself? How much better it would have been if the bullet had killed him instead of Helmuth! But now it was too late, now Ruzena was lying at the bottom of the river, staring with glazed eyes at the fishes darting over her in the grey water. Quite unexpectedly her drowned image blended again with that of the Italian at the opera; but that too vanished when Joachim discovered that the man under the water was really himself. Yes, in his own blue eyes was the unlucky evil glance that the Italians believed in, and it would serve those eyes right if the fishes were darting over them. Bertrand said: " Have you any idea where she might be? Let's hope that she has simply gone back to her home. I suppose she would have enough money for that? " Joachim felt annoyed by this question; it had a touch of the inquisitorial detachment of a doctor. What was Bertrand hinting at? Of course she had money on her. Bertrand did not remark his annoyance. " All the same, we'd better inform the police; it's not impossible that she may be wandering about." Of course they must inform the police; Bertrand was right, yet Joachim shrank from doing so; he would be questioned about his connection with Ruzena, and even though he told himself that it was unimportant, yet he feared that vague and mysterious consequences might follow. His connection with Ruzena had been all too long sinfully concealed; perhaps God had planned to have it brought to His notice by means of the police; perhaps this was another of the penances he must do, made still harder by the fact that the police office was situated in the Alexanderplatz, which he shrank more than ever from entering. Yet he rose to his feet. " I shall drive round to the police." " No, Pasenow, I'll arrange that for you; you're still too upset, and anyhow they'll suspect melodrama." Joachim was sincerely grateful. " Yes, but your arm ..." " Oh, that doesn't matter;

they're just going to discharge me here." " But I'll come with you." " All right, then, and I hope I'll still find *you* in the cab when I get into it again." Bertrand was once more gay, and Joachim felt secure. In the cab he begged Bertrand to tell the police to search the banks of the Havel. " Very well, Pasenow, but in my opinion Ruzena's long since back in Bohemia; a pity you don't know the name of her village, but we'll soon unearth it." Joachim himself was now surprised that he did not know the name of Ruzena's native village, scarcely, indeed, her family name. She had often in fun tried to make him pronounce these names, but he could never get his tongue round the foreign words and could not remember them. It occurred to him now that he had never really wanted to know them or to keep them in his memory; yes, almost as if he had been a little afraid of those harmless names.

He accompanied Bertrand through the corridors of the police building; he had to wait outside the door of an office. Bertrand soon came back. " They know it all right," and on a piece of paper he showed the name of a Czech village. " Did you direct them to the banks of the Havel? " Of course Bertrand had done so. " But, my dear Pasenow, there's something unpleasant for you to do this evening, for I can't do it because of my arm. You must get into mufti and hunt through all the cafés and cabarets. I didn't want to suggest that to the police; we can always do that later. They might pounce on poor Ruzena and arrest her in the middle of some dancing-floor." Joachim had not thought of such a vulgar and repulsive possibility. Bertrand was indeed a disgusting cynic. He looked at Bertrand. Did the man know more? Mephisto alone understood what Margaret had to do penance for. But Bertrand's face betrayed nothing. There was nothing for it but to submit and accept the task Bertrand had laid upon him as a further discipline.

He had entered upon his degrading pilgrimage, asking questions of waiters and barmaids, and was relieved to be told in the Jäger Casino that nothing had been seen of Ruzena. But on the staircase he met one of the plump dancing partners. " Looking for your sweetheart, I suppose, dearie; has she given you the slip? Well, come along, you can easily get another." What did the woman know of his connection with Ruzena? It was possible, of course, that she had met Ruzena somewhere, but the thought of asking her sickened him, and he hurried past her and into the next café. Yes, Ruzena had been there, said the woman at the buffet, yesterday or the day before, that was all she could tell him; perhaps the attendant in the ladies' toilet could give him more information. He had to continue his sorrowful quest, again and again overwhelmed with shame as he interrogated barmaids and lavatory attendants, and learned that she had been seen or had not been seen, that she had had a wash, that she had gone away once with a gentleman, that she had looked quite down-at-heels. " We all tried to persuade her to go home, for a girl in a state like that is no credit to any café, but she just sat and said nothing." Many of these people simply addressed him at once as " Herr Lieutenant," so that the suspicion awoke in him that Ruzena had taken them all into her confidence, and had betrayed his love to all these people. It was the lavatory attendants to whom he was always referred.

And it was in a toilet-room that he found her. She sat sleeping in the corner under a burning gas-jet; her hand, with the ring that he had given her, lay limp on the wet marble of the washstand. She had undone her boots, and over one foot, which showed beneath her skirt, the shapeless, unbuttoned top of the boot hung down, showing its grey lining. Her hat had slipped to the back of her head, dragging her hair with it by the hatpins. Joachim would have preferred to turn and go; she looked like a drunk woman. He touched her hand; Ruzena wearily opened her eyes; when she recognized him she shut them again. " Ruzena, we must go." She shook her head, keeping her eyes shut. He stood helplessly before her. " Give her a good kiss," the attendant encouraged him. " No! " shrieked Ruzena in terror, springing up and making for the door. She stumbled over her unbuttoned boots and Joachim caught hold of her. " But you can't go into the street with your boots and your hair like that," said the attendant; " the Herr Lieutenant isn't going to do you any harm." " Let go; let me go out, I say," panted Ruzena, and into Joachim's face: " All over, you know it, all over." Her breath smelt foul and stale. But Joachim still barred her way, so Ruzena turned round, tore open a lavatory door and locked herself in. " All over! " she screamed from behind the door. " Tell him must go away, all over." Joachim had sunk on to a chair beside the wash-basin; his mind could grasp nothing, he knew only that this too was one of the trials sent by God, and he stared at the half-open brown drawer of the toilet-table, in which the attendant's few possessions—handkerchiefs, a corkscrew, a clothes-brush—were bestowed higgledy-piggledy. " Is he gone? " he heard Ruzena's voice. " Ruzena, come out," he begged. " Fräulein, dearie, come out," begged the attendant, " this is the ladies' toilet and the Herr Lieutenant can't stay here." " He must go away," was Ruzena's answer. " Ruzena, please, do come out," implored Joachim once more, but behind her bolted door Ruzena was mute. The attendant drew him by the sleeve into the passage and whispered: " She'll come out when she thinks the Herr Lieutenant has gone. The Herr Lieutenant can wait for her downstairs." Joachim accepted her suggestion, and in the shadow of a neighbouring house he waited for a full hour. Then Ruzena appeared; beside her waddled a fat, bearded, soft-fleshed man. She peered cautiously round with a curiously fixed, malicious smile, and then the man hailed a cab and they drove away. Joachim had to fight against an inclination to vomit; he dragged himself home, scarcely knowing how he got there, and perhaps his worst torture was his inability to rid himself of the thought that the fat man should really be pitied, because Ruzena was unwashed and had a stale smell. The revolver was still lying on the chest of drawers; he examined it, two shots were missing. With the weapon in his clasped hands he began to pray: " God, take me to Thee like my brother; to him Thou wert merciful, be merciful also to me." But then he bethought himself that he still had to make his will; and he dared not leave Ruzena unprovided for, or else she would be justified in all she had done to him, incomprehensible as it was. He looked for pen and ink. Dawn found him fast asleep over an almost blank sheet of paper.

He concealed his misadventure with Ruzena, being ashamed before Bertrand and unwilling to grant him the satisfaction of having been right, and although the lie disgusted him he reported that he had found her in her own room. " That's all right," said Bertrand; " have you notified the police? If not, she might get into trouble with them." Of course Joachim had not thought of that, and Bertrand sent a messenger with the requisite information to the police. " Where has she been, then, for these three days? " " She won't say." " That's all right." Bertrand's dry indifference irritated him; he had nearly put a bullet through himself and the fellow merely said: " That's all right." But he had refrained from suicide because he had to provide for Ruzena, and for that he needed Bertrand's advice: " Listen, Bertrand, I expect I'll have to take over the estate now; but Ruzena needs some means of livelihood and an occupation, and I thought first of buying her a shop or something

of that kind . . ." (" Aha," said Bertrand) " but she won't hear of it.
So I'd like to settle some money on her. How does one do that? " " You
must make it over to her. It would be better, though, to allow her an
income for a certain time; otherwise she would go through all the money
at once." " Yes, but how does one do that? " " Well, of course I'd be
glad to arrange it for you, but it would be better to put my lawyer on
to it. I'll fix up an appointment with him for to-morrow or next day.
But, my dear chap, you're looking wretched." That didn't matter,
remarked Joachim. " Well, what is it that's pulling you down? You
really don't need to take this affair so much to heart," said Bertrand
with light good-humour. His ironical indiscretion and that flicker of
irony about his mouth are hateful, thought Joachim, and from afar the
suspicion again began to steal upon him that behind Ruzena's inexplicable behaviour and her instability were hidden Bertrand's intrigues, and
that Ruzena had been driven into this folly by her connection with
Bertrand. It was a minor satisfaction that, in a sense, she had betrayed
Bertrand too with the fat man. The sick disgust that had overwhelmed
him on the previous evening began to rise again. Into what a morass
had he fallen. Outside the autumn rain was pouring down the window-
panes. Borsig's factory buildings must now be black with running soot
and water, the paving-stones must be black, and the courtyard, that one
could see through the gateway, a sea of black, gleaming slime. He could
smell the smoke driven down by the rain from the blackened top of the
long red chimney-stack: it smelt foul, stale, sulphurous. That was the
morass; that was the natural setting for Ruzena and the fat man and
Bertrand; it was akin to the night haunts with their gas-jets and their
lavatories. The day had turned into night, as the night into day. The
word night-spirit occurred to him, a word, indeed, that conveyed no
clear meaning. Were there also light-spirits? He could hear the phrase,
" virginal shape of light." Ah, that was the opposite of night-spirit.
And he had a vision of Elisabeth, who was different from all the others,
hovering on a silver cloud high above the morass. Perhaps he had already
divined this when he first saw the white clouds of lace in Elisabeth's
room and had longed to watch over her slumbers. She would soon be
coming now with her mother, moving into the new house. Extraordinary
that there must be lavatories there too; he felt it was blasphemy to
think of this. But not less blasphemous was the fact that Bertrand was
lying here with his golden hair waved, lying in a white room like a

young girl. Thus darkness obscures its real nature and keeps its mystery intact. Bertrand, however, went on to say with friendly concern: " You are looking so wretched, Pasenow, that you ought to be sent on holiday, and a little travel would do you good, too. It would put other thoughts into your mind." He wants to get rid of me, thought Joachim; he has had his way with Ruzena and now he wants to ruin Elisabeth too. " No," he said, " I can't go just now. . . ." Bertrand was silent for a while, and then it was as though he had divined Joachim's thoughts and was himself forced to betray his evil designs on Elisabeth, for he asked: " Are the Baddensens in Berlin yet? " Bertrand was still smiling sympathetic- ally, almost frankly, but Joachim, with a gruffness unusual to him, answered curtly: " They'll probably remain at Lestow for some time to come." And now he knew that he must go on living, that chivalry demanded it of him, lest another destiny should be ruined by his fault and fall a prey to Bertrand; but Bertrand only gave him a gay good-bye, saying: " Well, I'll arrange things with my lawyer . . . and when Ruzena's affairs are settled you should take a holiday. You really need it." Joachim said nothing more; his decision was made, and he went off full of heavy thoughts. It was always Bertrand who aroused such thoughts in him. And with the slight straightening of the shoulders, almost as if at the word of command, by which Joachim von Pasenow sought to shake off his thoughts, suddenly it was as if Helmuth had taken his hand, as if Helmuth wanted to show him the way again, to lead him back into convention and order, to open his eyes again. That Bertrand, whose expedition the previous day to the police headquarters had certainly done him no good, was again fevered, Joachim von Pasenow did not observe in the least.

The news from his father's sick-bed remained persistently bad. The old man no longer recognized anyone: he was sinking into a lethargy. Joachim caught himself entertaining the hateful-pleasant thought that now one could, in all security, send any letter to Stolpin, and pictured the messenger with the post-bag entering the bedroom and the old man incomprehendingly dropping letter after letter, incomprehendingly letting them fall, though there might be a betrothal announcement among them. And that was a kind of relief, and a vague hope for the future.

The possibility of seeing Ruzena again filled him with dread, although many a time when he came off duty it seemed inconceivable that he should not find her in his rooms. In any case he was daily expecting to hear from her, for he had settled the matter of her income with Bertrand's lawyer, and could not but presume that she had been informed. Instead of a message from her, he got a letter from the lawyer to say that the money had been refused. This would never do; he set out for Ruzena's flat; the building, the staircase and the flat filled him with profound uneasiness, indeed with an almost anguished yearning. He feared that he would have to stand again before a locked door, perhaps even be turned away by some charwoman or other, and much as he shrank from forcing his way into a lady's room, he merely asked if she were at home, knocked at her door and walked in. The room and Ruzena were alike in a state of dirt and disorder, neglected and barbaric. She was lying on the sofa and made a defensive, weary gesture, as if she had known that he would come. Haltingly she said: " Not take nothing from you. The ring I keep, souvenir." Joachim could feel no sympathy rising within him; if on the very staircase he had still intended to point out that he literally did not understand what she had against him, he was now merely embittered; he could see nothing in her attitude but obstinacy. Yet he said: " Ruzena, I don't know what has really happened . . ." She laughed contemptuously, and his resentment of her obstinacy and instability, which had injured him and done him injustice, reasserted itself. No, there was no sense in trying to persuade her, and so he merely said that he could not bear the thought that she was not even half provided for, and that he would have done it long ago whether they had stuck to each other or not, only he could do it more easily now because—and he added this deliberately—he had to take over the estate and so had more money at his disposal. " You are good man," said Ruzena, " only you have bad friend." That was ultimately what Joachim believed at the bottom of his heart, but since he did not want to admit it he only said: " Why do you think that Bertrand is a bad friend? " " Wicked words," replied Ruzena. It was tempting to think of making common cause with Ruzena against Bertrand, but was it not just another temptation of the Devil's, another intrigue of Bertrand's? Obviously Ruzena felt so too, for she said: " Must beware him." Joachim answered: " I know his faults." She had raised herself up on the sofa, and they now sat side by side. " You are poor, good soul, can't know how bad peoples are." Joachim assured her that he knew it very well, and that he was not so easily deceived. And so they spoke for a while about Bertrand without mentioning his name, and since they did not want to stop speaking, they pursued the theme until the brackish melancholy that flowed behind their words rose higher and higher, and the words were drowned in it and blended with Ruzena's tears into a stream that broadened and slackened more and more. Joachim, too, had tears in his eyes. Both were helplessly delivered to the senselessness of Fate, now they were aware that they could no longer find comfort in each other. They did not dare to look at each other, and finally Joachim's woebegone voice said: " Please, Ruzena, please take the money at least." She made no reply, but she had grasped his hand. When he bent over her to kiss her she bowed her head, so that the kiss landed among her hairpins. " Go now," she said, " quick go," and Joachim silently left the room, in which it was already dusk.

He informed the lawyer, so that the deed of settlement could be drawn up again; this time Ruzena would surely accept it. But the kindness with which Ruzena and he had taken leave of each other depressed him more than the helpless resentment he had previously felt at her incomprehensible behaviour. It was indeed still as incomprehensible and dreadful as ever. His thoughts of Ruzena were full of sad yearning, full of that reluctant homesickness with which, in his cadet days, his mind had turned to his father's house and his mother. Was the fat man by her side now? He had to think of the jesting insult his father had put upon Ruzena, and here too he recognized the curse of his father, who, himself sick and helpless, had sent a deputy in his stead. Yes, God was fulfilling his father's curse, and all he could do was to submit.

Sometimes he made a feeble attempt to find Ruzena again; but whenever he was a few streets away from her flat he always turned back or took a side-street, landing in the slum quarter or in the turmoil of the Alexanderplatz, and once even going as far as the Küstriner Station. He was entangled all over again in the toils, and had lost hold of all the threads. His one firm certainty was that at least Ruzena's income should be assured, and Joachim now spent much time in the office of Bertrand's lawyer, much more time than was actually needful. But the hours he wasted there were a kind of consolation, and although these dull and somewhat pointless visits could not have been very agreeable to the lawyer, and although Joachim learned nothing of what he hoped to learn from Bertrand's representative, yet the lawyer did not spare himself

in going into the semi-relevant and almost private questions raised by
his aristocratic client, applying himself to them with a professional
interest which somewhat resembled a doctor's, but none the less did
Joachim good. The lawyer, a spare man and quite beardless although
he was Bertrand's legal representative, looked like an Englishman. When,
after ample delay, Ruzena's acceptance finally came, the lawyer said:
" Well, now we've got it. But if you'll take my advice, Herr von Pasenow,
you'll allow the lady in question the option of taking the capital sum instead of the interest on it." " Yes," interposed Joachim, " but I arranged
it so with Herr von Bertrand simply because . . ." " I appreciate your
motive, Herr von Pasenow, and I know too—if you'll excuse me—
that you are not much inclined to take any bull by the horns; but what
I advise is in the best interests of both parties: for the lady it's a pretty
sum of money, which in certain circumstances might set her up better
for life than an allowance, and for you, on the other hand, it's a definite
quittance." Joachim felt a little helpless; was it really a definite quittance
he wanted? The lawyer remarked his helplessness: " If I may touch on
the private aspect of the matter, my experience has taught me that the
best kind of settlement is one which enables one to regard a past obligation as non-existent." Joachim looked up. " Yes, as non-existent, Herr
von Pasenow. Convention, after all, is the safest guide." The word
" non-existent " stuck to Joachim. Only it was strange that through the
mouth of his representative Bertrand should signify such a change in
his opinions and even acknowledge a convention of feeling. Why did
he do it? The lawyer went on to say: " So think it over from that point
of view as well, Herr von Pasenow; and, of course, for a man in your
position the loss of the capital is of no importance." Yes, a man in his
position; Joachim's sentiment for his home welled up again, warm and
comforting. He left the lawyer's office this time in an exceptionally good
mood, one might almost say uplifted and strengthened. True, he did
not yet see his way clear before him, for he still felt bewildered in the
invisible tangle that seemed to net the whole city, a tangle of invisible
forces that could not be grasped and that made his dull, persistent
yearning for Ruzena insignificant, although bringing new elements of
anguish into it, yet that bound him in such a novel and unreal relation
to Ruzena and to all the world of the city that the net of false brightness
became a net of horror winding around him, within whose tangled
confusion lurked the threat that Elisabeth too, on returning to the city,

which was not her world, might be caught in it; that she, the innocent and untouched, might be caught and entangled in these devilish and impalpable coils, entangled by his fault, entrapped because of him, because he could not free himself from the invisible embrace of the Devil, so persistently did darkness threaten to cloud what was clear, darkness invisible, perhaps, and still far off, floating, perhaps, and uncertain, but as besmirching as what his father had done to the maids in his mother's house. In spite of that, however, Joachim felt as he left the lawyer's office that he had come to a turning-point, for it was as if Bertrand had denounced his lies through the mouth of his own representative; Bertrand it had been, Bertrand, who had tried to draw him into the invisible, impalpable net, and now his own representative had had to acknowledge that the position of a Pasenow was something other, something outside this city and its swarming creatures, provided only that one was willing to regard the whole mirage as non-existent. Yes, that was Bertrand's message by his representative, and so the Devil at last was loosening his grip of his own accord; even the Devil was still subject to the will of God, Who, in the person of a father, demands the annihilation and the non-existence of whatever lies under a father's curse. The Evil One had acknowledged defeat, and even though he had not expressly renounced his claims on Elisabeth yet, he had himself advised Joachim to obey his father's wishes. And without consulting Bertrand in person Joachim resolved to empower the lawyer to pay out the capital sum.

Similarly without consulting Bertrand, Joachim put on his dress-uniform and a new pair of gloves when he was informed that the Freiherr von Baddensen and his family had arrived, and drove to visit them at an hour when he could hope to find the Baron and the Baroness at home. They wanted to show him the new house at once, but he begged the Baron first for a private interview, and after the Baron had taken him into another room Joachim straightened himself with a jerk into a correct posture, standing stiffly as before a superior officer, and asked for Elisabeth's hand. The Baron said: " Delighted and honoured, my dear, dear Pasenow," and called the Baroness in. The Baroness said: " Oh, I have been expecting it; a mother sees ever so many things," and dabbed her eyes. Yes, he would be very welcome as their dear son; they could not think of a better, and were convinced that he would do his utmost to make their daughter happy. He would do that, he returned manfully.

The Baron had taken his hand: but now, first of all, they must speak to their daughter about it; he must understand that. Joachim replied that he understood; and thereupon they spent another quarter of an hour in half-formal, half-intimate conversation, in the course of which Joachim could not refrain from mentioning Bertrand's wound; then he took his leave briefly without having seen either the new house or Elisabeth, but that mattered little now, for he had all the rest of his life to see them in.

It surprised Joachim himself that he was not more passionately impatient for Elisabeth's consent and did not feel impelled to shorten the time of waiting, and often it amazed him that he could not imagine their future life together. He could see himself, indeed, leaning on a stick with a white ivory crook-handle, standing beside Elisabeth in the middle of the stableyard, but when he tried to visualize the scene more closely the image of Bertrand always intruded. It would not be easy to tell him of their betrothal; after all it was Bertrand against whom it was directed and Bertrand from whom Elisabeth had to be shielded, and, strictly regarded, it had a look of treachery about it, since in a manner of speaking he had once surrendered Elisabeth to him. And although Bertrand deserved nothing better, yet he shrank from inflicting such a hurt upon him. Of course that was no reason for postponing the betrothal; but suddenly it began to look as if the betrothal could not take place at all unless Bertrand were previously informed of it. He was still in duty bound to keep an eye on Bertrand, and could not comprehend how he had so completely forgotten him for days together, as if he were already exempt from all obligations. Besides, Bertrand was probably still an invalid. He drove to the hospital. Bertrand was, in fact, still lying there; they had had to operate on him; Joachim was genuinely upset to discover how he had neglected the patient, and now that he set himself to inform him of the approaching event he made it at the same time a kind of excuse for such remissness. " But, my dear Bertrand, I can't always be plaguing you with my private affairs." Bertrand smiled, and there was a hint of a consultant's or a woman's solicitude in his smile. " Go ahead, Pasenow, it's not so bad as all that; I enjoy listening to you." And Joachim related how he had proposed for Elisabeth. " I don't know whether she will, I dread still more that she won't, for then I should feel that I was irretrievably floundering again in all the awful complications of the past months which you have shared with me to a great extent, while with her by my side I hope to find a way into the open." Bertrand smiled again. " Do you know, Pasenow, all that sounds very fine, yet I wouldn't care to marry you on the strength of it; but you don't need to worry. I'm convinced that you'll soon be accepting congratulations." What repulsive cynicism; the man was literally a bad friend, he was no true friend at all, even though one had to admit in extenuation that he was both jealous and disappointed. Joachim therefore ignored the cynical remark and fell back on his own train of thought, asking: " What shall I do if she says no? " And Bertrand gave him the answer he desired: " She won't say no," averring it with such conviction and certainty that Joachim once more experienced that feeling of security which Bertrand so often evoked in him. It now seemed to him almost unfair that Elisabeth should attach her preference to him, the unsure one, and renounce the sure and steady leader. And as if to justify himself a voice within him said: " Comrades in the King's uniform." And suddenly he had a vision of Bertrand as a major. But from what source did Bertrand draw his confidence? How could he be certain that Elisabeth would not refuse? Why did he smile so ironically as he said so? What did this man know? And he regretted having confided in him.—

As a matter of fact Bertrand could have found many justifications for an ironical smile, or more precisely a knowing smile; yet his smile was one of simple friendliness.

On the previous day Elisabeth had abruptly descended upon him. She had driven to the hospital and asked for him in the reception-room. In spite of his aches and pains he had gone down immediately. It was an extraordinary visit, and certainly outraged convention, but Elisabeth did not take any pains to conceal its irregularity; she was obviously in distress and went straight to the point:

" Joachim has made an offer for my hand."

" If you love him, there isn't any problem."

" I don't love him."

" Then there isn't any problem either, for I suppose you'll refuse him."

" So you won't help me? "

" I'm afraid, Elisabeth, there's nobody who can do that."

" And I thought that you could."

" I didn't want to see you again."

" Have you no friendship for me? "

" I don't know, Elisabeth."

" Joachim loves me."

" Love needs some degree of cleverness, not to say wisdom. You must allow me to be somewhat dubious of his love for you. I warned you once already."

" You are a bad friend."

" No, but there are moments when one must be absolutely honest."

" Can one be too stupid to love? "

" I have just said so."

" Perhaps, then, I too am too stupid."

" Listen to me, Elisabeth, we won't touch on questions of that kind, for these are not the motives that decide our lives."

" Perhaps I do love him . . . there was a time when I wasn't unwilling to think of marrying him."

Elisabeth sat in the large invalid-chair in the small reception-room and looked at the floor.

" Why have you come here, Elisabeth? Surely not to ask for advice that nobody can give you? "

" You don't want to help me? "

" You have come because you can't bear to have anyone run away from you."

" I am serious in this . . . you mustn't make a joke of it . . . too serious to endure your saying more of your abominable things to me. I thought I should find some understanding. . . ."

" But I must tell you the truth. That's just why I must tell you the truth. You have come because you feel that I stand posted at some point outside your world, because you think that from my outpost there might be descried a third possibility beside the banal alternatives: I love him, I don't love him."

" Perhaps that is so; I don't know any longer."

" And you have come because you know that I love you—I told you that plainly enough—and because you want to show me what my somewhat absurd conception of love leads to," he gave her a side-glance, " perhaps to discover how quickly estrangement can turn into intimacy. . . ."

" That's not true! "

" Let us be honest, Elisabeth; the question between you and me now is whether you would marry me. Or, to be more exact, whether you love me."

" Herr von Bertrand, how dare you take advantage of the situation in such a way! "

" Ah, you shouldn't have said that, for you know perfectly well that it's not true. You have a decision for life in front of you, and you can't simply take refuge in convention. Of course the only question is whether a woman can think of her man as a lover, and not whether she is willing to set up house with him. If there is one thing I can't forgive Joachim for, it's that he didn't frankly discuss this essential point with you, but went with his so-called wooing to your parents, literally degrading you. Mark my words, he'll be on his knees next."

" You're trying to torment me again. I shouldn't have come here."

" No, you shouldn't have come, because I didn't want to see you again, but, my dear, you had to come, because you I——"

She stopped her ears.

" Well, more precisely, you are on the verge of believing that you might be able to love me."

" Oh, don't torment me; have I not been tormented enough already? " With her hands pressed to her temples she lay in the easy-chair, her head thrown back, her eyes shut; that was just how she used to sit in Lestow, and this relapse into old habit made him smile and feel almost tender. He was standing behind her. The arm in the sling pained him and made him awkward. But he succeeded in bending down and touching her lips with his. She started up: " This is madness! "

" No, it's merely a farewell."

With a voice as drained of life as her face she said: " You shouldn't, you, of all people . . ."

" Who should kiss you, Elisabeth? "

" You don't love me. . . ."

Bertrand was now walking up and down the room. His arm ached and he felt feverish. She was right, it was sheer madness. Suddenly he turned round and stopped close in front of her: without his intending it his voice sounded menacing: " I don't love you? "

She stood motionless with her arms hanging, and let him bend back her head. In her very face he repeated his threatening words: " I don't love you? " And she felt that he was going to bite her lips, but it turned into a kiss. And while most incomprehensibly the rigidity of her mouth relaxed into a smile, her hands, which had been hanging limp, now came to life and raised themselves, with the outflow of her feeling, towards his shoulders to clutch them, never more to let them go. At that he said: " Take care, Elisabeth, that's where I'm wounded."

Horrified, she loosened her grasp. But then her strength forsook her: she collapsed into the easy-chair. He sat on the arm of it, drew out the pins of her hat, and caressed her blond hair. " How lovely you are, and how much I love you." She was silent; she suffered him to take her hand; she felt the fevered heat of his, felt the heat of his face as he bent close to her again. When he hoarsely repeated " I love you " she shook her head, but yielded him her lips. Then at last the tears came.

Bertrand sat on the arm of the chair stroking her hair gently. He said: " I have such a longing for you."

She answered weakly: " It isn't true."

" I have such a longing for you."

She made no reply, staring into vacancy. He did not touch her again; he had risen to his feet and said once more: " I have an unspeakable longing for you."

Now she smiled.

" And you are going away? "

" Yes."

She looked up, questioning and incredulous; he repeated: " No, we shall never see each other again."

She was still unconvinced. Bertrand smiled: " Can you imagine me suing for you to your father? Giving the lie to everything I have said? That would make it all the most sordid comedy; the most barefaced imposition."

She grasped somehow what he meant, but yet could not understand:

" But why, then? Why . . . ? "

" I can't possibly ask you to be my mistress, to come with me . . . of course I could and you would end up by doing it too . . . perhaps out of romanticism . . . perhaps because you really care for me now . . . of course you do now . . . oh, my dear . . ." they lost themselves in a kiss . . . " but after all, I can't put you in a false position, even though it might perhaps mean more to you than . . . to put it frankly, than your marriage to Joachim."

She stared at him in amazement.

" You can still think of such a marriage? "

" Of course; it's only "—and to escape from the unbearable tension into raillery he looked at his watch—" twenty minutes since we were both thinking of it. Either the thought must have been unendurable twenty minutes ago, or it's still endurable."

" You shouldn't make a joke of it now . . ." then in fear, " or are you in earnest? "

" I don't know . . . that's something no man knows about himself."

" You're putting me off, or else you take a delight in tormenting me. You're a cynic."

Bertrand said seriously: " Am I to deceive you? "

" Perhaps you're deceiving yourself . . . perhaps because . . . I don't know why . . . but something doesn't ring true . . . no, you don't love me."

" I'm an egoist."

" You don't love me."

" I do love you."

She looked at him directly and seriously: " Am I to marry Joachim, then? "

" I can't, in spite of everything, tell you not to."

She freed her hands from his and sat for a long time in silence. Then she stood up, picked up her hat and put in the hatpins firmly.

" Good-bye, I'm going to get married . . . perhaps that's cynical, but you can't be surprised at that . . . perhaps we are both committing the worst crime against ourselves . . . good-bye."

" Good-bye, Elisabeth; don't forget this hour; it's my sole revenge on Joachim. . . . I shall never be able to forget you."

She passed her hand over his cheek. " You're feverish," she said, and went quickly out of the room.

That was what had happened, and Bertrand had paid for it with a severe bout of fever. But that seemed to him right and fitting, for it relegated yesterday to a greater distance. And made it possible for him to regard Joachim, who now sat before him in the same building—could it be the same?—with his usual kindness. No, it would have been too grotesque. So he said: " Don't you worry, Pasenow; you'll come to anchor all right in the harbour of matrimony. And the best of luck to it." An unchivalrous and cynical fellow, Joachim could not help thinking again, and yet he felt grateful and reassured. It might have been the memory of his father, or only the sight of Bertrand, but the thought of matrimony was mingled queerly with the vision of a quiet sick-chamber through which white-clad nuns flitted. Tender and nunlike

was Elisabeth, white on her silver cloud, and he recalled a picture of the
Madonna, an Assumption, which he believed he had seen in Dresden.
He took his cap from the hook. He felt hustled by Bertrand into this
marriage, and was struck now by the bizarre idea that Bertrand only
wanted to drag him back into civilian life, to strip him of his uniform
and his standing in the regiment, in order to be promoted as Major in
his stead; and as Bertrand gave him his hand in farewell he did not
observe how hot and feverish it was. Yet he thanked Bertrand for his
friendly words and took his leave, stiff and angular in his long regimental
coat. Bertrand could hear the faint jingle of his spurs as he went downstairs, and could not help thinking that Joachim was now passing the
door of the reception-room.

His suit was accepted. To be sure, wrote the Baron, Elisabeth did not
yet want an official betrothal. She had a kind of shrinking from the final
step; but Joachim was expected to supper next evening.

Even if it was not counted a definite betrothal, even if neither Elisabeth
nor his future parents-in-law addressed Joachim with the familiar " Du,"
yes, even if the tone at the supper-table was almost formal, there was
yet an unmistakable hint of festivity in the atmosphere, especially when
the Baron tapped on his glass and with many fine phrases elaborated
the idea that a family was an organic whole and could not easily admit a
newcomer into its circle; but when by the dispensation of Providence
a newcomer was admitted, then he should be admitted wholeheartedly,
and the love that united the family should embrace him also. The
Baroness had tears in her eyes, and took her husband's hand in her
own while he was speaking of love, and Joachim had the warm feeling
that he would be happy here; in the bosom of the family, he said to
himself, and the Holy Family occurred to him. Bertrand would probably
have smiled and made fun of the Baron's speech, but how cheap was
that kind of mockery! The obscure witticisms that Bertrand used to
fling about at table—how far away that was—were certainly more
offensive than the deep feeling that informed the Baron's words. Then
they all clinked their glasses until they rang, and the Baron cried:
" To the future! "

After supper the young people were left alone to open their hearts
to each other. They sat in the newly done-up music-room with
its black-silk chairs on which were sewed covers of lace made by the

Baroness and Elisabeth, and while Joachim was still trying to find the right words he heard Elisabeth say almost gaily: " So you want to marry me, Joachim; have you thought it over carefully? " How unladylike, he thought; it might almost have been Bertrand speaking. What was he to do? Should he get down on one knee to follow up his suit? Fortune was kind to him, for the tabouret on which he had set himself was so low that when he bent towards Elisabeth his knees were in any case almost on the floor, and his attitude, if one liked, could have been construed as kneeling. So he remained in this somewhat constrained posture and said: " May I venture to hope? " Elisabeth made no answer; she had thrown her head back, and her eyes were half shut. As he now gazed at her face he was disquieted to find that a section of landscape could be transferred within four walls; it was the very memory he had feared, it was that noonday under the autumn trees, it was that blending of contours, and he almost wished that the Baron's consent had been longer postponed. For more dreadful than a brother's apparition in a woman's face is the landscape that luxuriates over it, landscape that takes possession of it and absorbs the dehumanized features, so that not even Helmuth could avail to arrest their undulating flow. She said: " Have you taken your friend Bertrand's advice on this marriage? " That he could deny without violating the truth. " But he knew about it? " Yes, returned Joachim, he had mentioned the proposal to Bertrand. " And what did he say? " He had only wished him luck. " Are you very attached to him, Joachim? " Joachim was comforted by her voice and her words; they brought him back to the consciousness that it was a human being and not a landscape that he was regarding. Yet they were disquieting. What was in her mind about Bertrand? Where was this leading to? It was somehow unseemly to spend this hour talking about Bertrand, although it was a relief to find any topic of conversation at all. And since he could not abandon the topic, and since also he felt it his duty to be absolutely honest with his future wife, he said hesitatingly: " I don't know; I always have the feeling that he is the active element in our friendship, but very often it is I who seek him out. I don't know whether that could be called attachment." " Does he unsettle you? " " Yes, that's the right word . . . I am always being unsettled by him." " He is unsettled himself, and so unsettles others," said Elisabeth. Yes, that he was, replied Joachim, and feeling Elisabeth's look upon him could not help wondering anew that those transparent, rounded stars, set one on each side of a nose, could emit such a thing as a look. What is a look? He touched his own eyes, and at once Ruzena was there and Ruzena's eyes which he had felt with delight through her eyelids. It was unimaginable that he would ever be able to stroke Elisabeth's eyelids; perhaps it was true, as they said in the schools, that there was a cold so intense that it seared; the cold of outer space occurred to him, the cold of the stars. That was where Elisabeth hovered on a silver cloud, intangible her effluent, dissolving face, and he felt it as an agonizing impropriety that her father and mother had kissed her when the meal was ended. But from what sphere did Bertrand spring, whose slave and victim she had almost become? If Bertrand was a tempter sent to both of them by God, it was part of the discipline laid upon him that he should save Elisabeth from such earthly aggression. God was enthroned in absolute coldness, and His commands were ruthless, fitting into each other like the teeth on Borsig's cog-wheels; it was all so inevitable that Joachim felt it almost a comfort to know that there was even a single road to salvation, the straight path of duty, although he might be consumed in following it. " He's going to India soon," he said. " Oh yes, India," she replied. " I hesitated for a long time," he said, " for I can offer you only a simple country life." " We are different from him," she returned. Joachim was touched by that " we." " Perhaps his roots have been torn up, and he is longing to be restored." Elisabeth said: " Every man decides for himself." " But haven't we chosen the better part? " asked Joachim. " We can't tell," said Elisabeth. " Oh, surely," Joachim was indignant, " for he lives for his business, and he has to be cold and unfeeling. Think of your parents, think of what your father has just said. But *he* calls that convention; he hasn't got real inwardness, real Christian feeling." He fell silent: he hadn't expressed what he wanted to say, for what he expected from God and from Elisabeth was not a mere equivalent for Christian family life as he had been trained to understand it; yet just because he expected more from Elisabeth, he desired to confine his words to the neighbourhood of that celestial sphere in which she was to manifest herself as the tenderest of silvery, hovering Madonnas. Perhaps she would have to die before she could speak to him in the right way, for as she sat there leaning back, she looked like Snow-white in the glass casket and was so irradiated by that higher beauty and heavenly essence that her face had but little resemblance to the one he had known in life before it blended so dreadfully and irrevocably with the landscape. The wish that Elisabeth were dead and her voice imparting angelic comfort to him from the other side grew and grew, and the extraordinary tension it engendered, or out of which itself had sprung, attained such force that Elisabeth too must have been affected by the onrush of terrifying coldness, for she said: " He doesn't need the comforting warmth of companionship as we do." Yet she disappointed Joachim by these earthly words, and even though the need for protection that echoed in them moved his heart and awakened in him the vision of Mary wandering on earth before her assumption into heaven, yet he realized that his strength was hardly equal to affording such protection, and in his twofold disappointment he wished with twofold earnestness a kind and pleasant death for both of them. And since the mask falls from the face that is confronted by death, defenceless against the breath of the Eternal, Joachim said: " He would always have been remote from you," and this seemed to both of them a great and significant truth, although they had almost forgotten that it was Bertrand of whom they were speaking. Like yellow butterflies with black spots upon their serrated yellow wings, the ring of gas-jets blazed in the wreath of the chandelier over the black-silk catafalque on which Joachim still sat motionless with his body stiffly inclined and his knees bent, and the white-lace covers on the black silk were like copies of deaths' heads. Into that frozen stillness dropped Elisabeth's words: " He is more solitary than other people," and Joachim replied: " His demon drives him out." But Elisabeth almost imperceptibly shook her head: " He hopes to find fulfilment," and then she added, as if from a fixed recollection, " fulfilment and knowledge in solitude and remoteness." Joachim was silent; it was with reluctance that he took up this thought that hung cold and bewildering between them: " He is remote . . . he thrusts us all away, for God wills us to be solitary." " He does, indeed," said Elisabeth, and it was not to be determined whether she had referred to God or to Bertrand; but that ceased to matter, since the solitude prescribed for her and Joachim now began to encompass them, and froze the room, in spite of its intimate elegance, into a more complete and dreadful immobility; as they sat motionless, both of them, it seemed as if the room widened around them; as the walls receded the air seemed to grow colder and thinner, so thin that it could barely carry a voice. And although everything was tranced in immobility, yet the chairs, the piano, on whose black-lacquered surface the wreath of gas-jets was still reflected, seemed no longer in their usual places, but infinitely remote, and even the golden dragons and butterflies on the black Chinese screen in the corner had flitted away as if drawn after the receding walls, which now looked as if hung with black curtains. The gas-lights hissed with a faint, malicious susurration, and except for their infinitesimal mechanical vivacity, that jetted fleeringly from obscenely open small slits, all life was extinguished. She will die soon now, thought Joachim, and it was almost a confirmation of it that he heard her voice saying in the emptiness: " His death will be a lonely one "; it sounded like a doom and a pledge, a pledge that he fortified: " He is sick, and may die soon; perhaps this very moment." " Yes," said Elisabeth from the other side of beyond, and the word was like a drop that turned to ice as it fell, " yes, this very moment," and in the frozen featurelessness of that second in which Death stood beside them, Joachim did not know whether it was the two of them that Death touched, or whether it was his father, or Bertrand; he could not tell whether his mother was not sitting there to watch over his death, punctual and calm, as she watched in the milking-byre or by his father's bed, and he had a sudden near intuition, strangely clear, that his father was freezing and longed for the dark warmth of the cowshed. Was it not better to die now beside Elisabeth, and to be led by her into the glassy brightness that hovered above the dark? He said: " There will be frightful darkness around him, and no one will come to help him." But Elisabeth said in a hard voice: " No one should come," and with the same grey, toneless hardness she went on speaking in the emptiness, adding in the same breath, that yet was not a breath at all: " I will be your wife, Joachim," and was herself uncertain whether she had said it, for Joachim sat in unchanged stillness with his body inclined, and made no answer. No sign was given, and although it lasted no longer than the dulling and glazing of an eye, the tension was so charged with uncertainty and nullity that Elisabeth said again: " Yes, I'll be your wife." But Joachim did not want to hear her words, for they compelled him to turn back from that road on which there is no returning. With a great effort he tried to bend towards her; he barely succeeded, but his half-bent knee actually did touch the ground; his brow, beaded with cold sweat, inclined itself, and his lips, dry and cold as parchment, brushed her hand, which was so icy that he did not dare to touch her finger-tips, not even when the room slowly closed in again and the chairs resumed their former places.

So they remained until they heard the Baron's voice in the next room.
" We must go in," said Elisabeth. Then they entered the brightly lit
salon, and Elisabeth said: " We are engaged." " My child! " cried the
Baroness, and with tears enfolded Elisabeth in her arms. But the Baron,
whose eyes were not less wet, cried: " Let us be joyful and give thanks
to God for this happy day," and Joachim loved him for those heartening
words, and felt committed to his keeping.

Out of the apathetic doze into which his weariness declined amid the
rattle of the droshky wheels as he drove home, the thought emerged
more clearly that his father and Bertrand had died that day, and he was
almost amazed to find no announcement of their death awaiting him in
his flat, for that would have fitted in with the return of punctiliousness
to his life. In any case one should not conceal a betrothal from even a
dead friend. The thought continued to haunt him and next morning
strengthened into something like certainty, if not a certainty of their
death, a certainty of their non-existence at least: his father and Bertrand
had departed this life, and even although he was partly to blame for
their death, he remained sunk in quiet indifference and did not even
once find it necessary to decide whether it was Elisabeth or Ruzena of
whom he had robbed Bertrand. The task had been laid upon him to
catch Bertrand from behind, to keep an eye upon him, and the path
along which he was bound to pursue him had now come to an end, the
mystery was annulled; all that remained was to say farewell to his dead
friend. " Both good news and bad news," he said to himself. He had
plenty of time; he stopped the droshky to order bouquets for his fiancée
and the Baroness, and without haste proceeded to the hospital. But when
he entered the hospital no one made any reference to the catastrophe;
he was conducted in the usual manner to Bertrand's room as if nothing
had happened: it was only when he met the Sister in the corridor
that he learned that Bertrand had indeed had a bad night, but was now
feeling better. Joachim repeated mechanically: " He's feeling better . . .
yes, that's gratifying, very gratifying." It was as if Bertrand had betrayed
and deceived him yet again, and this became a firm conviction when he
was greeted by the gay words: " I take it you can be congratulated
to-day." How does he know that? Joachim asked himself, and in spite
of his annoyance was almost proud that his suspicions were, in a
way, justified by his new character as prospective bridegroom: yes, he

said, he was happy to be able to announce his engagement. Bertrand seemed, however, in a softened mood. " You know that I like you, Pasenow," he said—Joachim felt this as importunity—" and so it's with all my heart that I wish luck to you and your bride." Once more his words sounded warm and sincere, yet mocking: he—the man who always knew everything beforehand, he who had actually willed it and brought it about, although merely as the instrument of a higher power —was evading the issue, now that he saw his work accomplished, with a smooth and cordial congratulation. Joachim felt somehow exhausted; he sat down by the table in the middle of the room, looked at Bertrand, who was lying blond and almost girlish in his bed, and said gravely: " I hope that everything will turn out well," and Bertrand replied lightly with that offhand certainty which always laid its soothing and yet disquieting spell on Joachim: " Let me assure you, Pasenow, that everything will turn out for the very best . . . at least for you." Joachim repeated: " Yes, for the best . . ." but then he looked perplexed: " Why for me only? " Bertrand smiled and waved the question away with a faintly contemptuous gesture: " Oh, we . . . we're a lost generation," yet he explained himself no further, only adding abruptly: " And when's the wedding to be? " so that Joachim forgot to ask more, and at once said: well, there was still some way to go; his father's illness, above all, had to be considered. Bertrand eyed Joachim, who sat facing him with stiff propriety. " But getting married surely doesn't involve settling down on the estate at once? " he said. Joachim was shocked: apparently all his trouble had been wasted. After harping on the necessity for taking over the estate, after plunging Ruzena into despair, here was Bertrand now saying that he did not need to settle down on the estate, as if wishing to cheat him of his pride in its possession and even to deprive him of his home! With what devious cunning had Bertrand lured him on, and now he was shaking off all responsibility and actually disdaining the triumph he had scored in pulling him down to his own civilian level, repudiating him even there! It must have been sheer evil for evil's sake that Bertrand had wrought, and Joachim looked at him with indignant amazement. But Bertrand observed only the question in his eyes: " Well," he said, " you mentioned not long ago that you were just on the point of getting your captaincy, and you should stay on until you're promoted. Retired Captain sounds much better than retired Lieutenant "—now he's ashamed of himself, the Second Lieutenant, thought Joachim and straightened himself with a little jerk, as if on parade—" and during these few months your father's illness will have taken a decisive turn of some kind." Joachim would have liked to point out that married officers seemed to him an anomaly, and that he was longing for his native soil, but he did not venture to say so, remarking merely that Bertrand's suggested solution fitted in with the heartfelt desire of his future parents to see Elisabeth settled in the new west-end house. " Well, there you are, my dear Pasenow; everything turns out for the best," said Bertrand, and that was another gratuitous and abominable piece of presumption, " besides, you could certainly speed up your promotion if you were to tell your colonel that you mean to retire from the service as soon as you get your step." He was right in that, too, but it was annoying to have Bertrand interfering with even military arrangements. Joachim thoughtfully picked up Bertrand's stick from the table, scrutinized the handle, and ran his finger over the resilient black-rubber bulb at the point of it: a convalescent's stick. That the man was urging him into a headlong marriage filled him with new suspicion. What was behind it all? Yesterday evening he and Elisabeth had explained to her parents that they did not want to hurry on the marriage, and had enumerated all the obstacles; and now this Bertrand wanted simply to blow the obstacles away. " All the same, we can't precipitate the marriage," said Joachim obstinately. " Well," remarked Bertrand, " I'm only sorry that in that case I must be content with sending you a wire on the happy day, from India or somewhere. For as soon as I'm half set up again I'm going abroad. . . . This affair has pulled me down a bit." What affair? The slight wound to his arm? It was true that Bertrand looked ill, and convalescents always needed sticks, but what else had been happening? He shouldn't really let Bertrand go away until that was all cleared up, and Joachim wondered whether Helmuth, who had faced his enemy openly, hadn't been much more honourable than himself; was not the issue here the same: explanation or death? But Joachim wanted both of them, and yet neither. His father was right: he was dishonourable, as dishonourable as Bertrand, this friend of his, who could hardly be called his friend still. Yet that was almost gratifying, for it must have been in his father's mind that Bertrand should not be invited to the wedding.

None the less he listened quietly as Bertrand went on: " One thing more, Pasenow; I have the impression that the estate, except where your mother looks after it and where it runs itself, is in a fairly neglected condition. In his present state your father could possibly do it a great deal of additional harm. Excuse me for suggesting, as I feel bound to do, that you might have him declared incapable of managing it. And you should engage a good steward; he would anyhow earn his wages. I think you should discuss it with your father-in-law; after all, he's a land-owner too." Yes, Bertrand was talking like the vilest *agent provocateur*, and yet Joachim had to thank him for the advice, which he could see was just and well meant, and even had to express the hope that they would still see much of each other before Bertrand's full recovery. " Delighted," said Bertrand; " and give my humblest respects to your bride." Then he sank back exhausted on his pillow.

Two days later Joachim received a letter in which Bertrand announced that his health was much improved and that he had shifted into a hospital in Hamburg, so as to be nearer to his business. But they would certainly meet again before he started for the East. Bertrand's cool assumption that as a matter of course they would have another encounter made Joachim decide to avoid it at all costs. But he suffered from the knowledge that from now on he would have to do without his friend's sureness and lightness of touch, and his competence in the affairs of life.

Behind the Leipzigerplatz there is a shop which externally can hardly be distinguished from its neighbours, unless it should attract attention because there are no goods displayed in its windows and the eye is prevented from seeing what is inside by opaque-glass screens, beautifully etched with Pompeian and Renaissance designs. But this peculiarity is one which the shop shares with many banking houses and brokers' offices, and even the posters affixed to the screens, although they are an unpleasant interruption of the designs, have nothing unusual about them. On these posters the word " India " occurs, and a glance at the sign above the door informs one that inside the shop the Kaiser Panorama is on view.

On entering, one advances first into a light and cosily heated room in which an elderly and obviously good-natured lady acts as a kind of cashier behind a small table, selling tickets of admission to the establish-ment. Most of the visitors, however, pause at the table only to have their books of subscription tickets stamped and to exchange a few friendly words with the old lady. When the aged attendant appears from behind the black curtains that cut off one end of the room, and with a deprecating little gesture begs one to wait a minute or two, the visitor subsides with a faint sigh into one of the cane chairs and continues his conversation, mistrustfully watching the glass door that leads into the street, and if a fresh client appears regarding him with jealous and ashamed hostility. Then there is heard the faint scraping of chairs behind the curtains, and the man who emerges blinks a little in the light, and departs with a brief salutation to the old lady, going hurriedly, nervously, and without looking at anybody, as if he too were ashamed. The waiting client, however, springs quickly to his feet lest someone should push in ahead of him, breaks off his conversation without more ado, and vanishes behind the protecting curtains. It happens but seldom that clients speak to each other, although many must get to know each other by sight in the course of years, and only one or two shameless old men bring themselves to address the other waiting clients as well as the cashier, and to praise the programme; yet even then they are answered mostly in monosyllables.

Within, however, all is darkness, and one could suppose it an ancient, oppressive darkness that has been accumulating here for years. The attendant takes you gently by the hand and leads you carefully to a seat, a round seat without arms, that is waiting for you. In front of you are two bright eyes that look at you somewhat uncannily from a black screen, and under these eyes is a mouth, a hard rectangle softened by the dull light that fills it. Gradually you realize that you are set before a polygonal construction resembling a temple, and that the screen in front of which you are sitting is a part of it; you observe, too, that to right and left of you sits a worshipper who has applied his eyes to the eyes in the screen before him, and you do the same, after taking a look at the rectangle of light and noting that it says, " Government House in Calcutta." But as soon as you peer into the open eye, Government House vanishes to the tinkle of a sweet bell and with a mechanical rattle; you can still see it sliding away while another view comes sliding after it, so that you feel almost cheated; but another bell tinkles, the view gives itself a little shake, as if to set itself off to the best advantage, and comes to rest. You see palm-trees and a well-kept path: in the background, where it is shaded, a man in a light suit is sitting on a seat; a fountain throws a congealed, whiplike jet of spray into the air, but you are not content until a glance at the softly lit rectangle informs you: " View in the Royal Park, Calcutta." Then comes another tinkle, a sliding past of palms, seats, buildings, masts, a quiver into place, a tinkle of the bell, and in bright sunlight: " View of the Harbour, Bombay." The man who has just been sitting on the seat in Calcutta Park is now standing in a sun-helmet on the hewn stones of the mole in the foreground. He is propped on a walking-stick and does not move, because he is spellbound by the taut rigging of the ships, by their funnels and cranes, spellbound by the bundles of cotton bales on the quay, and gazes at them spellbound, and his face is in shadow and cannot be recognized. Yet perhaps he will advance into the magic space, enclosed in polished brown, that lies between you and the picture, a space that is but an abstract cube and yet a long journey; perhaps he will step out freely and magically upon the wooden floor, and you will recognize that it is Bertrand, airily and yet terribly warning you that he can never more be crossed out of your life, however far away he may be. But that may be only your imagination, for God has already rung the bell for him, and without a greeting, stiff and motionless, without taking even one step, he slides away again. You peep at your left-hand neighbour to see if that is where Bertrand has gone, but his lit rectangle reports: " Government House in Calcutta," and you can almost nurse the hope that Bertrand has appeared to you alone, to greet you only. But you have no time to reflect upon it, for when you turn quickly again to your own eyepieces a delightful surprise awaits you: the " Native Mother in Ceylon " is not only lit up by soft golden sunlight but represented in her natural colours; she smiles with white teeth between red lips and may be waiting for the white Sahib who has quitted the West because he despises European women. The " Temple Buildings in Delhi " also glow in all the colours of the Orient at the far end of the brown box: there the bad Christian may learn that even subject races know how to serve God. But did he not once say himself that it would devolve upon the black races to set up the Kingdom of Christ again? You look with horror at the swarm of brown figures, and are not ill-pleased to hear the signal with which they are dismissed, to give place to the "Elephant-hunting Expedition." Here stand the colossal quadrupeds, one of them gently lifting a forefoot. The square is full of fine white sand, and when you turn your dazzled eyes away for a moment you see above the rectangular title-plate a small button, which you twirl experimentally. At once, to your delight, the picture is suffused by soft moonlight, so that you can expedite the hunters at your pleasure by day or by night.

Well, since the sun-glare no longer blinds you, you seize the opportunity of examining the hunters' faces, and if your eye does not deceive you it is Bertrand, after all, who is sitting in the howdah behind the dusky mahout, his rifle at the ready in his right hand, promising death. You change the light, and once more it is an utter stranger who smiles at you, and the mahout lays his goad behind the elephant's ear to give the signal for the prescribed start of the expedition; they slide away into the jungle, yet you hear nothing of the trampling of the herds and the trumpeting of the bulls, but with a faint tinkle and a mechanical rattle landscape after landscape advances of its own accord and vanishes, and if the passing traveller seems to be really the man you are bound to seek for ever, the man you hunger for, the man who vanishes while you are still holding his hand, then the bell tinkles, and before you know where you are you are peering anxiously at your neighbour's title-plate on the right, and discovering the inscription: " Government House in Calcutta," so that you know your hour will be over soon. Then you give a cursory look to make sure that the palms of the Royal Park are due to follow, and since they follow on ruthlessly you scrape your chair, the attendant hurries up, and blinking a little, your collar turned up, a poor creature found indulging a pleasure he has never realized, you leave with a brief salutation the room in which others are already waiting, and in which the old lady is selling books of tickets.

Into this establishment Joachim and Elisabeth strayed, accompanied by Elisabeth's companion, when they were making purchases in the city for their house and the trousseau. For although they knew that Bertrand was still in Hamburg, and although they never mentioned his name again, the word India had a magic sound for them.

The wedding at Lestow was a quiet one. The condition of Joachim's father had become stationary; he lay in a coma, no longer recognizing the outer world, and one had to be reconciled to this lasting for years. True, the Baroness said that a quiet, intimate ceremony would be far more to the taste of herself and her husband than noisy display, but Joachim already knew the importance which his parents-in-law attached to their family festivals, and he felt to blame for his father, who robbed the occasion of its splendour. And he himself would perhaps have preferred a great and brilliant social setting to emphasise the social character of this marriage, into which mere love entered so little; yet on the other hand it seemed to him more in accordance with the gravity and Christian nature of the union that Elisabeth and he should approach the altar without any thought of the world. And so it was decided not to celebrate the marriage in Berlin, even although Lestow presented various difficulties not easy to overcome, more especially as Bertrand's advice was no longer to be had. Joachim rejected the idea of leading his bride home for the wedding night: the idea of passing that night in the house of sickness filled him with repugnance, but still more impossible to him was the thought that Elisabeth should retire to rest under the eyes of the domestic staff who knew him so well; so he suggested that Elisabeth should spend the night at Lestow, and he would fetch her next day. Strangely enough this proposal encountered the opposition of the Baroness, who found such a solution unseemly: " Even if we closed our eyes to it, what would the servants think? " Finally it was decided to hold the ceremony at such an early hour that the young couple could catch the midday train. " Then you'll be able to go straight to your own comfortable house in Berlin," said the Baroness, but Joachim would not hear of that either. No, it was too far out, for they would be leaving Berlin again early in the morning, and probably they might even be able to take the night train to Munich without stopping. Yes, night travel was almost the simplest solution of the marriage problem, a safeguard against the fear that someone might smile understandingly when he and Elisabeth had to retire for the night. Yet presently he doubted whether they really could set out for Munich straight off; after the excitement of the day could one really expect Elisabeth to undertake a night journey? And how could their day in Munich, in perpetual expectation of what was to come, be put in? It was clear that one could not have discussed such matters even with Bertrand, one had to come to a decision oneself; all the same, several things would have been appreciably simpler if Bertrand had been at hand. He considered what Bertrand would have done in such circumstances, and came to the conclusion that there was no harm in his booking rooms in the Hotel Royal in Berlin; if Elisabeth should wish it, they could still take the night train. And he was honestly proud of having found this adroit solution by himself.

It had now become quite wintry, and the closed carriages in which they drove to the church advanced only by slow stages through the snow. Joachim was in the same carriage as his mother; she sat there,

broad and complacent, and Joachim felt irritated when she reiterated:
" Father would have been delighted; well, it's a great pity." Yes, that was
all that was needed to fill his cup; Joachim was exasperated—nobody
would leave him in peace to gain that calm which was imperative at
this solemn hour, doubly imperative for him to whom this marriage
signified more than a Christian marriage, to whom it meant redemption
from the pit and the mire and a heavenly assurance that he was entering
the way of grace. In her wedding-robe Elisabeth looked more like
a Madonna than ever, looked like Snow-white, and he could not help
thinking of the legend of the bride who had fallen down dead before
the altar because she suddenly recognized in her bridegroom an incarnation of the Devil. The thought would not leave him and took such
complete possession of him that he heard neither the chant of the choir
nor the pastor's sermon: indeed he actually closed his ears to them out
of a fear that he might be compelled to interrupt them and tell those
people that a man unworthy, an outcast, stood before the altar, a man
who desecrated the holy state of matrimony; and he started in terror
when he had to pronounce the " Yes," in terror too at the thought that
the ceremony, which should have been for him the revelation of a new
life, had come to an end so quickly and almost without his being aware
of it. He found it actually comforting that Elisabeth should now be
called, without really being, his wife, but the thought that this state
would not last was appalling. During the drive back from the church
he took her hand and said: " My wife," and Elisabeth responded to
his pressure. But then everything was drowned in the tumult of good
wishes, the hurry of changing and setting out, so that only when they
reached the station did they realize what had happened.

He turned away while Elisabeth climbed into the compartment, so
as not again to fall a prey to impure thoughts. Now they were alone.
Elisabeth leant back wearily in her corner and smiled faintly at him.
" You're tired, Elisabeth," he said hopefully, glad that it was his privilege
and his duty to protect her. " Yes, I'm tired, Joachim." He did not
dare, however, to suggest that they should stop at Berlin, fearing that
she might interpret it as concupiscence. Her profile stood out sharply
against the window, beyond which stretched the grey winter afternoon,
and Joachim felt relieved that that oppressive and affrighting vision in
which her face changed into a landscape remained absent. But while
he was still regarding her he saw that the trunk, which had been placed

on the seat opposite, was outlined no less sharply against the grey sky, and he was overcome by the senselessly sharp fear that she might be a mere thing, a dead object, and not even a landscape. He got up hastily as though to do something to the trunk, but he merely opened it and took out the lunch-basket; it was a wedding present and a miniature miracle of elegance, suitable equally for train journeys and hunting expeditions: the ivory handles of the knives and forks were ornamented with decorative hunting scenes which were continued on the incised blades, and even the spirit-stove was not free from them; amid the ornamentation on each piece, however, one could recognize the inter-twined arms of Elisabeth and Joachim. The centre space of the basket served as a receptacle for food and had been solicitously filled by the Baroness. Joachim pressed Elisabeth to eat, and as they had not been able to wait for the wedding lunch she gladly acceded. " Our first married meal," said Joachim, and he poured the wine into the silver collapsible cups, and Elisabeth drank to him. In this way they passed the journey and Joachim was once more of the opinion that the train provided the best form of wedded life. He even began to understand Bertrand, who was at liberty to pass such a great part of his time in trains. " Shouldn't we go straight through to Munich this evening? " he asked; but Elisabeth replied that she felt really fatigued and would rather break the journey. So he could not but divulge to her that he had already provided for her wish and booked rooms.

He was grateful to Elisabeth for the fact that she had not lost her composure, even if it was probably only an assumed composure; for she lingered out the hour for retiring and asked for supper, and they sat for a very long time in the dining-hall; the band which played for the diners' entertainment had already put away their instruments, only a few guests were still left in the room, and grateful as any postponement of the hour was to Joachim, yet he felt again that cold, rarefied atmosphere diffusing itself through the room, that chill which on the evening of their betrothal had been like a dreadful foreboding of death. Perhaps even Elisabeth felt it, for she said that it was time now to retire.

So the moment had come. Elisabeth had parted from him with a friendly " Good-night, Joachim," and now he walked up and down his room. Should he simply go to bed? He regarded the bed, on which the sheets were folded down. Yet he had taken an oath to watch before her door, to guard her heavenly dreams, that for ever on her silvery cloud she might dream on; and now it had suddenly lost all sense and meaning, for everything seemed to point to the one conclusion, that he should make himself comfortable here. He glanced down at his clothes, and felt the long military coat as a protection; it was indecent for people to appear at weddings in frock-coats. All the same he must have a wash, and softly, as though he were committing an act of sacrilege, he pulled off his coat and poured water into the basin on the brown varnished washstand. How painful all this was, how senseless, unless it should be a link in the chain of trials laid on his shoulders; it would all have been easier if Elisabeth had locked the communicating door behind her, but out of consideration for him she had certainly not done that. Joachim vaguely remembered having been in the same position before, and now with crushing force came the memory of a locked door and a brown washstand under a gas-jet: dreadful because it was a memory of Ruzena, no less dreadful as raising the problem how, living with an angel, the thought of such a thing as a lavatory, no matter how discreetly it obtruded itself, was practically conceivable at all: in both cases a degradation of Elisabeth and a new trial. He had cleansed his face and hands gently and cautiously, so as to prevent the porcelain basin from making any sound against the marble top of the table, but now he was confronted with something quite inconceivable: for who could think of gargling in the immediate vicinity of Elisabeth? And yet he must immerse himself still more deeply in the purifying crystalline medium, must drown there, to walk forth from that utter purification as from baptism in Jordan. But how could even a bath help him here? Ruzena had recognized him for what he was and drawn the consequences. He slipped back hastily into his coat again, buttoned it up scrupulously, and walked up and down the room. There was no sound from the other room, and he felt that his presence must be an oppression to her. Why did she not scream at him to go away, as Ruzena had done behind the locked door? That time he had had the lavatory attendant at least to stand by him, but now he was alone and without support. All too prematurely he had rejected Bertrand and his easy assurance, and the fact that he had been capable of thinking it his duty to protect Elisabeth from Bertrand struck him now as hypocrisy. A terrible feeling of remorse came over him: it was not Elisabeth whom he had really wished to protect and save; he had merely hoped to save his own soul through her sacrifice. Was she kneeling on her knees in there praying that God might free her again from the fetters which she had assumed out of pity? Was it not his duty to say to her that he gave her her freedom, this very night, that if she commanded him he would drive her at once to her house in the west end, to her beautiful new house which was waiting for her? In great agitation he knocked at the communicating door and wished immediately that he had not done so. She said softly: " Joachim," and he turned the handle. She was lying in bed, a candle was burning on the commode. He remained at the door, almost as if he were standing at attention, and said hoarsely: " Elisabeth, I only wanted to tell you that I give you your freedom: I can't think of your sacrificing yourself for me." Elisabeth was astonished, but she felt relief that he did not accost her as a loving husband. " Do you think, Joachim, that I've sacrificed myself? " She smiled faintly. " Really you've thought of that a little too late." " It isn't too late yet; I thank God it isn't too late. . . . I didn't realize it until now. . . . Shall I drive you out to the west end? " Then Elisabeth could not help laughing: now, in the middle of the night! What would the people in the hotel think? " Why not just go to bed, Joachim. We can discuss all that in peace and quietness to-morrow. You must be tired too." Joachim said like an obstinate child: " I'm not tired." The flickering flame of the candle lighted up her pale face, which lay between her loosened hair on the snowy pillows. A peak of the bolster rose in the air like a nose, and its shadow on the wall was exactly the same shape as the shadow of Elisabeth's nose. " Please, Elisabeth, smooth down the corner of that pillow, to the left of your head there," he said from the door. " Why? " asked Elisabeth in surprise, putting up her hand towards it. " It casts such a horrible shadow," said Joachim; meanwhile another peak of the bolster had risen, showing another nose on the wall. Joachim was irritated, he wanted to set this matter right himself and took a step into the room. " But, Joachim, what's wrong with the shadows that they annoy you? Is it right now? " Joachim replied: " The shadow of your face on the wall is like a mountain range." " But that's nothing." " I can't stand it." Elisabeth was a little afraid lest this should be the prelude to putting out the candle, but to her pleasant surprise Joachim said: " We must have two candles for you, then there won't be any shadows and you'll look like Snow-white." And he actually went into his room and came back with the second lighted candle. " Oh, you're joking, Joachim," Elisabeth could not help saying, " where are you to put the second candle? There's no place for it on the wall. And besides, I would look like a corpse between two candles." Joachim studied the position. Elisabeth was right, so he said: " May I set it on the commode? " " Of course you may . . ." she paused for a moment, and said hesitatingly and yet with a slight feeling of reassurance, " you're my husband now." He held his hand in front of the flame and carried the candle over to the commode, reflectively contemplated the two lights, and the quietness and semi-darkness of this wedding night striking him he said: " Three would be more cheerful," as though with those words he were trying to excuse himself to Elisabeth and her parents for the quietness of the ceremony. She too gazed at the two candles; she had drawn the coverlet over her shoulders, and only her hand, caught at the wrist by a lace frill, hung languidly over the edge. Joachim was still thinking of the lack of display at their marriage; but he had held this hand in his in the carriage. He had become more composed, and had almost forgotten why he had come in here; now he remembered again and felt it his duty to repeat his offer: " So you don't want to go to your house, Elisabeth? " " But you're silly, Joachim; fancy my getting up now! I feel very comfortable here and you want to rout me out." Joachim stood irresolutely beside the commode; suddenly he could not comprehend the way in which things changed their nature and vocation; a bed was a pleasant article of furniture for sleeping on, with Ruzena it was a coign of desire and inexpressible sweetness, and now it was a thing unapproachable, a something whose edge he scarcely dared to touch. Wood was wood and nothing more, but still one shrank from touching the wood of a coffin. " It's so difficult, Elisabeth," he said suddenly, " forgive me." Yet he begged her forgiveness not merely, as she probably imagined, for expecting her to get up at that late hour, but because yet once more he had compared her with Ruzena, and—he admitted it to himself with horror —because he could almost have wished that Ruzena, and not she, were lying there. And he saw how deeply he was still stuck in the mire. " Forgive me," he said again, and he knelt down so as to kiss a goodnight on the white, blue-veined hand on the edge of the bed. She could not tell whether this might not mean the dreaded approach of intimacy, and remained silent. His mouth was pressed to her hand, and he became aware of his teeth, which were crushed against the inner side of his lips, as the frontier of the hard bony skull which was hidden beneath his own skull and was continued in the skeleton. He felt too the warm breath in the cavity of his mouth, and the tongue embedded in the trough between his lower teeth, and he knew that now he must quickly remove all these, so that Elisabeth might not become inwardly aware of them. Yet he would not concede Ruzena this quick triumph, and so in silence he remained stubbornly on his knees beside the bed, until Elisabeth, as though to indicate that he should go, very gently pressed his hand. Perhaps he intentionally misunderstood this hint, for it gave him a remote memory of Ruzena's caressing hands; so he did not free Elisabeth's hand, although he was actually very impatient to leave the room. He waited for the miracle, the token of grace which God must grant him, and it was as though fear stood between the gates of grace. "Elisabeth, say something," he begged, and Elisabeth replied very slowly, as though the words were not her own: "We aren't strange enough, and we aren't intimate enough." Joachim said: "Elisabeth, do you want to leave me?" Elisabeth answered gently: "No, Joachim, I think we'll go the same road together now. Don't be unhappy, Joachim, it will all turn out for the best yet." Yes, Joachim would have liked to answer, and that's what Bertrand said too; but he was silent, not merely because it would have been unseemly to suggest such a thing, but because in her mouth Bertrand's words were like a Mephistophelian sign from the demon and the Evil One, instead of the sign from God that he had expected and hoped for and prayed for. For a moment Bertrand's image was faintly visible as at the bottom of a brown box, visible and yet hidden, and it was the Devil incarnate whose face and form threw the shadow of a mountain range upon the wall. And immovable and frozen as it was when it appeared, and swiftly, as at the tinkling of a bell, as it vanished again, yet it was a warning that the Evil One was not yet overcome, and that Elisabeth herself was still in his power, seeing that with her own words she had called him up, and seeing that she had not succeeded in scaring away those phantoms and sick fancies with words from God. But even if this was disappointing, yet it was also good, filling him with a sense of the pathos of the earthly and the human and of human weakness. Elisabeth was his heavenly goal, but the way on earth to such a goal he had himself, in spite of his great weakness, to find out and prepare for both of them: and meanwhile where in this loneliness was a guide to be found to that knowledge? Where could he find help? Clausewitz's aphorism came into his mind, that men act only from a divination and instinctive feeling of truth, and his heart was prescient with the knowledge that in a Christian household their lives would be determined by the saving help of grace, guarding them so that they might not wander on the earth unenlightened, helpless and without meaning to their lives, and lose themselves in the void. No, that could not be called a mere convention of feeling. He straightened himself and ran his hand softly over the silk coverlet under which her body lay; he felt a little like a sick-room attendant, and distantly it was as though he were stroking his sick father, or his father's deputy. " Poor little Elisabeth," he said; it was the first endearment that he had ventured to utter. She had freed her hand, and now passed it over his hair: Ruzena had done that too, he thought. Nevertheless she said softly: " Joachim, we're not intimate enough yet." He had raised himself a little, and sat now on the edge of the bed and stroked her hair. Then with his head on his hand he contemplated her face, which still lay, pale and strange, not the face of a wife, not the face of his wife, on the pillow, and it so happened that gradually and without himself noticing it he found himself in a recumbent position beside her. She had moved a little to the side, and her hand, which with its befrilled wrist was all that emerged from the bedclothes, rested in his. Through his position his military coat had become disordered, the lapels falling apart left his black trousers visible, and when Joachim noticed this he hastily set things right again and covered the place. He had now drawn up his legs, and so as not to touch the sheets with his patent-leather shoes, he rested his feet in a rather constrained posture on the chair standing beside the bed. The candles flickered; first one went out, then the other. Now and then they heard muffled footsteps in the carpeted corridor, a door banged, and in the distance they could hear the sounds of the great city, whose gigantic traffic did not fully cease even at night. They lay motionless and gazed at the ceiling of the room, on which yellow strips of light from the slits of the window-blinds were pencilled, and they resembled a little the ribs of a skeleton. Then Joachim had fallen asleep, and when Elisabeth noticed it she could not help smiling. And then she too actually went to sleep.

IV

Nevertheless after some eighteen months they had their first child. It actually happened. How this came about cannot be told here. Besides, after the material for character construction already provided, the reader can imagine it for himself.

PART TWO
THE ANARCHIST
(1903)

I

THE 2nd of March 1903 was a bad day for August Esch, who was thirty years old and a clerk; he had had a row with his chief and found himself dismissed before he had time to think of giving notice. He was irritated, therefore, but less by the fact of his dismissal than by his own lack of resourcefulness. There were so many things that he could have flung in the man's face: a man who didn't know what was happening under his very nose, a man who believed the insinuations of a fellow like Nentwig and had no idea that the said Nentwig was pocketing commissions right and left—unless, indeed, he was shutting his eyes deliberately because Nentwig knew something shady about him. And what a fool Esch had been to let the pair of them catch him out like that: they had fallen foul of him over an alleged mistake in the books that wasn't a mistake at all, now that he came to think of it. But they had bullied him so insolently that it had simply turned into a shouting match, in the middle of which he suddenly found himself dismissed. At the time, of course, he hadn't been able to think of anything but guttersnipe abuse, whereas now he knew exactly how he could have scored. " Sir," yes, " Sir," he should have said, drawing himself up to his full height, and Esch now said " Sir " to himself in a sarcastic voice, " have you the slightest idea of the state your business is in . . . ? " yes, that's what he should have said, but now it was too late, and although he had gone and got drunk and slept with a girl he hadn't got rid of his irritation, and Esch swore to himself as he walked along beside the Rhine towards the town.

He heard steps behind him and, turning, caught sight of Martin, who was swinging along between his crutches with the foot of his game leg braced against one of them. If that wasn't the last straw! Esch would gladly have hurried on, at the risk of getting a wallop over the head from one of the crutches—serve him right too if he did get one over the head—but he felt it would be a low-down trick to play on a cripple, and so he stood waiting. Besides, he would have to look round for another job, and Martin, who knew everybody, might have heard of something. The cripple hobbled up, let his crooked leg swing free, and said bluntly: " Got the sack? " So he had heard of it already? Esch replied with bitterness: " Got the sack." " Have you any money left? " Esch shrugged his shoulders: " Enough for a day or two." Martin reflected: " I know of a job that might suit you." " No, you won't get me into your union." " I know, I know; you're too high and mighty for that. . . . Well, you'll join some day. Where shall we go? " Esch was going nowhere in particular, so they proceeded to Mother Hentjen's. In the Kastellgasse Martin stopped: " Have they given you a decent reference? " " I'll have to call for it to-day." " The Central Rhine people in Mannheim need a shipping clerk, or something in that line . . . if you don't mind leaving Cologne," and they went in. It was a fairly large, dingy room that had been a resort of the Rhine sailors probably for hundreds of years; though except for the vaulted roof, blackened with smoke, no sign now indicated its antiquity. The walls behind the tables were wainscoted in brown wood half-way up, to which was fixed a long bench that ran round the room. Upon the mantelpiece was an array of Munich quart-jugs, among which stood an Eiffel Tower in bronze. It was embellished with a red-and-black-and-white flag, and when one looked more closely the words " Table reserved " could be deciphered on it in faded gold-lettering. Between the two windows stood an orchestrion with its folding-doors open, showing its internal works and the roll of music. Actually the doors should have remained closed, and anyone who wished to enjoy the music should have inserted a coin in the slot. But Mother Hentjen did nothing shabbily, and so the customer had merely to thrust his hand into the machinery and pull the lever; all Mother Hentjen's customers knew how to work the apparatus. Facing the orchestrion the whole of the shorter back wall was taken up by the buffet, and behind the buffet was a huge mirror flanked on either side by two glass cabinets containing brightly hued liqueur bottles. When in the evening Mother Hentjen took her post behind the buffet, she had a habit of turning round to the mirror every now and then to pat her blond coiffure, which was perched on her round, heavy skull like a hard little sugar-loaf. On the counter itself stood rows of large wine and Schnapps bottles, for the gay liqueur bottles in the cabinet were seldom called for. And finally, between the buffet and the glass cabinet, a zinc washing-basin with a tap was discreetly let into the wall.

The room was unheated, and its coldness stank. The two men chafed their hands, and while Esch sat down dully on a bench Martin put his hand into the works of the orchestrion, which blared out *The March of the Gladiators* into the cold atmosphere of the room. In spite of the din they could presently hear a wooden stair creaking under someone's footsteps, and the swing door beside the buffet was flung open by Frau Hentjen. She was still in her morning working-garb, an ample blue-cotton apron was tied over her dress, and she had not yet donned her evening corset, so that her breasts lay like two sacks in her broad-checked dimity blouse. Her hair, however, was still as stiff and correct as ever, crowning like a sugar-loaf her pale, expressionless face, which gave no indication of her age. But everybody knew that Frau Gertrud Hentjen had thirty-six years to her credit, and that for a long, long time—they had reckoned a little while ago that it must certainly be fourteen years—she had been the relict of Herr Hentjen, whose photograph, yellow with age, gazed out over the Eiffel Tower between the restaurant licence and a moonlit landscape, all three in fine black frames with gold scroll-work. And although with his little goat's beard Herr Hentjen looked like a snippet of a tailor, his widow had remained faithful to him; at least nobody could say anything against her, and whenever anyone dared to approach her with an honourable proposal she would remark with disdain: "Yes, the business would suit him to a T, no doubt. No, I'd rather carry on alone, thank you."

"Morning, Herr Geyring. Morning, Herr Esch," she said. "You're early birds to-day." "We've been long enough on our legs, though, Mother Hentjen," replied Martin, "if one works one must eat," and he ordered wine and bread and cheese; Esch, whose mouth and stomach were still wry with the wine he had drunk yesterday, took Schnapps. Frau Hentjen sat down with the men and asked after their news. Esch was monosyllabic, and although he was not in the least ashamed of his dismissal, it annoyed him that Geyring should publish the fact so openly. "Yes, another victim of capitalism," the trade-union organizer concluded, "but now I must get to work again; of course the Duke here can spread himself at his ease now." He paid and insisted on settling for Esch's Schnapps at the same time—"One must support the unemployed"—grasped his crutches, which he had propped beside him, braced his left foot against the wood, and swung himself out through the door between his two supports with a great clatter.

After he had gone the two of them remained silent for a little; then

Esch jerked his chin towards the door: " An anarchist," he said. Frau Hentjen shrugged her plump shoulders: " And what if he is? He's a decent man." " He's a decent man, right enough," Esch corroborated, and Frau Hentjen went on: " but they'll lay him by the heels again sooner or later: he's done time for six months already . . ." then: " Well, it's all in his day's work." Once more they became silent. Esch was wondering whether Martin had been a cripple since his childhood; misbegotten, he thought to himself, and said: " He would like to land me among his socialist friends. But I'm not having any." " Why not? " asked Frau Hentjen without interest. " It doesn't suit my plans. I want to get to the top of the tree; law and order are necessary if you want to get to the top." Frau Hentjen could not but agree with that: " Yes, that's true, you must have law and order. But now I must go to the kitchen. Will you be having dinner with us to-day, Herr Esch? " Esch might as well dine here as anywhere else, and after all why should he wander about in the icy wind? " Strange that the snow hasn't come yet," he said, " the dust fairly blinds you." " Yes, it's dismal outside," said Frau Hentjen. " Then you'll just stay here? " She disappeared into the kitchen, the swing door vibrated for a little longer, and Esch dully followed its vibrations until it finally came to rest. Then he tried to sleep. But now the coldness of the room began to strike into him; he walked up and down with a heavy and rather unsteady tread and took up the newspaper that lay on the buffet; but he could not turn the pages with his stiff fingers; his eyes too were painful. So he resolved to seek out the warm kitchen; with the newspaper in his hand he walked in. " I suppose you've come to have a sniff at the saucepans? " said Frau Hentjen, suddenly remembering that it was cold in the eating-room, and as it was her custom not to put on a fire there until the afternoon she suffered him to bear her company. Esch watched her bustling about the hearth and had a longing to seize her beneath the breasts, but her reputation for inaccessibility checked his desire at once. When the kitchen-maid who helped Frau Hentjen with her work went out he said: " I can't understand your liking to live alone." " Aha! " she replied, " you're beginning that song too, are you? " " No," said Esch, " it isn't that. I was just wondering." Frau Hentjen's face had taken on a strangely frozen expression; it was as though she were disgusted at some thought, for she shook herself so violently that her breasts quivered, and then went about her work with the bored and empty face with which she always confronted her customers. Esch, sitting at the window, read his newspaper and afterwards looked out into the yard, where the wind was raising little cyclones of dust.

Later the two girls who acted as waitresses in the evening arrived, unwashed and unslept. Frau Hentjen, the two waitresses and the little kitchenmaid and Esch took their places round the kitchen table, stuck out their elbows, hunched themselves over their plates, and ate their dinner.

Esch had drawn up his application for the Mannheim post; he now needed only the reference to enclose with it. Actually he was glad that things had turned out as they had. It wasn't good for a man to vegetate all the time in one place. He felt he must get out of Cologne, and the farther the better. A fellow must keep his eyes open; as a matter of fact he had always done that.

In the afternoon he went to the office of Stemberg & Company, wholesale wine merchants, to get his reference. Nentwig kept him waiting at the counter, and sat at his desk, fat and slouching, totting up columns. Esch tapped impatiently with his strong finger-nails on the counter. Nentwig got up: " Patience, patience, Herr Esch," and he stepped to the barrier and said condescendingly: " Oh, about your reference?—that can't be so very urgent. Well? Date of birth? Date of employment here? " With his head averted Esch supplied this information and Nentwig took it down. Then Nentwig dictated to the stenographer and brought the reference. Esch read it through. " That isn't a reference," he said, handing the paper back. " Oh! Then what is it? " " You must certify to my ability as a book-keeper." " You—a book-keeper! You've shown us what you can do in that line." Now the moment of reckoning had come: " It's a very special kind of book-keeper that's needed for the inventories you draw up, I happen to know." Nentwig was taken aback: " What do you mean? " " I mean what I say." Nentwig changed his tune, became friendly: " You only harm yourself with your obstreperousness; here you had a good post, and you had to get into a row with the chief! " Esch tasted victory and began to roll it on his tongue: " I mean to have a talk with the chief later." " For all I care you can say what you like to the chief," Nentwig countered. " Well, what do you want me to put in your reference? " Esch decreed that he should be described as " conscientious, reliable and thoroughly versed in all

matters relating to book-keeping." Nentwig wanted to be rid of him.
" It isn't true, of course, but as far as I'm concerned——" He turned
again to the stenographer to dictate the new version. Esch grew red in
the face: " Oh, so it isn't true? . . . then please add: ' We heartily
recommend him to any employer who may be in need of his services.'
Have you got that?" Nentwig bowed elaborately: " Delighted, I'm
sure, Herr Esch." Esch read the new copy through and was appeased.
" The chief's signature," he commanded. But this was too much for
Nentwig, who shouted: " So mine isn't good enough for you?"
" If the firm authorizes you I'll let that pass," was Esch's large and
magnanimous reply, and Nentwig signed.

Esch stepped out into the street and made for the nearest pillar-box.
He whistled to himself; he felt rehabilitated. He had his reference,
good; it was in the envelope with his application to the Central Rhine
Company. The fact that Nentwig had given in showed that he had a
bad conscience. So the inventories were faked then, and the man should
be handed over to the police. Yes, it was simply one's duty as a citizen
to give him in charge straight away. The letter dropped into the post-
box with a soft, muffled thud, and Esch, his fingers still in the aperture,
considered whether he should go at once to the police headquarters. He
wandered on irresolutely. It had been a mistake to send off the reference,
he should have given it back to Nentwig; to force a reference out of a
man and then give him in charge wasn't decent. But now it was done,
and besides, without a reference he had little chance of getting a post
with the Central Rhine Shipping Company—there would be absolutely
nothing left for him but to go back to his old job in Stemberg's again.
And he saw a vision of the chief discovering the fraud, and Nentwig
languishing in prison. Yes, but what if the chief himself was involved
in the swindle? Then of course the public interrogation would bring
the whole concern toppling down. And then there would be another
bankruptcy, but no post for a book-keeper. And in the newspapers
people would read: " Revenge of a dismissed clerk." And finally he
would be suspected of collusion. And then he would be left without
a reference and without a job, for nobody would take him on. Esch
congratulated himself on the shrewdness with which he drew all the
consequences, but he was furious. " A fine bloody firm!" he swore
under his breath. He stood in the Ring in front of the Opera House,
cursing and swearing into the cold wind which blew the dust into his

eyes, and could not come to any decision, but finally resolved to postpone the affair; if he didn't get the post with the Central Rhine there would still be time left to act the part of Nemesis. He went through the darkening evening, his hands buried in the pockets of his shabby overcoat, actually went, indeed, as a matter of form, as far as the police headquarters. There he stood looking at the policemen on guard, and when a police wagon drove up he waited until all the prisoners had got out, and felt disappointed when the policeman finally slammed to the door without Nentwig's having put in an appearance. He remained standing for a few moments, then he turned resolutely and made for the Alt Markt. The two faint vertical lines on his cheeks had deepened. " Wine faker," he muttered in a fury, " vinegar tout." And morose and disillusioned over his poisoned victory, he ended the day by getting drunk again and sleeping with another girl.

In her brown-silk dress, which she was accustomed usually to don only in the evening, Frau Hentjen had been spending the afternoon with a woman friend, and now, as always on her return, she was put into a bad temper by the sight of the house and the restaurant in which for so long she had been compelled to pass her life. Certainly the business allowed her to lay by a little now and then, and when she was praised and flattered by her women friends for her capability she experienced a faintly pleasant sensation which made up for a good deal. But why wasn't she the owner of a linen-draper's shop, or a ladies' hairdressing saloon, instead of having to deal every evening with a pack of drunken louts? If her corset had not prevented her she would have shaken herself with loathing when she caught sight of her restaurant; so intensely did she hate the men who frequented it, these men that she had to serve. Though perhaps she hated still more the women who were always such fools as to run after them. Not a single one of her women friends belonged to the kind that took up with men, that trafficked with these creatures and like animals lusted for their embraces. Yesterday she had caught the kitchenmaid in the yard with a young lad, and the hand which had dealt the buffet still tingled pleasantly; she felt she would like to have it out with the girl again. No, women were probably still worse than men. She could put up only with her waitresses and all the other prostitutes who despised men even though they had to go to bed with them; she liked to talk to these women, she encouraged them to tell her their stories in detail, and comforted and pampered them to indemnify them for their sufferings. And so a post in Mother Hentjen's restaurant was highly prized, and her girls looked upon it as well worth the best they could give in return and did all they could to retain it. And Mother Hentjen was delighted with such devotion and love.

Her best room was up on the first floor; really too big, with its three windows on the narrow street it took up the full breadth of the house above the restaurant; in the back wall, corresponding to the buffet downstairs, there was an alcove shut off by a light curtain which was always drawn. If one drew aside the curtain and let one's eyes get used to the darkness, one could make out the twin marriage-beds. But Frau Hentjen never used this room, and nobody knew whether it had ever been used. For a room of such a size was difficult to heat except at a considerable cost, and so Frau Hentjen could not be blamed for choosing the smaller room above the kitchen as her bed- and sitting-room, employing the chill and gloomy parlour only for storing food that might go bad. Also the walnuts which she was accustomed to buy in autumn were stored here and lay strewn in heaps about the floor, upon which two broad green strips of linoleum were laid crosswise.

Still feeling angry, Frau Hentjen went up to the parlour to fetch sausage for her customers' suppers, and as anger makes one careless she stumbled into some of the nuts, which rolled before her feet with an exasperatingly loud clatter. It exasperated her still more when one cracked beneath her foot, and while she picked up the nut so that it might not be altogether wasted, and carefully detached the kernel from the splintered pieces of shell, and stuck the white fragments with the bitter pale-brown skin into her mouth, she kept meanwhile screaming for the kitchenmaid; at last the brazen trollop heard her, came stumbling up the stairs, and was received with a torrent of incoherent abuse: of course a girl that flirted with half-grown louts would be stealing nuts too—the nuts had been stored beside the window and now they were just inside the door, and nuts didn't walk across a floor of their own accord—and Frau Hentjen was preparing to raise her fist, and the girl had ducked and put up her arm, when a piece of shell caught in her mistress's teeth, who contented herself with spitting it out contemptuously; then, followed by the sobbing maid, she descended to the kitchen.

When she entered the restaurant, where already a thick cloud of tobacco smoke was hanging, she was overcome again, as almost every evening, by that apprehensive torpor which was so incomprehensible to her and yet so difficult to overcome. She went up to the mirror and mechanically patted the blond sugar-loaf on her head and pulled her dress straight, and only when she had assured herself that her appearance was satisfactory did her composure return. Now she looked round and saw the familiar faces among her customers, and although there was more profit on the drinks than on the food, she prized the eaters among her customers above the drinkers, and she stepped out from behind the buffet and went from table to table asking whether the food was to their liking. And she summoned the waitress almost with elation when a customer demanded a second helping. Yes, Mother Hentjen's cooking had no need to fear examination.

Geyring was already there; his crutches were leaning beside him; he had cut the meat on his plate into small pieces and now ate mechanically while in his left hand he held one of his Socialist papers, a whole bundle of which were always sticking out of his pocket. Frau Hentjen liked him, partly because, being a cripple, he did not count as a man, partly because it was not to shout and drink and make up to the waitresses that he came, but simply because his post demanded that he should keep in touch with the sailors and dock workers; but above all she liked him because evening after evening he had his supper at her restaurant and praised up her food. She sat down at his table. " Has Esch been here yet? " asked Geyring. " He's got the job with the Central Rhine, starts work on Monday." " And it's you that got it for him, I'm sure, Herr Geyring," said Frau Hentjen. " No, Mother Hentjen, we haven't got the length yet of filling posts through the union . . . no, not by a long way . . . well, that'll come too in time. But I put Esch on the track of it. Why shouldn't one help a nice lad, even if he isn't one of ourselves? " Mother Hentjen showed little sympathy with this sentiment: " You just eat that up, Herr Geyring, and you'll have an extra titbit from myself as well," and she went over to the buffet and brought on a plate a moderate-sized slice of sausage which she had garnished with a sprig of parsley. Geyring's wrinkled face of a boy of fourteen smiled at her in gratitude, showing a mouthful of bad teeth, and he patted her white, plump hand, which she immediately drew back with a slight return of her frozen manner.

Later Esch arrived. Geyring looked up from his paper and said: " Congratulations, August." " Thanks," said Esch. " So you know already?—there was no difficulty, a reply by return engaging me. Well, I must thank you for putting me on to it." But his face beneath the short, dark, cropped hair had the wooden empty look of a disappointed man. " A pleasure," said Martin, then he shouted over to the buffet: " Here's our new paymaster." " Good luck, Herr Esch," replied Frau Hentjen dryly, yet she came forward after all and gave him her hand. Esch, who wished to show that all the credit was not due to Martin, pulled his reference out of his breast-pocket: " It wouldn't have gone so smoothly, I can tell you, if I hadn't made Stemberg's give me such a good reference." He heavily emphasized the " made," and then added: " A measly firm." Frau Hentjen read the reference absently: " A splendid reference." Geyring too read it and nodded: " Yes, the Central Rhine must be glad they've got hold of such a first-class fellow. . . . I'll really have to get the Chairman, Bertrand, to fork out a commission for my services."

" An excellent book-keeper, excellent, what? " Esch preened himself. " Well, it's nice when anyone can have such things said about him," Frau Hentjen agreed. " You may feel very proud of yourself, Herr Esch; you've every right to: do you want anything to eat? " Of course he did, and while Frau Hentjen looked on complacently to see that he enjoyed his food, he said that now he was going farther up the Rhine he hoped to get one of the travelling jobs; that would mean going as far as Kehl and Basel. Meanwhile several of his other acquaintances had come up, the new paymaster ordered wine for them all, and Frau Hentjen withdrew. With disgust she noticed that every time Hede, the waitress, passed the table, Esch could not help fondling her, and that finally he ordered her to sit down beside him, so that they might drink to each other. But the score was a high one, and when the gentlemen broke up after midnight, taking Hede with them, Frau Hentjen pushed a mark into her hand.

Nevertheless Esch could not feel elated over his new post. It was as though he had purchased it at the cost of his soul's welfare, or at least of his decency. Now that things had gone so far and he had already drawn an advance for his travelling expenses from the Cologne branch of the Central Rhine, he was overcome anew by the doubt whether he shouldn't give Nentwig in charge. Of course in that case he would have to be present at the official inquiry, could not therefore leave the town, and

would almost certainly lose his new job. For a moment he thought of
solving the problem by writing an anonymous letter to the police, but
he rejected this plan: one couldn't wipe out one piece of rascality by
committing another. And on top of it all he was beginning to resent his
own twinges of conscience; after all he wasn't a child, he didn't give a
damn for the parsons and their morality; he had read all sorts of books,
and when Geyring had recently begged him yet again to join the Social
Democratic Party he had replied: " No, I won't have anything to do
with you anarchists, but I'll go with you this far: I'll turn Freethinker."
The thankless fool had replied that that didn't matter a damn to him.
That was what people were like: well, Esch wouldn't give a damn either.

Finally he did the most reasonable thing: he set off for Mannheim
at the appointed time. But he felt violently uprooted, he had none of his
accustomed pleasure in travelling, and as a safeguard he left part of
his belongings in Cologne: he even left his bicycle behind. Nevertheless
his travelling allowance put him in a generous mood. And standing
with his beer-glass in his hand and his ticket stuck in his hat on Mainz
platform, he thought of the people whom he had left, felt he wanted to
show them a kindness, and, a newspaper man happening to push his
barrow past at that moment, he bought two picture postcards. Martin
in particular deserved a line from him; yet one did not send picture
postcards to a man. So first he scribbled one to Hede: the second was
destined for Frau Hentjen. Then he reflected that it might seem insulting to Frau Hentjen, who was a proud woman, to receive a postcard
by the same post as one of her employees, and as he was in a reckless
mood he tore up the first one and posted only the one to Frau Hentjen,
containing his warmest greetings to her and all his kind friends and
acquaintances and Fräulein Hede and Fräulein Thusnelda from the
beautiful town of Mainz. After that he felt again a little lonely, drank a
second glass of beer, and let the train carry him on to Mannheim.

He had been instructed to report to the head office. The Central
Rhine Shipping Company Limited occupied a building of its own not
far from the Mühlau Dock, a massive stone edifice with pillars in front
of the door. The street in which it stood was asphalted, good for cycling;
it was a new street. The heavy door of wrought-iron and glass—it would
certainly swing smoothly and noiselessly on its hinges—stood ajar, and
Esch entered. The marble vestibule pleased him; over the stair hung
a glass sign-plate on whose transparent surface he read the words:

" Board Room " in gold letters. He made straight for it. When his foot
was on the first stair he heard a voice behind him: " Where are you
going, please? " He turned round and saw a commissionaire in grey
livery; silver buttons glittered on it and the cap had a strip of silver braid.
It was all very elegant, but Esch felt annoyed—what business was
it of this fellow's?—and he said curtly: " I was asked to report here,"
and made to go on. The other did not weaken: " To see the Chairman? "
" Why, who else, do you think? " replied Esch rudely. The stair led
up to a large, gloomy waiting-room on the first floor. In the middle of
it stood a great oaken table, round which were ranged a few upholstered
chairs. It was certainly very splendid. Once more a man with silver
buttons appeared and asked what he wanted. " The Chairman's office,"
said Esch. " The gentlemen are at a board meeting," said the attendant.
" Is it important? " Driven to the wall, Esch had to tell his business;
he drew out his papers, the letter engaging him, the receipt for his
travelling allowance. " I've some references with me too," he said, and
made to hand over Nentwig's reference. He was somewhat taken aback
when the fellow did not even look at it: " You've no business with this
up here . . . ground floor, through the corridor, then the second stair—
inquire down below."

Esch remained standing where he was for a moment; he grudged
the attendant his triumph and asked once more: " So this isn't the
place? " The attendant had already turned away indifferently: " No,
this is the Chairman's waiting-room." Esch felt anger rising up in him;
they made too much of a blow with their Chairman, their upholstered
furnishings and their silver-buttoned attendants; Nentwig too would
no doubt like to play this game; well, their fine Chairman was probably
not so very different from Nentwig. But, willy-nilly, Esch had to go
back the same road again. Down below the commissionaire was still at
his post. Esch looked at him to see whether he was angry; but as the
commissionaire merely gazed at him indifferently he said: " I want
the engagement bureau," and asked to be shown the way. After taking
a couple of steps he turned round, jerked his thumb towards the staircase, and asked: " What's the name of your boss up there, the Chairman? "
" Herr von Bertrand," said the commissionaire, and there was almost a
respectful ring in his voice. And Esch repeated, also somewhat respectfully: " Herr von Bertrand ": he must have heard the name at some
time or other.

In the engagement bureau he learned that he was to be employed as stores clerk in the docks. As he stepped out into the street again a carriage halted before the building. It was a cold day; the powdery snow, drifted by the wind, lay on the kerb and against the corners of the wall; the horse kept striking a hoof against the smooth asphalt. It was obviously impatient and with reason. " A carriage. no less, for the Chairman," Esch said to himself, " but as for us, we have to walk." Yet all the same he liked all this elegance, and he was glad that he belonged to it. After all, it was one in the eye for Nentwig.

In the warehouse of the Central Rhine Shipping Company the office was a glass-partitioned box at the end of a long line of sheds. His desk stood beside that of the customs officer, and at the back glowed a little iron stove. When one was bored with one's work, or felt lonely and forsaken, one could always watch the trucks being loaded and unloaded. The sailings were to begin in a few days, and on all the boats there was a great bustle. There were cranes which revolved and lowered their hooks as though to pick something or other cautiously out of the ships' entrails, and there were others which projected over the water like bridges that had been begun but never completed. Of course these sights were not new to Esch, for he had seen exactly the same in Cologne, but there he had been so used to the long row of storage sheds that he had never thought of them, and if he had forced himself to consider them, the buildings, the cranes and the landing-stages would have appeared almost meaningless, put there to serve human needs that were inexplicable. But now that he himself was concerned in these things they had grown into natural and purposive structures, and this gladdened him. While formerly he had at the most been surprised, occasionally indeed even irritated, that there should be so many export firms, and that the sheds, all alike, on the quays, should bear so many separate names, now the different businesses took on an individuality which one could recognize from the appearance of their stout or lean storekeepers, their gruff or pleasant stevedores. Also the insignia of His Majesty the Emperor of Germany's customs officers at the gates of the closed dock quarter flattered him: they made him vaguely conscious that here one lived and moved on foreign soil. It was both a constricted and a free life that one led in this sanctuary where wares could lie untaxed; it was frontier air that one breathed behind the iron gratings of the customs barriers. And even although he had no uniform to wear, and was, so to speak, only a private official, yet by virtue of his association with these customs and railway officials Esch had himself become almost an official figure, particularly as he carried in his pocket an official pass allowing him to wander at liberty through this exclusive province, and was already greeted with a welcoming salute by the watchman at the main gate. When he returned that salute he threw his cigarette away with a lordly sweep in obedience to the prohibition against smoking that was stuck up everywhere, and proceeded with long and important strides—a strict non-smoker himself, ready at any moment to come down upon any too familiar civilian for an infringement of the rule—to the office, where the storekeeper had already laid his list upon the desk. Then he drew on his grey-woollen mittens that left the finger-tips free, for without them his hands would have frozen in the musty coldness of the shed, looked over the lists, and checked the piled-up packing-cases and bales. Should a packing-case be in the wrong place he did not fail to throw the storekeeper, whose province it was to supervise the deliveries, a severe or at least an impatient look, so that he might give the docker responsible for it a proper talking-to. And when later the customs officer in his round stepped into the glass partition and said how warm it was in here, unfastening the collar of his tunic and pleasantly yawning in his chair, by that time the lists were checked and the contents copied into the books, and there was no difficulty about the rest; the two men sat at the table and lazily went over the papers. Then the customs officer, rapidly as ever, endorsed the lists with his blue pencil, took up the duplicates and locked them in his desk, and if there was nothing more to be done they proceeded together to the canteen.

Yes, Esch had made a good exchange, even if justice had suffered in the process. Still, he could not help wondering—and it was the only thing that disturbed his contentment—whether there mightn't be some way after all of duly giving Nentwig in charge; for only then would everything be in order.

Customs Inspector Balthasar Korn came from a very matter-of-fact part of Germany. He was born on the frontier-line between Bavaria and Saxony, and had received his earliest impressions from the hilly town of Hof. His mind was divided between a matter-of-fact desire for coarse amusements and a matter-of-fact parsimony, and after he had worked his way up to a sergeant's rank in active military service, he had seized the opportunity offered by a paternal Government to its faithful soldiers, and had obtained his transfer to the customs. A bachelor, he lived in Mannheim with his sister Erna, also unmarried, and as the empty best bedroom in his house was a standing offence in his eyes, he prevailed upon August Esch to give up his expensive room in the hotel and accept cheaper lodgings with him. And although he did not entirely approve of Esch, seeing that Esch as a Luxemburger could not boast of military service, yet he would not have been displeased to find in Esch a husband for his sister as well as an occupant for the spare bedroom; he was not sparing in unequivocal hints, and his sister, who was no longer young, accompanied them with bashful and tittering signs of protest. Indeed he actually went so far as to jeopardize his sister's good name, for he did not scruple to address Esch before the others in the canteen as " Herr Brother-in-Law," so that everybody must think that his friend already shared his sister's bed. Yet Korn did this not exclusively for the sake of having his joke; rather his intention was to compel Esch, partly by constantly accustoming him to the idea, partly through the pressure of public opinion, to transform into solid actuality the fictitious part which he was thus called on to play.

Esch had not been unwilling to move into Korn's house. Though he had knocked about so much he felt lonely. Perhaps the numbered streets of Mannheim were to blame, perhaps he missed the smells of Mother Hentjen's restaurant, perhaps it was that scoundrel Nentwig that still troubled him; at any rate he felt lonely and stayed on with the brother and sister, stayed on although he was quick to observe how the wind blew, stayed on although he had no intention of having anything to do with that elderly virgin; he was not impressed in the least by the great display of lingerie which Erna had gathered together in the course of the years, and which she showed him with considerable pride, nor did even the savings-bank book which she once let him see, showing a balance of over two thousand marks, attract him. But Korn's efforts to lure him into the trap were so amusing that they were worth taking some risk for; of course one had to be wary and not let oneself be caught. As for example: Korn would rarely let him pay for their drinks when they forgathered in the canteen before they went home together; and after they had heartily cursed the quality of the Mannheim beer Korn was not to be dissuaded from turning in for Munich beer at the Spatenbräu cellar. Then, if Herr Esch hastily put his hand into his pocket, Korn would again refuse to let him pay: " You'll have your revenge yet, Herr Brother-in-law." But when they were sauntering down Rheinstrasse the customs inspector would punctually halt before certain of the lighted shop-windows and clap Esch on the shoulder with his great paw: " My sister has been wanting an umbrella like that for a long time: I'll have to buy it for her birthday," or: " Every house should have a gas-iron like that," or: " If my sister had a wringer she would be happy." And when Esch made no reply to all these hints Korn would become as furiously angry as he had once been at recruits who refused to understand how to handle their rifles, and the more silent Esch was as they walked on, the more furious grew his burly companion's rage at the impudently knowing expression on Esch's face.

But it was by no means parsimony that made Esch dumb on those occasions. For although he was thrifty and fond of picking up small gains, yet the thorough and righteous book-keeping which in his soul he believed in did not allow him to accept goods without payment; service demanded counter-service, and goods must be paid for; nevertheless he thought it unnecessary to have a purchase forced on him in too great a hurry; indeed it would have seemed to him almost clumsy and inconsiderate to crown Korn's breezy demands with actual success. So for the time being he had hit upon a curious kind of revenge which allowed him to repay his obligations to Korn and at the same time show that he was in no hurry to marry; after dinner he would invite Korn out for a little evening's entertainment which took them to those beer-shops where there were barmaids, and unavoidably ended for them both in the so-called disreputable streets of the town. It sometimes cost a good deal of money to foot the bill for both of them—even if Korn could not get out of tipping his girl himself—yet the sight of Korn on the way home afterwards, walking along morosely, chewing at his black, bushy moustache, which was now limp and dejected, growling that this loose life Esch was leading him into must be put an end to: that was well worth all the expense. And besides, Korn was always in such a bad temper with his sister next morning that he went out of his way to wound her in her tenderest feelings, accusing her of never having been able to catch a man. And when thereupon she maintained hotly that she had had hosts of admirers, he would remind her contemptuously of her single estate.

One day Esch managed to wipe off his debt to a considerable extent. While he was on his way through the company's stores his vigilant eye was caught by the curiously shaped packing-cases and properties of a theatrical outfit, which were just being unloaded. A clean-shaven gentleman was standing by in great agitation, shouting that his valuable property, which represented untold wealth, was being handled as roughly as if it were firewood, and when Esch, who had been looking on gravely with the air of a connoisseur, threw a few pieces of superfluous advice to the labourers, and in this unmistakable fashion gave the gentleman to know that he was in the presence of a man of knowledge and authority, the formidable volubility of the stranger was turned upon him and they soon found themselves engaged in a friendly conversation, in the course of which the clean-shaven gentleman, raising his hat slightly, introduced himself as Herr Gernerth, the new lessee of the Thalia Theatre, who would be particularly flattered—in the meanwhile the work of unloading had been completed—if the Shipping Inspector and his esteemed family would attend the opening performance, and begged to present him with the necessary tickets at reduced prices. And when Esch agreed with alacrity, the manager put his hand in his pocket and actually wrote out three free tickets for him on the spot.

Now Esch was sitting with the Korns in the variety theatre at a table covered with a white cloth. The programme opened with a novel attraction, the moving pictures or, as they were called, the cinematograph. These pictures, however, did not meet with much applause from the audience, or indeed from the public in general at that time, not being regarded as serious and genuine entertainment, but merely as a prelude to it; nevertheless this modern art-form really held one's attention when a comedy was put on showing the comic effects of laxative pills, the critical moments being emphasized with a ruffle of drums. Korn roared with mirth and brought down the flat of his hand on the table; Fräulein Korn put her hand over her mouth and giggled, throwing stolen coquettish glances at Esch through her fingers, and Esch was as proud as though he himself were the inventor and producer of this highly successful entertainment. The smoke from their cigars ascended and melted into the cloud of tobacco smoke which very soon floated under

the low roof of the hall traversed by the silvery beam of the limelight
which lit up the screen. During the interval, which came after an act
imitating the whistling of birds, Esch ordered three glasses of beer,
though it cost considerably more here in the theatre than anywhere else,
but he was relieved when it proved to be flat and stale and they decided
to give no further orders, but to have a drink in the Spatenbräu after
the performance. He felt once more in a generous mood, and while the
prima donna was being passionate and despairing to the best of her
ability he said significantly: " Ah, love, Fräulein Erna, love." But when,
after the vociferous applause which greeted the singer from all sides, the
curtain rose again, the whole stage glittered as with silver, and little
nickel-plated tables stood about, and all the other glittering apparatus
of a juggler. On the red-velvet cloths with which the various stands
were either hung or completely draped stood balls and flasks, little flags
and banners, and also a great pile of white plates. On a ladder running
up to a point—it too shone with nickel-plating—hung some two dozen
daggers whose long blades glittered no less brilliantly than all the shining
metal round them. The juggler in his black dress-suit was supported by
a female assistant, whom he brought on, it was clear, simply to display
her striking beauty to the public, and also the spangled tights she wore
must have been designed merely to that end, for all that she had to do
was to hand the juggler the plates and the flags, or to fling them to him
in the midst of his performance whenever, as a signal, he clapped his
hands. She discharged this task with a gracious smile, and when she
threw him the hammer she emitted a short cry in some foreign tongue,
perhaps to draw the attention of her master to her, perhaps also to beg
for a little affection, which her austere tyrant, however, sternly denied
her. And although he must certainly have known that he ran the risk
of losing the audience's sympathy by his hard-heartedness, he did not
accord his beautiful helper even a single glance, and only when he had
to acknowledge the applause with a bow did he indicate by a casual
wave of his hand in her direction that he allowed her a certain percentage
of it. But then he walked to the back of the stage, and quite amicably,
as though the affront which he had just put upon her had never
happened, they lifted up together a great black board which, noticed
by nobody, had been waiting there all the time, brought it forward to
the waiting array of shining paraphernalia, set it up on end, and fastened
it securely to the ladder. Thereupon, mutually encouraging each other

with short cries and smiles, they pushed the black board, now set up vertically, to the front of the stage, and secured it to the floor and the wings with cords which suddenly appeared from nowhere. After they had seen to this with profound solemnity, the beautiful assistant once more emitted her short cry and skipped over to the board, which was so high that, stretching her arms upwards, she could scarcely touch the top edge. And now one saw that two handles were fixed into the board near the top, and the assistant, who stood with her back against the board, seized hold of those handles, and this somewhat constrained and artificial posture gave her, as she stood sharply outlined in her glittering and flimsy attire against the black board, the look of someone being crucified. Yet all the same she still went on smiling her gracious smile, even when the man, after regarding her with sharp half-shut eyes, went up to her and altered her position, altered it so slightly as to be unnoticeable, it is true, yet in such a way that the spectators became aware that everything depended on that fraction of an inch. All this was done to the subdued strains of a waltz, which immediately broke off at a slight sign from the juggler. The theatre became quite still; an extraordinary isolation, divested even of music, lay on the stage up there, and the waiters did not dare to walk up to the tables with the beer and food they were carrying, but stood, themselves tense with excitement, by the yellow-lighted doors at the back; guests who were on the point of eating put back their forks, on which they had already spitted some morsel, on their plates, and only the limelight, which the operator had directed full on the crucified girl, went on whirring. But the juggler was already testing one of the long daggers in his murderous hand; he bent his body back and now it was he who sent out the discordant exotic cry, while the dagger flew whistling from his hand, whizzed straight across the stage, and quivered in the black wood with a dull impact beside the body of the crucified girl. And now, faster than one could follow him, he had both hands full of glittering daggers, and while his cries became more rapid and more brutal, indeed, veritably bestial, the daggers whizzed in more and more rapid succession through the quivering air, struck with ever more rapid impact on the wood, and framed the girl's face, which still smiled, numb and yet confident, appealing and yet challenging, brave and yet apprehensive. Esch could almost have wished that it was himself who was standing up there with his arms raised to heaven, that it was himself being crucified, could almost have wished to station himself in front of that gentle girl and receive in his own breast the menacing blades; and had the juggler, as often happened, asked whether any gentleman in the audience would deign to step on to the stage and place himself against the black board, in sober truth Esch would have accepted the offer. Indeed the thought of standing up there alone and forsaken, where the long blades might pin one against the board like a beetle, filled him with almost voluptuous pleasure; but in that case, he thought, correcting himself, he would have to stand with his face to the board, for a beetle was never spitted from the under side: and the thought of standing with his face to the darkness of the board, not knowing when the deadly daggers might fly, transfixing his heart and pinning it to the board, had so extraordinary and mysterious a fascination for him, grew into a desire so novel, so powerful and satisfying, that he started as out of a dream of bliss when with a flourish of drums and fanfares the orchestra greeted the juggler, who had triumphantly dispatched the last of the daggers, and the girl skipped out of her frame, which was now complete, and both of them with a graceful pirouette, holding hands and executing spacious gestures with their free arms, bowed to the audience, now released from its ordeal. It was the fanfare of the Last Judgment, when the guilty were to be trodden underfoot like worms; why shouldn't they be spitted like beetles? Why, instead of a sickle, shouldn't Death carry a long darning-needle, or at least a lance? One always lived in fear of being awakened to the Last Judgment, for even if one had once upon a time almost thought of joining the Freethinkers, yet one had a conscience. He heard Korn saying: " That was great," and it sounded like blasphemy: and when Fräulein Erna remarked that, if they asked her, she would take good care not to be set up there almost naked and have knives thrown at her before the whole audience, it was too much for Esch, and in the most ungentle manner he flung away her knee, which was leaning against his; one shouldn't take people like these to see a superior entertainment; interlopers without a conscience, that's what they were; and he was not in the least impressed by the fact that Fräulein Erna was always running to her confessor; indeed the life of his Cologne friends seemed to him by far more secure and respectable.

In the Spatenbräu Esch drank his dark beer in silence. He was still in the grip of an emotion that could only be called yearning. Especially when it took shape as a need to send a picture postcard to Mother Hentjen. It was of course only natural that Erna should add a line: " Kind regards

from Erna Korn," but when Balthasar too insisted on contributing and
beneath his, " Regards, Korn, Customs Inspector," scored in his firm
hand a black definitively conclusive flourish, it was like a sort of homage
to Frau Hentjen, and it softened Esch so much that he became unsure
of himself: had he really quite fulfilled his obligation to give an honest
return for the Korns' kindness? Actually, to round off the evening, he
should steal across to Erna's door, and if he had not thrust her away
so ungently just now the door would certainly have been left unbarred.
Yes, properly regarded, that was the right and fitting conclusion to the
evening, yet he did nothing to bring it about. A sort of paralysis had
fallen on him; he paid no further attention to Erna, did not seek her
knee with his, and nothing happened either on the way home or afterwards. For some reason or other his conscience was troubling him, but
finally he decided in his mind that he had done enough after all, and
that it might even lead to trouble if he showed too much attention to
Fräulein Korn; he felt a fate hovering over his head with threateningly
upraised lance ready to strike if he should go on behaving like a
swine, and he felt that he must remain true to someone, even though he
did not know who it was.

While Esch was still feeling the stab of conscience in his back so
palpably that he declared he must have sat in a cold draught, and
every night rubbed himself as far as he could reach with a pungent
embrocation, Mother Hentjen was rejoicing over the two picture postcards which he had sent her, and stuck them, before they should go
for final preservation into her picture-postcard album, in the mirror
frame behind the buffet. Then in the evening she took them out and
showed them to the regular customers. Perhaps she did this also lest anybody might say of her that she was carrying on a secret correspondence
with a man; for if she let the postcards go the round of the restaurant then
they were no longer directed merely to her, but to the establishment,
which was only incidentally personified in her. For this reason too she
was glad that Geyring undertook the task of replying; yet she would
not hear of Herr Geyring going to any expense, so she herself procured
next day a particularly beautiful panorama card, as it was called, three
times the length of an ordinary postcard, showing the whole of Cologne
stretching along the dark-blue banks of the Rhine, and leaving space
for a great number of signatures. At the top she wrote: " Many thanks

for the beautiful postcards from Mother Hentjen." Then Geyring gave the command: " Ladies first," and Hede and Thusnelda signed their names. And then followed the names of Wilhelm Lassmann, Bruno May, Hoelst, Wrobek, Hülsenschmitt, John, the English mechanic Andrew, the sailor Wingast, and finally, after several more, all of which were not decipherable, the name of Martin Geyring. Then Geyring wrote out the address: " Herr August Esch, Head Book-keeper, Shipping Depot, Central Rhine Shipping Company Limited, Mannheim," and handed the finished product to Frau Hentjen, who, after reading it through carefully, opened the cash drawer to take from the large wire basket in which the bank-notes lay the necessary postage stamp. To her now the enormous card, with the long list of signatures, seemed almost too marked an honour for Esch, who had not been after all among the best patrons of the restaurant. But as everything she did she liked to do thoroughly, and as on the huge card there still remained, in spite of all the names, enough empty space not only to offend her sense of proportion, but also to provide the desired chance of putting Esch in his place by filling it in with a name of more humble rank, Mother Hentjen bore the card to the kitchen for the maid to sign her name, doubly pleased that in this way she could give pleasure to the poor girl without its costing anything.

When she returned to the restaurant Martin was sitting at his usual place in the corner near the buffet, buried in one of the Socialist journals. Frau Hentjen sat down beside him and said jestingly, as she often did: " Herr Geyring, you'll get my restaurant a bad name yet if you use it all the time for reading your seditious papers." " I'm disgusted enough myself with these scribblers," was the answer, " fellows like us do all the work, and these chaps only scribble a lot of nonsense." Once more Frau Hentjen felt a little disappointed in Geyring, for she had never given up the hope that he would yet come out with something revolutionary and full of hatred on which she might feed her own resentment against the world. She had often glanced into the Socialist papers, but really what she found there had seemed to her pretty tame, and so she hoped that Geyring's living speech would have more to give her than the printed word. So to a certain extent she was pleased that Geyring too did not think much of the newspaper writers, for she was always pleased when anyone did not think much of anyone else; yet, on the other hand, he still continued to disappoint her expectations. No, these anarchists didn't get you very far, there wasn't much help in a man like Geyring who sat in his trade-union bureau just like a police sergeant in his office, and Frau Hentjen was once more firmly convinced that the whole structure of society was simply a put-up job among the men, who laid their heads together to injure and disappoint women. She made one more attempt: " What is it that you don't like in your papers, Herr Geyring? " " They write such stuff," growled Martin, " turn the people's heads with their revolutionary rant, and then we've got to pay for it." Frau Hentjen did not quite understand this; besides, she was no longer interested. Mainly out of politeness she sighed: " Yes, life isn't easy." Geyring turned over a page and said absently: " No, life isn't easy, Mother Hentjen." " And a man like you, always on the go, always at it from early morning till late at night. . . ." Geyring said almost with satisfaction: " There won't be any eight-hour day for men like me for a long time yet: everybody else will get it first. . . ." " And to think that they try to make it harder for you! " said Frau Hentjen in amazement, shaking her head and throwing a glance at her coiffure in the mirror behind the buffet. " Yes, they can make a fine noise in the Reichstag and the newspaper, our friends the Jews," said Geyring, " but when it comes to the real work of organization they turn tail." Frau Hentjen could understand this: she agreed indignantly: " They're everywhere, these Jews; they have all the money and no woman is safe from them, they're just like bulls." The old expression of petrified loathing overspread her face. Martin looked up from his paper and could not help smiling: " It isn't as bad as all that, surely, Mother Hentjen." " So now you're sticking up for the Jews next? " there was a hint of hysterical aggressiveness in her voice, " but you always stick up for one another, you men," and then quite unexpectedly: " a girl in every port." " That may be, Mother Hentjen," laughed Martin, " but you won't find such good cooking as Mother Hentjen's anywhere in a hurry." Frau Hentjen was appeased: " Not even in Mannheim, maybe," she said, handing Geyring the picture postcard that he was to send off to Esch.

Gernerth, the theatre manager, now belonged to Esch's intimate circle of friends. For Esch, an impetuous man, had bought another ticket the very day after the first performance, not merely because he wanted to see that brave girl again, but also that he might look up a somewhat astonished Gernerth after the performance and introduce himself as a paying client; while doing this he once more thanked the manager for a lovely evening's enjoyment, and Gernerth, who saw a request for more free tickets in the offing, and was already preparing to refuse them, could not but feel touched. And heartened by his cordial reception Esch simply remained sitting; thus achieving his second object, for he was presented to the juggler Herr Teltscher and also to his brave companion Ilona, who, it turned out, were both of them of Hungarian birth, at least Ilona was, and she had very little command over German, while Herr Teltscher, whose professional name was Teltini, and who employed English on the stage, came from Pressburg.

Herr Gernerth, on the other hand, was an Egerlander, and this was a matter for great joy to Korn, the first time that the two men met; for the towns of Eger and Hof were close neighbours, and Korn could not but regard it as an extraordinary coincidence that two men who were almost landsmen should meet in Mannheim of all places. Still his expressions of joy and surprise were more or less rhetorical, for in less desirable circumstances the fact that he was meeting almost a landsman would have left him quite indifferent. He invited Gernerth to visit his sister and himself, partly perhaps because he could not bear the idea of his presumptive brother-in-law having private acquaintanceships of his own, and Herr Teltscher too was presently invited to a repast of coffee and cakes.

So now on a dull Sunday afternoon they all sat at the round table, on which beside the bulging coffee-pot the cakes, contributed by Esch, were piled up artistically in a pyramid, while outside the rain poured down the window-panes. Herr Gernerth began, trying to set the conversation going: " You've a very nice place here, Herr Customs Inspector, roomy, lots of light. . . ." And he looked out through the window at the dreary suburban street, in which lay great puddles of rain. Fräulein Erna remarked that it was really too small for their circumstances, yet a fireside of one's own was the only thing that could make life sweet. Herr Gernerth became elegiac: no place like home, yes, she might well say that, but for an artist it was an unfulfillable dream; no, for him there could be no home; he had a flat, it was true, a pleasant and comfortable flat in Munich, where his wife lived with the children, but he was almost a stranger to his family by this time. Why didn't he take them with him? It was no life for children, on tour all the time. And besides—— No, his children would never be artists, *his* children wouldn't. He was obviously an affectionate father, and Esch as well as Fräulein Erna felt touched by his goodness of heart. And perhaps because he felt lonely Esch said: " I'm an orphan, I can scarcely remember my mother." " Poor fellow! " said Fräulein Erna. But Herr Teltscher, who did not seem to relish this lugubrious talk, now made a coffee-cup revolve on the tip of his finger so that they could not help laughing, all but Ilona who sat impassively on her chair, recuperating, it seemed, from the perpetual smiles with which she had to embellish her evenings. At close quarters she was by no means so lovely and fragile as she had been on the stage, but might even have been called plump; her face was slightly puffy, there were heavy pouches covered with freckles under her eyes, and Esch, now become mistrustful, began to suspect that her beautiful blond hair, too, might not be genuine, but only a wig; yet his suspicions faded whenever he looked at her body, for he could not help seeing the knives whizzing past it. Then he noticed that Korn's eyes too were caressing that body, and so he tried to attract Ilona's attention, asked her whether she liked Mannheim, whether she had seen the Rhine before, with similar geographical inquiries. Unfortunately his attempts were unsuccessful, for Ilona only replied now and then and at the wrong point: " Yes, very nice," and wished, it seemed, to have nothing to do either with him or with Korn; she drank her coffee heavily and seriously, and even when Teltscher spluttered something at her in their sibilant native idiom, obviously something disagreeable, she scarcely listened. Meanwhile Fräulein Erna was telling Gernerth that a happy family life was the most beautiful thing in the world, and she gave Esch a little nudge with her toe, either to encourage him to follow Gernerth's example, or perhaps merely to withdraw his attention from the Hungarian girl, whose beauty, however, she praised none the less; for the greedy longing with which her brother was regarding the girl had not escaped her vigilant glance, and she considered it preferable that the lovely charmer should fall to her brother rather than to Esch. So she stroked Ilona's hands and praised their whiteness, rolled up the girl's sleeve and said that she had a lovely fine skin, Balthasar should only look at it. Balthasar put out his hairy paw to feel it. Teltscher laughed and said that every Hungarian woman had a skin like silk, whereupon Erna, who also had a skin of her own, replied that it was all a matter of tending one's complexion, and that she washed her face every day in milk.

Certainly, said Gernerth, she had a marvellous, indeed an international, complexion, and Fräulein Erna's withered face parted in a smile, showing her yellow teeth and the gap where one tooth was missing in her left upper jaw, and blushed to the roots of the hair at her temples, which hung down thin and brown and a little faded, from her coiffure.

Twilight had fallen; Korn's fist grasped Ilona's hand more and more firmly, and Fräulein Erna was waiting until Esch, or Gernerth at least, should do the same with hers. She hesitated to light the lamp, chiefly because Balthasar would have radically disapproved of the disturbance, but at last she was forced to get up so as to fetch the blue carafe of home-brewed liqueur which stood ostentatiously on the sideboard. Proudly announcing that the recipe was her own secret she served out the brew, which tasted like flat beer, but was applauded as delicious by Gernerth; in his admiration he even kissed her hand. Esch remembered that Mother Hentjen did not like Schnapps drinkers, and it filled him with particular satisfaction to think that she would have had all sorts of hard things to say of Korn, for he was tossing down one glass after another, smacking his lips each time, and sucking the drops from his dark, bushy moustache. Korn poured out a glass for Ilona too, and it may have been her imperturbable indifference and impassivity that made her allow him to lift the glass to her mouth and raise no objection even when he took a sip from it himself, dipping his moustache into it, and declaring that it was a kiss. Evidently Ilona did not understand what he had said, but on the other hand Teltscher must know what was happening. Incomprehensible that he should look on so calmly. Perhaps he was suffering inwardly, and was simply too well-bred to create a scene. Esch had a strong desire to do it for him, but then he remembered the rough tone in which Teltscher had ordered the brave girl to hand him things on the stage; perhaps he was deliberately trying to humiliate her? Something or other should be done, somebody ought to shield Ilona! But Teltscher merely clapped him jovially on the shoulder, calling him colleague and brother, and when Esch looked at him questioningly pointed to the two couples and said: " We must stick together, we young bachelors." " I'll have to take pity on you, I see," said Fräulein Erna, changing places so that she sat now between Gernerth and Esch, but Herr Gernerth said in an offended tone: " That's how we poor artists are always being slighted . . . for these commercial fellows." Teltscher declared that Esch shouldn't allow this, for it was only in the commercial class that solidity and breadth of vision were still to be found. The theatrical industry itself might even be regarded as a branch of commerce, and indeed as the most difficult of the lot with all respect to Herr Gernerth, who was not only his manager, but in a sense his partner, besides being in his own way a very capable man of business, even if he didn't exploit possible avenues of success as he might. He, Teltscher-Teltini, could see that very well, for before he felt drawn to an artist's life he had been in commerce himself. " And what's been the end of it all? Here I sit, when I might have lots of first-class engagements in America. . . . And I ask you, is my turn a first-class one, or isn't it? " A vague memory rose up rebelliously in Esch; what reason had they to praise up the commercial classes so much? The precious solidity they talked of wasn't so solid as they thought. He said so frankly, and ended: " Of course there's a great difference, for instance, between Nentwig and von Bertrand, the Chairman of our company; they're both in commerce, but the one is a swine and the other . . . well, he's something different, something better." Korn growled contemptuously that Bertrand was a renegade officer, everybody knew that, he needn't give himself airs. Esch was not displeased to hear this; so the difference between them wasn't so very great after all! But that didn't alter matters; Bertrand was something better, and in any case these were speculations which he had no desire to pursue too far. Meanwhile Teltscher went on talking about America; over there one could soon come to the top, over there one didn't need to work oneself to skin and bone for nothing as one did here. And he quoted: " America, you lucky land." Gernerth sighed: yes, if he had only had enough of the commercial spirit things would be different now; he had been very rich once himself, but in spite of all his business acumen he had kept the childlike trustfulness of the artist and had been cheated out of all his capital, almost a million marks, by pure fraud. Yes, Herr Esch might well look at him, Gernerth had once been a rich man! *Tempi passati*. Well, he would make his pile again. He had the idea of a theatrical trust, a huge limited liability company for whose shares people would yet be falling over one another. One had simply to march with the times and get hold of capital. And once more kissing Fräulein Erna's hand he asked his glass to be filled again, and said with the air of a connoisseur: " Delicious," still clasping her hand, which remained willingly and contentedly surrendered to him. But Esch, overwhelmed by all that he had heard, and now sunk in thought, scarcely noticed that Fräulein Erna's shoe was pressing against his, and saw only as from a distance and in the darkness Korn's yellow hand which lay on Ilona's shoulder and made it easy to guess that Balthasar Korn had put his powerful arm round Ilona's neck.

But then finally the lamp had to be lit, and now the conversation became general, only Ilona remaining silent. And as it was time to leave for the theatre, and they did not want to break up, Gernerth invited his hosts to attend the performance. So they got ready and took a tram to the theatre. The two ladies went inside and the men smoked their cigars on the platform at the back. Cold drops of rain spattered now and then into their heated faces, refreshing them pleasantly.

The name of the tobacconist from whom August Esch usually bought his cheap cigars was Fritz Lohberg. He was a young man about the same age as Esch, and this may have been the reason why Esch, who was always in the company of people older than himself, treated him as if he were a fool. Nevertheless the fool must have had some slight importance for him, and really it should have given Esch himself matter for thought that just in this shop he should feel so much at home as to become a regular customer. True, the shop lay on the way to his work, yet that was no reason why he should feel at home in it so immediately. Certainly it was very spick-and-span, a pleasant place to dawdle in: the light, pure fragrance of tobacco that filled it gave one an agreeable titillation in the nose, and it was nice to run one's hand over the polished counter, at one end of which, beside the glittering nickel-plated automatic cash register, invariably stood several open sample boxes of light-brown cigars and a little stand containing matches. If one made a purchase one received a box of matches free, a stylishly ample one. Further, there was a huge cigar-cutter which Herr Lohberg always had at hand, and if one wanted to light one's cigar on the spot, then with a sharp little click he snipped off the end that one held out to him. It was a good place to spend one's time in, bright and sunny and hospitable behind its plate-glass windows, and during these cold days full of a sort of pleasant smooth warmth that lay on the white floor-tiles and was a welcome change from the dusty, overheated atmosphere of the glass cage in the warehouse. But while that was sufficient reason for liking to come here after one's work or during the lunch-hour, it had no further significance. At these times one was full of praise for neatness and order, and grumbled at the filth one had to slave among; yet one did not intend this quite seriously, for Esch knew quite well that the perfect orderliness which he kept in his books and his goods lists couldn't be imposed on piles of packing-cases and bales and barrels, no matter how good the foreman might be at his job. But here in this shop, on the other hand, a curiously satisfying sense of order, an almost feminine precision, ruled, and this seemed all the stranger to Esch because he could scarcely picture to himself, or only with discomfort, girls selling cigars; in spite of all its cleanliness it was a job for men, a thing suggesting good-fellowship; yes, this was what friendship between men should be like, and not careless and perfunctory like the casual helpfulness of a trade-union secretary. But these were things which Esch really did not bother his mind about; they occurred to him only by the way. On the other hand, it was both funny and curious that Lohberg shouldn't be content with a job that suited him so well and in which he might have been happy, and still funnier were the grounds that he offered for his dissatisfaction, and in advancing which he showed so clearly that he was a fool. For although he had hung over the automatic cash register a board with the inscription: " Smoking has never harmed anybody "; although his boxes of cigars were accompanied by neat cards which displayed not only his business address and the names of the different brands, but also a little couplet: " Smoke good and pure tobacco every day, And you will have no doctors' bills to pay," yet he himself did not believe in these sentiments; indeed he smoked his own cigarettes simply from a sense of duty and because his conscience pricked him, and, in perpetual dread of so-called smoker's cancer, constantly felt in his stomach, his heart, his throat, all the evil symptoms of nicotine-poisoning. He was a lank little man with a dark shadow of a moustache and lifeless eyes which showed a great deal of white, and his somewhat coy charm and bearing were just as incompatible with his general principles as the business which he carried on and had no thought of exchanging for another; for he was not content to regard tobacco as a popular poison undermining the national well-being, perpetually reiterating that the people must be saved from this virus; no, he was also an advocate of a spacious, natural, genuinely German way of life, and it was a great disappointment to him that he could not live in the open air, a deep-chested, blond giant. For this deprivation, however, he partly compensated himself by

subscribing to anti-alcoholic and vegetarian associations, and so beside
the cash register there was always lying a pile of pamphlets on such
subjects, most of them sent to him from Switzerland. No doubt about
it, he was a pure fool.

Now Esch, who smoked cigars and drank wine and treated himself
to huge portions of meat whenever he had the chance, might not have
been so deeply impressed by Herr Lohberg's arguments, in spite of the
persuasive phrases about saving the people which always recurred in
them, if he had not been struck by a curious parallelism between them
and the principles of Mother Hentjen. Of course Mother Hentjen was
a sensible woman, even an unusually sensible woman, and so her opinions
had nothing in common with Lohberg's jargon. Yet when Lohberg,
true to the Calvinistic convictions which reached him from Switzerland
along with his pamphlets, inveighed like a priest against sensual indul-
gence and in the same breath pleaded like a Socialist orator addressing
a Freethinking audience for a free and simple life in the bosom of
nature; when in his own modest way he let it be understood that there
was something amiss with the world, a glaring error in the books which
could only be put right by a wonderful new entry, in all this confusion
only one thing was absolutely clear, that Mother Hentjen's restaurant
was in the same case as Lohberg's tobacconist shop: she had to depend
for her living on the men who boozed at her tables, and she too hated
her business and her customers. No doubt about it, it was a queer
coincidence, and Esch half thought of writing to Frau Hentjen to tell her
about it, it would interest her. But he dropped the idea when he reflected
that Frau Hentjen might think it odd, perhaps even feel insulted, to be
compared with a man who, in spite of all his virtues, was an idiot. So
he saved it up until he should see her; in any case he would soon have
to go to Cologne on business.

All the same the case of Lohberg was well worth mentioning; and
one evening, while Esch was sitting at dinner with Korn and Fräulein
Erna, he gave way to his desire to talk about it.

Of course the two Korns knew of Lohberg. Korn had already been
in his shop several times, but he had observed none of the man's peculiarities. " One wouldn't think it to see him," he said, after an interval
of silent thought, and agreed with Esch that the man was a fool. But
Fräulein Erna seemed to be seized with a violent aversion to this spiritual

double of Frau Hentjen, and inquired sharply whether Frau Hentjen perchance was Herr Esch's long and carefully concealed lady-love. She must be a very virtuous lady, no doubt, but Fräulein Erna thought all the same that she herself was just as good. And as for Herr Lohberg's virtuous scruples, of course it wasn't nice when a man made the curtains stink with his perpetual smoking as her brother did. Yet on the other hand one knew at least that there was a man about the house. " A man that does nothing but drink water . . . " she searched for words, " would sicken me." And then she inquired, did Herr Lohberg even know what it was to have a woman? " He's still an innocent, I suppose, the fool," said Esch, and Korn, foreseeing that there was sport to be had out of him yet, exclaimed: " A pure Joseph! "

Whether for this purpose, or because he wished to keep an eye on his lodger, or simply by pure chance, Korn too now became a regular customer of Lohberg's, and Lohberg shrank every time that the Herr Customs Inspector noisily entered his shop. His fear was not without cause. A few evenings later the blow fell; shortly before closing time Korn appeared with Esch and commanded: " Make yourself ready, my lad; to-night you're going to lose your innocence." Lohberg rolled his eyes helplessly and pointed to a man in the uniform of the Salvation Army who was standing in the shop. " Fancy dress? " said Korn, and Lohberg stammeringly introduced the man: " A friend of mine." " We're friends too," replied Korn, holding out his paw to the Salvation Army soldier. He was a freckled, somewhat pimply, red-haired youth, who had learned that one must be friendly to every soul one meets; he smiled in Korn's face and rescued Lohberg: " Brother Lohberg has promised to testify in our ranks to-night. I've come to fetch him." " So, you're going out to testify? Then we'll come too." Korn was enthusiastic. " We're all friends." " Every friend is welcome," said the joyful Salvation Army man. Lohberg was not consulted; he had the look of a thief caught in the act, and closed up the shop with a guilty air. Esch had followed the proceedings with great amusement, yet as Korn's high-handedness annoyed him he clapped Lohberg jovially on the shoulder, reproducing the very gesture that Teltscher had often expended on him.

They made for the Neckar quarter. In Käfertalerstrasse they could already hear the beating of the drums and tambourines, and Korn's feet, as if remembering their time in the army, fell into step. When they

came to the end of the street they saw the Salvation Army group standing at the corner of the park in the dying twilight. Watery sleet had
fallen, and where the group was gathered the snow had melted into
black slush which soaked through one's boots. The Lieutenant was
standing on a wooden bench and cried into the falling darkness: " Come
to us and be saved, poor wandering sinners, the Saviour is near! " But
only a few had answered his call, and when his soldiers, with drums
and tambourines beating, sang of the redeeming love and made their
chorus resound: " Lord God of Sabaoth save, Oh, save our souls from
Hell," hardly anybody in the crowd standing round joined in, and it
was obvious that the majority were merely looking on out of curiosity.
And although the honest soldiers sang on lustily, and the two girls
struck their tambourines with all their might, the crowd grew thinner
and thinner as the light faded, and soon they were left alone with their
Lieutenant, their only audience now being Lohberg, Korn and Esch.
Yet even now Lohberg was probably ready to join in the hymn, and
indeed he would certainly have done so without feeling either embarrassed
or intimidated by Esch and Korn if Korn had not kept on digging him
in the ribs and saying: " Sing, Lohberg! " It wasn't a very pleasant
situation for Lohberg, and he was glad when a policeman arrived and
ordered them to move on. They all set out for the Thomasbräu cellar.
And yet it was almost a pity that Lohberg hadn't joined in the singing,
yes, then perhaps a minor miracle might have happened, for it wouldn't
have taken much to make Esch too lift up his voice in praise of the
Saviour and His redeeming love; indeed only a slight impetus would
have been required, and perhaps the sound of Lohberg's voice would
have provided it. But one can never be sure of those things afterwards.

Esch himself could not make out what had happened to him at the
open-air meeting: the two girls had beaten their tambourines when the
officer standing on the bench gave the signal, and that had reminded
him strangely of the commands which Teltscher gave Ilona on the stage.
Perhaps it was the sudden dead silence of the evening that had affected
him, for there at the outskirts of the city the sounds of the evening
broke off as abruptly as the music in the theatre; perhaps it was the
motionlessness of the black trees that gazed up into the darkening
sky; and then behind him in the square the arc-lamps had flared out.
It was all incomprehensible. The biting coldness of the wet snow had
pierced through his shoes; but that was not the only reason why Esch

would have liked to be standing up there on the bench pointing out the way of salvation, for his old strange feeling of orphaned isolation had returned again, and suddenly it had become dreadfully clear to him that some time he would have to die in utter and complete loneliness. A vague and yet unforeseen hope had risen in him that things would go better, far better, with him if he could but stand up there on the bench; and he saw Ilona, Ilona in the Salvation Army uniform, gazing up at him and waiting for his redeeming signal to strike the tambourine and cry " Hallelujah! " But Korn was standing beside him, grinning out from between the great upturned collars of his damp customs cloak, and at the sight of him Esch's hopes had ignominiously melted away. Esch's mouth twisted wryly, his expression became contemptuous, and all at once he was almost glad to be orphaned and alone. In any case he too was relieved that the policeman had moved them on.

Lohberg was walking in front with the pimply Salvation Army man and one of the girls. Esch trudged behind. Yes, whether a girl like that beat a tambourine or threw plates, one only had to order her to do it, it was just the same, only the clothes were different. They sang about love in the Salvation Army as in the theatre. " Perfect redeeming love," Esch had to laugh, and he decided to sound the good Salvation Army girl on this question. When they were nearing the Thomasbräu cellar the girl stopped, planted her foot on a ledge projecting from the wall, bent down, and began to tie the laces of her wet, shapeless boots. As she stood there bent double, her black hat almost touching her knee, she looked lumpish and hardly human, a monstrosity, yet with a certain, as it were, mechanical effectiveness of structure, and Esch, who in other circumstances would have requited such a posture with a clap on the part most saliently exposed, was a little alarmed that no desire to do so awoke in him, and it almost seemed as though another bridge between him and his fellow-creatures had been broken, and he felt homesick for Cologne. That day in the kitchen he had wanted to take hold of Mother Hentjen under the breasts; yes, he would not have been put off had Mother Hentjen bent down and laced her shoes. But as all men have the same thoughts, Korn, who felt on good terms with all the world, now pointed to the girl: " Any chance with her, do you think? " Esch threw him a furious glance, but Korn did not stop: " Among themselves they're probably hot enough, the soldiers." Meanwhile they had reached the Thomasbräu cellar, and they walked into the bright, noisy room, which smelt pleasantly of roast beef, onions and beer.

Here, at any rate, Korn met with a disappointment. For the Salvation Army people were not to be prevailed upon to sit down at the same table; they said good-bye and gathered at one end of the room to distribute the *War Cry*. Esch too would have preferred not to be left alone with Korn; some remnant of hope still fluttered in his soul that these people might be able to bring back to him what he had felt under the darkening trees and yet had not been able to grasp. But it was a good thing, on the other hand, that they were now beyond the reach of Korn's raillery, and it would have been still better if they had taken Lohberg with them, for Korn was now anxious to get his own back and was beginning his joke at Lohberg's expense by trying to make the helpless fellow violate his principles with the aid of a portion of steak and onions and a great jug of beer. But the ninny stood his ground, merely saying in a quiet voice: " You shouldn't joke with a fellow's convictions," and touched neither the meat nor the beer, and Korn, once more disappointed, had to be content with morosely devouring them himself, so that they might not be wasted. Esch contemplated the dark residue of beer at the bottom of his jug; absurd to think that one's salvation could depend on whether one drank that up or not. All the same he felt almost grateful to the mild and obstinate fool. Lohberg sat there smiling meekly, and sometimes one almost expected tears to start to his great eyes with the exposed whites. Yet when the Salvation Army people in their round of the tables drew near again he stood up and it looked as though he were about to shout something to them. Against Esch's expectations he did not do so, but simply remained standing where he was. Then suddenly he uttered without warning or reason a single word, a word quite incomprehensible to everyone who heard it; he uttered loudly and distinctly the word " Redemption," and then sat down again. Korn looked at Esch and Esch looked at Korn. But when Korn put his finger to his brow and twirled it to indicate that Lohberg was weak in the head, the whole situation changed in the most extraordinary and terrifying manner, for it was as though the word of redemption, now set free, hovered over the table maintained in its detachment by an invisibly revolving mechanism, detached even from the mouth that had uttered it. And although Esch's contempt for Lohberg remained undiminished, yet it seemed now that the kingdom of salvation did exist, could exist, must exist, if only because Korn, that dead lump of flesh, was sitting on his broad hindquarters in the Thomasbräu cellar, quite incapable of sending his thoughts even as far as the next street corner, far less of losing them in the infinite spaces of freedom. And although, in spite of these ideas, Esch refused to act the prig, but instead rapped with his jug on the table and ordered another beer, yet he too became silent like Lohberg; and when on rising to leave Korn proposed that they should take the pure Joseph to visit the girls, Esch refused to second him, left a completely disappointed Balthasar Korn standing on the pavement, and escorted the tobacconist home, quite pleased that Korn should shout insults after them. It had stopped snowing, and in the warm wind that had risen Korn's rude words fluttered past like light spring blossoms.

Driven by that extraordinary oppression which falls on every human being when, childhood over, he begins to divine that he is fated to go on in isolation and unaided towards his own death; driven by this extraordinary oppression, which may with justice be called a fear of God, man looks round him for a companion hand in hand with whom he may tread the road to the dark portal, and if he has learned by experience how pleasurable it undoubtedly is to lie with another fellow-creature in bed, then he is ready to believe that this extremely intimate association of two bodies may last until these bodies are coffined: and even if at the same time it has its disgusting aspects, because it takes place under coarse and badly aired sheets, or because he is convinced that all a girl cares for is to get a husband who will support her in later life, yet it must not be forgotten that every fellow-creature, even if she has a sallow complexion, sharp, thin features and an obviously missing tooth in her left upper jaw, yearns, in spite of her missing tooth, for that love which she thinks will for ever shield her from death, from that fear of death which sinks with the falling of every night upon the human being who sleeps alone, a fear that already licks her as with a tongue of flame when she begins to take off her clothes, as Fräulein Erna was doing now; she laid aside her faded red-velvet blouse and took off her dark-green skirt and her petticoat. Then she drew off her shoes; but her stockings, on the other hand, as well as her white, starched under-petticoat, she kept on; indeed she could not even summon the resolution to undo her corsets. She was afraid, but she concealed her fear behind a knowing smile, and by the light of the flickering candle-flame on the bedside-table she slipped, without undressing further, into bed.

Now it came to pass that she heard Esch walking several times through the lobby, in doing which he made a greater noise than the necessary arrangements he was engaged in should have required. Perhaps these arrangements themselves were not indeed altogether necessary, for what need could there be to fetch water to his room twice? And the water-jug was surely not so heavy that he had to set it down with a bang in the passage immediately outside Erna's door. But every time that Fräulein Erna heard anything she resolved not to be outdone and made a noise too; stretched herself till the bed creaked, even pushed deliberately with her toes against the foot of it and sighed an audible " This is nice," as if she were sleepy; also she coughed and cleared her throat in pursuit of her purpose. Now Esch was an impetuous man, and after they had telegraphed to each other in this way for a little while he walked resolutely into her room.

There lay Fräulein Erna in bed and smiled knowingly and slyly and yet a little invitingly at him with her missing tooth, and really she did not attract him very much. All the same he paid no attention to her protest: " But Herr Esch, you mustn't stay here," but remained calmly where he was; and he did this not merely because he was a man of coarse appetites, like most men, he did it not merely because two people of different sexes living on intimate terms in the same house can scarcely escape the automatic functioning of physical attraction, and with the reflection " Why not, after all," will eventually yield casually to it, he did it not only because he divined that her feelings were much the same as his and so discounted her words, he did it therefore not simply in obedience to a low impulse, even if we add jealousy to it, the jealousy which any man might feel on seeing a woman flirting with Herr Gernerth; no, Esch did it because he was a man for whom it was essential that this pleasure, which people imagine one seeks for its own sake, should serve also a higher purpose, a purpose which he could scarcely name and yet felt bound to obey, but which nevertheless was nothing but the compulsion to put an end to a tremendous fear that extended far beyond himself, even if sometimes it might seem to be merely the fear that befalls the commercial traveller when, far from his wife and children, he lies down in his lonely hotel bed; the fear and desire of the traveller who resorts to the plain and elderly chambermaid, sometimes heart-broken by the squalor of the affair, and generally filled with remorse of conscience. Of course when Esch banged down his water-jug hard on the floor he was no longer thinking of the loneliness which had descended upon him since he had left Cologne, nor was he thinking of the isolation that had lain on the stage before Teltscher let fly the whistling, glittering daggers. Yet now that he sat on the edge of Fräulein Erna's bed and bent over her in desire, he wanted more from her than is currently construed as the satisfaction of an average sensual man's lust, for behind the very palpable, indeed banal, immediate object of desire, yearning was hidden, the yearning of the captive soul for redemption from its loneliness, for a salvation which should embrace himself and her, yes, perhaps all mankind, and most certainly Ilona, a salvation which Erna could not vouchsafe him, because neither she nor he knew what he wanted. So the rage which seized him when she refused him the final favour and gently said: " When we're man and wife," was neither merely the rage of the thwarted male, nor simple fury at the discovery of the trick she had played him in only half-undressing; it was more, it was despair, even if the words with which, sobered now, he rudely replied, were by no means high-sounding: " Well, it's all off, then." And although her refusal seemed to him a sign from God warning him to be chaste, he left the house immediately and went to a more willing lady. And that deeply wounded Erna.

From that evening there was open war between Esch and Fräulein Erna. She let no opportunity pass of provoking his desire, and he no less eagerly seized every pretext to renew his attempt and to lure the recalcitrant one into his bed without promise of marriage. The battle began in the morning when she brought his breakfast into his room before he was properly dressed, a lascivious kind of mothering that maddened him; and it ended in the evening in indifference, whether she had barred her door or let him in. Neither of them ever mentioned the word love, and the fact that open hatred did not break out between them, but was dissembled in spiteful jests, was due simply to the other fact that they had not yet possessed each other.

Often he thought that with Ilona things must be different and better, but strangely enough his thoughts did not dare to rise to her. She was something better, much in the same way as the Chairman of the company, Bertrand, was something better. And Esch did not even mind very much that one of Erna's tricks was to frustrate any chance of his meeting Ilona, indeed he was even glad of this, bitterly as he resented all her silly fuss and her tittering facetiousness. Meanwhile Ilona was about the place almost every day, and between her and Erna a sort of friendship had grown up, yet what they could find in each other was incomprehensible to Esch; if when he got home he smelt the cheap and powerful scent which Ilona used, and which always excited him, he was sure to find the two ladies in an extraordinary dumb dialogue; for Ilona knew scarcely a word of German and Fräulein Erna was forced to fall back on fondling her friend, stationing her before the mirror and admiringly patting and rearranging her coiffure and her dress. But generally Esch found himself excluded. For Erna now set herself to conceal from him even the presence of her friend in the house. So one evening he happened to be sitting quite innocently in his room when the door-bell rang. He heard Erna opening the door and would not have thought anything further about the matter if he had not suddenly heard the key of his door being turned. Esch made a spring for the door; he was locked in! The trollop had locked him in! And although he should simply have ignored the stupid joke, it was too much for him, and he began to bawl and bang on the door, until at last Fräulein Erna opened it and slipped into the room with a giggle. " Well," she said, " now I can attend to you . . . we have a visitor, I may say, but Balthasar is looking after her all right." Esch rushed out of the house in a rage.

When he returned late at night the lobby again reeked of Ilona's perfume. So she must have come back again, or rather she must still be here, for now he saw her hat hanging on the hat-rack. But where could she be? The parlour was dark. Korn was snoring next door. She simply couldn't have gone away without her hat! Esch listened at Erna's door; the agitating and oppressive thought came into his mind that the two women were lying in there side by side. He cautiously tried the door-handle; the door did not yield, it was barred as always when Fräulein Erna really wanted to sleep. Esch shrugged his shoulders and walked noisily to his room. But he could not rest in bed; he peered out into the passage; the perfume still hung in the air and the hat was still there. Something wasn't in order, one could feel that, and Esch stole through the house. It seemed to him that he could hear whispering in Korn's room; Korn wasn't the man to speak in a whisper, and Esch listened more intently: then suddenly Korn groaned, unmistakably he groaned, and Esch, a fellow who had no occasion to fear a man like Korn, fled back to his room in his bare feet as though something dreadful were pursuing him. He even felt he wanted to put his hands to his ears.

Next morning Erna awakened him out of a leaden sleep, and before he could bring out his question she said: "Hsh! I've a surprise for you. Get up at once!" He hastily put on his clothes, and when he walked into the kitchen, where Erna was busy, she took him by the hand and led him on tiptoe to her room, opened the door slightly and asked him to look in. There he saw Ilona; her round white arm, which still did not show any dagger wounds, was hanging over the edge of the bed, the heavy pouches under her eyes showed distinctly on her somewhat puffy face, and she was asleep.

Now Ilona frequently arrived at a late hour at the flat, and this lasted for a comparatively long time before Esch grasped the fact that she spent the night with Balthasar Korn and that Erna was shielding her brother's love affair, in a sense, with her own body.

Martin called on him at his work. It was extraordinary, the ease with which this pariah, whom every gate-keeper had orders to keep out, always managed to get himself admitted everywhere quite openly and swung at his ease on his crutches through places of business, nobody stopping him, many saluting him affectionately, partly no doubt because one was shy of appearing unkind to a cripple. Esch was not particularly pleased to receive a visit from a trade-union secretary at his work; Martin could just as well have waited for him outside, but on the other hand one could rely on his discretion; he knew the right time to come and the right time to go; he was a decent fellow. "'Morning, August," he said. "I just wanted to see how you were getting on. You've a nice job here, made a good exchange." Did the cripple want to remind him that he had him to thank for being in this accursed Mannheim? All the same Martin could not be held responsible for the affair between Ilona and Korn, and so Esch simply replied in a morose voice: "Yes, a good exchange." And somehow it rang true. For now that Martin reminded him of his former job and Nentwig, Esch was jolly glad that he had nothing more to do with Cologne. Like a thief he still kept Nentwig's misdemeanour concealed, and the fact that one might come across the man's ugly mug at any street corner in Cologne took away all pleasure at the thought of returning there. Cologne or Mannheim, there was nothing to choose between them. Was there really any place where one could be rid of all this rottenness? Nevertheless he asked how things were in Cologne. " Later," said Martin, " I haven't time just now; where are you having your dinner? " And as soon as Esch told him he swung himself hastily away.

By now Esch really felt glad at meeting Martin again, and as he was an impatient fellow he could scarcely wait for the dinner-hour to come. Spring had arrived overnight, and Esch left his greatcoat in the office; the flagstones between the sheds were bright with the cool sunshine, and in the corners of the buildings young tender grass had suddenly appeared between the cobbles. As he passed the unloading stage he laid his hand on the iron bands with which the clumsy grey wooden erection was clamped together, and the iron too felt warm. If he shouldn't be transferred to Cologne he must arrange to have his bicycle sent on soon. He breathed in the air deeply and easily, and the food had quite a different taste; perhaps because the windows of the restaurant were open. Martin related that he had come to Mannheim on strike business; otherwise he would have taken his time. But something was happening in the South German and Alsatian factories, and such things soon spread: " For all I care they can strike as much as they like, only we can't afford any nonsense just now. A strike of the transport workers would be pure madness at the moment . . . we're a poor union and there's no money to be had from the central office . . . it would be a complete wash-out. Of course it's no use talking to a docker: if a donkey like that makes up his mind to go on strike nothing will stop him. But sooner or later they'll have my blood yet." He said all this indulgently, without bitterness. " Now they're raising the cry again that I'm being paid by the shipping companies." " By Bertrand? " asked Esch with interest. Geyring nodded: " By Bertrand too, of course." " A proper swine," Esch could not help saying. Martin laughed. " Bertrand? He's a very decent fellow." " Oho, so he's a decent fellow? Is it true that he's a renegade officer? " " Yes, he's supposed to have quit the service —but that only speaks in the man's favour." Oho, that spoke in the man's favour, did it? Nothing was clear and simple, thought Esch in anger, nothing was clear and simple, even on a lovely spring day like this: " All I would like to know is why you stick to this job of yours." " Everybody must stay where God has put him," said Martin, and his

old-young face took on a pious look. Then he told Esch that Mother
Hentjen sent her greetings and that everybody was looking forward to
seeing him soon.

After dinner they went along to Lohberg's shop. They were in no
hurry, and so Martin rested in the massive oaken chair that stood
beside the counter and was as bright and solid as everything else in
the shop. Accustomed to pick up anything in print that came within
his reach, Martin glanced through the anti-alcoholic and vegetarian
journals from Switzerland. "Dear, dear!" he said, "here's almost a
comrade of mine." Lohberg felt flattered, but Esch spoilt his pleasure
for him: "Oh, he's one of the teetotal wash-outs," and to crush him
completely he added: "Geyring has a big meeting to-night, but a real
one—not a meeting of the Salvation Army!" "Unfortunately," said
Martin. Lohberg, who had a great weakness for public demonstrations
and oratorical performances, proposed immediately to go. "I advise
you not to," said Martin. "Esch at least mustn't go, it might go
badly with him if he were seen there. Besides, there's bound to be
trouble." Esch really had no anxiety about endangering his post, yet
strangely enough to attend the meeting seemed to him an act of treachery
towards Bertrand. Lohberg, on the other hand, said boldly: "I'll go
in any case," and Esch felt shamed by the teetotal ninny; no, it would
never do to leave a friend in the lurch; if he did he would never dare
to face Mother Hentjen again. But meanwhile he said nothing about
his decision. Martin explained: "I fancy that the shipping companies
will send an *agent provocateur* or two; it's all to their interest that the
strike should be as violent as possible." And although Nentwig was not
a shipper, but only the greasy head clerk in a firm of wine merchants,
to Esch it seemed that the rascal had his greasy fingers in this piece of
perfidy too.

The meeting took place, as was usual in such cases, in the public room
of a small tavern. A few policemen were standing before the entrance
keeping an eye on those who went in, who on their side pretended not
to notice the policemen. Esch arrived late; as he was about to enter
someone tapped him on the shoulder, and when he turned round he
saw it was the inspector of the dock police squad: "Why, what takes
you here, Herr Esch?" Esch thought quickly. Actually simple curiosity;
he had learned that Geyring, the trade-union secretary, whom he had
known in Cologne, was to speak, and as in a way he was connected with

shipping he felt interested in the whole business. " I advise you against
it, Herr Esch," said the inspector, " and just because you're in a shipping
firm; it will look fishy, and it can't do you any good." " I'll just look
in for a minute," Esch decided, and went in.

The low room, adorned with portraits of the Kaiser, the Grand Duke
of Baden, and the King of Württemberg, was crammed full. On the
raised platform stood a table covered with a white cloth, behind which
four men were sitting; Martin was one of them. Esch, at first a little
envious because he too was not sitting in such a prominent position,
was surprised next moment that he had noticed the table at all, so great
was the uproar and disorder in the room. Indeed it was some time before
he noticed that a man had mounted on a chair in the middle of the
hall and was shouting out an incomprehensible rigmarole, emphasizing
every word—he seemed to love particularly the word " demagogue "—
with a sweeping gesture, as though to fling it at the table on the platform.
It was a sort of unequal dialogue, for the only reply from the table was
the thin tinkle of a bell which did not pierce the din; yet it finally had
the last say when Martin, supporting himself on his crutches and the
back of his chair, got up, and the noise ebbed. True, it wasn't very easy
to grasp what Martin, with the somewhat weary and ironical fluency of
a practised speaker, was saying, but that he was worth twice all these
people bawling at him Esch could see. It almost looked as though
Martin had no wish to get a hearing, for with a faint smile he stopped
and let the shouts of " Capitalist pimp! " " Twister! " and " Kaiser's
Socialist! " pass over him, until suddenly, amid the whistling and cat-
calls, a sharper whistle was heard. In the sudden silence a police officer
appeared on the platform and said curtly: " In the name of the law I
declare this meeting closed; the hall must be cleared." And while Esch
was being borne through the door by the crush he had time to see
the police officer turning to Martin.

As if by arrangement the most of the audience had made for the
side-door of the tavern. But that did not help them much, for meanwhile the whole place had been encircled by the police, and every one
of them had either to explain his presence or go to the police station.
At the front entrance the crush was not so great; Esch had the good
luck to encounter the dock inspector again and said hastily: " You
were right, never again," and so he escaped interrogation. But the
affair was not yet ended. The crowd now stood before the place quite

quietly, contenting themselves with swearing softly at the committee, the union and Geyring. But all at once the rumour flew round that Geyring and the committee were arrested and that the police were only waiting for the crowd to disperse to lead them away. Then suddenly the feeling of the crowd swung round; whistles and cat-calls rose again, and the crowd made ready to rush the police. The friendly police inspector gave Esch a push: " You'd better disappear now, Herr Esch," and Esch, who saw that there was nothing else he could do, withdrew to the nearest street corner, hoping at least to run up against Lohberg.

Before the hall the noise still went on for a good while. Then six mounted police arrived at a sharp trot, and because horses, who although docile are yet somewhat insane creatures, exert on many human beings a sort of magical influence, this little equestrian reinforcement was decisive. Esch looked on while a number of workers in handcuffs were led away amid the terrified silence of their comrades, and then the street emptied. Wherever the police, now become rough and impatient, saw two men standing together, they drove them harshly away, and Esch, considering with good reason that he would be handled just as ruthlessly, vacated the field.

He went to Lohberg's house. Lohberg had not yet returned, and Esch remained waiting before his door in the warm spring night. He hoped that they hadn't led Lohberg away too in handcuffs. Although really that would have been a good joke. Lord! what would Erna say if she saw this paragon of virtue before her in handcuffs? Just when Esch was about to give up his watch Lohberg arrived in a terribly excited state, and almost weeping. Bit by bit, and very disconnectedly, Esch managed to discover that at first the meeting had proceeded quite quietly, even if the audience had shouted all sorts of abuse at Herr Geyring, who had spoken very well. But then a man had got up, obviously one of those *agents provocateurs* whom Herr Geyring himself had mentioned at dinner-time, and had made a furious speech against the rich classes, the State and even the Kaiser himself, until the police officer threatened to close the meeting if anything else of that nature was said. Quite incomprehensibly Herr Geyring, who must have known quite well what sort of a bird he had to deal with, had not unmasked the man as an *agent provocateur*, but had actually come to his assistance and demanded freedom of speech for him. Well, after that it grew worse and worse, and finally the meeting was broken up. The committee and Herr Geyring were under arrest; he could vouch for that, for he had been among the last to leave the hall.

Esch felt upset, indeed more upset than he would admit. All that he knew was that he must have some wine if he was to bring order into the world again; Martin, who was against the strike, was arrested by police who were in with the shipping companies and a renegade officer, police who, in the most infamous manner, had seized an innocent man —perhaps because Esch himself had not handed Nentwig over to them! Yet the inspector had acted in a very friendly way towards him, actually had shielded him. Sudden anger at Lohberg overcame him; the confounded fool was probably so taken aback simply because he had expected harmless and uplifting twaddle about brotherhood and did not understand that things could turn to deadly earnest. Suddenly all this brotherhood twaddle seemed disgusting to Esch; what was the use of all these brotherhoods and associations? They only made the confusion greater and probably they were the cause of it; he brutally let fly at Lohberg: " For God's sake put away that cursed lemonade of yours, or I'll sweep it off the table . . . if only you drank honest wine you would be able at least to give a sensible answer to a plain question." But Lohberg only looked at him with his great uncomprehending eyes, in whose whites little red veins now appeared, and was in no state to resolve Esch's doubts, doubts which next day became much worse when he heard that as a protest against the arrest of their union secretary the transport and dock workers had gone on strike. Meanwhile Geyring was sentenced to await his trial for the crime of sedition.

During the performance Esch sat with Gernerth in the so-called manager's office, which always reminded him of his glass cage in the bonded warehouse. On the stage Teltscher and Ilona were going through their act, and he heard the whizzing knives striking against the black board. Above the writing-table was fixed a little white box marked with a red cross, supposed to contain bandages. For a long time it had certainly contained none, and for decades nobody had even opened it, yet Esch was convinced that at any moment Ilona might be carried in to have her bleeding wounds bound. But instead Teltscher appeared, slightly perspiring and slightly proud of himself, and wiping his hands on his handkerchief said: " Real work, good honest work . . . must be paid for." Gernerth made some calculations in his notebook: "theatre rent, 22 marks; tax, 16 marks; lighting, 4 marks; salaries . . ." "Oh, stow that!" said Teltscher. "I know it all by heart already. I've put four thousand crowns into this business and I'll never see them again . . . I'll just have to grin and bear it. . . . Herr Esch, don't you know anybody who would buy me out? He can have a twenty-per-cent rebate, and I'll give you ten-per-cent commission over and above." Esch had already heard these outbursts and these offers and no longer paid any attention to them, although he would gladly have bought out Teltscher to get rid both of him and Ilona.

Esch was in an ill humour. Since Martin's imprisonment life had become radically darker: the fact that his skirmishing with Erna had grown burdensome and intolerable was really secondary; but that Bertrand had bribed the police, and that the police had behaved abominably, was more than exasperating, and Ilona's relations with Korn, no longer concealed either by them or by Erna, were repulsive in his sight. It was disgusting. The very thought of it repelled him: Ilona, after all, was something superior. Yes, better that he should know nothing about her, and that she should disappear out of his life for ever. And Bertrand as well, along with his Central Rhine Shipping Company. This became quite clear to Esch for the first time now that Ilona came in in her outdoor clothes and silently and seriously sat down without being accorded a glance by the two men. Korn would presently appear to take her away; lately he had been going in and out here quite at his ease.

Ilona had been overcome by a genuine passion for Balthasar Korn, perhaps because he reminded her of some sergeant whom she had loved in her youth, perhaps simply because he was such a complete contrast to the adroit, sickly, blasé Teltscher, who in spite of his sickliness was so essentially brutal. Frankly, Esch did not waste any thought on such things; enough that a woman whom he himself had renounced, because she was destined for a better fate, was now being degraded by a man like Korn. But Teltscher's attitude was quite inexplicable. The fellow was clearly a pimp, and yet that wasn't a thing to trouble one's head about. Besides, the whole business could not bring him in very much; Korn certainly was generous enough, and in the new clothes which he had given her Ilona really looked superb, so superb that Fräulein Erna no longer regarded her brother's expensive love affair with by any means the same favour as at first; but in spite of all this Ilona would accept no money from Korn, and he had literally to force his presents on her; so deeply did she love him.

Korn appeared at the door and Ilona flung herself on his uniformed breast with Eastern words of endearment. No, it was past endurance! Teltscher laughed: " See that you enjoy yourself," and as they went out together he shouted after her in Hungarian a few words, obviously spiteful, which earned him not only a glance full of hatred from Ilona, but also a half-joking, half-serious threat from Korn that he would give the Jewish knife-thrower a beating yet. Teltscher paid no attention to this, but returned to his beloved business speculations: " We must provide something that isn't too expensive and that will draw the crowd." " Oh, what an epoch-making discovery, Herr Teltscher-Teltini," said Gernerth, making calculations in his notebook again. Then he looked up: " What do you say to wrestling matches for women? " Teltscher whistled reflectively through his teeth: " Might be considered: of course that can't be done either without money." Gernerth scribbled in his notebook. " We'll need some money, but not so very much; women don't cost much. Then tights . . . we'll have to get someone interested in it." " I'm willing to teach them," said Teltscher, " and I can be the referee too. But here in Mannheim? " he made a contemptuous gesture, " there's no closing one's eyes to the fact that business is bad here. What do you say, Esch? " Esch had formed no definite opinion, but the hope rose within him that with a change of scene Ilona might be saved from Korn's clutches. And as it lay nearest to his heart, he replied that Cologne seemed to him a splendid place for staging wrestling matches; in the previous year wrestling matches had been given there in the circus, serious ones of course, and the place had been packed. " Ours will be serious too," Teltscher decided. They talked it over from all sides for a while longer, and finally Esch was empowered to discuss the matter, on his approaching visit to Cologne, with the theatrical agent, Oppenheimer, whom Gernerth would have written to in the interval. And if Esch should succeed in hunting up some money for the undertaking, it would not only be a friendly service, but he might get a percentage on it himself.

Esch knew at the moment of nobody likely to invest money. But in secret he thought of Lohberg, who might almost be regarded as a rich

man. But would a pure Joseph have any interest in wrestling matches
for women?

The arrests that had been made in advance of the strike had deprived
the dock labourers of all their leaders, yet after ten days the strike was
still lingering on. There were indeed some blacklegs, but they were too
few to handle the railway freights, and since shipping in any case was
partially paralysed, they were employed only on the most urgent work.
In the bonded warehouses a Sabbath quiet reigned. Esch was annoyed,
because it was unlikely that he could get away until the strike was over,
and he lounged idly round the sheds, leaned against the door-posts,
and finally sat down to write to Mother Hentjen. He gave her the details
of Martin's arrest and told her about Lohberg, but he did not even
mention Erna and Korn, for the mere thought of doing so disgusted
him. Then he procured a fresh batch of picture postcards and addressed
them to all the girls he had slept with in recent years, and whose names
he could remember. Outside in the shadow the foremen and stevedores
stood in a group, and behind the half-open sliding doors of an empty
goods truck some men were playing cards. Esch wondered whom he
should write to next, and tried to count in his head all the women he
had ever had. He could not be sure of the total, and it was as if a column
in his books would not balance properly, so to get it right he began to
make a list of the names on a piece of paper, entering the month and
year after each. Then he added them up and was satisfied, more especially as Korn came in boasting, as usual, what a fine woman Ilona was,
and what a fiery Hungarian. Esch pocketed his list and let Korn go on
talking; he would not be able to talk like that for much longer. Only
let the strike once come to an end, and the Herr Customs Inspector
would have to run all the way to Cologne for his Ilona, perhaps even
farther still, to the end of the world. And he was almost sorry for the
man because he did not know what was in store for him. Balthasar Korn
went on boasting happily of his conquest, and when he had said his
say about Ilona he drew out a pack of cards. In brotherly amity they
sought out a third man and settled down to play for the rest of the day.
In the evening Esch looked in on Lohberg, who was sitting in his
shop with a cigarette in his mouth before a pile of vegetarian journals.
He laid these aside when Esch came in and began to talk about Martin.
" The world," he said, " is poisoned, not only with nicotine and alcohol

and animal food, but with a still worse poison that we can hardly even recognize . . . it's just like boils breaking out." His eyes were moist and looked feverish; he gave one an unhealthy impression; it seemed possible that there really was some poison working within him. Esch stood, lean and robust, in front of him, but his head was empty after so much card-playing and he did not catch the sense of these idiotic remarks, he hardly realized that they referred to Martin's imprisonment; everything was wrapped in a fog of idiocy, and his only definite wish was to have the affair of the theatre partnership cleared up once and for all. Esch didn't like hole-and-corner methods: "Will you go shares in Gernerth's theatre?" The question took Lohberg quite by surprise, and opening his eyes wide he merely said: "Eh?" "I'm asking you, are you willing to go shares in the theatre business?" "But I have a tobacco business." "You've been lamenting all this time that you don't like it, and so I thought you might want a change." Lohberg shook his head: "So long as my mother's alive I'll have to keep on the shop; the half of it's hers." "Pity," said Esch, "Teltscher thinks that putting on women wrestlers would bring in a hundred-per-cent profit." Lohberg did not even ask what the theatre had to do with wrestling, but merely said in his turn: "Pity." Esch went on: "I'm as tired of my trade as you are of yours. They're on strike now and there's nothing to do but sit about, it's enough to make one sick." "What do you want to do, then? Are you going into the theatre business too?" Esch thought it over; that meant simply being tied to a stool in some dusty manager's office beside Gernerth and Teltscher. The artists didn't appeal to him now that he had been behind the scenes; they weren't much better than Hede or Thusnelda. He had really no idea what he wanted to do; the day had been so stale. He said: "Clear out, to America." In an illustrated journal he had seen pictures of New York; these now came into his head; there had been also a photograph of an American boxing match and that brought him back to the wrestling. "If I could make enough money out of it to pay my fare I'd go to America." He was himself astonished to find that he meant it seriously, and now began seriously counting up his resources: he had nearly three hundred marks; if he put them into the wrestling business he could certainly increase them, and why shouldn't he, a strong, capable man with book-keeping experience, try his luck in America as well as here? At the very least he would have seen a bit of the world. Perhaps Teltscher and Ilona might actually come to New York on that engagement Teltscher was always talking about. Lohberg interrupted his train of thought: " You have some knowledge of languages, but I haven't, unfortunately." Esch nodded complacently; yes, with his French he could manage somehow, and English couldn't be so very much of a mystery; but Lohberg didn't need to know languages in order to go shares in promoting wrestling bouts. " No, not for that, but for going to America," Lohberg replied. And although to Lohberg it was almost inconceivable that any man, let alone himself, should live in any town but Mannheim, both Esch and he felt almost like fellow-travellers as they discussed the cost of the voyage and how the money could be raised. This discussion brought them back, by a natural concatenation of thought, to the chances of making money through women wrestlers, and after much hesitation Lohberg came to the conclusion that he could quite well abstract a thousand marks from his business and invest them with Gernerth. Of course that wouldn't be enough to buy out Teltscher, but it was quite good for a start, especially when Esch's three hundred were counted in.

The day had ended better than it began. As he went home Esch brooded over the problem of raising the rest of the money, and Fräulein Erna came into his mind.

Strong as was Erna's temptation to bind Esch to her by financial obligations, she remained firm even here to her principle of parting with nothing except to her affianced husband. When she archly intimated this resolve Esch was indignant: what kind of a man did she think he was? Did she imagine he wanted the money for himself? But even as he said this he felt that it was beside the point; that it was not really the money that was in question, and that Fräulein Erna was much more in the wrong than she could ever be made to understand; of course the money was only a means of ransoming Ilona, of shielding defenceless girls from ever having knives hurled at them again; of course he didn't want it for himself. But even that was by no means all, for over and above that he wanted nothing from Ilona herself—not he, not at the cost of other people's money—and he was quite glad, too, to be in that position; he didn't give a fig for Ilona, he was thinking of more important things, and he had every right to be angry when Erna supposed him to be self-seeking, every right to tell her rudely: well, she could keep her money, then. Erna, however, took his rudeness as an admission of guilt, exulted in having unmasked him, and giggled that she knew all about that, thinking meanwhile of a commercial traveller in Hof, who had not only enjoyed her favours, but had involved her in the more serious loss of fifty marks.

It was altogether a good day for Fräulein Erna. Esch had asked her for something which she could refuse him, and besides she was wearing a pair of new shoes that made her feel gay and looked well on her feet. She was ensconced on the sofa, and as a saucy and slightly mocking gesture she let her feet peep from under her skirt, and swung them to and fro; she liked the faint creaking of the leather and the pleasant tension across her instep. She had no desire to abandon this delightful conversation, and in spite of the rude end that Esch had put to it she asked again what he wanted so much money for. Esch once more remarked that she could keep it; Lohberg had been glad enough to get a share in the business. " Oh, Herr Lohberg," said Fräulein Erna, " he has plenty, he can afford it." And with that waywardness which characterizes many phases of love, and in virtue of which Fräulein Erna would have given herself to any chance comer rather than to Herr Esch, who was to be granted nothing except in wedlock, she was very eager now to infuriate him by giving the money to Lohberg instead of to him. She swung her feet to and fro. " Oh, well, in partnership with Herr Lohberg, that's a different story. He's a good business man." " He's an idiot! " said Esch, partly from conviction and partly from jealousy, a jealousy that pleased Fräulein Erna, for she had reckoned on it. She turned the knife in the wound: " I wouldn't give it to *you*." But her remark was strangely ineffective. What did it matter to him? He had given up Ilona, and it was really Korn's business to redeem her from those knives. Esch looked at Erna's swinging feet. She would open her eyes if she were told that her money was really to be applied in helping her brother's affair. Of course even that wouldn't do what was needed. Perhaps it was really Nentwig who should be made to pay. For if the world was to be redeemed one must attack the virus at its source, as Lohberg said; but that source was Nentwig, or perhaps even something hiding behind Nentwig, something greater—perhaps as great and as securely hidden in his inaccessibility as the chairman of a company —something one knew nothing about. It was enough to make a man angry, and Esch, who was a strong fellow and not in the least afflicted with nerves, felt inclined to stamp on Fräulein Erna's swinging feet to make her quiet. She said: " Do you like my shoes? " " No," retorted

Esch. Fräulein Erna was taken aback. " Herr Lohberg would like them
. . . when are you going to bring him here? You've simply been hiding
him . . . out of jealousy, I suppose, Herr Esch? " Oh, he could bring the
man round at once if she was so anxious to see him, remarked Esch,
hoping privately that they would come to an understanding about the
theatre business. " No need for him to come at once," said Fräulein Erna,
" but why not this evening for coffee? " All right, he'd arrange that, said
Esch, and took himself off.

Lohberg came. He held his coffee-cup with one hand and stirred in it
mechanically with the other. He left his spoon in the cup even while he
was drinking, so that it hit him on the nose. Esch spread himself insolently,
asking if Balthasar and Ilona were coming, and making all kinds of tactless remarks. Fräulein Erna took no notice of him. She regarded with
interest Herr Lohberg's rachitic head and his large white eyeballs;
truly, he looked as if it would not take much to make him cry. And she
wondered if, in the heat and ardour of love, he would be moved to tears;
it annoyed her to think that her brother had pushed her into an unsatis-
factory relation with Esch, a brute of a man who upset her, while only
two or three houses farther away there was a well-established tradesman
who blushed whenever she looked at him. Had he ever had a woman,
she wondered, and to satisfy these speculations and to provoke Esch she
skilfully piloted the conversation towards the subject of love. " Are you
another of these born bachelors, Herr Lohberg? You'll repent it when
you're old and done and have nobody to look after you."

Lohberg blushed. " I'm only waiting for the right girl, Fräulein
Korn."

" And she hasn't turned up yet? " Fräulein Korn smiled encouragingly
and pointed her toe under the hem of her skirt. Lohberg set down his
cup and looked helpless.

Esch said tartly: " He hasn't tried yet, that's all."

Lohberg's convictions came to his support: " One can only love once,
Fräulein Korn."

" Oh! " said Fräulein Korn.

That was clear and unambiguous. Esch was almost ashamed of his
unchaste life, and it seemed to him not improbable that this great and
unique love was what Frau Hentjen had felt for her husband, and perhaps
that was why she now expected chastity and restraint from her customers.
All the same it must be dreadful for Frau Hentjen to have to pay for her

brief wedded bliss by renouncing love for ever afterwards, and so he said:
" Well, but what about widows, then? At that rate, a widow shouldn't
go on living . . . especially if she has no children . . ." and because he
was observant of what he read in the illustrated papers he added:
" Widows ought in that case really to be burned, so that . . . so that
they might be redeemed, in a manner of speaking."

" You're a brute, Herr Esch," said Fräulein Erna. " Herr Lohberg
would never say such things."

" Redemption is in God's hands," said Herr Lohberg, " if He grants
anyone the great gift of love it will last for all eternity."

" You're a clever man, Herr Lohberg, and lots of people would be the
better of taking your words to heart," said Fräulein Erna, " the very
idea of letting oneself be burned for any man! The impudence . . ."

Esch said: " If the world was as it should be it could be redeemed
without any of your silly organizations . . . yes, you can both look
incredulous," he almost shouted, " but there would be no need for a
Salvation Army if the police locked up all the people who deserved to
be locked up . . . instead of the ones that are innocent."

" I wouldn't marry any man unless he had a pension, or could leave
something for his widow, some kind of security," said Fräulein Erna,
" that's only what one is entitled to expect from a good man."

Esch despised her. Mother Hentjen would never think of talking in
such a way. But Lohberg said: " It's a bad provider who doesn't set his
house in order."

" You'll make your wife a happy woman," said Fräulein Erna.

Lohberg went on: " If God blesses me with a wife, I hope I can say
with confidence that we shall live in true Christian unity. We shall
renounce the world and live for each other."

Esch jeered: " Just like Balthasar and Ilona . . . and every evening she
gets knives chucked at her."

Lohberg was indignant: " A man who drinks cheap spirits can't
appreciate crystal-clear water, Fräulein Korn. A passion of that kind
isn't love."

Fräulein Erna took the crystalline purity as a reference to herself and
was flattered: " That dress he gave her cost thirty-eight marks. I found
that out in the shop. To fleece a man like that . . . I could never bring
myself to do it."

Esch said: " Things need to be set right. An innocent man sits in jail, and another runs around as he pleases; one ought either to do *him* in or do oneself in."

Lohberg soothed him down: " Human life isn't to be lightly taken."

" No," said Fräulein Erna, " if anyone should be done in it's a woman who has no feelings where men are concerned . . . as for me, when I have a man to look after I'm a woman of feeling."

Lohberg said: " A genuine Christian love is founded on mutual respect."

" And you would respect your wife even if she weren't as educated as yourself . . . but more a creature of feeling, as a woman should be."

" Only a person of feeling is capable of receiving the redeeming grace and ready for it."

Fräulein Erna said: " I'm sure you're a good son, Herr Lohberg, one that is capable of feeling gratitude for all his mother has done for him."

That made Esch angry, angrier than he knew: " Good son or no . . . I don't give *that* for gratitude; as long as people look on while injustice is being done there's no grace in the world . . . why has Martin sacrificed himself and been put in jail? "

Lohberg answered: " Herr Geyring is a victim of the poison that's destroying the world. Only when they get back to nature will people stop hurting each other."

Fräulein Erna said that she too was a lover of nature and often went for long walks.

Lohberg went on: " Only in God's good air, that lifts our hearts up, are men's nobler feelings awakened."

Esch said: " That kind of thing has never got a single man out of jail yet."

Fräulein Erna remarked: " That's what you say . . . but I say, a man with no feelings is no man at all. A man as faithless as you are, Herr Esch, has no right to put in his word. . . . And men are all the same."

" How can you think so badly of the world, Fräulein Korn? "

She sighed: " The disappointments of life, Herr Lohberg."

" But hope keeps our hearts up, Fräulein Korn."

Fräulein Erna gazed thoughtfully into space: " Yes, if it weren't for hope . . ." then she shook her head: " Men have no feelings, and too much brains is just as bad."

Esch wondered if Frau Hentjen and her husband had spoken in that strain when they got engaged. But Lohberg said: " In God and in God's divine Nature is hope for all of us."

Erna did not want to be outdone: " I go regularly to church and confession, thank God . . ." and with triumph she added: " Our holy Catholic faith has more feeling in a way than the Protestant religion—if I were a man I would never marry a Protestant."

Lohberg was too polite to contradict her:

" All ways to God are equally worthy of respect. And those whom God has joined will learn from Him to live peaceably together . . . all that is needed is good will."

Lohberg's virtue once more disgusted Esch, although he had often compared him with Mother Hentjen because of that same virtue. He burst out: " Any idiot can talk."

Fräulein Erna said with disdain: " Herr Esch, of course, would take anybody he came across, he doesn't bother about such things as feelings or religion; all he asks is that she should have money."

He simply couldn't believe that, said Herr Lohberg.

" Oh, you can take my word for it, I know him, he has no feelings, and he never thinks about anything . . . the kind of thoughts you have, Herr Lohberg, aren't to be found in everybody."

But if that were so he was sorry for Herr Esch, remarked Lohberg, for that meant he would never find happiness in this world.

Esch shrugged his shoulders. What did this fellow know about the new world? He said contemptuously: " First set the world right."

But Fräulein Erna had found the solution: " If two people worked together, if your wife, for instance, were to help you in your business, then everything else would be all right, even if the man was a Protestant and the wife a Catholic."

" Of course," said Lohberg.

" Or if two people should have something in common, a common interest, as they say . . . then they must stand by each other, mustn't they? "

" Of course," said Lohberg.

Fräulein Erna's lizard eye glanced at Esch as she said: " Would you have any objections, Herr Lohberg, if I joined you in the theatre business that Herr Esch was speaking of? Now that my brother has lost his senses I at least must try to bring in some money."

How could Herr Lohberg have any objection! And when Fräulein

Erna said that she would invest the half of her savings, say about a thousand marks, he cried, and she was delighted to hear it: " Oh! Then we'll be partners."

In spite of this Esch was dissatisfied. The fact that he had got his own way had all at once ceased to matter, maybe because in any case he had renounced Ilona, maybe because there were more important aims at stake, but perhaps only because—and this was the sole reason of which he was conscious—he suddenly had serious misgivings.

" Talk it over first with Gernerth, the manager of the theatre. I've only told you about it, I don't accept any responsibility."

" Oh yes," said Fräulein Erna, she knew well enough that he was an irresponsible man, and he didn't need to be afraid that he would be called to account. He wasn't much of a Christian, and she thought more of Herr Lohberg's little finger than of Herr Esch's whole body. And wouldn't Herr Lohberg come in now and then for a cup of coffee? Yes? And since it was getting late, and they had already got to their feet, she took Lohberg by the arm. The lamp above them shed a mild light upon their heads, and they stood before Esch like a newly engaged couple.

Esch had taken off his coat and hung it on the stand. Then he began to brush and beat it and examined its worn collar. Again he was conscious of some discrepancy in his calculations. He had given up Ilona, yet he was supposed to look on while Erna turned away from him and set her cap at that idiot. It was against all the laws of book-keeping, which demanded that every debit entry should be balanced by a credit one. Of course—and he shook the coat speculatively—if he chose he could keep a Lohberg from getting the better of *him*; he was easily a match for the man; no, August Esch was far from being such an ugly monstrosity, and he actually took a step or two towards the door, but paused before he opened it; tut, he didn't choose to, that was all. The creature across the passage might think he had come crawling to her out of gratitude for her measly thousand marks. He turned and sat down on his bed, where he unlaced his shoes. The balance was all right, so far. And the fact that he was at bottom resentful because he couldn't sleep with Erna, that was all right, too. One cut one's losses. Yet there was an obscure miscalculation somewhere that he couldn't put his finger on: granted that he wasn't going across the passage to that woman, granted that he was giving up his bit of fun, what was his real reason for doing so? Was it perhaps to escape marriage? Was he making the smaller sacrifice to escape the greater, to avoid paying in person? Esch said: " I'm a swine." Yes, he was a swine, not a whit better than Nentwig, who also shuffled off responsibility. His accounts were in a disorder which it would take the devil and all to clear up.

But disorderly accounts meant a disorderly world, and a disorderly world meant that Ilona would go on being a target for knives, that Nentwig would continue with brazen hypocrisy to evade punishment, and that Martin would sit in jail for ever. He thought it all over, and as he slipped off his drawers the answer came spontaneously: the others had given their money for the wrestling business, and so he, who had no money, must give himself, not in marriage, certainly, but in personal service, to the new undertaking. And since that, unfortunately, did not fit in with his job in Mannheim, he must simply give notice. That was the way he could pay his debt. And as if in corroboration of this con-clusion, he suddenly realized that he ought not to remain any longer with a company that had been the means of putting Martin in jail. No one could accuse him of disloyalty; even the Herr Chairman would have to admit that Esch was a decent fellow. This new idea drove Erna out of his head, and he lay down in bed relieved and comforted. Going back to Cologne and to Mother Hentjen's would, of course, be pleasant, and that diminished his sacrifice a little, but so little that it hardly counted; after all, Mother Hentjen hadn't even answered his letter. And there were restaurants a-plenty in Mannheim. No, the return to Cologne, that unjust town, was a very negligible offset to his sacrifice; it was at most an entry in the petty-cash account, and a man could always credit himself with petty cash. His eagerness to report his success drove him to see Gernerth early next morning: it was no small feat to have raised two thousand marks so quickly! Gernerth clapped him on the shoulder and called him the devil of a fellow. That did Esch good. Yet his decision to give up his job and take service in the theatre astounded Gernerth; he could not, however, produce any valid objection. " We'll manage it somehow, Herr Esch," he said, and Esch went off to the head office of the Central Rhine Shipping Company.

In the upper floors of the head office buildings there were long, hushed corridors laid with brown linoleum. On the doors were stylish plates bearing the names of the occupants, and at one end of each corridor, behind a table lit by a standard lamp, sat a man in uniform who asked what one wanted and wrote down one's name and business on a duplicate block. Esch traversed one of the corridors, and since it was for the last time he took good note of everything. He read every name on the doors, and when to his surprise he came on a woman's name, he paused and tried to imagine what she would be like: was she an ordinary clerk casting up accounts at a sloping desk with black cuffs over her sleeves, and would she be cool and offhand with visitors like all the others? He felt a sudden desire for the unknown woman behind the door, and there arose in him the conception of a new kind of love, a simple, one might almost say a business-like and official kind of love, a love that would run as smoothly, as calmly, and yet as spaciously and never-endingly, as these corridors with their polished linoleum. But then he saw the long series of doors with men's names, and he could not help thinking that a lone woman in that masculine environment must be as disgusted with it as Mother Hentjen was with her business. A hatred of commercial methods stirred again within him, hatred of an organization that, behind its apparent orderliness, its smooth corridors, its smooth and flawless book-keeping, concealed all manner of infamies. And that was called respectability! Whether head clerk or chairman of a company, there was nothing to choose between one man of business and another. And if for a moment Esch had regretted that he was no longer a unit in the smoothly running organization, no longer privileged to go out and in without being stopped or questioned or announced, his regret now vanished, and he saw only a row of Nentwigs sitting behind these doors, all of them pledged and concerned to keep Martin languishing in confinement. He would have liked to go straight down to the counting-house and tell the blind fools there that they too should break out of their prison of hypocritical ciphers and columns and like him set themselves free; yes, that was what they should do, even at the risk of having to join him in emigrating to America.

"But it's a pretty short star turn you've given us here," the staff manager said when he gave in his notice and asked for a testimonial, and Esch felt tempted to divulge the real reasons for his departure from such a despicable firm. But he had to leave them unsaid, for the friendly staff manager immediately bent his attention to other matters, although he repeated once or twice: "A short star turn . . . a short star turn," in an unctuous voice, as if he liked the phrase and as if he were hinting that theatrical life wasn't so very different from or even superior to the business that Esch was relinquishing. What could the staff manager know about it? Was he really reproaching Esch with disloyalty and planning to catch him unawares? To trip him up in his new job? Esch followed his movements with a suspicious eye and with a suspicious eye ran over the document that was handed to him, although he knew very well that in his new profession nobody would ask to see a testimonial. And since the thought of his work in the theatre obsessed him, even as he was striding over the brown linoleum of the corridor towards the staircase he no longer remarked the quiet orderliness of the building, nor speculated about the woman's name on the door he passed by, nor saw even the notice-board marked " Counting House "; the very pomp of the board-room and the Chairman's private office in the front part of the main building meant nothing to him. Only when he was out in the street did he cast a glance back, a farewell glance, as he said to himself, and was vaguely disappointed because there was no equipage waiting at the main entrance. He would really have liked to set eyes on Bertrand for once. Of course, like Nentwig, the man kept himself well out of the way. And of course it would be better not to see him, not to set eyes on him at all, or on Mannheim for that matter and all that it stood for. Good-bye for ever, said Esch; yet he was incapable of departing so quickly and found himself lingering and blinking in the midday sunlight that streamed evenly over the asphalt of the new street, lingering and waiting for the glass doors to turn noiselessly on their hinges, perhaps, and let the Chairman out. But even though in the shimmering light it looked as if the two wings of the door were trembling, so that one was reminded of the swing doors behind Mother Hentjen's buffet, yet that was only a so-called optical illusion and the two halves of the door were immobile in their marble framework. They did not open and no one came out. Esch felt insulted: there he had to stand in the glaring sun simply because the Central Rhine Shipping Company had established itself in a flashy new asphalt road instead of a cool and cellar-like street; he turned round, crossed the street with long, rather awkward strides, rounded the next corner, and as he swung himself on to the footboard of a tram that rattled past, he had finally decided to leave Mannheim the very next day and go to Cologne to start negotiations with Oppenheimer, the theatrical agent.

II

It was natural that Esch should be annoyed because Mother Hentjen had never answered his letter, since even business letters were always answered within a certain time, and a private letter deserved more consideration, not being a mere matter of business routine. Still, Mother Hentjen's silence was in keeping with her character. It was common knowledge that a man needed only snatch at her hand, or try to pinch her on the more protuberant parts of her body, to make her stiffen into that rigidity of disgust with which she silently checked the importunate; perhaps Esch's letter had provoked a similar reaction in her. After all, a letter is something the writer's fingers have dirtied, not unlike dirty body-linen, and Mother Hentjen might be depended on to see it in that light. She was quite different from other women; she was not the woman to walk into a man's room early in the morning before it had been tidied without showing embarrassment even if he was washing himself. She was no Erna: she would never have asked Esch to think of her sometimes and to write her nice, sentimental letters. Nor was she the woman to have an affair with a man like Korn, although she was a more earthly creature than Ilona. Of course, like Ilona, Mother Hentjen was something superior, only it seemed to Esch that on the earthly plane she had to maintain by artifice what Ilona had by nature. And if she was disgusted by his letter he could understand and approve her attitude; he had almost a yearning to be scolded by her: it seemed as if she were bound to know what he had been up to, and he could feel again the cold look with which she had always reproached him whenever he slept with Hede; not even that had she been willing to tolerate, and yet the girl was a member of her own establishment.

When he arrived in Cologne, however, and made it his first business to call on Mother Hentjen, Esch was received neither with the friendliness he had hoped for nor the reproach he had feared. She merely said: " Oh, there you are again, Herr Esch. I hope you're staying for some time," and he felt like an outsider, felt actually as if he were doomed for all eternity to vegetate forgotten in the Korn household. When Frau Hentjen did come to his table later she wounded him even more deeply by speaking only of Martin: " Yes, he's got what he was asking for, Herr Geyring "—she had warned him often enough. Esch answered in monosyllables; he had told her all he knew when he wrote. " Oh! I must thank you for your letter, too," said Frau Hentjen, and that was all. In spite of his disappointment he pulled out a parcel: " I've brought you a souvenir from Mannheim." It was a replica of the Schiller Memorial outside the Mannheim theatre, and Esch indicated the shelf from which the Eiffel Tower looked down with its black-white-and-red flag; it would perhaps go all right up there. And although he merely handed the thing over without further ado, Frau Hentjen accepted it with unexpected and genuine delight, for this was something she could show to her friends. " Oh no, I won't let anybody so much as look at it down here; it's too lovely for that; it's going upstairs into my parlour . . . but it isn't right of you, Herr Esch, to go to such expense for me." Her warmth put him in a good mood again, and he began to tell her about his life in Mannheim, not omitting to express certain edifying sentiments which, though really emanating from that fool Lohberg, would, he assumed, be acceptable to Mother Hentjen. With many interruptions, for she was often called to the buffet, he extolled to her the beauties of nature, especially of the Rhine, and said he was surprised that she stuck so closely to Cologne and never made an excursion to places so easily within her reach. " All very well for sweethearting couples," said Mother Hentjen contemptuously, and Esch answered respectfully that she could quite well go alone or with a woman friend. That sounded plausible and reassuring to Frau Hentjen, and she said that she might consider it some day. " Anyhow," she remarked, dismissing it for the present, " I knew the Rhine well enough when I was a girl." Hardly had she said this than she stiffened and stared over his head. Esch was not surprised, for he knew Mother Hentjen's sudden withdrawals. But there was a particular reason for her reserve on this occasion, a reason that Esch could not have surmised: it was the first time that Frau Hentjen had ever mentioned her private life to a customer, and she was so upset by the realization that she fled to the buffet to look in the glass and finger her sugar-loaf coiffure. She was angry with Esch because he had drawn confidences from her, and she did not return to his table although the Schiller Memorial was still standing there. She felt like telling him to take it away, especially as one or two of his friends had sat down beside him and were running it over with masculine eyes and masculine fingers. She fled still farther, into the kitchen, and Esch knew that he had unwittingly committed some blunder or other. But when she finally reappeared he rose and took the statuette to the buffet. She polished it clean with one of the glass-cloths. Esch, who remained standing because he did not know how to extricate himself, told her that in the theatre opposite the memorial the *première* —that was a word he had learned from Gernerth—the *première* of one of Schiller's plays had taken place. He himself had now various connections with the theatre, and if everything went well he would soon be able to get tickets for her. Really? He had connections with the theatre? Oh, well, he had always been something of a wastrel. For Mother Hentjen connections with the theatre simply meant relations with the vulgar actresses, and she remarked, contemptuously and indifferently, that she could not bear the theatre, for there was nothing in it but love, love, and that bored her. Esch did not venture to contradict her, but while Frau Hentjen carried her present into safety upstairs he began talking to Hede, who had barely looked at him, being obviously offended because he had not thought it worth his while to send her a postcard too. Hede seemed thoroughly ill-humoured, and ill-humour seemed to pervade the whole restaurant, in which the automatic instrument, set a-going by a reckless client, was now grinding out its tunes. Hede rushed to the instrument to turn it off, since music at such a late hour was against the public regulations, and all the men laughed at the success of the prank. Through the half-open window a stray night breeze wandered in, and Esch, who had got a whiff of it, slipped outside into the mild freshness of the night, quickly, before Hede could return, quickly, before he could encounter Frau Hentjen again; for she might get out of him that he had thrown up his job with the Central Rhine Shipping: and she certainly wouldn't be talked into believing that the promotion of wrestling matches was a respectable occupation; she wouldn't believe in its prospects, but would be sure to make adverse malicious comments— perhaps with justice. Still, he had had enough for one night, and so he took himself off.

In the black, cellar-like streets there was a chill stench, as always in summer. Esch was vaguely content. The air and the dark walls were familiar and comforting; a man did not feel lonely. He almost wished that he might meet Nentwig. He would have enjoyed giving the man a good hiding. And it exhilarated Esch to feel that life often provided quite simple solutions. Yet it was a lottery in which winning numbers were rare, and so he would just have to stick to the scheme for promoting wrestling matches.

Oppenheimer, the theatrical agent, possessed neither an antechamber with cushioned chairs, nor a reception clerk with forms for visitors to fill up. That was only to be expected. But nobody likes an exchange for the worse, and Esch had nursed a vague hope of finding an establishment not unlike that of the Central Rhine Shipping translated into theatrical terms. Well, it wasn't like that at all. After he had climbed a narrow dark staircase to the mezzanine floor, found a door marked " Oppenheimer's Agency," and knocked at it without getting any response, he was forced simply to walk in unannounced. He found himself in a room where an iron washstand was standing filled with dirty water and pigeonholes of all kinds were cluttered up with waste-paper. On one wall hung a large calendar issued by an insurance company, on the other wall, framed and glazed, was a picture of a ship of the Hamburg-Amerika line, the *Kaiserin Augusta Viktoria*, painted in gay colours with a swarm of smaller craft around her, as she left the harbour and clove the foaming blue waves of the North Sea. Esch did not give himself time to inspect the ship closely, for he had come on business, and since shyness was not one of his characteristics he pushed, although with some hesitation, into a second room. There he found a writing-desk that, in contrast to the disorder prevailing elsewhere, had nothing whatever upon it, not even any trace of writing materials, but was splotched with ink, its brown wood scored and nicked with old grey notches and new yellow ones, and its green-baize cloth torn in many places. There was no other door. In this room too, however, there were notable wall-decorations fastened to the wallpaper with drawing-pins, a collection of photographs that kindled Esch's interest, for there were many ladies in tights or spangles, in seductive and alluring poses, and he gave a glance round to see if Ilona was amongst them. But he thought it more proper to withdraw and inquire of somebody where Herr Oppenheimer might be found. There was no house porter, and so he rang at several doors until he was told, with a contempt that included himself, that Oppenheimer's office hours were highly irregular. " You can wait about for him if you've nothing better to do," said a woman.

So that was that. It was unpleasant to be treated in that way, and if his new profession were to expose him to such contempt it was hardly encouraging. Still, it couldn't be helped, he had taken it on for Ilona's sake (and the thought gave him a thrill of warmth about the heart); it was in any case his new profession, and so Esch waited. Fine office habits this Herr Oppenheimer had contracted! Esch had to laugh; no, this was not a job in which testimonials were likely to be asked for. He stood before the house door gazing down the street, until at length an insignificant, small, fair-haired, rosy man came towards the house and went up the stairs. Esch followed him. It was Herr Oppenheimer. When Esch explained his business Herr Oppenheimer said: " Women wrestlers? I'll fix it up, I'll fix it up all right. But what does Gernerth need you for? " Yes, what did Gernerth need him for? Why was he here? What had brought him here at all? Now that he had given up his post in the Central Rhine Shipping Company his visit to Cologne was by no means the official journey he had projected. Why had he come to Cologne, then? Surely not because Cologne was a stage nearer the sea?

When an honest man emigrates to America his relations and friends stand on the quay and wave their handkerchiefs to him. The ship's band plays, *Must I then, must I then, leave my native Town*, and although one might regard this, in view of the frequency with which ships make the voyage, as a show of hypocrisy on the part of the band-master, yet many of the listeners are moved. When the rope is once made fast to the tiny tug, when the ocean giant floats out on the dark, buoyant mirror of the sea, then fitful and forlorn over the water come faint gusts of more cheerful melodies with which the kindly bandmaster is trying to enliven the departing passengers. Then it becomes clear to many a man how dispersedly his fellows are scattered over the face of the sea and the earth, and how frail are the threads that bind them one to another. Thus, gliding out of the harbour into clearer waters, where the current of the river is no longer discernible and the tides of the sea actually seem to be setting backwards into the harbour, the great liner often swims in a cloud of invisible but tense anguish, so that many a spectator feels prompted to stop her. On she goes, past the ships that lie along the smoking, littered shores, rattling their cranes to and fro as they load and unload vague cargoes for vague destinations, past the littered shores that take on a dusty greenness towards the river-mouth and come to an end in scanty herbage, finally past the sand-dunes where the lighthouse comes into sight, on she goes, fettered like an outcast to her tiny escort, and on the ships and along the shores stand men who watch her go, raise their arms as if to stop her, yet summon up merely a half-hearted and awkward wave of the hand. Once she is out in the open sea and her hull is almost sunk below the horizon, so that her three funnels are barely visible, many a man peering out to sea from the coast asks himself if this ship is making for the harbour or forging her way into a loneliness that the longshoreman can never comprehend. And if he finds that she is heading for the land he is comforted, as though she were bringing home his sweetheart, or at least a long-expected letter that he had not known he was waiting for. Often in the light haze of that distant frontier two ships meet, and one can see them gliding past each other. There is a moment in which both the delicate silhouettes merge together and become one, a moment of subtle exaltation, until they softly separate again with a motion as quiet and soft as the distant haze in which they pair, and each one goes alone her own way. Sweet, never-to-be-fulfilled hope!

But the passenger out yonder on board the ship does not know that we have been anxious for him. He scarcely notices the undulating ribbon of the coast, and only when he vaguely divines the yellow ray of the lighthouse is he aware that there are those on land who are anxious for him and think of his danger. He does not understand the danger that in fact encompasses him, he is not conscious that a great mountain of water separates him from the sea-bottom that is the earth. Only the man who has an aim fears danger, for he is afraid of failure. But the passenger who walks on the smooth planks that run round the deck like a racing-track, and that are smoother than any path he has yet trod, the passenger on board ship has no aim, and can never complete his destiny; he is closed within himself. All his potentialities lie asleep. One who loves him can love him only for what he promises to be, for all that lies within him, not for what he will achieve or has achieved; he will never achieve it. So men on shore know nothing about love and mistake their fears for love. The sea-passenger, however, soon comes to this knowledge, and the threads that were spun from him to those on shore are broken before the coastline sinks out of sight. It is almost superfluous for the band-master to try enlivening melodies upon him, for the passenger is content to let his hand slide over the smooth brown polish of the railing and its glittering brass rings. The shining sea lies stretched before him; he is at peace. Mighty engines drive him on, and their humming shapes a path that leads nowhere. The eye of the passenger at sea is a different eye: it is the eye of an orphaned man that recognizes us no longer. He has forgotten what was once his daily task; he believes no longer in the correctness of addition sums, and if his way should take him past the telegraph operator's cabin and he should hear the ticking of the apparatus, he marvels maybe at the mechanism, but cannot convince himself that the operator is receiving messages from the land and sending messages to the land; indeed, if he were not a sober-minded man he might think that the operator was speaking to the cosmos. He loves the whales and the dolphins that play round the ship, and he has no fear of the icebergs. But if a distant coastline should come into sight he refuses to look at it and perhaps takes refuge in the belly of the ship until it has vanished again, for he knows that it is not love that awaits him there, not loose-footed freedom, but taut anxiety and the straight walls of his aim. For he who seeks love seeks the sea; he may perhaps speak of the land that lies beyond the sea, but he does not mean what he says, for he thinks of the voyage as endless, the voyage that nourishes in his lonely soul the hope of expanding and opening itself to receive that other who emerges free as air from the light haze and enters into him, that other whom he rightly recognizes as a potential, unborn immortal.

It is undeniable that none of these reflections occurred to Esch, although he remained obsessed by the thought of emigrating to America and taking the book-keepers of the Central Rhine Shipping Company as fellow-passengers. But whenever he came into Herr Oppenheimer's office he studied long and minutely the *Kaiserin Augusta Viktoria* as she clove the waves.

He had resumed his former life, occupied his old room, and often took his midday meal at Mother Hentjen's. He used his bicycle with zeal, but his daily routine took him now to Herr Oppenheimer's instead of to Stemberg & Company. Frau Hentjen had acknowledged the change in his vocation with a look that, in spite of her detachment, showed a blend of something like contempt, dissatisfaction, and perhaps even a hint of scorn, and although Esch had to admit that her concern was justified—indeed, maybe because of it—he exerted himself in painting to her in rosy colours the prospects and advantages of his new profession. He partly succeeded. Though she turned a deaf ear to his bold accounts of the greatness on the threshold of which he was now standing, and which would spread not only to America but over all the continents of the world, yet the compound of glittering riches, artistic success and joyous travel with which he tried to dazzle her, this destiny which another

was to achieve and not herself, this far-flung greatness aroused the envy
of the woman who had loathed for fifteen years the sordid narrowness
of her fate. She was filled, one might say, with a kind of malicious
admiration, for while on the one hand she maintained obstinately that his
ambitions were hollow and unattainable, on the other she surpassed him
in fantastic invention, gave him high-sounding advice, and encouraged
him to think that he might rise to become the Chief or, as he said, the
Chairman, of the whole gang of artists, performers and managers. " First
of all they must be brought under severe order and discipline," he used
to reply, " that's what they need most." Yes, he was convinced of that,
and this profound contempt for artists was founded not merely on his
distaste for Gernerth's greasy notebook and Oppenheimer's chaotic office,
but coincided so closely with Mother Hentjen's principles that in one
such moment of admiring assent—a world-embracing principle often de-
bouches into a domestic triviality—Frau Hentjen granted his request to
entrust her bills and accounts to his proficient supervision: she granted
it with a condescending smile, as if fully persuaded that her simple books
were kept in the most sensible and model manner. But scarcely had
Esch bent himself over the columns when Mother Hentjen cried that he
needn't put on such a superior air; she wasn't by any means impressed
by his smattering of book-keeping; he had much better turn his attention
to the theatrical business, which needed looking after much more than
hers. And she snatched the books from him.

Yes, the theatrical business! With the casualness of his profession
Oppenheimer was accustomed to accept lightly the accidents of chance,
and although the persistence of Esch left him defenceless, he laughed
over this man who came every day on his bicycle and behaved as if he
were a partner in the firm; but he put up with it on learning that Esch
was bringing new capital into the wrestling scheme, and even swallowed
the insults that Esch daily flung at the disorder in his office. They had
jointly bargained with the proprietor of the Alhambra Theatre for its
lease during June and July, and since Esch's zeal for work had to be
appeased, he was empowered to recruit the lady wrestlers.

Esch, experienced as he was in drinking dens, brothels and girls, was
the very man for this job. He combed out all the establishments, and
whenever he found likely girls who were willing to enter the lists, he
wrote down their names and qualifications in a notebook which he had
himself ruled and spaced, and in which he did not omit to enter after

each name, in a special column headed by the business-like word
" Observations," his judgment on the capabilities of the candidates
according to a rough-and-ready classification. He was especially partial
to girls with foreign-sounding names and of foreign race, for it was to
be an international wrestling tournament, and the only ones he excepted
were the Hungarians. It was often good enough fun trying the girls'
muscles, and sometimes even their stalwart charms seduced him. None
the less he did not really enjoy his task, and when he spoke of it to Mother
Hentjen in a disparaging and casual manner he was quite sincere: he
could no longer regard such an occupation as compatible with his dignity,
and he much preferred to sit at Oppenheimer's vacant desk or to inspect
the Alhambra.

He often betook himself there, traversing the empty grey auditorium
in which one's steps echoed on the floor-boards, and crossing the
teetering planks laid over the well of the orchestra up to the stage, whose
gigantic, naked grey walls were almost too overpowering for the flimsy
screens of the wings that would soon cover them. When he measured the
stage with long strides it was as if in triumph because no more knives
were to be hurled across it, and when he peeped into the managerial
office it was to wonder whether he couldn't already install himself there.
He reflected, too, that he must show Frau Hentjen round his new
kingdom. The air was oddly grey and cool, although the beer-garden
outside was glowing in the heat of the bright sun, and this self-contained
kingdom of dusty strangeness was like a remote island of the unknown
within a world of familiar things, it was a promise and an indication
of all the strange potentialities that lay in wait across the great grey sea.
In the evening, too, he often repaired to the Alhambra. But then the
beer-garden was illuminated, and a band played on the wooden platform
under the trees. The theatre lurked dark and almost unnoticed behind
the lights, filled to the very roof with darkness, and one could not imagine
how spacious and well arranged it was. Esch liked coming at such a
late hour, for he found it pleasant to think that it was reserved for him
and for no other to reawaken the life within that dark building.

When Esch visited the Alhambra again on one of the following mornings
he found the proprietor playing cards with friends at the bar. He joined
them and they played until late in the afternoon. By that time Esch
felt his face vacant and wooden, and was aware that the life he was

leading exactly resembled that in the Mannheim warehouses during the strike. It only needed Korn to come along and boast about Ilona's love-making. What was the sense of his having given up his job in the Central Rhine Shipping? Here he was frittering away his time in idleness, using up his money, and he had not even avenged Martin. If he had stayed in Mannheim he could at least have visited Martin in jail.

At supper he accused himself of having deserted Martin shamefully, but when Frau Hentjen replied that every man must look out for himself, and that Herr Geyring, who had been warned often enough by her, could not expect a friend of his to stay in Mannheim for his sake and give up a brilliant career, he flew into a rage and abused her so vehemently that she took refuge behind the buffet and fingered at her hair. He paid his bill on the spot and left the restaurant, infuriated because she had extolled his idleness as a brilliant career. He did not, however, admit to himself that that was the cause of his anger, but merely denounced her for cold heartlessness towards Martin, and he spent the whole night in brooding over ways and means of helping Martin.

Early in the morning he betook himself to Oppenheimer's office. He had procured writing materials for himself and spent the whole morning in composing a savage article in which he made it clear that that deserving union secretary, Martin Geyring, had fallen a victim to a diabolical intrigue between the Central Rhine Shipping Company and the Mannheim police. This article he carried forthwith to the editorial office of the Social Democratic *People's Guardian*.

The building in which *The People's Guardian* had its headquarters was no palace of journalism. Not a single marble vestibule or wrought-iron gate. In general it was not unlike Oppenheimer's office, only that it was much busier; but on Sundays, when the newspaper world was on holiday, it would be the exact double of his. The black iron railings of the staircase were sticky to the touch, the peeling, shabby walls bore the traces of frequent pictorial activity, and from a window one looked out on a small courtyard in which stood a dray loaded with rolls of paper. Printing machines were at work somewhere with asthmatic rattlings. One entered the editorial office through a door that had once been white and banged ruthlessly because its lock did not fit. Instead of an insurance calendar there was a timetable on the wall, instead of dancers' portraits a photograph of Karl Marx. Nothing else was different, and his incursion here seemed all at once so wholly superfluous that even his article, which had sounded powerful and sinister, suddenly appeared lame and superfluous too. The same crew everywhere, thought Esch with fury. The same crew of demagogues, living everywhere in the same disorder. It was a waste of time to put a weapon into the hand of any of them. In their hands it would droop ineffectually, for not one of them knew the ins and outs of anything.

He was directed to a second room. Behind a table that might have once been covered with cloth sat a man in a brown-velvet jacket. Esch gave him the manuscript. The editor skimmed it over hastily, folded it, and laid it in a basket beside him. " But you haven't read it," said Esch sharply. " Oh yes, I know what it's about . . . the Mannheim strike; we'll see if we can use it." Esch was amazed at the man's lack of curiosity about the article, and at his assumption that he knew all about it already. " Excuse me, these are facts that put the strike in an entirely new light," he insisted. The editor picked up the manuscript, but laid it down again immediately. " What facts? I saw nothing new in it." Esch felt that the other was trying to display his omniscience. " But I was an eyewitness; I was at the meeting! " " Well, our confidential agents were there too." " Have you made it public, then? " " As far as I know there was nothing special to make public." Esch was so astounded that he simply sat down on a chair, although he had not been asked to do so. " My dear comrade," the editor went on, " after all you can't expect us to wait until you choose to pitch in your report." " Yes, but," Esch was completely bewildered, "but why haven't you done something, then? Why do you let Martin," he corrected himself, " why do you let Geyring sit in jail though he's innocent? " " Oh, that's it? . . . all honour to your sense of justice," the editor glanced at the manuscript which bore Esch's name, " Herr Esch, . . . but do you really think we could get him out as easily as that? " He laughed. Esch was not to be put off with laughter: " It's the other side that should be in the lock-up . . . that was more than evident to anyone who was there! " " So you think that we should have the directors of the Central Rhine Shipping jailed instead of Geyring? " What a nasty laugh, thought Esch, and remained silent. Have Bertrand locked up? Why not Bertrand as well as Nentwig? After all, in the sober light of day there wasn't such an enormous difference between the chairman of a company and a Nentwig, except that the Mannheim chairman was something better than Nentwig, and the lock-up wouldn't be good enough for him. Absently he repeated:

" Have Bertrand locked up." The editor laughed more than ever. " That would just about put the lid on it." " And why? " asked Esch with irritation. " He's a decent chap, friendly and sociable," explained the editor amiably, " a first-class man of business, the kind of man one can get on with." " So you can get on with a man who's hand in glove with the police? " " Heavens above, of course the employers work with the police; if we were on top we'd do exactly the same." " And you call that justice? " said Esch indignantly. The editor raised his hands in amused resignation. " How can we help it? That's how justice is organized in the Capitalist State. Meanwhile a man who takes the trouble to keep his concerns going is of more use to us than one who simply shuts up shop. If you got your way and all the employers who are against us were put in jail we'd have an industrial crisis, and we'd get a lot of credit for that, wouldn't we? " Esch repeated with obstinate anger: " All the same, he should be locked up." The editor's mirth became more and more irritating. " Ah, now I see what you're getting at: you mean because he's a sodomite? . . . " Esch pricked up his ears, the editor became still more genial, " that bothers you, does it? Well, I can set your mind at rest on that point: he only does it down in Italy. And anyhow a gentleman like him isn't so easily nabbed as a Social Democrat." So that was it: cushioned chairs, silver lackeys, equipages, and a sodomite, and Nentwig could run about and do what he liked! Esch stared the mirthful editor in the face: " But Martin's locked up! " The editor had laid down his pencil and opened his arms a little: " My dear friend and comrade, neither of us can alter events. The strike in Mannheim was sheer stupidity, and the only thing we could do was to let things take their course and pocket our discomfiture. We can only be glad that Geyring's three months is good propaganda material for us. Many thanks for your article, my dear fellow, and if you ever have something else for us bring it sooner next time." He shook Esch by the hand, and Esch, in spite of his resentment, achieved an awkward bow.

June was approaching. Esch did Oppenheimer's errands to the printers and the poster-designers; everything was ready, and bold advertisements on pillars and hoardings informed the town that the strongest women of all the nations would be assembled in Cologne to try their strength; and the list of names appended would have convinced any sceptic: there was Tatiana Leonoff, the Russian champion, Maud Ferguson, winner of the New York Championship, Mirzl Oberleitner, holder of the Viennese Cup, to say nothing of the German representative, Irmentraud Kroff. The names for the most part were fanciful inventions of Oppenheimer, who found the girls' real names too tame and insipid. Esch had vainly striven against this piece of deception; had he taken all the trouble to find genuinely international girls simply for a Jew to mess about with their names? He took it as a fresh symptom of the anarchical condition of the world, in which no one seemed to know whether he was on the right or on the left, in the van or in the rear, and where it was ultimately of no importance whether Herr Oppenheimer called a person by this name or that; one had even to be thankful that Oppenheimer hadn't thought of a Hungarian name. Hungary had no business to exist, anyway, and it was equally unseemly for Oppenheimer to have included Italy in the list of competing nations. Was it so certain that there were women there at all? Italy seemed to be a haunt of sodomites. Still, he was not displeased as he regarded the placard with all its international names: the different countries stood shoulder to shoulder, and that whole world was in a sense his own creation, an earnest and a promise for his future career. He brought one of his posters into Mother Hentjen's and without asking permission pinned it up on the wooden panelling beneath the Eiffel Tower.

Frau Hentjen, however, was still resentful of the way he had abused her on Geyring's account, and she called out from the buffet that he would kindly stick up his posters only where he was asked to; it was for her to decide that kind of thing. Esch, who had long forgotten the incident, and was only reminded of it whenever he saw her angry face, made as if to obey her order. This submissiveness disarmed Mother Hentjen; she came from behind the buffet, still scolding, to have a look at the poster. As she deciphered the list of names she was overcome by sympathy and disgust: these females deserved the degradation of exposing themselves before the eyes of objectionable men, but she was at the same time sorry for them. Esch, who had engineered the whole thing, stood revealed as a pasha in the middle of a harem, and this seemed a situation of such surpassing wickedness, of such deep debauchery, that by comparison with the rest of her customers who sat around with their contemptible little lusts and vices Esch was raised to a different plane, even a higher one. His short, stiff hair, his dark head, his tanned, ruddy skin, pah! he gave her the creeps; no, she did not understand why she put up with the

man and his posters, and she started when he grasped her by the wrist.
Did it not look as if he meant to overpower her and have her at his mercy
and add her name to the list on the poster? She was almost disappointed
when nothing happened, except that Esch guided her obediently outstretched finger from one name to the other: " Russia, Germany, United
States of America, Belgium, Italy, Austria, Bohemia," he read out aloud,
and because it sounded grand, and not at all dangerous, Frau Hentjen
recovered her composure. She said: " But there's some missed out; for
instance, Luxemburg and Switzerland." None the less she presently
turned away from the poster with the list of feminine names as though
it had an evil smell: " How can you mix yourself up with all these women ! "
Esch replied by quoting Martin, that every man must stay where God
had put him, adding that anyhow it was Teltscher's business, not his,
to deal with the women; he was concerned only with the administrative
side.

Teltscher came to Cologne and inspected Esch's recruits in Oppenheimer's office. He sat the whole morning in judgment, dismissed some
of them outright, and appointed the others to meet him in the Alhambra
for a first lesson and a trial of their abilities.

It turned out to be a jolly entertainment. Teltscher had brought the
tights with him, and after Esch had called the roll from his notebook
Herr Teltini invited the ladies to enter the dressing-room and get into
their tights. Most of them refused to go until they had seen the others
first in that unusual costume. When the pioneers, stripped and highly
embarrassed, emerged from the dressing-room, there was a general outburst of laughter. The doors leading into the beer-garden were wide
open; the green trees looked gaily in, and sudden wafts of air brought
the warmth of the morning sun into the theatre. At the doors stood the
proprietor and all the cooks from the restaurant, and Teltscher climbed
up on the stage to give a demonstration, on the soft brown mat that was
laid out, of the rules governing the Græco-Roman style of wrestling.
Then he ordered up a couple to try it, but none of the girls would
come; they giggled and nudged each other, pushing forward now one,
now another, who resisted stoutly and took refuge in the crowd.

At long last two of them made up their minds to it; but when Teltscher
proceeded to show them the preliminary holds they only laughed and
let their arms hang and did not venture to touch each other. Teltscher
ordered up a third girl, but when the same thing happened he made

Esch call the roll again and attempted by jocose observations on each
name to create a bold and enterprising atmosphere. A French name he
hailed with praise of Gallic courage, and invited the "Pride of France"
to step up; then he announced the "Polish Giantess"; in brief, he
rehearsed all the honourable and inspiriting titles with which he intended
to introduce the wrestlers to the public. Some of the girls now appeared
on the stage, but others with shrieks of mirth called back that they
weren't having any and that they wanted to put on their clothes, which
Teltscher countered with expressions of regret and a pantomime of comic
despair. The whole thing was not to go off without an upset, however.
When Esch called out the name of Ruzena Hrushka and Teltscher added:
"Up with you, O Lioness of Bohemia," a plump, soft creature, still
dressed in her own clothes, pushed forward to the footlights and with
the hard sing-song cadence of her race screamed that no one would laugh
at her for dirty money. "I have throw away good money already because
I not let no one laugh over me," she screamed at Teltscher, and while
he was still trying to think of a joke that would save the situation she
lifted up her parasol as if to fling it at him. But then she fell silent, her
soft round shoulders began to heave, and it could be seen that she was
crying. When she turned round and went out between the silent ranks
of startled girls her eye fell on Esch, who was sitting at a table with his
lists. She bent over to him and spat out: "You, you are bad friend,
bring me here to shame me." Then she went out sobbing. Meanwhile
Teltscher had got the situation in hand again, and the incident was not
without its good effect; the girls, as if ashamed of their previous frivolity,
showed themselves now ready for serious work. Teltscher heartened them
with praise, and soon they had all forgotten the wild Czech woman.
Even Esch dismissed her reproaches from his mind, although he could
not but admit that he was a bad friend; yet in a little he would have
Martin out of confinement. Such were his thoughts as he went
home.

Frau Hentjen carefully blew her nose and regarded the result in her
handkerchief. Perhaps from a feeling of guilt Esch had told her of the
incident with the recalcitrant Czech woman, and Frau Hentjen had
rated him, saying that it would have served him right if the poor, abused
woman had scratched his eyes out. That was what came of degrading
himself to the level of such women. Didn't he have any proper pride?

The trollop should have been glad he had given her a chance to earn a little money. Yes, that was all the thanks he got. But the Czech woman was quite right all the same; that's how men should be treated. They deserved nothing better. To enjoy seeing a few poor drabs rolling over each other on the stage in tights! The poor things were ten times better than these men who took advantage of them. And she said cuttingly: "Put that cigar away for goodness' sake." Esch listened to all this respectfully, not merely because of the abundant dinner she gave him at a ridiculously low price, but also because he conceded her the right to show up his sinful way of life as it deserved. His affairs were in a bad state: of the three hundred marks that had been put aside for the wrestling project all he possessed now was a bare two hundred and fifty, and although his profits would begin to accumulate from the very first day's takings, yet he did not know where he was heading for. He must have a settled source of livelihood if the sacrifice which he had taken on himself for Ilona's sake, and which he had actually almost lost sight of by now, was not to come a cropper; he would have liked to talk the matter over but his vanity prevented him, for Mother Hentjen wasn't in a mood to see that even the most splendid careers must grow out of humble beginnings. So he simply said: " Better wrestling matches than knife-throwing." Frau Hentjen regarded the knife in Esch's hand; she did not really understand what he meant, but she felt uncomfortable, so she replied briefly: " Perhaps." " Nice meat," said Esch, bending over his plate, and she replied with the dignity of the expert: " Sirloin." "The grub poor Martin is getting now . . ." Frau Hentjen said: "Meat only on Sundays," and she added with a hint of satisfaction, " and the rest of the time turnips mostly, I reckon." For whose sake was Martin doomed to eat turnips? For whom was he sacrificing himself? Did Martin himself know? Martin was a martyr and yet regarded his martyrdom simply as an occupation, partly pleasant, partly disagreeable; all the same he was a decent fellow. Frau Hentjen said: " If you won't be led you must be driven." Esch did not reply. Perhaps Martin was keeping something to himself which nobody else knew of; a martyr had always to suffer for some conviction, for an inward certainty that determined all his actions. Martyrs were decent people. Frau Hentjen declared: " That's what comes of these anarchist papers." Esch agreed. " Yes, they're a set of swine, now they've left him in the lurch." Martin himself, of course, had sneered at the Socialist papers, although one would have thought that it was their duty to represent the Socialist point of view and advance it. Had Martin really any Socialist convictions, or had he none at all? Esch was annoyed at the thought that Martin had kept something from him. A man who possessed the truth could redeem his fellowmen; that was what the Christian martyrs had done. And because he felt proud of his education he said: " In the times of the Romans there were wrestling matches too, but with lions. Blood all over the place. Over in Trier there's a Roman circus still." Frau Hentjen said with interest: " Well? " But when no answer came she continued: " And I suppose you want to introduce that next, eh? " Esch silently shook his head. If Martin sacrificed himself and lived on turnips neither for his convictions, nor for his better knowledge, nor for anything else, then he probably just did it for the sake of the sacrifice itself. Perhaps one had to sacrifice oneself first, so that—how had that idiot in Mannheim put it?—so that one might feel the power of redeeming grace. But in that case perhaps Ilona too needed the daggers for her act of sacrifice; who could make head or tail of it? And so Esch said: " I don't want to do anything. Maybe all this wrestling business is pure idiocy." Yes, said Mother Hentjen, that it was. And again he felt a sort of respectful esteem for Mother Hentjen which gave him a sense of security.

The room smelt of food and tobacco smoke and the sweetish odour of wine. Mother Hentjen was right: the women didn't want things to be different. That was why Ilona had taken up with Korn. And if the wily cripple really did possess higher knowledge he didn't give it away, allowed nobody else to share in it. He ran about, quite happy, like a dog on three legs, then whipped suddenly round a corner into prison, and prison made as little impression on him as a beating did on a dog. " Perhaps it even amuses them to be beaten and to sacrifice themselves," he said absently. " Who? " asked Mother Hentjen with interest, " the women? " Esch reflected: " Yes, the lot of them. . . ." Mother Hentjen was pleased: " Shall I get you another slice? " She went to the kitchen. Esch was sorry for the Czech woman; she had cried so softly. But there too Mother Hentjen was probably right; the Hrushka woman herself did not want things to be different. And when Frau Hentjen returned with Esch's plate he suddenly said: " No doubt she's looking for a knife-thrower too, the Czech woman." " Well! " said Mother Hentjen. " Poor devil," continued Esch, and he himself did not know whether he meant Martin or the Czech woman. Mother Hentjen, however, took him to mean the Czech woman and retorted sarcastically: " Well, you can easily comfort her, seeing you're so sorry for her . . . you'd better run away to her now."

He made no reply: he had eaten well, and so he silently took up his newspaper and began to study the advertisement column, which had become to him the most important part of the paper since the announcement of the wrestling performances was to be found there. Yet the upright book-keeping of his soul demanded that for Frau Hentjen too an account should be opened; had she any less right to it, after all, than Ilona, who absolutely despised one's efforts to do her good? His eye was arrested by an announcement of a wine auction at Saint-Goar, and he asked Mother Hentjen where she bought her wine. She mentioned a wine-dealer in Cologne. Esch looked disdainful: " So you throw away your money on them! Why have you never asked me about it? I don't say that every firm is as bad as the set of swindlers our fine Herr Nentwig works for, but I bet you pay pretty well through the nose." She assumed a martyred expression: a weak woman fending for herself had to put up with lots of things. He suggested that he should go to Saint-Goar himself and buy wine for her. " Yes, and what about the expense? " she said. Esch became eager; the expense could easily be recouped in the price she charged, and if the quality was up to the mark the wine could be adulterated with a cheaper sort; he knew all about that. And besides he wasn't thinking of the expense; an excursion up the Rhine—Lohberg's idiotic twaddle about the joys of nature came into his mind—was always a pleasure, and she needn't refund him his expenses until she found she had made a profit on the transaction. " And I suppose you're going to take your Czech woman with you? " said Mother Hentjen suspiciously. The idea seemed to him not an unattractive one; yet he disavowed it loudly and indignantly; Mother Hentjen could see for herself by coming with him, why, she had said not so very long ago that she would like a day in the country—well, she could get both at the same time if she came with him, he added impatiently. She looked into his face, regarded his light-brown complexion, stiffened, and started back. " And who would look after the restaurant . . . ? No, it would never do."

Well, he wasn't so keen on it as all that himself; besides, his finances wouldn't stand a trip for two at present, so Esch said nothing further about it, and Mother Hentjen regained her confidence. She took up the newspaper, saw with reassurance that the auction was not to take place for a fortnight still, and said that she would think it over. Yes, she could think it over, said Esch dryly, getting up. He must go to the Alhambra, where Teltscher was having a rehearsal. He chose the route past the restaurant where the Czech woman was employed. But he trod on the pedal of his bicycle and rode past.

Gernerth had now arrived in Cologne, and Esch went down daily to the docks to inquire after the stage properties, which had been sent by boat down the Rhine, his expert knowledge of shipping affairs fitting him for this duty and his need for something to do making him zealous. And though perhaps he really went there to gaze at the sheds and nurse his regret at having given notice so prematurely to the Central Rhine Shipping Company, and to let the sight of the bonded wine-stores remind him that Nentwig was still a bitter thorn in his flesh, yet he saw and experienced all this not without satisfaction, for it proved to him visibly that his sacrifice could stand comparison with Martin's. Also the fact that Ilona had not come to Cologne, but had remained with Korn, fitted into the scheme and gave it a sort of higher significance. Yet it must not be imagined that Esch had become a man glorying in his sufferings. Not at all! To himself he did not scruple to call Ilona a whore, and even a filthy whore, and Teltscher a pimp and a scoundrel. And if he had met that rascal Nentwig between the piled-up rows of wine-barrels he would just have let fly at him. Yet whenever in passing the long row of warehouses belonging to the Central Rhine Company he caught sight of that hated sign bearing the firm's name, then high above all the swarm of petty scoundrels rose the splendid form of a man greater than life-size, the figure of a man of such high standing, a man so remote and lofty that he was almost more than human, and yet it was the figure of an arch-scoundrel; unimaginable and menacing rose that image of Bertrand, the rascally Chairman of this company, the sodomite who had got Martin thrown into prison. And that magnified figure, in essence unimaginable, appeared to subsume those of the two lesser scoundrels, and sometimes it seemed to Esch as though one had only to strike down this Antichrist to destroy as well all the pettier rascals in the world.

Of course it was stupid to bother one's head over such matters, for one had worse troubles; it was bad enough, in all conscience, to be loafing about these docks without pay. A man without a proper means

of livelihood deserved to be exterminated. Mother Hentjen herself
would agree with that, and it was curiously pleasant to picture this
eventuality to oneself. Yes, the best solution perhaps would be for a
super-murderer like that to come along and just do one in. And as Esch
strolled along the quay and encountered once more the sign of the
Central Rhine Shipping Company Limited he said loudly and distinctly:
" Either him or me."

Esch was looking down into the barge that had brought up the theatrical
properties, and supervising the unloading of its cargo. He saw Teltscher
approaching with his rosy-cheeked friend, Oppenheimer: they advanced,
so to speak, by stages, for every now and then they stopped, sometimes
one seizing the other in his eagerness by the lapel of his coat, and Esch
asked himself what they could have found to discuss so urgently. When
they were near enough he heard Teltscher: " And I tell you, Oppenheimer, this is no job for me—you wait, I'll send for Ilona yet, and if
in half-a-year's time I don't put on my turn in New York you can cut
off my head." Hoho, so Teltscher hadn't given up his claims on Ilona
even yet? Well, he would sing a different tune when things had been
put in order. And Esch no longer found any pleasure in the thought of
death. He snarled at the two of them: what did they want here? did
they fancy, perhaps, that he had never seen to a job like this in his life
before? or maybe they thought that he wanted to pinch something? or
perhaps the gentleman wished to supervise his work? Well, he regretted
bitterly that he had ever got other people to put their money into this
business, not to mention his own. Here he had been slaving for nothing
almost a whole month for this risky affair, and had put his last cent into
it, and why? because a certain Herr Teltscher, who was apparently
now intending to bolt, had wheedled him into it. Full of rage he began
unskilfully to mimic Herr Oppenheimer's Jewish intonations. " Why,
he's an Anti-Semite! " said Herr Oppenheimer, and Teltscher prophesied
that after the first report from the box-office the day after next the
Transport Director's spirits would rise considerably. And because he
himself felt in a good humour and wanted to tease Esch he walked
round the conveyance on which the properties were being loaded and
checked them carefully, then went up to the horses and offered them
a few lumps of sugar from his pocket. Esch, angry and offended, had
turned away from the Jews and was checking the packing-cases, but he
regarded the two men with the tail of his eye and was astonished at

Teltscher's amiability; yet he did not want to admit that it was genuine, and half expected that the horses would decline the gift with a shake of the head. But the horses, just like horses, took into their soft and friendly lips the sugar-lumps lying on Teltscher's flat palm, and Esch was annoyed; surely he himself might have thought of offering them a scrap of bread at least! But now that the work of loading was finished nothing remained for him but to give both the horses a sober clap on the crupper. Esch did so, and then, sitting on the packing-cases piled on the lorry, they all three drove into the town. Oppenheimer said good-bye at the Rhine Bridge; Teltscher and Esch drove on and got down at Mother Hentjen's.

Teltscher had been a few times in the restaurant and already put on the airs of an old and regular customer. Esch felt guilty at bringing such riff-raff to Mother Hentjen's place, instead of something better. He would have liked to fling the fellow off the lorry. A Judas like that to sit down in Martin's place, a lout who had no idea that there were better, more refined, more highly respectable men in the world; who had no idea that Martin had been struck down by the hand of a man who would think it beneath him even to spit on a mere knife-thrower! And this juggler, this pimp, gave himself the airs of a conqueror, as if Martin's seat belonged by rights to him. Conjurers' tricks; mere juggling with dead things, sterile labour full of lies and trickery.

They had arrived at Mother Hentjen's. Teltscher clambered down first from the lorry. Esch shouted after him: " Here! Who's to unload this stuff? Supervising and spying round, that suits you all right, but when it comes to real work you make yourself scarce." " I'm hungry," Teltscher retorted simply and pushed open the restaurant door. No use arguing with a Jew; Esch shrugged his shoulders and followed him. And to disclaim any responsibility for this sort of customer he said jestingly: " I've brought you a fine customer this time, Mother Hentjen, well, I couldn't find anything better at the moment." But suddenly everything seemed not to matter: Teltscher might sit in Martin's place, and Martin in Nentwig's; one could not make head or tail of it, and yet somewhere it was all as it should be. Somewhere it was not a matter merely involving human beings, for human beings were all the same and nothing was changed if one of them melted into another, or one of them sat in another's place—no, the world was not ordered according to good and evil men, but according to good and evil forces of some kind.

He looked furiously at Teltscher, who was performing conjuring tricks with his knife and fork, and now announced that he would extract a knife from Mother Hentjen's bodice. She started back with a shriek, but already Teltscher was holding up the knife between his thumb and first finger: " Mother Hentjen, Mother Hentjen, fancy you carrying things like that about in your bodice! " Then he proposed to hypnotize her and she became petrified at the mere suggestion. That was past the limit, and Esch let fly at Teltscher: " You should be locked up." " That's a new trick," said Teltscher. Esch growled: " Hypnotism is against the law." " An interesting chap," said Teltscher, jerking his chin towards Esch, and by this gesture inviting Frau Hentjen also to find the interesting chap a source of amusement; but she was still petrified with fear and mechanically fingered her coiffure. Esch silently digested the success of his intervention to rescue Mother Hentjen, and was satisfied. Yes, he had let one of them go, that man Nentwig, but it wouldn't happen a second time; even if it wasn't a matter of the individual, and even if people melted into one another, so that one fellow couldn't be told from the next; the wrong done existed apart from the doer, and it was the wrong alone that had to be expiated.

When later he accompanied Teltscher to the Alhambra he felt light-hearted. He had acquired a new kind of knowledge. And he almost felt sorry for Teltscher. And also for Bertrand. And even for Nentwig.

He had now managed at last to extort from Gernerth a guarantee of a hundred marks a month from the receipts in consideration of his collabora-tion—what would he have had to live on otherwise?—but the very first evening brought him in no less than seven marks. If that continued his revenue for the month would be doubled. Frau Hentjen had steadfastly refused to attend the opening performance, and next day at lunch-time Esch told her excitedly of its success. When he reached the most inter-esting, one might almost say the crucial, point of his narrative, and told how Teltscher had ripped up one of the girls' tights and only loosely tacked it together again, so that during the wrestling it could not help bursting at a certain prominent protuberance, and went on to say that this incident would be repeated evening after evening; while at the very memory of it he still found himself so overcome by laughter that repeatedly he had to help out his words with dumb show, suddenly Frau Hentjen got up and said she had had enough. It was scandalous that a man whom she had taken to be a decent fellow, a man who once had followed a respectable occupation, should sink so low. She withdrew into the kitchen.

Quite taken aback, Esch remained where he was and dried his eyes, still wet with laughter. In one corner of his heart he had a feeling of guilt, and in that corner he admitted that Mother Hentjen was right; the bursting tights on the stage were vaguely akin to the knives which no longer ought to be thrown there; yet Mother Hentjen certainly did not have the faintest suspicion of this, and her anger was really incomprehensible. He had a feeling of respect for her, he had no wish to swear at her as he did at that fool Lohberg, yet she would certainly have got on better with Lohberg, for as a matter of fact he wasn't so refined as Lohberg. He contemplated the portrait of Herr Hentjen over the mantelpiece to see whether it had any resemblance to Lohberg, and when he had looked long enough at the features of the late restaurant-keeper they did actually melt into those of the Mannheim tobacconist. Yes, wherever one looked it seemed that one figure melted into another and that one could not even distinguish the living from the dead. Nobody was what he thought he was; a man imagined he was a chap with his feet planted firmly on the earth, pocketing his seven marks a night and going wherever he pleased; and in reality he was just sometimes in one place, and sometimes in another, and even when he made a sacrifice it was not himself who made it. An irresistible desire overcame him to produce some proof that this was not so and that it could not be so, and even if it was impossible to prove it to anybody else he was resolved to show that woman in there that he wasn't to be confused either with Herr Lohberg or with Herr Hentjen. Without further ado he went through to the kitchen and said to Frau Hentjen that she mustn't forget the wine auction at Saint-Goar next Friday. " You'll get plenty to keep you company without me," responded Frau Hentjen from the hearth. Her opposition exasperated him. What did this woman want from him? Must he only say things to her that she herself prescribed and wanted to hear? He could not help thinking of the orchestrion, which anybody could set going. And yet she couldn't stand the orchestrion. If the kitchenmaid hadn't been there, for two pins he would simply have fallen on her as she stood there by the hearth, to convince her of his existence. So he simply said: " I've arranged everything; we take the train to Bacharach, then the steamer to Saint-Goar. We'll arrive there about eleven o'clock. in time for the auction.

In the afternoon we can walk up to the Lorelei." She stiffened a little under the firmness of his decision, yet she tried to give her reply a mocking inflection: " Great plans, Herr Esch." Esch was now sure of himself. " Only a beginning, Mother Hentjen: by the end of next week I expect to have made a hundred marks." Whistling to himself he left the kitchen.

In the restaurant he looked again through the newspapers he had brought with him and marked in red pencil the notices of the opening performance. When he found no word of it in *The People's Guardian* he felt irritated. Yes, they could let a comrade and friend of theirs who had sacrificed himself lie in prison. But they couldn't put in a measly little report of the wrestling performance. Here, too, things must be set in order. He felt within him the strength required for it and the faith that he would succeed in mastering and resolving the chaos in which everything was so painfully entangled, in which friend and foe, sullen and yet resigned, were so inextricably involved.

As he was walking through the theatre during the interval he suddenly caught sight of Nentwig, and he started so violently that it brought to his mind a phrase, " struck to the heart." Nentwig was sitting with four other men at a table, and one of the wrestlers, a bath-robe flung over her tights, was sitting with them. The bath-robe gaped and Nentwig was occupied in widening the opening by adroit movements of his pudgy hands. Esch walked past with his head averted, but the girl called out to him, so that he had to turn round. " Hallo, Herr Esch, what are you doing here? " he heard Nentwig's voice. Esch hesitated: then he said briefly: " 'Evening." Nentwig did not feel the rebuff, but lifted his glass to him, while the girl said: " You can have my chair, Herr Esch. I must go back to the stage now." Nentwig, who had been drinking, held Esch's hand firmly clasped, and while he poured out a glass of wine for him looked up at him with a sentimental, vinous gaze. " No, fancy meeting like this, it's quite an unexpected pleasure." Esch said that he too was needed on the stage, and Nentwig, still holding his hand, gurgled with laughter: " Aha! going to see the ladies behind the scenes. I'll come too, I'll come too." Esch tried to make Nentwig understand that he was here on business. At last Nentwig grasped it: " Oh? So you're employed here? A good post? " Esch's vanity would not allow him to admit this. No, he wasn't employed here; he was a partner in the concern. " Think of that, think of that," said Nentwig in astonishment; " a good business, a nice little business, obviously a nice little business "—he looked round at the well-packed hall—" and he forgets his good old friend Nentwig, who would always be glad to share in a thing like that." He became quite alert: " Who caters for the wine, Esch? " Esch explained that he had nothing to do with the catering; the proprietor looked after that. " Hm, but all the rest "—Nentwig made a grand comprehensive gesture embracing the hall and the stage—" you're concerned in all that? Come, drink a glass of wine anyway," and Esch could not avoid clinking glasses with Nentwig, and must shake hands with Nentwig's companions too, and drink to them. In spite of the cunning with which Nentwig had cornered him he could not summon up the hate he ought to have felt against Nentwig. He tried to bring to his mind again the sins of the head clerk; he did not succeed; there had been something fishy in the balance sheet, something very fishy, and Esch sat up a little straighter so as to keep his eye on the one policeman in the hall. But Nentwig's guilt had grown so strangely shadowy and contourless that Esch became aware at once of the senselessness of his intentions, and somewhat awkwardly and a little ashamed of himself he put out his hand for his wine-glass. Meanwhile Nentwig gazed with swimming eyes at his good old book-keeper, and it seemed to Esch as if along with those swimming eyes the whole plump form of Nentwig was dissolving into indeterminacy. This vinegar faker had treacherously accused him of erroneous book-keeping, had tried to deprive him of his livelihood and his existence, and would always go on conspiring against him. Yet one could hardly feel angry with him now. From the inextricable coil of happenings an arm projected, an arm with a threatening dagger in its hand, but if one were to discover that it was Nentwig's arm the whole thing would turn into a stupid and almost sordid episode. Death dealt by the hand of a Nentwig could scarcely even be called murder, and a sentence pronounced over Nentwig would be nothing but the shabbiest form of revenge for a mistake in book-keeping that was not a mistake at all. No, there was little point in handing over a head clerk to justice, for it was not a matter of striking down a hand, even if that hand held the threatening dagger, it was a matter of striking a blow at the whole thing, or at least at the head of the offence. Something inside Esch told him: " A man who sacrifices himself must be decent," and he decided to take no further notice of Nentwig. The fat little man had again sunk back into his drunken doze, and when

the strains of *The Gladiators' March* began, to which the wrestlers,
under Teltscher's direction, now came marching on to the stage, Nentwig
did not notice that Esch had disappeared.

When Esch walked into the manager's office Gernerth was sitting
with a glass of beer before him and lamenting: " A fine life this, a fine
life! . . . " Oppenheimer was toddling up and down wagging his head,
indeed his whole body wagged: " Can't see what there is to upset you
so much." Gernerth's notebook was lying before him: " The taxes
simply eat everything up. Why are we toiling and slaving here? To pay
the taxes! " They could hear the resounding smack of sweating women's
bodies coming to grips on the stage, and Esch felt indignant that this
man sitting here should talk of toiling and slaving, merely because he
was making calculations in a notebook. Gernerth went on with his
lament: " The children must go away for a holiday; that costs money
. . . where am I to get it? " Herr Oppenheimer evinced sympathy:
" Children are a blessing and children are a trial; don't you worry too
much, it'll come all right." Esch felt sorry for Gernerth, a good fellow,
Gernerth; all the same the affairs of the world became confused again
when you reflected that out there on the stage a pair of tights must
presently burst so that Gernerth's children might go away for a holiday.
Somewhere or other there was cause for Mother Hentjen's disgust at
the whole business, though not where she imagined it to be. Esch himself
could not tell where it lay; perhaps it was simply the muddle and confusion that filled him with disgust and rage. He went out; in the wings
some of the wrestlers were standing about, their bodies smelling of
sweat; to clear a passage for himself Esch seized them from behind by
the thick arms or by the breasts, hugging them tightly, until one or two
began to laugh wantonly. Then he stepped on to the stage and took
his place as clerk at the so-called jury bench. Teltscher, the referee's
whistle between his teeth, was lying on the floor peering sharply under
the arched body of one girl, who was resisting the efforts of another to
flatten her out, efforts ostensibly great, but only ostensibly, of course,
for the girl underneath was the German representative who was bound
to free herself forthwith by a patriotic upward heave from ignominious
captivity. And although Esch knew by heart this prearranged farce he
experienced a feeling of relief when the almost beaten wrestler got
on to her feet again: and yet he was filled with indignant pity for her
opponent when Irmentraud Kroff now sprang upon her and, amid the

patriotic acclamations of the audience, pressed the shoulders of the
enemy against the mat.

When Frau Hentjen got up the dawn was just breaking. She opened
the window to see how the day promised. The sky arched clear and
cloudless over the dark, grey yard, which lay below her in motionless
silence, a little rectangle within dark walls. The clean washtubs from
last washing day were still standing down there. A cool wind, imprisoned
between the walls, smelt of the city. She trailed up to the kitchenmaid's
room and knocked at the door; she didn't intend to leave without her
breakfast; on the top of everything else that would be the last straw.
Then she carefully began her toilet and drew on the brown-silk dress.
When Esch called for her she was sitting morosely at her morning coffee
in the restaurant. She said morosely: " Let's go," but at the house
door it occurred to her that Esch too might want some coffee; it was
got for him hastily in the kitchen, and he drank it standing. The sun
was already up, but the bright strips of sunshine that lay on the cobbles
between the long shadows of the house walls did not improve the temper
of either. Esch merely announced curtly and abruptly: " I'll get the
tickets," and then: " Platform five." In the carriage they sat side by
side in silence; but when they reached Bonn he leaned out, inquired
whether there were any fresh rolls to be had, and bought her one. She
ate it morosely and resentfully. After Coblenz, when the passengers as
usual crowded to the window to admire the Rhineland scenery, Frau
Hentjen too felt moved to follow their example. But Esch did not budge
from his place; he knew the neighbourhood so well that he was sick
of it, and besides he had not proposed to indicate the beauties of nature
to Frau Hentjen until they were on the steamer. Now he felt annoyed
at her for anticipating this pleasure and for listening to the edifying
explanations of the other people in the compartment. So every tunnel
that interrupted the view was a salve to his ill humour, and his
irritation mounted so high that at Ober-Wesel he peremptorily called
her away from the window: " I had a job myself once in Ober-Wesel."
Frau Hentjen looked out; there was nothing of interest to be seen in
the station. She replied politely: " Yes, you've been in lots of places."
Esch was not yet finished: " A wretched job it was, I stuck it out all
the same for a few months on account of a girl in the place . . . Hulda,
her name was." Then he could just get out and look for her, was Frau

Hentjen's furious rejoinder, he needn't trouble himself on her account.
But presently they arrived at Bacharach, and for the first time in his
life Esch experienced the helpless feeling which descends on the pleasure-
tripper who, standing in a railway station, has a vacant hour in front
of him. According to his programme they should have had a lunch on
the boat, but simply to cover his embarrassment he now suggested that
they should go to a restaurant that he knew. But as they were walking
through the narrow streets of the town which lay so quiet and peaceful
in the clear morning light, suddenly in front of one of the timbered
houses Mother Hentjen exclaimed: " That's where I would like to live,
that would be my ideal." Perhaps it was the flowers in the window-boxes
that touched her, perhaps it was simply the feeling of release that often
comes over people when they are on unfamiliar ground, or perhaps her
bad temper had simply exhausted itself—in any case the world had
become brighter; at peace with each other they gazed at everything,
climbed up as far as the ruins of the church, of which they could not
make very much, hurried too soon to the landing-stage for fear of missing
the boat, and did not mind in the least when they found that they must
wait for half-an-hour.

On the boat, it is true, they quarrelled more than once, for Frau
Hentjen's pride could not endure for long that Esch alone should know
the neighbourhood. She racked her memory for names of well-known
places, began in her turn to make conjectures and to provide information,
and was deeply insulted when he scrupulously refused to let any error
pass. Yet even this could not cloud their good humour, and, arrived at
Saint-Goar, they were sorry they had to leave the boat, indeed for a
moment they could not think why they were landing at all. The business
aspect of their journey had become in some way indifferent, and when
at the auction-rooms they learned that the sale of the cheap wines was
already finished it did not disturb them, but was almost like a deliverance from an obligation, for it seemed far more important to them that
they should be in time for the next journey of the ferry-boat, which
with outstretched sail was making for the sunny and alluring shores of
Goarshausen on the other bank. And when Esch, aping the precision
of a methodical business man, noted the prices the wines had reached
at the auction " for future reference," as he said, this affectation of
commercial zeal was a sham and gave him a queer kind of bad conscience
which made him diligently ignore the more favourable prices, and yet

on the other hand depressed him so acutely that when he was sitting in the ferry-boat he suddenly entered the missing prices in his list from memory, meanwhile regarding Frau Hentjen with a hostile glare.

Frau Hentjen sat on the sun-steeped wooden seat of the ferry-boat and contentedly dipped one finger into the water, very carefully, however, so as not to wet her cream-coloured lace mittens, and if she could have had her will she would simply have gone on sailing from one bank of the Rhine to the other, for the curiously light feeling of dizziness induced by the sight of water obliquely streaming past her was a pleasant one. But the day was already too far advanced, and it was pleasant enough under the trees in the inn garden on the bank of the river. They ate fish and drank wine, and smoking his cigar Esch revolved the question of establishing closer relations, earnestly considering whether Mother Hentjen, who sat there stout and magnificent, might not even expect it. Certainly she wasn't like other women, and so he began very cautiously to speak about Lohberg, who had really moved him to take this lovely trip, and he began to praise Lohberg, so that from this exordium he might in decorous terms lead up to an exposition of the vegetarian view of true love; but Frau Hentjen, who saw with anxiety where he was heading, broke off the conversation, and although she herself felt tired, and would rather have rested in peace, she referred him to his programme, according to which they must now climb up to the Lorelei. Esch felt indignant; he had done his best to speak like Lohberg and without effect. Evidently he was not yet refined enough for her.

He got up and paid the bill. While they were passing through the inn garden he noticed the summer visitors; among them were pretty young women and girls; and suddenly Esch could not understand why he was attached to this elderly woman, stately as was her appearance in the brown-silk dress. The girls were in light, gay, summer dresses, and Mother Hentjen's brown silk had become somewhat dusty and draggled on the roads. Nevertheless there seemed to be a certain amount of justice in it; one had a conscience, after all, and if one thought of Martin pining for the sun in his cell, after sacrificing himself for a base, ungrateful crowd, then one's own lot, all things considered, was still a long way too fortunate! And while he ploughed through the dust of the main road with Frau Hentjen, instead of lying in the grass with one of those pretty girls, it actually seemed to him quite fair that this woman should not feel any gratitude for his sacrifice. A man who sacrificed himself must be decent. He considered whether he could inform her with propriety that it was a sacrifice, but then he remembered Lohberg and refrained: a man of refinement suffered in silence. Some time or other, perhaps when it was too late, she would be bound to realize it. A painful agitation overcame him, and walking in front he took off first his coat and then his waistcoat. Mother Hentjen regarded with repulsion the two large wet patches where his shirt stuck to his shoulder-blades, and when after turning into a wood-path he remained standing and she caught up on him, she suddenly smelt the warm odour of his body and started back in alarm. Esch said good-humouredly: " Well, what is it, Mother Hentjen? " " Put on your jacket," she said severely, but she added in a maternal tone: " It's cold here, quite cold, you'll get a chill." " It's quite warm when you're walking," he replied, " you should let out a hook or two at the neck of your dress." She shook her head with the old-fashioned little hat perched on it; no, she wouldn't think of doing that, a fine sight she would be! " Well, there's nobody to see us here," said Esch, and this sudden open declaration that they were alone and together, in a seclusion in which they need not be ashamed before each other because nobody could see them, confused her. All at once she found it understandable that, as if in confidence, he should reveal his sweat to her; and if she still felt disgust she felt it no longer on the surface; it was dulled and muffled, as it were, hidden away; and even her fear of his strong white teeth now left her, and she accepted it as part of this strangely permitted and shameless freedom when he bared them laughingly again: " Forward, Mother Hentjen; it's no use saying you're tired." She felt offended that he should openly doubt whether she could keep up with him, and, a little short of breath, and supported on her fragile pink parasol, she again set herself in motion. Esch now remained by her side and at the steeper places attempted to assist her. She regarded him suspiciously at first, fearing a brazen approach to familiarity, and only after some hesitation finally took his arm, to relinquish this support immediately, however, indeed to push it away, as soon as she saw another traveller, or even a child, approaching.

They climbed slowly, and when with panting lungs they made a halt, gradually they became aware of the things round about them: the whitish clay of the wood-path cracked with the heat, the faded green plants sticking out of the dry soil, the roots which with their dusty fibres wandered over the narrow footpath, the dry, withered odour of the woods almost breathless under the heat, the shrubs among whose foliage hung black, lifeless berries, ready to shrivel at the touch of autumn. They took all this in, yet could not have described it, but presently they reached the first seat commanding a view and beheld the valley outspread before them, and although they were still a long way from the top of the Lorelei Rock it seemed to them, as they sank upon the seat, that they were already at their goal, from which they could drink in the scenery; and Frau Hentjen carefully smoothed out her dress so that her weight might not crease it. The air was so still that the sound of voices at the landing-stage and in the beer-gardens of Saint-Goar came over to them, as well as the drowsy, dull thud of the ferry-boat against the pier; and the unusualness of these impressions made them both a little uncomfortable. Frau Hentjen regarded the hearts and initials cut all over the bench and in a strained voice asked Esch whether he too had immortalized himself here with his Hulda from Ober-Wesel. When he jestingly began to look for his initials she told him he needn't bother: for whether in visible form or not, a man would always find his filthy past wherever he went. But Esch, who did not want to give up his jest, replied that maybe he might find her name too enclosed within a heart, and this made her really angry; what would he read next into people's words? thank God her past was pure and she could stand her ground with any young girl. Of course a man who all his life had been constantly running after loose women wouldn't understand that. And Esch, stricken to the heart by this accusation, felt common and despicable at having prized her less highly than the young girls in the inn garden, most of whom were probably unworthy to lace Mother Hentjen's shoes. And it did him good to know that here was a human being whose character was decided and unequivocal, a human being who knew her right hand from her left, who knew virtue from vice. For a moment he had the feeling that here was the longed-for rock, rising clear and steadfast out of the universal confusion, to which one might cling in security; but then the memory of Herr Hentjen and his portrait in the restaurant came to disturb him, and he could not get rid of the thought that somewhere a heart must be engraved that contained her initials and Herr Hentjen's lovingly interlaced. He did not trust himself to touch on this, however, but merely asked where her home had been originally. She replied curtly that she came from Westphalia; besides, that was nobody's business but her own. And as she could not

reach her coiffure she patted her hat instead. No, and she couldn't stand
people who stuck their noses into other people's affairs either, and it was
only men like Esch, who were incapable of imagining that some people
mightn't have a shady past, who would do that kind of thing. Wastrels,
who when they couldn't have a woman for themselves did their best to
fasten a past love affair on to her. In her indignation she shifted a little
farther away from him, and Esch, whose thoughts were still circling round
Herr Hentjen, was now certain that she must have been very unhappy.
His face took on an expression of bitter sorrow. Quite possible that
she had been driven into her marriage with kicks and blows. So he said
that he hadn't intended his question to be offensive. And, accustomed
to comfort by physical caresses women who cried or otherwise gave signs
of being unhappy, he took her hand and fondled it. Perhaps it was the
extraordinary stillness of everything round her, perhaps however it was
only her exhaustion, but she offered no resistance. She had expressed
her point of view, but her last words had fallen from her lips like a succession of meaningless sounds which she herself scarcely recognized, and
now she felt quite empty, incapable even of feeling repulsion or disgust.
She looked at the outspread valley without seeing it, and knew no longer
where she was. All those mechanical years in which her life had been
passed between the buffet in the restaurant and a few familiar streets
shrank to a tiny point, and it seemed to her that she had sat here for ever
in this unfamiliar place. The world was so unfamiliar that it was impossible
to grasp it, and nothing now connected her with it, nothing but the thin
twig with the pointed leaves which hung over the back of the seat and
which the fingers of her left hand occasionally touched. Esch asked himself whether he should kiss her, but he felt no desire to do so, and he
reflected also that it would not be refined.

So they sat on in silence. The sun was declining in the west and shone
on their faces, but Mother Hentjen did not feel its heat on her face, nor
the smarting of her stiff, reddened, dust-covered skin. And it almost
seemed as if this dreamlike, semi-conscious state were about to enclose
Esch too and clasp him in its embrace, for although he saw the lengthen-
ing and broadening mountain shadows in the valley as an alluring promise
of coolness he felt reluctant to move, and only with hesitation did he at
last take up his waistcoat, one of whose pockets contained his great silver
watch. It was time to go, and Frau Hentjen, now quite will-less, obeyed
his command. While descending she rested heavily on his arm, and he

carried the flimsy pink parasol over his shoulder; his waistcoat and jacket dangled from it. To ease the exertion of walking for her he undid two hooks on her high-necked dress, and Mother Hentjen submitted to it, nor did she push him away when other pedestrians approached; she did not see them. The skirt of her brown-silk dress trailed in the dust of the main road, and when in the station Esch deposited her on a seat while he went to quench his thirst she sat there helpless and will-less, waiting for him to return. He brought a glass of beer for her too, and she drank it at his bidding. In the dark compartment of the train he made a pillow for her head on his shoulder. He did not know whether she was asleep or awake, and she herself scarcely knew it. Her head rolled to and fro awkwardly on his hard shoulder. To his attempts to draw her to him her thick-set body in its casing of whalebone put up a stiff resistance, and the hatpins on her nodding head threatened his face. Impatient now, he pushed her hat back, which, sliding downwards along with her coiffure, gave her a drunken look. Her silk dress smelt of dust and heat; only now and then was one aware of the delicate lavender scent that still remained in the folds. Then he kissed her on the cheek as it slid past his mouth, and finally he took her round, heavy head in his hands and drew it to him. She responded to his kiss with dry, thick lips, somewhat like an animal which presses its muzzle against a window-pane.

Not until she was standing in the entrance hall did she find herself back in her world again. She gave Esch a push on the chest and with uncertain steps made her way to her place behind the buffet. There she sat down and stared out into the restaurant, which seemed to lie before her in a mist. At last she recognized Wrobek sitting at the nearest table and said: " Good-evening, Herr Wrobek." But she did not see that Esch had followed her into the restaurant, nor did she notice that he was among the last to leave. When he shouted good-night to her she replied non-committally: " Good-evening, gentlemen." Nevertheless as he stepped out of the restaurant Esch felt a strange and almost proud sensation: that of being Mother Hentjen's lover.

III

When a man has once kissed a woman the train of consequences follows inevitably and unalterably. One can hasten or delay it, but one cannot escape a law of nature. Esch knew that. Yet his imagination balked at picturing the course of his relationship to Mother Hentjen, and so he was relieved to have Teltscher beside him when he entered the restaurant next day at noon; that made it easier for him to meet Mother Hentjen, and simplified everything.

Teltscher had hit upon a new idea; they should get hold of a negress for the wrestling; that would make the final rounds peculiarly attractive; she could be called the " Black Star of Africa," and after two indecisive rounds would finally be beaten by the German. Esch was rather apprehensive that Teltscher would hold forth about this African scheme to Mother Hentjen, and he was not mistaken, for hardly was he inside the door before Teltscher paraded his new idea. "Frau Hentjen, our Esch is going to find a negress for us." She did not at first understand, not even when Esch truthfully declared that he didn't know where he was to get hold of a negress. No, Mother Hentjen simply refused to listen, taking refuge in biting sarcasm: " One woman more or less, that makes no difference to him." Teltscher jovially smacked him on the knee: " Of course, a man like him has so many women running after him, there's nobody that can put his nose out of joint." Esch glanced up at Herr Hentjen's portrait; there was a man who had put his nose out of joint. " Yes, that's the kind of fellow Esch is," repeated Teltscher. To Frau Hentjen this was a confirmation of her own judgment, and she sought to strengthen her alliance with Teltscher; she regarded the short bristles of Esch's hair, which were like a stiff dark brush above the yellowish skin of his head, and she felt that to-day she needed an ally. Turning her back on Esch she praised up Teltscher: it was only to be expected that a man who thought something of himself should avoid meddling with these women and should rather hand the job over to a man like Esch. Esch retorted huffily that most men would fall over each other to get jobs of that kind, but very few could handle them. And he despised Teltscher, who had not even managed to keep Ilona for himself. Still, she would soon be beyond anybody's reach. " Well, Herr Esch," said Frau Hentjen, " why don't you get on with it? Your negress is waiting;

away you go." Very well, he would go, he returned, and as soon as he had eaten his dinner he got up and left the somewhat disconcerted Frau Hentjen to Teltscher's society.

He dawdled about for a while. He had nothing to do. It annoyed him that he had left Frau Hentjen alone with Teltscher, and finally he was driven to return. It was hardly likely that Teltscher was still there, but he wanted to make sure. The restaurant was empty, nor could he find anybody in the kitchen. So Teltscher had gone, and there was nothing to hinder him from also taking himself off; but he knew that at this hour Frau Hentjen usually stayed in her own room, and suddenly he realized that that was why he had come back. He hesitated a moment and then quietly mounted the wooden stairs. Without knocking he entered the room. Mother Hentjen was sitting by the window darning stockings; when she caught sight of him she uttered a faint shriek and stood petrified. He went straight up to her, pressed her down into her chair again and kissed her on the mouth. She twisted and turned her heavy body in her efforts to evade him, and gasped hoarsely: " Go away . . . you've no business here." More keenly than his violence she resented the fact that he had come into her room, he, fresh from the arms of a Czech or a negress, into her room that no man had yet entered. She was fighting for her room. But he held her firmly, and at length with thick, dry lips she began to return his kisses, perhaps only as a concession to persuade him to go, for between the kisses she kept repeating with set teeth: " You've no business here." Finally she implored merely: " Not here." Esch, weary of the grim struggle, remembered that this was a woman to be treated with consideration and respect. If she wanted to change the scene of action, why not? He let her go, and she urged him to the door. When they were in the lobby he said gruffly: "Where, then?" She did not understand, for she believed that he would go now. Esch, with his face close to hers, again asked: " Where, then? " And since she made no move and gave no answer he grasped her again to push her back into the room. She was aware only that she must defend that room. Helplessly she gazed round, saw the door leading into the parlour, had a sudden hope that the primness of the parlour would bring him back to his senses and to decent behaviour, and indicated the door with her eyes; he made way for her, but followed with his hand on her shoulder as if she were a captive.

When they were inside she said uncertainly: " There, now perhaps you'll be sensible, Herr Esch," and strained towards the window to fling back the shutters. But he had seized her from behind, and Frau Hentjen could not move from the spot. She tried to wrest herself free, but they swayed and stumbled among the nuts, so that they almost fell. The nuts cracked under their feet, and as Frau Hentjen, anxious to save her stores, struggled backwards towards the alcove in search of firm footing and something she could get a purchase on, she had a momentary flash of dreamlike awareness, as if she were walking in her sleep: was it not her own doing that the man was being enticed into that corner? But that thought only made her angrier, and she hissed: " Go to your negress . . . you can get round these sluts, but you won't get round me." She clawed at the corner of the alcove, but instead caught hold of the curtain; the wooden rings on the curtain-pole rattled slightly, and being afraid of damaging the good curtain she let go, so that Esch was able to force her into the dark corner where the twin beds stood. He was still behind her and had recaptured her hands and pulled them close to him so that she could not but feel his excitement. Whether for that reason or because the sight of the marriage beds reduced her to defenceless immobility, she went limp under his passionate aggression. And as he tore impatiently at her clothing, and she was afraid that now her underlinen would be damaged, she herself helped him as a criminal might help the hangman, and it filled him almost with horror to note how smoothly things now took their course and in what a matter-of-fact way Mother Hentjen, when they fell on to the bed, laid herself on her back to receive him. And it filled him with a horror still more profound to see her lying rigid and motionless, as if submitting to a familiar duty, as if she were merely recapitulating an old and familiar act of submission, without interest, without enjoyment. Only her round head rolled to and fro on the bedcover as if in persistent negation. He felt the warmth of her body and whipped up his own lust to provoke and overmaster hers. He clutched her head between his hands as if to squeeze out of it the thoughts that were congealed within it, refusing to flow out to him, and his mouth followed the unlovely lines of her heavy cheeks and her low forehead that remained motionless and unresponsive, as unresponsive as the masses for whom Martin had sacrificed himself and who were still unfree. Perhaps Ilona might have the same feeling about Korn's massive insensitivity, and for a moment he was glad to think that his sacrifice was the same as hers, and that it was right, and that it was done for her and for redemption into righteousness. Oh, to release oneself, to strip oneself more and more, to annihilate oneself with all the sin that one had accumulated and bore about, yet to release her too whose mouth one sought for, to annihilate Time that had her in its grip, Time that had embedded itself in these ageing cheeks; oh, the desire he had to annihilate the woman who had lived in Time, to bid her be born again timeless, motionless and perforce at one with him! His seeking mouth had found hers, that was now pressed against his like the muzzle of an animal against a pane of glass, and Esch was enraged because she kept her soul tightly enclosed behind her set teeth so that he should not possess it. And when with a hoarse sound she opened her lips at last, he felt an ecstasy such as he had never yet experienced in a woman's arms, he flowed boundlessly into her, yearning to enter into possession of her who was no longer a woman to him but a re-won heritage wrested from the unknown, the matrix of life, annihilating his ego by transcending its confines till it was feature-less and submerged in its own enlargement. For the man who wills Goodness and Righteousness wills thereby the Absolute, and it was revealed to Esch for the first time that the goal is not the appeasement of lust but an absolute oneness exalted far above its immediate, sordid and even trivial occasion, a conjoint trance, itself timeless and so annihilating time; and that the rebirth of man is as still and serene as the universal spirit that yet contracts and closes round man when once his ecstatic will has compelled it, until he attains his sole birthright: deliverance and redemption.

How little it mattered, after all, that one was Mother Hentjen's lover! There are many men who think that life is centred in the existence of some particular woman. Esch had always known how to keep himself free from that prejudice. Especially now, even although Frau Hentjen often strangely usurped his thoughts. Especially now. His life was directed to greater and higher aims.

Near the New Market he came to a standstill in front of a book-shop. His eye fell on a picture of the Statue of Liberty stamped in gilt on green linen; beneath it was the title, *America To-day and To-morrow*. He had bought but few books in his life, and he was surprised at himself for going into the shop. Its smooth counters and the orderliness of its rectangular books reminded him vaguely of a tobacconist's. He would have liked to linger and talk, but since no one encouraged him he merely paid for the book and came out with a package in his hand that he did not know what to do with. A present for Frau Hentjen? She would certainly have not the slightest interest in it, and yet there was some inexplicable connection between her and his purchase. In his perplexity he came again to a standstill in front of the shop. Behind the glass pane on a line hung a bright array of foreign phrase-books, and on their covers waved the flags of their respective nations as if to cheer on aspiring students. Esch betook himself to his midday meal in the restaurant.

One is shy of producing an unsuitable gift, and so Esch carried his into the window-seat; that was where he always read the newspaper after dinner, so he might as well sit there with his book. It didn't take long for Mother Hentjen to call across the empty room: " Well, Herr Esch, of course you can afford to sit down and read books in the middle of the day." " Yes," he answered, " I'll show it you," got up and brought it to her at the buffet. " What's it for? " she said as he held the book out; he indicated by a jerk of the head that she was to look at it; she turned over a page here and there, regarded one or two pictures with closer attention, and simply handed the book back with a " very nice." Esch was disappointed; he had indeed suspected that she wouldn't be interested, for what did a woman like her know of the greater and higher aims of life! None the less he remained standing, expecting something else to happen . . . but all that happened was a remark from Mother Hentjen: " I suppose you're thinking of spending the whole afternoon over that stuff? " Esch retorted: " I'm not thinking of anything," and in a huff carried the book to his own room to read it in peace. And he came to the conclusion that he would emigrate by himself. By himself, all alone. Yet he could not help assuming again and again that his study of the American work was to benefit not only himself but Mother Hentjen.

He read a portion of it every day. At first he had contented himself with the illustrations, and now when he thought of America it seemed to him that the trees there were not green, the meadows not brightly coloured, the sky no longer blue, but that all American life was deployed against a polished and elegant chiaroscuro as in the brownish grey photographs, or against the sharp contours of the delicately limned pen-drawings. Later on, however, he became absorbed in the text. The recurring statistics certainly bored him, but he was too conscientious to skip them and succeeded in learning a good deal by heart. He was deeply interested in the American police system and the law courts, which, the book averred, were organized in the service of democratic freedom, so that any man able to read a book intelligently could gather that in America no cripples were thrown into jail at the bidding of wicked shipping firms; it would be as well therefore for Martin to go with him. Esch turned over the pages at random, and strangely enough the photograph of the giant liner at the landing-stage in New York revealed Mother Hentjen in her brown-silk dress, the light-pink parasol in her hands, leaning over the railing watching the swarm of strangers, while Martin with his crutch sat on a chest, and the air was filled with syllables of the English language.

And thoroughgoing as he was, Esch decided after some hesitation to visit once more the book-shop in which he had felt so much at home. Making light of the fresh expense he purchased the English phrase-book with the inviting Union Jack and forthwith set himself to learn the English words, behind each of which he saw the word " Liberty " in the elegant half-tones of a silky and glossy photograph, as if in this one word all that had ever existed in the past and been expressed in the old language must now be resolved and redeemed. He even made up his mind that they must speak English to each other, and that Mother Hentjen must be instructed in English to that end. But with his healthy contempt for all reverie he did not stop short at merely wishing for freedom: his profits were accumulating, and although the receipts for the last few days of the wrestling had fallen off somewhat, he had in any case a clear surplus of about two hundred marks, which he now definitely set aside as the nucleus of his travelling expenses; hence he could take action, he could escape from his prison, he could begin his new life. He was often drawn nowadays to the Cathedral. When he was on the steps overlooking Cathedral Square, and English-speaking tourists chanced to appear, it was like a breath of freedom invigorating him and caressing his brow as he stood with bared head in the warm summer wind. The very streets of Cologne began to take on another aspect, one might even say a more innocent aspect, and Esch regarded them with kindliness and almost with a hint of malicious triumph. Once he was on the other side, across the sea, they too would have a different look. And if he ever came back he would let the English-speaking guide show him over the Cathedral.—

After the performance he waited for Teltscher; the air was soft and
rainy as they walked through the night. Esch stopped suddenly: " Look
here, Teltscher, you've always been boasting about an American engagement: it's time you did something about it." Teltscher loved to discuss
his grand prospects: " If I've a mind to, I can get as many engagements
over there as I want." Esch dissented: " With your knife-throwing
stunt . . . h'm, well . . . don't you think wrestling or something of
that kind would go better over there? " Teltscher laughed scornfully:
" You're surely not thinking of taking our girls over! " " Well, why
not? " " You're an idiot, Esch, if you would take over that kind of
stuff. In any case . . . over there they expect real sporting turns, but
the kind of thing our girls do . . ." He laughed again. Esch suggested:
" But couldn't we get a good team together? " " Nonsense, people over
there aren't going to wait till we arrive," said Teltscher, " and where
could you find trained girls here? " . . . he reflected . . . " if these cows of
ours were anything to look at there might possibly be something in it.
But only in Mexico or South America." Esch did not grasp his meaning
at first, and Teltscher was provoked by his stupidity: " They're always
hard up for women out there . . . and if the wrestling wasn't a draw
the girls would at least be provided for, and we could keep all the
travelling expenses in our pockets." That seemed obvious enough. After
all, why not South America or Mexico? And the half-tone photographs
in Esch's mind took on a brilliantly coloured Southern luxuriance. Yes,
it was a convincing scheme. Teltscher said: " You've hit on a good
thing this time, Esch. Make it your job to fit out the circus with new
girls worth looking at. I know one or two fellows who could easily
arrange a tour for us over there. And then we'll set sail with the whole
cargo." Esch knew that the proposal savoured abominably of white
slave traffic. But he could ignore that knowledge, for the wrestling
matches were not illicit, and even if they gave any cause for suspicion
what did it matter? that would only pay off a few scores against a police
force that locked up innocent men. A police force that worked in the
cause of freedom and accepted no money from shipping firms wouldn't
need to be scored off. White slave traffic, of course, wasn't very refined,
but after all even Mother Hentjen's business was against her principles.
Nor did Lohberg approve of his shop. And in any case it was better to
take Teltscher to America with the circus than to leave him here throwing
knives. They passed a bored policeman who was patrolling his beat in

the rain, and Esch would have liked to assure him that the police would be none the worse off, for he would deliver Nentwig into their hands sooner or later! Esch was a man who upheld law and order and fulfilled his pledges, even though the other parties were swine. " Police swine," he growled. The wet asphalt shone like a photographic film, dark brown in the light of the yellow lamps, and Esch saw before him the Statue of Liberty whose torch consumed and released all the husks of one's past life, delivering into flame all that was dead and gone—and if that was murder, it was a kind of murder beyond the jurisdiction of the police: murder in the cause of redemption. His decision was taken, and when Teltscher advised him on parting: " And don't forget, it's always blonde girls they want out there, nothing but blonde," he accepted the fact that he was to seek out and provide blonde girls. He had only to settle up his old scores, and then they would set sail with their cargo of blondes. From the lofty deck of the ocean liner they would look down on the swarm of smaller craft. They would cry a farewell to the Old World, a final good-bye. Perhaps the blondes on the ship would strike up a farewell song in chorus, and when the ship on its taut tow-rope glided past the river shores perhaps Ilona would be walking on the bank and would wave a hand, herself a blonde, but rescued from all danger, and the level water would broaden between them.

Esch should really have admitted that his mistress stood on the same plane as himself: for if he kept love in a subordinate place Mother Hentjen ignored it. In that she was his match, although moved by other considerations than his. She regarded love as something so profoundly secret that she scarcely ventured to pronounce the word. She forgot again and again the existence of this lover who was now established and whom she could not prevent from stealing in upon her of an afternoon when she was taking her nap or at night when her last customers had departed, and again and again at his approach she was overwhelmed with petrified astonishment, a state of petrifaction that only began gradually to wear away when the dim parlour and the alcove had received them both: then it dissolved into a feeling of detached isolation, and the dark alcove in which she lay looking up at the ceiling began to float away till soon it seemed no longer a part of her familiar house, but was like a soaring chariot hanging somewhere in infinite space and darkness.

Only then did she realize that somebody else was there beside her, occupied with her, and it was no longer Esch, it was no longer even a man she knew, it was a Someone who had strangely and violently thrust himself into her isolation, and yet could not be reproached for his violence since he was a part of that isolation and could be found only within it, a Someone, quiet and yet threatening, demanding assuagement for his violence, and therefore one had to play the game with him that he demanded, and though the game was compulsory it was yet strangely guiltless, since it was engulfed in isolation and even God shut His eyes to it. But he with whom she shared the bed was little likely to suspect the nature of that isolation, and she was sternly on her guard to keep him from impinging upon it. A profound muteness enveloped him, and she would not let that disconcerting silence be assailed, even should he mistake it for insensibility or stupidity. Silence abolished shame, for shame was born only in speech. What she felt was not bodily lust but release from shame: she was so isolated that, as if alone for all eternity, she could no longer be ashamed of a single fibre in her body. He could not understand her muteness, and yet was disheartened by the shameless silence that invited and submitted to him in brutish immobility. She gave him barely a sigh, and he was all agonized expectation and hope that she would finally let her voice go in a cry of satisfied animal lust. Too often he waited in vain, and then he hated the solicitous crook of the arm with which she invited him to lay down his head and sleep on her plump, unmoved shoulder. But when she sent her lover away it was with hard abruptness, as if she suddenly wanted to annihilate both him and the knowledge he shared with her: she pushed him out through the door, and as he stole down the stairs he could feel her hatred at his back. That gave him an inkling that it was a strange, strange land he had been in, and in spite of himself the knowledge always impelled him back to her again with torment and increasing desire. For even in the bliss of losing himself, of sinking tranced and nameless in the shameless-ness of sex, the desire to overcome the woman kept stubborn vigil, the desire to force her to acknowledge him, to make the present moment flame up in her like a torch that burned up all else, so that in its glare she should be aware of her mate, and out of the silence of night that enveloped everything should let her voice ring out passionately, and say " du " to him and to him alone, as if he were her child. He no longer knew what she looked like, she was beyond beauty and ugliness, beyond youth and age, she was only a silent problem that he was set to master and to resolve.

Although in many respects Esch could not have wished for a better, and even had to admit that it was a lofty kind of love, surpassing ordinary standards, that had laid its spell upon him, yet it always annoyed him, time and again, that whenever he came into the restaurant Mother Hentjen, anxious lest the other customers should suspect something, was so markedly cold to him that against her will she made him conspicuous. Had it not been that he wanted to avoid further notice and even scandal, and had not his cheap and bountiful dinner been in question, he would simply have stayed away. As it was, he made an effort to be compliant and to strike the happy mean in his visits; but he could not manage it, he could not please Mother Hentjen whatever he did: if he appeared in the restaurant she put on a sulky face and obviously wished him gone, and if he stayed away she asked him spitefully if he had perhaps been off with his negress.

Teltscher thought that they could not decently refuse to give Gernerth a chance to share in the South American project. With that the plan would have acquired a certain solidity in Esch's eyes. But Gernerth declined, giving as an excuse his family, which he wanted to have with him when he took on his new contract in autumn. So the windbag Teltscher remained Esch's sole associate. He was certainly not much to depend on, but the project should not be postponed for all that; Esch began his canvassing at once, and set out on the search for women wrestlers fit for export. Perhaps in its course he might actually run across the negress whom they still wanted; that of course would be an extra piece of luck.

He again made his round of the dens and brothels, and if he sometimes felt a slight twinge of conscience in doing so, it was only because Frau Hentjen, if she should find out, would never believe that he devoted himself to such a task out of mere business considerations. So, as a kind of proof of his erotic indifference, as a moral though quite preposterous alibi, he extended his business researches to include the homosexual resorts, resorts which hitherto he had avoided almost apprehensively. Yet he felt vaguely that there must be another reason for his desire to visit them. What took place in them should have left him quite unmoved, and it was really queer, the horror that overcame him when he saw these men dancing with each other, cheek pressed against cheek. Then he

could not help thinking of his first visit to one of those filthy dens when
he was a mere lad at a loose end in the world, a lad who could scarcely
remember his mother, and how he had felt that he wanted to run away
to her the first time that he had caught sight of a male prostitute, tightly
laced and in long skirts, singing obscene songs in a falsetto voice. If he
forced himself to gaze at such abominations again, considering that the
sight of them almost made him vomit, Mother Hentjen would be compelled to realize, in spite of her prudishness, how little pleasure he got
out of his job. God knows, he would rather run to her than haunt such
places, searching for he knew not what, as if he were looking for his lost
innocence. Quite preposterous to think that one might run up against,
say, the chairman of a company, for these street boys were certainly
beneath the notice of a man like that. All the same, with such a queer lot
one had to be prepared for anything. And as in venturous situations one
exercises self-control, Esch did not bash in the painted mugs of these
little manikins when they spoke to him; on the contrary he was on his
best behaviour, treated them to sweet liqueurs, asked how they were
getting on and—if they became confidential—inquired also into their
source of income and the names of their kind uncles. True, he wondered
sometimes why he listened to all their chatter, but he pricked up his ears
when the name of Chairman Bertrand was mentioned; then the vague
picture that he carried in his mind of that great man, a picture scarcely
legible and yet larger than life-size, acquired gradually more colour, took
on strangely tender hues, and became at the same time a little smaller as
it grew more sharp and definite. Bertrand, it seemed, sailed up and down
the Rhine in a motor-yacht, and his crew were very handsome; everything
on this dream-boat was white and blue; once he had come to Cologne
and little Harry had had the great honour of finding favour in his eyes;
they had gone as far as Antwerp in the fairy yacht and in Ostend had
lived like gods; but usually he was too grand to pay any attention to the
kind of boys that came here. His castle stood in a great park in Badenweiler; deer grazed in the meadows and strange flowers scented the air;
he stayed there when he was not in distant lands; nobody had entry to
his castle, and his friends were Englishmen and Indians of fabulous
wealth; he owned a motor-car, and it was so huge that one could sleep
in it at nights. He was richer than the Kaiser.

Esch almost forgot his own work, so powerfully was he possessed by
the desire to find Harry Köhler; and when he succeeded, his heart beat

so fast and he bore himself so respectfully that one might have imagined
he did not know that the small youth was little better than a street boy.
He forgot his hatred, forgot that Martin had to suffer so that this lad
might lead a fine life; yes, he felt almost jealous because to this boy who
was accustomed to fine and well-to-do company he could not offer anything better than a visit to the wrestling performance, which, however,
he affably put at Herr Harry's disposal. But the boy, not in the least
impressed, simply refused with a disgusted " Pah! " so that Esch felt
ashamed of having suggested anything so unseemly; yet as he felt annoyed
too, he said rudely: " Well, I haven't a yacht to invite you to." " How?
What do you mean by that? " was the suspicious, yet strangely gentle
reply. Alfons, the fat, blond musician, who was sitting coatless at the table
in a gaudy silk shirt with rolls of fat beneath it that looked like a woman's
breasts, laughed, showing his white teeth: " He means—you know what
yourself, Harry." Harry looked offended: " I hope you don't intend to
insult anyone, my dear sir." God forbid, Esch replied glibly, that was
far from his thoughts; he was only sorry because he knew that Herr
Harry was used to finer things. With a smile of gentle resignation Harry
waved his hand languidly: " That's past." Alfons patted his arm: " Never
mind, my boy, there's lots here willing to comfort you." Harry shook
his head in gentle melancholy: " One can only love once." This fellow
talked like Lohberg, thought Esch, and he said: " That's true." For
although the Mannheim idiot wasn't very often right, in this case he
seemed to be right, and Esch said again: " Yes, that's true." Harry was
obviously pleased to find one who understood him, and looked at Esch
gratefully, but Alfons, who did not want to hear such sentiments, became
indignant: " And all the friendship we offer you, Harry, means nothing
to you? " Harry shook his head: " What does the little scrap of intimacy
amount to that you call friendship? As if love had anything to do with
friendship and intimacy! " " Well, my boy, you have your own views of
love," said Alfons tenderly. Harry spoke as though from memory: " Love
is great distance." While Alfons replied: " That's far too deep for a poor
devil of a musician, my boy," Esch could not but think of Frau Hentjen's
silence. The band was making a great din, and Harry, leaning over the
table so as not to have to shout, said mysteriously and in a low voice:
" Love is a matter of distance; here are two people, and each is on a
separate star, and neither can know anything of the other. And then
suddenly distance is annihilated and time is annihilated, and they have

flown together, so that they have no separate awareness of each other or of themselves, and feel no need of it. That is love." Esch thought of Badenweiler; of a remote love in that remote castle; something of the kind was perhaps preordained for Ilona. But while he was still brooding over this, a pang of rage and pain darted through him at the thought that never would he be able to discover whether it had been with this noble form of love or another that Herr and Frau Hentjen had loved each other. Harry continued as if he were reciting a verse from the Bible: " Only in a dreadful intensification of strangeness, only when the strangeness has become in a sense infinite, can the miracle happen, the unattainable goal of love: the mystery of oneness . . . yes, that's how it is." " Prosit! " said Alfons glumly, but to Esch it seemed that this boy had been given knowledge of higher things, and the hope awoke in him that that know-ledge might also hold the answer to his own questions. And although his thoughts were by no means in harmony with those which Harry had expressed, he said, as he had once said to Lohberg: " But in that case one could not go on living after the other," and he was filled with the half-joyful, half-bitter assurance that the widow Hentjen, seeing that she was still alive, could not have loved her husband. Alfons whispered to Esch: " For Heaven's sake, don't say such things before the boy," but he was too late, for Harry looked at Esch in horror and said tonelessly, just a trace more tonelessly than necessary: " I'm not really living now." Alfons pushed across a double glass of liqueur to him. " Poor fellow, ever since that affair he's talked like this . . . that man completely turned his head." Esch felt himself jerked back into reality; he put on an innocent air: " Who? " Alfons shrugged his shoulders. " Oh, him, the Lord God himself, the angel of purity . . ." " Hold your jaw, or I'll scratch your eyes out," panted Harry, and Esch, who felt sorry for the boy, said imperiously: " Leave him in peace." Suddenly Harry broke out into hysterical sobbing: " I'm not really living now, I'm not . . ." Esch felt rather helpless, for he could not employ here the methods which he was accustomed to use with girls when they cried. So that man had ruined this boy's life too, it seemed; Esch wanted to do something to comfort Harry and said abruptly: " We'll shoot this Bertrand for you." Harry screamed: " You'll do nothing of the kind! " " Why not? You should be pleased; he's earned it." " You shan't, you shan't do it . . ." the boy panted, glaring at him " . . . don't you dare to touch him. . . ." Esch was irritated at the boy for so stupidly misunderstanding his good intentions.

" A swine like that must be put away," he persisted. " He's not a swine," Harry said beseechingly, " he's the noblest, the best, the handsomest man in the world." In a sense the boy was certainly right, one couldn't injure such a man. Esch was on the point of giving his promise. " Hopeless," said Alfons dejectedly, drinking up his liqueur. Harry had leant his head between his hands, and nodding like an image he began to laugh: " Him a swine! Him a swine! " then his laughter suddenly changed into sobs again. When Alfons made to draw him to his fat, silken breast Esch had to interpose to prevent a fight. He told Alfons to clear out, and then turned to Harry: " Let's go. Where do you live? " Quite passive now, the boy obeyed him, and named his address. When they reached the street Esch took his arm as if he were a girl, and the one providing, the other accepting protection, they felt almost happy. A light wind was blowing from the Rhine. Before his door Harry clung to Esch, and seemed about to offer his face to be kissed. Esch pushed him through the door. But Harry slipped out again and whispered: " You won't do anything to him! " and before Esch knew what was happening the boy had embraced him, awkwardly kissed his sleeve, and vanished into the house.

The attendance at the wrestling performances was palpably falling off, and something had to be done in the way of publicity. Without consulting the others, Esch decided on his own responsibility to persuade *The People's Guardian* to insert a report. But before the dingy white door of the editorial office he recognized quite clearly that once more it was something else that had led him here. In itself this visit was quite meaningless and futile; the entire wrestling business had become indifferent to him, for it was not achieving anything even for Ilona, and so something more significant, more decisive, must be done for her, and he saw clearly too that *The People's Guardian* would not insert a report now, if they had omitted to do so hitherto because of some proletarian prejudice or other. Fundamentally the attitude of the Socialist paper was praiseworthy: at least it knew its right hand from its left, and drew a clear-cut distinction between the bourgeois and the proletarian points of view. One should really draw Mother Hentjen's attention to such strength of character: she might no longer disdainfully dismiss these people, who, although ordinary Socialists, yet condemned the wrestling business as much as she did herself, and she might no longer look askance at Martin either for being a Socialist. Esch was brought up with a start when he thought of Martin; the devil alone knew what he, August Esch, was doing here in this place! but it was clear that it had no connection with the wrestling. He was still brooding over this while he entered, and not until he was forced to jog the editor's memory by mentioning the strike—for the editor, most unflatteringly, had failed to recognize him—not until then did it dawn on Esch that he had come here on Martin's account. He said abruptly: " I have an important piece of news for you." " Oh, the strike! " with a wave of the hand the editor reduced that event to triviality, " that's ancient history." " Indeed! " replied Esch angrily, " but Geyring is still in prison." " Well? He got three months, didn't he? " " Something has got to be done," Esch heard himself saying in a louder voice than he had intended. " Well, don't shout at me like that—I didn't lock him up." Esch wasn't a man to be put off by such words. " Something has got to be done," he persisted grimly and impatiently, " I know some of the customers that your fine Herr Bertrand associates with . . . and they're here in Cologne, not in Italy! " he added triumphantly. " We've known that for several years, my dear friend and comrade. Or is that the piece of news you wanted to tell us? " Esch felt stunned. " Well, but why don't you do something, then? He's put himself in your hands." " My dear fellow," said the other, " you seem to have somewhat childish ideas of things. All the same you ought to know that we live in a civilized country." He waited now for Esch to take his leave, but Esch did not move, and so for a while the two men sat opposite each other, not knowing what to make of each other, not understanding each other, and each seeing only the other's naked moral unsightliness. Red spots of anger appeared on Esch's cheeks, and faded again into tan. The editor was once more wearing his light-brown velvet jacket, and his slightly plump face with the brown, drooping moustache was at once soft and strong like the velvet of his jacket. A slight trace of coquetry lay in this correspondence, reminding Esch of the finicking attire of the youths at the homosexual resort. He became aggressive: " So you're shielding that homosexual of yours, are you? And Martin can do time for it, for all you care? " He twisted his mouth into an expression of disgust, showing his strong teeth. The editor became impatient: " Look here, my dear sir, what business is it of yours anyway? " Esch grew red in the face: " You deliberately hinder anything that might get him out . . . you wouldn't print my article; you shield the scoundrel that got him thrown into prison, this Bertrand . . . and you, you give yourself out as a guardian of freedom!" He laughed bitterly. "With you freedom is in safe keeping!" A fool, evidently, thought the editor, and so he replied quietly: "Look here, technically speaking it's quite impossible for us to publish as news something that you bring us weeks and months too late; it's just . . ." Esch jumped up. "You'll get news that you don't like from me yet,' he shouted, rushing out and slamming the dingy white door behind him, which, however, did not remain shut, but went on banging.

When he reached the street he stopped aghast. Why had he blazed up like that? Could he alter the fact that these Socialists were swine? Once more Frau Hentjen had proved to be right in scorning the whole crew of them. "The corrupt Press," he kept on saying to himself. And he had gone there with the best intentions too, had wished to give them an opportunity to justify themselves in Frau Hentjen's eyes. Things as they were and things as they ought to be began anew to get entangled in a most exasperating confusion and chaos. Only one thing was certain, that the editor had behaved like a swine, firstly by his general attitude, and secondly because he sought to shield this Bertrand with all the resources of a corrupt Press, yes, a corrupt Press. And this chairman fellow himself was a proper swine, although the boy Harry would not admit it, and there was nothing one could do to put a stop to him. On the other hand what the boy had said about love was quite right. Nothing was simple! at most only one thing had come out clearly: Frau Hentjen could not have loved her husband; she must have been forced into marriage with that swine. And as Esch's thoughts filled with hatred of the world around him, and of the swine who should be done in, as such swine deserved, he began more and more definitely to hate the chairman Bertrand, to hate him for his blasphemies and his crimes. He tried to picture Bertrand sitting in a comfortable chair after dinner in his castle, surrounded by luxury, a fat cigar in his hand, and when that elegant figure at length emerged as from a cloud of tobacco smoke, it was somewhat like that of a dandified snippet of a tailor, strongly resembling the portrait of Herr Hentjen which hung over the mantelpiece in the restaurant.

For Mother Hentjen's birthday, which was duly celebrated every year by the regular customers, Esch had hunted out a small bronze Statue of Liberty, and the gift seemed to him ingenious, not only as hinting at their American future, but also as a happy pendant to the Schiller statue, with which he had scored such a success. At midday he put in an appearance with it.

Unfortunately the present failed of its effect. If he had handed it to her in dead secrecy she might have appreciated the beauty of the sculpture, but the panic fear into which any public familiarity, any sign of intimacy, threw her, so blinded her that she evinced but little delight, nor did she become any warmer in her manner when he apologetically added that the statue would probably go well with the Schiller monument. " Well, if you think so . . ." she said non-committally, and that was all. Of course the new present, too, would have served very well to embellish her room; but to show him that he must not flatter himself that he was entitled to claim such a privileged position for everything he brought her, and to prove to him once and for all that she still upheld the inviolateness of her room, she went upstairs and fetched the Schiller monument, and planted it along with the Statue of Liberty on the mantelpiece beside the Eiffel Tower. There were now collected the bard of freedom, the American statue and the French tower, as symbols of an attitude which Frau Hentjen did not share, and the statue stretched its arm upwards, stretched its torch upwards towards Herr Hentjen. Esch felt his gifts desecrated by Herr Hentjen's gaze, and he would have liked to ask that the portrait at least should be removed; yet what help would that have been? this restaurant in which Herr Hentjen had worked would remain the same, and it was almost more to his liking that everything should remain frankly and honestly where it was. Why try dishonestly to conceal something which it was impossible to conceal! And he made the discovery that what drew him here was not merely the excellence of the food dispensed to him under the eyes of Herr Hentjen, but that he also needed Herr Hentjen in some mysterious way as a strange and bitter seasoning to his food; it was the same inescapable bitter dose that he accepted in Mother Hentjen's moroseness, and that made him feel bound inescapably to her when she morosely whispered to him, as now, that he could come that night.

He spent the afternoon in lascivious thoughts of Mother Hentjen's natter-of-fact love rites. And once more he was tortured by that matter-of-factness, which contradicted so blatantly her customary aversion. In whose nightly embraces could she have contracted those habits? A hope in which he himself did not believe faintly dawned, promising that all this would fall away once they were in America, and the comfort of this hope mingled with the excitement which now came over him when he felt her house-door key in his pocket. Esch took out the key, held it in the palm of his hand, and felt the smooth metal of the handle. True, she had refused to learn English, but the wind of the future blew once more through the streets. The key to freedom, he thought. The cathedral rose grey in the late twilight, iron-grey soared the towers, and a breath of the new and the unfamiliar fanned them. Esch counted the hours until night. It was more important to hunt out girls for the South American journey than to go to the Alhambra. Five full hours, then he would be at the house door. Esch saw the alcove, saw her lying on the bed; and the thought of stealing in to her, the thought that at the touch of his aroused body her body would palpitate, made his breathing difficult and his mouth dry. For even last week, as during all the weeks before, she had received him in dull impassivity, and although that brief involuntary palpitation was insignificant in itself, yet it was a point at which the immense dead-weight of habit had been quickened, a tiny point, it was true, and yet a virginal one, and that was a herald of hope and of the future. And to Esch it seemed dishonourable to enter prostitutes' resorts on the evening of Mother Hentjen's birthday, so he betook himself to the Alhambra.

When afterwards he returned to the restaurant he could see from a long way off the yellow radiance on the uneven cobbles outside. The windows with their panes of bull's-eye glass were open, and inside he could see Mother Hentjen sitting, stiff in her silk dress, surrounded by her noisy customers; a bowl of punch stood on the table. Esch remained in the shadow; the thought of entering filled him with loathing. He turned away again, but not to go duteously in search of girls at their resorts; he strode in fury through the streets. On the Rhine Bridge he leant against the iron parapet, gazed down into the black water and across at the sheds on the quay. His knees were trembling, so intense had been his desire to burst the rigid bony construction in which that woman was encased; the whalebones would have cracked in the wild struggle. With an expressionless face he trailed back into the town, mechanically running his hand along the bars of the bridge railing as he went.

The house was dark. Mother Hentjen, a candlestick in her hand, was waiting for him at the top of the stairs. He simply blew out the candle-butt and seized her. But she had already taken off her corsets, nor did she defend herself, but instead gave him a tender kiss. And although this greeting took him quite by surprise, and was perhaps no less novel than that palpitation for which he was waiting so impatiently, yet from this kiss it was terribly and incontrovertibly clear that one of her old habits had been to conclude her birthday celebrations with a tender love rite, and when the longed-for moment now actually arrived, when that blissful palpitation ran through her body, the thought that the touch of Herr Hentjen's body, which in his present position Esch had no wish to picture, had also made her palpitate just like this, became a raging pain; the ghost which he had fancied was laid arose again, more mocking, more inconquerable than ever, and to conquer it and to show this woman that he, he alone was there, he flung himself upon her and sank his teeth into her plump shoulder. It must have hurt her, but she bore it in silence, although she made a wry face as though she had bitten on something sour, and when presently, exhausted, he made to leave her, she clasped him to her as in gratitude,—and yet her heavy awkward arm was like a vice—clasped him so fast that he could scarcely breathe and wrathfully struggled to free himself. She did not give way, but said—it was the first time that she had spoken to him in the alcove—in her usual business voice, in which nevertheless, had he been more sensitive, he might have heard a note almost of fear: " Why were you so late in coming? . . . because another year has been added to my age? " Esch was so stunned by her speaking at all that he did not grasp the meaning of her words; indeed, did not even attempt to grasp it, for the unexpected sound of her voice was to him like the termination of something, was like a sudden illumination after a long and painful process of thought, a sign that things could take on a different aspect. He said: " I'm sick of it, I'm going to finish it off." The blood froze in Frau Hentjen's veins; she had scarcely enough strength left to unclasp her arm from his shoulder; she felt leaden and icy, and her arm fell powerlessly of itself. All that she still knew was that she must not show her dismay before a man, that she must give him his marching orders before he went of his own accord, and summoning all her strength she brought out faintly: " Certainly, for all I care." Esch took no notice of this and went on: " Next week I'll go to Baden." What need had he to tell her this as well? She felt somehow flattered that his resolve to end the affair should shake him so deeply, it seemed, that it was driving him away from Cologne, out into the world. Yet he was pressing his lips again to her shoulder, and that was surely a queer way of showing that he wanted to finish with her. Or did he simply want to

indulge his lust up to the very last minute? men were capable of anything! Nevertheless she picked up hope again, and although her voice
was still difficult to control she asked: " Why? Is there another girl there
like the one in Ober-Wesel? " Esch laughed: " Yes, you might call it that,
a girl just like her." Frau Hentjen was indignant at his flippancy on the
top of everything else: " It's easy enough to make game of a weak woman."
Esch still thought she was referring to the person in Badenweiler: " Oh,
the one in Baden isn't so terribly weak as all that." This fed her
suspicions anew: " Who is it? " " A secret." She maintained an offended
silence, and submitted to his renewed caresses. Presently she asked:
" Why should you want another woman? " In spite of himself he
could not but secretly admit that this woman with her matter-of fact,
almost businesslike and yet so curiously reluctant and chaste surrender,
accorded him more intense pleasure and bliss than any other woman
could, and that he really wanted nobody else. She said again: " Why
should you want another woman? You've only to tell me if I'm not
young enough for you." He did not reply, for suddenly the fact that
she had spoken at last filled him with excitement and elation; she
who hitherto had lain silent in his arms, her head rolling in persistent
negation, so unalterably silent that her silence had always seemed to him
a legacy from the time of Herr Hentjen. She felt his happiness, and she
went on proudly: " You don't need any of those young things; I'm a
match for any of them." Nonsense, thought Esch, with a sudden stab
of pain, she must be lying. And with a stab of pain he remembered
Harry's words and repeated them: " One can only love once," and when
Frau Hentjen simply said " Yes," as if she meant to convey by this that
he was the man whom she loved, then it was clear what a liar she was;
pretended to be disgusted by men and yet sat drinking with them at her
table, and let them drink her health; pretended to love him now, and
yet was inconquerably matter-of-fact. But perhaps all this was wrong,
for she had no children. Once more his desire for the unambiguous, the
absolute, was brought up against an unscalable wall. If all this were
only past and done with! His journey to Badenweiler appeared to him
at that moment as a necessary prelude, an inevitable preliminary to the
journey to America. Evidently she guessed at these thoughts of travel,
for she asked: " What does she look like? " " Who? " " Why, the Baden
girl." Well, what did Bertrand look like? and more clearly than ever he
recognized that he could picture Bertrand only by calling up Hentjen's

portrait. He replied harshly: " The portrait must be taken away." She did not understand: " What portrait? " " That one below there," he could not bring himself to utter the name, " above the Eiffel Tower." She began to understand, but she rebelled against this attempt of his to mingle in her affairs: " Nobody has ever objected to it." " And that's just why," he persisted, and now it became quite clear to him that it was his affair with Hentjen that he had to settle with Bertrand, and he went on: " and besides, an end must be put to all this." " Well, perhaps . . . " she replied hesitatingly, and her rebellious feelings making her unwilling to understand, she added: " An end to what? " " We must go to America." " Yes," she said, " I know."

Esch had got up. He would have liked to walk up and down, as he was accustomed to do when anything occupied his mind, but there was no room in the alcove, and outside the nuts lay about the floor. So he sat down on the edge of the bed. And although he did his best to repeat Harry's words they changed when he tried to utter them:

" Love is only possible in a strange country. If you want to love really, you must begin a new life and destroy everything in your old one. Only in a new, quite strange life, where everything past is so dead that you don't even need to forget it, can two human beings become so at one that the past and even time itself no longer exist for them."

" I haven't a past," said Mother Hentjen in an offended voice.

" Only then," Esch made an angry grimace which in the darkness Frau Hentjen luckily could not see, " only then will there be no need any longer to deny anything, for then truth will reign, and truth is beyond time."

" I've never denied anything," said Mother Hentjen in defence.

Esch did not let himself be put off: " Truth has nothing to do with the world, nothing to do with Mannheim . . . " he almost shouted, " it has nothing to do with this old world."

Mother Hentjen sighed. Esch gave her a sharp glance:

" There's nothing to sigh over; you must free yourself from the old world, so as to become free yourself. . . ."

Mother Hentjen sighed uneasily: " What's to become of the restaurant? Shall we sell it? "

Esch said with conviction: " Sacrifices must be made . . . that's absolutely certain, for there's no salvation without sacrifice."

" If we go away we'll have to get married," and once more a little apprehensively: " . . . I suppose I'm too old for you to marry? "

Sitting on the edge of the bed, Esch regarded her in the light of the flickering candle. With his finger he wrote a " 37 " on the coverlet. He might have given her a cake with thirty-seven candles; no, better as it was, for she made a secret of her age, and would only have been annoyed. He contemplated her heavy, immobile features, and suddenly he would have liked her to be still older, a great deal older than she was. It seemed to him, although he did not know why, that that would have made things surer. If she were suddenly to become young and lie there in the fleeting semblance of youth, it would be all up with the sacrifice. And the sacrifice had to be, had to grow even greater along with his devotion to this ageing woman, so that the world might be put in order and Ilona might be shielded from the daggers, so that all living beings might be reinstated in their first innocence, and no one need any longer languish in prison. Well, one thing could be depended on, Mother Hentjen would soon grow old and ugly. The world seemed to him like a level, smooth, endless corridor, and he said absently:

" We must lay the restaurant with brown linoleum; that would look nice."

Mother Hentjen picked up hope: " Yes, and get it painted too; the whole place is going to ruin . . . all these years nothing's been done . . . but if you want to go to America . . .? "

Esch repeated the words: " All these years. . . ."

Mother Hentjen felt an apology was due: " One has to save, and one postpones a thing from year to year . . . and time passes . . ." and then she added: " . . . and one grows old."

Esch felt irritated: " When there are no children, saving is ridiculous . . . nobody ever saved up for me."

But Mother Hentjen was not listening. She merely wanted to find out whether it was worth while having the restaurant painted; she asked: " Are you going to take me to America with you? . . . or a young thing? "

Esch replied roughly: " What's all this eternal talk about young and old? . . . There will be no young and no old then, and there won't be any time then either . . ."

Esch was brought up short. An old woman could not have children. That perhaps was part of the sacrifice. But in a state of innocence nobody had children. Virgins had no children. And as he slipped back into bed

he added conclusively: " Then everything will be firm and sure. And
what you've left behind you can't do you any more harm."

He tugged the coverlet into position and also drew it carefully over
Mother Hentjen's shoulder. Thereupon he put out his hand for the
tin extinguisher that hung on the candlestick and that Herr Hentjen
too had employed on such occasions, and clapped it on the flickering
candle.

Mannheim lies on the way to Baden. And Esch remembered that a
man must do his duty by his friends. Something had been bothering
him for a long time and now he knew what it was: he could not leave
his friends' money in a losing business. They had earned more than fifty
per cent. on their investment so far and that was all right, but now
these profits must be secured. It was time to quit. His own three hundred
marks were on a different footing. Should he lose them it would serve
him right. For with a profit of fifty per cent. and two months' expenses
over and above that—and not a bad two months either—where did the
sacrifice come in which was to redeem Ilona? And to finance his flight
to America and liberty out of such ill-gotten gains would be another
falsification: it was high time to call off the wrestling matches, profits
and all. Mother Hentjen was right enough in her prophecy that he and
all his pack of women would end up in disgrace and scandal.

But meanwhile he had to secure the money for Lohberg and Erna.
It wasn't easy to buttonhole Gernerth on the matter: in the evenings
he kept grumbling about the empty theatre and in the daytime he
was hard to catch: he was never in the Alhambra, he never seemed to
enter his flat at all, and at Oppenheimer's place there was nothing but
two untidy rooms and no sign of anybody. Moreover, if one asked him
where he usually took his meals, Gernerth replied: " Oh, I just make
do with a sandwich, the father of a family can't spread himself much,"
which was, of course, hardly true, for one day when the English tourists
were crossing the Cathedral square, who should come out of the Cathedral
Hotel's marble vestibule but Herr Gernerth himself, looking well-fed
and with a fat cigar in his mouth? " Publicity, my dear friend, publicity,"
he had said, and made himself scarce, as if anybody would have taken
it amiss were he to live all the time in the Cathedral Hotel, and his whole
family with him. To-day, anyhow, he wouldn't get off: Esch would take
care of that!

So in the evening Esch opened the door of the manager's office, locked it behind him, grinning widely, pocketed the key, and with another wide grin presented to the trapped Gernerth a neatly ruled account of the profits to date due to Herr Fritz Lohberg and Fräulein Erna Korn on their invested capital of 2000 marks, amounting to 1123 marks, which with the capital made a sum-total of 3123 marks to be repaid, and under it was written " settled in full in the name of the said parties, August Esch." Besides that he demanded his own money. Gernerth shrieked murder and robbery. In the first place Esch had no legal power to sign a settlement, and in the second place the wrestling matches were still going on, and money couldn't be withdrawn from a going concern. They wrangled for some time, until at length with many lamentations Gernerth agreed to pay out the half of the sum due to Lohberg and Erna, while the other half was to remain invested and share in any further profits that arose. But for himself Esch could extract nothing save an advance of fifty marks for travelling expenses. Perhaps he had been too complaisant. In any case that was enough for the journey to Baden.

Frau Hentjen in her brown silk came to the station and peered round cautiously for any sign of an acquaintance who might see her and gossip about her. For although it was early there were swarms of people. At the other platform there stood a train going in the opposite direction, and several carriages for emigrants, Czechs or Hungarians, were being shunted on to it, and Salvation Army officials were running up and down. Now, Mother Hentjen's presence at the station was but right and proper: it was high time she gave up her stupid affectation of secrecy. All the same, Esch had a bad conscience when he saw the emigrants and the Salvation Army people. " Silly sheep! " he grumbled. He could not tell why he was so provoked. Apparently he had caught the absurd disease of secrecy from Mother Hentjen, for when one of the Salvation girls passed by he looked the other way. Frau Hentjen remarked it: " I suppose you're ashamed of my being here? Perhaps you've got another woman travelling with you? " Esch with some rudeness told her not to be a fool. But that was the last straw: " That's all one gets for compromising oneself . . . one can't touch pitch without being defiled." Once more Esch could not understand what bound him to this woman. As she stood there facing him in the daylight the remembrance of her sexual submission and of the dim alcove, the images that haunted him as soon as he was away from her, sank into oblivion as if they had never existed. With this same train he and she had travelled together to Bacharach; that was the beginning of the affair—perhaps to-day would see its end. Evidently she felt his detachment, for she said suddenly: " If you're unfaithful to me, I'll soon let you see. . . ." He was flattered and wanted her to go on; at the same time he wanted to hurt her: " All right, I'm going to do it this very day . . . what'll I see? " She stiffened and made no answer. That softened him, and he took her hand, which lay heavy and awkward in his. " Well, well, what'll happen then? " She said with a vacant eye: " I'll do you in." It was like a promise and a hope of redemption; yet he forced himself to laugh. She was not to be diverted, however, from her thoughts. " What else could I do? " After a pause: " You're probably going as far as Ober-Wesel? . . . to that woman? " Esch grew impatient: " Nonsense, I've told you a hundred times that I must settle up my affairs with Lohberg in Mannheim . . . aren't we going to America? " Frau Hentjen was not convinced: " Be honest about it." Esch impatiently waited for the signal to be given for the train's departure; he must on no account betray his intention to visit Bertrand: " Haven't I invited you to come with me? " " You didn't really mean it." But now that the signal was just going to be given it seemed to Esch that he really had meant the invitation to be taken seriously, and as he stood holding her plump arm he wanted to give her a kiss; she fended him off: " What, here before all these people! " And at that moment he had to climb into the train.

He had really intended to go straight through to Badenweiler, and it was only when he saw the name of Saint-Goar station that he definitely decided to get off at Mannheim. Yes, and from Mannheim he would write to her; that would soothe her down—and Esch smiled tenderly as he thought of her desire to kill him; he might really give her the chance. In any case his visit to Badenweiler was a bit of a venture, a risk that might lose him everything, and it was only decent to hand over other people's money first. The sentence " Human life isn't to be lightly taken " occurred to him, and wove itself into the rhythm of the rolling wheels. He saw Mother Hentjen lifting a dainty revolver, and then he heard Harry saying again: " You're not to do anything to him." Then Lohberg too, and Ilona and Fräulein Erna and Balthasar Korn appeared in a row before him, and he was amazed to think he had not seen them for so long; perhaps they hadn't been alive at all in the interval. They raised their arms in rhythmical measure to greet him, and it was as if an invisible and elegant showman were jerking them like marionettes on wires that suddenly revealed themselves. A third-class compartment is like a prison-cell, and up on the stage, high up on the left side where that tooth was missing, a grey screen from the side-wings suddenly came forward, a pasteboard screen behind which there was nothing save the dusty grey wall of the stage. But on the screen the word "Prison" appeared clearly, and although he knew that there was nothing behind it he knew all the same that there was Somebody in that prison, Somebody who did not exist and yet was the chief character in the play. But the stage, on which the pasteboard prison projected like a tooth, was cut off by an enormous back-drop on which a beautiful park was painted. Deer were grazing beneath mighty trees, and a girl dressed in shimmering spangles was plucking flowers. The gardener, in a wide-brimmed straw hat, his shining shears in his hand and a little dog beside him, was standing beside a dark lake whose fountain sent a crystal jet into the air like a glittering whip and spread coolness around. Far in the distance could be seen the lights and the ornamental outline of a magnificent castle with a black-white-and-red banner waving from the battlements. And that brought back all the uncertainty.

Now that Esch was approaching Mannheim it came into his head that Erna had certainly been sleeping with Lohberg, that pure Joseph. There was really no question about it, it was to be taken for granted and was hardly worth thinking over, it was to be taken for granted as much as the nose on one's face or the feet one walked on. Nothing and nobody could have shaken Esch's conviction that this was so; what else could the couple have found to do together? And yet he was mistaken. For even though life does not offer much variety, and though very little is necessary to bring two people of opposite sexes to an understanding, there are many things that are less to be taken for granted than one would think. A man like Esch who is still entangled in the earthly life of day after day, or has risen only a very little way above it, can easily forget that there is a Kingdom of Heaven whose stability throws all that is earthly into uncertainty, so that it can suddenly become doubtful whether one does actually walk on one's feet. In this case the fact was that Lohberg was restrained from crossing the boundary of idealistic and noble friendship partly by his shyness and partly by his unsleeping mistrust of the female sex, especially since sordid experience

had taught him to dread the poison of sordid disease, and since
he could not help remembering that Erna had been exposed to the
attentions of a professed rake, living cheek by jowl with her. Lohberg
was that kind of man. He merely went walking with Fräulein Erna Korn,
drank coffee with her, and regarded his acquaintance with her as a
time of probation and penance that would find its consummation only
when a sign from on high was given him, the sign, so to speak, of true
redeeming grace.

Esch, of course, knew that the idiot was virtuous, but was incapable
of conceiving the extent of his virtue, and even more incapable of realizing that he himself was still a cause of disquietude to Fräulein Erna,
that he still disturbed her blood, if not her heart, and that it was probably
on his account that she was in no hurry to give Lohberg the sign of
redeeming grace, nay, even deliberately delayed it, regarding such delay
as a proper preparation for the married state. These things Esch was
incapable of divining, and still less that the pair of them found much
pleasure in discovering grave defects in his character, and with their
usual enthusiasm even believed that their common interest in his failings
was a good foundation for a life-partnership.

Innocent of these developments, Esch had reckoned on a ceremonious
and joyous welcome. Instead of that, Fräulein Erna actually shrank
when he appeared in the doorway. Oh, she said, quickly pulling herself
together, it was indeed kind of Herr Esch to let his friends see him
again, oh, it was really kind of Herr Esch to condescend to remember
them after not having even taken the trouble to send them a line. And
then she said: "Who pays the piper calls the tune," with many other
scathing remarks, so that Esch didn't even get as far as the lobby. Korn,
however, who had heard their voices, came out of the living-room in
his shirt-sleeves, and since he was of coarser fibre than his sister and
had never bestowed a thought on Esch for the past two months, and
thus was not offended by his silence, but would rather have been blankly
astonished had it ever occurred to Esch to write to him, Korn was quite
overjoyed to see him, for not only did he remain attached to all that he
had once known, he also saw in the newly arrived Esch a source of
entertainment and a welcome provider of money for the use of the
empty room. And Korn shook his guest's hand with exclamations of
delight, and was inviting him simply to walk into his old room again,
which was waiting exclusively for him, when Fräulein Erna detained

him and half turning to her brother said: she didn't know if that arrangement would do. This roused Korn's anger: " Why shouldn't it do as it
did before? If I say it does, it does." Undoubtedly Esch, as a tactful
man, should then have taken his leave with expressions of regret, but
even if he had been tactful, which he was not, he was too intimate with
the family to prevent curiosity from getting the upper hand of tact;
what had been happening in his absence? And he simply stood rooted
in astonishment. Meanwhile Fräulein Erna, who was also accustomed
to plain speaking, satisfied his curiosity very quickly, for she hissed at
her brother that a woman who was about to make a respectable marriage
couldn't be expected to take a strange man under her roof; as it was,
she had enough disgrace to put up with in that house, and if her
future husband wasn't so magnanimous he would have made himself
scarce already. Korn, in his vulgar way, retorted: " Papperlapap, shut
your mouth. Esch is going to stay." But Fräulein Erna's hints drove
all else out of Esch's head, and he cried: " Well, what a surprise;
my heartiest congratulations, Fräulein Erna, who's the lucky man? "
Fräulein Erna could do no less than accept his congratulations and
intimate that she was on the point of coming to an agreement with Herr
Lohberg. She took Esch's arm and led him into the living-room. Yes,
and her fiancé, too, would be with them in a moment or so. And as they
stood talking of Lohberg Korn had the brilliant idea of hiding Esch
in a dark corner so that the unsuspecting Lohberg might get a shock
when Esch suddenly took part in the conversation like a ghost.

When the bell rang in the lobby and Erna went to open the door, Esch
obediently betook himself into a dark corner of the room. Korn, who
remained sitting at the table, made imperious signs that he was to tuck
himself still further in. For Korn was a man who set great store by
technical perfection and was apt to grow angry if a hitch occurred in his
arrangements. But it was not a fear of Korn's anger that made Esch hold
himself so still in his corner, no, he was not at all the man to be scared
into a corner, nor was it a place of humiliation and punishment for him;
of his own free will he flattened himself closer to the wall, heeding little
whether his sleeve grazed the distemper or not, for in that shadowy
retreat he became strangely and unexpectedly aware of a desire to increase
the distance between himself and the others at the table. The few minutes
that elapsed before Lohberg entered did not suffice for him to think it
out clearly, but it came into his head that he was slipping once more into

that curious isolation which was somehow connected with Mannheim, and which forbade him to make common cause with the others, an insistent isolation that was, however, so pleasant to him that it could not be too solitary, and if he could only have got far enough into his corner, would have made him a redeemed and noble hermit withdrawn from the world, a spirit commanding the company at the table, who were bound to the flesh. It was a state that could not have lasted long, for such reflections are indulged in only when time does not allow of their being thought out to a conclusion, not to say acted upon, and Esch had already forgotten them by the time that Lohberg came in according to programme and was so thoroughly confounded that he was even glad to see the newcomer. Esch certainly did not quite belong to the company, no more than Ilona did, but when they were all sitting round the table they were as one family and cross-questioned each other about many things. And since these questions soon reached money matters, Esch proudly drew out his note-case and laid 1561 marks and 50 pfennigs on the table. Fräulein Erna stretched out her hand delightedly to gather in, as she thought, her investment plus the profits, but when Esch explained that she would get as much in the end, but meanwhile had to share that sum with Lohberg since half of her money was still invested, she cried that that was a loss instead of a profit. And even when he tried to make it clear to her, she would not listen to reason, but swore she was not to be taken in, she could count as well as anybody: if you please—she got out paper and pencil—219 marks, 25 pfennigs, she made it, there it was in black and white, and raging, she thrust the paper under Esch's troubled nose. Lohberg kept his mouth shut, although as a business man he must have understood the situation well enough. Unwilling to get into trouble with his lady-love, the cowardly idiot. Esch said rudely: " I have my own sense of decency—apparently more than can be said of some people that are holding their tongues." And he grabbed Erna's arm, but not out of love; it was with most unloving anger and force that he banged her arm, paper and all, back on the table. Perhaps she had really understood the matter all along, or it might have been the firmness of Esch's grip; in short Fräulein Erna fell silent. Korn, hitherto a detached spectator, merely remarked that Teltscher, the Jew, must be a rogue. Well, then, retorted Esch, he should tell that to the police, for every rogue should be reported instead of having innocent men locked up. And since Lohberg's cowardly and disingenuous behaviour required punishment, he humiliated the fellow with the words: " As for innocent men, they're forgotten. Has Herr Lohberg, for instance, ever paid a visit to poor Martin? " Erna, who was still cowed but filled with healthy resentment, replied that she knew of other people who forgot their friends, yes, even ruined them, and that it was Herr Esch's business to bother about Martin. " That's what I've come here for," said Esch. " Aha," said Fräulein Erna, " if it hadn't been for that we should never have seen you again," and hesitatingly, almost timidly, as if only because she was bound not to abandon a good quarrel, she added: " nor our money either." Korn, however, who was a slow thinker, said: " You must have the Jew locked up."

That was, indeed, a remarkable solution of the problem, and although Esch had himself suggested it, he yearned to retort that it was merely a second-rate and partial solution compared with the much better, more radical, and as it were spiritual solution he now had an inkling of. What good would it do to lock up Teltscher for a month or two when Ilona would be exposed once more to knife-throwing? It struck him for the first time that Ilona wasn't present, although she really ought to have been there; almost as if it were intended that she should not see him until his task was accomplished. Anyhow, task or no task—here he was, promising to pay up profits in full, even while he was thinking of the great sacrifice he was to make! If the balance was ever to be truly struck the wrestling matches simply would have to be a dead loss. And since that implied that the wrathful Erna's money would be thrown away after all, he had a sense of guilt that was at bottom not at all unpleasant; but since it was no business of theirs he began to hector the others: so that was all the thanks he got, he was sorry he had ever troubled to bring the money, since that was how he was welcomed, but in any case he would write to Gernerth about the balance. He could do as he pleased, said Fräulein Erna spitefully. Then she would be good enough to write about it herself, for he had expressly disclaimed all responsibility. She certainly would not. Very well, then he would do it, for he was an honest man. " Indeed? " remarked Fräulein Erna. And so Esch demanded pen and paper and departed to his room without another look at those present.

In his room he strode up and down as was his habit when agitated. Then he began to whistle, so that the others might not think he was annoyed, and perhaps also because he was feeling lonely. Soon he heard Erna and Lohberg coming into the lobby. They were very subdued;

obviously Lohberg, coward that he was, was still trembling and rolling his pale eyes helplessly from side to side. As so often, Lohberg's image called up Mother Hentjen's. She, too, was helpless now, and had to submit to everything, poor woman. He listened to hear if Lohberg and Erna were abusing him. A fine predicament Mother Hentjen had landed him in with her silly jealousy; he needn't have been here, he might have been in Badenweiler hours ago. But in the lobby all was quiet. Lohberg must have gone; and Esch sat down and wrote in his clerkly hand: " To Herr Alfred Gernerth, Theatre Manager, Alhambra Theatre, Cologne. Kindly remit my capital of 780.75 marks, in return for which I shall send you a final quittance. Respectfully yours." With the letter in one hand and the inkpot and pen in the other he went straight across into Erna's room.

Erna, shuffling about in felt slippers, was just making down her bed, and Esch was amazed that she had managed to change her shoes so quickly. She was beginning to object to his intrusion when she remarked his equipment: " What are you doing with that rubbish? " He ordered her: " Sign here." " I'll sign no more for you. . . ." But meanwhile she had run her eye over the letter and went to the table with it: " All right," with a shrug; it wouldn't be of any use, the money was gone, thrown away, wasted, one would just have to put up with that; a man like Herr Esch, of course, didn't give a straw. Her abuse of him once more roused his curious feeling of guilt towards her; oh, what about it, he would help her to get her money, and he seized her hand to show her where to sign. When she tried to snatch it from him he was again annoyed; he grasped her hand more firmly with most unloving force, and for the second time it happened that Fräulein Erna grew silent and defenceless. At first he did not notice this, but merely guided her hand for the signature, then, however, her oblique lizard-like glance as she looked up at him struck him as an invitation. And when he embraced her she laid her cheek close to his breast. The fact that she did so did not trouble him at all; he was little disposed to ask whether it was merely the echo of her old fancy for him, or whether she wanted to revenge herself for Lohberg's lack of manliness, or—and that would have seemed most probable to Esch—whether she simply submitted because he happened to be there, because it was fated to happen, because they no longer had to wrangle over marriage. The situation had been cleared up: Erna had an admirer and he himself was going to America with Mother Hentjen; even his anger against Lohberg was allayed, and he almost felt a kind of tenderness for the idiot

who was like Mother Hentjen in so many respects, and since Fräulein
Erna must have taken over many of her wooer's qualities, being so intimate
with him, to embrace Erna was in a way, although in a far-off way, like
embracing a piece of Mother Hentjen, and couldn't be called unfaithfulness. Yet the recollection of their old quarrels was not yet quite banished,
they still hesitated, there was a flash, as it were, of hostile chastity, and
Esch was within an ace of returning to his own room, as of yore, without
achieving anything. But of a sudden she said: " Hush! " and drew away
from him: the main door outside had creaked, and Esch realized that
Ilona had come in. They stood motionless. But when the footsteps outside died away and the door into the living-room, behind which Korn's
bedroom lay, was locked, they too were locked in each other's arms.

As he crept later into his own bedroom he could not help thinking
of Mother Hentjen, and that he had got off at Mannheim only to allay
her jealous suspicions. That was all she got from her silly jealousy. Of
course it had been only in joke, his threat to be unfaithful to her that
very day. Yet it had turned out to be true, and it wasn't his fault. Besides,
it wasn't really unfaithfulness; one could not so easily be unfaithful to
a woman like that. All the same, it was a dirty thing to do. And why?
Because he should have made a clean sweep of things and gone straight
to the point; because in all decency he should have gone to Badenweiler
instead of pandering to a woman's silly jealousy. That was what he got
for it. A fine predicament, but it couldn't be helped now. Esch turned
his face to the wall.

He opened his eyes and recognized his old room; the bright morning
sun was streaming through the curtains, and like a lance the fear transfixed him: wasn't he late for the warehouse? but he remembered then
that he was quit of the Central Rhine Shipping Company, that he was
free and on holiday. Nobody had the power to waken him for judgment. He went on lying in bed, although it rather bored him, simply
because he could lie as long as he chose. It was very likely, too, that
Mother Hentjen would do him in, for she would never understand that
he had been true to her after all; she would want to kill him, in any
case, and that alone brought a comforting assurance of freedom. The
man who is about to die is free, and he who is redeemed into freedom
has taken death upon him. He could see the battlements of a castle on
which a black flag drooped quietly, yet it might have been the Eiffel

Tower, for who can distinguish the future from the past? In the park was a grave, the grave of a girl, the grave of a girl transfixed by a knife. In the face of death all things are permissible, free, gratis, so to speak, and strangely inconsequent. A man might make up to any woman in the street and ask her to sleep with him, and it would have the same pleasant inconsequence as sleeping with Erna, whom he would leave behind to-day or to-morrow when he journeyed into the darkness. He could hear her bustling about in the flat, the bony little creature, and he lay waiting for her to come in as she used to, for one must make hay while the sun shines. That the freedom to be unfaithful had first to be paid for by an act of unfathfulness, and that all the same one desired to be killed for it, was certainly more than Mother Hentjen would ever understand; what did she know of such complicated balancing? Or how could she ever trace the falsifications that are so cunningly insinuated into the world, that only a skilled accountant could dare to die a redeemer's death? For the slightest error if overlooked could make the whole structure of freedom totter. At that point he heard Fräulein Erna's voice from the kitchen: " May I bring my lord his coffee now? " " No," shouted Esch, " I'll be there in a minute," sprang out of his bed, had his clothes on in a twinkling, drank his coffee and was down at the tramway stop in no time, himself astounded at the speed with which he had moved. The tram bound towards the prison had not yet arrived, and it was only because he had to wait that Esch wondered whether it was merely the thought of his visit to Martin that had driven him out of bed so quickly, or whether it was Erna's voice that was responsible. It wasn't a pleasant voice, especially when she was scolding, as on the previous evening. But Esch wasn't the man to be spurred by a sharp tongue. So it couldn't have been her voice, or else he would have been driven out of the flat long ago, as on that occasion, for instance, when she had called him into the kitchen to look at the sleeping Ilona. As for Ilona, he had no need to set eyes on her again, neither here nor anywhere else. And it would be best to keep these things at a distance, to refuse to admit that he had probably fled from Erna and her evil lusts, from that inconsequent lust in which he was to be involved henceforward, but which could not face the daylight, since night alone was the time for freedom.

At the jail he discovered that visitors were allowed only three times weekly; he must apply again next day. What was he to do? Go on to

Badenweiler without further delay? He began to swear at this interference with the freedom of his movements. At length, however, he said: " Oh well, a reprieve," and the word "reprieve" stuck to him, haunting his mind, and gave him even a proud and comforting sense of brotherhood with a man so powerful as Bertrand, for the reprieve concerned both of them. He could not go off into the darkness without having seen Martin first, and it would have been ridiculous, even degrading, to let his visit to Mannheim mean nothing but a night with Erna. When a man takes a long journey he should leave no loose ends behind him, he should rather greet all his friends and say good-bye. So he went first down to the docks to look up his acquaintances in the warehouses and in the canteen. He felt almost like a long-lost relative returning from America, a little shy in case people should not know him again. For instance, it was quite possible that the watchman wouldn't even let him through the gates. But his reception was very amiable, perhaps because all those he met probably felt they no longer had a hold on him; the customs men at the gate welcomed him at once with light friendliness, and he had a short talk with them. Yes, they said, laughing, now that he wasn't with the Shipping Company he had no business there, and Esch said, he would soon let them see whether he had no business there, and they did not make the slightest attempt to prevent him from going in. Nobody hindered him from looking at all the sheds and cranes, warehouses and goods trucks, to his heart's content, and when he shouted in at the warehouse doors, the storekeepers and stevedores came out and stood like brothers before him. Yet he did not regret leaving it all, he merely impressed it with great clearness on his memory, sometimes caressing a goods wagon and sometimes a gangway, so that the feeling of dry wood clung to his hard palm. Only in the canteen was he disappointed; he looked for Korn but Korn was not there; Korn was stupid and kept out of the way, and Esch had to laugh, for he was no longer jealous of Ilona; Ilona would be spirited out of Korn's clutches into an inaccessible castle. So he merely drank a brandy with the policeman and betook himself along the accustomed street, no longer accustomed and yet more familiar than ever, till he came to a corner where the tobacco-shop regarded him expectantly, as if Lohberg had been waiting within for him with great impatience, waiting to have a chat.

Lohberg was really there behind his till with the large cigar-cutter in his hand, and as Esch came in he amiably laid the instrument down, for he had much to beg Esch's pardon for, and yet neither of them mentioned it, for Esch was ready to forgive and did not want Lohberg to burst into tears. Perhaps it was against the spirit of this agreement that Lohberg began to speak of Erna, but it was such a paltry infringement that Esch barely noticed it. Who could waken him until he chose? He was free! " She's a fine comrade," said Lohberg, " and we have many interests in common." And since Esch was free to say what he chose, he said: " Yes, she would never do you in." And he looked up at Lohberg's worried face that Mother Hentjen could have squashed merely with her thumb, and he was sorry for Erna because she wasn't big enough even to do that. Lohberg, however, smiled timidly, he was a little scared by the grisly jest, and under the eyes of his grim visitor he shrank and diminished. No, he was no fit opponent for a man like Esch; it is only the dead that are strong, though in life they may have looked like miserable snippets. Esch stalked about the shop like a ghost, sniffing the air, opening first one drawer and then another, and sliding the palm of his hand over the polished counter. He said: " When you're dead you'll be stronger than I am . . . but you're not the kind to be done in," he added contemptuously, for it struck him that even a dead Lohberg would be negligible; he knew the fellow too well, he would always be an idiot, and it was only those one didn't know, those who had never existed, who were omnipotent. Lohberg, however, still suspicious where women were concerned, said: " What do you mean? Do you mean would my widow be provided for? I've insured my life." That would certainly be a good reason for poisoning him off, said Esch, and could not help laughing so loudly that the laughter somehow stuck in his throat and hurt him. Mother Hentjen, now, that was a woman. She would have no truck with poison, she would simply spit a man like Lohberg on a pin as if he were a beetle. She was a woman to be regarded with consideration and respect, and it amazed Esch that he had ever thought of comparing her with Lohberg. And he was a little touched, because for all that she put on an air of weakness, and was probably quite right in doing so. Lohberg's skin prickled, and he rolled his pale eyes: " Poison? " he said, as if it were the first time he had ever heard the word, though it was always on his tongue, or at least as if it were the first time he had actually understood it. Esch's laughter became condescending and somewhat scornful: " Oh, she won't poison you, Erna's not that kind of woman." " No," said Lohberg, " she has a heart of gold; she wouldn't hurt a fly. . . ." " Or spit a beetle on a pin," said Esch. " I'm sure she wouldn't," said Lohberg. " But if you're ever unfaithful to her she'll do you in all the same," threatened Esch. " I'll never be unfaithful to my wife," announced the idiot. And suddenly Esch realized, and it was a pleasant and illuminating realization, why he had thought of comparing Lohberg and Mother Hentjen: Lohberg was merely a woman, after all, a kind of natural freak, and that was why it didn't matter if he slept with Erna: even Ilona had slept in Erna's bed. Esch rose to his feet, stood firmly and robustly on his legs, and stretched his arms like a man newly awakened from sleep or nailed to a cross. He felt strong, steadfast and well endowed, a man whom it would be worth while to kill. " Either him or me," he said, and felt that the world was at his feet. " Either him or me," he repeated, striding about the shop. " What do you mean? " asked Lohberg. " I don't mean you," replied Esch, showing his strong white teeth: " As for you, you're going to marry Erna," for that seemed right and proper: the fellow had a fine and highly polished shop, complete with life-insurance policy, and should marry little Erna and go on living in peace; he himself, on the other hand, had wakened up and accepted the task laid upon him. And since Lohberg went on singing Erna's praises, Esch said what was expected of him, and what the other had long been waiting for as a sign from on high: " Oh, you and your Salvation Army twaddle . . . if you hum and haw much longer she'll slip through your fingers. It's high time you took hold of her, you milksop." " Yes," said Lohberg, " yes, I think the time of probation is now fulfilled." The shop looked bright and friendly in the light of that dull summer day; its yellow-oak fittings made a solid and enduring impression, and beside the patent till lay a ledger with neatly added columns. Esch sat down at Lohberg's desk and wrote to Mother Hentjen that he had arrived safely and was well on the way to settle all his business.

His second night in Erna's bed he regarded as a formality that a free man was entitled to comply with. They had had a friendly talk about her marriage to Lohberg, and made love to each other almost tenderly and sentimentally, as if they had never fought tooth and nail. And after that long and wakeful night he rose with the pleasant feeling of having helped Erna and Lohberg to their joint happiness. For every man has many potentialities in him, and according to the chain of logic he

throws round them he can convince himself that they are good
or bad.

Immediately after breakfast he started for the prison. In Lohberg's
shop he bought some cigarettes for Martin; nothing else occurred to
him. The heat was sweltering, and Esch could not help thinking of that
afternoon in Goarshausen on which he had pitied Martin because of
the heat. In the prison he was shown into the visiting-room, which had
barred windows giving on the bare prison yard, across which the yellow-
washed buildings threw sharply cut shadows. The yard looked as if
the executioner's block might well be set up in the middle of it, that
block by which the criminal had to kneel and wait for the keen edge
of the axe that was to sever his head. When Esch had come to this
conclusion he did not want to look at the yard any longer, and
turned away from the window. He examined the room. In the middle
stood a yellow-painted table with splashes of ink on it that told
of previous use in an office; there were also one or two chairs.
The room was like an oven although it was in the shadow, for
the early morning sun had streamed into it and the windows were
shut. Esch became drowsy; he was alone and he sat down; he was
left to wait.

Then he heard footsteps in the paved corridor and the clacking of
Martin's crutches. Esch rose to his feet as if to greet a superior. But
Martin came in exactly as if he were coming into Mother Hentjen's.
If an orchestrion had been at hand he would have hobbled over to it
and set it going. He looked round the room and seemed pleased that
Esch was alone, went up to him and shook his hand. " 'Morning, Esch,
good of you to come and see me." He leaned his crutches against the
table, just as he always did in Mother Hentjen's, and sat down. " Come
on, Esch, sit down too." The warder who had escorted him was reminis-
cent of Korn in his uniform; he had remained standing by the door
according to regulations. " Will you not take a seat too, Herr Warder?
There's nobody coming and I certainly won't try to escape." The man
muttered something about the service regulations, but he came up to
the table and laid down his huge bunch of keys. " So," said Martin,
" now we're all comfortable," and then they were silent all three, sitting
round the table staring at the notches in it. Martin was rather yellower
than usual; Esch did not dare to ask how his health was. But Martin
could not help laughing at the embarrassed silence and said: " Well,

August, tell me all the news from Cologne, how's Mother Hentjen, and everybody else? "

In spite of his burning cheeks Esch felt himself redden, for suddenly it struck him that he had exploited the prisoner's absence to steal his friends from him. Nor did he know whether he should give them away before the warder. After all, few people care to be mentioned in connection with a criminal in the visiting-room of a prison. He said: " They're all getting on well."

Probably Martin had understood his constraint, for he did not insist on a more exhaustive answer, but asked: " And you yourself? "

" I'm on my way to Badenweiler."

" To take the waters? "

Esch felt that Martin had no need to make fun of him. He answered dryly: " To see Bertrand."

" Upon my soul, you're getting on! He's a fine chap, Bertrand."

Esch was not certain if Martin was still joking or being somehow ironical. A fine sodomite was what Bertrand was, that was the truth. But he couldn't say that in front of the warder. He muttered: " If he was really a fine chap you wouldn't be sitting here."

Martin looked a question.

" Well, you're innocent, aren't you? "

" I? I have it in black and white, and sworn to in a court of law, that I've already lost my innocence several times."

" Oh, stop making silly jokes! If Bertrand's such a fine chap he need only be told exactly what has happened to you. Then he'll see to it that you're let out."

" Is it you that's going to enlighten him? Is that why you're making for Badenweiler? " Martin laughed and stretched his hand out over the table to Esch: " My dear August, what an idea! It's a good thing you won't find him there. . . ."

Esch said quickly: " Where is he? "

" Oh, he's still on his travels, in America or somewhere."

Esch was dumbfounded: so Bertrand was in America! Had got there first, was basking before him in the light of freedom. And although Esch had always suspected that the greatness and liberty of that far country had a very significant though not fully comprehensible connection with the greatness and freedom of the man he could never reach, he felt now as if Bertrand's journey to America had annulled for ever his own plan of emigration. And because of this, and because everything was so remote and inaccessible, he fell into a rage with Martin: " A chairman of a company can get easily enough to America . . . but Italy would do him just as well."

Martin said peaceably: " Well, Italy, then, for all I care."

Esch reflected whether he should ask in the inquiry office of the Central Shipping where Bertrand was to be found. But suddenly that seemed to him superfluous, and he said: " No, he's in Badenweiler."

Martin laughed: " Well, you may be right, but even so they won't let you in . . . is there some girl or other behind all this, what? "

" I'll soon find ways and means of getting in," said Esch threateningly.

Martin scented trouble: " Don't do anything silly, August, don't worry the man; he's a decent chap and should be respected."

Obviously he has no idea of all that's hidden behind Bertrand, thought Esch, but he did not dare to mention it and merely said: " They're all decent enough; even Nentwig," and after some consideration he added: " All dead men are decent too, but one can only find out what that decency was worth by looking at the legacies they leave behind them."

" What do you mean? "

Esch shrugged his shoulders: " Nothing, I was just saying . . . yes, that it doesn't matter in the long run whether a man's decent or not; he's always decent on one side; and that doesn't come into question; the question is what did he do? " And he added angrily: " That's the only way to keep yourself from being at sixes and sevens."

Martin shook his head in amusement mingled with sorrow: " Look here, August, you have a friend here in Mannheim who's always prating about poison. Seems to me he must have poisoned you. . . ."

But Esch continued undismayed: " For we don't know black from white any longer. Everything's topsy-turvy. You don't even know what's past from what's still going on. . . ."

Martin laughed again: " And I know even less what's going to happen."

" Do be serious for once. You're sacrificing yourself for the future; that's what you told me yourself . . . that's the only thing left to do, to sacrifice oneself for the future and atone for all that is past; a decent man must sacrifice himself or else there's no order in the world."

The prison warder's suspicions were aroused: " You mustn't make revolutionary speeches here."

Martin said: " This man's no revolutionary, Herr Warder. You're more likely to be one yourself."

Esch was astounded that his remarks could be so construed. So he had turned into a Social Democrat, had he? Well, so be it! And obstinately he went on: " Let them be revolutionary, for all I care. Anyhow, you yourself have always preached that it doesn't matter whether a capitalist is a decent fellow or not, for it's as a capitalist he has to be opposed and not as a man."

Martin said: " Look at that, Herr Warder, do you think we should be allowed visitors? This man will poison me through and through with his heresies, and me just newly regenerated." And he turned to Esch: " You're the same old muddlehead, my dear August."

The warder said: " Duty's duty," and since he was in any case too hot, he looked at his watch and announced that their time was up.

Martin took his crutches: " All right, lead on." He gave Esch his hand. " And let me tell you again, August, don't do anything silly. And many thanks for everything."

Esch was not prepared for such a sudden break-up. He kept Martin's hand in his own and hesitated about shaking hands with the hostile warder. Then he offered the man his hand after all, because they had been sitting at the same table, and Martin nodded his approval. Then Martin departed, and Esch was again amazed because he went exactly as if he were only leaving Mother Hentjen's, and yet he was going into a prison cell! It seemed indeed as if nothing that happened in the world mattered at all. Yet there was nothing that wasn't significant: one had only to force it to be so.

Outside the prison gate Esch drew a deep breath; he dusted himself as if to convince himself of his own existence, discovered the cigarettes he had intended for Martin, and once more felt that inexplicable and terrible rage against him, and once more his mouth was filled with curses. He even called Martin a ridiculous tub-thumper, a demagogue, as they said, although there was really nothing he could reproach the man with except, at the very most, that he had carried himself as though he were the chief figure in the drama, while there were much more important characters. . . . But that was what demagogues were like.

Esch took a tram back to the town, was irritated by the sight of the conductor's uniform, and collected his things from Fräulein Erna's flat. She received him with every mark of affection. And in his rage at the

confusion of the world he treated her overtures with scorn. Thereupon
he took a brief farewell and hurried to the station to catch the night
train for Müllheim.

When desires and aims meet and merge, when dreams begin to fore-
shadow the great moments and crises of life, the road narrows then into
darker gorges, and the prophetic dream of death enshrouds the man who
has hitherto walked dreaming in sleep: all that has been, all aims, all
desires, flit past him once more as they do before the eyes of a dying man,
and one can well-nigh call it chance if that road does not end in death.

The man who from afar off yearns for his wife or merely for the home
of his childhood has begun his sleepwalking.

Many preparations, it may be, have already been made, only he has
not yet noticed them. As, for instance, when it strikes him on the way
to the station that houses are composed of regular rows of bricks, that
doors are made of sawn planks and windows of rectangular panes of
glass. Or when he remembers the editor and the demagogue, both of
whom pretend to know the difference between right and left, although
that is known only to women, and by no means to all women. But a
man cannot always be thinking of such matters, and so he quietly drinks
a glass of beer in the station.

Yet when he sees the train for Müllheim come roaring in, that great,
long serpent darting so surely towards its goal, he is again struck down,
suddenly struck by doubt of the engine's reliability, for it might take
the wrong road; struck by the fear that he, with evident and important
duties to fulfil on earth, might be diverted from these duties and cast
adrift perhaps even as far as America.

In his perplexity he would gladly approach some uniformed official,
as unpractised travellers do, and ask a question, but the platform is so
extended, so immeasurably long and bare, that he can scarcely race along
it, and must think himself lucky, breathless maybe but still lucky, to
reach the train at all, whatever its destination. Of course he strives to
make out the names of the towns posted on the carriages, but soon
realizes that it is a useless effort, for the names are mere words. And
the traveller hesitates a little uncertainly before his carriage.

Uncertainty and breathlessness are quite enough to make a hasty-
tempered man swear, still more when, startled by the signal for departure,
he has to scramble up the inconvenient steps at a breakneck pace into

the carriage, and barks his shin on one of them. He swears, he swears at the steps and their awkward construction, he swears at fate. Yet behind this rudeness there lurks a more relevant and even more maddening recognition, which the man could formulate if his mind were awake: mere human contrivances all these things are, these steps fitted to the bending and stretching of the human leg, that immeasurably long platform, these signboards with words upon them, and the locomotive's whistle, and the glittering steel rails—no end to the human contrivances, and all of them engendered in barrenness.

Vaguely the traveller feels that by such reflections he lifts himself above the trivial daily round, and he would like to stamp them on his mind for the rest of his life. For though reflections of that sort might be deemed general to the human race, yet they are more accessible to travellers, especially to hasty-tempered travellers, than to stay-at-homes who think of nothing, not even if they climb up and down their stairs ever so often daily. The stay-at-home does not observe that he is surrounded by things of human manufacture, and that his thoughts are merely manufactured in the same way. He sends his thoughts out, as if they were trusty and capable commercial travellers, on a journey round the world, and he fancies that thus he brings the world back into his parlour and into his own transactions.

But the man who sends himself out instead of his thoughts has lost this premature sense of security: his temper rises against everything that is of human manufacture, against the engineers who have designed the steps precisely to those measurements and not to others, against the demagogues who prate of justice, order and liberty as if they could rearrange the world according to their theories, against all dogmatists who claim to know better than others his anger rises, now that there is dawning within him the knowledge of ignorance.

He is painfully aware of a liberty allowing things to be otherwise. Imperceptibly the words with which things are labelled have lapsed into uncertainty: it is as if all words were orphan strays. Uncertainly the traveller walks up the long corridor of the carriage, a little bewildered to see glass windows like those in houses, and with his hand he touches their cool surfaces. The man who takes a journey can thus fall easily into a state of detached irresponsibility. And since the train goes roaring on at full speed, apparently darting towards a goal, apparently rushing into irresponsibility, and can be stopped in its career by nothing less than the emergency brake, and since beneath his very feet it is hurrying him off with great dispatch, the traveller who has not yet lost his conscience in the painful liberty of the open day makes an attempt to turn and walk in the opposite direction. But he arrives nowhere, for here there is nothing but the future.

Iron wheels roll between him and the good firm earth, and the traveller in the corridor thinks of ships with long passages in which cabin is ranged beside cabin, floating on top of a mountain of water high over the sea-bottom that is the earth. Sweet, never-to-be-fulfilled hope! what boots it to crawl into the belly of a ship when nothing but murder can bring liberty?—never, ah, never will the ship anchor beside the castle in which one's loved one dwells. The traveller in the corridor gives up his perambulations, and while he pretends to be looking at the landscape and the distant mountains he presses his nose flat against the window-pane as he used to do when he was a child.

Murder and Liberty, as closely akin as Birth and Death! And the man who is pitched headlong into liberty is as orphaned as the murderer who cries for his mother as he is led to the scaffold. In the rushing train only the future is real, for every moment is given to a different place, and the people in the carriages are as content as if they knew that they were being snatched from expiation. Those who are left behind on the station platform have made a last effort, by waving handkerchiefs and uttering cries, to rouse the conscience of their departing friends and summon them back to their duties, but the travellers cling to their irresponsibility, shut the windows on the pretext that the draught might give them stiff necks, and unpack the eatables which they need not now share with anyone.

Some of them have stuck their tickets in their hat-bands so that their innocence may be visible from afar, but the majority hunt with feverish haste for their tickets when the voice of conscience is heard and the uniformed official appears. The man who is thinking of murder is soon detected, and it avails him little that like a child he is gorging himself on a chaotic mixture of food and sweetmeats; it remains a meal in the shadow of the block.

They are sitting on benches which the designers, with shameless and perhaps premature knowingness, have made to fit the twice-curved form of the seated body, they are sitting eight in a row, packed tight in a wooden cage, they roll their heads and hear the creaking of wood and the light squeak of rods above the rolling, pounding wheels. Those facing the engine despise the others who are looking back into the past; they are afraid of the draught, and when the door is thrown open they fear that someone might come in and make them look over their shoulders. For the man whose head is turned the wrong way can no longer judge between guilt and atonement, he doubts that two and two make four, doubts that he is his own mother's child and not a changeling. So even their toes are carefully pointed forward in the direction of the business affairs that are to occupy them. For the occupations they follow bind them together in a community,—a community that has no power but is full of uncertainty and malice.

The mother alone can assure her child that he is no changeling. Travellers, however, and stray orphans, all those who have burned their bridges behind them, are no longer certain how they stand. Pitched headlong into freedom they must build up a new order and justice for themselves; they will no longer listen to the sophistries of engineers and demagogues, they hate the human factor in all political and technical constructions, but they do not dare to rebel against the stupidities of a thousand years and to invoke that terrible revolution of knowledge in which two and two will no longer be capable of addition. For there is no one present to assure them of their once lost and now recovered innocence, no one on whose bosom they may lay their heads, fleeing away into forgetfulness from the freedom of the open day.

Anger sharpens the wits. The travellers have carefully arranged their luggage on the rack, and now they plunge into angry and critical discussion of the political institutions of the Empire, of public order and the nature of law; they cavil at existing things and institutions with nice precision, although in words of whose reliability they are no longer sure. And in the bad conscience of their new liberty they are afraid lest they may hear the terrible crash of a railway accident, which might spit them bodily on the iron rods of the carriage. One is always reading about that kind of thing in the newspapers.

Yet they are like people who have been roused too soon from sleep into freedom, roused to catch the train in time. So their words become more and more uncertain and drowsy, and soon all conversation dies away in an indistinguishable muttering. One or the other remarks, indeed, that he would rather shut his eyes than go on staring at the racing landscape, but his fellow-travellers, escaping into their dreams, decline to listen. They doze into slumber with their fists clenched and their coats drawn over their faces, and their dreams are filled with rage against engineers and demagogues who, strong in the knowledge of infamy, call things by names that are false, so shamelessly false that the angry dreamer must give new and tentative names to everything, yet wistfully yearns that his mother could tell him the true names, and so make the world as secure as a settled home.

Everything is too remote and too near, as it is in childhood, and the traveller who has committed himself to the train and from afar off yearns for his wife, or merely for the home of his childhood, is like one whose sight is beginning to fail him, and feels stirring within him the terror of blindness. Many things around him are clouded, at least he thinks that they are as soon as he has covered his face with his coat, and yet a new knowledge burgeons within him, a knowledge that may have lain unnoticed for some time. He has begun his sleepwalking. He still follows the road laid down by the engineers, but he walks only on the extreme verge of it, so that one cannot but fear that he will be precipitated head-long. He still hears the voice of the demagogue, but it comes as a mere unmeaning murmur. He stretches his arms sideways and forwards like a poor tight-rope dancer who, high above solid earth, knows of a better support. Tranced and compelled his captive soul presses on, and the sleeper soars upwards to where the pinions of the loved one are ruffled by his breath like the down that is laid on a dead man's lips, and he desires to be asked, like a child, what his name is, so that in the arms of his woman, breathing deeply of home, he may sink into dreamlessness. He is not yet at a great height, but he is already on the first pinnacle of aspiration, for he knows no longer what his name may be.

> *The desire that someone should come to pay the debt of sacrificial death and redeem the world to a new innocence: this eternal dream of mankind may rise to murder, this eternal dream may rise to clairvoyance. All knowledge wavers between the dreamt wish and the foreshadowing dream, all knowledge of the redeeming sacrifice and the kingdom of salvation.*

Esch spent the night in Müllheim. When he climbed into the little local train to Badenweiler the vaporous light of morning still lay on the green hills of the Black Forest. The world looked clear and near like a dangerous toy. The engine was so short of breath that one felt one wanted to let out a few hooks at its throat; but whether it was pulling the train rapidly or

slowly it was impossible to tell. In spite of this Esch trusted himself to
it unthinkingly. When it stopped the trees greeted him with a greater
friendliness than ever before, and caressed by soft and fragrant airs a
kiosk arose beside the railway buildings offering a large assortment of
pretty picture postcards. Any of them would have looked effective in
Mother Hentjen's collection, and Esch chose one, a lovely card showing
the Schlossberg, stuck it in his pocket, and sought a shadowy seat that
he might write in peace. But he did not write. He remained calmly sitting,
like one who has nothing more to trouble about, and his hands rested
placidly on his knees. He sat like this for a long time, gazing through half-
closed lids at the green leaves of the trees, sat so long that when at last
he walked through the untroubled streets and saw human beings going
to and fro, in his astonishment he could not tell how he came to be there.
Before a house stood a sinister motor-car, and Esch regarded it closely
to see whether it was big enough to sleep in. He looked round lazily at
everything, for he felt the security and relaxation of the horseman who
has reached his goal, and, turning in his saddle, sees the others still a
long way behind; all his tension fell from him, and quite at his ease, almost
hesitatingly, he addressed himself to the last stretch, ardently longing,
indeed, for some unexpectedly high and difficult obstacle to rise before
him ere his goal was reached and he could grasp his secure triumph. So
it was almost a matter for grief to him—and propitious as the day was,
it was unpropitious to grief—that he should be making towards Bertrand's
house with such certainty: without knowing the place and without asking,
he knew all the turns to take. He climbed the gently winding avenue; the
breath of the woods met him, caressed his brow, caressed his skin beneath
his collar and shirt-cuffs, and to receive the coolness he took his hat in
his hand and opened the buttons of his waistcoat. Now he went in through
a park gate, almost unaffected by the discovery that the estate did not in
the least resemble the grandiose vision that had floated before him in
his dream pictures. And although in none of the high windows was Ilona
to be seen in shimmering spangles, the more lovely foil to this lovely
scene, already at her goal and languidly resting there, yet, though this
was a deep disappointment, the dream picture remained unscathed, and
it was as though what he saw palpably before him now were only a symbolical representation erected for a momentary and practical purpose, a
dream within a dream. At the top of the sloping deep green sward, which
lay in the morning shadow, stood the house, a villa executed in a severe

and solid style, and as though the wayward and evanescent coolness of
the morning, as though the symbolism of the scene wished once more to
duplicate itself, at the end of the slope rose an almost soundless fountain,
and its waters were like a crystalline draught which one longed to drink
simply because they were so limpid. Out of the lodge covered with honey-
suckle which stood behind the gate appeared a man in grey who asked
what Esch wanted. The silver buttons on his coat were not the appurten-
ances of a livery or uniform, for they glittered softly and coolly, as though
they had been sewed on expressly for this shimmering morning, and if
yesterday Esch had still felt for a moment his self-confidence sinking, and
doubted whether after all he would manage to penetrate to the Chairman,
now all his doubts vanished, and he felt he might almost claim to belong
to those who could go out and in here without hindrance. The behaviour
of the lodge-keeper, who made no attempt to enter his name and business
in a duplicate block, did not even surprise Esch, nor did it occur to him
that perhaps it would have been more fitting for him to wait at the door;
falling in step with the man he walked on by his side, and the man silently
allowed it. They entered a cool and shadowy ante-room, and while the
other vanished through one of the many white varnished doors, which
softly opened before and softly closed behind him, Esch felt the soft
yielding carpet under his feet and waited for the messenger, who presently
returned and led him through several apartments, until they came to
another door, at which with a bow his conductor left him. And although
he had now no more need of a guide, it seemed to him that it would have
been more fitting, and even more desirable, had the flight of rooms
extended for a long distance still, perhaps into eternity, into an unattainable eternity guarding the inner shrine, guarding the presence chamber
so to speak; and he almost imagined that in some miraculous and unseemly
and clandestine way he had indeed traversed an endless flight of endless
rooms when he now found himself in the presence of this man who held
out his hand to him. And although Esch knew that it was Bertrand, and
that there could be no doubt about it, now or at any time, yet it seemed
to him that this man was only the visible symbol of another, the reflected
image of someone more essential and perhaps greater who remained in
concealment, so simply and smoothly, so effortlessly did everything go.
And now he was looking at this man, who was clean-shaven like an actor
and yet was not an actor; the man's face was youthful, and his wavy hair
was white. There were a great many books in the room, and Esch sat

down beside the writing-table as if he were in a doctor's consulting-room. He heard the man's voice, and it was sympathetic like that of a doctor: " What brings you to me? "

And the dreamer heard his own voice saying softly: " I'm going to hand you over to the police."

" Oh! What a pity! " the reply came so quietly that Esch too did not dare after this to raise his voice. Almost as if speaking to himself he repeated:

" To the police."

" Why, do you hate me? "

" Yes," Esch lied, and was ashamed of the lie.

" That isn't true, my friend, you like me very well."

" An innocent man is sitting in prison in your place."

Esch felt that the other was smiling, and he saw Martin before him, smiling as he sometimes did in speaking. And the same smile was now in Bertrand's voice:

" But, my dear boy, in that case you should have given me in charge long ago."

One could make nothing of this man. Esch said defiantly: " I'm not a murderer."

Then Bertrand actually laughed, softly and inaudibly, and because the morning was so lovely, yes because the morning itself seemed so lovely, Esch could not summon up the annoyance natural in a man who is laughed at; he forgot that he had just spoken of murder, and had it not been unseemly in the circumstances he would have liked also to join in Bertrand's soft laughter. And although the two ideas he now had in his head did not really go together, or if they did, then only in some relation difficult to grasp, he summoned up all his seriousness and went on:

" No, I'm no murderer; you must set Martin free."

But Bertrand, who evidently understood everything, seemed to understand this too, though his voice, more serious now, still kept its tone of reassuring and light gaiety: " But Esch, how can anybody be so cowardly? Does one need a pretext for a murder? "

Now the word had been uttered again, even if it had only flitted by like a silent, dark-hued butterfly. And Esch thought that there was really no need for Bertrand to die now, seeing that Hentjen was already dead in any case. But then like a soft and clear illumination came the thought that a human being might die twice. And Esch said, marvelling that this thought had not come to him before: " You're at liberty to fly, of course," and he added temptingly, " to America."

It was as though Bertrand were not speaking to him: " You know, my dear fellow, that I shan't fly. I've waited too long already for this moment."

And now Esch felt a rush of love for this man who stood so much higher than himself and yet talked to him of death as though to a friend, to him, an obscure employee in his business and an orphan to boot. Esch was glad that he had kept the firm's books so well and rendered faithful and honest service. And he felt afraid to say that he understood how things stood with Bertrand, or to beg Bertrand to do him in: he simply nodded his head understandingly; Bertrand said: " No one stands so high that he dare judge his fellows, and no one is so depraved that his eternal soul can lose its claim to reverence."

Then Esch saw everything more clearly than ever before, saw too that he had deceived himself and others, for it was as though the knowledge that Bertrand possessed about him now flowed back to him: no, never had he believed that this man would set Martin free. But Bertrand, both judge and judged, said with a slightly disdainful wave of the hand: " And if I were to fulfil your craven hope and your unfulfillable condition, Esch, wouldn't we both feel ashamed of ourselves? You, who in that case would be only an ordinary little blackmailer, and I, for delivering myself into the hands of such a blackmailer? "

And although nothing escaped Esch, the overwakeful dreamer, neither the somewhat contemptuous gesture of the hand, nor the ironical curl that could now be seen on Bertrand's smiling lips, yet the hope refused to leave him that in spite of everything Bertrand would fulfil the condition or at least fly: Esch clung to this hope, for suddenly the fear had arisen in him that with Herr Hentjen's second death his desire for Mother Hentjen might die too. But that was his private affair, and to make Bertrand's fate dependent on it seemed to him as despicable as to extort money from Bertrand, and besides it did not accord with the purity of the morning. So he said: " There's no other way out—I must give you in charge."

And Bertrand replied: " Everyone must fulfil his dream, whether it be unhallowed or holy. Otherwise he will never partake of freedom."

Esch did not wholly understand this, and to reassure himself he said: " I must give you in charge. Otherwise things will get worse and worse."

" Yes, my dear chap, otherwise things will get worse and worse, and we must try to prevent that. Of us two I have certainly the easier part; I need only go away. The stranger never suffers, he is released from everything,—it is the one who remains behind in the coils that suffers."

Esch thought he could see again the ironical curl on Bertrand's lips: fatally entangled in the coils of that cold remoteness Harry Köhler could not but perish miserably, yet Esch could not feel angry with the man who brought such ruin on others. Indeed he too would have liked to dismiss the matter with a disdainful wave of the hand, and it was almost like a corroboration of Bertrand's words when he said: " If there was no expiation, there would be no past, present, or future."

" Oh, Esch, you make my heart heavy. You hope for too much. Time has never been reckoned yet from the day of death: it has always begun with the day of birth."

Esch, too, had a heavy heart. He was waiting for this man to give the command for the black flag to be hoisted on the battlements, and he thought: " He must make way for the other who will begin the new dispensation of Time."

But Bertrand did not seem to be saddened by the thought, for he said casually, as though in parenthesis: " Many must die, many must be sacrificed, so that a path may be prepared for the loving redeemer and judge. And only through his sacrificial death can the world be redeemed to a new innocence. But first the Antichrist must come— the mad and dreamless Antichrist. First the world must become quite empty, must be emptied of everything in it as by a vacuum cleaner— nothingness."

That was illuminating, like everything that Bertrand said, so illuminating and frank that the challenge to imitate his ironical tone became almost an obligation, almost a token of acknowledgment: " Yes, order must be established, so that one can begin at the beginning."

Yet even while he said this Esch felt ashamed, ashamed of the sarcastic inflection of his voice; he was afraid lest Bertrand should laugh at him again, for he felt naked in front of him, and he was grateful when Bertrand merely corrected him in a mild voice: " Your order, Esch, is only murder and counter-murder—the order of the machine."

Esch thought: " If he were to keep me here with him there would be order: everything would be forgotten, and cloudlessly the days would flow by in peace and clarity; but he will cast me out." And of course he would have to go, if Ilona were here. So he said: " Martin sacrificed himself, and yet he redeemed nobody."

Bertrand made a slight, somewhat contemptuous, hopeless gesture with his hand: " No one can see another in the darkness, Esch, and that cloudless clarity of yours is only a dream. You know that I cannot keep you beside me, much as you fear your loneliness. We are a lost generation. I too can only go about my business."

It was only natural that Esch should feel deeply stricken, and he said: " Nailed to the cross."

Now Bertrand smiled again, and because he had been repulsed, Esch could almost have wished Bertrand to die at that moment if the smile had not been so friendly, friendly and subdued, like Bertrand's words which divined everything: " Yes, Esch,—nailed to the cross. And in the hour of final loneliness pierced by the spear and anointed with vinegar. And only then can that darkness break in under cover of which the world must fall into dissolution so that it may become again clear and innocent, that darkness in which no man's path can meet another's —and where, even if we walk side by side, we will not hear each other, but will forget each other, as you too, my last dear friend, will forget what I say to you now, forget it like a dream."

He pressed a button and gave orders. Then they went into the garden which stretched away illimitably behind the house, and Bertrand showed Esch his flowers and his horses. Dark butterflies flitted silently from flower to flower, and the horses made no sound. Bertrand had a buoyant step as he walked through his property, and yet it sometimes seemed to Esch as though this light-footed man should be walking on crutches, for the heavens were in eclipse. Then they sat down together and ate; silver and wine and fruit decked the table, and they were like two friends who knew all about each other. When they had eaten Esch knew that the hour of parting was near, for the evening might unexpectedly overtake them. Bertrand accompanied him to the steps which led to the garden, and there the great red motor-car with the smooth red-leather seats, which were still hot with the rays of the midday sun, was already waiting. And now that their fingers touched in farewell, Esch felt an overwhelming desire to bow over Bertrand's hand and kiss it. But the driver of the car sounded his horn loudly, so that the guest had hastily to climb in. Hardly was the car in motion before a powerful, yet warm wind arose, so that house and garden seemed to be whirled away, and this wind did not subside until they reached Müllheim, where a lighted train with its engine snorting awaited the traveller. It was Esch's first drive in a motor-car, and it was very beautiful.

Great is the fear of him who awakens. He returns with less certainty to his waking life, and he fears the puissance of his dream, which though it may not have borne fruit in action has yet grown into a new knowledge. An exile from dream, he wanders in dream. And even if he carries in his pocket a picture postcard which he can gaze at, it does not avail him: before the Judgment he stands condemned a false witness.

Often it may happen that a human being never notices that the lineaments of his desire have altered in the course of a few hours. The change may consist merely in certain fine distinctions, nuances of light and shade which our average traveller is totally unaware of, yet his longing for home has unexpectedly been transformed into a longing for the promised land, and even if his heart is full of a vague dread, a dread of the darkness of his quiescent, waiting home, yet his eyes are already filled with an invisible radiance which has appeared from somewhere, invisible as yet, although one can divine that it is the radiance beyond the ocean, where the dark mists thin away: but if the mists should rise, then the radiant outspread rows of fields over there come into sight, and the gently sloping lawns, a land in which eternal morning is so embedded that the fearful traveller begins to forget women. The land is uninhabited, and the few colonists are strangers. They hold no intercourse with one another; every man lives alone in his stronghold. They go about their business and till the fields, sow and weed. The arm of justice cannot reach them, for they have neither rights nor laws. In their motor-cars they drive over the prairies and the virgin land, which has never yet been traversed by roads, and all that drives them on is their insatiable longing. Even when the colonists have made a home there they still feel strangers; for their longing is a longing for things afar off, and is directed towards far distances of an ever greater, never attainable radiance. And that is the strange thing about them, for they are a western people, that is to say a people whose gaze is turned towards the evening as though they awaited there not the night but the gates of dawn. Whether they seek this radiance because they wish to think clearly and definitely, or simply because they are afraid of the dark, remains disputable. All that is known is that they either settle where the forests are sparse, or clear the trees to make a spacious park; for though they love the coolness of the grove, they tell each other that they must protect their children from its uncanny gloom. Now whether this be true or not, it shows in any case that the ways of colonists are not so rude as those of colonists and pioneers are generally supposed to be, but resemble rather the ways of women, as their longing resembles the longing of women, which though ostensibly a longing for the man they love, is in reality a longing for the promised land into which he shall lead them out of their darkness. Yet one must be cautious in expressing such generalizations: for the colonists easily take offence, and then they withdraw into a still more impenetrable solitude. In the prairies, however, in the grass-lands which they love, rich in hills and veined with cooling streams, they are a cheerful race, although they are too shamefast to sing. Such is the life of the colonists, remote from care, and they seek it beyond the ocean. They die lightly and still young, even should their hair be already grey, for their longing is a perpetual rehearsal of farewell. They are as proud as Moses when he beheld the promised land, he alone in his divine longing, and he alone forbidden to enter. And often one may see among them the same somewhat hopeless and somewhat contemptuous gesture of the hand as in Moses on the mount. For irrevocably behind them lies the home of their race, and inaccessibly before them stretches the distance, and the man whose longing has been transformed without his knowledge sometimes feels like one whose sufferings have been merely deadened, and who can never fully forget them. Vain hope! For who can tell whether he is pressing towards the blessed fields, or straying like a lost orphan? Even though one's grief for the irretrievable becomes less and less the farther one presses into the promised land, even if many things thin away into vapour in the deepening radiance, and one's grief too becomes lighter, more and more transparent, perhaps even invisible, yet it does not vanish any more than the longing of the man in whose sleep-wandering the world passes away, dissolving into a memory of the darkness of woman, desirous and maternal, where at last it is only a painful echo of what had once been. Vain hope, and often groundless arrogance. A lost generation. And so many of the colonists, even when they appear cheerful and untroubled, suffer remorse of conscience, and are more prone to repentance than many who lead more sinful lives. Indeed it is possible that there may be some who can no longer endure the peace and clarity to which they have surrendered themselves, and although one may assume that their insatiable longing for far-off things has grown so great that of necessity it had to swing round to its opposite, to what may have been its original starting-point, yet it is none the less credible that colonists have been observed sobbing with their hands over their faces as though they were yearning for home.

And so, the nearer he approached Mannheim in the dimly breaking dawn, the more painfully was Esch overcome by dread, and he scarcely knew whether the train might not be carrying him straight to the restaurant in Cologne, or whether Mother Hentjen might not be waiting at Mann-heim to conceive a child by him. He was disappointed when all that awaited him was the letter on which in any case he had reckoned, and he felt disinclined to read it at all. Especially as he could see from the confounded letter that it had been written under Herr Hentjen's portrait. Perhaps for that reason, but perhaps too out of mere dread, Esch's hand trembled when, in spite of everything, he reached for the letter.

He gave Erna hardly a glance, ignored her reproachful looks, and went at once into the town, for he had a report to hand in at the police headquarters. Strangely enough, however, he landed first in Lohberg's shop, where he passed the time of day, and then he considered whether he should pay a visit to the docks. But he had already lost all desire even for that, and he would have liked best to take a tram out to the prison, although he knew quite well that there was no admittance before the afternoon. Loneliness threatened him, although it was still far off, and at last he stood before the Schiller monument, and would have been quite happy had he found the Eiffel Tower and the Statue of Liberty beside it. Perhaps it was merely the difference in the dimensions, but the life-size monument suggested nothing to him, and he found that he was no longer able even to picture Mother Hentjen's restaurant. Thus he frittered away the morning and wrestled with his memories; yes, he must hand in a report to the police, yet he was unable to formulate to himself the contents of that report. With a feeling of immense relief he gave up the plan at last when it dawned upon him that the Mannheim police, who had imprisoned Martin, were unworthy of receiving such a charge, and that he still remained under an obligation to provide the Cologne police with a substitute, as it were, for Nentwig. He felt irritated at himself: that might surely have occurred to him before, but now everything was in order, and he lunched in Lohberg's company with a good appetite.

Then he took a tram to the prison. Again it was a scorching day, again he found himself sitting in the visiting-room—had he ever left it? for everything had remained as it was, and nothing seemed to lie between that visit and this—again Martin entered with the warder, again Esch felt that agonizing feeling of emptiness in his head, again it was incomprehensible to him why he should be sitting in this official chamber, incomprehensible although it was happening for a definite end and after long premeditation. Fortunately he could feel the cigarettes in his pocket which he would take care this time to hand over to Martin, so that at least the visit might wipe off his former omission. But that was a pretext, yes a pretext, thought Esch, and then: a man's legs must work if his head won't. Everything exasperated him, and as they sat all three at the table again, this time it was Martin's ironically friendly air that exasperated him particularly—it reminded him of something that he did not want to admit to himself.

" So, back from your rest cure, August? You're looking first-rate, too. Have you run up against all your friends? "

Esch was not lying when he replied: " I've run up against nobody."

" Aha! So you weren't at Badenweiler after all? "

Esch could not answer.

" Esch, have you been playing the fool? "

Esch still remained silent, and Martin became serious: " If you've been up to any mischief I'm finished with you."

Esch said: " Things are too queer. What mischief could I be up to? "

Martin replied: " Have you a good conscience? Something isn't as it should be! "

" I have a good conscience."

Martin still regarded him searchingly, and Esch could not but think of the day when Martin had followed him in the street as though to strike him from behind with his crutch. But Martin was now quite friendly again and asked: " And what are you doing here in Mannheim still? "

" Lohberg is going to marry Erna Korn."

" Lohberg . . . oh, I remember now, the tobacconist fellow. And you're staying on because of that? " Martin's eyes had become suspicious again.

" I'm leaving to-day in any case . . . to-morrow at latest."

" And what's to happen to you after that? "

Esch wished he were somewhere else. He said: " I'm thinking of going to America."

Martin's aged boy's face smiled: " Well, well, you've wanted to do that for a long time . . . or have you some particular reason for wanting to leave the country now? "

No, Esch replied; he simply fancied that there were good prospects over there at present.

" Well, Esch, I hope I'll see you again before you leave. Better to be going because you have prospects than because you're running away from something . . . but if it shouldn't be so, you won't see my face again, Esch! " That sounded almost like a threat, and silence once more sank on the three men sitting at the ink-spotted table in the hot, airless room. Esch got up and said that he must hurry if he was still to catch the train that day, and as Martin once more regarded him questioningly and suspiciously, he pushed the cigarettes into Martin's hand, while the uniformed warder behaved as though he did not see anything, or maybe he had not really seen anything. Then Martin was led away.

On the way back to the town Martin's threat rang in Esch's ears, and perhaps indeed it had already come true, for all at once he could no longer picture Martin to himself, neither his hobbling walk, nor his smile, nor even that the cripple would ever enter the restaurant again. Martin had become strange to him. Esch marched on with long, awkward strides as though he had to increase as quickly as possible the distance between him and the prison, the distance between him and all that lay behind him. No, that man would never run after him again, so as to strike him from behind with his crutch; no man could really run after another, nor could the other send him away, for each was condemned to go his own lonely path, a stranger to all companionship: what mattered was to free oneself from the coil of the past, so that one might not suffer. One had simply to walk fast enough. Martin's threat had had singularly little effect, as if it were a clumsy work-a-day copy of a higher reality with which one had been already familiar for a long time. And if one left Martin behind, if one so to speak sacrificed him, that too was merely a work-a-day version of a higher sacrifice; but it was necessary if the past was to be finally destroyed. True, the streets of Mannheim were still familiar, yet he was making his way into a strange land, into freedom;

he walked as on a higher plane, and when next day he arrived at Cologne
he would no longer feel abashed before the city and the scenes it presented, he would find them submissive and humble, submissively ready
for transformation. Esch made a disdainful gesture with his swinging
hands, and even achieved an ironical grimace.

He was so deeply sunk in thought that he passed Korn's door without
noticing it; only when he was on the top floor did he realize that he
must descend one flight again. And when Fräulein Erna opened the
door he started back. He had forgotten her, and there she was looking
at him now through the slit of the partly opened door, showing her
yellowish teeth and making her demands upon him. It was the demon
of the past itself barring the gate of longing, the grimacing mask of the
work-a-day world, more invulnerable and mocking than ever, demanding
that one should for ever descend anew into the coils of dead-and-gone
things. And here a good conscience could not avail him, here it could
not avail him that at any moment he was at liberty to leave this place for
Cologne or America,—for a breathspace it seemed to him that Martin
had caught him up after all, and as though it were Martin's vengeance
that was pushing him down, down to Erna. But Fräulein Erna seemed
to know that there was no escape for him, for like Martin she smiled
all-knowingly and as in secret intelligence of a still obscure obligation
binding him to her world, an obligation that was inescapable and
threatening and yet of supreme importance. He gazed searchingly into
Fräulein Erna's face; it was the face of a withered Antichrist and gave no
answer. " When is Lohberg coming? " Esch asked the question abruptly
and as though in the vague hope that the answer would solve his problem;
and when Fräulein Erna slyly hinted that she had intentionally refrained
from inviting her fiancé, it was undoubtedly a flattering mark of preference,
and yet it made him furious. Without regarding her offended looks he ran
from the house to invite Lohberg for a visit that evening.

And indeed Esch felt comforted when he found the fool, so deeply
comforted that he at once begged for his company and purchased all
sorts of eatables and even two bouquets, one of which he stuck in
Lohberg's hand. Small wonder that at the sight of them Fräulein Erna
should clasp her hands and cry: " Why, here's two real cavaliers! "
Esch replied proudly: " A farewell celebration," and while she was
setting out the table he sat with his friend Lohberg on the sofa
and sang: *Must I then, must I then, leave my native Town*, which won

him disapproving and melancholy glances from Fräulein Erna. Yes, perhaps it was really a farewell celebration, a celebration of release from this work-a-day community, and he would have liked to forbid her to lay a place for Ilona. For Ilona too must be released by now and already at the goal. And this wish was so strong that in all seriousness Esch hoped that Ilona would stay away, stay away for ever. And incidentally he felt a little elated at the thought of Korn's disappointment.

Well, Korn really gave signs of being disappointed; though to be sure his disappointment expressed itself in coarse abuse of that Hungarian female, and in rabid impatience for immediate nourishment. Meanwhile he moved his broad bulk with astonishing agility through the room; addressed himself to the liqueur bottles, then to the table from which with his blunt fingers he lifted a few slices of sausage, and when Erna refused to allow this he turned upon Lohberg and with upraised hands shooed him from the sofa, which he claimed for himself by prescriptive right. The noise which the man Korn raised while doing this was extraordinary, his body and voice filled the room more and more, filled it from wall to wall; all that was earthly and fleshly in Korn's ravenously hungry being swelled beyond the confines of the room, threatening mightily to fill the whole world, and with it the unalterable past swelled up, crushing everything else out and stifling all hope; the uplifted and luminous stage darkened, and perhaps indeed it no longer existed. " Well, Lohberg, where's your kingdom of redemption now? " shouted Esch, as though he were seeking to deafen his own terrors, shouted it in fury, because neither Lohberg nor anybody else was capable of giving an answer to the question: why must Ilona descend into contact with the earthly and the dead? Korn sat there on his broad hindquarters and ordered brutally: " Bring in the food! " " No! " shouted Esch, " not till Ilona comes! " For though he was almost afraid of seeing Ilona again, everything was at hazard now, and suddenly Esch was full of impatience for Ilona to appear—as it were to be the touchstone of truth.

Ilona entered. She scarcely noticed the company, simply obeyed the signal of the silently chewing Korn and sat down beside him on the sofa, and in obedience to his equally silent command slung her soft arm languidly round his neck. But for the rest all that she saw was the good things on the table. Erna, who observed all this, said: " If I were you, Ilona, I would keep my hands off Balthasar while I was eating, at least." True, she was merely talking in the air, for Ilona obviously still did not understand a word of German, indeed must not understand it, just as she must not know of the sacrifices that had been made for her. Ignorant of their speech, she could hardly be regarded any longer as a guest at the table of the flesh-bound, but rather as a mere visitor to the prison of the work-a-day world, or as a voluntary captive. And Erna, who to-night seemed to know many things, made no further mention of earthly matters, and it was like an admission of a more subtle understanding when she lifted the bouquet from the table and held it under Ilona's nose: " There, smell that, Ilona," she said, and Ilona replied: " Yes, thank you," and it rang as from a distance which the munching Korn would never reach, rang as from a higher plane ready to receive her if only one did not grow weary in sacrifice. Esch felt light-hearted. Everyone must fulfil his dream, whether it be evil or holy, and then he will partake of freedom. And great pity as it was that the ninny should get Erna, and little as Ilona would ever guess that now the final line had been drawn under an account, it was a settlement and a turning-point, a testimony and the act of a new consciousness when Esch got up, drank to the company, and having briefly and heartily congratulated the betrothed couple, proposed a toast to their health, so that everybody, with the exception of Ilona for whose sake it was really done, looked quite dumbfounded. But as it expressed their secret wishes, their next emotion was gratitude, and Lohberg with moist eyes shook Esch's hand again and again. Then at Esch's request the happy couple gave each other the betrothal kiss.

Nevertheless what had been done did not yet appear to him final, and when the party was breaking up, and Korn had already retired with Ilona, and Fräulein Erna was preparing to put on her hat so as to keep Esch company in escorting her newly betrothed to his home, then Esch objected; no, he did not regard it as seemly that he, a bachelor, should spend the night in the house of Lohberg's fiancée, he would be very happy to seek a lodging for the night in Herr Lohberg's house or to exchange rooms with him; they should think it over again, for after their betrothal they must have a great many things to talk about; and thereupon he pushed the two of them into Erna's room and betook himself to his own.

In this way ended the first day of his release, and the first night of unaccustomed and unpleasant renunciation broke in.

The sleepless man who with moistened finger-tip has quenched the quiet candle beside his bed, and in the now cooler room awaits the coolness of sleep, with every beat of his heart approaches death without knowing it; for strangely as the cool room has expanded round him, just as stiflingly hot and hurried has time grown within his head, so stifling that beginning and end, birth and death, past and future, crumble to dust in the unique and isolated present, filling it to the brim, indeed almost bursting it.

Esch had considered for a moment whether Lohberg might not after all decide to go home and want his company. But with an ironical grimace he concluded that he might safely go to bed, and still grinning he began to take off his clothes. By the light of the candle he read again Mother Hentjen's letter; the copious items of news about the restaurant were boring; on the other hand there was one passage which pleased him: "And do not forget, dear August, that you are my only love in all the world and will always be, and that I cannot live without you, and would not rest in the cold grave without you, dear August." Yes, that pleased him, and now on Mother Hentjen's account too he was glad that he had sent Lohberg in to Erna. Then he moistened his finger-tip, put out the candle, and stretched himself on the bed.

A sleepless night begins with banal thoughts, somewhat as a juggler displays at first banal and easy feats of skill, before proceeding to the more difficult and thrilling ones. In the darkness Esch could not help grinning still at the thought of Lohberg slipping under the blankets to the coyly tittering Erna, and he was glad that he had no need to be jealous of the ninny. In truth his desire for Erna had now completely gone, but that was all to the good and as it should be. And in reality he only dwelt on the happenings in the other room to demonstrate how indifferent they left him, how indifferent it was to him that Erna was now caressing with her hands the meagre body of the idiot, and suffering such a misbegotten monstrosity beside her, and how totally indifferent what impressions, what phallic images—he employed a different term—she carried in her memory. So easy was it for him to picture all this that it seemed without importance, and besides with that pure Joseph one was not even certain that things would take such a course. Life would be an easy business if things of that kind left him just as indifferent in Mother Hentjen's case,— but the mere impact of the thought was so painful that he started violently, not entirely unlike Mother Hentjen at certain moments. He would gladly have sought refuge with Erna for himself and his thoughts, had not something barred the way, something invisible, of which he only knew that it was the threatening and inescapable presence of that afternoon. So he turned his thoughts to Ilona; all that was needed to establish order there was that the hurtling knives should be erased from her memory. As a preliminary rehearsal, so to speak, for more difficult feats, he tried to think of her, but he was unsuccessful. Yet when at last he managed to picture to himself, with rage and loathing, that at that moment she was languidly and submissively enduring the presence of Korn, that dead lump of flesh, regardless of herself, just as she had stood smiling in the midst of the daggers, waiting for one of them to strike her to the heart— oh, then he suddenly saw the end of his task; for it was self-murder that she was committing in such a curiously complicated and feminine fashion, self-murder that dragged her down into contact with earthly things. That was what she must be rescued from! His task was defined, but it had become a new task! Indeed, if it were not for that threatening something barring the way, he would simply dismiss Ilona from his mind, walk over to Erna's room, seize Lohberg by the collar, and curtly order him to take himself off. After that one would be able to sleep quietly and dreamlessly.

Yet just when he was on the point of picturing to himself how peaceful the world would be then, and already felt within himself the unequivocal desire for a woman, the sleepless Esch was pulled up by an idea which was at once a little comical and a little shocking: he dared not return to Erna, for then it would no longer be possible to tell who was the father of her child. So that was the inexplicable obligation, that was the threat which had made him start back when he saw Erna that afternoon! Yes, it all seemed to fit in; for there was one who had stepped aside to make place for another from whose advent the new dispensation of time was to begin, and it seemed right, too, that a messiah's father should be a pure Joseph. Esch tried again to summon his ironical grimace, but he was unsuccessful this time; his eyelids were too tightly shut, and no one can laugh in the dark. For night is the time of freedom, and laughter is the revenge of those who are not free. Oh, it was just and right that he should be lying here sleepless and wide awake, in a cold and strange excitement which was no longer the excitement of desire, lying in a semblance of death as in a vault, since the unborn was lying motionless and undreaming likewise. Yet how could one believe that Bertrand had been sacrificed, so that out of the paltry earthly vessel that was called Fräulein Erna new life should spring? Esch cursed to himself, as the sleepless sometimes are accustomed to do, but while he cursed he suddenly realized that after all it did not fit in, inasmuch as the magical hour of death should be the hour of procreation too. One could not be at the selfsame time in Baden-weiler and Mannheim; so the conclusion he had drawn was a premature one, and everything was perhaps more complex and more noble.

The darkness of the room was cool. Esch, a man of impetuous tempera-ment, lay motionless in his bed, his heart hammered time down to a thin dust of nothingness, and no reason could any longer be found why one should postpone death into a future which was in any case already the present. To the man who is awake such ideas may seem illogical, but he forgets that he himself exists for the most part in a kind of twilight state, and that only the sleepless man in his overwakefulness thinks with really logical severity. The sleepless man keeps his eyes closed, as though not to see the cold tomblike darkness in which he lies, not to see it, yet fearing that his sleeplessness may topple over into mere ordinary awakeness at the sight of the curtains which hang like woman's skirts before the window, and all the objects which may detach themselves from the dark-ness if he were to open his eyes. For he wants to be sleepless and not awake, otherwise he could not lie here with Mother Hentjen cut off from the world and safe in his tomb, full of a desire which is lust no longer; yes, he was robbed of desire now, and that too was good. United in death, thought Esch, lying in his semblance of death, yes, united in death, and in truth that would have been comforting, if he could but have refrained from thinking of Erna and Lohberg, who were also in a way united now in death. But in what a way! Well, the sleepless man has no inclination left for cynical witticisms, he wants, as it were, to let the metaphysical content of experience work upon him, and to estimate justly the extra-ordinary distance that separates his couch from the other rooms in the house, wishes in all seriousness to meditate on the attainable final com-munion, on the fulfilment of his dream which will lead him to consumma-tion; and as he cannot grasp all these things he becomes morose and aggrieved, becomes enraged and meditates now only on the question: how the dead can possibly give birth to the living. The sleepless man runs his hand over his closely cropped hair, a cool and prickling sensation remains in the palm of his hand; it is like a dangerous experiment which he will not repeat again.

And when by such means he has advanced to more difficult and remarkable feats, his rage waxes, and perhaps it is only the rage of impotent joyless desire. Ilona was committing self-murder in a peculiarly complicated and feminine fashion, suffering night after night the presence of a dead lump of flesh, so that her face was already puffy as though it had been touched by corruption. And every night that that image of obscene lust was imprinted on her the corruption must increase. So that was the reason why he had feared to see Ilona that afternoon! The knowledge of the sleepless man grows into a clairvoyant foreshadowing dream of death, and he recognizes that Mother Hentjen is already dead, that she, the dead woman, can have no child by him, that for this reason alone she has written him a letter instead of coming to Mannheim, written it under the portrait of the man from whose hands she accepted death, just as now Ilona is accepting death from that animal Korn. Mother Hentjen's cheeks too were puffy, time and death were embedded in her face, and the raptures of her nights were dead, dead as the automatic musical instrument which ground out its tune mechanically, one had only to press a lever. And Esch became furious.

The sleepless man does not know that his bed is standing in a certain position in a house in a certain street, and he refuses to be reminded of it. It is notorious that the sleepless are easily moved to anger; the rolling of a solitary tramcar through the night streets is enough to arouse them to fury. And how much stronger then must be their rage over a contradiction so colossal and so terrible that it cannot even be put down to a book-keeping error? In panic haste the sleepless man sets his thoughts flying to discover the meaning of the question which, coming from somewhere or other, from afar off, perhaps from America, now presses on him. He feels that there is a region in his head that is America, a region that is none other than the site of the future in his head, and yet that cannot exist so long as the past keeps breaking in so boundlessly into the future, the wrecked and annihilated overwhelming the new. In this storm that breaks in he himself is carried away, yet not only he, but everyone around him is swept away by the icy hurricane, all of them following the pioneer who has first flung himself into the storm, to be whirled away so that time may once more become time. Now there was no more time left, only an extraordinary amount of space; the sleepless man in his overwakefulness listens and knows that all the others are dead, and even if he shuts his eyelids ever so tightly so as not to see it, he knows that death is always murder.

So the word had appeared again, yet not flitting silently like a butterfly; but with the rattling clangour of a tramcar in the night streets the word murder had reappeared, and was shouting at him. The dead handed death on. There must be no surviving. As though death were a child, Mother Hentjen had conceived it by the dead tailor fellow, and Korn was imparting it to Ilona. Perhaps Korn too was dead; he was as fat as Mother Hentjen, and of redemption he knew nothing. Or if he were not dead already, he would die—faint comforting hope—would die like the snippet of a tailor, after he had consummated his murder. Murder and counter-murder, shock on shock, the past and the future broke upon each other, broke in the very moment of death which was the present. That must be thought out very vigilantly and very seriously, for only too easily might another book-keeping error slip in. And already how immeasurably difficult it was to distinguish sacrifice and murder from each other! Must all be destroyed ere the world could be redeemed to a state of innocence? Must the deluge break in, was it not enough for one man to sacrifice himself, for one to step aside? Esch still lived, although like all the sleepless he was dead to all appearance, Ilona still lived, although death had already touched her, and only one man was bearing the burden of sacrifice for the new life and the creation of a world in which daggers might no longer be flung. That sacrifice could never be undone now. And as all abstract and universally valid generalizations are to be found in the state of sleepless overwakefulness, Esch arrived at the conclusion: the dead are murderers of women. But he was not dead, and on him lay the obligation to rescue Ilona.

Again arose in him the desire, the impatient desire, to receive death from Mother Hentjen's hand, and the doubt whether it had not already happened. If he submitted himself to that death which came from the dead, he might propitiate the dead, and they might rest content with the one sacrifice. A comforting thought! And as the sleepless man can be more violently overcome with rage than the awake in their twilight state, so his happiness may be far more ecstatic, and he may experience it, one might almost say, with a sort of wild lightness of heart. Yes, that light and liberated feeling of happiness may become so bright that the very darkness behind the closed eyelids catches its radiance. For now it was absolutely certain that Esch, who was alive, a living man by whom women might conceive, if he resigned himself to Mother Hentjen and her body of death, must by this unprecedented measure not only consummate Ilona's redemption, must not only put her for ever beyond the reach of the daggers, must not only retrieve her beauty for her and cancel from her flesh all trace of mortality, cancel it so completely that she would regain a new virginity, but that by doing this he must also of necessity rescue Mother Hentjen from death, vivify again her loins, so that she might bear the one whose task it would be to renew Time.

Then it seemed to him as though his bed were returning with him from a great distance, until at last it rested again in a certain position in a certain alcove, and Esch, reborn in newly awakened longing, knew that he was at his goal, not, it was true, that final goal in which symbol and prototype return to their identity, yet none the less at that temporary goal with which earthly mortals must rest content, the goal that he termed love and that stood as the last attainable point on that coast beyond which lay the unattainable. And, as it were, in antithesis to the symbol and the prototype, women seemed curiously united and yet divided; Mother Hentjen might be sitting in Cologne waiting for him, Ilona might have receded into the unattainable and the invisible, and he knew that he would never see her again—but out there on that horizon where the visible and the invisible, the attainable and the unattainable became one, their ways crossed and their two silhouettes dissolved and merged into each other, and even if they were to separate, they would still remain united in a hope never to be fulfilled: the hope that, embracing Mother Hentjen in perfect love, bearing her life as his own, quickening and redeeming her from death in his arms, embracing in love this woman growing old, he might lift from Ilona the burden of approaching age and of memory, might create as a setting for Ilona's new and virginal beauty the higher plane of his desire; yes, widely separated as the two women were, they yet became one, the reflected image of one, of that invisible entity to which he could never turn back, and which yet was home.

The sleepless Esch was at his goal. In his overwakefulness indeed he had already foreknown the outcome, and he saw that he had merely been spinning a logical chain round it, and had remained wakeful merely because the chain had grown longer and longer; but now he permitted himself to forge the last link, and it was like a complicated book-keeping task which he had solved at last, indeed even more than a book-keeping task; it was the real task of love in all its absoluteness that he had taken upon him in submitting his earthly life to Mother Hentjen. He would gladly have made this conclusion known to Ilona, but in view of her imperfect mastery of the German language he would have to abstain.

Esch opened his eyes, recognized his room, and then went contentedly to sleep.

He had decided for Mother Hentjen. Finally. Esch did not look out through the carriage window. And when he turned his thoughts to this perfect and absolute love of his it was like a daring experiment; acquaintances and customers would be drinking in the brightly lit restaurant; he would enter, and regardless of all those eyewitnesses, Mother Hentjen would run to him and fling herself on his breast. But when he arrived in Cologne the picture seemed to have altered strangely; for this city was no longer a city that he knew, and his way through the evening streets seemed to stretch for miles and was strange to him. Incredible that he had been away for only six days. Time had stopped, and the house that awaited his entry was quite indefinite, the restaurant quite indefinite in shape and size. Esch stood in the doorway and looked across at Mother Hentjen. She sat enthroned behind the buffet. Above the mirror a light burned under a red shade, silence hung in the air, not a customer was to be seen in the forlorn room. Nothing happened. Why had he come here? Nothing happened; Mother Hentjen remained behind the buffet and said at last in her usual phlegmatic way: " Good-evening." And she glanced nervously round the room. Rage rose up in him, and all at once he could not understand why he had decided for this woman. So he too merely said, " Good-evening," for although he somehow approved of her proud coldness, and knew also that he had no right to repay her in the same coin, yet he felt angry; a man who had decided in his heart for unconditional love was entitled at any rate to be met on an equal footing,—he rapped out: " Thanks for your letter." She looked round the empty restaurant and said furiously: " What if anyone were to hear you? " and Esch, fully roused, replied with particular distinctness: " And what if they did . . . let this stupid mystery-mongering stop now, for heaven's sake! " said it without point or object, for the restaurant was empty, and he himself did not know why he was there. Mother Hentjen became silent with terror, and mechanically put up her hand to her coiffure. Since she had accompanied him to the train she had keenly regretted being so forward, giving herself away so completely, and after sending that imprudent letter to Mannheim she had actually fallen into a genuine panic; she would have been grateful to Esch now for not mentioning it. But now that with a set, implacable

face he openly exploited his advantage, she felt herself again defencelessly caught in a grip of iron. Esch said: " I can go, of course, if you
like," and now she would really have issued from behind her counter if
the first customers had not at that moment entered. So the two of them
remained standing where they were in silence; then Mother Hentjen
whispered in a contemptuous tone which was intended to show that
she merely wished to carry their quarrel to a finish: " Come back
to-night." Esch made no reply, but sat down at his table before a glass
of wine. He felt an orphan. His calculations yesterday, which had seemed
so clear, had now become incomprehensible to him; how could his
deciding for this woman help Ilona? he gazed round the restaurant
and still felt it strange; it meant nothing to him now, he had left all
those things too far behind. What was he doing in Cologne at all? he
should have been in America long ago. But then his glance caught Herr
Hentjen's portrait, hanging above the insignia of liberty, and it was
as though it suddenly reminded him of something; he asked for paper
and ink, and in his most beautiful clerkly script wrote: " I beg to bring
to the notice of the Chief Commissioner of Police that Herr Eduard
von Bertrand, resident in Badenweiler, Chairman of the Central Rhine
Shipping Company Limited in Mannheim, is guilty of illicit practices
with persons of the male sex, and I am prepared to appear as a witness
and furnish proof of my accusation."

When he was about to append his signature he stopped suddenly,
for he had been on the point of adding: " In the name of his bereaved
relatives and friends," and although he could not help smiling at this,
he was startled. Finally, however, he added his name and address to
the communication, and having carefully folded it, deposited it in his
pocket-book. Until to-morrow, he told himself, a last respite. The
picture postcard from Badenweiler was also sticking in his pocket-book.
He considered whether he could present it to Mother Hentjen that night,
and felt forlorn. But then he saw before him the alcove, saw her again
in her painfully submissive readiness to receive him, and as he passed
the buffet he said, and his voice was hoarse: " Well then, to-night."
She sat stiffly in her chair and seemed to have heard nothing, so that
filled with new rage, a different rage however from the first, he turned
back again, and raising his voice recklessly, said: " Be so good as to
remove that portrait over there." She still sat immobile, and he slammed
the door behind him.

When later he returned and made to open the house door he found it barred from inside. Without considering whether the maid might hear him, he rang the bell, and as nobody answered he went on ringing furiously. That did the trick; he heard footsteps; he almost hoped that it might be the little maid; he would tell her that he had forgotten something in the restaurant, but apart from that the maid would not disdain him, and that would be a lesson for Mother Hentjen. But it was not the maid, it was Frau Hentjen in person; she was still fully dressed and she was crying. Both circumstances increased his rage. They climbed the stairs in silence, and up in her room he fell upon her at once. When she submitted, and her kisses became tender, he asked threateningly: " Is that portrait going to be removed? " She did not know at first of what he was speaking, and when she did she did not quite understand for a moment: " The portrait? . . . oh, the portrait? why? don't you like it? " In despair before her inability to understand he said: " No, I don't like it . . . and there's a lot of things besides that I don't like." She replied complaisantly and politely: " If you don't like it I can easily hang it up somewhere else." She was so unutterably stupid that it would probably take a thrashing to make her understand. However, Esch restrained himself: " The portrait must be burned." " Burned? " " Yes, burned. And if you pretend to be so stupid much longer, I'll set fire to the whole place." She recoiled from him in terror, and, pleased with the effect of his threat, he said: " You should be glad; it isn't as if you had any great love for the place." She made no reply, and even if her mind was probably blank, and she only saw the flames rising from her roof-top, yet it was as though she were trying to conceal something. He said sternly: " Why don't you speak? " His harsh tone completely paralysed her. Could this woman not be driven by any means to drop her mask? Esch had risen and now stood threateningly at the entrance to the alcove as though to prevent her from escaping. One would have to call things by their real names, otherwise one would never make anything out of this lump of flesh. But when he asked: " Why did you marry him? " his voice was hoarse and strangled, for with the question so many wild and hopeless emotions surged up in him that in thought he had to fly to Erna for comfort. He had left her, though she did not torment him and it had been completely immaterial to him what phallic images she carried in her memory. And it had been equally immaterial to him whether she had children, or prevented them by artificial devices.

He dreaded Mother Hentjen's answer, did not want to hear it, yet he shouted: " Well? " And Mother Hentjen, her fear that she had given herself away too much reawakened, perhaps also dreading that the nimbus surrounding her, on whose account she imagined Esch loved her, might be in danger of vanishing, gathered herself together: " It's so long ago . . . you don't need to let that worry you." Esch pushed forward his under jaw and bared his strong teeth: " It shan't worry me . . . it shan't worry me . . ." he shouted, " it doesn't worry me in the least. . . . I don't give a hang for it." So this was how she requited his absolute and untiring devotion and his torments. She was stupid and callous; he, who had taken her fate upon him, he, who wanted to take upon him her life although it had been aged and defiled by death, he, August Esch, who was prepared to make the decision and give himself absolutely to her, who longed that all his strangeness might be merged in her, so that all her strangeness and all her thoughts, no matter how painful to him, might become his as it were by way of exchange: it needn't worry him! Oh, she was stupid and callous, and being so he had to beat her; he went up to the bed and hit out at her and struck her on the fat immobile cheek, as though by doing so he might reach the immobility of her spirit. She did not defend herself, but remained lying rigid, and even if he had flung knives at her, even then she would not have moved. Her cheek was red where he had struck her, and when a tear trickled down over it his anger was softened. He sat down on the bed, and she moved to the side to make room for him. Then he said imperiously: " We must get married." She simply answered, " Yes," and Esch was on the point of flying into a new rage, because she did not say that she was glad at last to be rid of the hated name. But the only reply she could think of was to put her arm round him and draw him to her. He was tired, and submitted; perhaps it was all right, perhaps it did not matter, for where the kingdom of salvation was concerned everything was uncertain, every hour uncertain, every figure and every reckoning. Yet he felt embittered again; what did she know about the kingdom of salvation? And did she even want to know about it? probably as little as Korn! it would certainly take some time to hammer it into her head. But meanwhile one must simply allow for that, must wait until she could understand it, must let her carry on her life as she was doing. In the land of justice, in America, it would be different; there the past would fall away like tinder. And when she asked him constrainedly whether he had stopped at Ober-Wesel, he was not annoyed, but shook his head seriously and growled: " Of course not." And so they celebrated their marriage night, and agreed to sell the business, and Mother Hentjen was grateful to him for not setting fire to anything. In a month's time they might be on the high seas. To-morrow he would see Teltscher and set the American project going again.

He remained longer than usual. Nor did they descend the stairs on tiptoe this time. And when she let him out there were already people in the streets. That filled him with pride.

Next morning he betook himself to the Alhambra. Of course nobody was there. He rummaged among the correspondence on Gernerth's desk, found an unopened envelope which bore his own handwriting, and was so taken aback for a moment that he did not recognize it: it was Erna's letter that he had himself written in Mannheim. Well, she would raise another fine outcry if she had received no reply all this time. And really not without justification. A careless lot, those theatre people.

At last Teltscher came wandering in. Esch was almost glad to see him again. Teltscher was in a gracious mood: " Well, high time for you to be back,—everybody disappears on private business and Teltscher is left to do all the measly work." Where was Gernerth? " Oh, in Munich with his precious family—grave illness in the family, they've got colds in the head or something." He would soon be back, Esch supposed. " He'll have to come back soon, the Herr Manager; last night there were scarcely fifty people in the theatre. We'll have to talk it over with Oppenheimer." " Right," said Esch, " let's go and see Oppenheimer."

They agreed with Oppenheimer that they would have to announce the end of the show. " Have I warned you, or haven't I? " said Oppenheimer. " Wrestling is all right, but nothing but wrestling! who would come to see that? " The decision suited Esch very well; all that he need do was to have his share paid to him when Gernerth returned, and the sooner the end came, the sooner they would get to America.

This time he asked Teltscher of his own accord to lunch with him, for now it was a matter of setting about the American project. Hardly were they on the pavement before Esch drew the list from his pocket and ticked off the girls whom he had earmarked for the journey. " Yes, I've got a few too," said Teltscher, " but first Gernerth must pay me back my money." Esch was surprised, for Teltscher should surely have been satisfied with Lohberg's and Erna's contributions. Teltscher said in exasperation: " And whose money have we been financing the wrestling matches with, do you think? Gernerth's money is tied up, don't you know that? He gave me the stage properties in pledge, but what can I do with them in America?" All this was somewhat surprising, but all the same when the business was liquidated Gernerth's money would be released, and then Teltscher could go to America. " Ilona must come too," decided Teltscher. That's where you make your mistake, my dear fellow, thought Esch, Ilona won't be mixed up with these things again; for though she might still be attached to Korn, that would not last much longer; soon she would be living in a distant, inaccessible castle, in whose grounds the deer grazed. He said that he must visit the police headquarters, and they made the necessary detour. In a stationer's shop Esch bought several newspapers and an envelope; he stuck the papers in his pocket, and with many flourishes addressed the envelope on the spot. Then he took out of his pocket-book the carefully folded sheet of paper, stuck it into the envelope and went over to the police buildings. As soon as he emerged again he continued his conversation; there was no need for Ilona to go with them. " Don't talk stuff," replied Teltscher, " in the first place, think of the splendid engagements we could get over there, and secondly, if the American idea should come to nothing, we must set to work here. She's idled long enough; besides, I've written to her already." " Nonsense," replied Esch rudely, " if you're dealing in young girls you can't take a woman with you." Teltscher laughed: " Well, if you think I shouldn't, you'll have to indemnify me for the damage to my prospects. You're a big capitalist now . . . and one generally brings back money from a business excursion, doesn't one? " Esch was alarmed; it seemed to him that Teltscher had glanced knowingly across at the police buildings—what could that mean? What did the Jewish conjurer know? he himself knew nothing of this business excursion; he turned on Teltscher: " Go to the devil! I haven't brought back any money." " No harm intended, Herr Esch, don't take it in that way, I didn't mean anything."

They turned into Mother Hentjen's restaurant, and to Esch it seemed again as though Teltscher possessed some secret knowledge, and might suddenly turn on him and say, " Murderer." He was afraid to look round the room. At last he raised his eyes and beheld a white patch, edged with cobwebs, where Hentjen's portrait had hung. He glanced across at Teltscher, but Teltscher said nothing, for he obviously had not noticed anything, had not noticed anything at all! Esch felt almost exultant; partly out of high spirits, partly to distract Teltscher's attention from the disappearance of the portrait, he went up to the orchestrion and set it noisily going; in response to the din Mother Hentjen appeared, and Esch felt a strong temptation to greet her with affectionate and tempestuous ardour; he would have liked to introduce her as Frau Esch, and if he refrained from this tender jest, it was not only because he felt grateful to her and prepared to respect her shyness, but also because Herr Teltscher-Teltini was quite unworthy of such a mark of intimacy. On the other hand Esch did not feel in the least bound to push discretion too far, and when after lunch Teltscher prepared to leave he did not accompany him as usual, to return afterwards by circuitous ways, no, he said quite openly that he would stay for a little and read his papers. He pulled the news-papers out of his pocket, put them back again, and remained sitting with his hands resting peacefully on his knees. He did not want to read. He contemplated the white patch on the wall. And when everything was quiet he went up the stairs. He felt grateful to Mother Hentjen and they had a pleasant afternoon. They spoke again of selling the business, and Esch thought that perhaps Oppenheimer might find a purchaser. And they tenderly discussed their marriage. There was a spot on the ceiling of the alcove that looked like a dark butterfly, but it was only dirt.

In the evening he dutifully set out on his search for girls. On his way it struck him that he should first look in to see what that lad Harry was doing. His search was in vain and he was about to leave the wretched place when Alfons entered. Fat Alfons presented a comical picture; his greasy dishevelled hair was sticking to his skull, his silk shirt was open, showing his white hairless breast, and one was reminded somehow of rumpled pillows. Esch could not help laughing. Alfons sat down beside a table near the door and groaned. Esch went up to him still laughing, yet in doing so it was as though he were trying to stifle something: " Hullo, Alfons, what's the matter? " The fat musician gazed at him with dull and hostile eyes. " Have a drink, and tell me what's wrong." Alfons drank a glass of brandy and remained silent. Finally he said: " Good God

. . . it's past belief . . . he's to blame for it himself, and he asks what's wrong! " " Don't talk nonsense. What is wrong? " " Good God! Why, he's dead! " Alfons put his hands under his chin and gazed in front of him; Esch sat down at the table. "Well, who is dead? " Alfons stammered: " He loved him too much." Now it sounded funny again. " Who loved whom? " Alfons's voice suddenly broke: "Don't talk like that; Harry's dead. . . ." So, Harry was dead. Esch could not really take it in and gazed somewhat blankly at the fat musician, down whose cheeks tears were running: " You put him quite beyond himself with your silly talk last time . . . he loved him too much . . . when he read it in the papers he locked himself in . . . this afternoon . . . and now they've found him . . . veronal." So, Harry was dead; in some way that fitted in, it was bound to come. Only Esch could not see how it fitted in. He said, " Poor chap," and suddenly he saw it and was filled with relief and joy because that forenoon he had handed in his letter at the police headquarters; here murder and counter-murder, debit and credit cancelled each other, here was for once an account that balanced itself perfectly. Funny to think that in spite of this he himself seemed to be in some way to blame. He said again: " Poor chap . . . why did he do it? " Alfons glared at him in blank astonishment: " But he saw it in the newspapers. . . ." " Saw what? " " There," Alfons pointed to the bunch of newspapers peeping from Esch's coat-pocket. Esch shrugged his shoulders—he had forgotten the newspapers. He pulled them out; there it was, in large letters, and with many circumlocutions, on the black-bordered last page, for all the firms with which he was connected, and his staff officials, and his workers, had insisted on the melancholy privilege of divulging the sad news that Herr Eduard von Bertrand, Chairman of the Board of Directors, a knight of various distinguished orders, etc., after a short serious illness had passed away. On the front page, however, along with a highly eulogistic obituary notice, was the information that, it was supposed in a sudden fit of mental aberration, the deceased had put an end to his life with a revolver shot. Esch read all this, but it did not very much interest him. It merely proved to him how right it was that the portrait had been removed that day. Funny that a man like this musician, who was not implicated at all, could make such a song about it. With a faint ironical grimace he clapped the fat musician benevolently and comfortingly on the flabby shoulder, paid for the brandy, and went back to Frau Hentjen. Stepping out complacently with long strides, he thought of Martin and reflected that now the cripple would no longer pursue him and menace him with his hard crutches. And that too was good.

Alone, Alfons put his head between his hands and stared in front of him. Esch seemed to him a bad man, like all men who sought women in order to possess them. He had learned by experience that all men of that type sowed evil. They seemed to him like savages running amok, raging through the world so that at their approach all one could do was to step aside. He scorned those men who rushed about in such a stupid fury, greedy not for life, which they obviously did not see, but for something which lay outside it, and to gain which they destroyed it in the name of this love of theirs. The musician was too dejected to think this out clearly; but he knew that although those men spoke with great ardour of their love, all that they meant by it was possession, or what is usually understood by that term. Of course he himself did not count, for at best he was a thoughtless chap, a poor devil of an orchestra player; but he knew that one did not attain the absolute by a long way when one decided for some woman. And he forgave the malignant rage of men, for he saw quite well that it sprang from fear and disappointment, saw that these passionate and evil men hid themselves behind a remnant of eternity to shield themselves from the fear that was always at their backs, telling them they must die. A stupid and thoughtless orchestra player he might be, but he could play sonatas from memory, and, versed in all kinds of knowledge, in spite of his sadness he could smile at the fact that human beings in their thirst for the absolute yearn for eternal love, imagining that then their lives can never come to an end, but will endure for ever. They might despise him because he had to play potpourris and polkas; nevertheless he knew that these hunted creatures, seeking the imperishable and the absolute in earthly things, would always find no more than a symbol and a substitute for the thing which they sought, and whose name they did not know: for they could watch others dying without regret or sorrow, so completely were they mastered by the thought of their own death; they furiously strove for the possession of some woman that they might in turn be possessed by her, for in her they hoped to find something steadfast and unchangeable which would own and guard them, and they hated the woman whom in their blindness they had chosen, hated her because she was only a symbol which they longed to destroy in their anger when they found themselves once more delivered over to fear and death. The musician felt pity for women; for although they wished for nothing better, yet they were not subject to that destructive and stupid passion for possession, they were less goaded by fear, and were thrilled more deeply when music was played to them, and stood in a more intimate and trustful relation to death: and in that women were like musicians, and even if one were oneself only a fat homosexual orchestra player, yet one could feel akin to them, could acknowledge that they had a faint divination that death was a sad and beautiful thing; for when they wept it was not because they had lost a possession, but simply because something that they had touched and seen had been good and gentle. Oh, those whose hearts thirsted for possession did not know the rapturous chaos of life, and the others knew little more of it; yet music divined it, music the melodious symbol of all that could be thought, music that annulled time so that it might be preserved in rhythm, that annulled death so that it might rise anew in sound. One who divined this, like the women and the musicians, might accept the disgrace of being thoughtless and stupid, and the musician Alfons ran his fingers over the rolls of fat on his body as though they were a good soft covering through which he could feel the presence of something precious and worthy of love; people could despise him and jeer at his effeminacy, well, he was only a poor devil, but nevertheless he was capable of surrendering himself more blissfully and passively and submissively to all the diverse manifestations of the eternal than those who jeered at him and yet made out of a tiny scrap of mortality the symbol and goal of their wretched striving. It was he who should despise the others. He was sorry even for Esch, and he could not help thinking of the heroic battle-music to whose strains the gladiators entered the arena, that the warrior, his courage stimulated, might forget that death stood at his back. He considered whether he should watch by Harry's bed, but he shuddered at the thought of the waxen face, and he decided instead to get drunk and watch the waiters and the customers, who moved about and yet bore on their faces the stamp of death.—

At the same hour that night Ilona rose from her bed and by the light of the tiny red lamp under the image of the Virgin regarded the sleeping form of Balthasar Korn. He was snoring, and when the sound ceased it was like the cessation of the music in the theatre before her act; and presently in the whistling of his breath the thin whizzing of the hurtling knives could be heard. Really she was not thinking of this at all, although she had received Teltscher's letter calling her back. She regarded Korn and tried to picture how he would have looked as a little boy and without his black moustache. She did not know clearly why she was doing this, but it seemed to her that then the Mother of God gazing from the wall would be readier to forgive her sin. For sin it was to have employed him for her unholy lust under the holy eyes of the Virgin, and if she had not been infected with disease as a young girl she too might have had children. That she had to forsake Korn left her indifferent, for she knew that someone else would succeed him; and that she had to return to Teltscher also left her indifferent; it did not give her a moment's thought that he was waiting for her in Cologne and counting on her; she simply knew that he needed her so that he might have someone at whom to throw his daggers. Also the fact that she was to go to America left her indifferent. She had travelled about too much already, and America was a place like any other place. She was without hope and without fear. She had learned to leave men, but for to-night she felt that she still belonged to Korn. She bore a scar on her neck, and she felt that the man to whom she had been unfaithful that time had been justified in trying to kill her. If Korn had been unfaithful to her, however, she would not have killed him, but merely thrown vitriol at him. Yes, in matters of jealousy such an apportionment of punishment seemed to her fitting, for if one possessed another one would want to destroy, but if one merely employed another one could content oneself with making the object unfit for use. That held good for everybody, even for a queen. For all human beings were the same, and no one could do any good to another. When she stood on the stage it was light, and when she lay with a man it was dark. One lived to eat, and ate to live. Once a man had killed himself because of her; it had not touched her very deeply, but she liked to remember it. Everything else sank into shadow, and in the shadow human forms moved like darker shadows which melted into one another and struggled to detach themselves again. Everybody did nothing but evil, it was as though they could not help punishing themselves for seeking enjoyment in one another. She was a little proud that she too had brought fatality, and when that man killed himself it had been like an act of expiation and a compensation from God for her barrenness. Many things were incomprehensible, indeed all. One could not brood over the meaning of happenings; but when children came into the world the shadows seemed to thicken and become corporeal, and then it was as though a sweet

music filled the world of shadows from end to end. That too perhaps
was why Mary bore the Christ-Child up there above the red lamp.
Erna would marry and have children: why had Lohberg not taken her,
instead of that skinny sallow little thing? She contemplated Korn and
found in his face nothing of what she sought; his hairy hands lay on
the sheet and had never been tender and young. She shuddered at the
sight of his red-lit fleshy face with the black moustache, and went softly
on her bare feet across to Erna's room, slipped gently and insinuatingly
in beside her, tenderly pressed herself against that angular body, and in
this posture fell asleep.

Esch now comported himself already almost as a prospective husband,
or, more correctly, a protector, for though they had not yet let fall any
hint of their engagement, Esch knew what was due to a weak woman,
and she allowed him to guard her interests. He was empowered to
deal not only with the man who brought the mineral water and ice, but
also with Oppenheimer, who at his suggestion had been entrusted with
the disposal of the business. For in addition to his theatrical work the
enterprising Oppenheimer undertook, whenever he got the chance, the
disposal of real estate, and acted for various kinds of agencies, and he
was of course delighted to devote all his attention to this matter. For
the moment, it was true, his mind was distracted by other cares. He
came to look over the house, but half way up the stairs he remained
standing and said: " Quite inexplicable, this business of Gernerth; I
hope to God nothing has happened to him . . . well, why should I bother,
it isn't my business." And although he repeated this again and again
as though to quiet his mind, he returned just as often to the fact that
Gernerth had now been away for eight days, now, at the very moment
when they were about to wind up the wrestling business and would
need the money for the salaries and the rent, which was in arrears. That
Gernerth, such a scrupulous fellow, should have allowed the rent to
get into arrears, he could never have believed it. And when they had
done so splendidly until recently, yes, quite splendidly. At present, of
course, they weren't even covering their expenses. Well, high time that
it was wound up. " And that ass Teltscher has let him go away without
even leaving the desk key, and can't do anything. And Gernerth has all
his money in the Darmstadt Bank! . . . too lofty and artistic, of course,
Herr Teltscher, to bother his head about such matters."

Esch had listened indifferently until now, especially as it seemed quite understandable to him that Teltscher should be more interested in the American project than in the wrestling, which was coming to an end. But now he pricked up his ears: money in the Darmstadt Bank? He flew at Oppenheimer: " My friends' investments are in that money in the Darmstadt Bank; it must be handed over! " Oppenheimer wagged his head: " Really it isn't any concern of mine," he said, " but to make sure I'll send a telegram to Gernerth in Munich. He must come and put things in order. You're right, there's no use in beating about the bush." Esch approved of the idea, and the telegram was sent off; they got no reply. Anxious now, they sent two days later a telegram to Frau Gernerth, reply prepaid, and learned that Gernerth had not returned to Munich at all. That was suspicious. And at the end of the week they must settle up all the accounts! There was nothing for it but to notify the police; the police discovered that three weeks before all the money that remained in the Darmstadt Bank had been lifted by Gernerth, and now no more doubt remained; Gernerth had absconded with the money! Teltscher, who had stuck up for Gernerth to the last moment, and now called himself the stupidest Jew in the world for being diddled again by a rotter, Teltscher was suspected of having played into Gernerth's hands. In view of the theatre properties which Gernerth had left him in pledge, it took him all his time to prove his innocence; but that he succeeded in doing so really helped him very little—he had hardly enough money left to tide him over the next few days. Helpless as a child, he blamed himself and the world at large, kept on repeating tiresomely that Ilona would have to come, and several times a day pestered Oppenheimer with requests for an immediate engagement. Oppenheimer took the blow more philosophically, for it was not his money that had been lost; he comforted Teltscher: things weren't so bad after all, as owner of the theatre properties a man with the name of Teltscher-Teltini would make a splendid theatre manager; if he could only get hold of some working capital everything would be all right again, and he would have many dealings yet with old Oppenheimer. Teltscher saw the idea at once, and recovered his old vigour so quickly and so completely that in a jiffy he had hatched out a new plan and straightway run with it to Esch.

But by the last turn of events Esch had been more than annoyed. Although he had always divined, yes even known, that the American journey would never come to anything, and although simply perhaps

because of this he had been so lax and casual in securing girls for it,
and although finally he actually felt a certain satisfaction at the fact that
his inner convictions had been justified: nevertheless his whole life had
been directed towards this American plan, and he felt now shaken to
the depths, for it seemed to him that the foundations of his connection
with Mother Hentjen had been undermined. Where was he to go with
her? and how did he stand in relation to this woman now? He had
wanted her to see him as the lord and master of a whole troupe of artists,
and now the whole lot had left him stranded in this measly fashion!
He felt ashamed to face Mother Hentjen.

It was while he was in this mood that Teltscher burst in upon him
with his plan: " Look here, Esch, you're a capitalist now, you could
come in as my partner." Esch stared at him as though he had gone out
of his wits: " A partner? Have you gone off your head? You know as
well as I do that it's all up with the American plan." " One can earn
a living in Europe," said Teltscher, " and if you want to invest your
money profitably . . ." " Money? What money? " shouted Esch. Well,
there wasn't any need to shout: he had heard casually that someone
had come in for a legacy, said Teltscher, and it made Esch quite furious:
" You've surely gone quite off your head," he shouted, " what is all this
drivel? Isn't it enough that I've been swindled once by you . . . ? " " If
that scoundrel Gernerth clears out, you can't hold me responsible for
it," said Teltscher in an offended voice, " I've lost more than you, and
because I'm down and out you needn't insult me when I bring you an
honourable proposal." Esch growled: " It's not a matter of my losses,
but the losses of my friends. . . ." " I offer you the chance of winning
the money back again." That was a hope, of course, and Esch asked
what Teltscher's proposals were. Why, with the theatre properties they
could start something, Oppenheimer thought that too, and Esch had
seen for himself that money could be made once one set about it with
any degree of skill. " And if I refuse? " Then of course there was nothing
for it but to store the theatre properties and secure an engagement
somewhere with Ilona. Esch became reflective; so Teltscher would have
to get an engagement with Ilona? . . . throw knives? . . . hm . . . he
would think it over.

Next day he made inquiries of Oppenheimer, for with Teltscher the
greatest caution was imperative. Oppenheimer confirmed Teltscher's
statements. " I see . . . then he'll have to get an engagement again with

Ilona. . . ." "He can count on me, I'll soon get an engagement for him," said Oppenheimer, "what else is there left for him to do?" Esch nodded: "And if he were to rent a theatre himself, he would need money . . . ?" "I don't suppose you have the few thousands needed?" said Oppenheimer. No, he hadn't. Oppenheimer wagged his head to and frc: it couldn't be done without money; perhaps they could interest somebody else in the matter . . . how about Frau Hentjen, for example, who wanted to sell her business and would have a lot of ready money at her disposal? He had no influence there, said Esch, but he would put the proposal to Frau Hentjen.

He did not like doing it, it was a new task, but there was no getting round it. Esch felt the victim of a most insidious attack. Quite possible that in spite of everything Oppenheimer and Teltscher were in league; the two Jews! Why should nothing remain for a bounder like that but to throw knives? as though there weren't honest and decent work to be had! And what was that he had drivelled about a death and a legacy? They had driven him into a cul-de-sac, it was as though they knew that nothing once done could be undone; that Ilona must be shielded from the knives and the world saved from injustice, that Bertrand's sacrifice must not have been in vain, any more than the removal of Herr Hentjen's portrait! No, nothing could be undone, nothing must be undone, for justice and freedom were involved, freedom, whose safety one dared no longer leave to the demagogues and the Socialists and the venal hirelings who wrote for the Press. That was his task. And that he had to retrieve Lohberg's and Erna's money seemed to him a part and a symbol of this higher task. And besides, if Teltscher could not rent a theatre, then the money would be lost for ever! There was no escape. Esch set the accounts against each other, made his calculations, and the sum gave the clear answer: he must induce Mother Hentjen to yoke herself like him to the task.

When he saw this clearly his uncertainty and anger faded. He mounted his bicycle, rode home, and sent Lohberg a detailed account of Herr Gernerth's incredible and revolting crime, adding that he had at once taken reliable measures to protect the investors, and begging the esteemed Fräulein Erna not to be disturbed.

So it was all up with America. Now he would have to stay in Cologne. The door of the cage had slammed to. He was imprisoned. The torch

of liberty was quenched. Strangely enough he could not feel angry with
Gernerth. For the real blame lay with a greater than Gernerth, with
one who in spite of all temptation and inducement had politely declined
to fly to America. Yes, that seemed to be the law, though it was not
justice; whoever sacrificed himself must give up his liberty first of all.
Nevertheless his position remained an incredible one. Esch repeated:
" Imprisoned," as though he had to convince himself of it. And
almost with a quiet mind, disturbed only by the merest twinge of conscience, he told Mother Hentjen that they would have to postpone the
American journey for the present, for Gernerth had sailed in advance
to make arrangements for them over there.

Really one could tell Mother Hentjen whatever one liked; she had
never shown the slightest interest either in the wrestling or in Herr
Gernerth, and besides in what happened around her she saw only what it
suited her to see. So now all that she saw was that the dreaded journey
to a strange and adventurous land was abandoned, and the knowledge
was like a warm and comforting bath into which her soul had been
unexpectedly dipped, and which she had to enjoy in silence for a little
before she said: " To-morrow I'll have in the painters, or winter will
be on us and then the walls won't dry properly." Esch was taken aback:
" The painters? But you want to sell the place! " Mother Hentjen put
her hands on her hips: " Oh well, it will be a good time yet before we
go,—I'll have the place painted, it must be kept in order." Esch shrugged
his shoulders and gave in: " Perhaps it will pay us, might get it back
in the price." " That's so," said Mother Hentjen. Nevertheless she
could not shake off a faint residue of uncertainty—who knew? perhaps
the American ghost had not been really laid—and she found it altogether
right and proper that she should pay something for her stability and
security. So Esch and Oppenheimer were very pleasantly surprised when
they found little trouble in persuading Frau Hentjen that the theatrical
business must be financed during Gernerth's absence; and she agreed
just as readily to a mortgage on the house, which Oppenheimer with
great foresight had brought with him. The transaction was concluded,
and Oppenheimer pocketed a commission of one per cent.

In this way did Mother Hentjen become a partner in Teltscher's new
theatrical venture; thanks to Oppenheimer's agency a theatre was
rented in the bustling town of Duisburg, and Mother Hentjen could
justly hope that she would share in really ample profits. Esch had in-

sisted on three conditions: first that he should retain the right to inspect the books, secondly that before the liquidation of the affair the remainder of Lohberg's and Erna's capital investment should be repaid (that was only just and reasonable, even if Mother Hentjen had no need to know anything about it), and thirdly he forced Herr Teltscher and Herr Oppenheimer by a clause in the contract to strike out the favourite knife-throwing act from any conjuring performance that might take place. " Off his jump! " said the two gentlemen; but Esch held to his point.

Thus far things had gone smoothly and in irreproachable order. The sacrifice which Mother Hentjen had made had now bound him to her for ever and rendered his decision irrevocable. True, the hated business was not yet sold, but the mortgage was in a way a first step towards the annihilation of the past. And in Mother Hentjen's bearing too there were things that might be read as signs of the beginning of a new life. She contested his marriage plans as little as she had contested the mortgage, and she was filled with a gentleness such as no one had seen in her hitherto. The autumn had come, premature and cold, and she wore again the grey dimity blouse, and was often without her corsets. Even her stiff coiffure seemed to have loosened; no doubt about it, she devoted no longer the old, cunning solicitude to her outward appearance, and in that too one could see the difference between the present and the past. Esch stamped through the house. If one were imprisoned and without anything to do, at least one should get something out of it. All the same, this couldn't be called a new life. At breakfast he sat in the restaurant, and at supper-time he was still sitting there. Mother Hentjen made sundry remarks about wastrels and ne'er-do-wells who liked to give themselves airs, but she fed him willingly. Esch put up with everything. He studied his newspaper, and sometimes examined the picture postcards sticking in the mirror frame, glad that among them there was none with his own handwriting. And he supervised the house-painters and whitewashers in case they should damage anything. It was easy for Mother Hentjen to talk. A fine lot she cared for the new life! With women it was a simple business anyway—Esch had to laugh—they could carry the new life about with them anywhere, under their hearts, that was to say. That of course was why they had no desire to go out into the new world, they had everything already within their four walls and thought that they had only to remain sitting in their cage to be innocent!

There they scrubbed and polished and fancied that by satisfying their petty mechanical instinct for order they had done the trick! The new life in a cage? as if it was as simple as all that!

No, with petty devices, with petty modifications, the new life, the state of innocence, was not to be brought about in captivity. The un-changeable, the already done, the earthly work-a-day world, was not so easy to circumvent. The house stood there unchanged, and no mark of that measly mortgage was to be seen on it. The streets, the towers, round which the autumn wind whistled, were unchanged, and of the breath of the future there was no longer any trace. And really to rouse from sleep Mother Hentjen's memories and Mother Hentjen's past life, one would need to set fire to the four corners of Cologne and raze it to the ground, until not one stone remained on another. For what good did it do him that Mother Hentjen now wore her hair a little less stiffly brushed back? she still strutted unchanged through the streets, and people lifted their hats to her, and everybody knew what name she bore. God knows, he had not thought it would be like this when, for the sake of the sacrifice, he had taken upon him her advancing years and her fading charms. Even if her hair were to grow grey overnight, if all at once she were to become a quite old woman who no longer could remember anything about her life, irrecognizable to all who had known her, a stranger attached by no bond to her accustomed surroundings,—even that might be the new life! And Esch could not keep back the thought that every fresh child aged the mother, and that childless women did not grow old: they were changeless and dead, with no hold on time. But when women were awaiting a new life, then they were filled with the hope that time would begin again for them, and it was as though the thing that aged them re-won for them a new virginity; it was to them a hope that all living beings might attain the state of innocence, a prophetic dream of death and yet new life, the coming of the kingdom of salvation in this ageworn world. Sweet, never-to-be-fulfilled hope.

Frankly, such thoughts would hardly have been to Mother Hentjen's taste. Anarchistic ideas, she would have called them. Perhaps even with justice. For one had revolutionary thoughts and made revolutionary speeches when one found oneself in prison. And did not even know that one was doing it. Esch clattered up and down the stairs, cursed the house, cursed the steps, cursed the workers. A fine appearance this new life of his had! The clean patch on the wall where the portrait had hung

was now painted over, so that one might almost imagine that the portrait
had been removed merely that the patch might be effaced. For no other
reason. Esch stared up at the wall. No, this was no new life at all that he
had begun; on the contrary, to all appearances Time had been put back
to where it was before. This woman seemed literally resolved to cancel
and undo everything. And one day after cleaning and dusting she came
down into the restaurant, sweating and blown and yet pleased with herself: " Ouf, you wouldn't believe how much the place was needing a
doing up." Esch asked absently: " When was it done up last? " but
suddenly it dawned on him that it must have been on the occasion of
her marriage; he brought down his fist on the table so that the plates
rattled, and shouted: " Of course the cage only needs to be painted each
time a new bird is put in it! " A little more, and he would have thrashed
her out there in the restaurant. He was tired of being forced to turn his
head the wrong way, always having to look back into the past. And on
the top of that she expected him to pay court to her; for she seemed in
no hurry with the marriage. On every side, unconquerable, the accustomed rose up again. And the substantial strand of settled habit was
palpable enough in all her new warmth and softness, and everything went
to show that not only did she contemplate taking up her old life again
and continuing it for all eternity, but it looked also as though she wished
to reduce love and lover alike to the rank of an ornamental accessory,
to a sort of painted wall decoration in the house of her life. And even
that semi-official intimacy which she had granted him as in a manner of
speaking a security for their bond, she was trying now to curtail again.
When he went off to Duisburg to supervise Teltscher's accounts, not
a word of appreciation did she vouchsafe him, and when he suggested
that she might perhaps go there with him some time, she talked of
impudence and retorted that he should stay there; that was the sort
of company that suited him.

    And Mother Hentjen was right! Yes, even in that! She was right to
show him that in her house he was no more than a merely tolerated
homeless orphan, one with whom nobody could have any real companionship. And yet she was not right! And that perhaps was the worst
of all. For behind her apparently justified coldness, behind her apparently righteous condemnation, the old senseless fear peeped out again
and again that he too—he, August Esch!—might simply have had his
eyes on her money in wanting to marry her. That became quite clear

when the deeds of mortgage arrived; Mother Hentjen pried about in
the papers for a while with an offended expression and at last said re-
proachfully: " Why, I never thought the stamp duty would be so high!
. . . I could easily have paid it out of my savings-bank account if I had
known," by which it became clear as the day that she possessed secret
reserves and preferred to conceal them, yes, preferred to accept a mortgage on her house rather than let him know anything about them. Not
to speak of putting them under his skilled supervision. Yes, that was
what this woman was like. She had learned nothing, knew nothing about
the kingdom of salvation, and desired to know nothing about it. And
the new life was a dead letter to her. She was striving again to return to
that commercial and conventional kind of love to which he had submitted
and yet could no longer endure: it was a vicious circle from which there
was no escape. What had been was inescapable and unalterable. Unassailable. And even if one were to annihilate the whole city—the dead
would still remain the mightier force.

And now Lohberg next made his appearance. He showed that his
suspicions were aroused because only the capital was to be repaid
without his and Erna's promised share of the profits. That was surely
the last straw. But when the fool hinted a little awkwardly and yet with
a certain pride that every penny would be a godsend to him, for Erna
was now well on the way, and they must seriously think of getting
married, it sounded to Esch like a voice from the beyond, and he knew
that his sacrifice was not yet complete. The faint and shabby hope that
this child, for which he disclaimed all responsibility, might after all be
Lohberg's, was swallowed up in the unearthly knowledge that for the
perfect love he had chosen an atonement must be made, atonement for
a blasphemy in which the menacing reverberation of murder could be
heard, so that his love was cursed with barrenness, while the child conceived in sin and without love would irrevocably come to birth. And
although he was full of anger at Mother Hentjen, who knew nothing
of this and thought only of getting her house painted instead of sharing
his terrors, he longed for such an atonement, and the wish that Mother
Hentjen might raise her arm to kill him again became strong. Yet in
spite of this he had to congratulate Lohberg, and shaking him by the
hand he said: " Your winnings will be paid if I can do it . . . as a christen-
ing gift." What else remained to be done? He passed his hand over his
stiff closely cropped hair, and a cool prickling sensation remained in

the palm of his hand. From Lohberg he learned also that Ilona was going to depart for Duisburg shortly. And he decided that beginning from the first of next month he must have Teltscher's books posted monthly to him in Cologne for supervision.

Yes, what else remained to be done? For it was all as it should be. Erna would have a child born in wedlock, and he would marry Mother Hentjen, and the restaurant would be freshly painted and laid with brown linoleum. And nobody guessed all that lay concealed behind the fine smooth surface, nobody knew by whom the child had been begotten who would now bear Lohberg's name, or that the perfect love in which he had sought salvation was nothing but a cheat and a lie, a blatant swindle to gloss over the fact that he was merely one among an indeterminate number of the snippety tailor's successors, he who had dreamt of flight and the joys of freedom, and yet now was condemned to rattle the bars of his cage. It was growing darker and darker, and the mists beyond the ocean would never thin away.

He began to avoid the house; it had become cramped and unfamiliar. He wandered along the banks of the Rhine, studied the rows of sheds, and gazed after the ships as they slowly floated down the river. He came to the Rhine Bridge, strolled on past the police headquarters to the Opera House, and reached the people's park. To stand on a seat and sing, with girls beating tambourines in front of one, yes, perhaps there was something in that, after all; to sing of the captive soul which could be set free through the power of redeeming love. Probably they were right, these Salvation Army idiots, in saying that first of all one must find one's way to this true and perfect love. Even the torch of liberty could not light one to redemption, for Bertrand, in spite of all his American and Italian journeys, had not been saved. It was simply no use trying to cheat oneself, one remained orphaned, one remained standing shivering in the snow, waiting for the redeeming grace of love gently to descend. Then, yes, then at last the miracle might descend, the miracle of perfect fulfilment. The home-return of the orphan child. The miracle of an ingemination of the world and of individual fate— and the child for whose sake Bertrand had stepped aside would not be a child of Erna's, but of another who in spite of everything would yet bring forth new life! Soon the snow would be coming, soft feathery snow. And the captive soul would be redeemed, hallelujah, would stand up on the bench, higher than he had stood who was accustomed to stand so high. And in his spirit Esch for the first time named that other who was to bear him the child by her Christian name: Gertrud.

Every time he came home he looked in her face. Her face was friendly, and her mouth conscientiously enumerated all the things that she had cooked that morning. And if August Esch had not any great hunger he turned away. It horrified him to think, and the knowledge was inescapable, that her womb was killed, or worse still that only a misbegotten monstrosity was to be expected from it. Only too well did he know the curse, only too well the murderous fury that was wreaked, and would continue to be wreaked, by the dead on women. Again the question tortured him so deeply that he did not dare to pose it . . . had children been denied to her, or had he and his predecessors only served her lust? His covetous rage against Mother Hentjen mounted, and once more he was in no state of mind to call her by the name by which the dead man called her, and he vowed that that name would not cross his lips until she had understood all that was involved. She did not understand, however. She received him submissively and matter-of-factly, and left him alone in his isolation. He tried to submit to fate; it was not perhaps a question of the child so much as of her readiness to have one, and he waited for some signs of that. But there too she failed him, and when, to prompt her, he dropped a hint that after their marriage they would want to have children, she merely returned a dry and matter-of-fact "Yes," but she did not give him the sign he was waiting for, and in their nights she did not cry that he must give her a child. He beat her, but she did not understand, and remained silent. Until he reached the knowledge that even that would not have availed; for even then the doubt would have remained, the ineluctable doubt whether she might not have begged Herr Hentjen too for a child, and the child whose father he longed to be might just as well have been one from Hentjen's loins as from his. No woman can hope to help a man caught in the despairing agonies of the unprovable. And deeply as he tormented himself, she could only look on in incomprehension; nevertheless it was only an unavailing gesture now, it was only, so to speak, a symbol and an intimation, when he beat her. His resistance was broken.

For he recognized that in the actual world fulfilment could never be achieved, recognized ever more clearly that even the farthest away places lay in the actual world, that all flight thither was senseless, as well as all hope of seeking there sanctuary from death, and fulfilment and freedom—and that the child itself, even if it came alive out of its mother's body, signified nothing more than the fortuitous cry of pleasure with which it was conceived, a dying and long since vanished cry which was of no significance for the existence of the lover who evoked it. The child would be a stranger, strange as that long past cry, strange as the past, strange as the dead and as death, wooden and empty. For unchangeable was the earthly though it might appear to change, and even were the whole world born anew, in spite of the Redeemer's death it would never attain a state of innocence in this life until the end of Time.

True, this knowledge was not very clear, but it sufficed to move Esch to organize his earthly life in Cologne, to seek a decent job and go about his business. Thanks to the excellent credentials which he possessed, he secured a prouder and more responsible position than he had yet occupied, and now once more earned all the pride and admiration which Mother Hentjen kept ready to expend on him. She had the restaurant laid with brown linoleum, and now that the danger of emigration seemed finally to be banished, she herself began to speak of their American castles in the air. He entered into her mood, partly because he felt that she was talking in this way to please him, and partly out of a sense of duty; for though he could hardly hope to see America now, he was resolved never to forsake the way that led towards it, never to turn back in spite of the invisible presence that followed him with the spear ready to strike, and an inward knowledge, hovering between dream and divination, told him that his way was now only a symbol and an intimation of a higher way which one had to walk in reality and in truth, and of which this one was only the earthly reflection, wavering and uncertain as a reflection in a dark pool. All this was not completely clear to him, indeed even the words of holy men, in which fulfilment and the absolute might be sought, did not help him. But he recognized that it was mere chance if the addition of the columns balanced, and so after all he could contemplate the earthly as from a higher coign of vantage, as from an airy castle rising from the plain, shut off from the world and yet open like a mirror to it; and often it seemed to him as though all that had been done or spoken or had come about was no more than a procession on a dimly lit stage, a representation which was soon forgotten and never palpably present, a thing already past which no one could lay hold on without increasing earthly suffering. For fulfilment always failed one in the actual world, but the way of longing and of freedom was endless

and could never be fully trod, was narrow and remote like that of the
sleepwalker, though it was also the way which led into the open arms
and the living breast of home. So Esch was strange in his love and yet
more at home in the earthly world than formerly, so that it made no
difference and everything still remained in the super-earthly, even if
for the sake of justice much still remained to be done for Ilona in the
sphere of the earthly. He talked to Mother Hentjen of America, the
land of freedom, and of the sale of the business, and of their marriage,
as to a child whom one wants to please, and sometimes he could call her
Gertrud again, even if she remained nameless to him in the nights when
he lay with her. They went hand in hand, although each walked a different
and endless road. When presently they got married, and the business
was knocked down for an absurdly low price, these were stations on
their symbolical road, yet at the same time stations on the road leading them nearer to the lofty and the eternal, which, if Esch had not
been a Freethinker, he might even have called the divine. But he knew
nevertheless that here on earth we have all to go our ways on crutches.

IV

When the theatre in Duisburg went bankrupt and both Teltscher
and Ilona were once more left destitute, Esch and his wife put almost
the whole of what remained of their means into the theatrical business,
and soon they had finally lost their money. Yet Esch now secured a
post as head book-keeper in a large industrial concern in his Luxemburg
home, and for this his wife admired him more than ever. They went
their way hand in hand and loved each other. He still sometimes beat
her, but less and less, and finally not at all.

PART THREE

THE REALIST
(1918)

CHAPTER I

HUGUENAU, whose forefathers might well have been called Hagenau before Alsace was occupied in 1692 by Condé's troops, had all the characteristics of the town-bred Alemanni. He was thick-set, inclined to be fat, and had worn glasses since his boyhood, or, to be more precise, since the time when he had attended the commercial school in Schlettstadt, and now that he was approaching his thirtieth year at the outbreak of the war he retained no trace of his youth either in face or behaviour. He did business in Baden and Württemberg, partly in branch establishments of his father's textile firm, André Huguenau, Colmar, Alsace, partly on his own account and as a representative of various Alsatian factories for which he acted as agent in that section of the country. In these provincial circles his reputation was that of an energetic, prudent and reliable man of business.

There is no doubt that with his capabilities he would have done better at smuggling, which the times made more profitable, than at soldiering. But he submitted without further ado when in 1917 his extreme short-sightedness was summarily ignored and he received a call to arms, as the phrase went. True, even while he was being trained in Fulda he did manage to wind up a tobacco business here and there, but soon enough he dropped everything. Not only because his military duties made him tired or inapt for other things. It was simply so pleasant not to have to bother about anything at all, and it reminded him vaguely of his schooldays; the boy who was once at school, Huguenau (Wilhelm), could still remember his last Speech Day in the Schlettstadt Academy, and how he and his class-mates had been dedicated by the Head to the serious issues of life, serious issues which hitherto he had coped with well enough and now had to abandon again in favour of a new schooling. Once more he was pinned down to an endless succession of duties that had been forgotten in the course of years, once more he was treated as a pupil and shouted at, had a similar attitude to the common lavatories as in his boyhood, and attached the same importance to food, while the ceremonies of respect and the ambitious competition in which he found himself involved gave a completely infantile stamp to the whole. As if that were not enough, he was quartered in a school building, and before falling asleep could see the two rows of lights with their green-and-white shades and the blackboard that had been left where it was. All this confused his schooldays and his soldiering days in an inextricable tangle, and even when the battalion set off at last to the Front, singing childish songs and bedecked with little flags, crowded into primitive sleeping-quarters in Cologne and Liège, Huguenau the fusilier could not get rid of the notion that he was on a school excursion.

It was evening when his company moved into the front line. They were posted in a fortified trench which was approached by long covered passage-ways. Unexampled filth reigned in the dug-outs, the floors were covered with spittle both fresh and dry, there were streaks of urine on the walls, and it could not be determined whether the prevailing stench was that of fæces or of corpses. In any case Huguenau was too tired to realize the actual sights and smells around him. Even while trotting in single file through the approach trenches all the men already had the feeling of being outcasts from the sheltering warmth of comradeship and common life, and hardened as they were to the complete lack of cleanliness, little as they missed the conventions of civilization with which humanity seeks to banish the stench of death and corruption, however surely the repression of their disgust advanced them one step towards heroism (a step that links heroism most strangely with love), long as most of them had been accustomed to live among horrors during the years of war, so that they merely joked and swore as they made their beds, yet there was not one among them who did not know that he was posted there as a solitary creature to live alone and to die alone in an overwhelmingly senseless world, so senseless that he could not comprehend it or rise beyond describing it as " this bloody war."

It was at a time when the various general staffs had reported that in the Flanders section complete quiet prevailed. The company that had just been relieved also asserted that there was nothing doing. And yet as soon as darkness fell the artillery on both sides began a cannonade that was severe enough to banish their weariness from the newcomers. Aching in every bone, Huguenau sat on a kind of camp-bed, and only after a fair length of time did he remark that his limbs were all trembling and twitching. The other men were in no better case. One of them was weeping. Some of the old soldiers, indeed, were merely amused: this was just a game the batteries played every night, it meant nothing, one soon got used to it; and taking no further notice of their weaker brethren they were actually snoring in a minute or two.

Huguenau would have liked to remonstrate with somebody: this was not at all what he had bargained for. Sick and faint as he was, he yearned for fresh air, and when his knees began to tremble less he tottered to the entrance of the dug-out, sat down there on a box and stared with vacant eyes at the firework display in the sky. Time and again he thought he saw the figure of a man flying up to Heaven with one hand raised in an orange cloud. Then he remembered Colmar, and that his school class had been taken one day to be lectured on art in the Museum; it had been rather boring, but there was one picture, standing like an altar in the middle of the floor, that had terrified him. It was, moreover, a Crucifixion. He detested crucifixions. That reminded him that years ago he had had to put in a Sunday in Nürnberg, between visits to customers, and had gone to see the torture chamber. Now that had been interesting. There was a fine collection of pictures too. One of them showed a man chained to a kind of camp-bed, a man who, the inscription said, had murdered a clergyman in Saxony by stabbing him repeatedly with a dagger, and now had to lie on that bed waiting to be broken on the wheel. To be broken on the wheel was a punishment sufficiently explained by other exhibits in the place. The man had a good-humoured expression, and it was just as unimaginable that he had stabbed a pastor and was doomed to be broken on the wheel, as that Huguenau himself should have to sit where he was, on a camp-bed in a stench of corpses. No doubt the man had ached all over too, and was bound to befoul himself since he was chained down. Huguenau spat, and said "Merde!" He went on sitting at the door of the dug-out like a sentry; he leaned his head against a post, he had turned up his coat-collar, he was no longer cold, he was not asleep, but neither was he awake. The torture chamber and the dug-out blended and sank more profoundly into the sordid and yet brilliant colours of Grünewald's altar-piece, and while in the palpitating orange light of the distant cannonade and the shooting rockets the boughs of naked trees stretched their arms towards Heaven, a man with uplifted hand soared through the illuminated vault of the sky.

When the first grey light of dawn came cold and leaden Huguenau noticed the tufts of grass at the lip of the trench and a few daisies that had survived from last year. So he simply crawled out and made off. He knew that he might be picked off at any moment by the English, and that similar attentions would be paid to him by the German outposts; but the world lay as if under a vacuum glass—Huguenau could not help thinking of a glass cover over cheese—grey, worm-eaten and completely dead in a silence that was inviolable.

CHAPTER II

Bathed in the limpid air that heralds the spring, the deserter made his way unarmed through the Belgian landscape. Haste would have served him little, prudent caution served him better, and weapons would not have protected him at all; it was, one might say, as a naked man that he slipped through the armed forces. His untroubled face was a better protection than weapons or hurried flight or forged papers.

For the Belgians were suspicious fellows. Four years of war had not improved their disposition. Their corn, their potatoes, their horses and cows had all had to suffer. And when a deserter came to them looking for sanctuary they examined him with twofold suspicion, lest he might be one of the men who had beaten on their doors with a rifle-butt. And even if the fugitive spoke passable French and gave himself out as an Alsatian, in nine cases out of ten that would have availed him little. Woe to the man who strayed into a village merely as a fugitive timidly imploring help! But a man who came like Huguenau with a ready jest on his lips, with a beaming and friendly face, found it easy enough to have beer smuggled to him in the barn, or even to sit with the family of an evening in the kitchen and tell tales of the Prussians' brutality and violence in Alsace; such a stranger was welcomed and got his share of the hoarded provisions; with luck he might even be visited in his bed of hay by one of the maids.

It was still more advantageous, of course, to get into the parsonages, and Huguenau soon discovered that he could manage this by way of the confessional. He made his confessions in French, skilfully grafting an account of his miserable plight on to the admission of his sin in breaking his oath of allegiance. To be sure, the results were not always pleasant. Once he hit upon a priest, a tall lean man so ascetic and passionate in appearance that Huguenau almost shrank from presenting himself at the parsonage on the evening after confession, and when he saw the severe figure busy at spring work in the orchard he felt inclined to turn tail. But the priest came quickly towards him. " Suivez-moi," he said harshly, and led him indoors.

For nearly a week Huguenau stayed there on meagre rations with a bed in the attic. He was given a blue blouse and set to work in the garden; he was awakened for Mass and permitted to eat in the kitchen at the same table as his silent host. Not a word was said of his escape, and the whole affair was like a penance that sat but ill on Huguenau. He had even made up his mind to quit the relative security of his asylum and continue his dangerous flight, when one day—eight days after his arrival —he found a suit of civilian clothes laid out in his attic. He was to accept the suit, said the priest, and he was free to go or to stay as he chose; only he could no longer be boarded there, for there was not sufficient food. Huguenau decided to go on farther, and as he embarked on a lengthy speech of thanks the priest cut him short: " Haïssez les Prussiens et les ennemis de la sainte religion. Et que Dieu vous bénisse." He lifted two fingers in benediction, made the sign of the Cross, and the deep-set eyes in his peasant face gazed with burning hate into a distant region inhabited, presumably, by Prussians and Protestants.

When Huguenau quitted that parsonage it became clear to him that he had to think out a definite plan of escape. Formerly he had often enough hung about in the neighbourhood of various corps headquarters where he passed without comment among the other soldiers, but that had now become impossible. He was really depressed by his civilian clothes; they were like an admonition to return to the work-a-day world of peace, and that he had donned them at the command of the priest seemed now a lapse into stupidity. The priest's offer was an unauthorized interference with his private life, and he had paid dear enough to secure his private life. Besides, even if he did not regard himself as belonging to the Kaiser's forces, yet as a deserter he had a peculiar, one might almost say a negative connection with them, and in any case he belonged to the war and he did not disapprove of the war. For instance, he had not been able to stomach the way in which men in the canteens abused the war and the newspapers, or asserted that Krupp had been buying up newspapers in order to prolong the war. For Wilhelm Huguenau was not only a deserter, he was a man of business, a salesman who admired all factory-owners for producing the wares that the rest of the world used. So if Krupp and the coal barons bought newspapers they knew what they were doing, and had a perfect right to do it, as much right as he had to wear his uniform as long as he pleased. There was no reason, therefore, why he should return to that background of civilian life which the priest with his suit of clothes had obviously destined for him, nothing to induce him to return to his native country in which there were no holidays, and which stood for all that was commonplace.

So he remained in the base lines. He turned southwards, avoiding towns and calling at villages, came through the Hennegau and penetrated to the Ardennes. The war by that time had lost much of its formality, and deserters were no longer closely hunted—there were too many of them, and the authorities did not want to admit their existence. Still, that does not explain how Huguenau got out of Belgium undiscovered; one can attribute it rather to the somnambulistic sureness with which he picked his way through the dangerous zone; he walked along in the clear air of early spring, walked light-heartedly as if under a glass bell, cut off from the world and yet in it, and he was untroubled by reflections. From the Ardennes he crossed into German territory, coming out on the bleak plateau of the Eifel where winter still prevailed and it was difficult to make headway. The inhabitants did not bother about him, they were surly, silent people, and they hated every extra mouth that sought a share of their scanty provender. Huguenau had to take to the train and break into his savings, hitherto untouched. The serious issues of life threatened him again in a new and different guise. Something had to be done to secure and prolong his holiday.

CHAPTER III

The little town lay girdled by vineyards in a tributary valley of the Moselle. The heights above were crowned by woods. The vineyards were all in trim, with the vine-stocks set in straight lines interrupted at places by outcrops of reddish rock. Huguenau observed with disapproval that many of the owners had not weeded their plots, and that the neglected patches stood out like rectangular yellow islets among the reddish grey soil of the others.

After the last days of winter in the Eifel highlands Huguenau had come down all at once into the real springtime. Like a promise of inalienable order and comfort the sun radiated gay well-being and light security into his heart. Any anxiety that might have lurked there could be thrown off. It was a satisfaction to him to see in the forefront of the town the stately District Hospital with its long facade lying in the morning shadow, he approved the fact that all its windows were open as if it were a southern sanatorium, and he found it pleasant to imagine the light spring airs blowing through the white wards. He approved, too, the large red cross marked on the roof of the hospital, and as he passed by he cast a benevolent glance at the soldiers in their grey hospital uniform, who were convalescing, some in shadow and some in the sun of the garden. Across the river lay the barracks, recognizable by its style of architecture, and a building resembling a monastery which he later discovered to be the prison. But the road sloped down towards the town in a friendly and comfortable manner, and as Huguenau passed through the mediæval town gate, a small fibre case in his hand just like the case of samples he used to carry, it did not even ruffle him that his entry reminded him strongly of similar entries into Württemberg towns which once upon a time—and how long ago it seemed—he had visited on his business rounds.

The streets, too, were so old-fashioned that they reminded him of his compulsory day of rest in Nürnberg. Here in Kur-Trier the war of the Palatinate had not raged with such ruthlessness as in the other regions west of the Rhine. The old fifteenth- and sixteenth-century houses were still intact, and so was the Gothic Town Hall in the market-place, with its Renaissance outworks and the tower before which stood the old pillory. And Huguenau, who had visited many a lovely old town on his commercial rounds, but had remarked none of them, was seized by a novel emotion which he could not have given a name to or traced to any known source, but which made him feel curiously at home in this town: if it had been described to him as an æsthetic emotion or as an emotion springing from a sense of freedom, he would have laughed incredulously, with the laughter of a man who has never had even an inkling of the beauty of the world, and he would have been right, in so far as nobody can determine whether it is freedom that opens the eyes of the soul to beauty, or beauty that gives the soul its vision of freedom, but yet he would have been wrong, for there was bound to be even in him a deeper human wisdom, a human longing for that freedom in which all the light of the world has its source and that finally creates the Sabbath that hallows life; and since this is so and cannot be otherwise, a gleam of the higher light may well have fallen on Huguenau in that very moment when he crawled out of the trench and shook himself free of human obligations, a gleam of that light which is freedom and which entered even into him and for the first time dedicated him to the Sabbath.

Far removed from speculations of this nature, Huguenau engaged a room in the hotel in the market-place. As if to assure himself that he was still on holiday, he set out to have a jolly evening. The Moselle wine was not rationed and in spite of the war had retained its quality. Huguenau treated himself to three pannikins full and sat long over them. There were citizens all round at the various tables; Huguenau was an alien among them, and here and there hasty questioning glances were directed at him. They all had their business and their pre-occupations, and he himself had nothing. None the less he was happy and contented. He was himself amazed: no employment and yet happy! so happy that he found pleasure in recapitulating to himself all the difficulties that would incontestably arise should a man like himself, a stranger without identification papers and without any connections in the town, attempt to set up business and obtain credit. It was extra-ordinarily funny to imagine the fix he would be in. Perhaps the wine was responsible. Huguenau, at any rate, as he climbed into bed with a somewhat addled head, did not feel like a worried commercial traveller, but like a merry and light-hearted tourist.

CHAPTER IV

When Gödicke, a bricklayer in the Landwehr, was unearthed from the ruins of his trench, his mouth, gaping as if for a scream, was filled with earth. His face was a blackish blue, and he had no discernible heart-beat. Had not the two ambulance men who found him made a bet about his survival he would simply have been re-buried immediately. That he was fated to see the sun again and the sunny world, he owed to the ten cigarettes which the winner of the bet was due to receive.

He could not be said to have revived under artificial respiration, although both men toiled and sweated over him, but they carried him off and observed him closely, abusing him from time to time because he so obstinately refused to solve the riddle of his life, the riddle of his death; and they were tireless in shoving him under the doctors' noses.

So the object of their bet lay for four whole days in a field hospital without moving and with a blackened skin. Whether during this time a dim flicker of infinitesimal slumbering life began to glimmer and was fanned with pain and anguish through the wreck of the body, or whether it was a faint and ecstatic pulsing on the verge of a great beyond, we do not know and Gödicke of the Landwehr could not have told.

For it was only piecemeal, half a cigarette at a time, so to speak, that the life returned to his body, and this slow caution was both proper and natural, since what his crushed body demanded was the utmost immobility. For many long days Ludwig Gödicke must have fancied himself the child in swaddling-clothes that he had been forty years before, constricted by an incomprehensible restraint and feeling nothing save the restraint. And if he had been capable of it he might well have whimpered for his mother's breast, and as a matter of fact he soon did begin to whimper. It was during the journey, and his whimpering was like the incessant mewling of a newly born child; nobody was willing to lie next to him, and one night another patient even threw something at him. That was during the time when everyone believed that he would have to die of hunger, since it was impossible for the doctors to find a way of introducing nourishment into him. That he went on living was inexplicable, and the Surgeon-Major's opinion that his body had nourished itself on all the bruised blood under the skin was scarcely worth calling an opinion, let alone a theory. The lower part of his body in especial was terribly injured. He was laid in a cold pack, but whether that alleviated his sufferings at all could not be determined. But it was possible that he had ceased to suffer so much, for the whimpering gradually died away. Until a few days later it broke out again more strongly: it was now—or one may imagine that it was—as if Ludwig Gödicke were recovering his soul only in single fragments, and as if each fragment came to him on a wave of agony. It may be that that was so, even though it cannot be proved; it may be that the anguish of a soul that has been torn and pulverized into atoms and must join itself together again is greater than any other anguish, keener than the anguish of a brain that quivers under renewed spasms of cramp, keener than all the bodily suffering that accompanies the process.

Thus Gödicke of the Landwehr lay in his bed on rubber air-cushions, and while it was impossible to nurse his battered body, while food was slowly injected in minute doses, his soul collected itself; to the bewilderment of Doctor Kühlenbeck, the Senior Medical Officer, to the bewilderment of Doctor Flurschütz, to the bewilderment of Sister Carla, his soul collected itself with agony around the core of his ego.

CHAPTER V

Huguenau woke up early. He was an energetic man. A decent bedroom; no garret such as he had had with the priest; a good bed. Huguenau scratched his leg. Then he tried to find his bearings.

A hotel; the market-place; and the Town Hall was facing him.

There were really many inducements for him to go back and take up the threads of his life again in the place where they had been dropped; there were many reasons why he should do his duty as a business man and pick up easy money as an agent for butter and textiles. Yet the very idea of casks of butter and sacks of coffee and bales of textiles was so repugnant to him that he was himself surprised,—and the repugnance was really a matter for surprise to a man who since his boyhood had thought and spoken of nothing but money and trading. And the thought of being on holiday from school came up again most amazingly. Huguenau found it pleasanter to meditate on the town he happened to be in.

Behind the town were the vineyards. And in many of them were weeds. The owner had probably been killed in the war or was a prisoner. His wife could not manage the work alone, or was running round with another man. Besides, the price of wine was controlled by the State. Unless one could sell wine on the sly it wasn't worth while to tend the vineyard. But the wines were of fine quality; they actually went a little to one's head.

A war widow like that would really be glad to sell her vineyard cheap.

Huguenau began to think of possible buyers for stocks of Moselle. One should be able to find them. One could make a good bit of commission on the deal. Wine-shippers were the people. Friedrichs' in Cologne, Matter & Co. in Frankfort. He had delivered pipes of wine to them before.

He jumped out of bed. His plan was made.

He tidied himself before the looking-glass. Combed his hair back. It had grown long since the company's barber had shaved it. Now when had that been? It seemed to be in a former life; if it weren't that hair grew slowly in winter he would have had a fine mane. When a man is dead his hair and nails go on growing. Huguenau took a strand of his hair and pulled it down over his forehead. It reached almost to the point of his nose. No, a man couldn't go about in that state. One always had one's hair cut just before a holiday. True, this wasn't a holiday. But it wasn't so very unlike one.

The morning was bright. A little chilly.

There were two yellow armchairs with black-leather seats in the barber's shop. The barber himself, a shaky old man, tied the not-very-clean overall round Huguenau's neck, and tucked a roll of paper into his collar. Huguenau moved his chin a little to and fro; the paper rasped him.

There was a newspaper hanging on a hook and Huguenau asked for it. It was the local *Kur-Trier Herald*, with a supplement on " Farming and Viniculture in the Moselle District." That was exactly what he needed.

He sat motionless, studying the paper, and then he looked at himself in the glass; he could easily have passed for one of the more solid citizens in the place. His hair was now cut as he liked it, short, respectable, and German. On top of his head a few strands of longer hair were left to make a parting. The next thing was to be shaved.

The barber whipped up a thin lather that spread cold and sparingly over Huguenau's face. The soap was no good.

" The soap's not up to much," said Huguenau. The barber made no reply, but stropped his razor. Huguenau was offended, but after a while said excusingly: " War goods."

The barber began to shave. With short, scraping strokes. He did it badly. Still, it was pleasant to be shaved. Shaving oneself was one of the conditions of war. Cheaper, too; but for once in a while it was pleasant to have it done for one. More like a holiday. There was a picture of a girl hanging on the wall with a lavish display of bosom, and beneath her were the words " Lotion Houbigant." Huguenau had laid back his head and let the paper hang in his idle hands. The barber was now shaving his chin and throat; was he never going to finish? Well, Huguenau didn't care; he had plenty of time. And to put off time a little longer he ordered a " Lotion Houbigant." What he got was eau-de-Cologne.

Freshly shaved, a clean-shaven spruce man with the scent of eau-de-

Cologne in his nose, Huguenau walked back to the inn. When he took off his hat he sniffed at the lining. It smelt of pomade, and that too was satisfactory.

There was no one in the dining-room. Huguenau got his coffee and the maid brought out a bread-card from which she snipped a portion. There was no butter, only a blackish syrupy kind of jam. Nor was the coffee real coffee, and while he sipped the hot liquid Huguenau reckoned up how much profit the manufacturers were making on their coffee-substitute; he reckoned it up without envy and approved it. In any case buying wine cheap in the Moselle district was just as profitable a venture, an excellent investment. And when he had finished his break-fast he set about drawing up an advertisement offering to buy wines of good quality. Then he took it along to the office of the *Kur-Trier Herald*.

CHAPTER VI

The District Hospital had become entirely a military hospital. Dr Friedrich Flurschütz was making his round of the wards. He was wear-ing a military cap with his doctor's white overall; a combination which Lieutenant Jaretzki characterized as absurd.

Jaretzki had been put into Officers' Room III. That had been pure chance, for these double-bedded rooms were supposed to be reserved for Staff Officers, but once he was in he stayed there. He was sitting on the edge of his bed with a cigarette in his mouth when Flurschütz came in, and his arm in its unwrapped bandage was lying on the bedside table.

" Well, how are we, Jaretzki? "

Jaretzki indicated his arm:

" The Surgeon-Major's just been in."

Flurschütz looked at the arm and touched it cautiously here and there:

" A bad business . . . gone a bit further? "

" Yes, an inch or so . . . the old man wants to amputate."

The arm lay there inflamed and reddish, the palm of the hand swollen, the fingers like red sausages, and round the wrist a ring of purulent blisters.

Jaretzki regarded his arm and said:

" Poor thing, look at it lying there."

" Don't worry about it, it's only the left."

" Yes, all you want to do is to cut things off."

Flurschütz shrugged his shoulders:

" Can't be helped; this century has been devoted to surgery and rewarded by a world-war with guns . . . now we're beginning to find out about glands, and by the time the next war comes along we'll be able to do wonders with these damned gas-poisonings . . . but for the present the only thing we can do is cut."

Jaretzki said:

" The next war? Don't tell me you believe that this one's ever going to come to an end."

" I don't need to be a prophet to do that, Jaretzki, the Russians have given it up already."

Jaretzki laughed bitterly:

" God preserve you in your childish faith and send us decent cigarettes. . . ."

With his sound right hand he had drawn a packet of cigarettes from the open shelf under the drawer of the table and now offered it to Flurschütz.

Flurschütz pointed to the ash-tray full of cigarette-butts:

" You shouldn't smoke so much. . . ."

Sister Mathilde came in.

" Well, do we bind it up again . . . what's your opinion, Doctor? "

Sister Mathilde was looking well. She had freckles on her forehead. Flurschütz said:

" It's a bad business, this gas."

He stayed to watch the Sister binding up the arm and then he went on his rounds again. At both ends of the broad corridor the windows were wide open, but no current of air could blow away the hospital smell.

CHAPTER VII

The house lay in Fischerstrasse, one of the side-streets leading down to the river, a timbered edifice in which, it was obvious, all sorts of handicrafts had been carried on for centuries. Beside the door there was a black battered tin plate with the words in faded gold-lettering: " *Kur-Trier Herald*, Editorial and Business Office (in the courtyard)."

Penetrating through the narrow passage-like entry, where in the darkness he stumbled over the trap-door leading down to the cellar, and passing an opening that gave on the stairs leading to the dwelling-house, Huguenau found himself in an unexpectedly spacious courtyard shaped somewhat like a horseshoe. A garden adjoined the courtyard; there a few cherry-trees were in blossom, and beyond the garden one's gaze was lost in the lovely mountain country.

The whole place witnessed to the semi-peasant character of its former possessor. The two wings had certainly served as granaries and stables; the left one had two storeys, and there was a steep and narrow wooden ladder on the outer wall; probably the top floor had once been the servants' quarters. The upper storey of the stable buildings on the right was a hayloft, and one of the stable doors had been displaced by a large business-like barred window, behind which a printing-press could be seen at work.

From the man at the printing-press Huguenau learned that Herr Esch was to be found on the first floor opposite.

So Huguenau climbed the wooden steps and found himself plump before a door with the inscription, " Editorial and Business Office," behind which Herr Esch, owner and publisher of the *Kur-Trier Herald*, exercised his functions. He was a lean man with a clean-shaven face in which, between two long and deep furrows running down the cheeks, a mouth as mobile as an actor's grimaced sarcastically, showing a set of strong yellowish teeth. He had something of the actor about him, something of the clergyman, and something of the horse.

The advertisement which Huguenau handed to him he scrutinized with the air of an examining magistrate considering a document. Huguenau took out his pocket-book, from which he extracted a five-mark note, as a hint, so to speak, that he was prepared to allot that sum for the insertion of the advertisement. But the other, paying not the least attention to this, asked abruptly: " So you're out to exploit the people round about here, are you? I suppose the poverty of our wine-growers is common talk already—heh? "

It was an unprovoked attack, and Huguenau decided that its purpose was to force up the price for inserting the advertisement. He produced therefore another mark, but that merely had the opposite effect from what he had wished: " Thanks . . . you can keep your advertisement. . . . Evidently you don't appreciate what it means to corrupt the Press

. . . let me tell you, you won't corrupt me with your six marks, nor with ten, nor with a hundred! "

Huguenau became more and more certain that he was dealing with a sharp business man. But simply for that reason it was imperative that he should not give way; perhaps the man was waiting for him to suggest going shares in the venture, and after all that arrangement would not be without its advantages.

" Hm, I've heard that these advertisement deals are sometimes made on a percentage basis—how about a half-per-cent commission on the results? Of course in that case you would have to insert the announcement three separate times at least . . . still, you're quite at liberty to insert it oftener than that, when it's a matter of generosity I impose no limits . . ." he risked a confidential laugh and sat down beside the rough kitchen table which served Herr Esch as a desk.

Esch paid no attention to him, but with a morose and suffering face walked from side to side of the room in a heavy awkward step which did not go with his lank appearance. The scrubbed floor creaked under his clumsy tread, and Huguenau contemplated the holes and loosened plaster between the two rooms, as well as Herr Esch's heavy black shoes, which were fastened, instead of with laces, with queer thongs that reminded one of saddle-straps; over the tops of the shoes bulged an expanse of grey darned sock. Esch communed aloud with himself: " The vultures are hovering over those poor people already . . . but when you try to draw public attention to all the misery, you find yourself up against the censorship."

Huguenau had crossed his legs. He regarded the things scattered on the table. An empty coffee-cup with brown stains, now dry, a bronze replica of the Statue of Liberty in New York (aha, a paper-weight), a paraffin lamp whose white wick behind the glass funnel reminded one distantly and dimly of a fœtus or a tapeworm preserved in spirits. Now Esch's voice boomed from the opposite corner:

" The censorship people should be made to look at all the misery and the distress themselves . . . it's to me that the people come . . . it would be simple treachery if . . ."

On a rickety shelf some manuscripts were lying, along with piles of newspapers tied together. Esch had resumed his prowling. In the middle of one of the walls, which were distempered in yellow, hung on a fortuitous nail a small faded picture in a black frame, " Badenweiler and the Schlossberg "; probably it was an old picture postcard. Huguenau reflected that a picture or a bronze statuette like that would look very well in his office. But when he tried to recall to his memory that office, and what he had done in it, he was unsuccessful, it seemed so remote and strange that he gave up the attempt, and his eyes sought again the excitable Esch, whose brown-velvet jacket and light cloth trousers went just as badly with his clumsy shoes as the bronze statuette on the kitchen table. Esch must have felt his glance, for he shouted:

" Damn it all, why do you go on sitting here? "

Of course Huguenau could have gone away—but where? it was not so easy to hit on another project. Huguenau felt that unknown powers had launched him on these new rails, and that he could not afford to leave them without a struggle, nor indeed without suffering for it. So he remained quietly sitting and polished his eyeglasses, as he was in the habit of doing during difficult commercial negotiations to maintain an air of composure. Nor did it fail of its effect this time, for Esch, exasperated now, planted himself in front of Huguenau and burst out anew:

" Where have you come from, anyway? Who sent you here? . . . you don't belong to this part of the country, and you needn't tell me that you intend to set up here as a wine-grower yourself. . . . You're just here to spy. Locked up, that's what you should be! "

Huguenau gazed at Esch's brown-velvet waistcoat, which was just at the level of his eye and showed a strip of leather belt beneath it, gazed at the light-coloured trousers spotted with grease. Past dry-cleaning, thought Huguenau, he'll have to have them dyed black, I should tell him so; what is he really after? if he really wants to throw me out he has no need to provoke a quarrel first . . . so he wants me to stay, then. There was something queer about it. Somehow Huguenau felt a sort of fellow-feeling with this man, and at the same time divined that there was some profit to be made. So returning to the attack he resolved to make certain:

" Herr Esch, I've offered you an honourable deal, and if you decide to refuse it that's your business. But if you merely want to swear at me, then there's no point in continuing our conversation."

He snapped his eyeglasses together and raised his bottom slightly from the chair, indicating by this movement that he was ready to go away—Esch had only to say the word.

But now Esch seemed really to have no wish to break off the conversation; he raised his hand propitiatingly, and Huguenau, once more using his bottom as an indicator, signified that he would remain:

" To tell you the truth, it's unlikely that I'll set up as a wine-grower here myself; perhaps you were quite right there—although even that isn't out of the question; a fellow longs for a quiet life. But I'm not here to exploit anyone," he wrought himself up, " a middleman has as much title to respect as anybody else, all that he's concerned with is to bring two parties together in a deal and satisfy them both, for then he has his reward too. Besides I must ask you to be a little more careful in the way you fling about expressions like ' spy,' that's a dangerous game in war-time."

Esch was put to shame:

" Come, come, I didn't intend any offence . . . but sometimes your disgust at things rises into your throat, and then you can't keep it from bursting out. . . . A Cologne builder, a thorough swindler, has been buy-ing up land here for a mere song . . . driven the people out of their homes . . . and the chemist here has been following his example . . . what use can Paulsen the chemist have for vineyards? can you tell me that, perhaps? "

Huguenau said again in an offended voice:

" A spy. . . ."

Esch had once more resumed his prowling:

" One should emigrate. Somewhere or other. To America. If I were younger I would fling everything up and start all over again . . ." once more he halted before Huguenau, " but you're a young man—why aren't you at the Front, eh? how do you come to be wandering about here? " Suddenly he had become aggressive again. Well, Huguenau had no desire to enter into that question; he evaded it; it was quite incomprehensible to him, he said, that a man in a distinguished position, the proprietor and editor of a newspaper, living amid lovely surroundings and enjoying the esteem of his fellow-citizens, and no longer young besides, should cherish thoughts of emigrating.

Esch grimaced sarcastically:

" Esteem of my fellow-citizens, esteem of my fellow-citizens . . . they snarl at my heels like a pack of curs. . . ."

Huguenau glanced at the picture of the Schlossberg, then he said:

" I can hardly believe that."

" Indeed! perhaps you're on their side? that wouldn't surprise me. . . ."

Huguenau steered his craft into safer waters:

" Again these vague accusations, Herr Esch. Won't you at least express yourself more precisely, if you have anything against me? "

But Herr Esch's desultory and irascible mind was not so easy to curb:

" Express myself precisely, express myself precisely, it's very easy to talk like that . . . as if a man can give a name to everything . . ." he shouted in Huguenau's face. " Young man, until you know that all names are false you know nothing; not even the clothes on your body are what they seem to be."

An uncanny feeling came over Huguenau. He didn't understand that, he said.

" Of course you don't understand it . . . but when a chemist snaps up land for a song, you can understand that all right . . . and it's quite understandable to you that a man who calls things by their real names should be persecuted and slandered as a communist . . . and be set upon by the Censor, what? that seems quite right to you? . . . and I suppose you think too that we're living in a just country? "

It was a disagreeable position to be in, said Huguenau.

" Disagreeable! One should emigrate . . . I'm sick of struggling against it."

Huguenau asked what Herr Esch thought of doing with the paper.

Esch waved his hand contemptuously: he had often said to his wife that he would like to sell the whole show, but he would keep the house —he had thoughts of opening a bookshop.

" The opposition must have damaged the paper a good deal, I suppose, Herr Esch? I mean to say, the circulation can't amount to very much now? "

Not at all, the *Herald* had its regular subscribers, the restaurants, the hairdressers, above all the people in the villages round about: the opposition was confined to certain circles in the town. But he was sick of squabbling with them.

Had Herr Esch any idea as to the price he wanted?

Oh yes . . . the paper and the printing-office were worth 20,000 marks, and a bargain at the price. In addition he would let the buyer have the use of the buildings rent-free for an extended period, say five years: and that would mean a big advantage for the buyer too. That was how he had figured it out, it was a decent offer, he didn't want to overreach anybody, he was simply sick of the whole business. He had often said so to his wife.

"Well," said Huguenau, "I didn't ask out of idle curiosity . . . as I said before I'm a middleman, and perhaps I may be able to do something for you. Mark my words, my dear Esch," and he patronizingly clapped the newspaper proprietor on the bony shoulder—"we'll do a little business deal together yet; you should never be in too great a hurry to throw anyone out. All the same you must put the thought of twenty thousand out of your head. Nobody pays fancy prices nowadays."

Self-assured and in excellent spirits Huguenau clattered down the wooden steps.

A child was squatting in front of the printing-shed.

Huguenau contemplated the child, contemplated the entrance to the printing-shed; he saw "No Admittance except on Business" on the door-plate.

Twenty thousand marks, he thought, and the little girl thrown in.

Well, he had no business in there yet, but from now on they could not refuse him admittance; if you were trying to sell a concern you had a right to see it. Esch would be obliged to show him round the printing-shed. Huguenau considered whether he should shout to him to come down, but then he decided, no: in a couple of days he would be returning here in any case, perhaps even with concrete proposals for buying the place,—Huguenau was quite certain of it, and besides it was dinner-time now. So he betook himself to his hotel.

CHAPTER VIII

Hanna Wendling was awake. She did not open her eyes, however, for there was still a chance that she might catch her vanishing dream. But it glided slowly away, and finally nothing remained but the emotion in which it had been immersed. As the emotion too drained away, Hanna voluntarily abandoned it just an instant before it completely vanished and glanced across at the window. Through the slats of the venetian blinds oozed a milky light; it must still be early, or else the sky was overcast. The striped light was like a continuation of her dream, perhaps because no sound entered with it, and Hanna decided that it must be very early after all. The venetian blinds stirred with a soft swaying motion between the open casements; that must be the dawn wind, and she inhaled its coolness by sniffing delicately, as if her nose could tell her what time it was. Then with closed eyes she reached out her hand to the bed on her left; it was not occupied; the pillows, the blankets and the eiderdown quilt were methodically piled up and covered by the plush counterpane. Before she drew back her hand, so as to return it along with her naked shoulder beneath the warm sheets, she ran it again over the yielding and slightly cold plush, and the action was like a corroboration of the fact that she was alone. Her thin nightgown had slipped up over her thighs and formed an uncomfortable bunch. Ah, she had slept badly again; as a sort of indemnification, however, her right hand was lying on her warm smooth body, and her finger-tips stroked softly and almost imperceptibly the soft downy curve of her bosom. She could not help thinking of some French rococo picture of dalliance; then she remembered Goya's portrait of the disrobed Maya. She remained lying in this position for a few minutes longer. Thereupon she smoothed down her nightgown—strange that a film-thin gown could warm one immediately like that—considered whether she should turn on her left or her right side, decided for the latter, as though she were afraid that the piled-up bed beside her would cut off the air, listened for a little longer to the silence of the street, and gave herself up to another dream, sought refuge in another dream, before any sound could reach her from outside.

When an hour later she once more found herself awake, she could no longer conceal from herself that the forenoon was already far advanced. For anyone who is bound only by very frail threads, threads that are scarcely palpable to him, to what other people or he himself calls life, getting up in the morning is always a hard task. Perhaps even a slight violation. And Hanna Wendling, who felt the unavoidable day once more approaching, got a headache. It began at the back of her head; she crossed her hands behind her neck, and when she tugged at her hair, which softly coiled round her fingers, for a moment she forgot her headache. Then she pressed against the place where the pain was; it was a throbbing which began behind her ears and ran down to the top of her spine. She was used to it. When she was in company, sometimes it seized her so violently that she became quite dizzy. With sudden resolution she flung back the bedclothes, slipped her feet into her high-heeled bedroom slippers, opened the venetian blinds without pulling them up, and holding her hand-glass behind her head contemplated the painful area at the back of her neck in the large mirror on her toilet-table. What was hurting her there? nothing could be seen. She turned her head from side to side; she could see the play of her spine under the skin; really she had a pretty neck. And her shoulders were pretty too. She would have liked to have had her breakfast in bed, but it was war-time; bad enough to have stayed in bed so late. Really she should have got up and taken her little son to school. Every day she made up her mind to do it. Twice she had actually done it, and then had left it again to the maid. Of course the boy should have had a French or an English governess long ago. Englishwomen made the best governesses. Once the war was over they would have to send the boy to England. When she was his age, yes when she was seven, she spoke French better than German. She searched for the flask with the toilet-vinegar, rubbed her neck and temples, and examined her eyes attentively in the mirror: they were golden-brown, in the left one a tiny red vein could be seen. That came from her restless night. She threw her kimono round her shoulders. And then she rang for the maid.

Hanna Wendling was the wife of Dr Heinrich Wendling, advocate. She was a native of Frankfort. For two years Heinrich Wendling had been in Roumania or Bessarabia or somewhere at the back of beyond.

CHAPTER IX

Huguenau sat down at his table in the dining-room. At a table not far from him a white-haired gentleman was sitting, a major. The waitress had just set down a plate of soup before him, and the old gentleman now went through a curious pantomime; with his hands folded and his reddish face piously composed he bowed his head a little over the table, and only after having ended this unmistakable grace did he break his fast.

Huguenau gaped at this unusual spectacle; he beckoned the waitress and asked without much ceremony who the strange officer was.

The waitress put her mouth to his ear; that was the Town Commandant, a high-born landowner from West Prussia who had been re-called to service for the duration of the war. His family were still living on the estate at home, but he got letters from them every day. Oh, and the Commandant's office was in the Town Hall, but the Herr Major had lived in the hotel ever since the beginning of the war.

Huguenau nodded, his curiosity satisfied. But then he suddenly felt a cold contraction in his stomach, and it struck him that the man sitting

over there embodied the power of the army, that the man needed only
to stretch out the hand now gripping a soup-spoon and he would be
done for, and that therefore he was, so to speak, living next door to his
own executioner. His appetite was gone! hadn't he better countermand
his order and take to flight?

But meanwhile the waitress had brought his soup, and as he mechanically spooned it up the paralysing coldness relaxed, passing over into an
almost comforting cool lassitude and defencelessness. Besides, he daren't
run away, he had to finish the deal with the *Kur-Trier Herald*.

He felt almost relieved. For although every man believes that his
decisions and resolutions involve the most multifarious factors, in
reality they are a mere oscillation between flight and longing, and the
ultimate goal of all flight and all longing is death. And in this wavering
of the soul and the spirit between the positive and the negative poles,
Huguenau, the same Wilhelm Huguenau who a moment before had
dreamt of flight, now felt himself strangely drawn to the old man
sitting at the other table.

He ate mechanically, not even noticing that to-day was meat day; he
drank mechanically, and in the extreme and as it were more clairvoyant
state of awareness to which he had had access for the past weeks, all
things fell asunder, flew apart and receded to the poles, receded to the
frontiers of the world where things once more regain their oneness and
distance is annihilated,—fear was changed to longing, and longing to
fear, and the *Kur-Trier Herald* coalesced into an extraordinarily indis-
soluble unity with the white-haired Major. The matter cannot be put
much more precisely or rationally than this, for Huguenau's actions
now developed in a world where all measurable distance was annihilated,
they were in a way short-circuited into irrationality without any time
for reflection; so while he waited for the Major to finish his meal, it was
not really waiting, it was a sort of simultaneity of cause and effect that
made him rise at the very moment when the Major, after another silent
grace, pushed back his chair and lit his cigar; forthwith and without
the slightest embarrassment Huguenau approached the Major, walked
up straight to the Major, quite unembarrassed although he had no
pretext whatever for such an intrusion.

Yet hardly had he duly introduced himself than he sat down without
being asked and the words began to flow effortlessly from his lips: he
took the liberty of respectfully announcing that he was from the Press

Bureau and had been sent here at its instructions. It seemed that there was a local sheet here called the *Kur-Trier Herald*, about whose policy all sorts of doubtful rumours were going round, and he had come, furnished with the fullest powers required, to study the position on the spot. Yes, and—what shall I say now? thought Huguenau—but his stream of eloquence flowed on; it was as though the words took shape in his mouth—yes, and seeing that the question of censorship fell to a certain degree and in a certain sense within the Town Commandant's province, he had considered it his duty to wait on the Herr Major and report himself.

In the course of this announcement the Major, drawing himself up with a little jerk, had assumed a formal attitude, and attempted to make the objection that the usual official channels were better suited to deal with such an affair; Huguenau, however, who could not afford to let his fluent stream of words run dry, scarcely listened to him, and summarily dismissed the objection by pointing out that he had approached the Herr Major not in an official, but merely in a semi-official capacity, since the full powers he had mentioned were not from the Government, but rather from the patriotic big industrialists—he need mention no names, they were well enough known—who had entrusted him with the mission of eventually purchasing doubtful newspapers if the price were reasonable, for they must of course prevent suspicious ideas reaching the people. And Huguenau repeated again the words, " suspicious ideas reaching the people," repeated them as though this return to his starting-point had given him absolute assurance, as though the phrase were a soft bed on which he could lie in comfort.

Apparently the Major did not understand what all this was leading to, but he nodded and Huguenau continued to revolve in his orbit: yes, it was a question of suspect newspapers, and in his own opinion, as indeed according to general opinion, the *Kur-Trier Herald* was a suspect paper, whose purchase he would unconditionally recommend.

He looked at the Major triumphantly, drummed with his fingers on the table, and it was as though he were awaiting the Town Commandant's admiration and praise for a successfully achieved feat.

" Very patriotic, no doubt," the Major at length agreed. " I thank you for the information."

With that Huguenau could have taken himself off, but it was necessary that he should achieve something more, and so he thanked the Herr

Major warmly for the good will he had shown him and, in view of that
good will, begged to add one more request, a small request:

" My employers naturally regard it as important that in buying a
newspaper such as this, which of course must be looked on more or less
as a local paper, local people interested should share in the transaction:
that of course is quite understandable, for the sake of local control and
so forth. . . . The Herr Major sees that? "

Yes, that was understandable, said the Major, not understanding in
the least.

Well, said Huguenau, the request he had to make was that the Herr
Major, who of course had the greatest prestige of anyone in the town,
should give him the names of a few reliable moneyed gentlemen among
the residents—of course in the strictest confidence—who might be
interested in the plan.

The Major remarked that the whole business really fell within the
province of the civil authorities and not of the military command, yet
he could give Herr Huguenau one piece of advice: to be here on Friday
evening, for on that evening he would always find a few town councillors
and other influential gentlemen in the place.

" Splendid! but the Herr Major will be here too, I hope," said
Huguenau, who was not to be put off so easily. " Splendid! If the Herr
Major will take the transaction under his patronage I can guarantee
that everything will go smoothly, especially as the capital required is
relatively small, and many of the gentlemen here will be interested no
doubt in the idea of getting into touch with the large industries, in being
admitted to partnership with them, so to speak. . . . Splendid! really
splendid! . . . May I smoke, Herr Major? " . . . and he pulled his chair
nearer, took a cigar out of his cigar-case, polished his eyeglasses, and
began to smoke.

The Major observed that certainly the auspices were very favourable,
and that he was sorry he was not a business man.

Oh, that didn't matter, said Huguenau, that didn't affect the matter
at all. And as he felt a need to repeat his performance again, perhaps
out of pure virtuosity, perhaps to establish his newly won confidence,
perhaps out of sheer wantonness, he pulled his chair yet a little nearer
to the Major, and begged permission to add a further piece of information, but only for the Herr Major's personal ear. In his dealings thus
far with the publisher of this newspaper—his name was Esch, the Herr

Major must certainly have heard of him—well he had got the definite impression that behind the paper there was a—how could he put it? a whole subterranean movement going on, a movement composed of suspicious and subversive elements. Something of this seemed to have leaked out already: but when the plan of buying the paper was actually realized, he would of course be in a position to get that insight into these obscure activities which it was desirable and necessary to have in the interests of the whole people.

And before the old gentleman could reply, Huguenan got up and said in conclusion:

" Please, oh, please, Herr Major! . . . it's simply my duty as a patriot . . . not worth mentioning. . . . So I'll take the liberty, then, of accepting your most flattering invitation for Friday evening."

He clicked his heels and went back with a light, almost jaunty step to his own table.

CHAPTER X

The fact that Herr August Esch's editorial duties filled him with such impatience and exasperation, and that he felt so strangely uncomfortable in his position, may be comprehensively referred back to the other fact that all his life he had followed the vocation of a book-keeper, having been, indeed, a head book-keeper for many years in a large industrial concern in his Luxemburg home, before—it was already in the middle of the war—he took possession of the *Kur-Trier Herald* and the buildings attached to it, as the result of an unexpected legacy.

For a book-keeper, and a head book-keeper in particular, is a man who lives within a strict and extraordinarily exact system of rules, rules so exact that he will never be able to apply them in any other kind of occupation. Supported firmly by such rules, he grows acclimatized to an all-powerful and yet modest world in which everything has its place, in which he himself is the point of reference, and where his glance remains unerring and undisturbed. He turns the pages of the ledger and compares them with the journal and the daybook; without a break numberless bridges stretch from the one to the other, giving security to life and the day's work. Each morning the janitor or the office girl brings the new book-keeping entries from the order office, and the head book-keeper summarizes them, so that the junior clerks may enter

them in the daybook. This done, the head book-keeper is at liberty
to reflect in peace on the more difficult problems, to examine the books
and give his decisions. Then if in his head he has disentangled and
straightened out a particularly difficult book-keeping problem, he sees
new and approved bridges once more stretching reciprocally from continent to continent, and this intricate maze of established connections
between account and account, this inextricable and yet so clearly woven
net, in which not a single knot is missing, is symbolized at last in a single
figure which he already foresees, though it may not go into the balance
sheet for months to come. Oh, sweet agitation of the final balance! no
matter whether it show a gain or a loss; for to the book-keeper all transactions bring gain and satisfaction. Even the monthly trial balances are
triumphs of power and skill, yet they are nothing when compared with
the general settlement of the books at the end of the half-year: during
those days he is the captain of the ship, and his hand never leaves the
helm; the young clerks in his department stick to their posts like galley
slaves, and no one heeds the dinner-hour, or thinks of sleep, until all
the accounts are balanced; but the drawing up of the profit and loss
account and the final balance sheet he reserves for himself, and when
he has achieved his task, and ruled the last line beneath the account,
he seals his labours with his signature. But woe if the balance is out
even by so much as a penny! A new, but bitter pleasure follows. Aided
by his chief assistant he goes through the suspected accounts with the
eye of a detective, and if that is of no avail all the entries of the last half-
year are ruthlessly scrutinized yet again. And woe to the young man in
whose books the error is found,—wrath and cold contempt will be his
portion, yea dismissal. If meanwhile, however, it is discovered that the
error has occurred not in the books but in the stocktaking in the storeroom, then the head book-keeper simply shrugs his shoulders, and his
lips wear a pitying or sarcastic smile, for the stocktaking lies outside
his province, and moreover he knows that in the store, as in life, that
perfect order can never be achieved which he maintains in his books.
With a contemptuous wave of the hand he returns to his office, and
when presently the days become more tranquil, not seldom it may be
the head book-keeper's good fortune, while flinging open a ledger,
smoothing out the page rapidly with his thumb, running down a column
of figures to check it, proud meanwhile of his skill which in spite of the
sureness of his smoothly proceeding calculations permits his thoughts

to stray freely to distant things—it may be his good fortune to realize
with delighted surprise, expected and yet enchanting surprise, that the
miracle of calculation still exists like a sure rock in an incalculable world.
But then, it may be, his hand slips down from the page, and sadness
steals into his heart as he thinks of the new system which it is one of
the duties of a modern book-keeper to inaugurate; and reflecting that
the new system is an affair of matter-of-fact cards instead of imposing
and massive tomes, superseding personal skill by adding-machines, he
is filled with bitterness.

Outside their work book-keepers are irritable. For the frontier between reality and unreality in life can never be clearly drawn, and a man
who lives within a world of precisely adjusted relations will refuse to
allow that there can be another world whose relations are incomprehensible and inscrutable to him: so when he steps out of his firmly
established world or is torn from it he becomes impatient, he becomes
an ascetic and passionate fanatic, even a rebel. The shadow of death has
touched him, and the one-time book-keeper—if he has grown old—is
really fit for nothing but the petty existence of the superannuated, and,
impervious to accident and all the life round him, can be content to
water his garden and attend to his fruit-trees; but if he is still vigorous
and eager for work, his life becomes a galling combat with a world of
reality which to him is unreal. Especially if fate or a legacy has deposited
him in such an exposed position as that of a newspaper editor, even
though it may be only a small provincial newspaper that he controls!
For there is certainly no occupation so dependent on the uncalculability
and uncertainty of the world's affairs as that of an editor, particularly
in times of war when report and counter-report, hope and despair,
heroism and misery, tread so closely on one another's heels that any
methodical keeping of the books becomes a sheer impossibility; only
by referring to the Censor's office can one establish what is to pass for
truth and what must remain in the realm of untruth, and each nation
lives enclosed in its own patriotic reality. Here a book-keeper is very
much out of place, for he may easily be tempted to write that our brave
troops are still posted on the left banks of the Marne awaiting orders
for a further advance, while in reality the French, on their side, have
long since pushed forward to the right bank. And if the censorship
should reprimand him for such falsehoods, the book-keeper, especially
if he is a man of impetuous moods, will inevitably get into a rage and

point out that while General Headquarters had indeed reported the fortification of the bridgehead on the left bank, nothing at all had been said of the withdrawal of the troops. This is only one instance among many, one may even say among hundreds, and they are sufficient to show amply how impossible it is to apply to entries in the annals of history that scrupulosity which is accepted as the first and absolute condition of the registration of business events, and how the inaccuracy of a war which it has become impossible to survey as a whole may nourish a spirit of rebellion, for which a precise and scrupulous man might have found excuse enough even in times of peace, but which now must develop of necessity into an inevitable struggle between authority and justice, between two unrealities, two violent forces, a struggle that is eternal, a renewal of Don Quixote's crusade against a world which refuses to submit to the demands of the law-bringing spirit. For ever the book-keeper will do battle for the right, since if a penny is out he will go over every item again should the integrity of his books require it, and without being actually a good man himself, he will rise as the advocate of oppressed justice as soon as he has recognized and registered the existence of injustice and wrong; unyielding and wrathful he will rise to give battle, a lean knight with lance in rest who must charge again and again for the honour of the accurate book-keeping that ought to be able to account for everything on earth.

So Herr Esch's editorial labours were by no means so easy as one might have supposed. True, the material for his half-weekly sheet was delivered by a Cologne news and article agency, and all that the editor really needed to do was to extract from among the sensational reports the most sensational, to choose from the elegant serials and articles the most elegant, and there was nothing left for him to deal with personally but the local news, which moreover consisted chiefly of paragraphs " from a correspondent." But simple as this looked, and simple indeed as it really was so long as Esch confined himself to the book-keeping, which he had established on a new basis (not of course on the American, but on the more modest Italian model), all sorts of complications set in when the acting editor was called up and Herr Esch found himself compelled, partly by his natural and book-keeping parsimony, partly by the increasing difficulty of the general situation, to take the editorship of the paper into his own hands. Then the fight began! the fight for precise evidence of the world's doings, and against the false or falsified book-keeping entries which people tried to fob off on him, the fight against the authorities who were indignant that the *Kur-Trier Herald* should give public currency to abuses at the Front and behind the lines, to sailors' revolts and unrest in munition factories, more, who refused to listen even to the paper's proposals for genuinely fighting these evils, but on the contrary found it suspicious—although only an ill-wisher could have found it suspicious—that such reports should be confided to Herr Esch, and already were seriously considering whether they should interdict him the exercise of his editorial calling, on the ground that he was a foreign subject (a Luxemburger) ; he had been repeatedly warned, and his relations with the Censor's office in Trier were becoming more uncomfortable from week to week. Small wonder, then, that Herr Esch, himself at odds with the world, should begin to feel a brotherly sympathy for his oppressed and downtrodden fellow-creatures, and should become an obstructionist and a rebel. But he did not actually admit it to himself.

CHAPTER XI

STORY OF THE SALVATION ARMY GIRL IN BERLIN (1)

Among the many intolerances and limitations which were so common in pre-war days, and of which we are now rightly ashamed, there must be reckoned our total lack of understanding when faced with phenomena that lay even a little way outside the confines of a seemingly rational world. And since we were then accustomed to regard only Western thought and culture as valid, and to depreciate all else as inferior, we were easily disposed to class as inferior and infra-European all phenomena that did not accord with simple reason. So when a phenomenon of that nature, such as the Salvation Army, made its appearance in the unimpressive garb of peace and fervent petition, it was met with endless ridicule. People demanded simplicity and heroism, something æsthetic in other words, believing as they did that such were the attributes of European man; for they were entangled in a misapprehension of Nietzsche's ideas, even although most of them had never heard his name, and the bogy which obsessed them was never laid until the world produced so many heroes that the sheer prevalence of heroism kept them from noticing it.

To-day, if I encounter a Salvation Army meeting in the street, I join it and am glad to put some money on the collection plate, and often I enter into conversation with the soldiers. Not that I have been converted by their somewhat primitive doctrine of salvation, but I feel that we who were once given over to prejudice are morally bound to repair our past errors wherever possible, even though these errors could be palliated as mere æsthetic decadence and had moreover the excuse of our extreme youth. Of course one's realization of these things came only gradually into consciousness, especially as during the war one seldom saw a Salvation Army soldier. I had indeed heard that they were developing a widely spread charitable organization, but I was almost surprised to meet a Salvation Army girl in one of the outlying streets in Schöneberg.

I suppose I must have looked somewhat lost and helpless, but my smile of friendly surprise encouraged her to accost me under a tactful pretext: she offered me a paper from the bundle under her arm. Perhaps she would have been disappointed if I had merely bought one, so I said: "I'm sorry, but I have no money." "That doesn't matter," she said, "come to us."

We traversed several typical suburban streets, passing derelict bits of ground, and I groused about the war. I believe she took me for a shirker, or even a deserter, who was forced by a kind of obsession to return to that theme, for she openly did her best to divert me to other topics. But I stuck to the war, I cannot now tell why, and went on grousing.

Suddenly we found that we had missed our way. We had taken a narrow road skirting a block of factory buildings, and as we rounded a corner we discovered that the block went on and on. So we turned left into a little path bounded by a slack and forlorn wire fence—it was incomprehensible why the path should be fenced off, since there was nothing on either side but rubbish-heaps, broken crockery, battered water-cans, and piles of jugs and pots that had been carted out to this remote and inaccessible spot for no discoverable reason—and the path finally came to an end in an open field, not a real field, for there was nothing growing in it, but a field that had at any rate once been ploughed, either before the war or in the previous spring. That was indicated by the hard-baked furrows, which looked like frozen waves of clay. But obviously nothing had ever been sown there. In the distance a train puffed slowly across the countryside.

Behind us lay the factories and the great city of Berlin. So our case was not desperate, although the afternoon sun blazed pitilessly down upon us. We debated what we were to do. Go on walking to the next village? "We're not fit to appear anywhere like this," I said, and she obediently tried to shake the dust off her dark uniform. It was of the same coarse stuff as the uniform of the tram-conductors, shoddy stuff with threads of paper woven through it.

Then I noticed a wooden post rammed into the earth like a boundary mark. We made for it. We sat in turn in the narrow shadow of the post, speaking little, except of my thirst. And when it grew cooler we found our way back to the city.

CHAPTER XII

DISINTEGRATION OF VALUES (1)

Is this distorted life of ours still real? is this cancerous reality still alive? the melodramatic gesture of our mass movement towards death ends in a shrug of the shoulders,—men die and do not know why; without a hold on reality they fall into nothingness; yet they are surrounded and slain by a reality that is their own, since they comprehend its causality.

The unreal is the illogical. And this age seems to have a capacity for surpassing even the acme of illogicality, of anti-logicality: it is as if the monstrous reality of the war had blotted out the reality of the world. Fantasy has become logical reality, but reality evolves the most a-logical phantasmagoria. An age that is softer and more cowardly than any preceding age suffocates in waves of blood and poison-gas; nations of bank clerks and profiteers hurl themselves upon barbed wire; a well-organized humanitarianism avails to hinder nothing, but calls itself the Red Cross and prepares artificial limbs for the victims; towns starve and coin money out of their own hunger; spectacled school-teachers lead storm-troops; city dwellers live in caves; factory hands and other civilians crawl out on reconnoitring duty, and in the end, once they are back in safety, apply their artificial limbs once more to the making of profits. Amid a blurring of all forms, in a twilight of apathetic uncertainty brooding over a ghostly world, man like a lost child gropes his way by the help of a small frail thread of logic through a dream landscape that he calls reality and that is nothing but a nightmare to him.

The melodramatic revulsion which characterizes this age as insane, the melodramatic enthusiasm which calls it great, are both justified by the swollen incomprehensibility and illogicality of the events that apparently make up its reality. Apparently! For insane or great are terms that can never be applied to an age, but only to an individual destiny. Our individual destinies, however, are as normal as they ever were. Our common destiny is the sum of our single lives, and each of these single lives is developing quite normally, in accordance, as it were, with its private logicality. We feel the totality to be insane, but for each single life we can easily discover logical guiding motives. Are we, then, insane because we have not gone mad?

The great question remains: how can an individual whose ideas have been genuinely directed towards other aims understand and accommodate himself to the implications and the reality of dying? One may answer that the mass of mankind have done nothing of the sort, and were merely forced towards death—an answer that is perhaps valid in these days of war-weariness; yet there undoubtedly was and still is, even to-day, a genuine enthusiasm for war and slaughter! One may answer that the average man, whose life moves between his table and his bed, has no ideas whatever, and therefore falls an easy prey to the ideology of hatred—which is in any case the most obviously intelligible of all, whether it concerns class hatred or national hatred—and that such narrow lives were bound to be subsumed in the service of any superpersonal idea, even a destructive one, provided that it could masquerade as socially valuable: yet even allowing for all that, this age was not devoid of other and higher super-personal values in which the individual, despite his narrow mediocrity, was already a participant. This age harboured somewhere a disinterested striving for truth, a disinterested will towards art, and had after all a very definite social feeling; how could the men who created these values and shared in them " comprehend " the ideology of war, unresistingly accept and approve it? How could a man take a gun in his hand, how could he march into the trenches, either to die in them or to come out again and take up his work as usual, without going insane? How is such adaptability possible? How could the ideology of war find any kind of response in these men, how could they ever come even to understand such an ideology and its field of reality, not to speak of enthusiastically welcoming it, as was not at all impossible? Are they insane because they did not go insane?

Is it to be referred to a mere indifference to others' sufferings? to the indifference that lets a citizen sleep soundly next door to the prison yard in which someone is being hanged by the neck or guillotined? the indiffer-ence that needs only to be multiplied to produce public indifference to the fact that thousands of men are being impaled on barbed wire? Of course it is that same indifference, but it goes further than that; for here we have no longer merely two mutually exclusive fields of reality, that of the slayer on one side and of the slain on the other; we find them co-existing in one and the same individual, implying that one single field can combine the most heterogeneous elements, among which, however, the individual apparently moves with the utmost naturalness and assurance. The contradiction is not one between supporters and opponents of war, nor is it a horizontal split in the life of the individual, on the supposition that after four years' semi-starvation he "changes" into another type and stands in complete contrast to his former self: it is a split in the totality of life and experience, a split that goes much deeper than a mere opposition of individuals, a split that cuts right into the individual himself and into his integral reality.

We know too well that we are ourselves split and riven, and yet we cannot account for it; if we try to cast the responsibility for it on the age in which we live, the age is too much for our comprehension, and so we fall back on calling it insane or great. We ourselves think that we are normal, because, in spite of the split in our souls, our inner machinery seems to run on logical principles. But if there were a man in whom all the events of our time took significant shape, a man whose native logic accounted for the events of our age, then and then only would this age cease to be insane. Presumably that is why we long for a "leader," so that he may provide us with the motivation for events that in his absence we can characterize only as insane.

CHAPTER XIII

Looked at from the outside, Hanna Wendling's life could have been described as idle passivity within a perfectly ordered system. And, curiously enough, this description would have fitted it from the inside view also. Probably she herself would have agreed with it. It was a life that from her uprising in the morning to her lying down at night hung like a slack silken thread, slack and curling through lack of tension. In her particular case life, which has so many dimensions, lost one dimension after another, it barely sufficed even to fill the three dimensions of space: one could safely assert that Hanna Wendling's dreams were more plastic and more alive than her waking states. But however closely this opinion

might have accorded with Hanna Wendling's, it leaves the heart of the
matter untouched, for it illumines only the large-scale view of that young
woman's existence, leaving almost unguessed-at the microscopic detail
which is alone significant: there is no one who knows anything about the
microscopic structure of his own soul, and unquestionably it is better
that he should not. Behind the visible slackness of Hanna Wendling's
life, then, there was a constant tension of its separate elements. If one
could have snipped off a small but sufficient portion of that apparently
slack thread, one would have discovered in it an extreme torsion, as if
every molecule, so to speak, were spasmodically cramped. The external
symptoms of this condition could best be covered by the popular term
" nervousness," in so far as that implies the exhausting guerrilla warfare
which during every second of its existence the ego has to wage against
even the minutest encroachments of the empirical world with which its
surface comes into contact. But although this term might account for
much in Hanna Wendling, the peculiar tension in her life did not arise
from nervous impatience with chance annoyances, such as dust on her
patent shoes, or the pressure of the ring on her finger, or even the mere
fact that a potato was not thoroughly cooked; it did not arise from that
kind of thing, for all such disturbances were an infinitesimal rippling of
the surface, like the shimmering of restless water in sunshine, and she
would have regretted their absence, since they kept her somehow from
being bored; no, it did not arise from that, but from the discrepancy
between this infinitely modulated surface and the still, immovable pro-
fundity of her soul, which like the bottom of the sea was extended at a
depth which no eye could ever penetrate: it was the discrepancy between
the visible limited surface and an invisible limitlessness, that discrepancy
which is the eternal setting for the most exciting drama ever played by
the soul; it was the immeasurable gulf that stretches between the obverse
and the reverse sides of darkness, a tension without equilibrium, a
fluctuating tension, one might say, since on the one side there was life,
but on the other that eternity which is the sea-bottom of the soul and
of all life.

Hanna Wendling's life was one largely emptied of all substance, and
perhaps for that reason purposeless. That it was the life of the insignificant spouse of an insignificant provincial lawyer makes very little
difference. For the significance of any one human life is not particularly
great. And even if the moral value of a slacker in a time of deadly war

is not to be rated very highly, one must not forget that not one single person who voluntarily or under compulsion fulfilled the heroic duties of war-time would have been sorry to exchange his ethically valuable activities for the ethically valueless existence of a slacker. And perhaps —although only perhaps—the increasing paralysis that gripped Hanna Wendling as the war progressed in severity was nothing but the expression of a highly moral revulsion from the horror to which mankind saw itself committed. And perhaps that revulsion, that horror, had already grown so strong in her that Hanna Wendling herself did not dare to be aware of it.

CHAPTER XIV

On one of the following afternoons Huguenau again visited Herr Esch. " Well, Herr Esch, what do you think: the thing's as good as done! "

Esch was correcting proofs and raised his head: " What thing? "

Imbécile, thought Huguenau, but he said:

" Why, the sale of your newspaper."

" Depends on whether I agree to it."

Huguenau became suspicious:

" Now, look here, you can't let me down . . . or are you negotiating with someone else? " Then he noticed the child whom he had seen outside the printing-office in the morning:

" Is that your daughter? "

" No."

" Indeed . . . well, then, Herr Esch, if I'm to sell your paper for you, you must at least show me round the premises. . . ."

Esch waved his hand to indicate the room in which they were sitting; Huguenau tried to draw a smile out of him:

" So the little girl's included, is she? . . ."

" No," said Esch.

Huguenau pressed his point; he did not really know why he was so interested:

" But the printing-shed, that's included . . . you must at least show me round the printing-shed. . . ."

" I don't mind," said Esch, getting up and taking the child by the hand, " let's go into the printing-shed, then."

" And what's your name? " asked Huguenau.

The child said:

" Marguerite."

" Une petite française," said Huguenau.

" No," said Esch, " only her father's French."

" Interesting," said Huguenau, " and her mother? ",

They were clambering down the ladder. Esch said in a low voice:

" Her mother's dead . . . her father was an electrician here in the paper factory, but now he's interned."

Huguenau shook his head:

" A sad business, very sad . . . and you've taken the child? "

Esch said:

" You're not inquisitive, are you? "

" I? no . . . but the child must surely live somewhere. . . ."

Esch said gruffly:

" She lives with her mother's sister . . . she only comes here sometimes for dinner . . . her people aren't well off."

Huguenau was content, now that he knew everything:

" Alors tu es une petite francaise, Marguerite? "

The child looked up at him, a glimmer of recollection played over her face, she let Esch go and took Huguenau's finger, but she made no reply.

" She can't speak a word of French . . . it's four years since her father was interned. . . ."

" How old is she, now? "

" Seven," said the child.

They went into the printing-shed.

" This is the printing-room," said Esch, " the press and the setting-plant alone are worth several thousands."

" A bit old-fashioned," said Huguenau, who had never seen a printing-press before. The composing-room was to the right. The grey-painted type cases did not interest him, but the printing-press took his fancy. The tiled floor, strengthened here and there with great patches of concrete, was saturated and brown with oil all round the press. The machine stood there heavy and stolid, its cast-iron parts lacquered black, its steel bars shining, and its joints and supports bound with rings of brass. An old workman in a blue blouse was rubbing up the steel bars with a handful of waste, paying no heed to the intruders at all.

Esch said:

" Well, that's all, let's go . . . come, Marguerite."

He went out without another word, leaving his visitor simply standing. Huguenau stared after the unmannerly lout, but was quite pleased; he could now examine things at his leisure. There was a pleasant effect of quietness and solidity. He took out his cigar-case, selected a cigar that was somewhat frayed, and offered it to the workman at the machine.

The printer looked at him incredulously, for tobacco was rare and a cigar at the best of times an acceptable gift. He wiped his hands on his blue garment, took the cigar, and because he was at a loss for adequate words of thanks he said:

" One doesn't often see these." " Yes," replied Huguenau, " it's a bad look-out for tobacco nowadays." " It's a bad look-out for everything," asserted the printer. Huguenau pricked up his ears: " That's just what your chief says." " It's what everybody says." The answer was not quite what Huguenau would have liked. " Well, light up," he ordered. The man bit off the end of the cigar with strong brownish teeth, somewhat as if he were cracking a nut, and lit up. His working blouse and his shirt were wide open, showing the white hair on his chest. Huguenau felt that he should get some return for the cigar; the man owed him something; so he encouraged him, saying: " A fine little machine." " It'll do," was the laconic answer. Huguenau's sympathies were with the machine, and he felt hurt by this grudging approval. And since he could think of no other way of breaking the silence, he asked: " What's your name? " " Lindner." Then silence settled definitely upon them, and Huguenau wondered if he shouldn't go away,—but suddenly his finger was clasped again by a childish hand; Marguerite had run in noiselessly on her bare feet.

" Tiens," he said, " tu lui as échappé."

The child looked up incomprehendingly.

" Oh, of course, you don't speak French . . . tut, tut, you'll have to learn it."

The child made a contemptuous gesture, the same gesture that Huguenau had already remarked as characteristic of Esch:

" The one upstairs can speak French too. . . ."

She said: the one upstairs.

Huguenau was pleased and said in a low tone:

" Don't you like him? "

The child's face grew sullen and her lower lip protruded, but then she noticed that Lindner was smoking.

" Herr Lindner's smoking! "

Huguenau laughed and opened his cigar-case.

" Would you like one too? "

She pushed the case away and answered slowly:

" Give me some money."

" What! It's money you want, is it? What do you want money for? " Lindner said:

" They begin young nowadays."

Huguenau had drawn out a chair for himself; he sat down and took Marguerite between his knees:

" I need money myself, you know."

" Give me some money."

" I'll give you some sweets."

She was silent.

" What do you want money for? "

And although Huguenau knew that " money " was a very important word, and although he could not get it out of his head, yet he was suddenly incapable of seeing any meaning in it, and had to ask himself with an effort:

" What does anybody want money for? "

Marguerite had braced her arms on his knees and stood very rigid. Lindner growled:

" Oh, send her away," and to Marguerite, " out you get, the printing-room is no place for children."

Marguerite gave him an angry side-glance. She clutched Huguenau's finger again and began to pull him to the door.

" More haste, less speed," said Huguenau, rising up. " It's quietly that does it, eh, Herr Lindner? "

Lindner was polishing his machine again without a word to spare, and all at once Huguenau felt that there was some vague kinship between the child and the machine, almost as if they were sisters. And as if his assurance might comfort the machine he said quickly to the child before he reached the door:

" I'll give you twenty pfennigs."

When she thrust out her hand he was again aware of that curious doubt about the value of money, and cautiously, as if the affair were a

mystery that concerned only the two of them and must not be overheard
by anyone, not even the machine, he pulled the child close to him and
whispered in her ear:

" What do you want the money for? "

The little one said:

" Give it to me."

But as Huguenau still delayed, she drew down reflective brows. Then
she said: " I'll tell you," escaped from his arm and pulled him out
through the door.

It had grown really cold by the time they were out in the courtyard.
Huguenau would gladly have carried in his arms the little girl whose
warmth he had so lately felt; it was not right of Esch to let a child run
round barefooted at this time of the year. He was a little embarrassed,
and polished his eyeglasses. Only when the child again thrust out her
hand and said " Give it to me," did he remember about the twenty
pfennigs. But he forgot to ask again what she wanted them for, opened
his purse and extracted the two coins. Marguerite grabbed them and
ran off, and Huguenau, left alone, could think of nothing else to do but
to run his eye once more over the yard and the buildings. Then he too
departed.

CHAPTER XV

As soon as Ludwig Gödicke of the Landwehr had gathered the most
essential parts of his soul round his ego, he discontinued the painful
struggle. It could be argued that all his life Gödicke had been a primitive
kind of creature, and that a further struggle on his part would not have
availed to increase the dimensions of his soul, since not even in the most
dramatic moments of his life had there been many elements at the
disposal of his ego. But that Gödicke was ever a primitive creature is a
mere assertion that cannot be proved—and this alone invalidates the
objection—nor could his new personality have been described as primitive; least of all, however, can one assume that the soul of a primitive
and the world he sees are meagre and, so to speak, rough-hewn. One
has only to remember how much more complicated is the structure of
a primitive language than that of civilized peoples, in order to see that
such an assumption is nonsensical. It is impossible to determine, therefore, whether Gödicke's choice among the elements of his soul was

comprehensive or not, how many he admitted into his new personality, and how many he excluded; all that can be said is that Gödicke went about with the feeling of having lost something that formerly belonged to him, something that was not absolutely essential to his new life, but something nevertheless that he missed and yet dared not find again lest it should kill him.

And that there really was something missing was easily discernible from the economy of his utterances. He could walk, although with difficulty, could eat, although without appetite, and his very digestion, like everything connected with the crushed lower part of his body, gave him severe trouble. Perhaps his difficulty in speaking was in the same category, for it often seemed to him that the same oppression lay on his breast as on his bowels, that the iron rings constricting his belly were also bound round his chest and hindered him from speaking. Yet his incapacity to bring out even the shortest of words certainly sprang from that very economy with which he had composed his ego, and that provided for only the minimum of activity, so that any further demand upon it, let it be only the breath required for a single word, would have meant an irreplaceable loss.

So he hobbled about the garden on two sticks, his brown beard down on his chest, and his brown eyes above the deeply pitted hairy furrows on his cheeks gazing into vacancy; he wore the hospital overall or his soldier's cloak according as the Sister laid out one or the other for him, and he was certainly unaware that he was in a hospital or living in a town the name of which he did not know. Ludwig Gödicke the brick-layer had, so to speak, built a scaffolding for the house of his soul, and as he hobbled about on his sticks he felt himself to be merely a scaffolding with supports and stresses on all sides; meanwhile he could not decide, or rather, it was a sheer impossibility for him, to assemble the tiles and bricks for the house itself, and all that he did, or more precisely all that he thought—for he did nothing—was concerned with the mere scaffolding, with the elaboration of that scaffolding and all its ladders and gangways, a scaffolding that grew more perplexing daily and needed careful underpinning: a scaffolding that existed in itself and by itself, though none the less its purpose was a real purpose, since invisibly in the centre of the scaffolding, and yet also in every single supporting beam, the ego of Ludwig Gödicke was precariously suspended and had to be preserved from dizziness.

Dr Flurschütz often thought of handing the man over to a mental
hospital. But the Senior Medical Officer, Surgeon-Major Dr Kühlenbeck,
was of the opinion that the patient's state of shock was merely the result
of his experiences, and not organic, and so would pass off in the course of
time. And since he was a quiet patient, easy to deal with, they agreed to
keep him until he had completely recuperated from his bodily injuries.

CHAPTER XVI

STORY OF THE SALVATION ARMY GIRL IN BERLIN (2)

There's much that can't be said except in verse,
despite the sneers of men who stick to prose;
the bonds of verse are less tight-drawn than those
of logic; song is fitter for a curse
or a lament, when day like a dark hearse
out-glooms the night, summoning ghostly woes,
and in a hymn the sad heart overflows,
even at a loud Salvation Army Meeting,
nor smiles when drums and tambourines are beating.—
Marie walked Berlin streets like a bold jade
and haunted drinking-dens in her poke-bonnet;
her girlhood was in flower, and yet upon it
the ugly uniform like a blight was laid;
her singing, when she sang before the Lord,
was a thin, empty piping—yet it soared.
Salvation Army Homes were Marie's setting,
where corridors were grey and reeked of stoves
burning foul coal, and old men sat in droves
with stinking breath and dirty feet a-sweating,
where even in summer chills played on one's back
and yellow soap stank strong from every crack.
Here was her dwelling-place, within that gate,
here in a brown deal alcove stood her bed
with a brown crucifix set at its head,
and here she knelt and thanked God for her fate,
waiting with rapt eyes for His heavenly grace,
and here she slept, and glory filled the place.

But she must rise at dawn and wash her face
with ice-cold water—hot water is forbidden
in such a house—while yet the sun is hidden,
while the expectant air is still and grey,
and sometimes heavy, as if the sky were chidden,
or a tarpaulin blotted out the day,
and that's an hour when one may be hag-ridden,
when hope may fail; for in the lonely dawn
how can one think that day will bring a friend?
or that the precious yesterday that's gone
will be affirmed again before day end?
Marie has no misgivings; she must fend
for all her charges; she puts coffee on,
she sweeps and scours; then, at the window dreaming,
she sees the grace of God on all things gleaming.

CHAPTER XVII

It was very seldom that Hanna Wendling went into the town. She hated the way there, not only the dusty main road, which would have been quite understandable, but the path along the river as well. Yet the path took barely twenty-five minutes, and the main road only a quarter of an hour. She had always had a deep dislike for the road into the town, even at the time when she was still daily calling for Heinrich at the office. Later there had been the car, but only for a few months, for then the war broke out. To-day it was Dr Kessel who had taken her to the town with him in his buggy.

She made some purchases. Her new frock reached only as far as her ankles, and she felt as if people were staring at her feet. She had an intuitive feeling for fashions, and had always had it; she anticipated a coming fashion somewhat as certain people know that they will awaken at a certain time without having to look at the clock. Fashion journals for her had always been merely a belated corroboration. And the fact that people were staring at her feet now was also a sort of corroboration. There are of course lots of people who are able to waken to the minute, and many women with an intuitive feeling for the immanent logic of fashion, yet the man or woman who possesses a gift of this kind generally regards himself or herself as unique. So Hanna Wendling was feeling a little proud of herself now, and even if she had only a vague inkling that her pride was unjustified, yet a slight feeling of guilt assailed her when she saw the haggard women standing in queues before the bakers' shops. But when she reflected that any woman with the smallest sense of fashion could quite well shorten her skirt, for it could be done practically without expense—the housemaid had fixed hers up in an hour in spite of the new edging—then her pride did not seem unjustified after all, and as pride puts one in a good humour Hanna Wendling was not irritated by the greengrocer's dirty finger-nails, nor by the flies buzzing round his shop, and for the moment even the fact that her shoes were covered with dust scarcely troubled her. As she strolled through the streets, stopping now at one shop window, now at another, she had incontestably that virginal or nun-like appearance—it was often to be remarked during the war— that is to be seen in women who have been parted from their husbands for a long time and have remained faithful to them. Yet simply because Hanna Wendling felt a little proud at the moment, her face had opened out, and that indefinable soft veil which can fall over such women's faces like a stealthy premonition of approaching age was drawn aside by some invisible hand. Her face was like the first spring day after a long and severe winter.

Dr Kessel, who had to make several visits to patients in the town and thereafter to drive out to the hospital, had promised to set her down again at her door; she had arranged to meet him at the chemist's. When she reached it the buggy was already standing before the door, and Dr Kessel was chatting with Paulsen the chemist. Hanna Wendling had no need to be told what to think of Paulsen; indeed, she probably possessed the knowledge, extending far beyond his particular case, that all men who know that they are betrayed by their wives are wont to display a conspicuous and curiously empty gallantry towards other women; and yet she felt flattered when he rushed up to her with the words: "What a charming visit! Like a fresh spring day." For ruthlessly as Hanna Wendling was accustomed to avoid and cut people in general, to-day, because she felt free and unconstrained she was susceptible even to the empty compliments of the chemist,—it was an oscillation from one extreme to the other, a vacillation between complete reserve and complete lack of it, an immoderation of bearing such as often appears in cramped natures and is not in the least the immoderation of the Renaissance popes, but simply the instability and insignificance of an ordinary bourgeois who lacks a sense of values. At least it may be asserted that it was the lack of a sense of values which now made Hanna Wendling, as she sat on the red plush-covered settle in the shop, shower dazzling and friendly glances on the chemist, and supply his lyrical phrases with a content in which she at once believed and did not believe. Indeed she felt quite cross with Dr Kessel, whose duty called him back to the hospital, when he was forced to suggest that they should leave, and when she sat beside him in the buggy the veil was once more drawn over her face.

She was monosyllabic on the way, monosyllabic at home. Once more she could not comprehend why she had refused so absolutely to return to her father's house in Frankfort for the duration of the war. The objection that food was easier to procure in the little town, that she could not leave the house standing empty, that the air here would be better for the boy; these were subterfuges which merely served to cloak the curious state of estrangement into which she had fallen, and to which she could not shut her eyes. She was shy of people, she had said so to Dr Kessel; "Shy of people," she repeated the words, and as she uttered them it was as though she were putting the responsibility for her shyness on Heinrich, just as she had blamed him when the brass pan in the kitchen had to be given up to be melted down for the war. Even with regard to the boy she was not immune from this mysterious feeling of estrangement. When she woke up in the night she found it difficult to realize that he was sleeping in the next room, and that he was her son. And when she struck a few chords on the piano, it was no longer her hands that did it, but unfeeling fingers which had become strange to her, and she knew that she was losing even her music. Hanna Wendling went to the bathroom to wash away her morning in the town. Then she contemplated herself carefully in the mirror, looking to see whether the face there was still hers. She found it, but she found it curiously veiled, and although she was in reality pleased by this, nevertheless she blamed Heinrich for it.

Moreover she often discovered now that his name did not come to her at once, and then even to herself she called him by the same name that she employed before the servants: Dr Wendling.

CHAPTER XVIII

STORY OF THE SALVATION ARMY GIRL IN BERLIN (3)

I had lost sight of Marie, the Salvation Army girl, for some weeks. Berlin at that time resembled—well, what did it resemble? the days were hot; the asphalt soft, even gaping in places, for nothing was repaired; women were everywhere in charge as conductresses and the like; the trees in the streets wilted in the very spring-time, looking like children with old men's faces, and whenever the wind blew, dust and scraps of paper went whirling; Berlin had grown more countrified, more natural, as it were, and yet that made it all the more unnatural, as if it were an imitation of itself. In the house where I lodged there were two rooms occupied by Jewish refugees from the neighbourhood of Lodz, whose number and relationship to each other I was never able to make out; there were old men in Russian boots and ritual curls, and one that I happened to meet had buckled shoes and white stockings to the knee under his caftan, in the fashion of the eighteenth century; there were men who merely wore their coats rather long to suggest the caftan, and young men of remarkably mild appearance with woolly blond beards growing like false theatrical beards. Now and then a man in service grey uniform turned up, and even his uniform had a hint of the caftan about it. And sometimes there came a man of indefinite age, in ordinary town clothes, and his brown beard was shaven to a square fringe like Oom Paul Kruger's, and left unshorn only at the temples. He always had a stick with an old-fashioned crook handle, and a pince-nez on a black cord. I took him at once for a doctor. Of course there were women too, and children, matrons with false fronts, and young girls dressed, curiously enough, in the height of fashion.

In time I picked up a few words of the Yiddish German they spoke. But I never, of course, really understood it. Still, they seemed to think that inconceivable, for whenever I drew near they broke off the guttural gibberish that came so queerly from the mouths of such dignified ancients, and regarded me with sidelong shyness. In the evenings they mostly sat together in their unlighted rooms, and when in the mornings I came into the hall that was always crammed with garments of all kinds, in the middle of which the maid brushed shoes, I often used to find one of the older men standing at the window. He had his phylacteries bound on brow and wrists, he swayed his torso in time to the shoe-brush, and from time to time kissing the fringes of his cloak, recited at passionate speed with his faded lips faded, passionate prayers out of the window. Perhaps because the window faced east.

I was so fascinated by the Jews that I spent many hours daily quietly observing them. In the hall there hung two chromolithographs of rococo scenes, and I could not help wondering if the Jews could really see these pictures and many other things with the same eyes as ours, and read the same meaning into them. And obsessed by such preoccupations I completely forgot Marie of the Salvation Army, although in some way I felt that she was not unconnected with them.

CHAPTER XIX

Lieutenant Jaretzki's arm had been amputated. Above the elbow. When Kühlenbeck did a thing he did it thoroughly. What was left of Jaretzki sat in the hospital garden beside the shrubbery, regarding the blossoming apple-tree.

A round of inspection by the Town Commandant.

Jaretzki rose to his feet, felt for his diseased hand, felt nothing but emptiness. Then he stood to attention.

" Good-morning, Herr Lieutenant: well on the road to recovery, I see? "

" Yes, sir, but there's a good bit of me missing."

It almost seemed that Major von Pasenow felt himself responsible for Jaretzki's arm as he said:

" It's a terrible war . . . won't you sit down again, Herr Lieutenant? "

" Thank you, Herr Major."

The Major said:

" Where were you wounded? "

" I wasn't wounded, sir . . . gas."

The Major glanced at the stump of Jaretzki's arm:

" I don't understand . . . I thought gas suffocated a man. . . ."

" It can do this kind of thing too, sir."

The Major thought it over for a while. Then he said:

" An unchivalrous weapon."

" Quite so, sir."

Both of them remembered that Germany too was employing that unchivalrous weapon. But they did not mention it.

The Major said:

" How old are you? "

" Twenty-eight, sir."

" When the war began there wasn't any gas."

" No, sir, I believe not."

The sun illumined the long yellow wall of the hospital. A few white clouds hung in the blue sky. The gravel of the garden-path was firmly embedded in the black earth, and at the edge of the lawn crawled an earthworm. The apple-tree was like an enormous nosegay.

The Senior Medical Officer in his white overall came out of the house towards them.

The Major said:

" I hope you'll be all right soon."

" Thank you very much, sir," said Jaretzki.

CHAPTER XX

DISINTEGRATION OF VALUES (2)

The horror of this age is perhaps most palpable in the effect that its architecture has on one; I always come home exhausted and depressed after a walk through the streets. I do not even need to look at the house-fronts; they distress me without my raising my eyes to them. Sometimes I fly for consolation to the so highly commended " modern " buildings, but—and here I'm certainly at fault—the warehouse designed by Messel, who is none the less a great architect, strikes me only as a comic kind of Gothic, and it is a comic effect that irritates and depresses me. It depresses me so much that looking at buildings in the classical style scarcely suffices to restore me. And yet I admire the noble clarity of Schinkel's architecture.

I am convinced that no former age ever received its architectural expressions with dislike and repugnance; that has been reserved for ours. Right up to the development of classicism building was a natural function. It is possible that people never even noticed new buildings, much as one scarcely notices a newly planted tree, but if a man's eye did light upon them he saw that they were good and natural; that was how Goethe still saw the buildings of his time.

I am not an æsthete, and unquestionably never was one, although I may unwittingly have given that impression, and I am just as little addicted to the sentimentality that yearns for the past, transfiguring dead-and-gone epochs. No, behind all my repugnance and weariness there is a very positive conviction, the conviction that nothing is of more importance to any epoch than its style. There is no epoch in the history of all the human race that divulges its character except in its style, and above all in the style of its buildings; indeed no epoch deserves the name except in so far as it possesses a style.

It may be objected that my weariness and irritation are the results of my under-nourishment. It may be pointed out that this age has its own very suggestive machine-and-cannon-and-concrete style, and that some generations must pass before it will be recognized. Well, every age has some stylistic claim; even the experimental ages in spite of their eclecticism had a kind of style. And I am even willing to admit that in our day technique has simply outrun creative effort, that we have not yet wrested from our new material its adequate forms of expression, and that all the disquieting lack of proportion arises from imperfectly mastered purpose. On the other hand, no one can deny that the new kind of building, whether because its material is recalcitrant or its builders incapable, has lost something, has even quite deliberately abandoned something that it could not help abandoning, the lack of which distinguishes it fundamentally from all previous styles: the characteristic use of ornament. Of course that renunciation can be praised as a virtue, on the assumption that we are the first to discover principles of structural economy that enable us to dispense with ornamental excrescences. But is not that term " structural economy " merely a modern catchword? Can it be maintained that the Gothic or any other style was not built with structural economy? To regard ornament as merely an excrescence is to mistake the inner logic of structure. Style in architecture is logic, a logic that governs the whole building from the plan of its foundation to its skyline, and within that logical system the ornament is only the last, the most differentiated expression on a small scale of the unified and unifying conception of the whole. Whether it is an inability to use ornament or a renunciation of it makes no difference; the result is that the architectural structures of this age are sharply distinguished from all previous styles.

But what does it avail to recognize this? Ornament can neither be fashioned by eclecticism nor artificially invented without falling into the

comic absurdities of a Van der Velde. We are left with a profound dis-
quiet and the knowledge that this style of building, which is no longer
a style, is merely a symptom, a writing on the wall proclaiming a state
of the soul which must be the non-soul of our non-age. Simply to look
at it makes me tired. If I could, I would never leave my house again.

CHAPTER XXI

Apart from the fact that the food at the hotel was expensive and that
Huguenau was unwilling to allow himself such a luxury until he had
established himself in a new position, he had the distinct feeling that
it might endanger his impending transactions if the Major saw too much
of him. Further discussions would only spoil the effect he had made and
gain nothing, and it seemed more advantageous that the Major should
forget about him until they met again on Friday. So Huguenau took
his meals in a humbler establishment, and appeared in the dining-hall
again only on the Friday evening.

He had not reckoned in vain. There sat the Major, and he looked
completely surprised when Huguenau approached him briskly and
cordially and thanked him anew for his very friendly and flattering
invitation. " Oh yes," said the Major, who now remembered at last.
" Oh yes. I'll introduce you to the gentlemen."

Huguenau once more thanked him and sat down modestly at another
table. But when the Major had finished his supper and looked up,
Huguenau smiled over at him and rose slightly, to show that he was
at the Major's disposal. Thereupon they went together into the little
adjoining room, where was held the Friday gathering of the gentlemen
of the town.

The gentlemen were present in full force, even the burgomaster himself was there. Huguenau was quite unable to catch all their names. As
soon as he entered he had a feeling of being greeted with warm sympathy,
and a premonition of complete success. This feeling did not deceive
him. The majority of the company already knew of his presence in the
town and the hotel; obviously he had become a theme for speculation,
and they now evinced the warmest interest in his proposals, as he
later informed Esch. The evening ended with unexpectedly positive
results.

That was indeed nothing to be surprised at. The company had the impression that they were taking part in a secret conventicle, which was moreover at the same time a sort of summary court held on the rebel Esch. And if Huguenau got such an exceptionally gracious hearing from his listeners, that was not merely because of his intense desire to win it, nor because of his somnambulistic sureness, but also because he was not in the least a rebel, being rather a man fending for himself and his own interests, and speaking consequently a language which the others understood.

Huguenau could with ease have got the gentlemen to the point of subscribing the 20,000 marks demanded by Esch. But he did not do so. A secret fear admonished him that everything must remain tentative and no more than just plausible, because real security always hovers beyond or above the actual, and any too great solidity is dangerous and like an inexplicable oppression. This may appear meaningless, yet as every absurdity admits of some shred of reasonable explanation, so Huguenau's explanation here was perfectly reasonable and led strangely enough to the same conclusion: it was that if he demanded or accepted too much money from these people, one of them might be struck with the idea of inquiring into his credentials; but if he was standoffish and declined large subscriptions, retaining for his own legendary group the greater share of the invested capital, then they could not doubt that they beheld in him the genuine representative of the most highly capitalized industrial group in the Empire (Krupp's). And indeed no one doubted this, and in the end Huguenau himself finished by believing it. He declared that he was not in a position to offer his esteemed friends a greater share of the proposed 20,000 marks than a third—in other words 6600 marks in all; nevertheless he was prepared to enter into negotiations again with his group to find out whether instead of the two-thirds majority they would be content with a simple one of 51 per cent., and he would be glad also to accept suggestions in advance for later capital expansion; for the moment, however, the gentlemen must content themselves with the small sum mentioned.

The gentlemen were naturally disappointed, but there was no help for it. It was agreed that they should receive interim share certificates in return for their payments as soon as Huguenau had completed the purchase of the *Kur-Trier Herald,* and that after further sounding of the central group the consolidated undertaking would be established as a limited liability company or perhaps even as a syndicate. The prospective shareholders dreamed of future meetings of directors, and the evening closed with cheers for the allied armies and His Majesty the Kaiser.

CHAPTER XXII

When Huguenau awoke he put his hand under the pillow; there he was accustomed to keep his pocket-book for safety of nights. He had a pleasant sense of owning 20,000 marks, and although he knew that his pocket-book did not contain even the 6600 marks which he would receive from the local gentlemen only when the purchase of the *Herald* was completed, but that all that was left in it was a balance of 185 marks, yet he stuck to it that he had 20,000. He possessed 20,000 marks, and that settled the matter.

Against his usual custom he remained lying in bed for a little. If he had 20,000 marks it would be a piece of madness to give them to Esch, simply because the man asked so much for his measly rag. Every price allowed for give-and-take, and he would be able to beat Esch down a bit, Esch could depend on that. At 14,000 marks the paper would still be too dear, and that left a private profit of 6000. The matter had merely to be cleverly managed, so that nobody might know that Esch was not getting his full 20,000. One could put it down as capital reserve, or give out that the industrial group were content with a bare majority instead of the decisive two-thirds preponderance, or something like that. Something was certain to occur to him! and Huguenau leapt cheerfully out of bed.

When he appeared at the office of the *Herald* it was still quite early. And he fell upon the dumbfounded Herr Esch with the most violent reproaches for having let his paper fall so low. It was shocking, the things that he, Wilhelm Huguenau, who after all was not in the least responsible for Herr Esch, had had to listen to about the paper during those last two days. As a middleman, of course, that might have left him quite indifferent, but it broke one's heart, yes, it was heart-breaking to look on and see a good business wantonly being ruined; a newspaper lived by its reputation, and when its reputation was bankrupt, then it was itself bankrupt too. As things stood, it seemed that Herr Esch had managed things so that the *Kur-Trier Herald* was now a wretched unsaleable proposition. " You must see yourself, my dear Esch, that you should actually pay something to anyone who'll take over the paper, instead of demanding money from him."

Esch listened with a woebegone face; then he grimaced contemptuously. But Huguenau was not to be put out of countenance by that: " It's not a smiling matter, my dear friend, it's deadly serious, apparently far more serious than you think." The idea of making a profit was out of the question, and if one nevertheless did not give up all hope of that, it would be made possible only with the help of tremendous sacrifices, yes sacrifices, my dear Esch. If among his friends, as he hoped and believed, there were some self-sacrificing men prepared to take up this quite sense-less, because idealistic scheme, then Herr Esch could simply call it luck, a piece of luck such as one did not encounter more than once in a lifetime; for thanks to singularly favourable circumstances, and his own very efficient abilities as a negotiator, he might eventually get together in spite of everything a round sum of 10,000 marks for Esch, and if Esch didn't snatch at that, then he was only sorry that he had thrown away his time on Esch's affairs, which didn't concern him in the least, no, not in the very least.

" Then leave them alone!" shouted Esch, striking the table with his fist.

" Pardon me, of course I can leave them alone . . . but I don't quite see why you should jump into a rage when a man doesn't accept straight off your fantastic ideas of what the paper's worth."

" I haven't made any fantastic demands. . . . The paper's a bargain at twenty thousand."

" Well, but don't you see that I actually accept your valuation? For you'll admit that the buyer will have to spend a further ten thousand at least in getting the paper on its legs again . . . and thirty thousand would really be exorbitant, don't you agree? "

Esch became thoughtful. Huguenau felt that he was on the right lines:

" Now, I see that you're going to be reasonable . . . I don't want to press you, of course. . . . You should just sleep on it. . . ."

Esch paced up and down the room. Then he said:

" I would like to talk it over with my wife."

" Do that by all means . . . only don't be too long in considering it . . . money talks, my dear Herr Esch, but it doesn't wait."

He got up:

" I'll call on you again to-morrow . . . and meanwhile please give my respects to your good lady."

CHAPTER XXIII

Dr Flurschütz and Lieutenant Jaretzki were walking from the hospital towards the town. The road was pitted with holes made by the motor-lorries, which ran on iron tyres now, for there was no rubber left.

A closed-down roofing-asphalt factory stretched thin black-zinc pipes up into the still air. Birds twittered in the woods.

Jaretzki's sleeve was fastened by a safety-pin to the pocket of his army tunic.

" Extraordinary," said Jaretzki, " since I've got rid of my left arm, the right one hangs down from my shoulder like a weight. I almost feel as if I would like it amputated too."

" You're a symmetrical fellow, it seems . . . engineers have a feeling for symmetry."

" Do you know, Flurschütz, sometimes I forget altogether that I ever was an engineer. . . . You won't understand that, for you've stuck to your profession."

" No, one can hardly say that . . . I was really more of a biologist than a doctor."

" I've sent off an application to the General Electric, there's a shortage of skilled workers everywhere now of course . . . but I simply can't picture myself sitting at a drawing-board again . . . what do you really think, how many have been killed altogether? "

" Can't say, five millions, ten millions . . . perhaps twenty before it comes to an end."

" I'm quite convinced that it can never come to an end . . . it will go on like this for all eternity."

Dr Flurschütz stopped:

" Look here, Jaretzki, can you understand how we can be walking about so peacefully here, how life itself can run on so quietly here, while only a few miles away they're blazing away merrily at each other? "

" Well, there's lots of things I don't understand . . . besides we've both done our bit out there. . . ."

Dr Flurschütz mechanically felt under the peak of his cap for his bullet scar:

" That wasn't what I meant . . . that was at the start, when one rushed into it because one felt ashamed to be left . . . but now one should by rights be going off one's head."

" It hasn't come to that yet . . . no, thanks, better to drink oneself blind. . . ."

" Well, you follow the prescription rather thoroughly."

The wind carried a smell of tar to them from the closed-down factory.

Thin and bent, with his fair pointed beard and his eyeglasses, Dr Flurschütz looked somewhat awkward in his uniform. They were silent for a while.

The road descended. The scattered bungalows that had sprung up outside the town gates during recent years presently drew together in a continuous line; they looked very peaceful. In all the front gardens wretched-looking vegetables were growing.

Jaretzki said:

" Not very pleasant to live all the year round in this smell of tar."

Flurschütz replied:

" I was in Roumania and Poland. And do you know . . . everywhere the houses had just the same peaceful look . . . with the same trade signs as here, master-builder, locksmith, and so forth . . . in a dug-out near Armentières I once saw a shop sign, it was one of the roof props, ' Tailleur pour Dames ' . . . perhaps it's silly, but the complete madness of the whole war really only dawned on me then for the first time."

Jaretzki said:

" With my one arm I suppose I could get myself taken on for some job in the army as an engineer."

" You would like that better than the General Electric? "

" No, I'm past liking anything better . . . perhaps I'll just report for service again with my remaining arm . . . for throwing hand-grenades one arm would be enough . . . lend me a hand to get this cigarette lit."

" What have you been drinking to-day, Jaretzki? "

" Me? nothing worth speaking of, I've kept sober for the sake of the wine I'm presently going to introduce you to."

" Well, how about the General Electric? "

Jaretzki laughed:

" To be quite honest, merely a sentimental attempt to get back into civilian life, with a career to look forward to, no more of this drifting about, perhaps get married . . . but you believe as little in that as I do."

" Why on earth shouldn't I believe in it? "

Jaretzki punctuated his reply with his cigarette:

" Because . . . the . . . war . . . can . . . never . . . come . . . to . . . an . . . end . . . how often must I tell you that? "

" That too would be a solution," said Flurschütz.

" It is the only solution."

They had reached the town gate. . . . Jaretzki put up his foot on the curbstone, drew his handkerchief out of his pocket, and, his cigarette aslant in his mouth, flicked the dust of the road from his shoes. Then he stroked his dark moustache smooth, and passing through the cool arch of the gate they stepped into the still and narrow street.

CHAPTER XXIV

DISINTEGRATION OF VALUES (3)

The primacy of architectural style among the things that characterize an epoch is a very curious phenomenon. But, in general, so is the uniquely privileged position that plastic art has maintained in history. It is after all only a very small excerpt from the totality of human activities with which an age is filled, and certainly not even a particularly spiritual excerpt, and yet in power of characterization it surpasses every other province of the spirit, surpasses poetry, surpasses even science, surpasses even religion. The thing that endures through thousands of years is the work of plastic art; it remains the exponent of the age and its style.

This cannot be due merely to the durability of the material employed; the bulk of the printed paper from the last few centuries has survived, and yet any Gothic statue is more " medieval " than the whole of medieval literature. No, that would be a very inadequate explanation,—if there should be one, it must be found in the intrinsic nature of the concept of style itself.

For certainly style is not a thing confined to architectural and plastic art merely; style is something which uniformly permeates all the living expressions of an epoch. It would be against all reason to regard the artist as an exception among mankind, as a man leading a sort of peculiar existence within the style which he himself produces, while the others remain excluded.

No, if there is such a thing as style, then all human manifestations are penetrated by it, so that the style of a period is as indubitably present in its thought as in every other human activity of the period. And only

by starting from this fact, which must be so, because it is impossible that
it should be otherwise, can we find an explanation for the remarkable
fact that precisely those activities which manifest themselves in spatial
terms have become of such extraordinary and in the real sense of the
word visible significance.

Perhaps it would be idle to consider this too curiously if behind it
there did not stand the problem which alone justifies all philosophizing:
our dread of nothingness, our dread of Time, which conducts us to
death. And perhaps all the disquietude which bad architecture evokes,
causing me to hide in my house, is nothing else than that dread. For whatever a man may do, he does it in order to annihilate Time, in order to
revoke it, and that revocation is called Space. Even music, which exists
only in time and fills time, transmutes time into space, and it is in the
utmost degree probable that all thought takes place in a spatial world,
that the process of thought represents a combination of indescribably
complicated many-dimensional logically extended spaces. But if that
be so, then it also becomes clear why all those activities which are
immediately related to space achieve a significance and an obviousness
that can never be achieved by any other human activity. And in this
also can be seen the peculiar symptomatic significance of ornament.
For ornament, detached from all purposive activity, although produced
by it, becomes the abstract expression, the "formula" of the whole
complex of spatial thought, becomes the formula of style itself, and with
that the formula of the entire epoch and its life.

And in this, it seems to me, lies the significance, a significance that I
might almost call magical, of the fact that an epoch which is completely
under the dominion of death and hell must live in a style that can no
longer give birth to ornament.

CHAPTER XXV

Had it not been for the prospect of building the new house they were
to live in, Hanna Wendling might perhaps never have become engaged
to the young provincial advocate. But in 1910 all young girls in the
better-class bourgeois families read *The Studio*, *Interior Decoration*,
German Art and Decoration, and owned a work called *English Period
Furniture*, and their erotic preconceptions of marriage were in the
most intimate manner bound up with problems of architectonics. The

Wendlings' house, or "Rose Cottage," for such the quaint lettering on its gable designated it, conformed in a modest degree to these ideals; it had a deep roof with low eaves; majolica cherubs at either side of the front door displayed symbols of love and fertility; there was an English hall with a rough tiled stove, and a chimneypiece with brass knick-knacks standing on it. It had given her a great deal of labour and pleasure to find for every piece of furniture its appropriate position, so that a general architectonical equilibrium might be inaugurated; and when all was finished Hanna Wendling had the feeling that she and she alone was aware of the perfection of that equilibrium, even though Heinrich too had a share in the knowledge, even though a great part of their married happiness consisted in this mutual awareness of the secret harmony and counterpoint exemplified in the arrangement of the furniture and pictures.

Now the furniture had not been moved since that time, on the contrary, strict care had been taken not to alter the original arrangement by an inch; and yet it had become different: what had happened? can equilibrium suffer depreciation, can harmony become threadbare? In the beginning she was not conscious that apathy was at the back of this,— her positive emotion simply relapsed into neutrality, and only when it transformed itself into a negative condition did it become perceptible: it was not that the house or the arrangement of the furniture had now become repellent to her, for that might have been got over at a pinch by changing the disposition of the furniture; no, it was something that went deeper; the curse of the fortuitous and the accidental had spread itself over things and the relations between things, and one could not think out any arrangement that would not be just as fortuitous and arbitrary as the existing one. In all this there lay doubtless a certain confusion, a certain darkness, indeed almost a danger, particularly as there seemed no reason why this insecurity in architectonics should stop at other matters of sentiment, even for instance at questions of fashion: this thought was particularly alarming, and although Hanna Wendling knew very well that there were far more important and difficult problems, yet perhaps nothing was more alarming to her than the thought that even the fashion journals might lose their attraction for her, and that one day she might regard without delight, without interest, without comprehension, the English journal *Vogue* itself, which she had missed so sorely during these four years of the war.

When she caught herself indulging in those thoughts she told herself that they were fantastic, although in fact they were far more essentially sober than fantastic, filled with a kind of disenchantment which was only fantastic in so far as no intoxication had preceded it, rather indeed a subsequent and additional disenchantment supervening on a state that was already sober and almost normal, so that in a sense it became still more normal and landed in negation. Such evaluations must always of course be relative in a certain degree; the border-line between sobriety and intoxication cannot always be established, and whether for instance the Russian love for humanity should be regarded as an intoxication, or whether it is to be taken as a standard for normal social relations, indeed whether the whole panorama of existence is to be regarded as drunk or sober; all these questions in the final resort are not to be resolved. Nevertheless it is not impossible that sobriety implies an ultimate state of entropy or an absolute zero, an absolute zero towards which all movement perpetually and of necessity strives. And there were many indications that Hanna Wendling was moving in this direction, and in essentials perhaps she was simply as usual anticipating a coming fashion; for the entropy of man implies his absolute isolation, and that which hitherto he has called harmony or equilibrium was perhaps only an image, an image of the social structure, which he made for himself, and could not help making, so long as he remained a part of it. But the more lonely he becomes, the more disintegrated and isolated will things seem to him, the more indifferent he must become to the connections between things, and finally he will scarcely be able any longer to see those connections. So Hanna Wendling walked through the house, walked through her garden, walked over paths which were laid with crazy-paving in the English style, and she no longer saw the pattern, no longer saw the windings of the white paths, and painful as this might well have been, it was scarcely even painful any more, for it was necessary.

CHAPTER XXVI

Huguenau now turned up daily in Fischerstrasse to see Herr Esch. Often, employing a well-tried business ruse, he did not even mention the transaction that had brought him, but waited for his opponent's move, talking meanwhile about the weather, the crops, and the latest victories. When he saw that Esch did not want to hear anything about the victories, he dropped the victories and confined himself to the weather.

Sometimes he found Marguerite in the courtyard. The child was confiding, clung to his finger, and begged him to take her into the printing-room again. Huguenau said:

"Aha! you're after another twenty pfennigs, are you? But Uncle Huguenau isn't rich enough yet, everything takes its time."

Nevertheless he gave her ten pfennigs for her money-box:

"Well, what will we do when we're both rich . . .?"

The child stared at the ground and did not reply. At last she said hesitatingly:

"Go away."

For some reason Huguenau felt pleased by this:

"So that's what you need the money for . . . well, when we're rich we can both go away together. . . . I'll take you with me."

"Yes, do," said Marguerite.

Whenever he went up to see Esch she generally stole up after him, sat down on the floor and listened. Or if she did not do this she would at least put her head in at the door and laugh. Huguenau would say then, because it was an unfailing topic for conversation:

"I'm fond of children."

Esch seemed to like that; he smiled complacently:

"A little ruffian . . . she would do one in if it came up her back."

Haïssez les Prussiens, Huguenau could not help thinking, although Esch was not a Prussian at all, but a Luxemburger. Esch went on:

"I've often thought of adopting the little rascal . . . we haven't any children of our own."

Huguenau was surprised:

"Another man's child. . . ."

Esch said:

"Another's or your own . . . it's much the same . . . a pretty thin life without one."

Huguenau laughed:

"Well, yes, you can't be too sure even of your own children."

Esch said:

"Her father's interned. . . . I've talked over the question of adopting her with my wife . . . after all she's practically an orphan."

Huguenau said reflectively:

" Hm, but then you would have to provide for her."

" Of course," said Esch.

" If you had any spare cash, or could get hold of some, by selling out, for instance, you could take out a life insurance policy for your family. . . . I have connections with several insurance companies."

" Indeed," said Esch.

·' I'm still a single man, thank God, in difficult times like these that's an immense advantage . . . but if I should ever set up house, I'll safeguard my family by a settlement of capital or something of the kind . . . well, you're in the enviable position of being able to do that. . . ."

Huguenau went away.

Marguerite was waiting for him in the courtyard.

" Would you like to stay here always? "

" Where? " asked the child.

" Why, here, with Uncle Esch."

The child gazed at him with hostility.

Huguenau winked at her and wagged his head:

" Rather not, what? "

Marguerite laughed too.

" Well, you would rather not . . .? "

" No, I don't want to."

" And you don't care much for him either . . . he's very strict with you, eh? " and Huguenau brought his arm down as if smacking someone.

Marguerite made a contemptuous grimace:

" No. . . ."

" And the other one . . . Aunt Esch . . .? "

The child shrugged her shoulders.

Huguenau was satisfied:

" Well, you won't need to stay here . . . we'll run away, the two of us, to Belgium . . . come, let's go and see Herr Lindner in the printing-room."

Together they went up to the printing-press and watched Herr Lindner as he fed it with sheets of paper.

CHAPTER XXVII

STORY OF THE SALVATION ARMY GIRL IN BERLIN (4)

The feeling that the Jews had been taking stock of me proved to be justified. For two days I had felt rather out of sorts, had scarcely touched my breakfast and gone out for only half-an-hour. On the evening of the second day there came a knock at the door of my room, and to my surprise the little man entered whom I had always taken to be a doctor. And indeed he actually revealed himself as one.

" You must be ill," he said.

" No," I said, " and if I am it's nobody's business."

" It won't cost you anything, I haven't come for the sake of the money," he said timidly, " one must help."

" Thanks," I said, " I'm quite well."

He stood before me, holding his walking-stick tightly pressed to his bosom.

" Fever? " he asked imploringly.

" No, I'm quite well, I'm just going out."

I got up and we left the room together.

In the hall one of the young Jews was standing, one of those with the downy stage beards.

The doctor now introduced itself:

" My name is Dr Litwak."

" Bertrand Müller, doctor of philosophy," I gave him my hand; the young Jew also offered me his hand. It was dry and cool, and as smooth as his face.

They attached themselves to me as though it were the most natural thing in the world. I wasn't going anywhere in particular, but I walked very fast. The two of them, one on my right and the other on my left, kept step with me and conversed with each other in Yiddish. I became seriously annoyed:

" I don't understand a word you're saying."

They laughed:

" He says he doesn't understand a word."

After a while:

" Really, you don't know any Yiddish? "

" No."

We reached the end of Reichenbergerstrasse, and I set my course for Rixdorf.

Well, and then we encountered Marie.

She was leaning against a lamp-post. It was already quite dark, but the gas was being used sparingly. All the same I recognized her at once.

Moreover the windows of the restaurant opposite gave a little light.

Marie recognized me too; she smiled to me. Then she asked:

" Are these friends of yours? "

" Neighbours," I replied.

I suggested a visit to the restaurant, for Marie seemed to be exhausted and in need of something to eat. But the two Jews refused to enter the restaurant. Perhaps they were afraid that they might be forced to eat pork, perhaps they were afraid of being jeered at or something or other. In any case one could have made it a pretext for getting rid of them.

But an extraordinary thing happened: Marie ranged herself on the side of the Jews, said that she was not in the least hungry, and as though it were an unavoidable arrangement, she went on in front with the young Jew, while I followed with Dr Litwak.

" Who is he? " I asked the doctor, pointing at the young Jew, the tails of whose grey coat swung in front of me.

" He's called Nuchem Sussin," said Dr Litwak.

CHAPTER XXVIII

Dr Kühlenbeck and Dr Kessel had been in the operating-theatre. Generally Kühlenbeck spared Dr Kessel as much as possible, for Dr Kessel, although at the disposal of the hospital, was overworked attending to his panel patients; just now, however, the new offensive had brought in fresh material for treatment, and Kühlenbeck had no choice. It was fortunate that only lighter cases had been sent. Or at least what were called lighter cases.

And because the two men were genuine doctors, they sat talking over their cases later in Kühlenbeck's room. Flurschütz too had come in.

" A pity that you weren't there to-day, Flurschütz, you would have enjoyed it," said Kühlenbeck. " It's astonishing how much you learn . . . if we hadn't operated, the man would have been a cripple for the rest of his life . . ." he laughed, " but now he'll be able to go out and be shot at again in six weeks' time."

Kessel said:

" I only wish my poor panel patients were as well looked after as the men here."

Kühlenbeck said:

" Do you know the story of the convict who swallowed a fish-bone and had to be operated on so that they might be able to hang him next morning? That's our job at the moment."

Flurschütz said:

" If the doctors in all the combatant countries went on strike, the war would soon be over."

" Well, Flurschütz, you can make a beginning."

Dr Kessel said:

" I feel jolly well inclined to send the ribbon back . . . you should feel ashamed of yourself, Kühlenbeck, playing an old colleague such a dirty trick."

" What could I do? I had to give you your medicine . . . the civilians are all wearing the black-and-white now."

" Yes, and you're just running round palming it off on them. . . . You've been down on the list too for a long time now, Flurschütz."

Flurschütz said:

" At bottom it just comes down to this, that we all sit about here discussing cases that are more or less interesting, without thinking of anything else . . . we haven't time as a matter of fact to think of anything else . . . and it's the same everywhere. You get swallowed up, swallowed up by what you're doing . . . simply swallowed up."

Dr Kessel said:

" Damn it all, I'm fifty-six, what is there left for me to think about? . . . I'm glad when I get into bed at night."

Kühlenbeck said:

" Would you care for a drink at the regiment's expense . . .? We'll be getting another twenty men or so in by two o'clock . . . will you stay to receive them? "

He had got up and walked over to the medicine cabinet beside the window, from which he now took a bottle of cognac and three glasses. As he stood in profile against the window reaching up his hand to the shelf in the cabinet, his beard was outlined against the light and he looked gigantic.

Flurschütz said:

" We're all being pumped dry by the profession we're stuck in . . . and even soldiering and patriotism are nothing more than professions . . . we're simply past understanding what is happening in any province but our own."

" Thank God for that! " said Dr Kühlenbeck, " doctors don't need to be philosophers."

Sister Mathilde entered. She smelt of scented soap. Or at least one felt that she must smell of it. Her narrow face with the long nose contrasted with her housemaid's red hands.

" Dr Kühlenbeck, the station people have rung up to say that the transport train has arrived."

" Good, one more cigarette before we go . . . you're coming too, Sister? "

" Sister Carla and Sister Emmy have gone to the station already."

" Excellent . . . well, shall we be going, Flurschütz? "

" Straining at the leash," remarked Dr Kessel, but without real gusto.

Sister Mathilde had remained standing at the door. She liked to dawdle in the doctors' room. And as they all went out, Flurschütz's eye caught the gleam of her white throat, noted the freckles where her hair began, and he felt a little touched.

" 'Day, Sister," said the Chief.

" Good-day, Sister," said Flurschütz too.

" Gott mit uns," said Dr Kessel.

CHAPTER XXIX

Trees and houses appeared before the eyes of the bricklayer Gödicke, the weather changed, sometimes it was day and sometimes night, people moved about and he heard them speaking. Food was brought and set before him on objects, mostly round, made of tin or earthenware. He knew all this, but the way that led to a knowledge of these things, or by which they reached him, was a laborious one: the bricklayer Gödicke had now to work harder than he had ever done in his hard-working life. For it was by no means a simple and self-evident action to lift a spoon to one's mouth when one was not clear in one's mind who it was that was being fed, and the frightful strain of making this clear turned it into a torment of despairing labour and impossible duty; for nobody, least of all Gödicke himself, could have provided a theory to explain the structural elements that composed his personality. For of course it would have been erroneous to assert that the man Gödicke was made up of several Gödickes, including for instance a boy Ludwig Gödicke who had played in the street with his friends and made tunnels in the ash-heaps and sandpits, a boy who was called in every day to dinner by his mother and made to carry his father's dinner afterwards to the building where he was working, since he too had been a bricklayer; to assert that that boy Ludwig Gödicke represented a constituent part of the man's present self would have been just as erroneous as to recognize another constituent part of it, say, in the apprentice Gödicke who had envied the Hamburg carpenters so intensely on account of their broad-brimmed hats and the mother-of-pearl buttons on their waistcoats that he had not rested until, to spite them all, he had seduced the bride of the carpenter Gürzner among the bushes by the riverside, although he was merely a bricklayer's apprentice; and it would be erroneous again to assert that yet another part was the man who during a strike had put the concrete-mixing machine out of action by unscrewing the cylinders, and in spite of that had left the union when he married the servant-girl Anna Lamprecht, and that simply because she cried so much on account of the baby that was coming: no, such a longitudinal splitting as this, such a quasi-historical section, can never give the constituent elements of a personality, for it cannot go beyond the biographical. The difficulties with which the man Gödicke had to contend, then, were certainly not caused by the fact that he felt this whole series of persons living within him, but rather sprang from the sudden interruption of the series at a certain point, from the fact that there was no connection between the earlier biography and himself, though he himself should obviously have been the last link in the chain, and that being cast adrift in this way from something which he could hardly any longer describe as his life, he had lost his own identity. He saw these figures as through smoked glass, and although when he lifted the spoon to his mouth he would have liked well enough to be feeding the man who had lain with Gürzner's fiancée under the bushes—indeed, that would have given him great pleasure—nevertheless he simply could not bridge the gap, he remained as it were on the farther bank and could not lay hold of the man on the other side. And yet perhaps in spite of all that he might have bridged the gap if he could only have known for certain who it really was that remembered Gürzner's girl: for the eyes that had looked at the bushes by the riverside then were not the same eyes that gazed at the trees along the avenue now, nor again were these quite the same as those which looked round the room. And beyond doubt there was one Gödicke who could not bear that that other man should be fed, and who refused to feed him, that man who was even now still prepared to sleep with Gürzner's girl. And the Gödicke who was enduring these pains in his abdomen might be with equal probability either the one who issued the refusal, or the one against whom it was directed, but he might just as well be a quite different Gödicke altogether. It was a highly complicated problem, and the bricklayer Gödicke could not see his way through it at all. It had probably arisen through his reluctance to resume all the scattered fragments of his soul in returning to consciousness, but perhaps it might also have been the cause why he was not in a condition to do so. True, if he could have peered within himself now, one could not exclude the possibility that in each fragment of his ego which he had admitted he might have recognized a separate Gödicke, somewhat as though each of those fragments were an independent nucleus. For it may be that the same thing happens with the soul as with a piece of protoplasm, in which by dissection one can produce a multiplication of nuclei and therewith new regions of autonomous, intact and separate life. However that may be, and however it may have come about, in Gödicke's soul there existed several autonomous and integral separate existences, to each of which one might have ventured to give the title of Gödicke, and it was a laborious and almost impossible task to subsume them all in one personality.

This task the bricklayer Gödicke had to accomplish entirely by himself; there was no one who could help him.

CHAPTER XXX

When after a politic interval of two days Huguenau once more appeared in Esch's office, he found a broad-hipped person of uncertain age, devoid equally of sex and charm, sitting in the basket-chair beside Esch's desk. It was Frau Esch, and Huguenau knew that now the game was his. He had only to make a favourable impression on her:

" Oh, your good lady is going to give us the benefit of her assistance in these difficult negotiations. . . ."

Frau Esch drew back a little:

" I know nothing about business matters, that's my husband's affair."

" Ah, yes, your husband, he's a real business man *comme il faut*; he's a tough nut to crack, I can tell you, and lots of people will break their teeth on him yet."

Frau Esch smiled faintly, and Huguenau felt encouraged to go on:

" A splendid idea of his to take advantage of the market and get rid of the paper, which brings him only worry and annoyance, you might say, and business going from bad to worse."

Frau Esch said politely:

" Yes, my husband has a great deal of worry with the paper."

" I'm not going to give it up, all the same," said Esch.

" Come, come, Herr Esch, if your health is of no account to yourself, I'm sure that your good lady will have a word or two to say about that . . . besides," Huguenau considered, " . . . if you don't want to sever your connection entirely with the paper, you can make your further collaboration a condition of the deal, the group I represent will only be too glad if I secure them such valuable assistance."

Well, that might be considered, Esch thought, but under 18,000 marks it couldn't be done, he and his wife had just come to that decision.

Well, it was a hopeful sign that Herr Esch had already somewhat qualified the fancy price he had asked; still, if he wanted to retain his connection with the business, he must surely make some allowance for that too.

To what extent, asked Herr Esch.

Huguenau felt that something concrete was demanded:

" The simplest way, really, would be to draw up a trial contract and go over the different points by the way."

" All right, I don't mind," said Esch, taking out a sheet of paper, " dictate."

Huguenau seated himself in the appropriate posture:

" Well, right then; Heading: Memorandum of Contract."

After much desultory discussion, which took up the whole forenoon, the following contract resulted:

1. *Herr Wilhelm Huguenau, as representative and executor of a group of combined interests, hereby enters into partnership with the private company owning the* Kur-Trier Herald *on the following terms, the property of the firm to be allocated as follows:*

10 per cent. to remain in the possession of Herr August Esch.

60 per cent. to be held by the " Industrial Group " represented by Herr Huguenau.

30 per cent. to be held by the group of local interests also represented by Herr Huguenau.

Esch's original claim to half-ownership was turned down by Huguenau: " That would be against your own interests, my dear Esch, the bigger your share, the less you'll realize in cash . . . you see, I'm keeping an eye on your interests."

2. *The firm's assets consist of the publishing and other rights, together with the office furnishings and complete printing plant. Interim share certificates shall be issued, covering the new distribution of share capital.*

The Statue of Liberty and the view of Badenweiler were claimed by Herr Esch as his private property and not included among the firm's assets. " Certainly," said Huguenau magnanimously.

3. *The net profits shall be distributed among the shareholders in proportion to the number of share certificates held, except for any sum that may be carried to the reserve fund. The losses shall be borne in the same proportion.*

The clause regarding the losses was inserted in the contract at Herr Esch's request, as Herr Huguenau had not entertained the possibility of losses. The reserve fund too was Esch's suggestion.

4. *As representative and executor of the new group of shareholders Herr Huguenau brings into the firm capital amounting to 20,000 marks (say twenty thousand marks). One-third of this amount to be paid up immediately; the two further instalments of one-third may be paid, if the shareholders desire, within the next six months or twelve months respectively. On deferred payments the firm shall charge interest at the rate of 4 per cent. per half-year. The share certificates shall be allotted in proportion to the money paid in.*

As the share certificates were to be issued immediately on payment, and the high rate of 4 per cent. was a grave deterrent, Huguenau was not greatly afraid of the local subscribers taking advantage of the deferred payment; but even if they did, some means or other would easily enough be found of tiding over the emergency. Nor was he worried by the question of how he himself was to get together the deferred payments of his legendary industrial group—the first instalment did not fall due for another half-year, at the beginning of 1919, that was to say, and it was a long time until then, and lots of things might happen; the war conditions created a great deal of confusion, perhaps peace might have come by then, perhaps the paper itself might have brought in the sum required, in which case it would of course be necessary to conceal those gains by the creation of imaginary losses and thus wipe them off, perhaps Esch would be dead by that time—one would find some way of getting over the difficulty and coming out on top.

> 5. *The payments made by Herr Wilhelm Huguenau, in all 20,000 marks, shall be allocated to two accounts: viz. 13,400 marks to the account of the Huguenau " Industrial Group," and 6600 marks to the account of the local subscribers.*

But now came the most difficult point in the negotiations. For Esch insisted on his 18,000 marks, while Huguenau maintained that first of all 10 per cent., that was 2000 marks, had to be deducted on account of the shares retained by Esch, but that in addition the rebate had to be doubled in consideration of the increased capital put into the business, thus making in all 4000 marks; so that Esch, even accepting his own valuation, would have only 14,000 coming to him; but even that was still far too much; he, Huguenau, as a middleman, had to be unbiassed, and he would never be able to get such a price as that out of his group, delighted as he would be to do so for Esch and his charming wife's sake; no, that would be simply impossible, for he must have a serious proposal to lay before his clients, and he had no wish to be laughed out of court; in this matter he was not in the least a partisan, but quite objective, and as an impartial judge he could offer 10,000 marks for the remaining 90 per cent. of the business, but not a penny more.

No, Esch shouted, he wanted his eighteen thousand.

" How can anyone be so hard of hearing? " Huguenau turned to Frau Esch, " I've just proved to him that according to his own valuation all that he can ask is fourteen thousand."

Frau Esch sighed.

Finally they agreed on 12,000 marks and on the following clause:

> 6. *As former sole proprietor Herr August Esch shall receive:*
> (a) *A final quittance of 12,000 marks, of which a third, that is to say, 4000 marks, shall be paid immediately to Herr Esch by the*

*company, and the two further instalments of 4000 each on 1st January
and 1st July 1919 respectively. Interest at the rate of 4 per cent. will
be charged on the two outstanding instalments;*

(b) *A contract engaging him for a period of two years as assistant
editor and head book-keeper with a monthly salary of 125 marks.*

Perhaps Esch might not still have given in, even though Huguenau
adroitly diverted the dispute to the subordinate concession of the interest
payable to Esch, intending only after a hotly contested sham fight to
allow the 4 per cent. to be wrung from him; no, Esch might not even
then have given in, had not the prospect of such complicated book-
keeping so dazzled and enchanted him that it never entered his head
that the outstanding instalments—and he had not the slightest idea
that their payment presupposed nothing less than a miracle—might
never be settled, or that the difference between the 12,000 marks and the
20,000 marks might flow, in spite of all those book-keeping prospects
which so allured him, into Huguenau's fraudulently open pockets. To
tell the truth, Huguenau thought just as little of such sordid matters,
so unconscious was he that once the payments were made by the local
subscribers the *Kur-Trier Herald* became *via facti* a pure gift to him;
he fought with all sincerity for the interests of his hypothetical clients
and said at last in an exhausted tone: " Ouf, well, as far as I'm concerned, let us make it 12,000 marks and 4 per cent. as you say, to settle
the matter for good. I'll take the responsibility on my own shoulders . . .
but I must get something out of it too. . . . "

7. *Reciprocal rights and duties:*

(a) *Herr Huguenau shall act as publisher and editor. The commercial
and financial conduct of the enterprise rests exclusively in his hands.
He has furthermore the right to accept and reject articles for the paper
as he thinks fit. In return for these services the firm guarantees him
a minimum salary of 175 M. per month, that is to say, 2100 M. yearly.*

(b) *During the period covered by his contract Herr Esch shall for
his part keep the books of the firm and act as assistant editor.*

Esch had to agree to the limitation of his editorial powers out of consideration for the industrial group; his book-keeping powers represented
a sort of compensation.

8. *The rooms in Herr Esch's house hitherto employed in the pro-
duction of the paper shall be placed at the disposal of the firm for a*

period of three years. Furthermore Herr Esch shall put at the disposition of the editor for the same period two comfortably furnished front rooms with breakfast in the aforesaid house. Herr Esch shall receive from the firm's revenues a reimbursement of 25 marks per month for these services.

9. Should the company be converted at a later stage into a limited liability or joint stock company, the gist of the aforesaid conditions shall be respected.

With this projected conversion of the business into a company compelled to audit its accounts, Huguenau's house of cards of course would fall to pieces. But Huguenau did not worry his head about such trifles; for him the whole thing was a perfectly legitimate piece of business, and the only item that struck him as verging on sharp-practice was the one giving him a present of free quarters with his breakfast thrown in, but he was elated at bringing it off. Esch, on the other hand, was grieved because the contract had not run to ten clauses. They thought for a while and then they found the tenth:

10. Any difference of interpretation which may arise out of this contract shall be decided by public arbitration.

So in an astonishingly short time—it was the 14th of May—Huguenau was able to report that the purchase had been smoothly settled. The local subscribers did not hesitate to pay up their full capital investment of 6600 marks; of this 4000 was allotted to Herr Esch in accordance with the terms of the contract; as a prudent and solid business man Herr Huguenau allocated 1600 marks for working expenses, while as for the remaining 1000, he embellished it with the title of floating capital and employed it for his own uses. The interim share certificates were issued to the shareholders, and in a few days it was duly announced that from the first of June the paper would appear under its new editorship and in a new make-up. Huguenau had managed to induce the Major to inaugurate the new era with a leading article, and the festal number was also embellished partly with patriotic, partly with political-economical, but in greater part with patriotic-economical pronouncements from the pens of the local subscribers.

But to celebrate the new epoch Huguenau installed himself in the two rooms prepared for him in Esch's house.

The style of an epoch, it is certain, affects not merely the artist; it penetrates all contemporary activities, and crystallizes itself not only in works of art but in all the values which make up the culture of the age, and of which works of art constitute only an insignificant part; yet one is fairly at a loss when confronted by the concrete question: in how far is the style of an age incarnated in the average man, in a business man, for example, of the type of Wilhelm Huguenau? Has the man who deals in pipes of wine or textiles anything in common with the feeling for style that is evident in the shops built by Messel, or Peter Behrens's turbine power-houses? His private taste will certainly run to pinnacled villas and rooms cluttered with knick-knacks, and even if it should not, he remains a member of the public, which, however it may comport itself, is separated by a great gulf from the artist.

Yet when one regards more closely a man such as Huguenau, one sees that the gulf between him and the artist does not affect the real point at issue. One may certainly assume that in epochs which had a supreme feeling for style the lack of understanding between the artist and his contemporaries was less strongly marked than it is to-day, that for instance a new picture by Dürer in the Sebaldus Church excited general joy and admiration among even the Huguenaus of the time; for there is plenty of evidence that at that period the artist and his public were bound together in a very different kind of community, and that the painter understood the clothier and the saddler at least as profoundly as they enjoyed looking at his pictures. Of course this cannot be verified, and it may be, too, that many revolutionary spirits received but little recognition from their contemporaries; perhaps that was the case with Grünewald. But such exceptions are not particularly relevant, and in any case whether an understanding between the artist and his contemporaries ruled in the Middle Ages or not becomes a matter of indifference in face of the fact that misunderstanding and understanding alike are just as truly expressions of the legendary " Time Spirit " as a work of art in itself or any other contemporary activity.

But if this be so, then it is also a matter of indifference what direction is taken by the architectural or other taste of a business agent of

Huguenau's type, and the fact that Huguenau had a certain æsthetic pleasure in machinery is likewise without importance; the sole question of any moment is whether his ordinary actions, his ordinary thoughts, were influenced by the same laws that in another sphere produced a style devoid of ornament, or evolved the theory of relativity, or led up to the philosophical conclusions of neo-Kantianism,—in other words, whether even the thought of an epoch is not a vehicle for its style, governed by that same style which attains visible and palpable expression in works of art; which amounts to the assertion that truth, the ultimate product of thought, is equally a vehicle for the style of the epoch in which it has been discovered and in which it is valid, precisely like all the other values of that epoch.

And indeed it cannot be otherwise. For it is not merely that, seen from a certain standpoint, truth is just a value among other values; truth also governs all the actions of mankind, which are, one may say, steeped in truth : whatever a man does is plausible to him at every moment, he justifies it to himself with reasons which in his eyes represent the truth, he proves it to himself logically, and—at least in the very moment of action —his actions are always justifiable. If his actions, then, are dominated by the style of his age, so must his thoughts be; we need not decide (from the practical or epistemological standpoint) whether the act has preceded the thought or the thought the act, the motion of life the motion of reason, the *sum* the *cogito*, or the *cogito* the *sum*—all we can take into account is the rational logic of thought, for the irrational logic of action, in which style is embodied, can be perceived only in the finished product, in the result.

But with this extremely intimate connection between the substance of logical thought and the positive and negative values which action embodies, the scheme of thought which governs a man like Huguenau and compels him to act in one particular way, which determines his business methods for him and makes him draft contracts from a certain standpoint—that is to say, all the inner logic of a man like Huguenau—is given its own place in the whole logical framework of the epoch, and brought into essential relation with whatever logic permeates the productive spirit of the epoch and its visible style. And even although that rational thought, that rational logic, may be nothing but a thin and as it were one-dimensional thread which has to be wound round and round the multiplicity of dimensions presented by life, nevertheless that thought, projected in the abstraction of logical space, is an abbreviated expression of life's multiplicity and prevailing style, much in the same way as ornament is an abbreviated spatial expression of the visible style-product,—a projected abbreviation of all the works that embody style.

Huguenau is a man who acts with singleness of purpose. He organizes his day with singleness of purpose, he carries on his business affairs with his eye singly on his purpose, he evolves and concludes his contracts with his eye singly on his purpose. Behind all his purposefulness there lies a logic that is completely stripped of ornament, and the fact that this logic should demand the elimination of all ornament does not seem a too daring conclusion to draw; indeed it actually appears as good and just as every other necessary conclusion. And yet this elimination of all ornament involves nothingness, involves death, and a monstrous dissolution is concealed behind it in which our age is crumbling away.

CHAPTER XXXII

The rebel must not be confused with the criminal, though society may often stigmatize the rebel as a criminal, and though the criminal may sometimes pose as a rebel to dignify his actions. The rebel stands alone: the most faithful son of that society which is the target of his hostility and rejection, he sees in the world he combats a totality of living relationships whose threads have merely been tangled in confusion by some diabolical wickedness, and it is his chosen task to disentangle them and order them according to his own better ideas. Thus did Luther make his protest against the Pope, and so Esch might with justice be called a rebel.

This is by no means, however, a sufficient cause to asperse Huguenau, on the other hand, as a criminal. That would be not only to slander him, but also to do him grievous injustice. From the military standpoint a deserter is of course a criminal, and undoubtedly there are convinced militarists who loathe the deserter with the same intensity as, let us say, a farmer loathes a chicken thief, and like the farmer they will recognize nothing less than the death penalty as a just punishment for such a transgressor. Nevertheless there is here a principal and objective distinction: the essence of a crime lies in the fact that it can be repeated; and the fact that it can be repeated characterizes it as nothing else than a social profession. Criminalism is directed only in a very loose sense against the existing social order, even when its battle against law and order assumes American forms; to the thief and the coiner the slogans of communism cannot mean very much, and the burglar who goes about his work of nights on noiseless rubber soles is a handworker like any other handworker, he is conservative like all handworkers, and even the profession of the murderer, who with his knife between his teeth climbs up the unaccommodating wall, is not directed against the whole community, but is simply a private affair which he has to settle with his victim. There is no attempt to upset the existing regime. Proposals for the improvement or amelioration of the penal laws have never emanated from the criminal classes, closely as these things may concern them above all others. If it had been left to the criminals, we should still be hanging thieves and coiners on the gallows, and we should not even have got to the point of distinguishing murder from manslaughter, in spite of the fact that criminals usually show a fine feeling for the nuances of their professional exploits, and are delighted when the penal code adapts itself to their fine-drawn distinctions and exactions; but the very fact that they demand a corresponding distinction of penalties, the gallows for one crime, the wheel and the red-hot brand for another, the cat-o'-nine tails or the stocks for a third,—this simple and clumsy desire for recognition, in reality nothing but the groping aspiration of uneducated men who cannot express themselves properly, and who awkwardly, in symbol as it were, demand something that represents only a small fraction of what their hearts are set on, though they scarcely know what it is; this very fact betrays the goal of their aspiration: which is that the border-land they live in, that border-land on the frontier of a world full of good ordinances, should be admitted into that greater, that good, that almost beloved order which they do not want to alter; and if criminals can conceive of such an admittance and acknowledgment only within a framework of regulated and severe penalties, yet that proves them to be aspiring and social by nature, men who are moved simply by the desire to avoid frontier friction, to go about their vocation in peace and quiet, and to accommodate themselves more and more uncomplainingly, inconspicuously and sensitively to their calling, whose point of reference is the whole structure of society and the existing order.

Rebel and criminal, they both bring their own order, their own conceptions of value into the existing regime. But while the rebel wants to subjugate the existing regime, the criminal seeks to fit himself into it.

The deserter belongs neither to the one category nor the other, or perhaps he belongs to both. Huguenau may have felt this, now that he was faced with the task of setting up his own little world of reality on the outposts of that greater order and of adapting the one to the other, and even if he agreed that deserters should be sentenced to death by rifle fire, that was irrelevant for the time being, and the fact that the *Kur-Trier Herald* represented in his eyes a part of a great machine, say, a brass-plated joint where the bars met and were clamped together, a point at which the country where his own law ruled met that other one whose laws he reverenced and loved, into which he was resolved to make his way and in which he wished to dwell; this fact was not merely nonsensical; it was no more nonsensical than the language of his dreams. And all these motives were jointly responsible for the need that Huguenau felt to get hold of the *Kur-Trier Herald*; they also provide an explanation for the complete success of his transaction.

CHAPTER XXXIII

(Leading Article in the *Kur-Trier Herald* of 1st June 1918.)

THE TURNING-POINT IN THE DESTINY OF THE GERMAN PEOPLE.

Reflections by
Town Commandant Major Joachim von Pasenow.

Then the devil leaveth him, and, behold, angels came and ministered unto him.—MATTHEW iv. 11.

Although the change in the editorial policy of this paper is but a trifling occurrence compared with the mighty event whose anniversary we may soon be seeing for the fourth time, yet it seems to me that, as so often is the case, we must here too regard the smaller event as a mirror of the greater.

For we too and this paper of ours stand at a parting of the ways, we too have the desire to take a new and better path which will lead us nearer to the truth, and we nurse the faith that as far as it is permitted to human powers we shall   .   .   .   .   .

.   .   .   .

.   .   .   .

.   .   .   .

where is the devil whom we must drive out from amidst us, where the
angel whom we can call to our aid?

It beseems an old soldier to speak his mind bluntly, even at the risk
that what he says may seem untimely to many people   .   .

.   .   .   .

.   .   .   .

.   .   .   .

to free ourselves from the iron embrace of the enemy nations, but also
to release the Fatherland and with it the whole world from the unclean
spirit which   .   .   .   .

.   .   .   .

.   .   .   .

.   .   .   .

not to be wondered at that the nations should be visited with hundredfold dissension and thousandfold disunion. For in the member with which
you have sinned shall you be punished.

I hear someone objecting that in that case we should simply submit to the
punishment, endure the scourge, and turn the other cheek to the persecut-

.   .   .   .

.   .   .   .

.   .   .   .

just as Luther's struggle against a Popedom which had grown corrupt
was a justified struggle. And does not our master Clausewitz teach
us that the spirit of righteousness is one of the weapons of war, which

.   .   .   .

.   .   .   .

.   .   .   .

it shall be said of our struggle: " His foes fled in terror before him,
the evil-doer was abashed, and salvation was in his hands " (Maccabees
iii. 6), yet we must not fix our thoughts on the pursuit of the flying
foe, but on salvation, the salvation of our own as of other nations.
We have been shortsighted, and in very truth all our sacrifices will have
been in vain, if they are regarded frivolously, and God's   .   .

.   .   .   .

.   .   .   .

.   .   .   .

possesses that outward freedom which we have to fight for, only when
at the same time that inward and truly divine freedom is vouchsafed

to it. And we shall achieve that freedom not on our battlefields, victorious as we may be there, but we shall find it only in our hearts. For that inward freedom is commensurate with the faith which the world stands now in danger of losing. So the war is not only   .   .

.   .   .   .

.   .   .   .

.   .   .   .

according to the Scriptures? " Good and pious works will never make a man good and pious, but a good and pious man will do good and pious works," asserted Luther, writing of Christian freedom, and he goes on: " But if works can make no man pious, and a man must be pious before he can do good works, then it is evident that only the faith granted us by infinite grace through Christ . . .   .

.   .   .   .

.   .   .   .

.   .   .   .

and John says (iii. 30) " He must increase, but I must decrease," and so it was with the war, which had to increase that our faith might de-crease, and until our faith is re-born to blossom anew, until that happens this war may not be able to come to an end. Evil for the mere sake of evil

.   .   .   .

.   .   .   .

.   .   .   .

and it almost seems to us that first the black hordes will have to be let loose on the whole world, so that out of the fires of the Apocalypse the new brotherhood and fellowship may arise, so that once more the kingdom of Christ may be established, and new and glorious   .   .

.   .   .   .

.   .   .   .

.   .   .   .

the black troops, armed with unchivalrous weapons, sent out against us, yet these are only the vanguard. They shall be followed by the black hosts, by the terrors of the Johannine Apocalypse. For as long as the white races are incapable of overcoming this inertia of feeling, and casting from them   .   .   .   .   .   .

.   .   .   .

.   .   .   .

.   .   .   .

embraces honour, it is a lost generation and the dreadful darkness will be round it, and no one will come to help it and its   .   .   .

.   .   .   .

.   .   .   .

.   .   .   .

the venom of the blasphemer and the adventurer, which infects not only the insolent capitals of the enemy, but has not spared our Fatherland. Like an inextricable network it lies invisibly over our cities

.   .   .   .

.   .   .   .

.   .   .   .

just as first our glorious campaign of 1870 had to come so as to unite the dispersed tribes of the German people, so it will be the glory of this far greater and more dreadful war not merely to have united whole races in brotherhood, but in a sense   .   .   .   .

.   .   .   .

.   .   .   .

.   .   .   .

and the Christian faith and the grace of freedom be ours again. Then we shall be able to say: " A Christian is a faithful servant of all things and subject to every man," no less than: " A Christian is a free master over all things and subject to no man "; for both will be true, and that is how we should think of true freedom.

I do not know whether I have been able to make myself thoroughly understood, for I myself have had to wrestle for a long time in order to arrive at these truths, and am convinced that they are still fragmentary. But here too the words of General Clausewitz may apply: " The heart-rending spectacle of danger and suffering may easily make our feelings prevail over our reasonable convictions, and in the twilight of appearance it is so hard to gain a profound and clear insight into things that vacillation is understandable and excusable. *It is always out of a mere inkling and foreboding of the truth that man acts.*"

Thus did Major von Pasenow come to grips with the problem of the war and the future of Germany, and he found it hard work. War, for which his upbringing had been a preparation, war, for whose sake he had worn a uniform during the years of his youth and donned it again four years ago, war had suddenly become no longer a matter of uniform, no longer a matter of red regimentals or blue regimentals, no longer an affair between gallant enemies who chivalrously crossed swords; no, war had proved neither the crown nor the fulfilment of a life in uniform, but had invisibly and yet more and more palpably shaken the foundations of that life, had worn threadbare the ties of morality holding it together, and through the meshes of the fabric grinned the Evil One. Spiritual forces trained in the cadet school of Culm were not adequate for the subjugation of the Evil One, and that was not surprising, since the Church itself, although much better equipped, has failed to overcome once and for all the antinomy of original sin. But the idea that once hovered before Augustine's mind as the salvation of the secular world, the dream that the Stoics had dreamed before him, the idea of a religious State embracing within it all that bears the lineaments of mankind, this exalted idea shone through the picture of heart-rending danger and suffering, and had awakened—more as a feeling, it is true, than as a reasoned conviction, rather a vague divination than a profound and clear intuition—it had awakened in the soul of the old officer too; and so a connection, hazy, indeed, and sometimes misconceived, but continuously traceable, ran from Zeno and Seneca, perhaps even from the Pythagoreans, to the thoughts of Major von Pasenow.

CHAPTER XXXIV

DISINTEGRATION OF VALUES (5)

Logical Excursus.

Although it cannot be denied that the style of thinking prevailing, say, in the Royal Prussian Cadet School at Culm is quite different from that in a Roman Catholic seminary, yet the concept " style of thinking " is so vague that it reminds one of the vagueness of those philosophical and historical tendencies which find the crux of their methodology in the word " intuition." For the *a priori* unambiguity of thought and logic permits of no stylistic gradations, and so cannot countenance any other intuition than the mind's *a priori* apprehension of itself, discarding everything else as empirical and pathological abnormality more fitted for psychological and medical research than for philosophy. An argument for the insufficiency of the human brain's work-a-day and empirical thinking in face of the absolute logic of the self, the absolute logic of God.

Or it could be argued that the absolute formality of logic is unassailable and cannot be changed even by human agency; all that changes being the content of its propositions, their interpretation of the nature of the world; so that the question of style is at most an epistemological question and can never be a logical one. Logic, like mathematics, is devoid of style.

But is the form of logic actually so independent of its content? For somewhere, curiously enough, logic itself is identified with content, and nowhere more clearly than in so-called formal concatenations of proof; for not only are the links of these chains axioms or axiomatic propositions —such as the principle of non-contradiction—which form an impassable limit to plausibility (until one fine day that limit is passed, all the same, as for instance in the principle of the excluded middle), and whose evidence is no longer based on formal proof but only on actual content, but more than that, there would be no syllogisms at all, the whole logical machinery of drawing and proving conclusions would not even work, without the application of extra-logical principles to set the whole in motion, principles that in the long run, however far one pushes the limit of definition, are ultimately metaphysical and substantive. The structure of formal logic thus rests on substantive foundations.

The idealism of intuitional psychologizers presupposes a " feeling for truth " which provides the resting-point in which every line of inquiry, beginning with the wondering question: " What is that? " and proceeding by posing reiterated " whys? " finally comes to an end with the assertion of an axiomatic plausibility: " That is so and not otherwise." Now although in reference to the immutability of an *a priori* and purely formal logic this feeling for truth is a superfluous importation, yet in reference to the substantive element in logical proof it has claims to more reasonable respect. For the resting-points of evidence at the end of the lines of inquiry and chains of proof have detached themselves from formal immutability and yet are supposed to have a determining influence on the process of logical proof itself and on its form. The problem which this raises: " In what way can substantive content, be it a logical axiom or non-logical in its nature, so affect formal logic as to admit of variation in style of thinking while maintaining intact the invariability of form?" this problem is no longer empirical and psycho-logical, but methodological and metaphysical, for behind it stands in all its *a priority* the first question of all ethics: How can God permit error, how is it that a madman is allowed to live in God's world?

One can imagine a line of inquiry that never comes to a conclusion at all. All inquiries into ultimate origins obviously have this peculiarity; the problem of matter, which advances from one fundamental concept to another, from primal substance to the atom, from the atom to the electron, from the electron to the quantum of energy, and each time reaches only a temporary resting-place, is an example of such an infinite line of inquiry.

Now the point at which such a line of inquiry terminates is obviously conditioned by a feeling for truth and evidence, conditioned, therefore, by whatever axioms prevail. The doctrine of Thales, for instance, that the terminal point, the point of plausibility for the inquiry into the origin of matter, was the substance " water " permits us to infer that for Thales there was an accepted system of axioms within which the watery nature of matter seemed probable. Here it is substantive and not logically formal axioms that stop the line of inquiry, axioms of the prevailing cosmogony,—but these substantive axioms must have some relation to those of formal logic, they must at the very least be incapable of formal contradiction, for if the substantive development of the evidence did not agree with the formal there would be no plausibility in the conclusion. (And yet the possibility of disagreement between substantive and logical axioms can be discovered in the doctrine of twofold truth.) Moreover, even if one were to take up a position of complete scepticism and say *Ignorabimus*, and, denying the existence of a plausibility depend-ing on cosmogony and of its concomitant axioms, were to assume the non-terminable nature of inquiries and regard their termination at any fixed point as a purely purposeful and yet fictitious piece of arbitrariness, still it is clear that even the plea *Ignorabimus* as such possesses a definite attribute of plausibility, which again is supported by a definite frame of logic and a definite system of logical axioms.

Perhaps the number of axioms implicit and effective in any view of the world could provide some kind of conception of these relationships, a reasonable conception extending beyond the limits of pure intuition.

Naturally the precise quantity could neither be produced nor enumerated —one could only indicate the comparative multiplicity or dearth of axioms in extreme cases. The cosmogony of a primitive people, for instance, is of the utmost complexity; every object in the world has a life of its own, is in a sense *causa sui*; each tree is inhabited by its own god, each thing by its own demon; it is a world of an infinite number of things, and every line of inquiry relating to the objects in that world advances only a few steps, perhaps one step only, before stopping short at one of these axioms. In contrast with such a multiplicity of short chains of ontological reasoning, mostly chains of only one link, the chains of reasoning in a monotheistic world are already much lengthened, although not lengthened into infinity; they are lengthened, that is, to the point where they all converge in the sole First Cause, God. So that if one considers merely the ontological axioms of cosmogony—leaving out of account the others, those that are purely logical—in the two extreme cases represented by the polarized cosmogonies of primitive magic and of monotheism, the number of axioms varies from infinity to one.

In so far as language is an expression of logic, in so far as logic appears to be immanent in the structure of language, one could draw from the language of a people a conclusion about the number of its ontological axioms, the nature of logic and the variability of its " style." For the complicated ontological system of a primitive race, its widely distributed system of axioms, is what is reflected in the extraordinary complication of the structure and syntax of its language. And just as little as the change in our metaphysical view of the world can be explained on practical grounds—nobody would maintain that our Western metaphysic is more " practical " than, say, the Chinese, which stands at least on an equally high pinnacle of development—just as little can the simplification and fundamental changes in the style of languages, including their tendency to obsolescence, be explained exclusively by practical considerations, quite apart from the fact that no practical explanation suffices to account for a great number of changes and syntactical peculiarities.

But the part played by a system of axioms, whether ontological or logical, in relation to a purely logical structure, the manner in which it stamps a particular " style " on a formal logic that yet remains immutable, can be made conceivable by reference to a diagram. In certain geometrical figures an infinitely distant point is arbitrarily assumed to lie within a given finite plane, and then the figure is constructed as if this assumed point were really at an infinite distance. The relation of the various parts to each other in such a figure remain the same as if the assumed point were really at an infinite distance, but all the masses are distorted and foreshortened. In somewhat similar fashion we may conceive that the constructions of logic are affected when the logical point of plausibility is moved from the infinite to the finite: the purely formal logic as such, its methods of inference, even its substantive associative relations, remain unaltered,—what is altered is the shape of its masses, its " style."

The farther step taken beyond the monotheistic cosmogony has been taken almost imperceptibly, and yet it is of greater significance than any preceding one: the First Cause has been moved beyond the " finite " infinity of a God that still remained anthropomorphic, into a real infinity of abstraction; the lines of inquiry no longer converge on this idea of God (they no longer converge on any point, one may say, but run parallel to each other), cosmogony no longer bases itself on God but on the eternal continuance of inquiry, on the consciousness that there is no point at which one can stop, that questions can for ever be advanced and must for ever be advanced, that there is neither a First Substance nor a First Cause discoverable, that behind every system of logic there is still a meta-logic, that every solution is merely a temporary solution, and that nothing remains but the act of questioning in itself: cosmogony has become radically scientific, and its language and its syntax have discarded their " style " and turned into mathematical expressions.

CHAPTER XXXV

Esch and Huguenau were crossing the market-place; it was Tuesday, the fourth of June, and a rainy day. Plump and rotund, Huguenau swaggered along with his overcoat thrown open. Like a conqueror, thought Esch venomously.

When they turned the corner by the Town Hall they met a melancholy procession; a German soldier, handcuffed and escorted by two men with fixed bayonets, was being conducted—probably from the railway station or the courts of justice—to the prison. It was raining, the drops were splashing on the man's face, and to wipe them away he had to lift his fettered hands every now and then and rub them against his face; it was both a clumsy and a pathetic gesture.

"What's he been doing?" said Esch to Huguenau, who seemed to be as affected as himself.

Huguenau shrugged his shoulders and muttered something about murder and robbery and child violation:

"Or he's stabbed a parson perhaps . . . with a kitchen knife."

Esch repeated:

"Stabbed with a knife."

"If he's a deserter he'll be shot," said Huguenau, closing the subject, and Esch saw the court martial sitting in the familiar court of justice, saw the Town Commandant sitting in judgment, heard him pronouncing the pitiless sentence, and saw the man being led out into the prison yard in the spattering rain, and while he faced the firing squad wiping for the last time with his fettered hands his face, down which ran in a mingled stream rain, tears and icy sweat.

Esch was a man of impetuous moods; he saw the world divided into black and white, he saw it dominated by the play of good and evil forces. But his impetuosity often made him see an individual where he should have seen a system, and he was already on the point of blaming the Major instead of a cold and brutal militarism for the inhumanity presently to be wreaked on the poor deserter, and was just going to say to Huguenau that the Major was a swine, when suddenly it ceased to be valid; suddenly he did not know what to think, for suddenly it was quite incomprehensible that the Major and the author of that article should be the same person.

The Major wasn't a swine, the Major was something superior, the Major had suddenly moved from the black to the white side of the world.

Esch saw the leading article quite clearly before him, and the Major's somewhat hazy but noble thoughts seemed clear and great to him, like an exposition of man's high duty to strive for freedom and justice in the world; and that was all the more remarkable as he found in it a restatement of his own task and his own aims, though transmuted, indeed, into such lofty, radiant and soaring language that all that he himself had hitherto thought or done appeared now dull, narrow, ordinary and purblind.

Esch stopped.

"One must pay for things," he said.

Huguenau was disagreeably affected by the words:

" It's easy for you to talk, you aren't going to be shot."

Esch shook his head and made a disdainful and slightly despairing gesture with his hand:

" If it was only a question of that . . . it's a question of one's self-respect . . . do you know that at one time in my life I wanted to join the Free-thinkers? "

" And what of it? " said Huguenau.

" You shouldn't talk like that," said Esch, " there's something in the Bible, all the same. Just you read the Major's article."

" A fine article," said Huguenau.

" Well? "

Huguenau considered:

" He's not likely to write any more articles for us . . . we must look out for something else. . . . But of course I'll have to attend to that myself as usual, you never think of anything. And yet you fancy yourself at bringing out a paper! "

Esch gazed at him despairingly; quite obviously you could not get any further with a lump of flesh like that, the fellow couldn't understand or didn't want to understand. Esch would have liked to thrash him. He shouted at him:

" If you're to set up as the angel sent to serve him, then I would rather be the devil."

" We're none of us angels," replied Huguenau sagely.

Esch gave it up; they had reached the office in any case.

In the entry Marguerite was playing with a few boys from the neigh-bourhood. She looked up crossly at being disturbed, but Esch, paying no attention, seized her and set her on his shoulders, holding her fast by the legs.

" Look out for the doors! " he shouted, bending low at the threshold.

Huguenau entered behind them.

As they climbed the steps and Marguerite, teetering high above the banister, looked down on the courtyard, now so strangely enlarged, and on the garden that swayed before her eyes, she was seized with fear; she grabbed Esch's forehead with her hard little hands and tried to fix her fingers in his eye-sockets.

" Be quiet up there," Esch ordered, " look out for the door." But it was in vain that he stooped; Marguerite made herself rigid, threw her body back, bumped her head against the lintel of the door and began to howl. Esch, from old habit accustomed to comfort weeping women with physical caresses, let the child slide down to kissing height, but now she struggled with all her strength and flew again at his eyes, so that willy-nilly he had to set her down and let her go. Marguerite wanted to escape, but Huguenau blocked the way, making signs as though to catch her. He had looked on with pleasure as she tried to struggle away from Esch, and if she had now stayed with him instead, it would have been a great satisfaction. All the same when he saw her darkened face he did not dare to hold her back, but straddled his legs and said: " Here's the door." The child understood him, laughed, and crept on all-fours through the door.

Esch followed her with his eyes: " She could do you in like a shot," it sounded as if he were moved to tenderness, " the little black rascal." Huguenau sat down opposite him: " Well, she seems to suit your taste pretty well . . . but I'll have to get a desk of my own installed here fairly soon now." " I can't prevent you," Esch growled, " and anyhow, it's about time you began to do some editorial work." Huguenau's thoughts were still with the child: " That kid's always about the place too." Esch smiled slightly: " Children are a blessing and a trial, Herr Huguenau, but you don't understand that yet." " I understand well enough that you're crazy about her . . . otherwise why should you want to adopt somebody else's brat? " " Your own or somebody else's, it doesn't matter: I've already told you that." " Oh, it matters all right, when another man's had the pleasure." " You don't understand that," shouted Esch, jumping up.

He prowled up and down the room a few times, then went to the corner where the files of newspapers were piled up, pulled out a paper— it was the special issue—and began to study the Major's article.

Huguenau regarded him with interest. Esch held his head clasped in his hands, his short grey brush of hair escaped from between his fingers, —he had a passionate, almost an ascetic appearance, and Huguenau, desirous of banishing some vague, unpleasant memory, said cheerfully: " You just see, Esch, we'll make a great thing of the paper yet." Esch replied: " The Major is a good man." " That may be," said Huguenau, " but it would be better for you to be thinking of what we can make out of the paper," he had stepped up to Esch, and, as though to waken him up, tapped him on the shoulder, " The Herald must be asked for in Berlin and Nürnberg, and it must be on show in the Hauptwache Coffee

House in Frankfort too, you know Frankfort, don't you? . . . it must become a paper for the whole world."

Esch paid no attention. He indicated with his finger a passage in the article: " But if works can make no man pious, and a man must be pious before he can do good works . . . do you know what that means? it means that the child doesn't matter, but only your feeling about it; another's or your own, it's all one, do you hear, it's all one! "

Huguenau felt disappointed somehow: " All I know is that you're a fool and that you've brought the paper to ruin with your feelings," he said and left the room.

The door had slammed long since, but Esch still sat there staring at it, sat and thought. It was not by any means clear, but Huguenau might be right all the same about one's feelings. Nevertheless it looked as if there was some hope of order at last. The world was divided into good and evil, debit and credit, black and white, and even if a book-keeping error should happen to creep in, then it must be expunged, and it would be expunged. Esch had grown calmer. Peacefully his hands rested on his knees, he sat placidly staring through closed eyelids at the door, saw through closed lids the whole room, which now strangely transformed itself into a landscape—or was it a picture postcard?—and was like a kiosk among green trees, the trees of the Schlossberg at Badenweiler; he saw the Major's face, and it was the face of a greater and higher being. And Esch sat for so long that at last, filled with wonder, he knew no longer where he had got to, and only with an effort did he manage to return to his reading. True, he could have recited the article by heart, word for word, yet he forced himself to read on, and now he knew once more what side he belonged to in this world. For the reflections which the Major had addressed to the German people had made an impression on one part of the German nation, even if it was not a very important part; they had made an impression on Herr Esch.

CHAPTER XXXVI

Four women were scrubbing the hospital ward.

Surgeon-Major Kühlenbeck entered and looked at them for a moment. " Well, how are things with you? "

" What can you expect, Herr Surgeon-Major . . . ? "

The women sighed, then they went on scrubbing again.

One of them raised her head:

" My man's coming home on leave next week."

" Great, Tielden . . . the bed will fairly bounce then."

Frau Tielden blushed under her brown leathery skin. The others laughed heartily. And Frau Tielden laughed with them.

All at once a noise, somewhat like a bark, was heard from one of the beds. It was not so much a bark, however, as a breathless, heavy and very painful expulsion of something that was scarcely a sound and came from far within.

Gödicke of the Landwehr sat up in his bed; his features were painfully distorted, and it was he who had laughed in such a strange fashion.

It was the first sound that had been got out of him ever since his arrival in the hospital (if one does not take into account his first whimperings).

" A lewd rascal," said Surgeon-Major Kühlenbeck, " why, he can laugh! "

CHAPTER XXXVII

STORY OF THE SALVATION ARMY GIRL IN BERLIN (5)

The sickly spring-time of an adamant law,
The sickly spring-time of a Jewish bride,
The sickly din of the city, that yet tongue-tied
Lies trapped and netted in invisible snares,
A summer day of stone no warmth can thaw,
A sickly sky looks down on asphalt squares,
On streets like chasms, on a stony waste that wears
Out like a scabby sore the earth's grey hide.
O city of lying light, O city of lying prayers,
The penitent desires no verdant tree,
He seeks but penitential caves, where he
Implores the Law to yield him holiness
Uprising like a fountain from deep thought,
From holy words, from doubts, from fear distraught.
It is the city of exiles, of penitents in distress,
The city of the people chosen by God,
A race that breeds for duty, passionless,
And only counts its sons, whose old men nod

Praying at windows, a monk-bearded race
Bound ever to its God with fasts and thongs,
The while its women knead the unleavened bread
And votive oil flames raise their pallid tongues:
A race that marries to beget in bed
The pallid youth with the actor's beard and face,
The youthful Jacob to whom angels bend,
Whom truth guides on a journey that will end
At that far well by which the angels sank,
At that far well where Rachel's wethers drank.
Grey city, the pallid nomads' halting-place
Upon their road to Zion, their way to God,
A godless city in an invisible net,
A vacant mass of stone with curses laden
And sorrow; where the Salvation Army maiden
Tinkles her tambourine, so that the sinner yet
May find the true way and return to grace,
The way to Zion, to love's holy place.—
In this town of Berlin, in these spring days
Did Nuchem Sussin meet the girl Marie,
And for a while they felt a sweet amaze
And each fell down in spirit on one knee;
The uplifted hand of Fate they did not see,
Zion they saw; their hearts were filled with praise.

CHAPTER XXXVIII

For almost two years Heinrich Wendling had not been home on leave.
Yet in spite of this Hanna was surprised, as surprised as though some
irrational and incomprehensible event had burst in upon her, when the
letter arrived in which he announced his homecoming. The journey
from Salonika would take six days at least, probably even longer, but
in any case it was only a matter of days. Hanna dreaded his arrival as
though she had a secret lover to conceal from him. Every day's delay
was to her like an act of grace, yet every evening she went through
her night toilet even more scrupulously than usual, and she lay in bed
each morning too even longer than usual, waiting, dreading lest the
returning wanderer might take possession of her immediately, filthy and

unshaven as he was. And even though she felt she should be ashamed of such fancies, and for that very reason hoped that some offensive or other accident might cancel his leave, yet she felt as well the presence of a still stronger, a very strange hope that lurked somewhere, a vague presentiment that she did not want to acknowledge and indeed did not acknowledge, and which was like one's sensation before a grave operation: one had to submit to it in order to be protected from something fatal towards which one was involuntarily striving; it was like a last terrifying refuge, and dark as it was, yet it rescued one from a profounder darkness. To dismiss as masochism such an attitude of hopeful dread and terrified waiting would be to leave unexplored all but the mere surface of the spirit. And the only explanation that Hanna could find for her state, in so far as she was aware of it at all, was very like the fatuous conviction of old women that marriage is the sole means of putting an end once and for all to the various sufferings of anæmic girls. No, she could not dare to examine it more closely, it was a tangle into which she had no wish to penetrate, and though with one part of her she expected that as soon as Heinrich came in everything would be the same again, quite naturally, yet she divined with equal intensity that never would things be the same again.

Summer had really come at last. " Rose Cottage " did honour to its name, although in deference to the times vegetables were cultivated rather than flowers, and although the semi-invalid jobbing gardener was incapable of attending properly to his business. But the crimson ramblers did not allow even the war to restrain them and had climbed up to the cherubs at each side of the door; the beds of peonies were pink and white, and the rows of heliotrope and stock on the border of the lawn were in full blossom. In front of the house the green landscape stretched peacefully, the spacious sweep of the valley held one's gaze and carried it to the edge of the woods; the forester's house, exposed to the eye in winter so that every one of its windows could be seen, was again smothered in green; the vineyards too had greened over, the woods lay dark, darker than ever now that black clouds were approaching from the mountains.

In the afternoon Hanna had taken her chair outside. She lay back in it beneath the chestnut-trees and gazed at the advancing clouds, whose shadows marched across the fields, transforming the bright clear green into a dark and strangely restful greenish violet; as the shadow stretched across the garden and the air suddenly became cool and cellarlike, the flowers, until now sealed up by the heat, began all at once to exhale their perfumes as though their breath had been released. Or perhaps it was the sudden coolness that now gave Hanna leisure to feel their scent; yet it was so sudden, so unique, so vehement, this breaking wave of sweet perfume, cool and magical as an evening in a southern garden, as the falling dusk on the rocky beach of a Tyrrhenian sea. So the earth lay on the shore of a sea of cloud that broke in waves of rain, the soft, thick rain of thunder-showers, and Hanna, standing at the open veranda door, could smell the south; and even though she breathed in almost greedily the soft humidity that felt so cool and fresh in her nostrils, yet with the memory of that southern fragrance there had also been wafted to her the fear which she had felt for the first time during her honeymoon, standing on the seashore one rainy evening in Sicily; the hotel lay behind her, the flowers in the hotel garden perfumed the air, and she did not know who the strange man was that stood beside her —he was called Dr Wendling.

She started; the gardener had hurried across the path to put the garden implements in a place of safety out of the rain; she started, because she could not help thinking that it was a burglar who had broken in, although she knew quite well what the man was about. If Walter had not come out to her she would have fled into the house and locked the door. Walter had seated himself on the door-step; he stretched out his naked legs into the rain and occupied himself in cautiously loosening the dried crust of a scar on his knee, afterwards contentedly stroking the new pink skin. Hanna too sat down on the door-step; she clasped her hands round her legs, her beautiful slender legs—she too wore no stockings when she was in the house or the garden—and her smooth shins felt cool to the touch.

By now the rain had beaten down the scent of the flowers which it had awakened at first, and the air smelt only of moist earth. The brown-flecked tiled roof of the garden-house gleamed with wet, and when the gardener once more trudged down the path the gravel no longer crunched dryly under his feet, but rattled its wet and separate pebbles. Hanna put her arm round her son's shoulders,—why couldn't they remain always sitting like this, calmly at rest in a cool and cleanly world? only a very little of her fear was left. All the same she said: " If there's more thunder like this during the night, Walter, you can come in beside me."

CHAPTER XXXIX

When Surgeon-Major Kühlenbeck and Dr Kessel entered the dining-room of the hotel, the Major was already sitting at his accustomed place. He was reading the *Cologne News*, which had just arrived. The two gentlemen said good-evening, and the Major rose and invited them to sit at his table.

The Surgeon-Major most tactlessly referred to the newspaper:

" Are we to have the pleasure, Herr Major, of reading you in other papers too ? "

The Major simply shook his head, handed the paper across the table, and indicating the column containing the reports from the Front said:

" Bad news."

Dr Kühlenbeck glanced over the reports:

" Really no worse than usual, Herr Major."

The Major looked up questioningly.

" Herr Major, all news is bad except one thing, and that is—peace."

" You're right there," said the Major, " but it must be an honourable peace."

" Right," said Kühlenbeck, lifting his glass, " then here's to peace."

The other two gentlemen clinked glasses with him and the Major repeated again:

" To an honourable peace . . . otherwise what should all those sacrifices have been made for ? " As though he wanted to say something more, he still held his glass in his hand but remained silent; at last, however, he shook off his immobility and said: " Honour is by no means a mere convention . . . once upon a time poison-gas would have been rejected as a weapon of warfare."

The gentlemen made no reply, and went on drinking their wine.

Then Dr Kessel said:

" What's the good of all those beautiful theories about war-time food? . . . When I come home at night I can scarcely stand on my legs; for a man well on in years the food simply isn't enough."

Kühlenbeck said:

" You're a defeatist, Kessel: it's been demonstrated that diabetes has been reduced to a minimum, and with carcinoma it seems to be the same . . . it's only your personal misfortune that you're not a diabetic . . .

besides, my dear chap, if you do feel pains in your legs . . . we're none of us getting younger."

Major von Pasenow said:

" Honour isn't mere inertia of feeling."

" I don't quite understand, Herr Major," said Dr Kühlenbeck.

The Major gazed into vacancy:

" Oh, it was nothing . . . as you know . . . my son fell at Verdun . . . he would be twenty-eight now. . . ."

" But he wasn't your only son, Herr Major? "

The Major did not reply at once, it may be that he regarded the question as an indiscretion. Finally he said:

" Yes, there's my younger son . . . and the two girls . . . the boy will soon be called up too . . . one must render unto Cæsar the things that are Cæsar's . . ." he stopped, then he went on: " You see, the cause of all the evil is that we don't render to God the things that are God's."

Dr Kühlenbeck said:

" We don't even render to human beings the things that are theirs . . . it seems to me we should begin with that first."

" God first," said Major von Pasenow.

Kühlenbeck threw out his chin; his dark grey beard jutted out into the air:

" We doctors are blatant materialists, I'm afraid."

The Major said deprecatingly:

" You mustn't say that."

Dr Kessel too dissented; a true doctor was always an idealist. Kühlenbeck laughed:

" It's true, I forgot your panel patients."

After a while Dr Kessel said:

" As soon as I have half a chance I'll take up my chamber music again."

And the Major remarked that his wife too loved her playing. He thought for a little and then he added: " Spohr, an excellent composer."

CHAPTER XL

Since it had been rumoured that Gödicke had laughed, his room-mates had tried everything possible to make him laugh again. The grossest stories were dished up to him, and as he lay in bed hardly anyone passed without hopefully shaking the bed until it bounced up and down. But it was of no avail. Gödicke did not laugh again. He remained dumb.

Until one day Sister Carla brought him a postcard: " Gödicke, your wife has written to you . . ." Gödicke did not stir, " I'll read it to you." And Sister Carla read out to him that his faithful wife had heard nothing from him now for a long time, that she and the children were well, and that they all hoped he would soon be coming back. " I'll answer it for you," said Sister Carla. Gödicke gave not a sign of comprehension, and one might have thought that he had really understood nothing. And probably he would actually have succeeded in concealing from any eye-witness the tempest in his soul, that tempest which jumbled together the constituents of his ego and in rapid succession heaved them to the surface to submerge them just as rapidly again in the dark waves, he might have succeeded in calming the storm and gradually laying it altogether, had not the practical joker of the ward, Josef Settler the dragoon, passed by at that moment and as usual caught hold of the foot of the bed to make it oscillate a little. At that Gödicke of the Landwehr gave a cry which by no means resembled the laugh that was expected of him and that he was really under an obligation to provide; he gave an angry and heavy cry, sat up, by no means so slowly and laboriously as he was accustomed to do, and he snatched the postcard from Sister Carla, and he tore the postcard to pieces. Then he sank back, for the violent move-ment had started his pains again, and clasped his abdomen with his hands.

So there he lay looking up at the roof, and tried to reinstate a minimum of order among his thoughts. He was conscious of having acted rightly; he had with full justification turned away the intruder. That this intruder was the servant-girl Anna Lamprecht with her three children was almost immaterial, and could be quickly forgotten again. Indeed he was very glad that the Gödicke who had made an honest woman of the servant-girl Lamprecht had been so expeditiously called to order and relegated to his place behind the dark barrier,—there he would have to wait until he was summoned. Nevertheless with that the matter was not settled; an intruder who comes once may come again, even though he is not summoned, and once one door is opened, then every other door may fly open of itself. With terror he felt, though he could not have formulated it, that this intrusion into one part of his soul had affected all the other parts by sympathy, indeed that through it they were all being changed. It was like a humming in his ears, a humming of the soul, a humming of the ego that hummed so violently that he could feel it in all his body; but it was also as though a clod of earth had been pushed under one's tongue, a stifling clod that deranged all one's thoughts. Or perhaps it was something else, but in any case it was something beyond one's power, something before which one felt helpless. It was as though one wanted to spread the mortar before laying a brick, and the mortar hardened on the trowel. It was as though a foreman were there driving one to work at an illegal and impossible speed, and causing the bricks to be piled with furious haste on the scaffolding, so that they towered in great heaps and could not be worked off. The scaffolding must collapse if one did not at once put the winch and the concrete-mixing machine out of action to stop the whole business. Best of all if one's eyes could grow together again and one's ears be sealed again: the man Gödicke must see nothing, hear nothing, eat nothing. If the pain were not so bad now he would go into the garden and fetch a handful of earth to stop up all the holes. And while he clasped his sore abdomen, from which his children had issued, while he pressed his hands down on it as though never again must anything issue from him, while he clenched his teeth and bit his lips so that not even a sigh of pain might escape them, it seemed to him that thus his powers were increased, and that those waxing powers must raise the scaffolding to ever higher and airier heights, that he himself was omnipresent on every level and storey of that scaffolding, and that at last he would manage to stand quite alone on the topmost storey, at the summit of the scaffolding; that he would be able to stand there, dare to stand there, released from all pain, singing as he had always sung when he was up aloft. The carpenters would be working beneath him, hammering and driving in nails, and he would spit down, as he had always spat, spit down in a wide arc over them, and where the spittle struck and rebounded trees would grow up, which, no matter how high they grew, would never reach the height where he stood.

When Sister Carla came with the washing basin and the towels, he was lying peacefully, and peacefully too let himself be packed into the compresses. For two whole days he again refused meat and drink. And then an incident happened that made him begin to speak.

CHAPTER XLI

STORY OF THE SALVATION ARMY GIRL IN BERLIN (6)

To my own surprise I had again begun to occupy myself with my thesis on the disintegration of values. Although I hardly ever left the house, my work proceeded but slowly. Nuchem Sussin often came to see me, seating himself on the grey tails of his frock-coat. He never unbuttoned it; it was probably a kind of shame that prevented him. I often asked myself how these people could put any trust in Dr Litwak, whose short jacket flouted all their prejudices. Until I came to the conclusion that the walking-stick he carried before him might represent a sort of substitute for his lack of coat-tails. But that, of course, was a mere assumption.

It took me a long time to find out what Sussin was really after. When he seated himself he never neglected to say " With your kind permission," and after a short embarrassed silence he would then bring up some juristic problem: whether the Government was empowered to confiscate food or fat that was already in one's house or on one's plate; whether the maintenance allowance received by soldiers' wives could be applied to taking out a life insurance policy . . . .one simply could not tell what he was trying to get at, he seemed to be pulling wires at random, and yet one had the feeling that out of all this real problems were emerging, or that in his mind a juridical landscape lay outspread, which one was challenged to survey through these artificial and distorted lenses.

Even when he took up a book and held it in front of his shortsighted eyes, he seemed to be reading quite other things out of it. He had an immeasurable respect for books, but he could laugh uproariously over a few lines of Kant, and was astonished when I did not join in. So it seemed to him an extraordinarily good joke when he found this maxim while looking over Hegel: *The principle of magic consists in this, that the connection between the means and the effect shall not be recognized.* He certainly despised me for not seeing the funny side of things as he did, and strangely enough I was inclined to ascribe to him a truer, if also more complicated, insight than I myself possessed. In any case it was only at things such as these that I had ever seen him laugh.

And he had some feeling for music. A much-beribboned lute hung in my room. I imagine that it had belonged to my landlady's son: he was either in captivity or missing. Every time he came Sussin begged me to " play something " and would not believe me when I said I couldn't. He thought I was too shy. But by way of this he managed at last to reach his real theme:

" Have you ever heard the people playing . . . the ones in uniform? . . . very beautiful."

He meant the Salvation Army, and smiled guiltily at my guessing it.

" I'm going this evening to listen. Will you come too? "

CHAPTER XLII

Huguenau's delight in the paper had not lasted long, not even for a whole month. It was still June, and Huguenau was sick of the whole business. In his first enthusiasm he had succeeded in bringing off the great idea of the special number and the Major's leading article; but as nothing fresh had immediately occurred to him he had lost interest. It was as though he had flung a toy into the corner; he no longer liked it. And even although this dislike perhaps masked an intuition that one really could not make a great newspaper out of a provincial rag, yet he was merely aware of boredom, he simply did not want to hear anything more about it, and felt the independent reality of the newspaper routine as an interference with himself. If at one time he could not get quickly enough to his work, he now loved to linger in bed, dawdled unconscionably over his breakfast, and only with repugnance could drag himself to the backyard where the office was; indeed quite often it happened that he got no farther than the kitchen, where he discussed the price of food with Frau Esch. And if he finally did reach the editorial office, generally he clattered down the steps again in a little while and stole in to look at the printing-press.

Marguerite was playing in the garden. Huguenau shouted across the courtyard to her: " Marguerite, I'm in the printing-shed."

The child came running, and they went in together. " 'Morning," said Huguenau curtly, for since Lindner and the assistant compositor had become his subordinates he had set himself to be as curt as possible with them. The two men, however, did not seem to worry much about that, and he had once more the feeling that they looked down on him as a man who knew nothing about machines. At present they were working in the case-room, and Huguenau, with the child hanging on to his hand, did his best to look over their shoulders with the air of an expert, but was relieved when he was out of the case-room again and back beside his printing-press.

For he still loved the printing-press. A man who all his life has sold commodities produced by machines, but for whom factories and the possessors of machines remain in a class above him, a class he can never attain, such a man will assuredly regard it as a wonderful experience if he himself suddenly becomes the possessor of a machine; and it may well be that there will dawn in him that affectionate attitude to machines which one almost always finds in boys and in young races, an attitude that glorifies the machine and projects it into the exalted and free plane of their own desires and of mighty and heroic deeds. For hours the boy can watch the locomotive in the station, deeply content that it should shunt the trucks from one line to another; and for hours Wilhelm Huguenau could sit before his printing-press and watch it affectionately with the serious and vacant gaze of a boy behind his glasses, quite satisfied because it was in motion, because it ate up paper and gave it out again. And the ardour of his love for that living entity filled his being so completely that it left room neither for ambition nor even for any desire to understand that incomprehensible and marvellous mechanical function; admiringly and tenderly, almost timidly, he accepted it as it was.

Marguerite had crawled up on to the paper bales, and Huguenau sat on the rough bench which stood beside them. He gazed at the machine, gazed at the child. The machine was his property, it belonged to him, the child belonged to Esch. For a while they tossed to each other a sheet of paper rolled into a ball; then Huguenau grew tired of the game, he crossed his legs, wiped his glasses, and said:

" Something more could be made out of the advertising side."

The child went on playing with the paper ball.

Huguenau continued:

" It's worse even than I imagined. The paper was too dear at the price . . . all the same, we own the press; you like the printing-press, don't you? "

" Yes, let's play at printing-presses, Uncle Huguenau! "

Marguerite came down from her paper bales and climbed on to his knee. Then they took each other by the arms, threw their bodies rhythmically backwards and forwards, and punctuated the motion with:
" Pum, pum."

Huguenau put on the brake. Marguerite remained sitting stridelegs on his knees. Huguenau was a little short of breath:

" The paper was too dear . . . if things go well, we'll bring the circulation up to four hundred . . . but if we can get two pages of advertisements it will pay and we'll grow rich. Won't we, Marguerite? "

Marguerite jumped up and down on his knee, and Huguenau set her in brisk trotting motion; she laughed, for it made her words come in jerks:

" Yes, you'll get rich, you'll get rich."

" Are you glad, Marguerite? "

" Then you'll give me lots of money."

" Oho? "

" Lots of money."

" I tell you what, Marguerite, we'll hire some boys, they'll collect the advertisements . . . in the villages . . . all over the place. For a commission."

The child nodded gravely.

" I've thought it all out already, marriage announcements, sales, and so forth and so forth . . . just fetch the lay-outs from Herr Lindner," and he shouted across to the case-room: " Lindner, the advertisement lay-outs."

The child ran over and brought them back.

" Look here, we'll give our agents a copy of these . . . you'll see what a draw that'll be." He had taken her on his knee again and they studied the lay-outs together. Then Huguenau said:

" So, you want the money so as to run away from them . . . where do you want to go? "

Marguerite shrugged her shoulders:

" Anywhere."

Huguenau considered:

" If you go through the Eifel country you'll come to Belgium. There's good people there."

Marguerite asked:

" Will you come too? "

" Perhaps . . . yes, perhaps later."

" When later? "

She snuggled against him, but Huguenau said suddenly and brusquely: " That's enough," lifted her up and set her on the press. Strangely clear there rose up again the picture of that murderer, that violator of children chained to his pallet, and it disturbed him. " Everything in its time," he said, contemplating the girl, who sat, slender and animated, on the solid inanimate machine, and yet in some way belonged to it. If the machine were set in motion it would swallow up Marguerite just as it did the paper, and he made quite certain that the belt was not on. Almost fearfully he repeated: " Everything in its time, the time will come all right . . . he doesn't disturb us here at any rate."

And while he was wondering what it was that the time would come for, he remembered Esch with his big teeth, that lean insufferable pedagogue who would never leave him in peace and was always insisting on the terms of the contract and trying to push editorial duties upon him,—insisting on the terms of the contract and demanding that he should sit there all day and work, probably expecting him, too, to put on a blue overall. Stand on his rights, the fellow could do that, but as for ideas, he hadn't a single one! And now Huguenau was filled with extraordinary satisfaction at the thought that his schoolmaster had not once yet succeeded in forcing him to work.

As he folded up the advertisement lay-outs he said:

" We'll pay out the schoolmaster yet, Marguerite—what do you say? "

" Lift me down," said the child.

Huguenau went up to the printing-press, but when the little girl put her arm round his neck he remained standing for a moment in silent reverie, for now he had found what he had been looking for: in secret he was actually set above the schoolmaster! for he had himself offered to exercise a surveillance over the dangerous fellow, and the Major had approved of it! It dawned on Huguenau that he had been led here simply in order to find his real goal in life, and that his life would be completely fulfilled if he could succeed in completely unmasking Herr Esch's secret machinations. Yes, that was it, and Huguenau gave Marguerite a hearty kiss on her cheek that was smeared with printing-ink.

But Herr Esch sat upstairs in the editorial office, relieved that he could continue his labours and not give them up to Huguenau. For among other things he was convinced that Huguenau would never be capable of running the paper on the lines laid down by the Major, and he was bent on doing so himself, for in that way he might serve the Major and the good cause.

CHAPTER XLIII

Dr Flurschütz was examining Jaretzki's arm stump in the operating-theatre:

" Looks splendid . . . the chief will be sending you off one of these days . . . if you agree to it . . . to a convalescent home."

" Of course I agree to it; high time one was out of this."

" I think so too, or we'll have you on our hands next with delirium tremens."

" Well, what is there to do but drink? . . . it's here that I really learned to do it."

" Didn't you ever drink before? "

" No . . . well, a little, just like everybody else. . . . I was in the polytechnic in Brunswick, you know . . . where did you get your degree? "

" Erlangen."

" Oh well, you must have drunk a bit in your time too . . . one always does in small towns . . . and what with sitting about as one has to here, it comes back of itself . . ." Flurschütz was still probing and fingering the arm stump " . . . look there, that one bad spot simply won't heal . . . how about my artificial arm? "

" Been ordered . . . we shan't send you off without the arm."

" Right, but see that it comes soon . . . if you hadn't your work to do here, you would start drinking again too."

" Couldn't say . . . I might find something else to do . . . really, I've never seen you with a book yet, Jaretzki."

" Look here, tell me honestly: do you actually read all those piles of books that you keep lying about in your room? "

" Yes."

" Extraordinary . . . and has that any meaning or object? "

" Not the slightest."

" That's a relief . . . look here, Dr Flurschütz . . . all right, I'll keep still . . . you've dispatched a good few people in your time, that's part of your job of course, but when one has deliberately done in a few . . . well it seems to me one hasn't any need to look into a book for all the rest of one's life . . . it's a sort of feeling I've got . . . one has achieved everything . . . and that's the reason too why the war will never end. . . ."

" A daring speculation, Jaretzki; what have you been drinking to-day? "

" I'm as sober as a new-born babe. . . ."

" Well, that's finished . . . we'll give the artificial arm a trial in a fortnight at latest . . . then you must really go into one of those schools where they teach you to use it . . . you want to draw, don't you? "

" Yes, I suppose so, only I simply can't imagine it to myself."

" And what about the General Electric? "

" Oh, very well, let it be the artificial-arm school . . . sometimes it seems to me that you snicked off the thing quite unnecessarily . . . simply out of a sense of justice, so to speak, because I once flung a hand-grenade between a Frenchman's legs. . . ."

Flurschütz looked at him attentively:

" I say, Jaretzki, pull yourself together. You're quite alarming . . . how many have you really had to-day? "

" Nothing worth speaking of . . . besides I'm really grateful to you for your sense of justice, and the operation was very well done . . . I feel on much better terms with the world now . . . on bloody good terms, every-thing settled . . . and the General Electric's simply pining for my arrival."

" Seriously, Jaretzki, you should go there."

" But I just want to tell you . . . it was the wrong arm you took . . . this one here," Jaretzki tapped with two fingers on the plate-glass cover of the instrument-case, " this one here was the one I flung the hand-grenade with . . . probably that's why I feel it hanging from my shoulder like a dead weight."

" That will soon be all right, Jaretzki."

" Oh, everything's all right as it is."

CHAPTER XLIV

DISINTEGRATION OF VALUES (6)

The logic of the soldier demands that he shall throw a hand-grenade between the legs of his enemy:

the logic of the army demands in general that all military resources shall be exploited with the utmost rigour and severity, resulting, if necessary, in the extermination of peoples, the demolition of cathedrals, the bombardment of hospitals and operating-theatres:

the logic of the business man demands that all commercial resources shall be exploited with the utmost rigour and efficiency to bring about the destruction of all competition and the sole domination of his own business, whether that be a trading house or a factory or a company or other economic body:

the logic of the painter demands that the principles of painting shall be followed to their conclusions with the utmost rigour and thoroughness, at the peril of producing pictures which are completely esoteric, and comprehensible only by those who produce them:

the logic of the revolutionist demands that the revolutionary impulse shall be pursued with the utmost rigour and thoroughness for the achievement of a revolution as an end in itself, as, indeed, the logic of politicians in general demands that they shall obtain an absolute dictatorship for their political aims:

the logic of the bourgeois climber demands that the watchword " enrichissez-vous " shall be followed with the most absolute and uncompromising rigour:

in this fashion, in this absolute devotion to logical rigour, the Western world has won its achievements,—and with the same thoroughness, the absolute thoroughness that abrogates itself, must it eventually advance *ad absurdum*:

war is war, *l'art pour l'art*, in politics there's no room for compunction, business is business,—all these signify the same thing, all these appertain to the same aggressive and radical spirit, informed by that uncanny, I might almost say that metaphysical, lack of consideration for consequences, that ruthless logic directed on the object and on the object alone, which looks neither to the right nor to the left; and this, all this, is the style of thinking that characterizes our age.

One cannot escape from this brutal and aggressive logic that exhibits itself in all the values and non-values of our age, not even by withdrawing into the solitude of a castle or of a Jewish dwelling; yet a man who shrinks from knowledge, that is to say, a romantic, a man who must have a bounded world, a closed system of values, and who seeks in the past the completeness he longs for, such a man has good reason for turning to the Middle Ages. For the Middle Ages possessed the ideal centre of values that he requires, possessed a supreme value to which all other values were subordinate: the belief in the Christian God. Cosmogony was as dependent on that central value (more, it could be scholastically deduced from it) as man himself; man with all his activities formed a part of the whole world-order which was merely the reflected image of an ecclesiastical hierarchy, the closed and finite symbol of an eternal and infinite harmony. The dictum " Business is business " was not permitted to the medieval merchant, competitive struggle being forbidden to him; the medieval artist knew nothing of *l'art pour l'art*, but only that he must serve his faith; medieval warfare claimed absolute authority only when it was waged in the service of the faith. It was a world reposing on faith, a final not a causal world, a world founded on being, not on becoming; and its social structure, its art, the sentiments that bound it together, in short, its whole system of values, was subordinated to the all-embracing living value of the faith: the faith was the point of plausibility in which every line of inquiry ended, the faith was what enforced logic and gave it that specific colouring, that style-creating impulse, which expresses itself not only in a certain style of thinking, but continues to shape a style characterizing the whole epoch for so long as the faith survives.

But thought dared to take the step from monotheism into the abstract, and God, the personal God made visible in the finite infinity of the Trinity, became an entity whose name could no longer be spoken and whose image could no longer be fashioned, an entity that ascended into the infinite neutrality of the Absolute and there was lost to sight in the dread vastness of Being, no longer immanent but beyond the reach of man.

In the violence of this revolution caused by the radical application, one might even say by the unleashing, of logic, in this removal of the point of plausibility to a new plane of the infinite, in this withdrawal of faith from concrete life, the simple sufficiency of existence was also destroyed. The style-creating force seems to vanish from concrete expression at this point, and beside the mass of the Kantian structure and the flames of revolution all that we find is rococo and an Empire degenerated over- night into Biedermeyer. For even although the Empire, and shortly after it the romantic movement, recognizing the discrepancy between this spiritual revolution and the existing forms of concrete expression, looked to the past for help, calling in the antique and the Gothic, yet the new development could not be checked: immanent Being had been analysed into pure function, the physical world itself had been analysed into such abstraction that two generations later even Space could be eliminated from it; the decision for pure abstraction was already irrevocable. And the infinite remoteness, the inaccessible noumenal remoteness of that point towards which all lines of inquiry and chains of probability were now destined to strive, rendered impossible at one stroke the binding of all single value-systems to a central value; the abstract ruthlessly invaded the logic of every single value-making activity, stripping its content bare, and not only forbade it to deviate at all from the form determined by its function, insisting on purely functional structure whether in architecture or in any other constructive activity, but has also radicalized so thoroughly the single value-systems that these, being thrown back on themselves and referred to the Absolute, have separated from one another, now run parallel to each other, and, since they can no longer combine in the service of a supreme value, claim equality one with the other: like strangers they exist side by side, an economic value-system of " good business " next to an æsthetic one of *l'art pour l'art*, a military code of values side by side with a technical or an athletic, each autonomous, each " in and for itself," each " unfettered " in its autonomy, each resolved to push home with radical thoroughness the final conclusions of its logic and to break its own record. And woe to the others, if in this conflict of systems that precariously maintain an equilibrium one should gain the preponderance and overtop all the rest, as the military system does in war, or as the economic system is now doing, a system to which even war is subordinate,—woe to the others! For the triumphant system will embrace the whole of the world, it will overwhelm all other values and exterminate them as a cloud of locusts lays waste a field.

But man, who was once the image of God, the mirror of a universal value created by himself, man has fallen from his former estate: he may still have some dim remembrance of his one-time security, he may still ask himself what is this superimposed logic that has perverted his life; yet he is driven out into the horror of the infinite, and, no matter how he shudders at the prospect, no matter how romantically and sentimentally he may yearn to return to the fold of faith, he is helplessly caught in the mechanism of the autonomous value-systems, and can do nothing but submit himself to the particular value that has become his profession, he can do nothing but become a function of that value—a specialist, eaten up by the radical logic of the value into whose jaws he has fallen.

CHAPTER XLV

Huguenau had arranged with Frau Esch that she should give him his midday meal every day. That suited his convenience in all sorts of ways, and Frau Esch did her best for him, she had to be given credit for that.

One day when he went up for his dinner, he found Esch sitting at the newly laid table absorbed in a black-bound book. Huguenau looked inquisitively over his shoulder and recognized the woodcuts of a Bible. As he seldom allowed himself to be surprised at anything, except perhaps when someone overreached him in business, and that happened rarely enough, he merely said: " Aha! " and waited for his food to be served up.

Frau Esch, broad-hipped, sexless, dowdy, passed through the room; her indeterminately fair hair was caught untidily in a knot. But in passing she touched her husband's bony shoulder with an uncalled-for gesture, and Huguenau suddenly had the feeling that of nights she must know very well how to avail herself of her conjugal state. The thought was unpleasant, and so he asked:

" Well, Esch, are you preparing to go into a monastery? "

Esch glanced up from his book:

" That's just the question, whether any escape is permissible," adding with his accustomed rudeness, " but you don't understand that."

Frau Esch brought in the soup, and Huguenau's disagreeable thoughts would not leave him. The two of them lived together like lovers, without desiring children, and it was probably to cloak this that they wanted to adopt the girl Marguerite. Actually he was sitting on the chair where their son should have been. So with simple guile he took up the joke again and told Frau Esch that her husband was going into a monastery. Whereupon Frau Esch asked whether it was true that in all the monasteries there were suspicious goings-on among the monks. And she laughed over some dissolute fancy that rose in her mind. But then her eyes turned slowly and suspiciously towards her husband:

" Yes, you're capable of anything."

This was obviously painful to Herr Esch; Huguenau noted that he flushed and returned her glance with anger. Nevertheless, resolved not to lose his prestige in front of his wife but rather to enhance it, Esch declared that after all it was simply a matter of habit, but that everybody knew well enough that even in a monkery there wasn't the slightest need to take refuge in these practices, on the contrary, he flattered himself that even if he wore a cowl he would be able to give a good account of himself.

Frau Esch had stiffened into expressionless gravity. She mechanically patted her hair to rights and said at last:

" Is the soup good, Herr Huguenau? "

" Splendid," said Huguenau, supping it up.

" Would you like another plateful? " Frau Esch sighed. " I've nothing very grand to follow to-day in any case, only a tart."

She nodded in satisfaction when he let his plate be filled again. But meanwhile Huguenau stuck to his theme: apparently Herr Esch was already sick of the war rations; there were no meat and flour cards in the monasteries, one could still live there as if it were peace-time; but considering how much land the priests owned that wasn't surprising. They still stuffed their bellies full in these places. When he was in Maulbronn an employee of the monastery had told him . . .

Esch interrupted him: if the world became really free again, there would be no need for anyone to eat prison fare. . . .

" Turnips and cabbages," said Frau Esch.

" But not fresh cabbage," said Huguenau, " what do you call being really free? "

Esch said:

" The freedom of a Christian soul."

" By all means," said Huguenau, " but I would like to know what that has to do with cabbage."

Esch seized the Bible:

" My house shall be called the house of prayer; but ye have made it a den of murderers."

" Hm, and murderers are given stale cabbage," grinned Huguenau; then he became serious: " So you think the war is a kind of murder, murder with robbery in a way, as the Socialists say."

Esch paid no attention to him; he went on turning over the leaves:

" And besides it's stated in Chronicles second book . . . sixth chapter, eighth verse . . . here it is: ' Forasmuch as it was in thine heart to build an house for my name, thou didst well in that it was in thine heart: Notwithstanding thou shalt not build the house; but thy son which shall come forth out of thy loins, he shall build the house for my name.' " Esch's face had grown red: " That's a very important passage."

" It may be," said Huguenau, " but why? "

" Murder and counter-murder . . . many must sacrifice themselves that the Redeemer may be born, the son who shall build the house."

Huguenau asked cautiously:

" Do you mean the future Socialist State? "

" Trade unions alone can't do it."

" I see . . . that's from the Major's article, I suppose? "

" No, that's in the Bible, only nobody has gathered its meaning yet."

Huguenau threatened Esch with an upraised finger:

" You're a sly dog, Esch . . . and you fancy that the old Major will never notice what you're up to now under cover of the Bible? "

" What's that? "

" Why, communistic propaganda."

Esch grinned, showing his strong yellow teeth:

" You're an idiot."

" It's easy to be rude . . . what's your idea of the future state, then? "

Esch thought hard:

" It's impossible to make you understand anything . . . but one thing I can tell you: when people begin again to understand how to read the Bible, then there won't be any more need of Communism or Socialism . . . and there won't be any French Republic or German Emperor either."

" Well, but that's plain revolution . . . just tell that to the Major."

" I'd tell him, too, without any hesitation."

" He'll be delighted to hear it, no doubt . . . and what will happen next, after you've got rid of the Emperor? "

Esch said:

" The Redeemer will reign over all men."

Huguenau winked across at Frau Esch:

" Your son, do you mean? "

Esch too gazed at his wife: it looked almost as if he were startled:

" My son? "

" We have no children," said Frau Esch.

" But you said that your son would build the house," Huguenau grinned.

That, however, was too much for Esch:

" You're blaspheming, sir . . . you're so dense that you can't help blaspheming or twisting one's words. . . ,"

"He doesn't mean it like that," said Frau Esch appeasingly, "the food will grow quite cold if you two quarrel."

Esch sat in silence and accepted his portion of tart.

"Oh, I've often sat at table with a silent parson," said Huguenau.

Esch still made no reply, and Huguenau challenged him again:

"Well, what about this reign of the Redeemer, then?"

Frau Esch assumed an expectant look:

"Tell him."

"It's a symbol," growled Esch.

"Interesting," said Huguenau, "do you mean the priests are to reign?"

"God in Heaven . . . it's hopeless to get anything into your head . . . the sovereignty of the Church is something you never heard of, I suppose . . . and yet you call yourself an editor."

Now Huguenau on his side was honestly indignant:

"So that's what your communism is . . . if that's what it really is . . . you want to hand everything over to the priests. That's why you want to go into a monastery . . . so that the priests may live still better . . . then there won't be even stale cabbage for us . . . to throw the hard-earned money of this company into the maw of these gentry . . . no, I much prefer my honest business to your communism in that case."

"Devil take it, then go about your business! but if you refuse to learn anything you shouldn't persist in wanting to run a paper with your narrow-minded—yes, I repeat, narrow-minded views. It can't be done."

Whereupon Huguenau triumphantly retorted that Esch should be jolly glad to have found him; the advertising side of the paper, as a certain Herr Esch had run it, would have brought the *Herald* to ruin within a year, anybody could prove that in his sleep. And he blinked expectantly at Frau Esch, assuming that she would give him support on this practical question. But Frau Esch was clearing the table and seemed in a softened mood: once more Huguenau was forced to note with disapproval that she had laid her hand on her husband's shoulder; she did not listen to what was said, but simply stated that there were things which you and me, dear Herr Huguenau, find it difficult to grasp. And Esch, rising from the table in apotheosis, closed the discussion:

"You must learn, young man; learn to open your eyes."

Huguenau left the room. Priests' gabble, he thought. *Haïssez les ennemis de la sainte religion.* Oh, yes, merde, blagueurs, he was willing enough to hate, but he refused to have it laid down for him whom he was to hate. D'ailleurs je m'en fous. The clattering sound of washed plates and the stale smell of dishwater accompanied him down the wooden stairs and reminded him with strange vividness of his parents' house and his mother in her kitchen.

CHAPTER XLVI

A few days later the following epistle flowed from Huguenau's pen:

To the TOWN COMMANDANT MAJOR JOACHIM VON PASENOW. *Local.*

Secret Report No. 1.

MOST ESTEEMED HERR MAJOR,

With reference to the conversation which I was privileged to have with you regarding above, I respectfully beg to report that I was present yesterday at a meeting between the said Herr Esch and several suspicious elements. As already mentioned, Herr Esch meets certain subversive elements several times every week in the Palatine Tavern, and yesterday he kindly invited me to accompany him. In addition to a foreman in the paper factory, a certain Liebel, there were present a worker in the aforesaid factory whose name was uttered with intentional indistinctness so that I did not catch it, also two inmates of the military hospital who had been given leave to go out—viz.: a corporal of the name of Bauer and an artilleryman with a Polish name. Somewhat later there arrived a volunteer belonging to a bomb-throwing section. He was called Betge, Betzge, or something resembling that, and was addressed by the aforesaid Herr E. as " Herr Doctor." The conversation soon switched on to the war even without my suggesting it, and a great deal was said especially about the possibility of the war ending. The aforesaid volunteer in particular asserted that the war was nearing its end, because the Austrians were slackening. He had heard from some of our allies passing through in an armoured train that a great munition factory near Vienna had been blown into the air by Italian fliers or by treachery, and that the Austrian fleet had gone over to the enemy after murdering their officers, and that they were only prevented from doing this by German submarines. The artilleryman replied that he could not believe this, because the German sailors too were sick of the war. When asked by me who had informed him of that he said that he had learned it from a girl in the town brothel, who had been told it by a naval paymaster here on leave. After the glorious Skagerrak sea-fight she said, as reported afterwards by the artilleryman, the sailors had refused to obey further orders, claiming also that the men's food was bad. Every one agreed thereupon that an end must be made of the war. In this connection the works foreman maintained that the war brought profit to nobody except the big capitalists, and that the Russians had been the first to recognize this. These subversive ideas were also advocated by E., who drew his support in doing so from the Bible, but from my experiences with Herr E., I think I can say with certainty that he is pursuing hypocritical ends by such means, and that the properties of the Church are a thorn in his flesh. Obviously to serve as a cloak for the plot that is being hatched, he proposed that a Bible Society should be founded, but all the same this was greeted with scorn by most of those present. So as to learn more of him on the one hand, and of the paymaster on the other, we visited the brothel at my suggestion after the two inmates of the hospital and the factory worker had left. I could not gather much information, however, about the paymaster at the brothel, but on the other hand the conduct of Herr E. seemed more and more suspicious to me. For the " Doctor," who beyond doubt is a regular customer of the house, introduced me with the words: " This is a gentleman from the Government, you must treat him gratis," from which I deduced that E. had certain suspicions regarding me, and accordingly had warned his accomplices to be cautious in my presence. Consequently I was unsuccessful in my attempt to induce Herr E. to drop his reserve, and although he drank a great deal at my invitation and my expense, he refused in spite of every encouragement to go upstairs, but remained apparently quite sober, which state he employed to make noisy harangues in the waiting-room on the un-Christian and blasphemous nature of such establishments. Only when the volunteer " Doctor " explained to him that these houses were allotted to the army on sanitary grounds by the military authorities, and consequently must be regarded as military institutions, did he give up his antagonistic standpoint, which he once more took up, however, on the way home.

As I have nothing further to report to-day, I beg to send you my profoundest respects and to declare myself eagerly willing for further service.

Yours respectfully,

WILH. HUGUENAU.

P.S.—I beg respectfully to add that during our conversation in the Palatine Tavern Herr Esch made mention of the fact that in the prison in this town one or more deserters are lying at present, preparatory to their being shot. Thereupon everyone, including Herr Esch, loudly expressed the opinion that there was no object in shooting deserters now that the war is nearing its end (which these people seem to count on), seeing that enough blood had already been shed without that. Herr Esch was of the opinion that steps should be taken for this purpose. Whether by this he meant violent or other steps he did not say. I should like once more to respectfully insist that I consider the said E. as a wolf in sheep's clothing, who conceals his subversive aims behind pious phrases. Once more with profoundest respects,

W. H.

After concluding this report Huguenau gazed into the mirror to see whether he could bring off an ironical grimace like that which had so often exasperated him in Esch. Yes, his letter was a masterly achievement; it did one good to put a spoke in Esch's wheel, and Huguenau was so delighted with this pleasant thought that he could not help picturing the satisfaction which the Major would feel on receiving the letter. He considered whether he should deliver it personally, but then it seemed more fitting to him that it should reach the Major's hands by the official postal delivery. So he sent it by registered post, not however without first writing in huge letters on the envelope " Personal," and underlining it thrice.

Huguenau had deceived himself, however; the Major was by no means pleased when he found the letter among the correspondence lying on his desk. It was a dull thundery morning, the rain poured down the window panes of his office and the air smelt of sulphur or of soot. Something ugly and violent was concealed behind this letter, something subterranean, and even though the Major did not know, and even though it was not his duty to know, that there must always be violence and violation when one man tries to force his way into the reality of others and to graft his own on to it, yet the word " Night-birds " came into his mind, and it seemed to him that he was called upon to protect himself, to protect his wife and children from something which was not of his world, but belonged to the pit. Hesitatingly he took up the letter again; at bottom one could not blame this man, whose violence was only, so to speak, an insignificant kind of violence, who merely fulfilled his duty as a patriot and made his report, and if he did it in the loathsome and dishonourable manner of an *agent provocateur*, yet one could not take that amiss in an uneducated man. Yet because all this was really incomprehensible and beyond his grasp, the Major felt only a rush of shame at having reposed confidence in a man of low mind, and his face under his white hair became a little redder with shame. Nevertheless the Town Commandant could not consider himself justified in simply relegating the communication to the wastepaper-basket; rather did his office oblige him to continue to regard the suspicious Herr Esch with due mistrust, to keep watch on him, so to speak, from the distance, so that any danger that might possibly threaten the Fatherland from Herr Esch's activities might be prevented.

CHAPTER XLVII

Surgeon-Major Kühlenbeck rang up Dr Kessel on the telephone:

" Can you come at three this afternoon to operate, a small bullet extraction . . .? "

Dr Kessel thought he could hardly manage it, his time was so taken up.

" Too simple for you, I suppose, fishing out a bullet, for me too . . . but one mustn't ask too much . . . this isn't a life or the type of work a man can stand for long, I admit, and I'll throw it up some day or other, too . . . but to-day there's no help for it. . . . I order you to come. I'll send a car for you, it won't take longer than half-an-hour."

Kühlenbeck put back the receiver and laughed:

" Well, that's two hours of his time accounted for."

Flurschütz was sitting beside him:

" I had been wondering, I must admit, why you asked Kessel to come for such a trifle."

" Poor old Kessel is always trying to give me the slip. We'll take out Kneese's appendix at the same time."

" You really intend to operate on him? "

" Why not? The man must be allowed his pleasures . . . and me too."

" Why, does he want to be operated on? "

" Come, Flurschütz, you're becoming as naïve as our old friend Kessel—have I ever asked anybody that? Afterwards they were all thankful enough. And the four weeks' sick-leave that I get for every one of them . . . well, just think for yourself."

Flurschütz made to say something. Kühlenbeck put up his hand:

" Oh, leave me in peace with your secretion theories . . . my dear chap, if I can look into a man's belly I have no need of theories . . . follow my example and become a surgeon . . . the only way of keeping young."

" And am I to throw up all the work I've done on glands? "

" Throw it up with a good conscience . . . you operate quite neatly as it is."

" Something must be done about Jaretzki, sir . . . the man's going to pieces."

" Suppose we try a trepanning operation on him."

" But you've already discharged him . . . with his nerves in the condition they're in he should be sent to a special institution."

" I've reported him for Kreuznach, he'll soon pull himself together there. . . . You're a fine generation! a little boozing and you break down and must be sent to an institute for neurotics. . . . Orderly! "

The orderly appeared in the doorway.

" Tell Sister Carla that we shall operate at three . . . oh yes, and Murwitz in room two and Kneese in room three are to be given nothing to eat to-day . . . that's all . . . what do you say, Flurschütz, we won't really need poor old Kessel, we'll manage quite nicely by ourselves . . . it's hardly worth while calling in Kessel, he only complains that his legs are paining him: real sadism of me to drag him out . . . well, what do you say, Flurschütz? "

" With all respect, sir, I can act for Kessel this time, but this can't go on indefinitely . . . and then it won't be possible any longer simply to order a medical man to operate."

" Insubordination, Flurschütz? "

" Merely theoretical, sir . . . yes, it seems to me that in no very long time medicine will have specialized itself so completely that a consultation between a physician and a surgeon or a dermatologist will lead to no result at all, simply because there will be no means of making one specialist understand another."

" Wrong, quite wrong, Flurschütz, very shortly there will be nothing but surgery . . . that's the only thing that will be left of this whole wretched art of medicine . . . man is a butcher and whatever he may do he remains a butcher, he can't understand anything else . . . but he understands that to a T." And Dr Kühlenbeck regarded his great hairy skilful hands with the nails cut quite short.

Then he said reflectively:

" Do you know, a man who refused to come to terms with that fact might actually go off his head . . . one must take the matter as it is and get what pleasure one can out of it . . . so be advised, Flurschütz, swop horses and become a surgeon."

CHAPTER XLVIII

One had to fight for every bale of paper that one asked to be delivered, and although Esch was furnished with a certificate from the authorities empowering him to receive the supply required by the *Kur-Trier Herald*, he had to go out to the paper factory every week. And almost every time there was a row with old Herr Keller or the factory manager.

The men were just leaving for the day when Esch left the factory. He overtook the foreman Liebel and the mechanic Fendrich on the road. He really couldn't stand Liebel, with his fair-haired conical head and the thick vein across his brow. He said:

" 'Evening."

" 'Evening, Esch, have you been praying all this time with the old man? "

Esch did not understand.

" Why, to get him to deliver your paper."

" Bloody nonsense," said Esch.

Fendrich stopped and showed the soles of his shoes; they were in holes:

" That'll cost six marks . . . that's how your rises in wages go."

This provided Esch with a starting-point:

" You can't do much by simply raising your wages, that's the mistake all the unions make."

" What's this, Esch? Are you thinking of mending Fendrich's boots with the Bible too? "

" Bloody nonsense," repeated Esch.

Fendrich's eyes glowed feverishly in their dark cavities; he was tuberculous and could not get enough milk to drink. He said:

" Religion too is probably a luxury that only the rich people can afford."

Liebel said:

" Majors and newspaper editors."

Esch said somewhat apologetically:

" I'm only an employee of the paper, like yourself," then he flared up, " besides that's all nonsense, as if the unions had ever taken the vow of poverty! "

Fendrich said:

" It would be all very fine if one could believe."

Esch said:

" I've discovered something: religion has to renew itself too, and get a new life . . . it says in the Bible that only the son can build the house."

Liebel said:

" Of course the next generation will have a better time, that isn't news to me. . . . I simply can't live now on my hundred and forty marks, even reckoning in the bonus . . . the old man won't admit that . . . and I'm supposed to be foreman, too."

" I haven't any more than that myself," said Esch, " counting in the house and all. . . . I've two tenants, but I can't decently ask anything from them, poor devils . . . my rent account is passive."

The evening wind freshened. Fendrich coughed.

Liebel said:

" Well? Any news? "

Esch admitted:

" I've been seeing the priest. . . ."

" What for? "

" About that passage in the Bible, the idiot didn't even listen . . . mumbled something about prayer and the Church, and that was all. The bloody priest . . . one must help oneself."

" That's right," said Fendrich, " nobody helps you."

Liebel said:

" If you stick together, you help one another . . . that's the advantage of the unions."

" The doctor says I must go to the mountains, and he's applied ten times already to the sick-fund . . . but if you don't come from the Front you've got to want, these days, and my cough just goes on and on."

Esch put on his ironical expression:

" With your unions and your sick-funds you won't get much further on than me with my priests. . . ."

" You have to die by yourself," said Fendrich, coughing.

Liebel asked:

" What really are you after? "

Esch considered:

" I used to think that one only had to clear out . . . to America . . . across the wide ocean on a ship . . . so as to begin a new life . . . but now . . ."

Liebel waited for the end of the sentence:

" And now? "

But Esch answered unexpectedly:

" Perhaps the Protestants are nearer it . . . the Major is a Protestant after all . . . but one must think the matter over first oneself . . . one must get together with other people and read the Bible to get some clear light . . . when one's alone, one keeps on doubting, no matter how much one broods on the subject."

" When one has friends, everything's easier," said Fendrich.

" You come and see me," said Esch, " I'll show you the passage in the Bible."

" All right," said Fendrich.

" And what about you, Liebel? " Esch felt obliged to ask.

" You must tell me first what you've concocted together."

Fendrich sighed:

" Everybody can only see things through his own eyes."

Liebel laughed and went away.

" He'll come yet, all right," said Esch.

CHAPTER XLIX

STORY OF THE SALVATION ARMY GIRL IN BERLIN (7)

My memory has not retained much of the evening that I spent with Nuchem Sussin at the Salvation Army meeting. I was occupied with more important things. No matter how one may estimate philosophical activity, it has at any rate the effect of making the external world insignificant and less worthy of notice. And apart from that even the most noteworthy things escape one's notice while one is experiencing them. In short, all that I can remember is Nuchem Sussin walking along beside me with his grey frock-coat buttoned up, his trousers flapping about his legs, they were so short, and his absurdly small velour hat perched on his head. All these Jews, when they're not rigged out in black caps, wear those velour hats that are too small for them, even the ostensibly fashionable Dr Litwak does this, and I could not forbear asking Nuchem the rude question where he had got that hat of his. " I just got it," was the answer.

Besides, the whole affair was not worth mentioning. It took on some colour of importance only because of Dr Litwak, who came in to see me yesterday. He has the unpleasant habit of simply walking in on me; he did the same thing on the occasion of my so-called illness. So he appeared before me again as I lay on the chaise-longue; he had the indispensable walking-stick in his hand and the absurd little velour hat on his head. That is to say, the hat itself was by no means small, it had a broad brim, but it sat on the very top of his skull without covering it. It occurred to me at that moment that Dr Litwak too must have had a milk-white complexion in his youth. Now it reminded one unquestionably of yellow cream.

" You will be able to tell me about Sussin."

I said, because it conformed with the truth:

" He is my friend."

" Friend, very good . . ." Dr Litwak pulled over a chair for himself, " his people are anxious, they asked me to come . . . you understand? "

In reality I was under no obligation to understand him, but I wanted to shorten the proceedings:

" He has a right to go where he likes."

" Oh, who has the right, who hasn't the right. . . . I'm not reproaching you of course . . . but why is he running about with this goy girl? "

It dawned on me only then that on that evening I had asked Marie and Nuchem into my room. People who haven't money can't sit about in restaurants.

I could not help laughing.

" You laugh, and his wife is sitting up there crying."

Well, that was certainly news to me; all the same I might have remembered that these Jews get married at fifteen. If I had only known which was Nuchem's wife: one of the stylish girls? or one of the matrons with their hair parted in the middle? the latter seemed the more probable.

I held Dr Litwak by the cord of his eyeglasses:

" Has he children as well? "

" Why, what do you expect him to have? Kittens? "

Dr Litwak put on such an indignant expression that I had to ask him what his first name was.

" Dr Samson Litwak," he introduced himself anew.

" Well then look here, Dr Samson, what do you really want of me? "

He reflected for a while:

" I'm an enlightened man . . . but this is going too far . . . you must stop him."

" Stop him from what? from wanting to go to Zion? Leave him that harmless pleasure."

" He'll get himself baptized yet . . . you must stop him."

" But whether he reaches Jerusalem as a Jew or a Christian is surely a bagatelle."

" Jerusalem," he repeated, as if a bonbon had been put into his mouth.

" Well, then," said I, hoping that he would retire now.

He was still obviously rolling the name on his tongue:

" I'm an enlightened man . . . but nobody ever got there by singing songs and beating drums . . . that's for a different kind of people. . . . I must visit everybody, I'm a doctor, it needn't matter to me whether one is a Jew or a Christian . . . there's decent people everywhere, will you stop him? "

This persistence got on my nerves:

" I'm a great Anti-Semite," he smiled incredulously, " I'm an agent of the Salvation Army, I'm quartermaster in Jerusalem."

" A joke," he said appreciatively, although he was visibly disconcerted, " a joke, *nebbich*."

There he was certainly right; a joke, *nebbich*, that was for the time being the attitude to life into which I had fallen. What could be held responsible for it? The war? I did not know, and probably do not know even to-day, although many things have changed since.

I still held Dr Litwak by the cord of his eyeglasses. He said:

" But you're an enlightened man too. . . ."

" Well? "

" Why don't you leave people their . . ." he brought out the word only with difficulty, ". . . their prejudices? "

" So, you call such things prejudices! "

Now he was quite thrown into confusion.

" They're not really prejudices of course . . . what do you mean by prejudices? . . . " and finally becoming calm again: " but in reality they're not prejudices."

When he had gone I went over in my mind that evening of the Salvation Army meeting. As I have said, it had passed without making the slightest impression on me. Now and then I had regarded Nuchem Sussin as he sat there with a somewhat lifeless smile round the curved Jewish lips in his milk-white face, listening to the singing. And then I had asked them both up to my room, or more correctly Marie only, for Nuchem of course lived in the house,—well, and then they had both sat in my room silently listening while I talked. Until Nuchem once more pointed to the lute and said: " Play something." Then Marie had taken the lute and sung: " We're marching on to Zion's gate, A host so great and true, All cleansed in the Redeemer's blood, And there is room for you." And Nuchem listened with a somewhat lifeless smile.

CHAPTER L

Huguenau waited for eight days, expecting some sign of approval or at least a reply from the Major. He waited for ten days. Then he became uneasy. The report had obviously not come up to the Major's expectations. But was it his fault that that cretin Esch provided him with no material? Huguenau considered whether he should follow up the first report with a second, but what was he to say in it? That Esch was colloguing as usual with the vine-growers and the factory workers was nothing new; that would only bore the Major!

The Major mustn't be bored—Huguenau racked his brains to find some proposal to lay before the Major. Something simply must be done; Esch reigned supreme in the office and acted as though the real editor of the paper were non-existent, and in the printing-shed everything was dreary beyond endurance. Huguenau looked through the great newspapers for stimulation, and found it when he made the discovery that all these journals were labouring in the service of national charities, while the *Kur-Trier Herald* had undertaken nothing, absolutely nothing at all. So that was what Herr Esch's warmth of heart amounted to, that warmth of heart which could not endure the spectacle of the misery among the vine-growers. But as for himself he knew now what to do.

On Friday evening, after a long absence, he appeared again at the hotel and proceeded at once to the room where the notabilities sat, for that was his place by right. The Major was sitting at his table in the outer dining-room, and Huguenau greeted him formally and curtly in passing.

By good luck the gentlemen were already there in force, and Huguenau announced that he was glad to find so many of them, for he had an important matter to discuss, and at once, before the Major came in. And in a fairly long speech he pointed out that the town lacked,

painfully lacked, any proper charitable organization such as had already
existed for years almost everywhere else for the alleviation of hardships
caused by the war, and he moved that such an organization should be
established at once. As for its objects, he would content himself with
mentioning, among other things, the preservation of soldiers' graves,
the provision for soldiers' widows and orphans and so on; further, he
would like to point out that the money for these lofty objects must be
raised, and that in this connection an " Iron Bismarck," [1] for instance,
could be erected in the market-place, nails at ten pfennigs per nail,
besides it was a crying scandal that this town alone should lack such
a monument—and finally that charitable appeals of various kinds, not
to speak of public collections, would always help to increase their funds.
And that this organization, for which he begged to suggest the title of
" The Moselle Memorial Association " should appear under the patronage
of the Town Commandant. He himself and his paper—of course within
the limits of their modest powers—stood at all times and free of cost
at the disposal of the association and its lofty aims.

It need scarcely be said, of course, that the proposal was greeted
with universal applause and was accepted unanimously and without
discussion. Huguenau and Herr Paulsen the chemist were nominated
as delegates to convey the proposal to the Herr Major, and smoothing
down their coats they strode with a certain solemnity into the dining-
room.

The Major looked up with some surprise, then he drew himself up
with a little jerk as though on parade and listened attentively but without understanding to the phrases of the two gentlemen. These phrases
crossed one another and raced one another, and the Major heard something about an Iron Bismarck and war widows and a " Moselle Memorial "
and did not understand. At last Huguenau was intelligent enough to
resign all speech to the chemist; it seemed to him also that that was
the more modest course, and so he sat still and regarded the clock on
the wall, the picture of *The Crown-Prince Friedrich after the Battle of
Gravelotte*, and the Spatenbräu sign (with the spade) which hung on
a cord beside the picture of the Crown-Prince. Where could one get
Spatenbräu now! Meanwhile the Major had grasped what Paulsen was
saying: he thought, he said, that there were no military grounds against

[1] A wooden statue, into which the public were encouraged to hammer nails
until the wood was covered.

his acceptance, he welcomed this patriotic proposal, he could only thank them most cordially, and he rose in order to convey his thanks to the gentlemen in the next room. Paulsen and Huguenau followed, proud of their accomplished achievement.

They sat for a long time together, for it was in a sense an inaugural celebration. Huguenau waited for an opportunity to get hold of the Major, and it came presently when they drank to the health and success of the new association and its patron, not forgetting, of course, the man who had originated the splendid idea, Herr Huguenau.

Huguenau, his glass in his hand, went the round of the table and in this manner reached Major von Pasenow:

" I hope Herr Major is satisfied with me to-night."

He had never had any cause for dissatisfaction, replied the Major.

" Come, Herr Major, my report seems to have rather missed fire . . . but I hope you'll take into consideration that the circumstances were very difficult. And then I have been working early and late reorganizing the paper; I hope you will not set it down to negligence that I haven't been able to send you a second report. . . ."

The Major said firmly:

" I think it is scarcely worth while pursuing the matter any further; you have done already all that you were in duty bound to do."

Huguenau was taken aback.

" Oh, not at all, not at all," he muttered, and assured the Major that he would take up his work of surveillance really in earnest now.

As the Major made no reply to this, Huguenau went on:

" We'll print the appeal for ' The Moselle Memorial ' at once, to-morrow . . . in honour of the occasion will not the Herr Major pay our concern the honour of a visit, after so graciously standing god-father to it . . . that would be the most splendid propaganda for the new association."

The Major replied that he would be only too delighted to pay the *Kur-Trier Herald* a visit; for the next day, however, all his arrangements were already made, but he presumed any day would suit equally.

" The earlier the better, Herr Major," Huguenau ventured. " The Herr Major won't find anything very remarkable to inspect . . . everything quite modest . . . and of course there aren't many outward signs of the work that has been put into reorganizing it, but I can say with all modesty that the printing arrangements are in perfect order . . ."

Suddenly he had a new idea:

" The printing-press, for instance, would do splendidly for any printing required by the military authorities," he caught fire, he would have liked to seize the Major by the coat-button. " You see, Herr Major, you see how Esch has neglected the business . . . it needed me to hit on that idea. We must get the custom of the army authorities, now that the paper is, so to speak, under your direct patronage, and we have put so much money into it . . . how else am I to squeeze a dividend out of it for the shareholders . . . considering the state I found the business in ? " he said in despair, and he felt honestly embittered.

The Major replied somewhat helplessly:

" But that isn't my province . . ."

" Quite, quite, Herr Major, but if the Herr Major seriously desired it . . . and once the Herr Major has seen the printing-office, he will certainly desire it. . . ."

He gazed at the Major alluringly and seductively and despairingly all in one. But then he pulled himself up, wiped his glasses, and cast a glance round the table: " It is obviously in the interests of all the gentlemen sitting here too . . . all you gentlemen are invited to inspect the place, of course that's understood."

But most of them knew Esch's den already. Only they did not say so.

CHAPTER LI

Since Heinrich Wendling had announced that he was coming home on leave, more than three weeks had passed. And although she still lay long in bed of mornings, Hanna scarcely believed now that Heinrich would really come. He suddenly arrived, however, neither in the evening, nor in the morning, but in the broad light of day. He had spent half the night in Coblenz station, and then had come on with a dawdling transport train. And as he was telling her this they stood opposite each other on the paved garden-path; the noonday sun shone down, and in the middle of the lawn a red garden-umbrella glowed warmly beside the camp-chair on which she had been lying; they could smell the hot, red cotton, and the leaves of her book, which had slipped down, fluttered in the light wind. Heinrich did not touch her, he had not even reached out his hand to her, but stared immovably in her face, and she, knowing that he must be searching for a picture which he had carried in his mind for more than two years, kept quite still under his searching glance; and she too looked into the face turned towards her, seeking in her turn not, indeed, for a picture she had harboured, for there was no longer any picture in her mind, but for the traits because of which she had once been compulsively drawn to love that face. Strangely unaltered that face seemed to her now, she knew and recognized again the line of the lips; the arrangement and shape of the teeth, the dimple on the chin had remained unchanged, and the space between the eyes was a little too wide on account of the breadth of the skull. " I must see your profile," she said and he turned his head obediently. And it was the same straight nose and long upper lip that she saw again, only every trace of softness had vanished, that was all. One had really to acknowledge that he was a handsome man, yet she did not find what had once so intensely delighted and attracted her. Heinrich asked: " Where's the boy? " " He's at school . . . won't you come in? " They went into the house. Yet even now he still did not touch her, still did not kiss her, but simply gazed at her. " I must have a thorough wash first of all . . . haven't had a bath since leaving Vienna."

" Yes, we'll turn on a bath."

The two maids appeared to bid the master welcome. Hanna did not quite like that. She went up with him to the bathroom, and herself laid out the bath towels.

" Everything's still in its old place, Heinrich."

" Oh, everything's still in its old place? "

She left the bathroom; there were all sorts of things to arrange and rearrange; she attended to them wearily.

She cut roses in the garden for the dinner-table.

After a while she returned softly to the bathroom door and listened to the splashing inside. She could feel her usual headache coming on. Supporting herself on the banister she descended once more to the hall.

At last the boy returned from school. She took him by the hand. At the bathroom door she cried: " May we come in now? " " Of course," the reply came in a somewhat astonished voice. She opened the door a little, and peeped in through the opening: Heinrich was standing half dressed before the mirror, and she thrust one of the roses into the unwillingly opened hand of the child, pushed him in and ran away.

She waited for the two of them in the dining-room, and could not help averting her eyes when they entered. They looked absurdly alike, with the same eyes set wide apart, the same movements, the same crop of brown hair, except that Heinrich wore his quite short now. It was as though she had had no share at all in the child. A terrible mechanism; oh, it was terrible to have been loved. And at that moment her life seemed to her like one long imbecility, a despairing imbecility, which nevertheless she would never be able to change.

Heinrich said: " Home again " and sat down at his old place. Perhaps his words seemed stupid to him; he smiled uncertainly. The boy regarded him attentively and distantly.

There he sat, the father of the family, and spoilt everything.

The maid too could not keep her eyes off him; there was a hint of admiration and envy in her glance; and when she entered again Hanna said very distinctly:

" Should I telephone to Röders . . . about this evening? "

The advocate Röders was Wendling's colleague in the office; he was over fifty and exempt from military service.

The English clock in its mahogany case struck a deep gong-like stroke.

With her little finger Hanna lightly touched the back of Heinrich's hand, as though by the caress she were begging forgiveness for thinking of spending the evening with Röders, but warning him at the same time that she desired to avoid physical contacts.

Heinrich said:

" Of course, I'll have to ring up Röders . . . I'll fix it up, then."

Hanna said:

" We'll go out walking with papa in the afternoon and show ourselves."

" Yes, let's do that," said Heinrich.

" Isn't it lovely to have papa sitting here with us again? "

" Yes," said the boy after some hesitation.

" You must look over his school books . . . he can write and count already. He wrote his letters to you quite by himself."

" They were splendid letters, Walter."

" They were only postcards," said Walter shyly.

That they were appealing to the child between them, so as to find each other across his brown head, seemed to them both like an abuse of the child. Certainly it would have been more honest to say: we will not kiss each other until our longing has become intolerable. But that longing was not really longing, it was only intolerable expectation.

They went up to the nursery, on whose panelled walls a childish fresco, intentionally gay, was painted. And with that second and clearer and somewhat wry intelligence which can arise from intensified expectation or from an agonizing headache, Hanna knew that all these lacquered furnishings and all this whiteness was also an abuse of the child, knew that it had nothing to do with his own life and nature, but that a symbol had been set up in this room, a symbol of her white breasts and of the white milk which they would produce after successful embraces. It was a very remote and very vague thought, and yet in it lay the reason why she had never been able to stay long in the nursery and had preferred that the boy should come to her. She said: " You must show papa your new toys too." Walter brought the new box of bricks and the soldiers in field-grey. There were twenty-three men and an officer, who with one knee bent waved his drawn sword towards the enemy. None of the three noticed that Dr Heinrich Wendling also wore the field-grey uniform of an officer; each, it is true, had a different motive for not noticing it: Walter, because he felt that his father was an intruder, Heinrich, because it was impossible for him to identify the heroic gestures of the tin soldiers with real war, Hanna because, to her own horror, she suddenly saw this man naked before her, naked, and isolated in his nakedness. It was the same isolation as she had remarked in the pieces of furniture about her, that stood as though naked, with no connection with their surroundings, no relation to each other, strange and disturbing.

He too could not but feel it. And when they went out walking they took the child between them, and although Hanna held the boy's hand and swung it gaily, and Heinrich often took the other hand, he was a barrier separating them. They did not look at each other, they were embarrassed, as if ashamed, they gazed straight ahead or at the fields where dandelions and purple clover, wild pinks and lilac scabious, were growing in the grass. The day was warm and Hanna was not used to walking in the afternoon. Yet it was not solely the heat that made her feel such an urgent need for a bath when she returned; every wish of hers now reached down in the most curious way to a deeper stratum of consciousness: it was as though the immersion of her body in the water would spread a great solitude around her, as if she had visions of that magical rebirth which one experiences in the isolation of the water. More definite, certainly, than these thoughts was her repugnance at the idea of visiting the bathroom at bedtime in Heinrich's presence. On the other hand the maid would think it queer if she were to take a bath in the middle of the day, and on the pretext that she had to change for the evening she asked Heinrich if he would order a car meanwhile and look after Walter. Then she went to the bathroom, intending to have a shower-bath at least. But when she got into the tub, to which a few drops from the midday bath still clung, for the douche was dripping, her knees grew weak and she had to let the cold water run over her until her skin was like glass and the points of her breasts grew quite hard. After that it was more endurable.

It was late when they drove over to Röders'; Heinrich dismissed the car since it was such a lovely evening, and Hanna was thankful for the suggestion that they should walk home—the later that happened, the better. And it was actually midnight when they left Röders! But when they were crossing the silent market-place on which nobody was to be seen except the sentry on duty at military headquarters, when the empty place surrounded by the dark houses, in which scarcely a light was burning, lay before them like a crater of isolation, like a crater of silence out of which recurring waves of peace flowed over the sleeping town, then Heinrich Wendling took his wife's arm, and at that first physical contact she closed her eyes. Perhaps he too had closed his eyes and saw neither the deep summer night sky nor the white ribbon of the road that stretched in front of them as they walked in its dust, perhaps each of them saw a different firmament, both of them sealed like their eyes, each in a separate isolation, and yet united in the renewed knowledge of their bodies, which yielded at last to a kiss; and the veils dropped from their faces, that were lascivious in the consciousness of sex, yet chaste in the pain of a separation that could never end, that could never be abolished again no matter how tender they were with each other.

CHAPTER LII

After Samwald's funeral Gödicke of the Landwehr began to speak.

Samwald, a volunteer, was the brother of Friedrich Samwald the watchmaker, who had a shop in Römerstrasse. After a mass attack accompanied by a heavy bombardment, young Samwald had suddenly begun to cough and collapsed. He was a nice brave lad of nineteen, everybody liked him, and so he had managed to get sent to the hospital of his native town. He did not arrive even in a hospital transport, but alone, like a man on leave, and Surgeon-Major Kühlenbeck said: " Well, as for you, my lad, we'll soon put you to rights." And although Dr Kessel never came to the hospital without looking up young Samwald, and although Samwald seemed quite restored to health, he was suddenly seized with another hæmorrhage and in three days he was dead. In spite of the brilliant sun smiling down from the sky.

Since the hospital was one only for light cases, death was not hushed up there as in larger hospitals. On the contrary it was treated as a solemn event. Before the coffin was borne to the cemetery it was laid on the bier in front of the entrance to the hospital, and there consecrated. Those patients who were not confined to bed put on their uniforms and formed up in order, and there were a good many people from the town. The Surgeon-Major pronounced a stirring eulogy, the priest stood beside the coffin, a boy in a red soutane with a white tunic swung the censer. Then the women knelt, many of the men too, and once more they told over their rosaries.

Gödicke had remained in the hospital garden. When he noticed the crowd assembling he hobbled up on his two sticks and joined it. The spectacle he now saw was familiar to him, and consequently he refused to countenance it. He thought deeply; he wanted to destroy what he saw, to tear it to bits as one tears to bits a piece of paper or cardboard—and how that was to be done had to be vigilantly and keenly thought out. When the women plumped down on their knees like charwomen, a laugh rose into his throat, but he dared not make a sound, that was forbidden him. Supported on his two sticks, he stood in the midst of the kneeling women, he stood there like a scaffolding, and rammed his supports into the ground and pressed the sound back into his throat. But now the women had finished their Paternoster and their three Aves and came to the passage, " descended into Hell, and rose again from the dead on the third day "; then—it seemed in a lower storey of the scaffolding, and as though spoken by a ventriloquist he had once heard—words began to form just above his tortured and compressed abdomen, and instead of roaring them out, so reluctantly did the words emerge that it was perhaps inaudibly that the bricklayer Gödricke said: " Arisen from the dead," and immediately fell silent again, so terrified was he at what had taken place in the lower storey of his scaffolding. No one was regarding him; they had raised the coffin; the coffin with the crucifix fastened to it swayed on the bearers' shoulders; the watchmaker Samwald, small and a little bent, fell in with the other relatives behind the bearers; then followed the doctors; then came the rest of the procession. Last of all hobbled the bricklayer Gödicke on his sticks, wearing his hospital overall.

Sister Mathilde caught sight of him as they were going along the boulevard. She made straight for him: " But, Gödicke, you can't come like this . . . what are you thinking about, in your overall . . ." but he paid no attention to her. Even when she fetched the Surgeon-Major to support her he refused to be shaken, but simply stared steadily through them both and went straight on. At last Kühlenbeck said: " Oh, let him come, war is war . . . if he gets tired one of the men must stay with him and take him back."

It was a long road that Ludwig Gödicke travelled in this way; the women round about him were praying, and there were bushes beside the road. When one group reached the end of their Aves, another took them up, and from the wood came the cry of a cuckoo. Some of the men, the little watchmaker Samwald among them, wore black suits like carpenters. Many things came nearer and closed up, especially when at the turnings the procession slowed down and the mourners' bodies were pressed closely together; and the women's skirts were like his own over-all; their skirts struck against their legs when they walked; and a woman away in front was walking with her head bowed and her handkerchief before her face. And even if Gödicke did not look at anything, but held his eyes immovably fixed on the wheel tracks in front of him, trying, indeed, every now and then actually to keep his eyes closed just as firmly as his teeth were clenched, so that the parts of his soul crowded together still more closely, threatening to stifle his ego; yes, though he would actually have preferred to come to a stop, to ram his crutches into the ground and force all these people to keep still and say nothing, or to scatter them all to the four winds; nevertheless he was drawn on, borne on, and he swam and floated, himself a swaying coffin, on the wave of ever-recurring prayer that accompanied him.

In the cemetery, when the body had once more been consecrated, and over the opened grave into which it was lowered the litany once more began: "Arisen from the dead," and while the little watchmaker Samwald stood rigid, gazing into the hole and sobbing, and one by one the people went up to fling a spadeful of earth on the dead warrior and to shake the watchmaker by the hand, suddenly, uplifted before the eyes of all, the gigantic form of Gödicke, supported on his two sticks, in his long grey hospital overall, his long beard waving, appeared on the edge of the grave beside the little watchmaker and ignored the hand offered him, but said with a great effort, yet clearly enough for everybody to understand, his first words: "Arisen from the dead." And thereupon he laid his sticks aside, yet not to take the spade and throw a little earth down into the grave; no, he did not do that, he did something quite different and unexpected; he addressed himself to the task of climbing down into the hole, he began laboriously and systematically to clamber down into it, and already by good luck had one leg over the edge. Naturally his intentions were incomprehensible to all the bystanders; they thought that without the support of his sticks he had simply fallen down out of sheer weakness. The Surgeon-Major and a few others rushed across, pulled him out of the hole and carried him to one of the benches. Perhaps by now the man Gödicke was really forsaken by his strength; in any case he offered no resistance, but sat there quite quietly with his eyes shut and his head a little to one side. But the watchmaker Samwald, who had run to him with the others and would have gladly helped to carry him, now stayed beside him; and as a great sorrow may sometimes shake up a man's soul, Samwald divined that something very strange had happened to his companion; sitting beside the bricklayer Gödicke, he spoke to him comfortingly as to one who was bearing a sorrow, a heavy sorrow, and he spoke too of his own dead brother, who had had a beautiful and early and painless death. And Gödicke listened to him with his eyes shut.

Meanwhile the local celebrities advanced to the grave, among them, as was fitting, Huguenau in a blue suit, a stiff black hat in one hand, a wreath in the other. And Huguenau looked about him in extreme indignation because the deceased's brother was not at hand to admire the wreath, a beautiful garland of oak-leaves sent by "The Moselle Memorial Association," a really beautiful wreath with a ribbon on which could be read: "From the Fatherland to its brave soldier."

CHAPTER LIII

STORY OF THE SALVATION ARMY GIRL IN BERLIN (8)

Like the quick sperm of future shining seas
the iridescent foam holds, one by one,
these quivering golden shafts cast by the sun—
a spirit moving on the water's face—
and to the far horizon's edge they gleam
where the bright sky begets itself again,
itself a mirror of the glassy plain,
sinking to rest in Aphrodite's dream:
was this the hour in which he was beset?
was this the hour in which the anguish fell,
twisting him in the throes and pains of hell,
bringing forth natural need's unnatural get?
Was it a wood like this, beside a field,
that sank beneath his feet so that he reeled?
for in a blinding rain of fire there spoke
a voice of thunder; headlong he was hurled,
nor did his senses waken till he whirled
far down in sulphurous chasms of glowing rock,
dashed on the stones, the void beneath his feet,
breaking himself as, impotent, he strove
to rise again to that lost land above,
to that lost land of shade and cypress grove,
where tangled bushes dip in waters fleet,
where night and day in one green twilight meet,
where delicate sharp odours drift and twine
along the glimmering aisles of beech and pine,—
this was the hour he sought and seeks for ever
to win again, the hour for ever lost,
ere like a leaf by sudden tempest tossed
that dread voice whirled him off, the hour for him
of new-won knowledge, filling to the brim
his cup of being, even while it drained
all meaning from the draught, and nought remained
but knowledge big with doubt in a waste land,

a land unending: did the cypress stand
beside him? Was there sea? He cannot tell.
He only knows he heard the voice resound,
the voice that hurled him headlong into hell,
the voice that masters him and holds him bound.
Were that hour once re-won, then, purged of sin,
he would find long-forgotten things break in,
bringing the tang of brine on grass and tree,
the mirrored shore beside the shining sea.—
But new-born knowledge drives him on from doubt
to doubt in anguish, hounds him through the wastes
to seek the voice that he can never find,
the voice he flees when it pursues behind
yet conjures still to stop, as on he hastes,
by that great oath he falsely swore to One
who in days past once chose him as a son,
him, the betrayer; and a shriek bursts out
from his despairing mouth, a shriek that wrongs
and deafens knowledge, a cry from the abyss,
a cry that shivers into nothingness,
cry of the helpless animal at bay,
cry of the wild beast trapped by fiery tongues;
O cry of amazement! cry of dire dismay!
Do I feel it, this wonder of amazement? or is it myself
    that is amazed?
From what far country comest thou by right
to me, O thought, profoundest Almost-but-not-quite?
in the blankness of death I hover,
Ahasuerus, crying in despair for ever!
In hell's sleepless, bloodshot, yellow light
my hands are withered and blinded my sight,
I, Ahasuerus, born to cry for ever!
banished my home, by cliffs hemmed about,
nourished in knowledge and ravaged by doubt,
sowing dry stones and fed on dry dust,
fashioned in knowledge and hollow with lust,
blessed by many, by one voice chidden,
the sanctified sower of fruit forbidden.

CHAPTER LIV

The Major was somewhat disagreeably surprised when the orderly reported that Herr Editor Esch wished to see him. Was this newspaper man an ambassador of Huguenau? an emissary of the pit and the underworld? This question made the Major almost forget that Huguenau had drawn a distinct line between himself and the presumably politically suspect Esch, and since a few moments' reflection suggested nothing decisive he said at last:

" Well, it doesn't matter . . . tell him to come in."

Esch certainly looked like neither an emissary from hell, nor a politically suspect individual; he was embarrassed and confused, like a man who was already regretting the step he had taken:

" Herr Major, my business is . . . Herr Major, in short, your article made a deep impression on me. . . ."

Major von Pasenow told himself that he must not allow himself to be taken in by hypocritical speeches, gratifying as it might be to believe that his words had had an effect.

" And if by the devil who must be driven out, the Herr Major meant me . . ."

Whereupon the Major found it necessary to make clear that a Biblical quotation implied no personal point or insinuation, for that would indeed be a degradation of the Bible, and that at every turning-point of our lives, if it was for the better, we had to put behind us a part of the devil. So that if Herr Esch had come to demand explanation or satisfaction, he could rest content with this statement.

While the Major was speaking Esch had regained his composure:

" No, Herr Major, that was not what I came about. I would even take that about the devil on my own shoulders, but not because my paper has been confiscated repeatedly," he made a disdainful gesture, " no, Herr Major, I can't be reproached for ever having run my paper less decently than I do now. I've come with another request."

And he demanded no more and no less than that the Major should point out the way of salvation to him and his friends, or the brethren, as in his excitement he called them.

As he stood there before the Major's desk, his hat in his hands, a red flush of excitement showing on each cheek-bone, a red that ebbed into the brownish hollows beneath, Esch reminded the Major of his estate steward. What right had a steward to talk about religion? and the Major had the feeling that concern with religious questions was a prescriptive right of landowners. Pictures of the religious life he knew rose up in him, he saw the church to which he and his family drove in the high-wheeled coach over the dusty summer roads, in the low sledge well covered with furs during winter; he saw himself holding the usual Bible service for his children and the servants at Christmas and at Easter, saw the Polish maids walking in their red head-cloths and wide skirts to the Catholic Church in the neighbouring village, and as that church reminded him that Herr Esch belonged to the Roman Catholic persuasion, Esch was thus brought into an unpleasantly close relationship with the Polish land-workers and that disturbing atmosphere of unreliability with which, partly from personal experience, partly because of their politics, partly out of pure prejudice, he was accustomed to accredit the Polish nation. And as it is a fact that questions of conscience in a fellow-man very often throw us into embarrassment, as though he were exaggerating something that is not nearly so important to him as he makes out, the Major, while inviting Esch to be seated, did not make any reference to the theme he had opened, but merely inquired after the well-being of the paper.

Esch, however, was not a man to be so easily deflected from his purpose. " For the sake of the paper itself, Herr Major, you must listen to me"— and in answer to the Major's questioning look—" . . . yes, you, Herr Major, have prescribed a new policy for the *Kur-Trier Herald* . . . even though I've always said myself that order must be made in the world and that even an editor must do his part in it, that is, if he doesn't want to be an anarchist and a conscienceless swine . . . Herr Major, everybody seeks salvation, everybody is afraid of evil poison, everybody is waiting for redemption to come and injustice to be destroyed."

He had begun to shout and the Major looked at him in surprise. Esch pulled himself together again: " You see, Herr Major, Socialism is only one sign among many others . . . but since your article in the new issue . . . Herr Major, it's freedom and justice in the world that's at stake . . . one mustn't take human life lightly, something must happen, otherwise all the sacrifice will have been in vain."

" All the sacrifice in vain . . ." repeated the Major as though out of an old memory. But then he collected himself. " Perhaps you want,

Herr Esch, to steer the paper back into the Socialist stream? And do you actually expect me to support you in that? "

Esch's bearing was contemptuous and disrespectful:

" It's not a question of Socialism, Herr Major . . . it's a question of the new life . . . of decency . . . of searching together for the faith . . . my friends and I have started a Bible class . . . Herr Major, when you wrote your article you meant every word of it in your heart, and you can't reject us now."

It was clear: Esch was presenting an account, even although only a spiritual one, and the Major could not but think again of his steward sitting opposite him in the office with his accounts, and he thought too of the Polish farm-labourers, who were always trying to get the better of him. Was this man not threatening him with his Socialism? Perhaps it was something long forgotten that he repeated when he said:

" Someone always rejects us, Herr Esch."

Esch had got up and, yielding to habit, had begun to walk with awkward strides up and down the room. The sharp vertical folds at either side of his mouth were still deeper than usual; how careworn he looks, thought the Major, incredible that this earnest man should be a tavern frequenter or a visitor to disreputable resorts, an emissary from the underworld. Can he be such a hypocrite? It was as impossible to imagine as that underworld itself.

Esch planted himself directly in front of the Major:

" Herr Major, to put it quite frankly . . . how can I fill my position when I'm not even clear whether our path might not be made plainer by accepting the Protestant faith. . . ."

Now the Major could of course have responded that it was not one of an editor's duties to solve theological problems,—but he was too much alarmed by Esch's direct question to find any answer at all: it was not so unlike Huguenau's entreaties to be given the army printing, and for a moment the figures of the two men seemed about to blend together again. The Major put up his hand to the Iron Cross on his breast and his bearing became official: was it fitting that he, an officer in a prominent position, should make proselytes? The Catholic Church counted after all as a sort of ally, and he would not have taken it upon him to induce an Austrian or a Bulgarian or a Turk to give up the ties binding him to his own state in favour of Germany. It was really annoying, the way that this Esch insisted on his pound of flesh, and yet again it was flattering and alluring; in this appeal to him was there not something of the faith that for ever renews and regenerates religion? But the Major still resisted, and begged to point out that, himself a Protestant, he did not feel competent to counsel a Catholic in matters of belief.

Esch once more made a disdainful gesture with his hand,—that was beside the question: in the Major's article it said that Christian must stand by Christian—so there was no difference between Catholic and Protestant Christianity, and the town priest paid little enough attention to such scruples.

The Major did not reply. Was it really a net made out of his own words that was being drawn round him? with which this man wished to drag him down into the darkness and the pit? And yet it was as though a gentle hand were stretched out to lead him forth to the peaceful banks of quiet waters. He could not help thinking of the baptism in Jordan, and almost against his will he said:

"There's no rule in matters of faith, Herr Esch; faith is a natural fountain that springs up, as we are told in the Bible," and then he added reflectively, "every one must come to know divine grace by himself."

Esch had turned his back discourteously on the Major; he stood at the window with his forehead pressed against the window pane. Now he turned round: his expression was grave, almost imploring:

"Herr Major, it isn't a question of rules . . . it's a question of trust . . ." and after a little: "otherwise it would be . . ." he could not find the right word, "otherwise the paper would be no better than all the other papers . . . a corrupt Press . . . eyewash for demagogues . . . but you, Herr Major, wanted something different. . . ."

Once more Major von Pasenow felt the sweetness of yielding, of being carried away; it was as though a silvery cloud sought to catch him up, floating over the spring streams. The security of trust! No, that man standing so seriously before him was no adventurer, no traitor, no unreliable Pole, not a man to carry your confidence over to the other side and there shamelessly and openly expose it. So at first hesitatingly, but becoming warmer as he went on, the Major began to speak of Luther's teaching, in following which nobody need despair, nobody, Herr Esch! for everyone carried the divine spark somewhere in his soul, and—the strength with which Major von Pasenow felt this he was unable even to express—no one was shut out from grace, and everyone who was granted grace might go forth to preach redemption. And any man who looked deeply into his own heart would recognize the truth and the way; and Esch too would find his way to the light and follow it. " Be comforted, Herr Editor," he said, " it will all turn out for the best." And he would be glad to talk to Herr Esch again if Herr Esch should desire it and his own scanty leisure permitted—the Major had risen and reached Esch his hand across the desk—besides he would be coming presently to have a look over the publishing office of the *Kur-Trier Herald*. He nodded to Esch. Esch remained irresolutely standing, and the Major feared a speech of thanks. But he received no thanks, for Esch asked almost roughly: " And my friends? " The Major once more became slightly official: " Later, Herr Esch, later perhaps." And Esch bowed awkwardly and retired.

Nevertheless for a man so radically impetuous as Esch there was no hanging back after this. When a few days later—to the astonishment of everybody who heard of it, and that was presently the whole town— he joined the Protestant Church, it seemed to his ardent soul an act of homage to the Major at the same time.

CHAPTER LV

DISINTEGRATION OF VALUES (7)

Historical Excursus.

That criminal and rebellious age known as the Renaissance, that age in which the Christian scheme of values was broken in two halves, one Catholic and the other Protestant, that age in which with the falling asunder of the medieval organon a process of dissolution destined to go on for five centuries was inaugurated and the seeds of the modern world planted, that age at once of sowing and of first blossoming cannot be comprehensively subsumed either under its Protestantism or its individualism or its nationalism or its joyous sensuousness, or even under its revival of humanism and natural science: if that age, which in its style presented such an obvious appearance of unity, and is now regarded as a coherent whole, possessed a homogeneous spirit commensurable with that unity and producing that style, it is certainly not to be found in any one phenomenon selected from its various manifestations, not even in a phenomenon of such profound revolutionary force as Protestantism; rather must all these phenomena be referred to a common denominator, they must all possess a common root, and that root must have lain in the logical structure of thought itself, in that specific logic which penetrated and informed all the activities of the epoch.

Now it may be asserted with some confidence that a sweeping revolution in the style of thinking—and the revolutionary aspect of all these phenomena entitles us to infer such a complete revolution in thinking—invariably results from the fact that thought has reached its provisional limit of infinity, that it is no longer able to resolve the antinomies of infinity by the old methods, and so is compelled to revise its own basic principles.

We have before our own eyes a very clear example of such a process in the research into first principles of modern mathematics, which, starting from the antinomies of infinity, has achieved a revolution of mathematical method whose extent cannot yet be estimated. True, it is impossible to decide whether here we are dealing with a new revolution in thought, or with the final and definitive liquidation of medieval logic (probably with both). For not only has a residue of medieval values survived right up to our time, giving room for the assumption that its concomitant ways of thinking have also survived; it is to be remarked as well that the paradox of all antinomies and the very essence of the antinomies of infinity is the fact that they derive from the deductive method: but that means that they derive from theological method, for there is no world system of theology that is not deductive, in other words that does not seek by reason to deduce all phenomena from a supreme principle, from God; and in the last resort every form of Platonism is thus deductive theology. So even if the Platonic-theological content in the system of modern mathematics is not immediately visible, and perhaps must even remain invisible while mathematics remains an adequate expression of the logic that prevails over mathematics as well as over everything else, yet there is a striking affinity between the antinomies of infinity postulated by mathematics and those of medieval scholasticism. The medieval discussion of the infinite, of course, did not take place on the mathematical plane (or only parenthetically, in cosmic speculations), but the " ethical " infinite, as one may venture to call it, such as is implied in the perennial problem of the infinite attributes of God, includes all the questions about actual and potential infinity and posits the same structural limitations that puzzle modern mathematics and provide its antinomies. In both cases the substance of the antinomy arises from the absoluteness with which logic is applied, an absoluteness that cannot be avoided so long as logic prevails, and that can be recognized only when the antinomian limits are reached. Among the scholastics this misleading absolutism found expression chiefly in the interpretation of symbols: the concreteness of the Church in its earthly and finite form that nevertheless claimed to be absolute could not but draw in its train a finite limitation of all symbolic forms, and though the result was a system of marvellous symbol-mirages, a system rising from symbol to symbol, overshadowed and bound in a magical unity by the heavenly-earthly, infinite-finite symbol of the Eucharist, yet it could not stave off inevitable collapse; for at its antinomian limits of infinity scholastic thought had to break down, to turn back and solve once more through dialectic the now finite Platonic idea, that is to say, to prepare the reaction towards Positivism, and to enter on that automatic development whose beginnings were already visible in the Aristotelian formation of the Church, and whose further progress, in spite of manifold attempts by the scholastics to hold it up (the theory of twofold truth, the quarrel between nominalists and realists, Occam's new formulation of the theory of knowledge) could no longer be checked; scholastic thought had to founder on its own absolutism, its own antinomies of infinity,—its logic was abrogated.

But thought corresponds to reality only for so long as its logicalness remains undisputed. This applies to all thinking, not merely to deductive dialectic (all the more as it is impossible to distinguish how much deduction is inherent in any act of thinking). It would be wrong, however, to say that deduction became suspect because people had suddenly learned to look at facts with different and better eyes; the exact reverse is the case: things are only regarded with different eyes once dialectic has broken down, and that breakdown occurs not at the point where thought interprets reality, since reality would go on indefinitely submitting itself to such interpretation, but anterior to that, in thought's own province of logic, namely in face of the problems raised by infinity. The patience with which mankind suffers the authority of logic is simply inexhaustible and can be compared only to the imperturbable patience with which it submits to the art of medicine: and just as the human body confides itself to the most nonsensical medical cures, and is actually cured by them, so reality submits to the erection of the most impossible theoretic structures,—and so long as the theory does not itself declare its bankruptcy it will be supported with confidence, and reality will remain tractable. Only after bankruptcy has been openly declared does man begin to rub his eyes and look once more at reality; only then does he seek the source of knowledge in living experience instead of in ratiocination.

These two phases of spiritual revolution can be clearly perceived in the declining years of the Middle Ages: the bankruptcy of scholastic dialectic, and thereafter the—truly Copernican—rotation of attention to the immediate object. Or, in other words, it is the change from Platonism to Positivism, from the speech of God to the language of things.

Yet with this change from the centralization of an ecclesiastical organon to the multifariousness of direct experience, with this transition from the Platonic pattern of medieval theocracy to the positivist contemplation of the empirically given and endlessly shifting world, with this atomizing of a former whole, there had to be a concurrent atomizing of value-systems in so far as these were related to object-systems. In short, values are no longer determined by a central authority, but take their colouring from the object: what matters is no longer the conservation of Biblical cosmogony, but the " scientific " observation of natural objects and the experiments that can be carried out on them; the politician is no longer concerned to model a divine state, but to manage a newly autonomous political unit that makes inevitable the emergence of new and efficient political methods in the shape of Machia-vellianism; the warrior is no longer concerned with absolute war, such as took concrete shape in the Crusades, but with earthly squabbles carried on with new-fangled and unchivalrous weapons, such as fire-arms; no longer is it Christendom as a whole that is in question, but only certain empirical groups of men held together by the external bond of national language; nor is it man as the member of an ecclesiastical organon that the new individualism studies, but man as an individual in himself with his individual significance; and lastly the aim of art is no longer solely and finally the glorification of the community of saints, but the faithful observation of the external world, that faithfulness of representation which constitutes the naturalism of the Renaissance. Yet worldly as this obsession with the immediate object may seem, even purely pagan as it perhaps struck people at the time, so pagan that the newly discovered ancients were joyfully invoked as confeder-ates, the inner object forced itself upon men's attention with no less violence than the outer, indeed the immediacy of experience in the

Renaissance is perhaps most immediate of all in its introspection: with this inward turning of the eye, with this discovery of the divine spark in the soul, God, who hitherto had been allowed to manifest Himself only through the medium of an ecclesiastical Platonic hierarchy, now became the object of immediate mystical apprehension, the re-won assurer of divine grace,—and this extraordinary juxtaposition of the most extreme pagan worldliness with the most unconditional inwardness of Protestant mysticism, this co-existence of the most disparate tendencies within the same province of style, would certainly be quite inexplicable were it not that it can be referred to the common denominator of immediacy. Like all other phenomena of the Renaissance, and perhaps in still greater measure than the others, Protestantism is a phenomenon of immediacy.

But yet another and very decisive characteristic of that epoch may here find its determining cause: the glorification of " action," the phenomenon of the " deed," which is so conspicuous in all expressions of life in the Renaissance, and not least in Protestantism; that nascent contempt for the word which tries to confine the function of language as far as possible to its autonomous realms of poetry and rhetoric, refusing it access to other spheres and substituting for it as sole operating factor the man who acts; that movement towards a dumbness which was to prepare the way for the dumbness of a whole world: all this stands in a relation which cannot be ignored to the disintegration of the world into separate value-systems, and follows from that changing-over to the language of things which, to keep the metaphor, is a dumb language. It is almost like a testimony to the fact that any understanding between the separate value-systems was superfluous, or as though such an understanding might falsify the severity and singleness of the language of things. The two great rational vehicles of understanding in the modern world, the language of science in mathematics and the language of money in book-keeping, both find their starting-point in the Renaissance, both arise from that single and exclusive concentration on a single value-system, from that esoteric theory of expression, which might be called ascetic in its severity. Yet such an attitude had little in common with the asceticism of Catholic monks, for unlike the latter it was not a means to an end, not a device for summoning ecstatic " aid," but sprang from the singleness of action, of that " action " which was thenceforth accounted the sole unambiguous language and the sole determining force. So Protestantism also by its origin and its nature is an " action "; it presupposes a religiously active man, seeking God, finding God, a man endowed with the same positive activity as the new scientific researcher, or, indeed, the new type of soldier or politician. Luther's religion was through and through that of a man of action, and at bottom anything but contemplative. But even in the heart of the action, at the core of this matter-of-fact sense of actuality, there lay the same severity, the same categorical imperative of duty, the same exclusion of all other value-systems; that literally iconoclastic asceticism of a Calvin which one might almost call an epistemological asceticism, and which drove Erasmus to the point of insisting that music should be excluded from the service of God.

Yet the Middle Ages too had recognized the force of action. And no matter how violently the new positivism recoiled from Platonic scholasticism, in referring the individual to the solitary authority of his ego it also laid bare the " positivist roots " of Platonism. The new Christianity did not merely protest, it reformed as well, it looked upon itself throughout as a Renaissance of the Christian idea; and although at first it had no theology, it developed later, on a more autonomous and restricted basis, a purely Platonic and idealistic theology: for that is what Kantian philosophy amounts to. So the orientation of values, the ethical imperative directing action, remained the same as in the Middle Ages, and indeed could not have changed, for value consists only in the effective will to value and to unconditionality—there are no values save absolute values. What had changed was the delimitation of the value-producing action: hitherto the intensity of human aspiration towards the absolute had been concentrated on the total value of the Christian organon; now, however, all the radicality of a self-dependent logic, all the severity of autonomy, was directed to each system of values separately, each value-system was raised to an absolute value of its own, and that vehemence was engendered which was to maintain these absolute values side by side in isolation without reference to each other, that vehemence which gives the age of the Renaissance its characteristic colouring.

Of course it could be objected that the general style of the age embraced indifferently all the disparate value-systems, that the personality of Luther, for instance, was by no means ascetically limited to one single system, but strikingly united in a characteristic fashion both religious and worldly impulses. In return it could be just as reasonably asserted that we are dealing here with the mere beginnings of a movement that needed five hundred years for its full development, that the age was still full of yearning for the medieval synthesis, and that it was precisely a personality like Luther's, a personality subsuming in itself the most disparate tendencies, not by force of logic but by virtue of its human breadth, that met the needs of the age half way, and dominated and influenced it to an incomparably greater degree than the more " logical " Calvin. It is as if the age were still full of fear in face of the new " severity " and the approaching dumbness of the world, as if it wanted to shout down that dreadful approaching dumbness, and for this reason, perhaps, had to bring to birth the new language of God, the new polyphonic music. But these are assumptions that cannot be proved. On the other hand it can be taken for granted that this uncertain state of the age, this confusion of inchoate impulses, made possible the Counter-reformation; that the fear of approaching loneliness and isolation opened the way for a movement which promised to regain the lost unity. For the Counter-reformation took upon itself the gigantic task of gathering in again the value-systems excluded by the narrow and ascetic religiousness of Protestantism, of attempting a new synthesis of the world and all its values, and, under the guidance of the new Jesuit scholasticism, of once more striving towards the lost medieval wholeness, so that, enthroned as the supreme value, the Platonic unity of the Church might maintain for ever its divine position above all other values of the world.

CHAPTER LVI

The watchmaker Samwald often came out to the hospital now. He lingered at the places where his brother had been tended, and, wishful to show his gratitude, not only regulated the clocks of the hospital free of cost, but also offered to repair gratis the inmates' watches. And then he went to see Gödicke of the Landwehr.

Gödicke looked forward to these visits. Since the funeral many things had become clearer and less disturbing to him: the earthly part of his life had become more solid, and yet it seemed to be growing loftier and airier, without losing any of its stability. He knew now quite clearly that he need no longer be terrified at the looming darkness behind which stood that other Gödicke, or more precisely the many Gödickes of yore, for that dark barrier was nothing but the period during which he had lain in the grave. And should anyone come up and try to remind him of what was on the other side, of what had happened before his burial, he need no longer have any fear, but could, as it were, dismiss it with a shrug of the shoulders, knowing that it had ceased to be of any consequence. All that he had to do was to bide his time, for he need not dread the life that was condensing round him now, even when it pressed quite close upon him; for he had already put death behind him, and everything that came would simply serve to build the scaffolding yet higher. True, he still did not utter a word, nor did he listen when the sisters of his ward-mates addressed him; but his deafness and dumbness were now far less a defence of his ego and his solitude than an advertisement of his contempt for those who disturbed his peace. The watchmaker Samwald was the only one he tolerated, indeed he looked forward to his coming.

Samwald certainly made things easy for him. Even though Gödicke walked with his body bent, leaning on his two sticks, he could look down on the little watchmaker; but that was not what mattered most. More important was the fact that Samwald, as though he knew whom he was dealing with, made not the slightest attempt to question him or to remind him of anything that he, Ludwig Gödicke, did not like. In truth Samwald was not a great talker at any time. As they sat together on a seat in the garden he would show Gödicke a watch that he had taken over for repair, making the cover fly open so that one could see the works, and trying to explain where the defect lay. Or he would speak of his dead brother, who, so he said, was to be envied, for he had got over his troubles and was now in a happier land. But when the watchmaker Samwald went on to speak of Paradise and its heavenly joys, on the one hand that was to be discountenanced, for it pertained to the confirmation class attended by a long-discarded Ludwig Gödicke, yet on the other hand it was a sort of homage to the man Gödicke, like a question addressed to one who was already on the farther side and knew all about it. And when Samwald spoke of Bible gatherings which he was in the custom of attending and from which he derived much enlightenment, when he maintained that the misery of this war must finally lead to a brighter day of salvation, Gödicke did not bother to listen; yet it was vaguely a kind of corroboration of his new-won life, and a challenge to take up in that life a fitting and as it were a post-mortem position. The little watchmaker seemed to him then like one of the lads or women who carried the hods of bricks to the wall, and whom one never talked to civilly but merely ordered about, yet whom one needed nevertheless. This too may have been the reason why he once interrupted the little watchmaker in his stories with the order: " Bring me a beer," and when the beer did not promptly arrive he stared in front of him in incomprehending indignation. For many days he was angry with Samwald and refused to look at him, and Samwald racked his brains trying to find some way of propitiating Gödicke again. That was difficult enough. For Gödicke did not himself know that he was angry with Samwald, and he suffered a great deal from the fact that under the compulsion of an unknown decree he had to turn his face away whenever Samwald appeared. And it was not that he regarded Samwald as the originator of the decree; but he blamed him most bitterly for the fact that the decree was not rescinded. It was a sort of laborious search for each other that arose between the two men, and it was almost an inspiration of the watchmaker's when one day he seized Gödicke by the hand and led him away.

It was a fine warm afternoon, and the watchmaker Samwald led Gödicke the one-time bricklayer by the sleeve of his tunic, cautiously, step by step, taking care to avoid the jagged flint-stones on the road. Sometimes they rested. And when they had rested for a while Samwald tugged at Gödicke's sleeve, and Gödicke got up and they went on again. In this way they arrived at Esch's house.

The ladder leading up to the editorial office was too steep for Gödicke, so Samwald deposited him on the bench in front of the garden and ascended alone: he came back presently with Esch and Fendrich. " This is Gödicke," said Samwald. Gödicke made no sign. Esch led them towards the summer-house. But in front of the two forcing frames, whose glass covers were open, for Esch had been sowing for the autumn crop, Gödicke remained standing, gazing into their depths at the bottom of which lay the brown mould. Esch said: " Well? " But Gödicke still went on staring into the frames. So they all remained standing, bareheaded and in their dark suits, as though they were gathered round an open grave. Samwald said: " It was Herr Esch who started the Bible class . . . we are all seeking guidance from Heaven." Then Gödicke laughed, he did not laugh scornfully, it was only perhaps a somewhat noisy laugh, and he said: " Ludwig Gödicke, arisen from the dead," he did not say it very loudly, and he looked triumphantly at Esch, more, he straightened himself from his humble and bowed posture and was almost as big as Esch. Fendrich, who carried the Bible under his arm, regarded him with the feverish eyes of a consumptive, and then he softly touched Gödicke's uniform, as though he wished to make certain that Gödicke was really present in the flesh. But for Gödicke that seemed to finish the matter, he had done his part, it had not even been a very great strain, he could afford to rest now, and so he simply let himself down on the wooden edge of the frame, waiting for Samwald to sit down beside him. Samwald said: " He's tired," and Esch went with long strides back into the courtyard and shouted up to Frau Esch at the kitchen window to bring some coffee. Then Frau Esch brought out coffee, and they fetched Herr Lindner too from the printing-shed to drink coffee with them, and they stood round Gödicke while he sat on the edge of the frame, and gazed at him sipping his coffee. And none of them saw what Gödicke saw. And after Gödicke had been refreshed by the coffee Samwald once more took him by the hand, and they set out on their way back to the hospital. They went cautiously, and Samwald saw to it that Gödicke did not step on the jagged flints. Sometimes they rested. And when Samwald smiled at his companion, Gödicke no longer turned his eyes away.

CHAPTER LVII

Yes, Huguenau was in a very bad humour. The printed appeals for the Iron Bismarck had been wretchedly botched. That the printing-office did not possess a block of Bismarck's head was perhaps excusable, but not even a proper Iron Cross with laurel wreath complete was to be found in the place, and so there had been nothing for it but to embellish each of the four corners of the appeal with one of the little Iron Crosses usually employed to mark the death notices of soldiers killed in the war. He wouldn't have gone personally with the miserable sheet to the Major at all if he hadn't had a piece of good news as well: a firm of carvers in Giessen, whose advertisement he had discovered and to whom he had immediately wired, were prepared to supply a Bismarck statue within two weeks. But naturally enough the Major must have been deeply disappointed by the tasteless appeal; at first he had not even listened to Huguenau, and had dismissed his excuses with an ill-humoured and indifferent: " It doesn't matter." And even though he had finally condescended to fix his visit for to-day, yet he had spoilt it immediately by inquiring after Esch. That was all the more unjust, seeing that Esch himself was to blame for the lack of decent blocks in the printing-office.

His hands in his trousers-pockets, Huguenau strolled up and down the courtyard and waited for the Major. As for Esch, he had manœuvred him out of the way quite nicely. It had been quite a sly move to dissuade him the day before from going out to the paper factory—and then to-day one found that it had been a mistake after all, and that strangely enough there was a shortage of paper, and so the Herr Editor had just had to go. Unfortunately the lout had considered it necessary to take his bicycle, and if the Major put off coming for very much longer the whole manœuvre would be up the spout, and the two of them would meet after all.

It was a warm sultry day. Huguenau looked now and then at his watch, then he went into the garden, surveyed the fruit, which hung on the branches still unripe, and estimated the crop. Well, in these times things would never be allowed to ripen; long before that everything would be stolen. One fine morning Esch would find his garden cleared out. It wouldn't be long either; on the sunny side the plums were already reddening, and Huguenau put up his hand and tested the fruit between his fingers. Esch should put barbed wire round his garden; but the crop was certainly not worth so much expense. After the war barbed wire would be cheap enough.

Waiting is like barbed wire stretched inside one. Huguenau looked once more up into the branches, blinked up at the grey clouds; where the sun should be they brightened to a dazzling white. He whistled for Marguerite several times; but she did not appear and Huguenau became annoyed; of course she was down at the river again with those boys. He felt inclined to go and fetch her. But he had to wait for the Major.

Suddenly—he was just on the point of whistling for her again—Marguerite stood before him. He said severely: " Where have you been hiding again? There's visitors coming." Then he took her hand, and crossing the courtyard they went through the entry hall to the street and kept watch for the Major. I sent Esch off too soon, Huguenau could not help telling himself again and again.

At last the Major appeared round the corner; he was accompanied by the aged commissariat officer, who also filled the rôle of adjutant to the Town Commandant. Although Huguenau had reckoned on having the Major to himself, he felt nevertheless flattered that the visit should take such an official form. Really it had been stupid to let Esch go, the whole staff should have formed up in line and Marguerite in a white dress should have presented a bouquet of flowers. In some way or other Esch was responsible for this omission too, but there it was, anyhow, and Huguenau's ceremonial fervour had to be confined to a few low bows when the two officers stopped in front of the house.

Fortunately the commissariat officer said good-bye at the door, so that the occasion ceased to be official and became private, and when the Major crossed the threshold Huguenau fairly shone with affability and devotion. " Marguerite, make a curtsy," he commanded. Marguerite stared into the strange man's face. The Major ran his fingers through her black curls: " Well, won't you say how do you do, little Tartar? " Huguenau apologized: " It's Esch's little girl. . . ." The Major raised Marguerite's chin: " So you're Herr Esch's daughter? " " She's only staying here—a sort of foster-child," Huguenau said. The Major stroked her curls again: " Little black Tartar," he repeated as they passed through the entry to the courtyard. " French by birth, Herr Major . . . Esch intends to adopt her eventually . . . but that's unnecessary, she has an aunt in any case . . . wouldn't Herr Major like to see the printing-office straight away? please step this way, to the right. . . ." Huguenau ran in front. " Very well, Herr Huguenau," said the Major, " but I should like to say good-day to Herr Esch first." " Esch will be here in a few minutes, Herr Major, I thought that the Herr Major would like to look over the printing-shop first without being disturbed." " Herr Esch does not disturb me in the least," said the Major, and Huguenau was dashed by his somewhat sharp tone. Esch must have been intriguing somehow . . . well, he would soon get on his track yet and then there would be a full-flavoured secret report number 2. And because such a report was a certainty, Huguenau felt reassured, for no one can endure this inner stream of events to be held up or dammed by external forces. And so Huguenau said formally: " Herr Esch unfortunately had to go to the paper factory . . . I had to make sure that the paper would be delivered . . . but perhaps the Herr Major would like to inspect the printing-shop meanwhile."

The press was set in motion in honour of the Major, and in honour of the Major Huguenau quite gratuitously had a section of the appeal for " The Moselle Memorial Association " run off. He still held Marguerite by the hand, and when Lindner drew off the first sheets of the appeal, Huguenau lifted the uppermost one and held it out to the Major. He felt compelled to apologize once more: " It's a very simple make-up,

I'm afraid; at the very least it should have had a proper Iron Cross
with a laurel wreath . . . in a matter under the immediate patronage of
the Herr Major."

The Major had put up his hand to the Iron Cross at his buttonhole
and seemed reassured to find it still hanging there. " Oh, the Iron Cross
—you don't need another, surely that would be superfluous." Huguenau
bowed: " Yes, the Herr Major is quite right, in such difficult times a
modest make-up will have to do, I can only agree with the Herr Major
there, but a modest little block wouldn't have added much to the outlay
. . . of course that's a matter of indifference to Herr Esch." The Major
did not seem to have heard. But after a while he said: " I think, Herr
Huguenau, that you do Herr Esch an injustice." Huguenau smiled
politely and a little scornfully. But the Major was not looking at him,
but at Marguerite: " I would have taken her for a Slav, this little black
Tartar girl." Huguenau felt called upon to mention once more that the
child was French by birth. " She only comes here." The Major bent
down to Marguerite: " I've a little girl like you at home too, she's a
little bigger, it's true, fourteen . . . and not as black as a little Tartar
either . . . her name is Elisabeth . . ." and after a while he said: " So,
a little French girl." " She can only speak German," said Huguenau,
" she's forgotten everything." The Major asked: " And do you love
your foster-parents very much? " " Yes," said Marguerite, and Huguenau
was astonished that she could tell such a lie, but as the Major seemed
absent-minded he repeated distinctly: " She stays with her relations."
The Major said: " Driven from home . . ." that really sounded somewhat absent-minded, he was an old gentleman after all, and Huguenau
said in corroboration: " Quite true, Herr Major, the right phrase, driven
from home. . . ." The Major looked at Marguerite attentively. Huguenau
said alluringly: " The case-room, Herr Major, you haven't seen the
case-room yet." The Major passed his hand over the child's brow:
" You mustn't look so cross, you mustn't wrinkle up your brow like
that . . . " the child considered earnestly and then said: " Why not? "
The Major smiled, passed his fingers lightly over her eyelids, under
which the hard eyeballs rested, smiled and said: " Little girls mustn't
have furrows on their brows . . . that's a sin . . . hidden and yet visible,
that's what sin always is." Marguerite recoiled and Huguenau remembered how she had broken away from Esch; she was quite right, he
thought. The Major now passed his hand over his own eyes: " Well, it

doesn't matter . . ." and Huguenau felt that the Major too was struggling to break away, though with feeble powers, and he was actually glad when he saw Esch on his rather too low bicycle, which made him look bandy-legged, riding into the courtyard and springing off by the outside ladder.

They all went into the courtyard to greet Esch; the Major stood between Huguenau and the little girl.

Esch leant his bicycle against the wall beneath the ladder and went slowly up to the group. He showed no trace of surprise at finding the Major there, so little surprise did he show and so calmly did he greet the guest, that Huguenau began to suspect that this lean schoolmaster already knew of the visit. So he gave vent to his ill-humour:

"What do you say to this unexpected honour? Aren't you even surprised?"

"I'm very glad," said Esch.

The Major said:

"I'm very glad that you've returned in time, Herr Esch."

Esch said gravely:

"Perhaps at the eleventh hour, Herr Major."

Huguenau said:

"It isn't so very late yet . . . would the Herr Major like to see the other offices too? the ladder, I'm afraid, is a little awkward."

Esch said:

"It was a long way."

The child said:

"He came on his bicycle."

The Major said dreamily:

"A long way . . . and he is not yet at the goal."

Huguenau said:

"We've the worst already behind us . . . we've two pages of advertise-ments already . . . and if we could secure the orders of the military authorities as well . . ."

Esch said:

"It's not a question of advertisements."

Huguenau said:

"We haven't even a block of an Iron Cross—I suppose you think that doesn't matter either!"

The child pointed at the Major's chest:

" There's an Iron Cross."

The Major said:

" The true badge of honour is always invisible, only sin is visible."

The child said:

" Lying is the greatest sin."

Esch said:

" The invisible is at our backs, we come out of falsehood, and if we do not find the way we must lose ourselves in the darkness of the invisible."

The child said:

" Nobody hears you when you tell a lie."

The Major said:

" God hears it."

Huguenau said:

" Nobody hears a deserter, nobody recognizes him, even if all he says is right."

Esch said:

" Nobody can see another in the darkness."

The Major said:

" Visible, and yet hidden from each other."

The child said:

" God doesn't hear it."

Esch said:

" He will hear again the voices of His children."

Huguenau said:

" It's best for nobody to hear one, one must fight one's way by oneself . . . we'll bring it off yet."

The Major said:

" We have forsaken Him and He has left us to ourselves . . . so alone that we can no longer find each other."

Esch said:

" Imprisoned in our loneliness."

The child said:

" No one will be able to find me."

The Major said:

" The one we forsake we must seek for ever."

Huguenau said:

" Do you want to hide? "

" Yes," said the child.

The milky grey sky began to break up; in several places it became blue. Barefooted and inaudible, the little girl had flitted away. Then the men went too. Each in a different direction.

CHAPTER LVIII

STORY OF THE SALVATION ARMY GIRL IN BERLIN (9)

Well, they were with me again yesterday, Nuchem and Marie, and we sang together. At my suggestion we sang first of all the hymn:

> To battle out we march elate,
> Firm faith our dauntless gage,
> We do not fear the Devil's hate,
> And laugh at all his rage.
> Our banner proudly waves before
> And fills our souls with might;
> Still in the forefront as of yore,
> It leads us to the fight.

> *Chorus*
> We will be faithful to our King,
> Till death we will be true,
> And follow on through everything
> Our flag gold, red and blue.

We sang it to the air of Andreas Hofer's song, Marie accompanied it on the lute, Nuchem hummed and beat time with his soft smooth hands. During the singing they exchanged glances a few times, but it may have been that I only fancied so, for Dr Litwak's talk had made me suspicious. At any rate I bawled out the song as loud as I could, and that for various reasons. For on the one hand I wanted to reassure Nuchem's family, who doubtless were assembled outside my door by this time: the children in the very front, probably, with their ears pressed against the door panel, then the white-bearded grandfather with his body bent forward, his hand forming an ear-trumpet, while the women kept more in the background, perhaps one of them weeping quietly to herself, the whole bunch gradually drawing nearer, yet not daring to open the door,—yes, on the one hand I wanted to reassure them, but on the other hand it was a sadistic pleasure to me to know that they were out there, and to allure and repulse them at the same moment. But by bawling so loudly I wished also to say to Nuchem and Marie: don't stand on ceremony, my children, you see that I'm occupied with myself and my voice, unbutton your frock-coat, Nuchem, lift the tails of your coat and make a bow to the lady, and you, Marie, throw off your prudishness, lift your skirt with two fingers, and dance, both of you, dance to Jerusalem, dance in my bed, make yourselves at home. And so I no longer even sang Marie's words to the air, but my own, the authentic ones: " To Mantua in chains was led, Brave Hofer leal and true," unfortunately that was all I knew, but I modulated these lines to the tune and found that they went beautifully.

At last, however, Marie concluded the song with the flourish that always rounds off songs sung to the lute, and she said:

" We did that splendidly, now as a reward we'll have a little prayer too."

And already she had slipped down on her knees before her chair, raised her clasped hands to her face, and begun the hundred and twenty-second psalm :

" I was glad when they said unto me, Let us go into the house of the Lord. Our feet shall stand within thy gates, O Jerusalem. Jerusalem is builded as a city that is compact together: Whither the tribes go up, the tribes of the Lord, unto the testimony of Israel, to give thanks unto the name of the Lord."

I could not have stopped her except by smashing the lute over her head. So I knelt down too, stretched my arms out and prayed: " Let us make tea for the daughters and young men of Israel, let us pour rum into the tea, war-rum, hero's rum, synthetic rum, that we may forget our loneliness, for our loneliness is too great, whether it be in Zion or in the holy city of Berlin." But while I was uttering these words and beating my breast with my fists, Nuchem had got up: he planted himself before me, he turned his bottom to me, and with his praying countenance fixed on the open window, at which the greasy and torn curtains fluttered in the night breeze like a faded gold, red and blue army banner, he set his swaying body in motion. Oh, that was indecent, that was indecent of Nuchem, who after all was my friend.

I sprang to the door, tore it open and shouted:

" Come in, Israel, drink tea with us, behold the obscene postures of my friend and the unveiled face of the lady."

The lobby, however, the lobby was empty. They had slipped away, they had scattered into their rooms, the women tumbling over the children, the rheumatic grandfather, who could not straighten himself, along with them.

" Splendid," said I, closing the door and turning once more to my familiar spirits, " splendid, my children, now give each other the kiss of Zion."

But the two of them stood there with their arms hanging, and did not dare to seize each other or to dance; smiling sheepishly they simply stood there. And finally we sat down and drank tea.

CHAPTER LIX

THE SYMPOSIUM OR DIALOGUE ON REDEMPTION

Incapable of communicating himself to others, incapable of breaking out of his isolation, doomed to remain the mere actor of his life, the deputy of his own ego—all that any human being can know of another is a mere symbol, the symbol of an ego that remains beyond our grasp, possessing no more value than that of a symbol; and all that can be told is the symbol of a symbol, a symbol at a second, third, nth remove, asking for representation in the true double sense of the word. Therefore it will raise no difficulty for anyone, and will at least make for brevity, if we imagine that Herr and Frau Esch together with the Major and Herr Huguenau find themselves in a scene on the stage, involved in a performance which no human being can escape: that of play-acting.

At the table in ESCH'S *summer-house are sitting* FRAU ESCH, *on her right the* MAJOR, *on her left* HUGUENAU, *opposite her (with his back to the audience)* HERR ESCH. *The evening meal is over. On the table are the bread and the wine, the latter of which* HERR ESCH *has procured from a vineyard proprietor who advertises in his paper.*

Darkness is beginning to fall. In the background the contours of the mountains can still be discerned. Two candles burn within glass globes to protect them from the breeze: moths flutter round them. The jerky asthmatic pounding of the printing-press can be heard.

ESCH: May I fill your glass again, Herr Major?

HUGUENAU: Tip-top wine, no doubt about it . . . we Alsatians must take a back seat after this when our wine is mentioned. Does the Herr Major know our Alsatian wine?

MAJOR (*absently*): I don't think so.

HUGUENAU: Well, it's a harmless wine . . . we Alsatians are altogether harmless . . . an honest tipple you could call it, all frank and above-board (*he laughs*) and all it does to you is to make you simply and naturally tight . . . you go to sleep when you've had enough, that's all.

ESCH: To be drunk is never natural, it's a poisoned state.

HUGUENAU: Well, well, I can remember occasions when you were quite willing to take a glass or two over the score . . . for instance . . . well, may I mention the Palatine Tavern, Herr Esch? . . . besides (*he regards* ESCH *attentively*) you don't strike me as being so free from poison as all that.

MAJOR: Your attacks on our friend Esch are very regrettable, Herr Huguenau.

ESCH: Don't mind him, Herr Major, he's not in earnest.

HUGUENAU: Yes, I am in earnest . . . I always say straight out what I think . . . our friend Esch is a wolf in sheep's clothing . . . yes, I stick to that . . . and, by your leave, he has his little orgies in private.

ESCH (*contemptuously*): No wine has ever upset my applecart yet. . . .

HUGUENAU: That's you all over, Herr Esch, trying to keep sober so that you don't give yourself away.

ESCH: . . . now and then I may take a drop too much, yes, and then the world becomes so simple that you would think it was made of nothing but truth . . . as simple as in a dream . . . simple and yet brazenly full of false names . . . the right names for things aren't to be found. . . .

HUGUENAU: You'd better drink consecrated wine, then you'd soon find those names of yours . . . or the future Socialist State, if that's what you're after.

MAJOR: One shouldn't blaspheme even in jest . . . even wine and bread are symbols of the divine.

(HUGUENAU *notices his mistake and reddens.*)

FRAU ESCH: Oh, Herr Major, it's always like this when Herr Huguenau and my husband are together . . . chaff may be a sign of friendship, but sometimes it's really past endurance, the way he drags in the mud everything that is holy to my poor husband.

HUGUENAU: Holy! Pure sham! (*He has once more regained his composure and ceremoniously relights his cigar which has gone out.*)

ESCH (*possessed by his train of thought*): The truth that comes to you in dreams walks on crutches . . . (*he strikes on the table*) the whole world goes on crutches . . . a hobbling monstrosity . . .

HUGUENAU (*interested*): An invalid?

ESCH: . . . if there is even one single error in the world, if at any point at all the false passes for true, then . . . yes, then the whole world is false . . . then everything becomes unreal . . . diabolically conjured away. . . .

HUGUENAU: Abracadabra, it's gone. . . .

MAJOR (*without paying any attention to* HUGUENAU): No, friend Esch, it's the opposite way about: there need be only one righteous man among a thousand sinners . . .

HUGUENAU: . . . the great magician Esch. . . .

ESCH (*rudely*): What do you know about magic? (*shouts at him*) I should think you're more like a conjurer, a juggler, a knife-thrower. . . .

HUGUENAU: Herr Esch, you are in company, remember yourself.

ESCH (*more calmly*): Magic and juggling are devil's work, they're the real evil, they make the confusion still worse . . .

MAJOR: Where knowledge fails, that is where evil begins. . . .

ESCH: . . . but first the man must come who will blot out every error and bring order, who will take upon him the sacrificial death, that the world may be redeemed to a new innocence, so that from the dead new life may arise. . . .

MAJOR: The one who will take the penance upon him . . . (*with assurance*) but He has already come: it was He who destroyed false knowledge and drove out the magicians . . .

ESCH: . . . the darkness still remains, and in the darkness the world is collapsing . . . nailed to the cross and in the hour of final loneliness pierced by the spear. . . .

HUGUENAU: Hm, very unpleasant.

MAJOR: A dreadful darkness was round Him, a half-light of heavy uncertainty, and no one approached Him in His loneliness to help Him . . . yet He took man's sin upon Him, He redeemed the world from sin . . .

ESCH: . . . there has been nothing until now but murder and counter-murder, and order will only come when we awaken. . . .

MAJOR: We must take the penance upon us, we must be awakened out of our sin . . .

ESCH: . . . nothing is decided yet, we are still in prison and we must wait . . .

MAJOR: . . . we are encompassed by sin, and our light is darkness . . .

ᴇꜱcʜ: . . . we are waiting for the Judgment, we still have a respite and can still begin a new life . . . evil has not yet triumphed . . .

ᴍᴀᴊᴏʀ: . . . when we are delivered from the darkness, delivered by grace . . . then evil will vanish as if it had never been . . .

ᴇꜱcʜ: . . . like an evil magic, a corrupt magic . . .

ᴍᴀᴊᴏʀ: . . . evil is always outside the world, outside its frontiers: only the man who steps over the world's frontiers and steps out of the truth can fall into the abyss of evil.

ᴇꜱcʜ: . . . we are standing on the edge of the abyss . . . on the edge of the dark gully . . .

ʜᴜɢᴜᴇɴᴀᴜ: That's too deep for us, what, Frau Esch?

(ꜰʀᴀᴜ ᴇꜱcʜ *smooths her hair back, then lays a finger on her lips as a sign to* ʜᴜɢᴜᴇɴᴀᴜ *to be silent.*)

ᴇꜱcʜ: Many must still die, many must sacrifice themselves, so that room may be made for the son who shall build the house anew . . . only then will the mists thin away and the new life will come, radiant and innocent.

ᴍᴀᴊᴏʀ: The evil we see is only an illusion, it takes many shapes, but it is never really there itself . . . a symbol of nothingness—only divine grace is real.

ʜᴜɢᴜᴇɴᴀᴜ (*who does not intend to be relegated to the part of a silent listener*): Well, if robbery or child-rape or desertion or embezzlement are only illusions, it's a very cheerful outlook.

ᴍᴀᴊᴏʀ: Evil is non-existent . . . divine grace has redeemed the world from evil.

ᴇꜱcʜ: The harder the tribulation, the deeper the darkness, the sharper the whizzing knives, the nearer is the kingdom of redemption.

ᴍᴀᴊᴏʀ: Only the good is real and true . . . there is only one sin: not to desire the good, not to desire knowledge, not to have good-will. . . .

ʜᴜɢᴜᴇɴᴀᴜ (*eagerly*): Yes, Herr Major, that's right . . . myself for instance, I'm certainly no angel . . . (*reflectively*) . . . there's this to be said, in that case one couldn't punish anyone . . . a deserter, for instance, who had good-will couldn't be shot simply to make an example of him.

ᴇꜱcʜ: No one stands so high that he dare judge his fellows, and no one is so depraved that his eternal soul can lose its claim to reverence.

ʜᴜɢᴜᴇɴᴀᴜ: Quite right.

ᴍᴀᴊᴏʀ: The man who desires evil can desire good at the same time, but the man who does not desire good has made divine grace bankrupt . . . it is the sign of obstinacy, inertia of feeling.

ESCH: It's not a matter of good or bad works. . . .

HUGUENAU: I beg your pardon, Herr Major, but that doesn't seem quite to fit the case . . . once I lost six hundred marks in Reutlingen through a man going bankrupt, a tidy sum of money, and why? because the man was mad, he had religious mania, of course I wasn't to know that . . . and right enough, he was acquitted and stuck in a lunatic asylum. But my money was gone.

ESCH: What do you want to infer from that?

HUGUENAU: Why, there you have a good man, and yet he did evil works . . . (*grinning*) and if you were to do me in, Herr Esch, you would be acquitted on the plea of religious mania, but if I were to do you in I would lose my head . . . what do you say to that, Herr Esch, with your sham piety? Hm? (*He glances at the* MAJOR, *seeking approval.*)

MAJOR: The madman is like the dreamer; his truth is a false truth . . . he curses his own child . . . nobody can be the mouthpiece of God without suffering for it . . . he is singled out. . . .

ESCH: He lives in a false reality . . . we are all still living in a false reality . . . by rights we should all be madmen, mad in our loneliness.

HUGUENAU: Yes, but I'll be shot and he won't! I beg your pardon, Herr Major, but that's just where he shows his hypocrisy . . . (*becoming heated*), ah, merde, la sainte religion et les curés à faire des courbettes auprès de la guillotine, ah, merde, alors. . . . I'm an enlightened man, but that's a bit too much for me!

MAJOR: Come, come, Herr Huguenau, this Moselle seems to be dangerous to a man of your temperament (HUGUENAU *makes an apologetic gesture*) . . . to take the penance and the chastisement voluntarily upon us, as we have had to take the war, because we have sinned . . . that isn't hypocrisy.

ESCH (*absently*): Yes, to take men's sins upon you . . . in the final hour of loneliness. . . .

The printing-machine stops: the pounding falls silent; the chirping of the crickets can be heard. A wind stirs the leaves of the fruit-trees. Round the moon a few white irradiated clouds can be seen. In the sudden silence the conversation falls away and ceases.

FRAU ESCH: How good the silence is.

ESCH: Sometimes it seems as if the world were only one huge dreadful machine that never stops . . . the war and everything . . . it runs by laws that we don't understand . . . impudent self-assured laws, engineers' laws . . . every man must do what is prescribed for him, without turning his head to right or left . . . every man is a machine that one can only see from outside, a hostile machine . . . oh, the machine is the root of evil and the Evil One is the machine. Their order is the void that must come . . . before Time can begin again. . . .

MAJOR: Not evil, a symbol of evil. . . .

ESCH: Yes, a symbol.

HUGUENAU (*listening complacently to the sounds from the printing-shop*): Lindner is putting in fresh paper now.

ESCH (*in sudden fear*): Oh, God, is there no possibility of one human being reaching another? is there no fellowship, is there no understanding? Must every man be nothing but an evil machine to his fellows?

MAJOR (*lays his hand comfortingly on* ESCH'S *arm*): But, Esch . . .

ESCH: Oh, God, who is there that doesn't think evilly of me?

MAJOR: Anyone who knows you, my son . . . only knowledge can overcome estrangement.

ESCH (*his hands covering his face*): God, let it be by Thee that I am known.

MAJOR: Only to him who has knowledge will knowledge be given, only he who sows love will reap it.

ESCH (*his hands still clasped before his face*): Since I acknowledge Thee, oh, God, Thou wilt not be angry with me any more, for I am Thy beloved son, rescued by Thee from orphanhood. . . . He who submits himself to death has found love . . . only he who flings himself into a dreadful intensification of estrangement and death . . . will find unity and understanding.

MAJOR: And the divine grace will descend on him and take away his fear, the fear that he is wandering on the earth without meaning or purpose, and must go to the grave unenlightened and helpless and without meaning or purpose. . . .

ESCH: So knowledge will grow to love, and love to knowledge, and every soul that is chosen as the vessel of grace will be inviolable; uplifted by love to join the communion of souls, where each is inviolable and alone and yet united in knowledge—the highest law of knowledge not to wound a living creature: if I have known Thee, God, then I shall live eternally in Thee.

MAJOR: Let mask fall after mask until your heart
And face are open to the eternal breath. . . .

ESCH: I will become an empty vessel drained
Of all desire and solace, I will take
The chastisement upon me, plunge myself
In nothingness and die, but oh, the fear
Is terrible!

MAJOR: Fear is the fruitful sign
Of heavenly grace, fear is God's word inscribed
Upon the gate that leads to your salvation,—
Step through.

ESCH: Accept me, Lord, in my great need.
When the fore-dream of death descends upon me,
A wanderer in life's dream, the fear of death
Leaps on me, I am helpless and alone,
And doomed to die alone, forsaken by all.

(HUGUENAU *listens incomprehendingly and* FRAU ESCH *fearfully to her husband's words.*)

MAJOR: You are not alone, even though you die alone,
Released from evil, fear will leave you too,
You shall decrease that His will may increase,
And as you are known, so also you shall know
The mighty world arisen and manifest.

ESCH: If I could know Thee, Lord, in love through Him
Who knew me in His love, the waste would turn
Into a garden of eternal light,
Boundless the meads, the sun would never set. . . .

MAJOR: Garden of grace encircling all the world,
Basking in soft spring zephyrs, home where all
Fears shall have ceased.

ESCH: I have been a sinner,
Sinful and evil, evil in conscious fear,
Knowing the false way, skirting the edge of the pit,
Face and hands withered, hounded through wastes and gorges,
Fleeing in terror from the dagger's point,
With at my back Ahasuerus' fear,
And in my feet Ahasuerus' dread,

And in my eyes Ahasuerus' lust
For One whom I have lost time and again,
For One I never saw, One I betrayed
And yet who chose me broken and tempest tossed
In the icy tempest of the starry legions,
And sank His grace into me, where it grew,
Grew to redemption, set me free. . . .

MAJOR: Oh, be my brother, the brother that I lost,
Be as a brother to me. . . .

(The two of them chant in antiphony, somewhat in the style of the Salvation Army. The MAJOR *in baritone,* HERR ESCH *in bass.)*

Lord God of Sabaoth,
Take, oh, take us to Thine altar,
Bind us all in one firm band,
Lead us on with Thine own hand,
Lord God of Sabaoth,
Guide our feet lest we may falter,
Lead us to the Promised Land,
Lord God of Sabaoth.

(HUGUENAU, *who until now has beaten time on the table, strikes in (tenor))*:

Keep us safe from axe and halter,
Keep us safe from wheel and brand,
Lord God of Sabaoth.

ALL THREE: Lord God of Sabaoth.

FRAU ESCH *(strikes in (no voice at all))*:

Thou hast given me food and shelter,
All is Thine, if Thou command,
Lord God of Sabaoth.

ALL TOGETHER (HUGUENAU *and* ESCH *beating time on the table)*:

Lord God of Sabaoth,
Save my soul, my spirit,
Save my soul from utter death,
Let not torment sear it,
Let it be in grace baptized,
Nor in sin be e'er chastised,
Keep it whole in merit,

Fan its spark with Thine own breath,
Till it flame in burning faith,
Lord God of Sabaoth,
Save, oh, save Thou me from death.

(*The* MAJOR *has laid his arm round* ESCH'S *shoulder.* HUGUENAU, *his drumming fists still on the table, now slowly lets them fall. The candles have burned down.* FRAU ESCH *pours the last of the wine into the men's glasses, being careful that each receives the same share; the final tiny residue she pours into her husband's glass. The moon is somewhat overcast, and out of the dark landscape the wind blows more coolly now, as though out of a cellar door. Now too the printing-machine once more resumes its pounding, and* FRAU ESCH *touches her husband's arm*): " Shouldn't we go to bed now? "

TRANSFORMATION

Before ESCH'S *house. The* MAJOR *and* HUGUENAU

Huguenau, jerking his thumb towards the window of the Eschs' bedroom:

" Now they're getting into bed. Esch could very well have stayed with us a little longer . . . but she knows what she's after. . . . Hm, will the Herr Major permit me to accompany him for a few steps? A little exercise does one good."

They go through the silent medieval streets. The house entries are like black holes. In one of them, pressed against the door, stand a pair of lovers, from another a dog detaches itself and runs on three legs up the street; at the corner it vanishes. Behind some of the windows a faint light is still burning—but what is happening behind the unlighted ones? perhaps a dead man is lying there, stretched out on his bed, his peaked nose in the air, and the coverlet makes a little tent over his upward-pointing toes. Both the Major and Huguenau gaze up at the windows, and Huguenau would like to ask the Major if he too cannot help thinking of dead men,—but the Major walks on in silence, almost as though he were troubled; probably his thoughts are with Esch, Huguenau tells himself, and he is indignant that Esch should go to bed with his wife and so trouble the good old chap's mind. But devil take it, why should the Major be troubled at all? he makes friends with Esch on the spot instead of keeping that officious hypocrite at arm's-length! A nice friendship, that, between the two of them, between these two fine gentlemen who evidently have forgotten that without him they would never have met each other; who was it, then, that had a prior right to the Major? and if the Major was troubled now, it served him right. More than that, according to his deserts he should be a good deal more troubled, and along with his beloved Herr Esch the Herr Major ought to suffer richly for his treachery. . . . Huguenau stopped short—a daring and seductive idea had arisen before him with clairvoyant lucidity: the idea of entering into a new and venturous relation with the Major that would enable him in a manner of speaking to betray Esch, at present lying with his wife, with the Major, and to land the Major himself in a humiliating situation! yes, a brilliant, a promising idea, and Huguenau said:

" The Herr Major will remember my first report in which I described my visit to the ki . . ." Huguenau clapped his hand over his mouth, " pardon, the public brothel. Herr Esch is sleeping respectably in his matrimonial bed now, but he made one of the party that night, all the same. Since then I've been investigating the matter further, and I think I've found a clue. I would like to have another glance into the place . . . if the Herr Major is interested in the matter and in, how shall I put it, the most interesting milieu, I would most respectfully suggest that he should make a visit of inspection."

The Major let his gaze run once more over the window fronts, over the house doors, which looked like entries to black cellar-caves, and then, to Huguenau's surprise, he said without further ado: " Let us go."

They turned back, for the house lay in the opposite direction and outside the town. The Major again strode on in silence beside Huguenau, he looked perhaps even more troubled than before, and Huguenau, greatly as he longed for a light and confidential tone, dared not even risk starting a conversation. But a still worse disappointment awaited him: when they reached the house, over whose portal a great red lantern shone, the Major abruptly said " No " and held out his hand. And when Huguenau stared at him dumbfounded, he gave a forced smile: " I think you'd better make your researches by yourself to-night." The old man turned back once more towards the town. Huguenau gazed after him in rage and bitterness; but then he remembered Esch, shrugged his shoulders, and opened the door.

He left the house in less than an hour. His spirits had improved; the fear that had weighed upon him was gone, he had put something right, and although he could not have given it a name, yet he felt definitely that he had retrieved his personality and his clear common sense. The others could do what they liked, they could give him the cold shoulder, he snapped his fingers at them. He stepped out vigorously, a Salvation Army song that he must have heard somewhere came into his mind, and with every step he beat time with his walking-stick on the ground to the words: " Lord God of Sabaoth."

CHAPTER LX

Victory Celebration of " The Moselle Memorial Association " in the beer-hall " Stadthalle " in commemoration of the Battle of Tannenberg

Jaretzki was prowling about in the garden of the " Stadthalle." In the big hall they were dancing. Of course one could dance even lacking an arm, but Jaretzki felt shy. He was glad to find Sister Mathilde standing at one of the doors of the dancing-hall:

" So you're not dancing either, Sister? "

" Of course I'm dancing; shall we have a try, Lieutenant Jaretzki? "

" Until I get that thingummy-jig, that artificial arm, there's nothing much I can do . . . except drinking and smoking . . . will you have a cigarette, Sister Mathilde? "

" Why, what are you thinking of? I'm here on duty."

" I see, it's duty that makes you offer to dance. Then duty bids you take pity on a poor one-armed cripple . . . do sit down and bear me company for a little."

Jaretzki sat down somewhat heavily at the nearest table.

" Do you enjoy all this, Sister? "

" Yes, it's very nice."

" Well, I don't like it."

" But the crowd are enjoying themselves, one mustn't grudge them their pleasure."

" Look here, Sister, perhaps I'm a little muzzy as it is . . . but that doesn't matter. . . . I tell you that this war can never stop . . . or what do you think? "

" Why, it must stop some time or other. . . ."

" What shall we do with ourselves then, when there's no more war . . . when no more cripples are turned out for you to nurse? "

Sister Mathilde considered:

"After the war . . . well, you know yourself what you're thinking of doing then. You told me of some job you've been offered. . . ."

"With me it's different . . . I've been at the Front . . . I've killed people . . . forgive me, it sounds a bit confused perhaps, but it's quite clear to me all the same . . . for me it's all over . . . but there are all those others . . ." he waved his hand towards the garden, "they must all face the music yet . . . the Russians are supposed to be forming women's battalions already. . . ."

"The things you say are quite terrifying, Lieutenant Jaretzki."

"Me? not at all . . . I'm finished with the whole business. . . . I'll go back home . . . find myself a wife . . . night after night the same one . . . no more philandering . . . I'm afraid I must be a little drunk, Sister, . . . but you see it isn't good for a man to be alone, it isn't good for a man to be alone . . . it says so in the Bible. And you think a great deal of the Bible, Sister, what?"

"What do you say, Lieutenant Jaretzki, wouldn't you like to go back to the hospital now? Some of our people are wanting to leave . . . you could go with them. . . ."

She felt his alcoholic breath on her face:

"I tell you this, Sister, that the war can't stop because every man out there has found himself alone . . . because one after another, they all find themselves alone . . . and every man who is all alone must kill some other man . . . you think I've drunk too much, Sister, but you know I can carry a lot . . . no reason at all for sending me to bed . . . but it's true, what I've been telling you."

He got up:

"Funny music, what? . . . God knows what kind of dancing this is, but shall we watch it for a little?"

Dr Ernst Pelzer, the volunteer from the trench mortar division, ran slap into Huguenau in one of the hall doorways:

"Hey, look out, Herr Grand Master of Ceremonies . . . you're a regular whirlwind . . . chasing the ladies, as usual?"

Huguenau did not listen at all; with beaming importance he indicated two gentlemen in dress-suits who had just come into the garden:

"The Burgomaster has arrived!"

"Aha—flying after higher game . . . well, good hunting to you, tally-ho! and yoicks! and all the rest of it, my noble sportsman. . . ."

"Thanks, thanks, Herr Doctor"; Huguenau, who had not heard a word, cried his thanks over his shoulder and was already getting into position for the official speech of welcome.

Surgeon-Major Kühlenbeck should really have been sitting at the table of honour. But he did not remain there long.

"Let joy be unconfined," he said, "we are mercenaries in a conquered town."

He steered for a group of young girls. He carried his head high, his beard stuck almost horizontally into the air. As he passed Fusilier Kneese, who was leaning, sad and bored, against a tree, he clapped him on the shoulder: "Well, mourning still for your appendix? You're fine soldiers, I must say, you're here to get the women with child. . . . I'm ashamed of such milksops . . . forward, my lad!"

"Very well, sir," said Kneese, standing to attention.

Kühlenbeck hooked himself on to Berta Kringel, squeezing her arm to his ribs:

"I'll dance a round with you all . . . the one that dances best will get a kiss."

The girls shrieked. Berta Kringel tried to free herself. But when he enclosed her stub-fingered hand in his soft masculine fist, he felt her fingers growing weak and nestling into his.

"So you won't dance . . . you're all afraid of me, that's what it is . . . all right, I'll take you over to the tombola . . . children like to play at such games."

Lisbeth Wöger cried:

"You're only poking fun at us again, Herr Kühlenbeck . . . a Surgeon-Major doesn't dance."

"Well, Lisbeth, you'll come to know me better yet."

And Surgeon-Major Kühlenbeck captured Lisbeth too by the arm.

While they were standing at the tombola-table, Frau Paulsen the wife of the apothecary Paulsen approached, took her stand beside Dr Kühlenbeck, and whispered with pale lips:

"Aren't you ashamed . . . with these callow creatures. . . ."

The huge man gazed at her a little apprehensively from behind his glasses; then he laughed:

"Oh, dear lady, I promise the first prize to you."

"Thanks," said Frau Paulsen, taking herself off.

Lisbeth Wöger and Berta stuck their heads together:

"Did you see how green she was with jealousy?"

Although Heinrich's presence had to a certain degree broken through her hermit existence, Hanna Wendling had not come to the celebration willingly. But as one of the town's prominent citizens and also as an officer, Advocate Wendling had felt it his duty to attend. So they had driven over with Röders.

They sat in the dancing-hall; Dr Kessel kept them company. At the upper end of the room stood the table of honour, gleaming with napery and decked with flowers and festoons of leaves; there presided the Burgomaster and the Major, and Herr Editor Huguenau had also his place there. When he caught sight of the newcomers he steered his way across to them. That he was on the committee could be seen from the badge in his buttonhole, but still more clearly was it written on his brow. No one could fail to remark Herr Huguenau's dignity. Huguenau had known of course for a long time who this lady was: he had noticed her several times in the town, and a very little inquiry had discovered that she was Frau Advocate Wendling.

He made straight for Dr Kessel:

"May I beg you, Herr Doctor, to do me the great favour of introducing me to your friends?"

"Yes, with pleasure."

"A great honour, a great honour," said Herr Huguenau, "a great privilege; the gracious lady lives in such retirement, and if it were not for the great good fortune of her husband being here on furlough I feel sure that we wouldn't have had the pleasure of welcoming her in our midst to-night."

The war had made her rather shy of people, replied Hanna Wendling.

"That's the wrong way to take it, dear lady. It's just in such grave times that one needs cheering up. . . . I hope that you're both staying for the dance."

"No, my wife is a little tired, so unfortunately we must go soon."

Huguenau was honestly hurt:

"But, Herr Advocate, you and your charming wife must really grant us the honour for once, our festivities really must be graced by such a beautiful lady . . . and it's for a philanthropic object, so won't the Herr Lieutenant close one eye and put mercy before justice?"

And although Frau Hanna Wendling was perfectly aware of the shallowness of these flatteries, her face opened and she said:

"Well, as a favour to you, Herr Editor, we'll stay for a little longer."

In the middle of the garden a long table had been set up for the soldiers, and "The Moselle Memorial" had presented them with a small cask of beer, which stood on its two trestles beside the table. The beer had been finished long ago, but a few of the men still loitered round the empty table. Kneese had joined them, and now he was drawing designs with a finger-tip in the pools of beer on the wooden boards:

"The Surgeon-Major says that we're to give them children."

"Who?"

"The girls here."

"Tell him he must lead the way."

Guffaws.

"He's doing that as it is."

"It would be more sense if he let us go home to our wives."

The lamps swayed in the night wind.

Jaretzki wandered alone through the garden. When he met Frau Paulsen he bowed:

"So lonely, dear lady?"

Frau Paulsen said:

"You seem to be lonely too, Herr Lieutenant."

"Doesn't mean anything in my case, I'm finished with everything."

"Come, shall we try our luck at the tombola, Herr Lieutenant?"

Frau Paulsen attached herself to Jaretzki's sound right arm.

Huguenau met Surgeon-Major Kühlenbeck walking with Lisbeth and Berta under the trees.

Huguenau exclaimed in greeting:

"A happy evening, Herr Surgeon-Major, a happy evening, young ladies."

And he was gone.

Dr Kühlenbeck was still holding stub-fingered bourgeoise hands in his great warm paws:

" Well, do you like that elegant young fellow? "

" No . . ." the two girls tittered.

" Indeed? Why not? "

" There's others better than him."

" I see. Who, for instance? "

Berta said:

" There's Lieutenant Jaretzki walking with Frau Paulsen over there."

" Leave them to themselves," said the Surgeon-Major. " I'm going to stick to you."

The band blew a flourish. Huguenau stood beside the conductor on the platform, which on one side projected into the hall, on the other, in the form of a pavilion, into the garden.

Making a speaking trumpet with his hands, Huguenau shouted over the tables standing in the garden:

" Silence."

In the garden and the hall there was dead silence.

" Silence," crowed Huguenau once more into the stillness.

Captain von Schnaack of Room VI.—he had a shot wound in the lung which was now healed—stepped up beside Huguenau on the platform and now unfolded a sheet of paper :

" Victory at Amiens. 3700 English prisoners, 3 enemy aeroplanes shot down, two of them by Captain Blöcke, who thus achieves his twenty-third air victory."

Captain von Schnaack raised his arm: " Hip, hip, hooray! " The band struck up the national anthem. All rose to their feet; the most of them joined in the singing. When it had died away again, someone shouted from a shadowy corner:

" Hurrah, hurrah, hurrah, long live the war! "

Everybody turned and looked.

There sat Lieutenant Jaretzki. A bottle of champagne was standing before him, and he was trying to embrace Frau Paulsen with his sound arm.

The walls of the dancing-hall were decorated with portraits of the allied generals and rulers decked with oak-leaves and paper garlands and hung with banners. The patriotic and ceremonious part of the celebration was now over, and Huguenau could dedicate himself to pleasure. He had always been a good dancer, had always been able to flatter himself that in spite of his stoutness and short stature he cut a good figure; but to-night more was at stake, to-night more was in question than the elasticity and agility of a stout little man; here under the eyes of the military commanders the dance became a celebration of victory.

The dancer is removed beyond the reach of this world. Wrapped in the music, he has renounced his freedom of action, and yet acts in accordance with a higher and more lucid freedom. In the rigorous security of the rhythm that guides him he is safely sheltered, and a great relief comes to him from that security. Thus music brings unity and order into the confusion and chaos of life. Cancelling Time it cancels death, and yet resurrects it anew in every beat of the rhythm, even in the rhythm of that dreary and endless potpourri which, calling itself *A Selection of Music from All Countries*, is now being played, and consists of a particoloured assortment of German folk-songs and enemy dances such as the cakewalk, the matchiche and the tango. The dancer's partner hums, then, growing more ardent, she sings. And her emotional and unschooled voice sings the barbarous words of these melodies, all of which she knows without exception, her soft zephyr-like breath brushing his cheek when he bends over her in the tango. But soon he straightens himself again, his warlike spirit reawakened he gazes fixedly and sternly through his eyeglasses, gazes into the distance, and dauntlessly he and his partner defy hostile powers when the music breaks triumphantly into an heroic march; but now with the changing rhythm they fall into the artful contortions of the one-step, and shuffle with curious swayings on one spot, almost without progressing, until the long waves of the tango once more roll up and their movements once more become catlike and soft, with a yielding suppleness of leg and body. Should they pass the table of honour, behind whose flower-filled vases the Major sits side by side with the Burgomaster, then with a sweep of the arm the dancer snatches up a glass from the board—for he himself belongs to this table—and without interrupting the dance, like a tight-rope dancer who carelessly and smilingly devours a succulent meal while still high up in the air, he drinks to the seated company.

He scarcely guides his partner now; one hand, gallantly enveloped in

his pocket-handkerchief, rests delicately beneath the low-cut back of her
dress, but his left arm hangs carelessly by his side. Only when the music
changes over to a waltz do they join their free hands; stiffly, in reciprocal
tension, they brace their outstretched arms, and with their fingers locked
the pair whirl round the hall. Glancing round the hall, he sees that the
ranks of dancers have thinned. Only one other pair is still dancing, they
come nearer, almost brush him, recede, glide away again along the walls.
The others have withdrawn among the spectators; unequal to the alien
dance rhythms, they stand and admire. Should the music cease, the
spectators and dancers alike clap their hands, and it begins once more.
It is almost like a trial of strength. Huguenau scarcely sees his partner,
who with head flung back in surrender has resigned herself to his strong
and yet hardly visible guidance; he does not know that the music has
released in his partner a more delicate and disciplined artistry of sex, a
bacchantic feminine power which will remain for ever unknown to her
husband, to her lover, even to herself, nor does he see the ecstatic smile
with which the other lady hangs in her partner's arms; he sees only his
rival, sees only the other hostile dancer, a lean wine-agent in evening
clothes with a black tie and an Iron Cross on his chest, who in elegance
and military distinction outshines himself in his plain blue suit. So might
Esch himself, with his long lank limbs, dance here, and therefore, to filch
the lady from him, Huguenau holds her with his eye as she glides past
with her partner, and he keeps on doing this until she returns his gaze,
gives herself to him with her glances, so that he, Wilhelm Huguenau,
now possesses both the women, possesses them without desiring them,
for it is not the favour of women that matters to him, though he may be
competing for it now—the pleasures of love do not matter to him; on the
contrary this celebration and this spacious hall concentrate ever more
exclusively around the white-decked table over there, and his thoughts
are directed more and more unconditionally on the Major who sits, white-
bearded and beautiful, behind the flowers watching him, him, Wilhelm
Huguenau in the middle of the floor; he is a warrior dancing before his
chieftain.

But the Major's eyes were filling with growing horror. This hall with
these two men shamelessly shuffling, shamelessly hopping, more shameless
even than the women with whom they were coupled; it was like a house
of ill fame, it was the pit of corruption itself. And that a war could be
accompanied by such celebrations of victory turned war itself into a

bloody caricature of corruption. It was as though the world were becoming featureless, featureless every face, a pit where nothing could be distinguished, a pit from which there was no longer any rescue. Seized with horror, Major von Pasenow caught himself wishing that he, a Prussian officer, could tear the banners from the walls, not because they were desecrated by the festive abominations, but because they were incomprehensibly bound up with these abominations and this diabolical display, in an incomprehensibility behind which all the unchivalry of unchivalrous weapons, treacherous friends and broken pledges was concealed. And as he sat in a strange icy immobility, the dreadful desire arose in him to destroy this demoniacal rabble, to exterminate them, to see them lying crushed at his feet. But motionless and gigantic as a towering mountain range, as the shadow of a mountain range on the wall, there rose grave and solemn above the rabble the image of a friend, perhaps it was that of Esch, and to Major von Pasenow it seemed that it must be for this friend's sake that the Evil One had to be crushed and cast into nothingness. Major von Pasenow longed for his brother.

Sister Mathilde was searching for Dr Kühlenbeck. She found him among a crowd of prominent business men. Kringel the merchant, Quint the hotelkeeper and pork-butcher, Herr Salzer the architect, and Herr Westrich the postmaster, were all sitting there. And their wives and daughters were sitting beside them.

" A moment, Herr Surgeon-Major."

" Another woman that's cocked her eye at me."

" Just one moment, sir."

Kühlenbeck got up:

" What's wrong, my child? "

" We must get Lieutenant Jaretzki out of here. . . ."

" Yes, I fancy he's had about enough."

Sister Mathilde smiled in agreement.

" I'll come and see to him."

Jaretzki's sound arm was lying on the table, his head was resting on it, and he was asleep.

The Surgeon-Major looked at his watch:

" Flurschütz is relieving me. He should be arriving at any moment now with the car. He can take Jaretzki back with him."

" Can we leave him here asleep like this, sir ? "
" There's nothing else for it. War is war."

Dr Flurschütz blinked through somewhat inflamed eyes at the lighted
garden. Then he went into the dancing-hall. The Major and the other
guests of honour had already left. The long table had been removed and
the whole room set free for the dancing, which proceeded on its crowded,
steaming, sweating, shuffling course.

It was some time before he caught sight of his chief; with grave expression and upward-pointing beard Kühlenbeck was revolving with Frau
Chemist Paulsen in a waltz. Flurschütz waited for the dance to end,
and then he reported himself.

" Well, here at last, Flurschütz: you see what childish follies you have
driven your worthy superior officer to with your lateness . . . but now
there's no excuse for you; when the chief dances, the next in command
must dance too."

" Insubordination, sir, I refuse to dance."

" And this is the younger generation . . . it seems to me that I'm younger
than the lot of you . . . but now I must go, I'll send the car back for you.
Bring Jaretzki with you; he's blind to the world for the moment . . .
one of the sisters will return with me, you bring the other."

In the garden he unearthed Sister Carla:

" Sister Carla, I'll take you back with me, I can manage four wounded
men too. Round them up, will you, but be quick."

Then he packed in his passengers. Three men were got into the back
seat, Sister Carla and another man in the front seat, and he himself took
his place beside the chauffeur. Seven crutches stared into the dark air
(the eighth lay somewhere in the car), stars hung in the black tent of the
sky. The air smelt of petrol and dust. But from time to time, particularly
at the turns of the roads, one felt the nearness of the woods.

Lieutenant Jaretzki got up. He had a feeling as though he had fallen
asleep in a railway carriage. Now the train was stopping at one of the
bigger stations; Jaretzki resolved to visit the buffet. There were a great
many people and a great many lights on the platform. " Sunday traffic "
Jaretzki told himself. He had got quite cold. Round about the region
of the stomach. Something warm would do him good. Suddenly his
left arm was missing. Must have left it lying on the luggage-rack. He

steered his way through tables and people. At the tombola counter he halted.

" A grog," he commanded.

" It's a good thing that you're here," said Sister Mathilde to Dr Flurschütz, " it won't be an easy job to deal with Jaretzki to-night."

" We'll manage it all right, Sister . . . enjoyed yourself? "

" Oh yes, it was quite jolly."

" Isn't it a little spectral to you too, Sister? "

Sister Mathilde tried to understand, and did not answer.

" Well, could you have pictured anything like this to yourself years ago? "

" It reminds me somewhat of our annual fair."

" A somewhat hysterical fair."

" Well, perhaps, Dr Flurschütz."

" Empty forms that still live . . . looks like a fair, but the people in it don't know any longer what's happening to them."

" It will all soon come right again, Herr Doctor."

She stood before him, straight and sound.

Flurschütz shook his head:

" Nothing has ever come right yet . . . least of all on the Judgment Day . . . doesn't this look a little bit like it? what? "

" The ideas you have, Doctor! . . . but we must get our patients together."

The volunteer Dr Pelzer caught up Jaretzki in his wandering course near the music pavilion.

" You seem to be looking for something badly, Herr Lieutenant."

" Yes, a grog."

" That's a famous idea, Herr Lieutenant, winter is coming, I'll fetch you a grog . . . but sit down . . . until I get it." He rushed away and Jaretzki sat down on a table, swinging his legs.

Dr Wendling and his wife, just leaving, passed by. Jaretzki saluted:

" Allow me, Herr Lieutenant, I'm Second Lieutenant Jaretzki, Hessian Light Infantry Battalion No. 8, Army of the Crown Prince, lost left arm as result of gas-poisoning at Armentières, beg to introduce myself."

Wendling looked at him in astonishment:

"Delighted," he said. "Lieutenant Dr Wendling."

"Diploma engineer Otto Jaretzki," Jaretzki now felt obliged to add, this time standing to attention before Hanna, so as to show that the introduction also included her.

Hanna Wendling had already encountered a great deal of admiration during the evening. She said graciously:

"But that's horrible, about your arm."

"Quite right, gracious lady, horrible but just."

"Come, come, Herr Comrade," said Wendling, "one can't talk of justice in such things."

Jaretzki raised one finger:

"It isn't legal justice that I mean, Herr Comrade . . . we've been given a new kind of justice, a man doesn't need so many members when he's alone . . . you'll agree with that, I'm sure, gracious lady."

"Good-evening," said Wendling.

"A pity, a horrible pity," said Jaretzki, "but of course everyone is pledged to his loneliness . . . good-evening." And he returned to his table again.

"Queer man," said Hanna Wendling.

"Drunken fool," replied her husband.

The volunteer Pelzer passing with two glasses of grog stood to attention.

Huguenau hurried out of the ballroom. He wiped the sweat from his brow, and tucked his handkerchief inside his collar.

Sister Mathilde stopped him:

"Herr Huguenau, you could help us by gathering the patients together."

"A great honour, gracious lady, shall I order a flourish to be blown?" —and he turned at once towards the band.

"No, no, Herr Huguenau, I don't want any fuss, we can manage without that."

"As you please . . . been a splendid evening, hasn't it, gracious lady? The Herr Major has expressed his pleasure in the most gracious terms."

"Certainly, a lovely evening."

"The Herr Surgeon-Major seemed to be very pleased too . . . he was in splendid spirits . . . may I beg you to give him my humble regards . . . he left us so suddenly that I couldn't see him off."

"I wonder, Herr Huguenau, if you would let the soldiers in the ballroom know that Dr Flurschütz and myself are waiting for them at the door."

" It shall be done, it shall be done at once . . . but it isn't right of you, gracious lady, to leave us so soon . . . not a sign, I hope, that you haven't enjoyed yourself . . . well then, I shan't regard it as that."

His handkerchief tucked inside his collar, Huguenau hastened back into the ballroom.

" What about the officers, Sister? " asked Flurschütz.

" Oh, we don't need to bother about them, they've made arrangements themselves for being driven back."

" Good, then everything seems to be coming right after all . . . but we've still got Jaretzki on our shoulders."

Jaretzki and Dr Pelzer were still sitting in the garden beneath the music pavilion. Jaretzki was trying to look at the illuminations through his brown grog-glass.

Flurschütz sat down beside them:

" How about going to bed, Jaretzki? "

" I'll go to bed if I can find a woman, if I can't find a woman I won't go to bed . . . the whole thing began with the men going to bed without women and the women going to bed without men . . . that was a bad arrangement."

" He's right there," said the volunteer.

" Possibly," said Flurschütz, " and that's only occurred to you now, Jaretzki? "

" Yes, this very moment . . . but I've known it for a long time."

" Well, you'll certainly save the world with that idea."

" It would be enough if he saved Germany," said the volunteer Pelzer.

" Germany . . ." said Flurschütz, looking round the empty garden.

" Germany . . ." said Pelzer, " when it began I volunteered straight off for the Front . . . now I'm glad to be sitting here."

" Germany . . ." said Jaretzki, who had begun to weep, " too late . . . " he wiped his eyes, " Flurschütz, you're a nice fellow, I love you."

" That's good of you, I love you too . . . shall we go home now? "

" We haven't a home to go to, Flurschütz . . . I'll have a shot at getting married."

" It's too late for that too, at this time of day, I fancy," said the volunteer.

"Yes, it's rather late, Jaretzki," said Flurschütz.

"It's never too late for that," bawled Jaretzki, "but you've cut it off, you swine."

"Come, Jaretzki, it really is time now that you wakened up."

"If you cut mine off, I'll cut yours off . . . that's why the war must go on for ever . . . have you ever tried to do it with a hand-grenade . . .?" he nodded gravely, ". . . now I, I have . . . fine eggs, the hand-grenades . . . rotten eggs."

Flurschütz took him under the arm:

"Well, Jaretzki, probably you're quite right . . . yes, and probably it's actually the only way left of coming to a mutual understanding . . . but now come along, my friend."

At the outside door the soldiers were already assembled round Sister Mathilde.

"Pull yourself together, Jaretzki," said Flurschütz.

"Righto!" said Jaretzki, and as he appeared before Sister Mathilde he straightened himself to attention and reported: "A lieutenant, a medical officer and fourteen men present . . . I beg to report that he has cut it off . . ." he made a short pause for effect, and then drew the empty sleeve out of his pocket and waved it to and fro under Sister Mathilde's long nose: "Chaste and empty."

Sister Mathilde cried:

"Those who want to drive back can do so; I am going on foot with the others."

Huguenau came rushing out:

"I hope everything has gone all right, gracious lady, and that we're all here . . . may I wish you a safe journey home?"

He shook hands with Sister Mathilde, with Dr Flurschütz, with Lieutenant Jaretzki, and with each of the fourteen soldiers, being careful to introduce himself in each case as "Huguenau."

CHAPTER LXI

STORY OF THE SALVATION ARMY GIRL IN BERLIN (10)

What really do I want of Marie? I invite her here, I ask her to sing, I couple her in all chastity with Nuchem, the Talmudist, the renegade Talmudist, I suppose I should say, and I let her go away again, let her disappear within the walls of her grey hostel. What do I want of her? and why does she lend herself to this game? is she resolved to save my soul, is she resolved to take on the endless, the ultimately impossible task of capturing the Talmudist soul of this Jew and leading it to Jesus? What does Nuchem think about it anyway? Here I am with these two human beings apparently in the hollow of my hand, and yet I know nothing about them, not even what they are thinking and what they will eat this evening; man is such an isolated creature that nobody, not even God Who created him, knows anything about him.

The whole thing disturbed me extraordinarily, especially as I had never been able to look upon Marie except as a creature filled to the brim with hymns and Bible texts, and in my uneasiness I set out for the hostel.

I had to go there twice before I found her. She was out on a round of sick-visiting, and did not return until the evening. So I sat and waited in the common-room, contemplated the Bible texts on the walls, contemplated the portrait of General Booth, and once more considered all the various possibilities. I recalled to my mind my first meeting with Marie, also her first chance encounter with Nuchem, I made myself visualize everything that had happened since, I impressed all this very thoroughly on my mind, not even excepting my situation at the moment; I examined the common-room with the greatest attention, walking about in the slowly increasing dusk, for the sky had darkened; outside heavy raindrops were falling, hastening the twilight. I asked myself whether the two old men who were also sitting in the room like myself were to be included in my memory, and I included them—best to make certain. They were very feeble, their thoughts were impenetrable, I was empty air to them.

It was quite late when Marie arrived. Meanwhile the two old men had been led out, and I had been almost afraid that I would be treated in the same way. In the barely lit room she did not recognize me at once; she said: " God send you His blessing," and I responded: " That is only a symbolic figure of speech." Recognizing me now she replied on her side: " It isn't a figure of speech, may God send you His blessing." Now I said for my part: " With us Jews everything is a symbol." Thereupon she replied: " You aren't a Jew." To which I answered: " The bread and the wine are only symbols, none the less; besides, I live among Jews." She said: " The Lord is our eternal home." That was completely in character, that was just as I had imagined it to myself, a sacred text for every eventuality; now she was delivered once more into my hand, and raising my voice I said: " I forbid you ever to enter my Jewish home again," but it had an empty sound in that place. I must have her in my flat again, it seemed, if I was to talk reasonably to her; so I laughed and said: " A joke of mine, *nebbich*, a joke." Yet though with that Yiddish word I may have been seeking to take refuge from my own speech in that of an alien, an utterly alien people, and to shelter myself under the ægis of a God alien to me, it was of no avail, I did not recover my assurance. It may be that I was really too broken by my long wait, grown old like the two old men who had finally been led out of the waiting-room; I had been humiliated by my wait, a creature instead of a creator, a disthroned God. Almost humbly I had to bring out: " I wanted to save you from scandal, Dr Litwak has been pointing out the danger to me." Now that was of course a distortion of the case, for Litwak had feared the danger simply for Nuchem's sake. And to call in such a ridiculous half-baked Freethinker as a confederate! truly I could not have given a more painful wound to my self-respect. And simple as was the retort which she found in reply, it was a reproof: " When your heart is filled with the joy of the Lord, you're safe from scandal." My patience gave under this humiliation, and I did not notice that now I was actually serving the old grandfather's and Dr Litwak's purposes: " You mustn't carry on any more with the young Jew; he has a fat wife and a swarm of children." Oh, could I have read in her soul, could I have known whether with these words I had hurt and wounded her, torn that heart which gave out that it was filled with the joy of the Lord, —but there was no sign of that, perhaps she had not even understood what I said. She merely said: " I'll come to see you. We'll sing together." I acknowledged myself beaten. " We can go now," I said with a last remnant of hope that I might still manage to decide her course. She replied: " I would love to, but I must go back to my sick patients."

So I was compelled to set off for home again with everything still unsettled. Only a soft rain was falling now. In front of me marched a very young pair of lovers; they were clasping each other and their free arms swung to the rhythm of their march.

CHAPTER LXII

DISINTEGRATION OF VALUES (8)

Religions arise out of sects and in their decadence lapse again into sects, returning to their original status before falling into complete dissolution. At the beginning of the Christian era there were the several Christ- and Mithras-cults, at its close we find the grotesque American sects and the Salvation Army.

Protestantism was the first great sect-formation in the decay of Christianity. A sect, not a new religion. For it lacked the most important characteristic of a new religion, that new theology which binds together into a new harmony the new experience of God and a new cosmogony. Protestantism, by its very nature undeductive and untheological, refused to venture beyond the sphere of the autonomous inward religious experience.

Kant's attempt to establish a retrospective Protestant theology did indeed wrestle with the task of transferring the substance of religious Platonism to the new positivistic science, but it was far from seeking to set up a universal theological canon of values on the Catholic pattern.

The defence of Catholicism against a progressive disintegration into sects was organized by the Jesuits of the Counter-reformation in a draconic, even a military, centralization of values. That was the time when even the survivals of heathenish folk-customs were pressed into the service of the Church, when folk-art received its Catholic colouring, when the Church of the Jesuits blossomed into an unheard-of splendour, aspiring towards and achieving an ecstatic unity which was no longer, indeed, the mystic symbolical unity of the Gothic, but none the less was its heroic-romantic counterpart.

Protestantism has had to dispense with that kind of defence against sectarianism. It does not absorb the non-religious values, it only tolerates them. It despises extraneous " aids," for its asceticism insists on the radical inwardness of religious experience. And although it acknowledges ecstasy to be the source and the crown of religion, yet it exacts that the ecstatic value shall be independently wrested from the sphere of pure religion, remaining absolutely uncontaminated, uncompromised, and autonomous.

This attitude of severity is what governs the relationship of Protestantism to the non-religious social values, and what it depends on also to ensure its own stability as a Church on earth. In its exclusive and single-minded devotion to God it must of necessity fall back on the sole extant emanation of God's spirit on earth, the Holy Scriptures,—and so fidelity to the Scripture becomes the highest earthly duty of the Protestant, and all the radicality, all the severity of the Protestant method is applied to maintaining it.

The most characteristically Protestant idea is the categorical imperative of duty. It is in complete opposition to Catholicism: the extraneous values of life are neither subsumed in a creed nor included in a theological canon, but are merely strictly and somewhat bleakly supervised on the authority of Scripture.

If Protestantism had chosen to follow the other line of development, the Catholic, in order to achieve in its turn an organic system of Protestant values, such as Leibniz envisaged, for example, it would perhaps have preserved itself not less successfully than Catholicism against a further splitting-up into sects; but it would have been compelled to lose its essential character. It found itself—and still finds itself—in the situation of a revolutionary party that runs the danger, once it has risen to power, of being forced to identify itself with the old order it has been opposing. The reproach of disguised Catholicism levelled against Leibniz was not quite without foundation.

There is no severity that may not be a mask for fear. But the fear of lapsing into sectarianism would be much too insignificant a motive to account for the severity of Protestantism. And the flight to punctilious fidelity, to the written word, is pregnant with the fear of God, that fear which comes to light in Luther's *pœnitentia*, that " absolute " fear of the " ruthlessness " of the Absolute which Kierkegaard experienced and in which God " is enthroned in sorrow."

It is as if Protestantism by clinging to the Scripture wished to preserve the last faint echoes of God's Word in a world that has fallen silent, a world where only things speak dumbly, a world delivered over to the silence and ruthlessness of the Absolute,—and in his fear of God the Protestant has realized that it is his own goal before which he cowers. For in excluding all other values, in casting himself in the last resort on an autonomous religious experience, he has assumed a final abstraction of a logical rigour that urges him unambiguously to strip all sensory trappings from his faith, to empty it of all content but the naked Absolute, retaining nothing but the pure form, the pure, empty and neutral form of a " religion in itself," a " mysticism in itself."

There is a striking correspondence between this process and the structure of the Jewish religion: perhaps the Jews have carried to a still more advanced stage the neutralization of religious experience, the stripping of all emotional and sensory elements from mysticism, the elimination of the " external " aids to ecstasy; perhaps they have already got as near to the coldness of the Absolute as the ordinary man can bear —but they too have preserved the utmost rigour and severity of the Law as the last vestige of a bond with religious life on the earthly plane.

This correspondence in the process of intensification, this correspond·ence in the form of religious structure, which is asserted to extend even to the point of causing a corresponding similarity of character between orthodox Jews and Swiss Calvinists or British Puritans, this correspondence could, of course, be attributed also to a certain similarity in the external circumstances of these religions: Protestantism being a revolutionary movement, and the Jews an oppressed minority; they are both in opposition; and it could even be alleged that Catholicism itself when driven into a minority, as for instance in Ireland, exhibits the same characteristics. Yet a Catholicism of that stamp has as little in common with the Catholicism of Rome as the original Protestant faith has with the Romanizing tendencies of the High Church. They have simply inverted their distinguishing signs. And however these empiric facts are expounded, their explanatory value is but little, since the facts would not be available at all were it not for the determining religious experience behind them.

Is it this radical religiosity, dumb and stripped of ornament, this conception of an infinity conditioned by severity and by severity alone, that determines the style of our new epoch? Is this ruthlessness of the divine principle a symptom of the infinite recession of the focus of plausibility? Is this immolation of all sensory content to be regarded as the root-cause of the prevailing disintegration of values? Yes.

The Jew, by virtue of the abstract rigour of his conception of infinity, is the really modern, the most " advanced " man *kat' exochen*: he it is who surrenders himself with absolute radicality to whatever system of values, whatever career he has chosen; he it is who raises his profession, even though it be a means of livelihood taken up by chance, to a hitherto unknown absolute pitch; he it is who, unconditionally and ruthlessly following up his actions without reference to any other system of values, attains the highest summit of spiritual enlightenment or sinks to the most brutal absorption in material things: in good as in evil a creature of extremes—it looks as though the current of the absolute Abstract which for two thousand years has flowed through the ghettoes like an almost imperceptible trickle beside the great river of life should now become the main stream; it is as if the radicality of Protestant thought had inflamed to virulence all the dread ruthlessness of abstraction which for two thousand years had been sheltered by insignificance and reduced to its minimum, as if it had released that absolute power of indefinite extension which inheres potentially in the pure Abstract alone, released it explosively to shatter our age and transform the hitherto unregarded warden of abstract thought into the paradigmatic incarnation of our disintegrating epoch.

Apparently a Christian can only decide between two alternatives: either to seek the still available protection of the Catholic harmony of values, in the literally motherly bosom of the Church, or courageously to accept the absolute Protestantism which involves abasement before an abstract God,—and wherever this decision has not been taken, fear of the future lies like an oppression. And in fact it is the case that in all countries where men are still undecided this fear is latent and constantly active, though it may find expression merely in a fear of the Jews, whose spirit and mode of living are felt, if not recognized, to be a hateful image of the future.

In the idea of a Protestant organon of values there certainly exists a

desire for the reunion of all Christian churches, the kind of reunion
envisaged by Leibniz, and that Leibniz, who comprehended completely
the values of his age, was bound to think of it can now be seen as almost
inevitable; but it was equally inevitable that a man like him, a man
centuries ahead of his time, who foresaw the *lingua universalis* of logic,
must have also envisaged in that final reunion the abstraction of a *religio
universalis*, an abstraction of a coldness that perhaps he alone was capable
of enduring, being as he was the most profound mystic of Protestantism.
But the Protestant line of development postulated first the immolation
of life; so it was Kant's philosophy, not Leibniz's, that engendered
Protestant theology; and the rediscovery of Leibniz was reserved,
significantly enough, for Catholic theologians.

The numerous sects that have split off one after another from
Protestantism, and have been treated by it with that ostensible tolerance
which is peculiar to every revolutionary movement, have all developed
in the same direction; they are all a rehash, a whittling away and
levelling down of that old idea of a Protestant organon of values; they
are all on the side of the " Counter-reformation ": for instance, to leave
out of account the grotesque American sects, the Salvation Army not
only resembles the Jesuit movement of the Counter-reformation in its
military organization, but also exhibits very clearly the same tendency
to centralize all values, to draw everything into its net, to show how
popular art of every kind, down to the street song, may be reclaimed
for religion and reinstated as " ecstatic aids." Pathetic and inadequate
expense of spirit.

Pathetic and inadequate expense of spirit, deceptive hope, to think
of saving the Protestant idea from the horror of the Absolute. It is a
touching cry for help, a cry summoning all the resources of a religious
community, even though that may be seen only as the pale reflection of
what was once a great fellowship. For at the door in rigid severity stand
silence, ruthlessness and neutralization, and the cry for help mounts
more and more urgently from the lips of all those who are not capable
of accepting what is bound to come.

CHAPTER LXIII

On the Sunday afternoon following the celebration in the Stadthalle, Major von Pasenow, to his own surprise, decided to avail himself of Esch's invitation to visit the Bible class. It came about in the following way: actually he had not been thinking of Esch at all, and what turned the scale was perhaps simply the walking-stick which he suddenly saw leaning in the hall-stand, a walking-stick with a white ivory crook-handle, which in some way had got smuggled in among his other things and evidently must have been hidden until now in some cupboard. Of course he remembered the stick quite well, nevertheless it was strange to him. For a moment it seemed to Major von Pasenow as though he must change into mufti and visit one of those ambiguous pleasure resorts which an officer is not allowed to enter in uniform. And so to speak as a concession, he did not buckle on his sword, but took the stick in his hand and left the hotel. He remained standing hesitatingly for a little in front of the hotel, then set out in the direction of the river. He walked slowly, supporting himself on the stick, somewhat like a wounded or an invalid officer at a health resort,—and he could not help remembering vaguely that the indiarubber bulb at the point of the old stick needed to be replaced. So at a moderate pace he reached the outskirts of the town, and he had the slight agreeable sense of freedom that a man has who can turn back at any moment, like an officer on furlough. And in fact he presently did turn back—it was like a happy and reassuring, yet disconcerting return to one's home—and as though remembering an urgent promise which he had to redeem at once, he took the shortest way to Esch's dwelling.

Since the number of Esch's disciples had increased, and as during the summer months there was no need in any case for a heated room, the meetings were held in one of the empty store-rooms opening on the courtyard. A carpenter who belonged to the circle had provided rude benches; a little table with a chair behind it stood in the middle of the room. As there was no window the door was left open, and the Major, entering the courtyard, knew at once what direction to take.

Now that the Major appeared framed in the doorway and paused for a little to accustom his eyes to the twilight, everybody stood up; it almost gave the impression of an expected visit of inspection by a superior officer on his rounds, and this impression was strengthened by the uniforms of the soldiers present. This transformation, even though merely figurative, of his unusual situation into the dignified terms of the office to which he was accustomed, mitigated the shock of it for the Major; it was as though a light and yet firm hand had held him back from stepping down dark ways, it was a fleeting intimation of a danger overcome, and he raised his hand in salute.

Esch had sprung up along with the others, and now he escorted the guest to the chair behind the table. He himself remained standing beside it, rather like a guardian angel allotted to the Major. And the Major had somewhat that feeling about it, more, it was as though the object of his visit were already fulfilled, as though he were surrounded by an atmosphere of security, a simplified area of life which was waiting to receive him, the returned wanderer. Even the silence that surrounded him was like an end in itself, it might have endured as it was for ever; no one spoke a word, the room, filled with the silence, strangely emptied by the silence, seemed to extend beyond its own walls, and the yellow sunlight outside the open door flowed past like an eternal immeasurable river on whose banks they were sitting. Nobody knew how long this silent motionless state lasted, it had as it were the frozen timelessness of those seconds when men are faced with death, and although the Major knew that it was Esch who stood beside him, he felt to the full the fraternal presence of death, felt its menace as a sweet support. And when he made to turn round to Esch, it required all the effort which one needs when one awaits something decisive, knowing at the same time that one must maintain one's calm to the very last instant. With a great effort he turned round to him and said: " Please continue."

But nothing at all happened, for Esch gazed down on the Major's white hair-parting, he heard the Major's low voice, and it was as though the Major knew all about him, as though he knew all about the Major, like two friends who know each other well. He and the Major were there as on an uplifted and radiant stage, they were seated in the places of honour, the audience were still as though a bell had commanded silence, and Esch, who dared not lay his hand on the Major's shoulder, leaned on the back of the chair, although that too was undeniably presumptuous. He felt strong, steadfast and firm, as strong as in the best days of his youth, at once secure and gentle, as though he were delivered from all the works of man, as though the room were no longer made of bricks laid one on another, the door no longer of sawn planks of wood, as though all were the work of God and the words in his mouth were God's words.

He opened the Bible and read from the sixteenth chapter of the Acts of the Apostles:

" And suddenly there was a great earthquake, so that the foundations of the prison were shaken: and immediately all the doors were opened, and every one's bands were loosed.

" And the keeper of the prison awaking out of his sleep, and seeing the prison doors open, he drew out his sword, and would have killed himself, supposing that the prisoners had been fled.

" But Paul cried out with a loud voice, saying, Do thyself no harm: for we are all here."

Clearing his throat cautiously, Esch waited, his finger between the pages of the closed book. He waited for the foundations of the house to tremble, he waited for a great revelation now to manifest itself, he waited for One to give the command that the black flag should be hoisted, and he thought: I must make way for him who shall create time anew. He thought all this and waited. But for the Major the words he had heard were like drops which turned to ice while they fell; he kept silence and all kept silence with him.

Esch said:

" All flight is meaningless, of our own free will we must accept our imprisonment . . . the invisible shape with the sword stands behind us."

As the Major saw very clearly for a moment, Esch had interpreted the sense of the passage in part correctly, in part in the most obscure and fantastic way; but the old man did not linger over this reflection, and it was blotted out by an emerging picture which, though resembling a memory, was yet scarcely a memory, for it presented everything corporeally before him; the old reservists of the Landsturm and the young recruits were changed into apostles and disciples, members of a community met together in some greengrocer's cellar or dark cave, speaking a strange dark language that was yet as comprehensible as a language one had known in childhood, and over them shone a celestial silvery cloud—and the disciples, like himself, were gazing up to heaven with trust and resolute ardour.

" Let us sing," said Esch, and he began:

> " Lord God of Sabaoth,
> Take, O take us to Thine altar,
> Bind us all in one firm band,
> Lead us on with Thine own hand,
> Lord God of Sabaoth."

With the sole of his boot Esch beat time; many of the others did the same, rocking themselves in time and singing. The Major may have joined in the singing, but he did not know it, the singing seemed rather to be inside him, a singing behind his closed eyes, like a crystalline drop that falls singing from a cloud. And he heard the voice say: " Do thyself no harm: for we are all here."

Esch let the singing die away, and then he said:

" It is of no avail to flee from the darkness of the prison, for we flee only into outer darkness . . . we must build the house anew when the time has come."

A voice began again:

> " Fan its spark with Thine own breath,
> Till it flame in burning faith,
> Lord God of Sabaoth."

" Shut up," said another voice.

A neighbouring voice responded:

> " Baptize us, Jesus, with thy fire,
> Let the fire descend!
> To fiery baptism we aspire,
> Let the fire descend!
> O Lord our God, of Thee we crave
> Let the fire descend!
> Nothing else can bless and save.
> Let the fire descend! "

" Shut up," repeated the other voice, a slow voice, but resonant as a vaulted crypt, and it was the voice of a man in Landwehr uniform, a man with a long beard who stood up leaning on two sticks. And despite the effort it cost him, he went on to say: " Anyone who hasn't been dead should shut up . . . whoever has been dead is baptized, but not the others."

But the first singer had also sprung to his feet and his voice rang out again, singing:

> " Save, O save my soul from death,
> Lord God of Sabaoth."

" Let the fire descend," added the Major at this moment in a low voice that was yet audible enough to make Esch bend down towards him. It was in a sense an incorporeal approach, at least the Major felt it to be so; there was an element of assurance in it, both reassuring and disconcerting, and the Major studied the ivory crook of his stick that was lying before him on the table, studied the white cuff that projected a little beyond the sleeve of his uniform coat,—it was in a sense an incorporeal serenity, a kind of etherealized, luminous, almost white serenity that expanded in the dark room and spread over the confusion of voices, like a network of tinkling glass in a strangely abstract simplification. The stream of sunlight shimmered outside like a sharp fiery sword; they were safe as in a haven of refuge, in a cave, a cellar, a catacomb.

Perhaps Esch was expecting the Major to say something more, for the Major twice lifted his hand in time with the measure of the song as if desiring to make some acknowledgment,—Esch held his breath, but the Major let his hand sink again. Then Esch said, as though to quicken into life something that was dead:

" The torch of liberty . . . the blaze of illumination . . . the torch of true freedom."

But for the Major everything was so fused and blended into one experience that he could not have told whether he actually saw the fiery crests of torches or heard the voice of the man who was continually intoning " Let the fire descend," or whether it was Esch's voice or the wailing of Samwald the little watchmaker that rose in a thin piping from the background:

> " Illumine our darkness, lead us into the joys of paradise."

But the Landwehr man, gasping as he drew himself upright, waved one of his sticks and emitted hoarse sounds, bawling:

" Arisen from the dead . . . anyone who hasn't been buried must shut up."

Esch showed his strong teeth and laughed:

" Shut up yourself, Gödicke."

These were rude words: Esch himself could not help laughing so loudly that the laughter somehow stuck in his throat and hurt him, as if he were laughing in his sleep. The Major, indeed, perceived neither the rudeness of the words nor Esch's overloud laugh, for in his clearer knowledge he saw through the surface coarseness without even remarking it; indeed it seemed to him that Esch would be able with a light touch to set everything right, that Esch's features, almost unrecognizable in the dusk, were blending with the whole room into a strangely dim, blurred landscape, and through the resonant laughter he saw the glimmer of a soul leaning out of a neighbouring window with a smile, the soul of a brother, yet not an individual soul, nor yet in actual proximity, but a soul that was like an infinitely remote homeland. And he gave Esch a smile. That knowledge, however, filled Esch too, and he too understood that the smile they exchanged raised them together to a high peak; it was as if he had come whirling from a remote distance on the wings of a roaring wind that swept away all the dead past, as if he had come in a fiery red chariot to an appointed goal, a high pinnacle on which it no longer mattered by what name a man was called or whether one figure blended with another, a goal where there was no longer any to-day or to-morrow,—he felt the breath of liberty stir on his forehead, a dream within a dream, and Esch, unbuttoning his waistcoat, stood there drawn up to his full height as if he were about to set his foot on the outer stairway of the castle.

Yet in spite of it all he had not been able to cow Ludwig Gödicke, who now hobbled forward almost up to the table and screamed pugnaciously:

" You can't say anything till you've crawled under the ground . . . down there . . ." he bored the point of his stick into the earthen floor, " . . . down there . . . crawl down there yourself first."

Esch had to laugh again. He felt strong, steadfast and robust, firm on his legs, a fine fellow whom it was worth anyone's while to do in. He stretched his arms out like a man waking from sleep or nailed on a cross:

" Are you maybe thinking of knocking me down, eh? . . . with your crutches . . . you and your crutches, you misbegotten object."

There was some shouting that he was to leave Gödicke alone, Gödicke was a holy man.

Esch made a gesture of sweeping denial:

" No one is holy . . . there's no one holy but the son who will build the house."

" I build all kinds of houses," roared Gödicke the bricklayer, " all kinds of houses have I built . . . higher and higher . . ." and he spat contemptuously.

" Skyscrapers in America, I suppose," sneered Esch.

" He can build skyscrapers too," wept Samwald the watchmaker.

" Scraper yourself . . . scraping down walls is all he's fit for."

" From the earth beneath to the very skies. . . ."

Gödicke had raised his arms in the air with his two sticks; he looked menacing and powerful, " . . . arisen from the dead! "

" Dead! " screamed Esch, " the dead believe that they're powerful . . . yes, powerful they are, but they can't awaken life in the dark house . . . the dead are murderers! Murderers, that's what they are! "

He stopped abruptly, scared by the echo of murder that was now fluttering in the air like a dark butterfly, but scared and silenced no less by the Major's behaviour: for the Major had risen to his feet with a queer, stiff jerk, and had repeated the word, had woodenly repeated " murderers," and now was gazing at the open door and the courtyard outside as if he were expecting something dreadful to appear.

All the men fell silent and stared at the Major. He did not move but went on gazing spellbound at the door, and Esch also turned his eyes towards it. There was nothing there out of the ordinary; the air quivered in the sunlight, the house wall on the other side of that sunny flood— the wall of a quay, the Major could not help thinking—was a blinding white rectangle standing out against the brown box of the doorway and the two wings of the door. But the illusion began to lose its intoxicating immediacy, and when Esch, seizing his opportunity in the silence, read again from the Bible: " and immediately all the doors were opened " the door became for the Major once more an ordinary barn door, and nothing remained except that the ordinary courtyard outside bore a far-off resemblance to his old home and the great farmyard among the byres and stables. And when Esch concluded: " Do thyself no harm, for we are all here " even the serenity vanished, leaving only fear, the fear that in a world of illusion and semblances nothing but evil could take on bodily form. " We are all here," repeated Esch, and the Major could not believe it, for these were no longer apostles and disciples before his eyes, only men of the Landsturm and recruits, men of the rank and file, and he knew that Esch, lonely as he himself, was like him staring in terror at the door. So they stood side by side.

And then it happened that in the depths of the dark box, in the frame of the doorway, a figure came into sight, a round, thickset figure that advanced over the white gravel of the yard without causing the sun to darken. Huguenau. With his hands linked behind him, a passer-by taking an amiable stroll, he walked across the courtyard and paused in the doorway, blinking as he peered in. The Major and Esch were still standing immovably, for although it seemed an eternity to them it was only a matter of a few seconds, and as soon as Huguenau had ascertained what was going on he took off his hat, entered on tiptoe, bowed to the Major and sat down modestly at the end of a seat. "The devil incarnate," murmured the Major, "the murderer . . ." but perhaps he did not say it, for his throat was drawn together and he looked at Esch almost as if imploring help. Esch, however, smiled with a hint of sarcasm, although he himself felt Huguenau's intrusion as a treacherous attack or an assassination, as a blow bringing the inevitable death that one yet longs for, even when the arm holding the dagger is merely that of a despicable agent,—Esch smiled, and, since the man who faces death is released into freedom and all is permitted to him, he touched the Major's arm: "There's always a traitor among us." And the Major answered in an equally low voice: "He should get out . . . get out . . ." and as Esch shook his head he added: ". . . naked and exposed . . . yes, naked and exposed are we on the other side," and then he said finally: " . . . well it doesn't matter . . ." for in the wave of disgust that he felt suddenly rising within him there was a broad and dominant current of indifference, of weariness. And wearily and heavily he lowered himself again into his seat by the table.

Esch, too, would have liked to hear and see no more. He would have liked to dismiss the meeting. But he could not let the Major depart in such an inharmonious frame of mind, and so, somewhat indecorously, he banged the Bible on the table and announced:

"We shall read again in the Scriptures. Isaiah, chapter forty-two, verse seven: To open the blind eyes, to bring out the prisoners from the prison, and them that sit in darkness out of the prison house."

"Amen," responded Fendrich.

"It is a fine allegory," said the Major.

"An allegory of redemption," said Esch.

" Yes, an allegory of redemption through repentance," said the Major, and drew himself up with a little jerk, as if on parade, " a fine allegory . . . shall we now bring the service to a close for to-day? "

" Amen," said Esch, and buttoned up his waistcoat.

" Amen," said the congregation.

As they left the barn and were still standing irresolutely in quiet conversation in the courtyard, Huguenau pushed his way through the groups till he reached the Major, but was taken aback by that officer's discouraging aloofness. Still, he was unwilling to abandon the encounter, all the more as he had a joke ready to fire off: " So the Herr Major has come to assist at our fine new minister's first celebration? " The curt, aloof nod with which he was answered informed him that their relationship was under a cloud, and this became still more obvious when the Major turned round and said with loud emphasis: " Come along, Esch, you and I will take a walk outside the town." Huguenau was left standing in a state of mingled incomprehension, wrath and vaguely questioning guiltiness.

The other two took the path through the garden. The sun was already inclining towards the western heights. That year it seemed as if the summer were never coming to an end: days of shimmering golden stillness followed each other in equal radiance, as if by their sweetness and peace they wanted to make the war, now in its bloodiest period, appear doubly insensate. As the sun dipped behind the chain of mountain peaks, as the sky paled into tenderer blue, as the road stretched away more peacefully and all life folded in upon itself like the breathing of a sleeper, that stillness grew more and more accessible and acceptable to the human soul. Surely that Sabbath peace lay over the whole of the German fatherland, and in a sudden uprush of yearning the Major thought of his wife and children whom he saw walking over the sunset fields. " I wish this were all over and done with," and Esch could not find any word of comfort for him. Hopeless and dreary this life seemed to both of them, its sole meagre return a walk in the evening landscape which they were both contemplating. It's like a reprieve, thought Esch. And so they went on in silence.

CHAPTER LXIV

It would be false to say that Hanna longed for the end of Heinrich's furlough. She feared it. Night after night this man was her lover. And her daytime life, that even hitherto had been only a blurring and fending-off of consciousness, a darkening directed towards evening and towards bed, was now much more unambiguously directed to that end, with a lack of ambiguity that was startling and could scarcely be attributed to love, with such hardness, such unsentimentality, was it all dominated by the knowledge that she was a woman and he a man: it was a rapture that did not smile, a literally anatomical rapture that was in part too godlike for a lawyer and his wife and in part too base.

Her life was certainly a fading into darkness. Yet this obscuration proceeded only by layers, so to speak; it never deepened into complete unconsciousness, but rather resembled a too-vivid dream in which one is painfully aware that one's will is paralysed; and the more helplessly she was committed to it, the wilder the flora and fauna she accepted, the more did that layer of consciousness awaken which lay immediately above the dream. Only it could not be put into words, not because shame prevented it, but rather because words can never penetrate to the ultimate nakedness that arises from action as the night arises from the day,—her words, too, had fallen into layers, as it were, into at least two layers of language, a night-language closely bound to the event, stammering in its utterance, and a day-language that was detached from the event and went round it in a wide circle, closing in upon it circuitously—the method that the rational always follows until it finally surrenders itself in the screaming and sobbing of despair. And often this day-language was a feeling and seeking for the ultimate cause of the disease that afflicted her. " When the war's over," Heinrich would say almost every day, " everything will be different again . . . the war has made us all more primitive somehow." " I can't understand it," was Hanna's usual answer to that, or: " One simply can't think it out, it's all so inconceivable." These rejoinders were ultimately a refusal to discuss things with Heinrich as if he were on the same level; he was a guilty party and ought to defend himself instead of surveying things from above. Therefore she said as she stood before the mirror and loosened the light tortoiseshell

comb from her fair hair: " That queer man in the Stadthalle talked about
our loneliness." Heinrich dismissed him: " The fellow was drunk."
Hanna combed her hair and could not help thinking that her breasts were
drawn up more tightly when her arms were raised. She could feel them
under the silk of her chemise, on which they were outlined like two small
pointed tents. She could see them in the mirror that was lit on each side
by a small electric candle under a softly patterned pink shade. Then she
heard Heinrich say: " It's as if we had been shaken through a sieve . . .
crumbled to dust." She said: " In a time like this no children should be
born." She thought of the boy who looked so like Heinrich, and it seemed
unimaginable to her that her blonde body should be fashioned to receive
a man's seed, to be a woman. She had to shut her eyes. He said: " It's
possible that a new generation of criminals is growing up. . . . There's
no guarantee that we mightn't have a flare-up at any moment just like
Russia . . . well, we'll hope not . . . but our only comfort lies in the extraordinary vitality of inherited tradition. . . ." Both of them felt that the
conversation was tailing off into irrelevancy. It was almost as if a prisoner
in the dock were to say: " Lovely weather to-day. A spacious court-
room," and Hanna relapsed into silence for a moment, letting herself go
on that wave of hatred which made her nights more sordid, more profound and more lustful. Then she said: " We'll have to wait and see . . .
it has certainly some connection with the war . . . but not in that way
. . . it's as if the war were only the second thing." " How the second
thing? " asked Heinrich. Hanna made a furrow between her eyebrows:
" We are the second thing and the war is the second thing . . . the first
thing is something invisible, something that we have given off. . . ." She
remembered how she had longed for the end of their honeymoon to come,
so that—as she then believed—she might fling herself with enthusiasm
into the arrangement of their home. Their present situation was not so
unlike that; a honeymoon is a kind of furlough too. What she had felt
then must have really been a premonition of approaching isolation and
loneliness,—perhaps, it dawned on her now, perhaps loneliness was that
first thing, perhaps loneliness was the root of the disease! And seeing that
it had begun immediately after her wedding—Hanna sent her thoughts
back: yes, it had begun even while they were in Switzerland—and seeing
that everything fitted in, she felt her suspicion grow keener that Heinrich
in those days must have committed some irreparable mistake in his
relation to her, some injustice or other that could never be undone but

only made greater, a gigantic injustice that had helped in some way to let the war loose. She had applied her face-cream and carefully rubbed it in with her fingers, and now she examined her face in the mirror with jealous attention. The girlish face of those days had vanished, had turned into a woman's face through which that of the young girl now only glimmered. She did not know why all these things were connected, but she concluded her silent train of thought, saying: " The war is not the cause, it's only a secondary thing." And then she realized: the war is a second face, a night face. It was a disintegration of the world, a night face crumbling into cold and bodiless ash, and it was the disintegration of her own face, that disintegration she felt when Heinrich kissed her in the hollow of her shoulder. He said: " Why, certainly, the war is only the result of our mistaken policy," and perhaps he might actually have been able to understand that even policy is only a secondary matter in so far as there is a cause which lies deeper. But he was content with his explanation and Hanna, as she sprayed herself sparingly with the French perfume, now irreplaceable, and sniffed its fragrance, was no longer listening: she had bent her head for a kiss on the nape where the faint silvery hairs grew, and she obtained it. " Another," she said.

CHAPTER LXV

Esch was a man of impetuous moods. So any trifle was capable of provoking him to self-sacrifice. His desire was for simple directness: he wanted to create a world so strong in its simplicity that his own loneliness could be bound fast to it as to an iron stake.

Huguenau was a man who had braved many winds; even when he came into a stuffy room he was braving winds.

There was a man who fled from his own loneliness as far as India and America. He wanted to solve the problem of loneliness by earthly methods; but he was an æsthete, and so he had to kill himself.

Marguerite was a child, a child engendered by a sexual act, burdened with original sin and left alone to sin: someone might happen to give her a nod and ask what her name was—but such fleeting sympathy could not avail to save her.

There is no symbol that does not necessitate a further symbol,—does the immediate experience stand at the beginning or at the end of the series of symbols?

In a medieval poem the series of symbols begins in God and returns to God again—it is poised in God.

Hanna Wendling wanted things to be ordered so that in their poised equilibrium symbols would return to themselves again as in a poem.

One says Farewell, the other deserts—but they all desert from chaos; yet only he who was never bound can escape being shot.

There is nothing more despairing than a child.

He who is mentally lonely can always escape into romanticism, and from spiritual loneliness there is always a way of escape into the intimacy of sex—but for ultimate loneliness, for immediate loneliness, there is no longer any escape into symbols.

Major von Pasenow was a man who yearned passionately for the familiar assurance of home, for an invisible assurance in visible things. And his yearning was so strong that layer by layer the visible sank for him into the invisible, but the invisible, on the other hand, layer by layer became visible.

" Ah," says the romantic, drawing on the cloak of an alien value-system, " ah, now I am one of you and am no longer lonely." " Ah," says the æsthete, drawing on the same cloak, " I am still lonely, but this is a lovely cloak." The æsthete is the serpent in the romantic Garden of Eden.

Children are intimate at once with everything: the thing is both immediate and at the same time a symbol. Hence the radicality of children.

When Marguerite wept it was only from rage. She did not sympathize even with herself.

The lonelier a man becomes, the more detached he is from the value-system in which he lives, the more obviously are his actions determined by the irrational. But the romantic, clinging to the framework of an alien and dogmatic system, is—it seems incredible—completely rational and unchildlike.

The rationality of the irrational: an apparently completely rational man like Huguenau cannot distinguish between good and evil. In an absolutely rational world there would be no absolute value-system, and no sinners, or at most, mere detrimentals.

The æsthete too does not distinguish good from evil: in that lies his fascination. But he knows very well what is good and what evil, he merely chooses not to distinguish them. And that makes him depraved.

An age that is so rational that it must continually take to its heels.

CHAPTER LXVI

STORY OF THE SALVATION ARMY GIRL IN BERLIN (11)

I draw back from the Jews as much as possible, but I find myself as before compelled to go on observing them. So I cannot help wondering again at the confidence they repose in Samson Litwak, that half-free thinker. It is obvious that the man is a blockhead who was allowed to study merely because he was incapable of following a proper occupation —one has only to compare his bare unwrinkled face, that has looked out on the world from its fringe of beard for more than fifty years, with the furrowed thought-creased faces of the old Jews—and yet he seems to have a kind of oracular prestige among them which they invoke on all occasions. Perhaps it is a survival of the old belief in the half-wit as the mouthpiece of God, for it cannot be respect for scientific knowledge; they are too conscious of possessing the higher knowledge. It is hardly credible that I am mistaken. Dr Litwak, indeed, tries to put me off the scent, but he does it very badly. This tale of his "enlightenment" is pure fabrication: his reverence for the Jews' knowledge is too great, and if he gives me a friendly greeting in spite of the way I treat him, that is doubtless because I have refused to dismiss the Talmudic wisdom of the Jewish ancients as " prejudice." Obviously he has taken this as encouragement to hope that I will keep Nuchem on the right path; and so he submits to my continual snubbing of him and his attempts at familiarity.

To-day I met him on the stairs. I was going up and he was coming down. Had it been the other way about I could simply have dashed past him; it's not so easy to stop a man who is rushing down. But I was climbing up too slowly, what with the heat of the city and my half-starved condition. He barred my way jokingly with his walking-stick. Probably he wanted me to jump over it like a poodle (I catch myself in these last ᵈays becoming touchy, far too touchy; that too may be the result of semi-starvation). I raised the stick with two fingers so as to get past it.

Oh, how I loathed his grinning familiarity! He nodded to me:

" What do you say to it now? everybody's quite upset."

" Yes, it's very hot."

" If it were only the heat! "

" Well, the Austrians are held up in Transylvania."

" Who's speaking of Transylvania? . . . what do you really say to it now? he says one must have joy in the heart."

My condition makes me enter into the most idiotic discussions:

" That sounds quite like a psalm of David . . . have you any objection? "

" Objection? I only object . . . I only say the old grandfather's right, old people are always right."

" Prejudice, Samson, prejudice."

" You won't have *me* on toast! "

" Well, what does dear Grandpapa say? "

" Now listen! He says, a Jew must have joy not in the heart but here. . . ." He tapped himself on the forehead.

" In the head, then? "

" Yes, in the head."

" And what do you do with your hearts when you're joyful in the head? "

" With the heart we must serve . . . *uwchol levovcho, uwchol nawschecho, uwchol meaudecho,* that means, with all one's heart, with all one's soul, and with all one's might."

" Does Grandpapa say that too? "

" Not only the grandfather says it, it is so."

I tried to look at him pityingly, but it did not quite come off:

" And you call yourself enlightened, Herr Dr Samson Litwak? "

" Of course I'm an enlightened man . . . just as you are an enlightened man . . . of course, but is that any reason for upsetting the law? "

He laughed.

" God bless you, Dr Litwak," said I and went on climbing.

He replied: " A hundredfold," he was still laughing, " but no man can upset the law, not you, not I, not Nuchem. . . ."

I went on ascending the sordid stair. Why did I stay here? In the Army hostel I would be better accommodated. Texts on the walls instead of oleographs, for instance.

CHAPTER LXVII

STORY OF THE SALVATION ARMY GIRL IN BERLIN (12)

He said: my mule, quick-trotting, carries me
and thee together through our dream of Zion,
with jingling bells and purple bridle flying.
He said: I called to thee.
He said: my heart is open to the miracle
of the great Temple with its thousand stairs,
the city where my fathers said their prayers.
He said: we two shall build a tabernacle.
He said: till now I have waited for release
sunk in my book, waiting till I awoke.
He said: this joy I have longed for, and this peace . . .
he did not speak, it was his heart that spoke.
She too said nothing. Deep in silence lapped
so they went on, and yet their hearts were rapt.
So they went on, and yet their hearts were rapt
in silence, inner yearning, hidden glory,
so they went on and heeded not the story
of the mean streets they passed, the dens of shame.
She said: in the most secret part of me
the spark is fanned and rises into flame,
a blaze of light, a splendour without name.
He said: I thought of thee.

She said: my heart is kindled in a glow,
from me, a sinner, thou dost not turn aside.
He said: bright gleams the road to Zion that we go.
She said: for us thou once wert crucified.
They said no more: light dazzled what was said.
They did no more: the deed was perfected.

CHAPTER LXVIII

"What, are you thinking of going out at this late hour, Lieutenant Jaretzki?"

Sister Mathilde was sitting near the porch of the hospital, and Lieutenant Jaretzki, standing in the illuminated doorway, lit himself a cigarette.

"It was too hot to-day to go out . . ." he clicked his lighter shut, "a good invention, these petrol lighters . . . you know, don't you, that I'm going away next week, Sister?"

"Yes, so I heard. To Kreuznach, to a convalescent home? . . . You must be glad to get out of here at last. . . ."

"Oh, well . . . I suppose you're glad to get rid of me."

"You haven't been exactly a good patient."

Silence.

"Come for a little walk, Sister, it's cool now."

Sister Mathilde hesitated:

"I have to go in again soon . . . but, if you like, let's take a short turn."

Jaretzki said reassuringly:

"I'm quite sober, Sister."

They went out into the road. The hospital with its two rows of lighted windows lay to their right. The outline of the town beneath them was just discernible, its mass was a little blacker than the blackness of the night. A few lights were burning there, and on the hills, too, a light now and then gleamed from some solitary farmhouse. The town clocks struck nine.

"Wouldn't you like to be leaving too, Sister Mathilde?"

"Oh, I'm quite happy. . . . I have my work."

"It's really frightfully decent of you to come for a walk with a good-for-nothing down-and-out like me, Sister."

" Why shouldn't I go for a walk with you once in a way, Lieutenant Jaretzki? "

" Why not, indeed. . . ." After a while: " So you want to stay here all your life, do you? "

" Not exactly . . . not when the war's over."

" Then you're going home? . . . to Silesia? "

" How do you know that? "

" Oh, one soon finds out these things . . . and you think that it'll be a simple matter just to go home . . . as if nothing had happened? "

" I haven't really thought about it . . . things always turn out differently."

" Do you know, Sister . . . now, I'm quite sober . . . but it's my firm conviction that none of us will ever really get home again."

" But we all want to get home again, Lieutenant; what should we have been fighting for, if not for our homes? "

Jaretzki stood still.

" What have we been fighting for? What have we been fighting for . . . you'd better not ask, Sister . . . besides, just as you said, things always turn out differently in any case."

Sister Mathilde made no reply. Then she said:

" What do you mean exactly, Lieutenant? "

Jaretzki laughed:

" Well, should you ever have expected to be going for a walk with a boozing, one-armed engineer? . . . you're a Countess, aren't you? "

Sister Mathilde did not answer. She was not a Countess, but she was certainly a *von* and her grandmother was a Countess.

" Perhaps it doesn't matter a rap . . . if I'd been a Count I should just have been the same, I should have had to booze just the same . . . you see, we're all much too lonely for a thing like that to make much difference to us . . . you're not offended, are you? "

" Oh, why should I? . . ." she saw his profile against the darkness and was afraid that he might try to seize her hand. She crossed to the other side of the road.

" Time to turn back now, Lieutenant."

" You must be lonely too, Sister, or else you couldn't stick it out . . . let's be glad that the war isn't coming to an end."

They were once more at the iron gate of the hospital. Most of the windows were now dark. One could see the lowered lights in the sick wards.

"Well, now I'm going to have a drink, all the same . . . you wouldn't join me in any case, Sister."

"It's high time I was in, Lieutenant Jaretzki."

"Good-night, Sister: thank you very much."

"Good-night, Lieutenant."

Sister Mathilde felt somehow disappointed and depressed. She called after him:

"Don't be too late in coming back home, Lieutenant."

CHAPTER LXIX

Since that walk through the evening fields with Esch the Major often found himself going through Fischerstrasse after his day's work was done, indeed he often caught himself slowing down a street or two farther on, standing uncertainly for a moment, and then turning back. One could have literally affirmed that he went slinking round and round the office of the *Kur-Trier Herald*. Perhaps he would actually have gone in had he not feared an encounter with Huguenau, and he did not want to meet Huguenau; the mere prospect of meeting him in the street filled him with embarrassment. But when Esch suddenly appeared instead of Huguenau, he could not tell at first whether he had not feared this encounter even more. For there he was, the Town Commandant in full uniform, his sword at his side, standing with a newspaper civilian fellow, standing in his uniform in the open street, and he had not only offered the fellow his hand but, instead of leaving it at that, he was actually filled with happiness, forgetting all decorum, because the man showed signs of accompanying him. Still, Esch had removed his hat most respectfully, and the Major was staring at close-cropped bristling grey hair,—and it was like an assurance, like a sudden evocation of Bible classes at home, and at the same time it was the reaffirmation of that afternoon's brotherhood, bringing with it the need to say something kind to this man who was almost a friend, even if it were only that Esch might cherish a happy memory of him; he hesitated a little longer and then said: "Come along."

As a result, these walks became frequent. Not so frequent, indeed, as the Major or even Esch would have liked. For not only were the times becoming more exacting—troops were continually being billeted and withdrawn again, columns of motor transport rattled through the streets, and the Town Commandant had often to work all through the night— but Major von Pasenow could not bring himself to the point of haunting the *Herald* office again, and it was some time before Esch realized this. When he did, however, he began to make allowances; he waited discreetly near the Major's headquarters, and when practicable took Marguerite with him. " The little monkey insists on coming with me," he would say; and though the Major was not quite certain whether the child's insistence was to be considered delightful or intrusive, he accepted it kindly and stroked Marguerite's black curls. Then the three of them would wander over the fields or down the path beside the bushes on the river-bank, and often it was as if there stirred a yearning of farewell, a gentle and wistful flowing of the heart, a living ebb of resignation; it was like that certitude of the end in which every beginning has its source. But gentle as it was, it contained a trace of dejection, perhaps because Esch had no part in this farewell, perhaps because it was proper that he should be so excluded, perhaps, however, because Esch remained inscrutable on these points, persisting in a disappointing silence. That was somehow dark and secretive, for there was still a fading hope that everything could be made right and simple if Esch would only speak. Alas, it was amazingly difficult to determine precisely what he expected Esch to say; still, Esch ought to have known what it was. So they went on in silence, in the silence of the evening light and of a growing disappointment, and the radiance lying on the fields became a misleading and weary brightness. And when Esch took off his hat to let the wind blow through his short bristling hair, that gesture took on such an unseemly intimacy that the Major almost pitied the little girl for having fallen into the power of such a man. Once he said: " Little slave-girl," but that too died out in weary indifference. Marguerite, however, ran on ahead and did not concern herself about the two men.

They had climbed to the top of the valley ridge and were following the edge of the forest. The short dry grass crackled under their shoes. Stillness lay over the valley. One could hear the creaking of the carts on the road below, the stubble-fields revealed the brown soil, and the wind blew cool from the dusky depths of the foliage. The vineyards hung green on the slopes, in the rustling of the trees the silvery, metallic sharpness of autumn was already discernible, and the stiff stems by the forest edge with their black and red berries were ready to shrivel up. Over the western flanks of the hills the sun was sinking, blazing like fire in the windows of the valley houses. Each house was standing on a long carpet of shadow pointing east; one could look down on the roofs of the prison buildings, flecked with red and black, and see right into the bleak, waste courtyards where there were also gloomy sharply cut shadows.

A small field-path led down the slope and entered the main road close by the prison. Marguerite, running on ahead, had turned down it, and the Major took this as a sign from God: " We'll turn back," he said listlessly. But when they were about half-way down they both came to a stop and listened: a curious brumming noise assailed them in rhythmic jerks; it came from below, but one simply could not tell from what quarter. Nothing could be seen but a car coming speeding from the town with its engine humming in the usual way and its horn hooting every minute or so; a long cloud of dust trailed behind it. The uncanny noise had nothing to do with the car. " An ominous sound," said the Major uneasily. " Some kind of machine," said Esch, although it sounded not at all like a machine. The car followed the windings of the road and with much tooting of its horn arrived at the prison. Esch's sharper eyes observed that it was the Commandant's official car, and he became uneasy when he noted that it did not appear again on the other side of the prison buildings. But he said nothing, only hurrying his steps. The curious sound grew harder and more sharply accentuated, and when they came in sight of the prisoⁱ gate they could see the car halted there among a crowd of excited people. " Something has happened," said the Major, and now they could hear welling from the barred and railed-in windows of the prison a frightful chorus beat out in bars of three phrases: " We're hungry, we're hungry, we're hungry. . . . We're hungry, we're hungry, we're hungry. . . . We're hungry, we're hungry, we're hungry . . ." and from time to time the chorus was interrupted by a conglomerate farmyard howl. The chauffeur came running to meet them: " Please, sir, it's a rebellion . . . we have been looking for you everywhere . . ." then he ran back to summon the gatekeeper.

The people made way for the Major, but he had come to a stop. The air was still vibrating with the threefold chorus, and now Marguerite began to dance in time to it: " We're hungry, we're hungry, we're hungry," she carolled. The Major gazed at the building with the dreadful impenetrable windows, he gazed at the dancing child whose laughter seemed to him strangely mechanical, strangely evil, and horror overwhelmed him. Implacable destiny, inevitable trial! The chauffeur was still pulling at the iron bell and beating on the gate, but at last the grille was opened and the gate turned creaking and heavy on its hinges. The Major was leaning against a tree and his lips murmured: " This is the end." Esch moved as if to help—the Major waved him off. " This is the end," he repeated, but he drew himself up, touched the ribbon of his Iron Cross, and then, his hand on his sword-hilt, advanced quickly towards the prison gate.

He vanished inside it. Esch sat down on the small escarpment beside the road. The air was still shattered by the syncopated cries. A single shot rang out, followed by a renewed howling. Then a few last cries like the last drops from a turned-off water-tap. Then there was silence. Esch watched the gate that had closed behind the Major—" This is the end," he echoed, and went on waiting. But the end did not come, no earthquake broke out, no angel descended, and the gate was not opened. The child squatted beside him, and he would have liked to take her in his arms. Like the wings of a stage scene the prison walls towered up to the bright evening sky, like teeth with gaps between them, and Esch felt far away from himself, far away from what was happening around him, far away from everything; he shrank from changing his posture and was no longer aware how he came to be there. Beside the gate hung a notice-board that could no longer be deciphered; of course it was a list of visiting-hours, but they were only words. For even the demagogues and murderers and deformed creatures that were imprisoned would come out of their prison into a new and more enlightened community in a Promised Land. He heard the child say: " There's Uncle Huguenau," and he saw Huguenau pass by at the double, saw him and was not surprised, so soundless was everything, soundless the step of Huguenau, soundless the movements of the people by the gate, soundless as the movements of artistes and rope dancers when the music has ceased, soundless as the paling of the clear evening sky. Remote beyond recovery lay the distant horizon before the dreamer, yet he was no dreamer but an orphan seeking vainly for his home; and he was like a man whose desire has transformed itself without his knowing it, like one who has merely deadened his pain but cannot forget it. The first stars came out in the sky, and it was to Esch as if he had sat for days and years in that self-same spot, wrapped in a padded and spectral silence. Then the movements of the waiting crowd became more infrequent, more shadowy, died away completely, and there remained a soundless waiting black mass before the gate. And finally Esch was aware only of the damp grass resting against the palm of his hand.

The child had vanished; perhaps she had gone off with Huguenau; Esch did not bother, but stared at the gate. At last the Major appeared. He walked quickly with an unusually undeviating air, it almost looked as if he had a limp and were trying to conceal it. He made straight for the car. Esch had sprung to his feet. The Major was now standing in the car, he stood there drawn up to his full height and looked over Esch's head, over the heads of the crowd that were pressing in silence round the car; he looked along the white road ahead of him and over at the town, in which lights were already twinkling from the windows. In the near vicinity a red light shone out; Esch knew where that was. Maybe the Major had observed it too, for he now looked down at Esch and said, gravely holding out his hand: "Well, it doesn't matter." Esch said nothing; he shouldered his way quickly through the crowd and took the path over the fields. Had he turned round, however, and had it not been so dark, he could have seen that the Major remained standing in the car, looking after him as he vanished into the night.

After some time he heard the engine starting and saw the headlights of the car following the windings of the road.

CHAPTER LXX

Huguenau had trotted home from the prison as fast as he could, with Marguerite running behind him. In the printing-shed he bade the press be stopped: "Some important news, Lindner," and then he betook himself to his room to do some writing. When he had finished it he said "Salut," and spat in the direction of the Eschs' living-rooms. "Salut," he said again, as he passed the kitchen door, and then he handed his composition to Lindner, "Among the news of the town, in small type," he ordered. And next day the following appeared in small type among the news of the town in the *Kur-Trier Herald*:

Incident at the Prison.—Yesterday evening there were some regrettable scenes at the prison. Some of the inmates believed that they had grounds for complaint about the inferior quality of the prison fare, and the unpatriotic elements among them seized on this as a pretext for abusing the authorities and causing an uproar. The prompt intervention of the Town Commandant, Major von Pasenow, who behaved with great courage and composure, soon quelled the disturbance. The rumour that this was really an attempt to escape on the part of alleged deserters now under lock and key pending execution is, we are informed on the best authority, quite without foundation, as there are no deserters in this prison. No one was injured.

It was another of these lucid inspirations of his, and Huguenau could hardly sleep for pure joy. He kept on reckoning it all up:

firstly, that bit about the deserters would annoy the Major, but the reference to the inferior food could not leave a Town Commandant complacent either, and if there was a man who deserved to be annoyed it was the Major;

secondly, the Major would hold Esch responsible, especially because of that hint about information on the best authority; for nobody would believe that Esch knew nothing of it,—and that would certainly put an end to the walking excursions of these two gentlemen;

thirdly, when one considered how furious the skinny Esch would be, the horse-faced Reverend, it was a sweet and gratifying thought;

fourthly, it was all so law-abiding—he was the editor and could put in what he liked, and the Major would have to be grateful to him, besides, for the compliments he had worked in;

fifthly and sixthly, there was no end to the gratifying consequences, it was, in a word, a highly successful stroke, it was, in a word, a *coup*, —and besides, it would make the Major respect him: the reports of a Huguenau had the knack of striking home, even if one did despise them;

yes, fifthly and sixthly and seventhly, one could go on and on, there was ever so much more of it, although to be sure there was a suggestion of unpleasantness somewhere that it was better not to think about.

In the morning Huguenau read the article in the printing-shed and was again delighted. He looked out of the window and cast a glance up at the office, twisting his face ironically. But he did not go up there. Not, of course, that he was afraid of the Reverend. When a man was only standing on his rights he had no need to be afraid. And a man must stand on his rights when he is persecuted. Even if it should bring everything about his ears a man must stand on his rights. All a fellow wants is to be left in peace and quiet; he only wants his due. And so Huguenau went to the barber's, where he studied the *Herald* yet once more.

To be sure, his dinner remained a problem. It would be unpleasant to sit at the same table with Esch, who would in some way, although without any justification, feel himself the injured party. One knew these high and mighty looks that priests gave; enough to take away a man's appetite. And this Reverend was a Communist himself, and wanted to socialize everything, and yet always behaved as if it were the other fellow who was trying to smash up society, just because he wouldn't let himself be put upon.

Huguenau went for a walk and thought it over. But he could not hit on a good idea. It was like going to school: let one be as inventive as anything, the only final course is to sham sick. So he turned back so as to get home before Esch, and climbed the stairs to see Mother Esch (for he had recently taken to calling her that). And with every step that he mounted his indisposition became more genuine. Perhaps he was really rather unwell, and it might be better to eat nothing at all. Yet, after all, his board and lodging were included in his salary, and he needn't make Esch a present of any of it.

" Frau Esch, I'm not well."

Frau Esch looked up and was touched by Huguenau's pathetic appearance.

" I don't think I can eat anything, Frau Esch."

" But, Herr Huguenau . . . a little soup, I'll make you some nice soup . . . that never did anyone any harm."

Huguenau considered. Then he said gloomily:

" A bouillon? "

Frau Esch was startled.

" Yes, but . . . I haven't any beef in the house."

Huguenau grew gloomier.

" Oh, no beef? . . . I think I'm in a fever . . . just feel how hot I am, Mother Esch. . . ."

Frau Esch came nearer and hesitatingly laid a finger on Huguenau's hand.

Huguenau said:

" Perhaps an omelette would be the thing."

" Hadn't I better make you some herb-tea? "

Huguenau suspected economy:

" Oh, an omelette could surely be managed . . . you must have eggs in the house . . . say, three eggs."

Thereupon with dragging feet he left the kitchen.

Partly because it was the right thing for an invalid to do, partly because he had to make up for the sleep he had lost in the night, he lay down on the sofa. But there was little chance of sleep, for his excitement over

the successful journalistic *coup* was still vibrating. In a kind of waking
doze he looked up at the mirror above the washstand, looked at the
window, listened to the noises in the house. There were the usual kitchen
noises: he could hear a bit of meat being beaten—so she had swindled
him after all, the fat madam, so that that blighter might have all the
meat to himself. Of course she would argue she couldn't make bouillon
out of pork, but a nice bit of lightly fried pork never hurt anyone, not
even an invalid. Then he heard a short, sharp chopping on a board, and
diagnosed it as the cutting of vegetables,—he had always been scared as
he watched his mother chopping up parsley or celery with quick-cutting
strokes, scared for fear she would chop off her finger-tips. Kitchen
knives were sharp. He was glad when the chopping noise ended and
mother wiped her unharmed fingers on the kitchen towel. If one could
only go to sleep: it might be better to get into bed, and then the Esch
woman could sit beside him and knit or give him hot fomentations. He
felt his hand; it was really hot. The thing to do was to think of something
pleasant. Women, for instance. Naked women. That was the stair creaking, someone coming up. Strange, for father wasn't usually so early.
Oh, it was only the postman. Mother Esch was speaking to him. The
baker used always to come up, but he never came now. That was just
nonsense: it was impossible to sleep while one was hungry.

Huguenau blinked again at the window, and noted outside the chain
of the Colmar mountains; the castellan of the royal castle was a Major,
the Kaiser himself had appointed him. Haïssez les Prussiens et les
ennemis de la sainte religion. Somebody laughed in Huguenau's ear;
he heard words in Alsatian dialect. A cooking-pot boiled over; it hissed
on the stove. Now someone was whispering, " we're hungry, we're
hungry, we're hungry." That was too stupid. Why couldn't he have
his dinner with the others? he was being treated worse and worse.
Perhaps they would give his seat to the Major? The stair was creaking
again—Huguenau flinched, it was his father's step. Oh, stuff, it was
only Esch, the would-be Reverend.

A swine that Esch; served him right if he was annoyed. Tit for tat.
You can't play with knives and not be cut. Esch had managed to turn
Protestant; next thing he'd turn Jew and have himself cut, circumcised;
must remember to tell the madam that. Finger-tips. Knife-tips. Best
of all just to get up and go over to the office and ask him if he was
thinking of turning Jew. All nonsense to be afraid of him; I'm only too

lazy. But she should bring me my dinner, and be quick about it . . . before that sanctimonious blighter gets his.

Huguenau listened intently to hear if they were sitting down to table. No wonder a man grew thinner and thinner with that Esch bagging everything. But that was what he was like. A Reverend had to have a belly. Pure fraud, his parson's black coat. An executioner had a black coat too. An executioner had to eat a lot to keep up his strength. One never knew whether people were coming to lead one to the block or merely bringing one's dinner. From now on he would go to the hotel and eat meat at the Major's table. That very evening. If that omelette was much longer in coming there would be a good row. An omelette only took five minutes to make!

Frau Esch came quietly into the room and set the plate with the omelette on a chair and pushed the chair up to the sofa.

" Hadn't I better make you some tea as well, Herr Huguenau, some herb-tea? "

Huguenau looked up. His irritation had almost vanished; her sympathy did him good.

" I'm rather fevered, Frau Esch."

She ought at least to pass her hand over his forehead to feel if he had fever; he was vexed because she did not.

" I think I'll go to bed, Mother Esch."

Frau Esch, however, stood stolidly before him and insisted on giving him tea: it was a very special kind of tea, not only an ancient recipe but also a famous remedy; the herbalist, who had inherited the secret from his father and great-grandfather, had become very rich, he owned a house in Cologne, and people went to consult him from all over the country. She had seldom said so many words in one breath.

None the less Huguenau resisted:

" Some cherry-brandy, Frau Esch, would do me good."

She primmed up her face with disgust: spirits? No! Even her husband, whose health was not of the most robust, had been won over to her tea.

" That so? Does Esch drink the tea? "

" Yes," said Frau Esch.

" All right, then, for the love of God make me some too," and with a sigh Huguenau sat up and ate his omelette.

CHAPTER LXXI

Heinrich's departure had passed off with remarkable ease. In so far as physical and spiritual effects can be separated, it might have been called a purely physical experience. As Hanna came home from the station she herself felt a little like an empty house where the blinds have been drawn down. But that was all. Besides, she knew for certain that Heinrich would return unharmed from the war. And this conviction of hers, which kept the departing soldier from turning into a martyr, not only obviated the sentimental outburst she had dreaded at the station, but had the more far-reaching effect of neutralizing and displacing her wish that he might never return. When she said to her son: " Daddy will soon come back," they probably both knew what she meant.

The physical experience, for as such she was entitled to regard this six-weeks' furlough, now presented itself to her mind as a contraction of her vital powers, a contraction of her ego; it had been like a damming-in of her ego within the limits of her body, like the foaming narrowing of a river within a ravine. In the past, now that she thought of it, she had always had the feeling that her ego was not bounded by her skin and could radiate through that tenuous covering into her silken underclothing, and it had been almost as if even her gowns were informed by an emanation from her ego (that was probably why she had such infallible taste in matters of fashion), yes, it had been almost as if her ego stretched far beyond her body and enveloped rather than inhabited it, and as if she did not think in her head but somewhere outside it, on a higher watch-tower, so to speak, from which her own bodily existence, however important it might be, could be observed and regarded as a trivial irrelevancy; but during these last six weeks of physical experience, during that head-long rush through the ravine, of all that diffused spaciousness nothing had survived but a shining vapour above the tossing waters, a rainbow glitter that was in a way the last refuge of her soul. Now, however, that the kindly plain once more spread before her and she felt as if released from fetters, her feeling of relief and smoothness turned at the same time into a wish to forget the troubled narrows. This forgetfulness, however, encroached upon her only a little at a time. All her personal memories vanished with relatively great rapidity; Heinrich's bearing, his voice, his words, his walk, all that very soon disappeared; but the general memories

persisted. To use a highly improper analogy: the first to disappear was
his face, then his movable extremities, his hands and feet, but the un-
moving, rigid body, the torso reaching from the breast-bone to the thigh,
that lascivious image of the male, persisted in the depths of her memory
like the statue of a god embedded in the soil or washed by the surf of a
Tyrrhenian sea. And the farther this encroaching forgetfulness advanced
—and that was the frightful part of it—the more that statue of the god
was shortened, the more emphatic and isolated became its indecency, an
indecency on which forgetfulness encroached more and more slowly,
filching smaller and smaller portions—paralysed by that indecency. That
is only a metaphor, and like all metaphors coarsens the real truth which
is always shadowy, a play of undefined ideas, a mingled current of half-
remembered memories, half-thought thoughts and half-wished desires,
a river without banks, over which rises a silvery vapour, a silvery emanation that spreads to the very clouds and the black sky of stars. So the
torso in the mud of the river was no mere torso, it was a hewn boulder,
it was an isolated piece of furniture, household rubbish jettisoned in the
stream of events, a lump abandoned to the surf: wave succeeded wave,
day was woven into night and night into day, and what the days trans-
mitted to each other was inscrutable, sometimes more inscrutable than
the dreams that followed each other, and at times it included something
that recognizably suggested the secret knowledge of schoolgirls yet at
the same time somehow aroused a secret wish to flee from such infantile
knowledge, to flee into the world of the individual and to disinter
Heinrich's face once more from forgetfulness. But that was only a wish,
and its fulfilment admitted of about as much possibility as the complete
restoration of a Greek statue found in the soil: that is to say, it could not
be fulfilled.

At first sight it might seem irrelevant whether the individual or the
general prevailed in Hanna's memories. But in an age when the general
is everywhere so obviously dominant, where the social bonds of humanity
that are spun only from individual to individual have been loosened in
favour of collective concepts of hitherto undreamed-of unities, where a
de-individualized state of ruthlessness prevails such as is natural only to
childhood and old age, in such a time the memory of an individual cannot
escape subjection to the general law, and the isolation of a highly insignificant woman, be she ever so pretty and ever such an excellent
bedfellow, cannot be explained simply as the result of an unfortunately

complete deprivation of sexual intercourse, but forms a part of the whole and mirrors, like every individual destiny, a metaphysical necessity that is laid upon the world, a physical event, if one likes to call it that, and yet metaphysical in its tragedy: for that tragedy is the isolation of the ego.

CHAPTER LXXII

STORY OF THE SALVATION ARMY GIRL IN BERLIN (13)

Can this age, this disintegrating life, be said still to have reality? My passivity increases from day to day, not because I am exhausted by struggling with a reality that may be stronger than myself, but because on all sides I encounter unreality. I am thoroughly conscious that the meaning and the ethos of my life can be found only in activity, but I begin to suspect that this age no longer has time for the contemplative activity of philosophizing, which is the sole real activity. I try to philosophize—but where is the dignity of knowledge to be found to-day? Is it not long defunct? Has Philosophy itself not disintegrated into mere phrases in face of the disintegration of its object? This world without Being, this world without repose, this world that can find and maintain its equilibrium only in increasing speed of movement, this world's mad racing has become the pseudo-activity of mankind and will hurl it into nothingness—is there any resignation deeper than that of an age which is denied the capacity to philosophize? Philosophy itself has become an æsthetic pastime, a pastime that no longer really exists but has fallen into the empty detachment of evil and become a recreation for citizens who need to kill time of an evening! nothing is left us but number, nothing is left us but law!

It often seems to me as if the state I am now in, the state that keeps me here in this Jewish house, is beyond resignation and is rather a kind of wisdom that has learned to come to terms with a completely alien environment. For even Nuchem and Marie are alien to me, even these two on whom I had set my last hope, the hope that they were my creations, the sweet, unrealizable hope that I had taken their fate into my own hands and could determine it. Nuchem and Marie are not my creatures and never were so. Treacherous hope, to take the liberty of shaping the world!

Does the world have an independent existence? No. Do Nuchem and

Marie have an independent existence? Certainly not, for no being exists in itself. But the moments that determine destinies lie far beyond the range of my thinking or my powers. I myself can only fulfil my own law, supervise my own prescribed business; I am in no case to penetrate farther, and even although my love for Nuchem and Marie is not extinguished, even though I do not relax in the struggle for their souls and their fate, yet the moments by which they are determined are beyond my reach, remain hidden from me, as hidden as the white-bearded grandfather whom I meet, to be sure, now and then in the hall, but who takes on his real shape only in the living-room from which I am always excluded, and who treats with me only through his delegate Litwak; they remain as hidden from me as the white-bearded General Booth whose picture hangs in the reception-room of the hostel. And when I consider it objectively, it is not a combat that I am engaged in, neither with the grandfather nor the Salvation Army General, rather do I strive to see justice done to them, and my wooing of Nuchem and Marie applies also to them; yes, sometimes I believe that my aim is exclusively to win through my actions the love of these old men, to win their blessing so that I may not die lonely. For reality is to be found in them that have laid down the law.

Is this resignation? Is it a revulsion from all æsthetic? Where did I stand of yore? My life is darkening behind me and I do not know if I have lived or if my life was a tale told to me, so far has it sunk in remote seas. Did ships bear me to the shores of the farthest east and farthest west? was I a cotton-picker in American plantations, was I the white hunter in the elephant jungles of India? Everything is possible, nothing, not even a castle in a park, is improbable; heights and depths, all are possible, for nothing permanent has survived in this dynamic activity that exists for its own sake, this activity that is manifest in work, in quietness and serene clarity: nothing has survived—flung to the winds is my ego, flung into nothingness; irrealizable my yearning, unattainable the Promised Land, invisible the ever-brightening but constantly receding radiance, and the community that we grope for is devoid of strength yet full of evil will. Vain hope, and often groundless pride—the world has remained an alien enemy, or even less than an enemy, merely an alien entity whose surface I could explore but into which I could never penetrate, an alien entity into which I shall never penetrate, lost as I am in ever-increasing strangeness, blind in ever-increasing blindness, failing and falling asunder in yearning remembrance of the night of home, to become at last merely a vanishing breath of what has been. I have traversed many ways to find the One in which all the others are conjoined, but they have only diverged more and more from each other, and even God has not been established by me but by my fathers.

I said to Nuchem:

" You are a suspicious people, an angry people; you are jealous even of God and are constantly pulling Him up even in His own Book."

He answered:

" The law is imperishable. God is not until every jot and tittle of the Law has been deciphered."

I said to Marie:

" You are a brave but a thoughtless people! You believe that you need only be good and strike up music in order to draw God near."

She answered:

" Joy in God is God, His grace is inexhaustible."

I said to myself:

" You are a fool, you are a Platonist, you believe that in comprehending the world you can shape it and raise yourself in freedom to Godhood. Can you not see that you are bleeding yourself to death? "

I answered myself:

" Yes, I am bleeding to death."

CHAPTER LXXIII

DISINTEGRATION OF VALUES (9)

Epistemological Excursus.

Can this age be said still to have reality? Does it possess any real value in which the meaning of its existence is preserved? Is there a reality for the non-meaning of a non-existence? In what haven has reality found its refuge? in science, in law, in duty or in the uncertainty of an ever-questioning logic whose point of plausibility has vanished into the infinite? Hegel called history " the path to the liberation of spiritual substance," the path leading to the self-liberation of the spirit, and it has become the path leading to the self-destruction of all values.

Of course the question is not whether Hegel's interpretation of history has been overthrown by the World War; that had been done already by the stars in their courses; for a reality that had grown autonomous through a development extending over four hundred years would have ceased in any circumstances to be capable of submitting any longer to a deductive system. A more important question would be to inquire into the logical possibilities of this emergent anti-deductive reality, into the logical grounds for such anti-deductiveness; in short, to examine " the conditions of possible experience " in which this development of the spirit has become inevitable—but a contempt for all philosophy, a weariness of words, are themselves inherent in this reality and in this development, and it is only with a complete mistrust of the coercive suasion of words that we can pose the urgent methodological questions: what is an historical event? what is historical unity? or, to go still further: what is an event at all? what principle of selection must be followed to weld single occurrences into the unity of an event?

Autonomous life is as indissolubly and organically knit to the category of value as autonomous consciousness is knit to the category of truth,— one could find other names for the phenomena of truth and value, but as phenomena they would remain as irrefutable as *Sum* and *Cogito*, both of them drawn out of the isolated autonomy of the Self, both of them activities as well as surrounding products of that Self; thus value can be split up into the value-making activity, which in the widest sense creates worlds, and into the formed, spatially discernible and generally visible value-product, and the concept of value splits into the corresponding categories: into the ethical value of the activity and the æsthetic value of the product, the obverse and reverse sides of the same medal, and it is in combination and only in combination that these give the most general concept of value and the logical co-ordinates of all life. And, indeed, this is borne out by history: for the writing of history in antiquity was already governed by its concepts of value, the moralizing historians of the eighteenth century applied theirs with full deliberation, and in Hegel's scheme the concept of an absolute value is most clearly revealed in the ideas of a " World-spirit " and a " High Court of History." It is not surprising that the post-Hegelian philosophy of history occupied itself chiefly in considering the methodological function of the concept of value, bringing about incidentally the fateful splitting-up of the whole realm of knowledge into a philosophy of nature unaffected by values and a philosophy of spirit conditioned by values— which, if one likes, may be considered the first declared bankruptcy of philosophy, since it confined the identity of Thought and Being to the realm of logic and mathematics, allowing all the rest of knowledge to dispense with what is the main idealistic task of philosophy or to relegate it to the vagueness of intuition.

Hegel levelled against Schelling the (justified) reproach that he had projected the Absolute into the world "as if it were a bullet from a pistol." But that applies with equal force to the concept of value projected by Hegelian and post-Hegelian philosophy. Simply to project a concept of value into history and summarily to describe as "values" all that history has preserved may be permissible at a pinch for the purely æsthetic values of the creative arts, but is otherwise so sweepingly false that it drives one in contradiction to maintain that history is a conglomeration of non-values, and to deny outright that there is any value-reality in history.

First Thesis:

history is composed of values, since life can be comprehended only in the category of value—yet these values cannot be introduced into reality as absolutes, but can only be thought of in reference to an ethically-motived value-positing subject. Hegel's absolute and objectified "world spirit" was such a subject introduced into reality, but the all-embracing absoluteness of its operation could not but result in a *reductio ad absurdum*. (This is another example of the impassable limits imposed on deductive thinking.) These values are not absolutes, but only finite postulates. Where a concrete and *a priori* finite subject comes into question, that is to say, an actual person, the relativity of values, their dependence on the subject, becomes immediately clear; the biography of any person is composed of all the value-contents which have been important to him. In himself he may be a person of no value, even a destroyer of values, such as a bandit leader or a deserter, but as the centre of his own system of values he is yet a ripe subject for biography and history. And the same is true of the fictive centres of value such as a state, or a club, or a nation, or the German Hanseatic League, historically considered; indeed, even the histories of inanimate objects, as for instance the architectural history of a house, are made up from a selection of those facts which would have been important to the respective subjects if they had had a will to create values. An event without a value-positing centre dissolves into nebulosity—the battle of Kunersdorf consists not of an army list of the Grenadiers who took part in it, but of the reality-formations which were determined by the plans of the commander. Every historical unity depends on an effective or fictive centre of value; the " style " of an epoch would not be discernible unless a unifying principle of selection were assumed at its centre, or a " spirit of the age " which serves as a standard for judging the value-positing and style-creating forces in operation. Or, to fall back on a hackneyed expression, culture is a value-formation, culture can be conceived of only in terms of style, and in order to be conceivable at all it needs the assumption of a style- and value-producing " culture-spirit " at the centre of that circle of values which it represents.

Does this mean that all values are made relative? That one must abandon all hope of the logical Absolute ever manifesting itself in reality through the unifying of thought and being? that one must abandon all hope of ever even drawing near to the path that leads to the self-liberation of the spirit and of humanity?

Second Thesis:

the ripeness for history or for biography of the value-positing action is conditioned by the absoluteness of the Logos. For the actual or fictive value-positing subject can be imagined only in the isolation of its selfhood, in that inevitable, complete, and Platonic isolation whose pride it is to depend exclusively on the precepts of logic, and whose compulsion it is to state all activity in terms of logical plausibility; but this means that one must postulate, in the complete Kantian sense, not only the good will which shapes the work for the work's sake, but also the rule that all consequences must be drawn from the autonomous code of the Self, so that the work, uninfluenced by any dogma, shall spring from the pure originality of the Self and of its law. In other words, whatever does not arise purely in accordance with its own laws vanishes out of history. But however contemporary this individual force of law may be in any age, that is to say, however it may be conditioned by the spirit and style of its age, it can never be anything else than a reflection of the superposed Logos, of that Logos which is active to-day and which is thought itself, a merely earthly reflection, it is true, even in our day, but a reflection through which there gleams that which has a lasting claim to transcend all ages and alone makes it possible for stylized thinking to be projected into another ego. And this formal ultimate unity is continuously and with complete clearness revealed again and again in the narrower sphere of created work and of generally applied æsthetics, for instance in all art, but most obviously in the undying persistence of art forms.

From this we can draw the following comprehensive conclusion, the *Third Thesis:*

the world is a product [1] of the intelligible Self, for the Platonic idea has never been abandoned nor ever can be. But this product is not projected " like a bullet from a pistol," for nothing can be posited but value-making subjects, which in their turn reflect the structure of the intelligible Self and in their turn fashion their own value-products, their own world-formations: the world is not an immediate but a mediate product of the Self, it is " a product of products," " a product of products of products," and so on in infinite iteration. This process, the positing of " products of products," provides the world with its methodological organization and hierarchy, a relative organization, certainly, but yet absolute in form, since the ethical imperative postulated for the effective or fictive value-positing subjects remains undiminished in its force, together with the immanent validity of the Logos within the created product: the logic of things remains unshaken. And even though the logical advance of history must be arrested time and again whenever it reaches the limits of infinity inherent in its metaphysical construction, and though the Platonic view of the world must time and again màke way for a positivistic examination of data, yet the reality of the Platonic idea remains invincible, for with every access of Positivism it merely touches its mother earth again to rise anew, upborne by the bathos of experience.

Every conceptually comprehensible unity in the world is " product of a product," every concept, every thing; and this methodological function of knowledge, of knowledge as an integrator that can comprehend a thing only by regarding it as an autonomous and value-positing subject, probably extends right into mathematics, thus abolishing the distinction between mathematical scientific abstraction and empirical abstraction. For, methodologically regarded, to define a thing as the " product of a product " is nothing else than to introduce the ideal observer into the field of observation, as has been already done long since by the empirical sciences (by physics, for example, in the Theory of Relativity) quite independently of epistemological considerations: and further, research into mathematical first principles, pursuing the questions " what is number? " and " what is unity? " has reached a point at which it has found itself compelled to accept intuition as the

[1] Product = Setzung.

only way out of its difficulties: now the principle of "product of a product" provides intuition with its logical legitimation, for the infiltration of the Self into a hypostatized value-positing subject can be justifiably termed the methodological structure of the act of intuition.

That this principle has been so long unrecognized may perhaps be explained by its obviousness, even its primitiveness. For it is indeed primitive. And the pride of man seems to find insuperable difficulty in admitting the validity of a primitive attitude. For even though this view of everything as the "product of a product" guarantees the presence of the intelligible self in every object throughout the world, yet, if one ignores for a moment this Platonic background, it amounts to a kind of animism that reanimates the whole of nature, nay, the whole of the world in its totality, an animism that introduces a value-subject into everything, into every concept however abstract, and that can be compared only to the animism of primitive peoples: it seems as if the development of logic has an ontogenesis of its own that keeps alive, even in the most highly developed logical structures, all previous and apparently obsolete thought-formations, including that of the simple animism which shortened to one link all chains of plausibility; an ontogenesis that preserves in every new advance of thought the form if not the content of primitive metaphysics—indubitably a stumbling-block for the rationalists, but a consolation to pantheistic feeling.

And yet there is consolation even for the rationalists. For if the principle of "product of products" in its dependence on the governing Logos may be interpreted as the logical structure of the intuitive act, it may also be regarded as the "condition of possible experience" for the otherwise inexplicable fact of the mutual understanding between man and man between one isolated self and another; so it provides not only an epistemological structure that accounts for the translatableness of all languages, be they ever so different from each other, but far beyond that, infinitely far, it provides in the unity of thought a common denominator for all human speech, a warrant for the unity of mankind and of a humanity that even in its self-laceration remains the image of God—for in every thought and in every unity that man creates, the Logos, mirror of himself, shines out upon him, the Word of God shines out as the measure of all things. And even if all that is created in this world were to be annihilated, if all its æsthetic values were abolished and resolved into a function, dissolved in scepticism of all law, nay more, in the imperative duty to question and to doubt, there would yet survive untouched the unity of thought, the ethical postulate, the rigorous operation of ethical value as pure function, the real duty of its most strict observance: all these would survive and with them a continuing unity of the world, a unity of mankind, illuminating all things, still surviving and imperishable through all eternities of space and time.

CHAPTER LXXIV

Dr Flurschütz was helping Jaretzki to fit on his artificial arm. Sister Mathilde too was in attendance.

Jaretzki was jerking at the straps:

" Well, Flurschütz, aren't you heart-broken that I'm leaving you so soon . . . not to speak of Sister Mathilde! "

" Do you know, Jaretzki, I would really like to keep you here for a while longer under observation . . . you're at a highly questionable stage of your development."

" Can't say . . . wait a minute," Jaretzki endeavoured to wedge a cigarette between the fingers of the artificial hand, " . . . wait a minute, how would it do if we added a kind of cigarette-receiver to this . . . or a permanent cigarette-holder . . . that would be quite an ingenious idea . . .? "

" Stand still just for a minute, Jaretzki," Flurschütz fastened the straps, " . . . there, how do you feel? "

" Like a newly-born machine . . . a machine at a fine stage of development . . . if the cigarettes were better it would be still finer."

" Couldn't you let this smoking of yours alone altogether . . . and the other thing too, of course."

" Love? Oh yes, like a shot."

Sister Mathilde said quite superfluously:

" No, Dr Flurschütz meant that you should give up drinking."

" Oh, I see, I didn't understand . . . when one is sober, it's so hard to understand things. . . . I'm surprised that that has never struck you, Flurschütz: it's only when people are drunk that they can understand one another."

" That's a daring attempt at self-justification! "

" But just cast your mind back, Flurschütz, and remember how gloriously drunk we all were in August 1914 . . . it seems to me as though that was the first and the last time that people felt a real sense of fellowship."

" Scheler says something like that. . . ."

" Who? "

" Scheler. *The Genius of War* . . . not much of a book."

" Oh, I see, a book . . . that doesn't count . . . but I tell you this, Flurschütz, and I say it in all seriousness: give me some other, some new drunkenness, it doesn't matter what as far as I'm concerned, morphia or patriotism or communism or anything else that makes a man drunk . . . give me something to make me feel we're all comrades again, and I'll give up drinking . . . to-morrow."

Flurschütz reflected; then he said:

" There's something in what you say . . . but if you must have intoxication and fellowship, there's a simple enough remedy: fall in love."

" Under doctor's orders, certainly . . . have you ever fallen in love under doctor's orders, Sister? "

Sister Mathilde blushed; two red patches appeared amid the freckles that covered her neck.

Jaretzki averted his eyes:

" A bad stage of development for falling in love . . . it seems to me we're all in a bad way . . . even love's no more use . . ." he tested the joints of the artificial arm, " . . . we should really be given instructions for using this thing . . . there must surely be a special joint for cuddling somewhere in it."

Flurschütz strangely enough felt shocked. Perhaps because Sister Mathilde was present. Sister Mathilde blushed still more deeply:

" What ideas you have, Herr Jaretzki! "

" How? they're quite good ideas . . . artificial limbs for making love . . . yes, quite a splendid idea, special models for staff officers, from colonels upwards . . . I'll set up a factory."

Flurschütz said:

" Must you always play the *enfant terrible*? "

" Not at all, I simply have ideas for the armament industry . . . now let's take it off." Jaretzki began to undo the straps; Sister Mathilde helped him. He straightened the joints of the metallic fingers: " There, now it only needs a glove . . . little finger, ring finger and that's the thumb that picks out the plum."

Flurschütz examined the scars on the naked arm stump.

"I think it fits quite all right, only be careful at the beginning that it doesn't rub your arm sore."

"Let the good charwomen rub and scrub . . . this one picks out the plums."

"Well, Jaretzki, as far as you're concerned at any rate, there really seems no hope of common understanding."

CHAPTER LXXV

Huguenau's dodging Esch at the dinner-hour had of course availed nothing. That very same evening there was a violent scene. Nevertheless Esch was soon disarmed, for Huguenau not only took his stand in his documented rights as a publisher, which fully authorized him to insert any article that he liked, but he also employed Esch's own arguments: "My dear friend," he jeered, "you've complained often enough about people queering your pitch when you wanted to unmask public abuses . . . but when someone else has the courage actually to do it you draw in your horns . . . of course one doesn't fling away the favour of a high and mighty Town Commandant in a hurry . . . must always trim your coat to suit the fashion, what?" Yes, Esch had to listen to things like that, and although it was a vile and cowardly attack with which the fellow had taken him in the rear, he could find nothing better as a retort but guttersnipe abuse, and after that had held his tongue.

But Huguenau had thereupon adroitly changed his tactics. He had gone to Frau Esch and complained bitterly that her husband had treated abominably a conscientious partner, simply because said partner had conscientiously and selflessly tried to do his duty. That had not been without its effect, and when next day Esch came up to his dinner he found a sulky and offended Huguenau and a wife who with conciliating words spoke up for Herr Huguenau's innocence, so that before they knew where they were they were reconciled and all supped their soup in peace together, much to the satisfaction of Frau Esch, who was anxious not to lose a patron so generous with his praise.

But perhaps Esch too was actually glad that he had avoided having to show Huguenau the door: one couldn't tell what attacks against the Major this fellow might still have in mind . . . it was best in any case not to let

him out of one's sight. So Huguenau stayed where he was, although these
meals were none too sociable, especially as Esch now took to glaring at
Huguenau across the dishes, mustering him with suspicious eyes.

To Huguenau's credit it must be said that he did his best to brighten
matters: but his efforts met with scant success. Even a week later Esch
was still in his most bearish mood. And to the hesitant inquiries of his
spouse he replied only in a growl: " Emigrate to America. . . ." After
which nothing more was said. Finally, however, Huguenau leant back
satiated, and broke the uncomfortable silence with these auspicious words:

" Mother Esch," he said, lifting one finger, " Mother Esch, I've hunted
up a farmer who will deliver flour to us, maybe a gammon occasionally
too."

" Indeed? " said Esch mistrustfully, " where have you picked him up? "

Of course this farmer was non-existent, but what is non-existent may
one day come to life, and Huguenau was annoyed that his good will was
never recognized. Yet he did not want to get into a squabble with Esch
so soon again, on the contrary he wanted to say something conciliatory:

" We must lighten things a little for Mother Esch if we can . . . four
mouths . . . I'm surprised that she manages it at all . . . for one must
count in the kid as well."

Esch smiled:

" Yes, the little one."

Huguenau said forthcomingly:

" Where has she been hiding herself? "

Frau Esch sighed:

" You're right, nowadays it's no trifle to fill four mouths . . . it would
have been better if my husband hadn't saddled us with the worry of the
child."

" I refuse to listen to a word about that," Esch burst out. He looked
angrily across at his wife, who sat there with a curiously frigid smile, as
though conscious of guilt. Esch was somewhat mollified: " When there's
no new life, everything's dead."

" That's so," said Frau Esch, " that's so."

Huguenau said:

" But she runs about the streets all day . . . with the boys; you mark
my words, she'll run away yet."

" Oh, it suits her quite well to stay with us," said Frau Esch. And
Esch, almost warily, almost as though he were touching a pregnant

woman, gripped his wife above the elbow by the thick arm: " And I say that she likes to stay with us, do you hear? "

Huguenau was exasperated by the two of them. He said:

" It suits me too to stay with you, Mother Esch . . . wouldn't you like to adopt me as well? " He would have liked to add that Esch then would have the son that he was always raving about and that was to build the house—but for some reason incomprehensible even to himself he felt deeply indignant, and the whole business seemed to him no longer a matter for jest. If Esch had suddenly sprung up and threatened him Huguenau would not have been surprised. No doubt about it, it would be better to slip away and look for Marguerite; she would probably be down in the courtyard. The best thing would be to fly from the place and take Marguerite with him.

Frau Esch too seemed terrified by the unreasonable request that Huguenau had made to her. She felt her arm clasped by her husband's bony hand, and with her mouth open she stared at Huguenau, who meanwhile had risen; only when he had reached the door did she stammer: " And why not, Herr Huguenau? . . ."

Huguenau heard her, but it did not lessen his bitter indignation against Esch. He found Marguerite below and presented her with a whole mark. " For your travels," he said, " but you must dress yourself properly for going away . . . warm knickers . . . let me see . . . it seems to me you're almost naked . . . in autumn it's cold."

CHAPTER LXXVI

It was already past nine when Dr Kessel's door-bell rang. Kühlenbeck was sitting in the corner of the sofa smoking his cigar: " Well, Kessel, is this another patient? " " What else can it be? " replied Kessel, who had risen automatically, " what else . . . not a single night that one can sleep in peace." And he walked wearily into the next room to fetch his bag.

Meanwhile the maid had come up: " Herr Doctor, Herr Doctor, the Herr Major is below." " Who? " shouted Kessel from the next room. " The Herr Major." " It must be something for me," said Kühlenbeck. " I'm coming at once," cried Kessel, and, his black bag still in his hand, he hurried out to receive the guest.

Presently the Major appeared in the doorway; he smiled a little awkwardly:

" I knew that you two gentlemen were here together . . . and as you so kindly invited me once, Herr Doctor Kessel . . . I thought that you two gentlemen were perhaps having a musical evening."

" Well, thank God there's nothing happened. I thought something had gone wrong again," said Kühlenbeck, " . . . well, all the better."

" No, nothing has gone wrong," said the Major.

" No more revolts? " said Kühlenbeck, with his usual tactlessness, an'd went on: " Who really was it that put that idiotic article in the *Herald*? Esch, or that clown with the French name? "

The Major did not reply; he had been unpleasantly affected by Kühlenbeck's question. He regretted having come. Kühlenbeck however went on:

" Well, prison can't be exactly comfortable for these gentry . . . but they're safely away from the Front and that should be enough to keep them contented. They must have forgotten what a sheer stroke of luck it is to be alive, simply to live, no matter how shabbily . . . human beings have short memories."

" These newspaper people," said the Major, although it was not a real answer at all.

" I was afraid that it was another summons to a patient," said Kessel, " it's to be hoped that there won't be anybody to-night."

Kühlenbeck went on talking:

" An unheard-of luxury for the State to keep prisons going these days . . . superfluous in any case . . . the whole world is a prison . . . but it can't last for much longer . . . besides the prison here should have been evacuated long ago . . . what will we do with these people when we've all got to shift? "

" It hasn't come to that yet," said the Major, " and with God's help it won't come to that either." He said this, but he did not believe it. Only that afternoon he had received another secret order with instructions in case of the possible evacuation of the town. Orders and counter-orders were coming in pell-mell and one did not know what the next hour would bring. It was a veritable pit.

Kühlenbeck regarded his great capable surgeon's hands.

" If the French come across here . . . take my word for it, we'll strangle them with our bare hands."

Kessel said:

" Sometimes I think it a good thing that my wife is not alive to see these times." He gazed at the photograph which hung over the piano surrounded by a wreath of immortelles and a band of *crêpe*.

The Major too gazed up at it: "Your wife was musical too?" he asked at last. Beside the piano stood the 'cello in a grey-linen case on whose cover a red lyre and two crossed flutes were embroidered. Why had he come here? Why had he come to see these doctors? did he feel ill? and he couldn't stand doctors, they were all Freethinkers and unreliable. Had no sense of honour. There sat the Surgeon-Major with his head laid back on the corner of the sofa, blowing smoke rings up towards the ceiling, sticking his pointed beard into the air. It was all unseemly. Why had he come here? yet better to be here all the same than in the lonely hotel bedroom, or in the dining-hall where any moment that fellow Huguenau might appear. Kessel had rung for another bottle of Berncastler, and the Major hastily drank a glass. Then he said: "I thought that you would be having some music."

Kessel smiled absently:

"Yes, my wife was very musical."

Kühlenbeck said:

"What do you say, Kessel? why not fetch out your 'cello for once? . . . it will do us all good."

The Major felt that Kühlenbeck was wanting to show him a kindness, even if it was perhaps a little too familiar of him. So he merely said: "Yes, that would be splendid."

Kessel went over to the 'cello and with a glance at the photograph took out the instrument. But then he stopped: "Yes, but who will play the accompaniment for me?"

"You'll manage all right by yourself, Kessel," said Kühlenbeck, "pluck does it." Kessel still hesitated a little: "Yes, but what shall I play?" "Something with feeling," said Kühlenbeck, and Kessel drew in a chair and seated himself beside the piano, as though there were someone there accompanying him; he struck a note, ran his hand tenderly over the strings of the bow and tuned the instrument. Then he closed his eyes.

He played Brahms' 'cello sonata in E flat, Op. 38. His mild face had a curious inward look, the grey moustache above his compressed lips was no longer a moustache, but a grey shadow, the furrows in his cheeks had altered their contours, it was no longer a face, it was almost invisible

perhaps a grey autumnal landscape waiting for the snow to come. And
even when a tear trickled down his nose, it was no longer a tear. Only
the hand was still a hand, and it was as though the stroke of the bow
had drawn all life into itself, rising and falling on the waves of the soft
brown stream of sound which became broader and broader, flowing
round and enclosing the player, so that he was cut off and very alone.
He played. Probably he was only a dilettante, but that could well be a
matter of indifference to him, as it was for the Major and even perhaps
for Kühlenbeck: for the clamorous silence of that time, its tumult of
dumb impenetrable noise raised up between one human being and
another, a wall through which the human voice cannot penetrate, so
that it has to falter and die—the terrifying silence of that time was
cancelled, Time itself was cancelled and shaped itself into space which
enclosed them all while Kessel's 'cello rang out, uprearing sound,
upbuilding space, fulfilling space, fulfilling them also.

When the music had died away and Dr Kessel once more became
Dr Kessel, the Major gave himself a little jerk so as to conceal his
emotion under a prescribed military bearing. And he waited for Kessel
now to say something comforting—surely one might say it now! But
Dr Kessel merely bent his head and one could see the meagre locks—
not at all like Esch's grey stiff brush of hair—that sparsely covered the
top of his head. Almost with shame he put the instrument away, shoving
it into its linen case, which gave one almost an unseemly impression,
and Kühlenbeck from his sofa corner merely muttered " Ay." Perhaps
they were all three ashamed.

At last Kühlenbeck said:

" Ay, doctors are a musical lot."

The Major searched his memory. In his youth he had had a friend,
or was it a friend? who had played the violin, but he was not a doctor,
although he . . . perhaps, indeed, he was a doctor or had wanted to be
one. Memory stopped there, memory froze, movement froze, and the
Major saw nothing but his own bare hand resting on the black cloth
of his army trousers. And independently of his own will his lips said
" Naked and exposed. . . ."

" I beg your pardon! " said Kühlenbeck.

The Major turned towards him: " Oh, nothing . . . these are bad times
. . . I thank you, Herr Doctor Kessel."

Now Kessel said at last:

" Yes, music is a comfort in these times . . . there's not much else left in the way of comfort."

Kühlenbeck brought his hand down on the table:

" Don't whine, Kessel . . . for let the world be full of devils, we dare not despair . . . let peace only come and we'll raise our heads again."

The Major shook his head:

" Against foul treachery one is powerless." The image of Esch rose before him, that tanned brown face with the challenging smile, yes, challenging was the right word, that face which nevertheless seemed somehow to be asking for forgiveness and now had the reproachful expression of a horse that has fallen and cannot get up again.

" We Germans have always been betrayed," said Kühlenbeck, " and we're still alive in spite of it." He raised his glass: " Long live Germany! "

The Major too raised his glass, and he thought, " Germany," thought of the order and security which Germany had hitherto meant to him. He could no longer see Germany. In some way or other he held Huguenau responsible for the misfortunes of the Fatherland, for the marching through of troops, for the contradictory orders of the Army Command, for the unchivalrous weapons of this war of gas, for the growing and general disorder. And he would actually have liked the image of Esch to melt and blend into one with that of Huguenau, proving that they were both emissaries of the Evil One, both adventurers who had emerged out of that inextricable turmoil filled with business affairs and faces which one did not understand, both unreliable and contemptible, loaded with guilt, demoniacally loaded with guilt for the disastrous conclusion of the war:

Kessel said:

" I'm finished with it. . . . I'll do my duty, but I'm finished with it."

An inextricable maze was life, the net of evil lay over the world, and the dumb, stupendous din had begun again. Whoever strayed from the strict path of evangelical Christian duty was a sinner, and the hope that divine grace might fulfil itself here below had been a sinful hope, though proclaimed by the voice of the friend who had shattered the silence and rigidity that encased him and released him from his isolation in a blissful outpouring of the soul. And the Major said: " We have strayed from the path of duty and must bear the penalty."

" Well, well, Herr Major," laughed Kühlenbeck, " I don't agree with you there, but I do agree that it's time we were striking the path for home, so that our exhausted friend Kessel may get to his little bed." He had got up, his army coat hung somewhat loosely on his massive body. A disguised civilian, the Major could not help thinking—that wasn't the King's uniform. Major von Pasenow had also risen. Why had he come here, he, an officer in the King's uniform? Earthly duty was a reflection of divine ordinance, and the service of something greater than oneself obliged a man to subordinate his life to higher ideas, demanded from him that he should give up even the last thin strip of personal freedom left him, if it was necessary. Voluntary obedience, yes, that was the attitude laid down by God; all the rest was to be regarded as non-existent. The Major pulled down his coat so that it hung straight, touched the ribbon of his Iron Cross, and in the punctilious military correctness with which he took his leave he found again that serenity and security which duty and a uniform bestow on men.

Dr Kessel had escorted them downstairs. At the door the Major said with a certain formality: " I thank you, Herr Doctor Kessel, for the artistic treat which you have given us." Kessel hesitated a little in replying and then he said in a low voice: " I should thank you, Herr Major . . . this is the first time since the death of my dear wife that I have touched my 'cello." The Major, however, did not hear and merely held out his hand with a certain stiffness. He went with Kühlenbeck through narrow streets, they crossed the market-place, a thin autumnal rain blew slantingly in their faces, they both wore the grey overcoat of an officer, both wore officers' caps, and yet they were not comrades in the King's uniform. The Major noted this inwardly.

CHAPTER LXXVII

STORY OF THE SALVATION ARMY GIRL IN BERLIN (14)

Perceptions which are attained through fastings and self-mortifications certainly lack a final logical sharpness. I think I may say with certainty that about this time a change took place in my perceptive states. I regarded this transformation, however, with the utmost distrust, as it went hand in hand with long-continued under-nourishment; indeed I was almost prepared to agree with Dr Litwak's diagnosis and admit that I was sick, especially as the change consisted in a feeling of great physical lucidity rather than in a sharpening of my perception of the world round me. For instance if I put the old question to myself whether my life still possessed any intelligible reality, it was this physical feeling that provided me with the answer and gave me the certitude of living in a sort of second-grade reality, giving rise to a kind of unreal reality, of real unreality, which sent through me a thrill of strange gladness. It was a state, as it were, hovering between knowledge not yet grasped and knowledge grasped, a symbol that had found another symbol for itself, a sleep-walking that led towards the light, a fear that annulled itself and yet rose reborn again from itself; it was like a hovering above the sea of death, a winged rising and falling over the waves without touching them, so light had I become,—it was an almost physical intuition by which I seized the higher Platonic reality of the world, and all my being was filled with the certainty that I needed take only a small step to transform this physical intuition into a rational one.

In this wavering reality things streamed towards me and streamed into me and I had no need to raise a finger. What had formerly looked like passivity now found its meaning. If formerly I had stayed inside to give free rein to my thoughts, to hold philosophical monologues and now and then to jot down the heads of them, now I stayed in my room like an invalid who is obedient to his doctor and his malady. Everything turned out as Dr Litwak had prophesied. He visits me now regularly, and sometimes I myself actually call him in; and when, suddenly changing his opinion, he sets out to prove to me that I am not ill at all, " You're just a little anæmic and more than half-crazy," he seems to be right in that too, for I feel as though there were very little blood in my veins. I don't want to think any longer, not, however, because I would be incapable of it; no, I don't think any longer simply because I despise thinking. It is not that I have become so very wise as all that, I make no claim whatever to have reached the final plane of knowledge, or to have surmounted knowledge—alas, I know too well that I am far below the plane of knowledge; what keeps me from thinking is rather the fear of losing this hovering state, a fear that conceals itself behind contempt for the word. Or is it the suddenly awakened conviction that the unity of thought and being can be realized only within the most modest limits? Both thought and being reduced to their minimum!

Marie sometimes visits me, brings me gifts of food as she does to her other invalids, and I accept them. Recently she arrived when Litwak and

Nuchem were with me. According to her normal custom she greeted them with a friendly " God bless you " and Litwak responded with his usual answer: " A hundredfold." Marie coughed and he put on a solicitous face: " You should be careful," he said, from which it remained uncertain whether he meant the presumable presence of lung trouble in Marie or the danger of infection to which he saw Nuchem exposed. He offered also to examine Marie free of charge, and when she declined he said: " You should at least go out walking as much as you can in the fresh air . . . and take him with you, he's anæmic." Nuchem stood about and glanced through my books. For the rest, Litwak was always prescribing new medicines for me, and when he handed me the prescription he would laugh: " You won't take it in any case, but a doctor must prescribe something." We had arrived at a kind of mutual understanding.

What was the point of contact between us? why had I to stay with these people? why had this provisory Jewish domicile become a permanency for me, which I could no longer imagine myself leaving? why did I yield so obediently to those Jews? everything was provisory, these refugees were provisory, yes, so was their whole existence, and Time itself was provisory too, as provisory as the war, which was lingering on past its own end. The provisory seems to have become the definitive; incessantly it cancels itself and yet remains. It pursues us and we come to terms with it, in a Jewish house, in a hostel. But it lifts us above the past, it holds us suspended in a happy, almost euphorian hovering state in which everything looks towards the future.

Finally I obeyed Dr Litwak and went out for walks whenever Nuchem or Marie could accompany me.

These autumn days were very beautiful and I sat with Marie under the trees. And as everything had a radiant candour, and as words were of no consequence, I asked her:

" Are you a fallen woman? "

" I was one," she replied.

" And are you chaste now? "

" Yes."

" You know that you'll never save Nuchem? "

" Yes, I know."

" Then you love him? "

She smiled.

Mirror of itself, symbol of a symbol! to what bourne can the continuous chain of symbols lead us if not to death!

" Listen, Marie, I've made up my mind to kill myself, to shoot myself or jump into the Landwehr Canal . . . but you must go with me, by myself I won't move a step."

That sounded like a joke, but it was seriously meant. She must have guessed that, for without smiling, almost matter-of-factly, she replied:

" No, I won't do that, and you mustn't kill yourself either."

" But your love for Nuchem is quite hopeless."

She was unable to draw any consequences from that; she simply fixed her eyes questioningly on me, searching for the possibility of an understanding between us. Her eyes were colourless.

It was not a very pleasant game that I was playing with her, and yet the understanding between us must have been already established, for she said:

" We are in the joy of the Lord."

I said:

" Nuchem will not kill himself, he daren't, he is under the law, but we are in the joy of the Lord . . . we can dare to do it."

Perhaps the thought that Nuchem was preserved from all danger of suicide reassured her, for now she smiled again, yes, she even crossed her legs like a lady and the superior complacency of a lady was written on her face:

" We too are under the law."

I could not take offence at her Salvation Army phrases, it may be because while one is in a provisory state every phrase loses its meaning, it may be because then it takes on a new meaning beforehand and fits the case. It may be that words too can hover between the past and the future, that they too hover between the law and the joy of the Lord, taking refuge from the contempt which is their deserved fate in a new meaning in the unstable flux.

Yet I did not want to hear anything about the law, for it had recalled me back to reality; I did not want to hear anything about the law, I wanted to maintain intact my own state of suspension, and I asked:

" You're happy, in spite of your hopeless love? "

" Yes," she said.

Irretrievably lost is our home, inaccessibly stretches the distance before us, but our grief is eased more and more, becomes more and more transparent, perhaps even invisible; nothing remains but a painful echo of what has once been. And Marie said:

" The sorrow in the world is great, but the joy of the Lord is greater."

I said:

" Oh, Marie, you have known what estrangement is and yet you are happy . . . and you know that death alone, that your last moment alone, will annul that estrangement, and yet you desire to live."

She replied:

" Whoever lives in Christ is never alone . . . come to us."

" No," I said, " I belong to my Jewish quarters, I'm going to Nuchem."

But that no longer made any impression on her.

CHAPTER LXXVIII

A man whose arms have been amputated is a torso. This thought was the bridge which Hanna Wendling was accustomed to employ when she endeavoured to find her way back from the general to the individual and the concrete. And at the end of this bridge stood not Heinrich, but, swaying a little, Jaretzki with his empty sleeve tucked into the pocket of his army coat. It took a long time before she was able to recognize this fancy clearly, and still longer before she grasped that it might in some way correspond to an actual reality. And then another considerable time passed before she summoned the decision to ring up Dr Kessel.

This extremely retarded process was certainly not caused by a particularly strong moral sense; no, it was simply that she had lost any feeling for time or tempo, it was a slowing down of the life-stream, yet not at all a damming up of it, but rather an evaporation into nothingness, an oozing away into a completely porous ground, a vanishing without remembrance of her thoughts as she thought them. And when Dr Kessel as arranged called for her in his buggy to take her to the town, it seemed to her that she had called in the doctor on account of some strange anxiety, which she could not formulate, about her son, and only with an effort did she manage to get her memory to work. Then, it is true, she asked at once in sudden apprehension, which she immediately forgot again— they were just crossing the garden—who the one-armed lieutenant in the hospital really was. Dr Kessel was at a loss for a moment, but when he had helped her into the buggy and groaning a little sat down beside her he suddenly recollected: " Of course, you mean Jaretzki, of course . . .

poor young fellow, he's to be sent to an institution for nervous cases now, I believe." With which the Jaretzki episode was finished for Hanna. She dispatched her purchases in the town, sent off a parcel to Heinrich, absolved a visit to Röders. She had asked Walter to meet her there; then they were to walk home together. Her inexplicable anxieties about Walter were all at once gone. It was a mild and peaceful autumn evening.

It would not have been surprising if Hanna Wendling had dreamt that night of a Greek torso buried in the river mud or a block of marble or—even that would have sufficed—a pebble washed by the stream. But as she remembered no such dream it would be neither honest nor relevant to express any opinion on the matter. On the other hand it is certain that she passed a restless night and often awoke and peered across at the open window, waiting for the venetian blinds to be raised and the masked head of a burglar to appear. Next morning she thought of furnishing the storeroom beside the kitchen for the use of the gardener and his wife, so that there should be at any rate a man in the house whom one could summon in case of anything happening, but she rejected the plan, for the weakly little gardener would be really no protection, and all that remained was a residue of violent indignation against Heinrich for putting the gardener's house at such a distance from the villa; also he had neglected to have bars fixed over the windows. Yet she herself had to admit that all this uneasiness had hardly anything to do with real fear; it was not so much fear as a sort of exasperation at the lonely and isolated position of the villa, and although Hanna would certainly have felt and expressed a repugnance to any house where she was in closer contact with her neighbours, yet the empty space which surrounded the villa was so empty, the dead landscape, which looked as though it had been patched together out of scraps and bits, was so dead, that it became as it were a ring of vacancy which coiled itself more and more closely round her loneliness, a ring which could be broken only by a violent stroke, by bursting it, by an assault from inside or an invasion from outside. Shortly before she had read something in the newspaper about the Russian Revolution and the soviets, under the heading " The Invasion from Below "; she had remembered this phrase during the night and it returned again and again to her mind like the refrain of a popular song. In any case it would be well to get an estimate for affixing bars to the windows from Krahl the locksmith.

The nights grew longer and the cold moon lay in the sky like a pebble.

In spite of the piercing cold Hanna could not summon up the resolution to close the window. Still more than the appearance of a noiseless burglar she dreaded the crash that would be made if the window panes were forced in, and this strange tension, which was not actually fear, yet was on the point at any moment of toppling over into panic, betrayed her into quasi-romantic gestures. So now almost every night she leaned against the open window and gazed out at the dead zone of the autumn, curiously attracted, almost drawn out of herself into the vacancy of the landscape, and her fear, which by that attraction was denuded of all fear, became a light bubble—her heart bore itself as lightly as a flower, and the rigidity of her isolation opened out in the released freedom of her breathing. And that was almost like a blissful infidelity towards Heinrich, it was a state which she experienced as the diametrical opposite of another and past state . . . yes, but what state? and then she became aware that it was the opposite of what she had once called the physical experience. And the best of it was that at those moments the physical experience was completely forgotten.

CHAPTER LXXIX

Esch's fears were destined to be realized: Huguenau got the Major into fresh trouble. It must be admitted, however, that Huguenau's rôle at first was a passive one.

At the beginning of October there arrived on the Major's desk one of those lists which the Army Command issued from time to time in its attempt to track down all soldiers missing from their regiments, including suspected deserters; and among the names there was that of a certain Wilhelm Huguenau from Colmar, a private in the Fourteenth Fusiliers.

The Major had already laid the list aside when he grew aware that something was bothering him. So he picked it up once more; being far-sighted he held it out at arm's-length, turning it to the light, and read again: "Wilhelm Huguenau," a name that he surely had heard before. He looked up questioningly at the orderly whose duty it was to wait while the day's post was examined; he was just able to see that the man, obviously expecting some order, had drawn himself up at attention, and was just able to collect his strength sufficiently to say, "You may go," but once he was alone he sank forward over the desk with his face buried in his hands.

From this blank confusion he started up with the thought that the orderly was still standing by the door and that the orderly was Esch. At first he did not dare to look and see, but when he finally assured himself that there was no one there he said aloud in the empty room: "Well, it doesn't matter . . ." as if that settled it. But that did not settle it, the image of Esch still stood by the door gazing at him, gazing at him as if it had just discovered that he was a branded man. It was a stern reproachful look that rested upon him, and the Major was ashamed because he had watched Huguenau dancing. But that remembrance died away and suddenly he heard Esch's voice: "There's always a traitor among us."

"There's always a traitor among us," repeated the Major. A traitor is a dishonourable man, a traitor is a man who betrays his fatherland, a traitor is a man who is false to his fatherland, false to his fatherland and his comrades . . . a deserter is a traitor. And while in this manner his thoughts were gradually drawing closer to some veiled and hidden preoccupation, suddenly the veil was rent and all at once he knew everything, everything: he himself was the traitor, he himself, the Town Commandant, had allied himself with a deserter and had looked on while the man danced, he had allied himself with a deserter so that he might be invited into an editorial office, so that the deserter might pave the way for him into civilian affairs, into friendships with men who were not comrades . . . the Major put his hand up to the Iron Cross and tore at its ribbon: a traitor had no right to a decoration, a traitor must be deprived of his decoration, could not be buried with it on his breast . . . a deed of dishonour could be paid for only with a pistol bullet . . . one had to take the punishment on one's own shoulders . . . and the Major, rigidly immobile, with a frozen look in his eyes, said: "The unchivalrous end."

His hand was still touching the buttons of his uniform; mechanically he assured himself that they were all fastened, and that was a strange reassurance, a kind of hope that one could still return to duty, to one's own secure life, even although Esch's image had not yet vanished. It was a glittering and uncanny image, it stood in the other world and yet in this, it was both good and evil, it was bright and assured and yet had all the unreliability of the civilian, of the man who has his waistcoat open at the neck and lets his shirt be seen. And the Major, his fingers still on his uniform buttons, drew himself up, smoothed the

wrinkles out of his coat, passed his hand over his forehead and said:
"Phantasms."

He would have liked to send for Esch; Esch was the man to clear
everything up . . . he longed to do it, but that would be a fresh deviation
from the path of duty, a fresh deviation into civilian affairs. That must
not happen. Besides . . . one must decide things for oneself: all these
suspicions might prove groundless . . . and, on reflection, it was certain
that this Huguenau had always behaved in a correct and patriotic manner
. . . perhaps everything would be cleared up yet and turn out well.

With hands that still trembled a little the Major held the list again
before his eyes, then he laid it down and addressed himself to the other
letters that had come in. Yet, strong as was the effort he made to bring
his thoughts under control, it was not strong enough to master the contradictory orders and service instructions before him; he was incapable
of resolving the contradictions. Chaos was invading the world on every
side and chaos was spreading over his thoughts and over the world,
darkness was spreading, and the advance of darkness sounded like the
agony of a painful death, like a death-rattle in which only one thing was
audible, only one thing certain, the downfall of the Fatherland—oh,
how the darkness was rising and the chaos, and out of that chaos, as if
from a sink of poisonous gases, there grinned the visage of Huguenau,
the visage of the traitor, the instrument of divine wrath, the author of
all the encroaching evil.

For two whole days the Major endured the torment of an indecision
that the pressure of precipitate events kept him from realizing. In face
of the general disorder it would have been quite natural had he simply
let the matter drop, for a desertion was of little account; but it was just
as natural for the Town Commandant not even to consider the possibility of such an easy way out. For the categorical imperative of duty
cannot allow evasion to be piled upon evasion; and on the second day
the Major gave instructions for Huguenau to be summoned.

At the sight of the traitor all the Major's repressed disgust broke out
with renewed force. Huguenau's friendly greeting he countered with
officia reserve, and reaching the list across the table pointed silently to
the name "Wilhelm Huguenau," which was marked with a red line.
Huguenau realized that everything was now at stake, and face to face
with imminent danger drew again upon the lucid assurance that had
hitherto preserved him. The tone that he adopted was light enough, but

behind the flashing eyeglasses the firmness of his look was an indication
to the Major that here was a man who knew very well how to defend
himself.

" I have been expecting something like this for a long time, my dear
Major, the disorder in the army, if you will allow me to say so, is daily
increasing . . . yes, you may shake your head, but so it is; I am, unfortunately, a living witness to it; when I reported at the Central Press
Office the sergeant on duty took all my papers from me, in order, as he
said, to send particulars to my regiment; I suspected at once that I
would have grave difficulties, since it isn't the thing to send a soldier
anywhere without his papers—you agree with me there, of course—
but I was reassured when they told me that they would send on the
papers after me. All that I got was a provisional travelling-permit for
Trier, you understand, I had nothing in my pocket but that permit,
otherwise I was left to my own resources! Well, and I had to give up
the permit, of course, to the military police at the station . . . that's the
whole story. Of course I must admit that I shouldn't have kept on
forgetting about it, but you know better than anyone, sir, how over-
burdened I am with work, and when the authorities are so remiss one can't
blame a simple taxpayer who's doing his best to defend his country. At
least, one would think so. But instead of setting their own house in
order they find it naturally much easier to brand a respectable man as a
deserter. If my patriotic duty did not forbid me, sir, I would gladly
expose such incredible conduct in the Press! "

All that sounded plausible; the Major was again undecided.

" If I might venture to suggest it, sir, you should take up this line;
inform the army police and the regiment—sticking to the truth—that
I am in charge here of the official newspaper for the region, and that I
shall send on as soon as possible the missing papers, which I shall
meanwhile try to procure."

The Major's ill-humour fastened on the phrase " sticking to the
truth." What language the man dared to use!

" It's not for you to prescribe to me what reports I am to make.
Besides, to stick completely to the truth: I don't believe you!"

" You don't believe me? Has it perhaps occurred to you, sir, to find
out whether the informer who laid this accusation is trustworthy?
And that it can be only the work of some informer—and a stupid and
malicious one at that—is as clear as daylight. . . ."

He stared triumphantly at the Major, who, surprised by this new attack, did not even remember that for this particular accusation no informer had been necessary. And triumphantly Huguenau continued:

" How many people, after all, know that I have had trouble about my papers? only one, so far as I know, and that one has often enough abused me as a traitor, pretending that he was speaking in joke, or symbolically, as he chooses to put it; you have only to cast your mind back, sir. . . . I know these sham-pious jokers . . . religious mania's what people call it, and a poor man like me can lose all his money because of it, not to speak of his head. . . ."

The Major interrupted him with unexpected suddenness; he even rapped on the table with the paper-knife:

" Will you have the goodness to leave Herr Esch out of the question? He is an honourable man."

Perhaps it was not wise of Huguenau to persist in hanging on, for his house of cards threatened every minute to collapse. He knew that, but something within him said " va banque " and he could not do otherwise:

" I beg respectfully, sir, to point out that it is you and not I who mention Herr Esch by name. So I'm not mistaken, and he's the fine informer, is he? Ah, if that's the way the wind's blowing, and it's to please Herr Esch that you do his dirty work for him, then all I ask, my dear sir, is to be arrested."

This shaft went home. The Major pointed a finger at Huguenau and stammered with difficulty:

" Out you get . . . out you get . . . I'll have you thrown out."

" As you please, Herr Major . . . quite as you please. I know what I have to expect from a Prussian officer who adopts such means to remove a witness of his defeatist speeches in communistic gatherings; it's all very well to trim your sails to the wind, but it's not my habit to denounce the trimmer. . . . Salut."

These last words, which were really sheer nonsense and only added by Huguenau to embellish his rhetoric, were not even heard by the Major. He kept on murmuring tonelessly: " Out you get . . . he's to get out . . . the traitor " long after Huguenau had left the room and disrespectfully banged the door behind him. It was the end, the unchivalrous end! he was branded for ever!

Was there still a way of escape? no, there was none . . . the Major drew his army revolver from the drawer of his desk and laid it before him.

Then he took a sheet of letter-paper and laid it also before him; it was to be his petition for a successor to relieve him. He would have preferred simply to ask to be cashiered in disgrace. But the punctual performance of official duties must go on. He would not leave his place until he had handed everything over in a regular manner.

Although the Major believed that he was doing all this with prompt and soldier-like dispatch, his actions were extremely slow and every movement cost him a painful effort. And it was with an intense effort that he began to write: he wanted to write with a firm hand. Perhaps the very intensity of the strain he put upon himself prevented him from getting further than the first words: " To the . . ." he had traced upon the paper, in letters that seemed unrecognizable even to himself, and there he stuck —the pen-nib was splintered, it had torn the paper and made an ugly splutter. And firmly, even convulsively, clutching the pen-handle the Major slowly crumpled up, no longer a Major but a worn old man. He attempted again to dip the broken nib into the ink but without success, he only knocked over the inkpot, and the ink ran in a narrow stream over the top of the desk and trickled on to his trousers. The Major paid no attention to it. He sat there with ink-stained hands and stared at the door through which Huguenau had vanished. But when some time later the door opened and the orderly appeared he managed to sit up and stretch out his arm commandingly: " Get out," he ordered the somewhat flustered man, " get out . . . I am staying at my post."

CHAPTER LXXX

Jaretzki had gone off with Captain von Schnaack. The sisters were still standing in front of the gate waving after the carriage that was taking both men to the station. When they turned to re-enter the house Sister Mathilde looked peaked and old-maidish. Flurschütz said:

" It was really terribly decent of you to take him under your wing last night . . . the fellow was in an awful state . . . where on earth did he get hold of the vodka? "

" An unfortunate man," said Sister Mathilde.

" Have you ever read *Dead Souls*? "

" Let me think . . . I believe I have. . . ."

" Gogol," said Sister Carla, with the pride of ready information, " Russian serfs."

" Jaretzki is a dead soul," said Flurschütz, then, after a pause, pointing to a group of soldiers in the garden, " . . . that's what they all are, dead souls . . . probably all of us, too; it's touched all of us somewhere."

" Can you lend me the book? " asked Sister Mathilde.

" I don't have it here . . . but we can get hold of it . . . as for books . . . do you know, I can't read anything now. . . ."

He had sat down on the seat beside the porch and was staring at the road, at the mountains, at the clear autumnal sky that was darkening in the north. Sister Mathilde hesitated a moment, then she too sat down.

" You know, Sister, we really need to discover some new means of communication, something beyond speech . . . all that is written and said has become quite dumb and meaningless . . . something new is needed, or else our chief is absolutely in the right with his surgery. . . ."

" I don't quite understand," said Sister Mathilde.

" Oh, it's not worth bothering about, it's just . . . I only meant that if our souls are dead there's nothing for it but the surgical knife . . . but that's just nonsense."

Sister Mathilde thought of something:

" Didn't Lieutenant Jaretzki say something like that when his arm had to be amputated? "

" Very possibly he did, he's infected with radicalism too . . . of course he couldn't be anything but radical . . . like every trapped animal. . . ."

Sister Mathilde was shocked by the word " animal ":

" I believe he was only trying to forget everything . . . he once hinted at that; and all that drinking . . ."

Flurschütz had pushed his cap back; he felt the scar on his forehead and passed his finger over it.

" Well, I shouldn't be surprised if we were entering on a time when people will do nothing but try to forget, only to forget: to sleep and eat and sleep and eat . . . just like our fellows here . . . to sleep and eat and play cards. . . ."

" But that would be dreadful, to live without ideals! "

" My dear Sister Mathilde, what you are seeing here is scarcely the war, it's only a miniature edition of the war . . . you haven't been out of this place for four years . . . and all the men keep a shut mouth even when they're wounded . . . keep a shut mouth and forget about it . . . but you can take my word for it, not one of them has brought back any ideals."

Sister Mathilde got up. The thunder-clouds were now outlined against the clear sky like a broad black wall.

" I'm going to apply for a field hospital again as soon as I can," he said.

" Lieutenant Jaretzki believes that the war is never going to come to an end."

" Yes . . . perhaps that's just why I want to get out there again."

" I suppose I ought to go out there too. . . ."

" Oh, you're doing your bit here, Sister."

Sister Mathilde looked up at the sky.

" I must bring in the deck-chairs."

" Yes, you'd better do that, Sister."

CHAPTER LXXXI

It was Saturday; Huguenau was paying out the week's wages in the printing-room.

Life had gone on in the usual manner; not for a moment had it occurred to Huguenau that as an openly advertised deserter who was already being tracked down he really should take to flight. He had simply stayed where he was. Not only because he was already too much bound up with local affairs, not only because a business conscience cannot bear to see any enterprise abandoned in which a considerable sum of money has been invested, whether one's own or another's—it was rather a feeling of general indefiniteness that kept him where he was and prevented him from admitting defeat, a feeling that compelled him to assert his reality against that of the others. And though it was somewhat nebulous, yet it resolved itself into a very definite idea: that the Major and Esch would get together behind his back and sneer at him. So he stayed where he was, only making an agreement with Frau Esch that meals he did not consume were to be made up to him, thus enabling him to avoid without material loss the hateful midday dinners.

Of course he knew that the trend of affairs was not favourable to the taking of action against a single insignificant Alsatian deserter; he felt himself relatively secure, and moreover he had positively a strangle-hold on the Major. He knew that, but he preferred not to know it. On the contrary he played with the thought that the luck of war might take another turn, that the Major might again be a power in the land, and that the Major and Esch were only waiting until then to crush him. It was for him to foil them in good time. Maybe it was sheer superstition, but he could not afford to fold his hands, he had to use every minute of his time, he had far too many urgent things to settle; and although he could not have told precisely whither this urgency was driving him, yet he consoled himself with the reflection that it was only their own fault if he laid counter-mines against his enemies.

Now he was paying out the wages. Lindner regarded the money, counted it over again, looked at it once more and left it lying on the table. The apprentice compositor was standing by, equally silent. Huguenau was puzzled:

" Well, Lindner, why don't you pick up your money ? "

Finally, with obvious reluctance, Lindner brought out the words:

" The Union rate's ninety-two pfennings."

That was something new. But Huguenau was not at a loss:

" Yes, yes, in large printing-works . . . but not in a tight squeeze like this . . . you're an old, experienced workman and you must know the condition we're in. With enemies on every hand, nothing but enemies . . . if I hadn't set the paper on its legs again there wouldn't be any wages at all to-day . . . that's all the thanks I get. Do you imagine I wouldn't be glad to give you twice as much . . . but where am I to get it from? Perhaps you think we're a Government paper bolstered up with subsidies . . . then, of course, there would be some sense in your joining the Union and asking for Union rates. I would join it myself; I'd be much better off."

" I haven't joined the Union," muttered Lindner.

" How do you know the Union rate, then ? "

" One soon gets to hear of it."

Huguenau had meanwhile considered the matter. Of course Liebel was at the bottom of this with his workshop propaganda. So he was an enemy too. But Liebel was a man to keep in with for the present. He said therefore:

" Well, we'll manage some arrangement . . . let's say, from November the new rate, and until then we'll see what can be done."

Both men professed themselves content.

In the evening Huguenau went to the Palatine Tavern to look for Liebel. The Lindner affair was really only a pretext. Huguenau was not at all ill-natured; he looked with clear eyes at the world; only a man has to know who are his enemies so that he can make a change of front when necessary. Oh, he knew well enough who his enemy was. They had managed to shut down the brothel and two outlying pubs . . . but when he offered to help them in their fight with the real subversive elements the Major had turned tail. Well, to-morrow he would butter the old man up again in the newspaper, this time for having closed the brothel. And Huguenau hummed to himself: " Lord God of Sabaoth."

In the Palatine he found Liebel, Doctor Pelzer, who had volunteered as a private, and a few more. Pelzer asked at once:

" And where have you left Esch? we never see him at all nowadays."

Huguenau grinned:

" Bible class for the Holy Sabbath . . . he'll be getting himself circumcised next."

They all roared with laughter, and Huguenau swelled with pride. But Pelzer said:

" All the same, Esch is a fine chap."

Liebel shook his head:

" It's almost incredible, the stuff that people swallow. . . ."

Pelzer said:

" It's just in times like these that everyone has his own ideas. . . . I'm a Socialist, and so are you, Liebel . . . but that's just why, all the same, Esch is a fine chap. . . . I like him very much."

Liebel's forehead, which rose up not unlike a tower, reddened, and the vein running over it stood out:

" In my opinion that kind of thing just makes people besotted and should be stopped."

" Quite right," said Huguenau, " destructive ideas."

Someone at the table laughed:

" O Lord, how even the big capitalists are changing their tune! "

Huguenau's eyeglasses flashed at the speaker:

" If I were a big capitalist I wouldn't be sitting here, but in Cologne, if not in Berlin."

" Um, you're not exactly a communist either, Herr Huguenau," said Pelzer.

" Nor that either, my dear Herr Doctor . . . but I know what's just and what's unjust . . . who was the first to expose the state of things in the prison? eh? "

" Nobody denies the services you've rendered," conceded Pelzer, " where would we have got such a fine Iron Bismarck but for you? "

Huguenau became genial; he clapped Pelzer on the shoulder:

" Pull your grandmother's leg, my dear fellow! "

But then he proceeded to let himself go:

The services he had rendered were neither here nor there. Of course he had always been a good patriot, of course he had acclaimed the victories of his Fatherland, and would anybody venture to blame him for that? but he had always known very well that that was the only way of rousing the bourgeoisie, who kept a tight hand on their ill-gotten gains, to do something for the children of the poor proletarian victims of the war; as far as he remembered it was he who had managed that! but what thanks had he got? it wouldn't surprise him to find that secret police orders were already out against him! but he wasn't afraid, let them do their worst, he had friends who would get him out of prison if necessary. This secret service work must in any case be put a stop to. " A man disappears, nobody knows how, and the next thing you hear is that he's been buried in the prison yard; God only knows how many are still languishing in prison! No, we don't get justice, we get only police justice! and the worst of it all is the sham piety of these police butchers; they have their Bibles always in their hands, but only to hit people ove. the head with. And they say grace before and after meat, but other people can starve to death, grace or no grace. . . ."

Pelzer had listened approvingly, but now he interrupted:

" Seems to me, Huguenau, you're an *agent provocateur*."

Huguenau scratched his head:

" And do you imagine that I haven't had offers of that kind made to me? if I could only tell you . . . well, never mind. . . . I was always an honest man and I'll remain an honest man if it should cost me my head . . . only I can't stand that sham hypocrisy."

Liebel said in agreement:

" This Bible stuff is only a stunt . . . the masters simply love to see the people fed on Bible texts."

Huguenau nodded:

" Yes, first a text and then a bullet . . . there are plenty who had a hand in the shooting affair in the prison . . . well, I'd better say nothing. But I'd rather go to quod than to one of their Bible classes."

So Huguenau aligned his position in the struggle then beginning between the upper and lower orders. And although Bolshevist propaganda was a matter of complete indifference to him, and he would have been the first to call for help if his own possessions had been in danger, although indeed it was only with great uneasiness that he reported in the *Kur-Trier Herald* the increasing number of inroads on property, yet he said now with honest conviction:

" The Russians are great fellows."

And Pelzer said:

" I believe you, my boy."

As they left the inn Huguenau shook his finger at Liebel:

" You're another of these sham-pious Johnnies . . . egging on my good old Lindner against me, and yet I'm only working for the people . . . and you know it, too. Well, I suppose we'll come to an understanding yet."

CHAPTER LXXXII

An eight-year-old child has resolved to wander alone out into the world.

She walks along the narrow strip of grass between the wheel-ruts and sees the pale purple of fading clover-heads that have strayed there, dried cakes of cow-dung, hoary with age, that have grass growing in their cracks, and the prickly burrs that cling to her stockings. She sees many other things too, the meadow-saffron growing in the fields and two dun cows grazing on the valley slopes, and since she cannot be always looking at the landscape she looks also at her frock and sees the little wild roses printed on its black cotton: over and over again a fully opened flower and a bud together on one bright green stalk between two small green leaves; in the middle of the opened rose there is a yellow point. She wishes that she had a black hat in which a rose with a bud and two leaves could be pinned—that would go well with the frock. But she has only a grey woollen cloak with a hood.

As she wanders along the river like this, one hand on her hip and the other clutching a mark to defray her expenses, she is in well-known country. She is not afraid. She walks through the landscape as a house-wife might walk through her dwelling, and if the pleasant feeling in her big toe induces her to kick a stone off the strip of grass, that is only a kind of tidying up. All around her everything is clear. She can see the clumps of trees that stand clearly modelled in the transparent air of the early autumn afternoon, and the landscape has no mystery for her:

behind the transparent air is the bright blue sky, among the transparent
green leafage there appears from time to time, as if it could not be otherwise, a tree with yellow leaves, and often, although there is not a breath
of wind, a yellow leaf comes fluttering from somewhere and slowly
circling settles on the path.

When she turns her eyes to the right, yonder where the willows and
bushes fringe the shore of the river, she can see the white boulders in
the river-bed, she can even see the water; for the foliage of the bushes
has thinned out with the autumn and reveals the brown branches, it is
no longer the impenetrable green wall of summer. But if she turns her
eyes to the left she sees the marsh-meadow: uncanny and malicious it
lies there, and if one sets a foot in its grass the water plashes up and
seeps into one's shoes; one dare not try to cross a marsh like that, for
who knows? one might sink and be smothered in the bog.

Children have a more restricted and yet a more intense feeling for
nature than grown-ups. They will never linger at a beautiful prospect
to absorb the whole of a landscape, but a tree standing on a distant hill
can attract them so strongly that they feel as if they could take it in
their mouths and must run to touch it. And when a great valley spreads
before their feet they do not want to gaze at it, but to fling themselves
into it as if they could fling their own fears in too; that is why children
are in such constant and often purposeless movement, rolling in the grass,
climbing trees, trying to eat leaves, and finally concealing themselves
in the top of a tree or deep in the dark security of a bush.

Much, therefore, of what is generally ascribed to the sheer inexhaust-
ibility of a youth's unfolding powers and to its purposeless yet purposeful
exuberance is really nothing else than the naked fear of the creature that
has begun to die in realizing its own loneliness; a child rushes to and fro
because in so many senses it is wandering about at the beginning of its
course; the laughter of a child, so often censured by adults as idle, is the
laughter of one who sees himself surprised and mastered by loneliness:
so it is not only comprehensible that an eight-year-old may decide
to go out into the world in an extraordinary, one might almost say, an
heroic and final attempt to concentrate her own loneliness and conquer
within that the greater loneliness, to challenge infinity by unity and unity
by infinity—not only is that comprehensible, but it is also comprehensible
that in an enterprise of this kind the motives influencing her will be
neither ordinary nor weighed by ordinary standards; a mere butterfly,

that is to say a thing of such little weight that it cannot come into consideration at all, may have a determining influence on the whole course of her adventure—for instance, let the butterfly that has fluttered for some time ahead of her suddenly leave the path to vanish across the marshes, and it is only in the eyes of an adult that that will seem irrelevant, for adults cannot see that it is the soul of the butterfly, not the butterfly itself, and yet itself, that has deserted the child. She comes to a stop; she takes her hand from her hip and with a wild swoop doomed beforehand to failure she tries to catch the creature that is already far away.

She does, indeed, continue on her original path for some time. She comes almost to the great iron bridge that carries across the river the main road from the east towards the town. The path by the shore which she has been following would here climb up the road embankment and cross it to descend on the other side. But the child does not get so far as that. For in face of the familiar bridge with its grey lattice-work that cuts the black pine-forest into multitudinous black rectangles when one looks through it, a sight that has always terrified her, and of the surprising and apparently unending familiarity of the country, she now quite suddenly decides to leave the valley. No sooner thought than done. And even although when she wandered off from home she may have hoped that what was familiar and homelike would vanish only gradually, merging almost painlessly, as it were, into what was strange, yet the painfulness of this sudden farewell to the valley is drowned in her strong desire to cross to the other side of the marsh, to where the butterfly vanished.

It is only a moderately high bluff that rises over there, but it is high enough for the child to see nothing of the house on its summit save the roof, and nothing of the trees that grow there save their tops. Perhaps her most sensible course would be simply to tackle the ascent from the main road. But her impatience is too great: under the bright blue sky, that cool-warm sky of the Indian summer, under the rays of the sun that burn her back, she begins to run; she runs along the edge of the marsh looking for a ford or a raised path, the narrowest of paths will do; but while she is searching she has run right round the marsh and is already at the foot of the hill, just as if the hill had run to meet her like a camel and was kneeling down for her to climb up on it. This twofold haste, her own and that of the hill, is a little uncanny, and she really hesitates now that she is about to set foot on the imperceptible swell that marks the transition from the flat marshland to the steep hill. If she now lifts her head the farmhouse up there has quite vanished from sight and only a few tree-tops are visible. But the higher she clambers the more the little settlement up there grows to meet her eye, first the trees in their rich green as if spring were calling to her, then the roof from which the chimney rises like a candle, and finally the white walls of the house gleam through the trees: it is some kind of farmhouse set in a very green garden, and the last slope, so steep that she scrambles up on all-fours, is likewise so green that she advances her arms until she is stretched flat on her belly, her face in the grass, and only then slowly lets her knees follow.

Now that she is really at the top and the farmyard dog barks and tugs at his chain, the springtime she hoped to find is wanting. The landscape, indeed, is strange and unfamiliar, and even the valley, into which she now casts a glance, even that is no longer the valley out of which she came. A twofold transformation! a transformation that is certainly heightened by melancholy, but none the less is not decisive, for the transformation can be attributed to the change in the light: with that swiftness peculiar to autumn the clear purity of the light has become opaque and milky, and the whitening shield of the sky looks down on another sky, for the valley is beginning also to fill with cloud that is equally white. It is yet afternoon, ah, yet afternoon, but the evening of strangeness has already invaded it. Far into the infinite distance stretches the road on which the farm is set, and in the quickly mounting cold the butterflies droop and die. And that is decisive! She is suddenly aware that there is no fixed goal for her, that her casting about and seeking for a goal has been in vain, that only the infinite distance itself can be a goal. The child does not formulate this thought, but she answers with her actions the question she has not posed, she flings herself into the strangeness, she flees along the road, she flees along the road that stretches without end, she loses her wits and cannot even weep in her breathless race that is like a suspension of movement between the moveless masses of cloud. And when the evening really steals upon her through the clouds, when the moon becomes a bright patch in the cloudy roof, when the clouds are then washed away by some noiseless force and all the stars are vaulted above her, when the stillness of dusk is superseded by the immobility of night, she finds herself in an unknown village, stumbling through silent alleys in which here and there a cart is standing without its horses.

It is almost a matter of no account how far Marguerite will penetrate, whether she will ever be brought back or whether she will fall a prey to some wandering tramp—the sleepwalking of the infinite has seized upon her and never more will let her go.

CHAPTER LXXXIII

STORY OF THE SALVATION ARMY GIRL IN BERLIN (15)

O autumn year, O new year of starvation,
O gentle stars that warmed the autumn leaves,
O agony of the long day! agony of barren sheaves,
O agony of farewell, when in sad resignation
they said farewell, and in their eyes, grief-stricken,
was nought but tearless seeking to hold fast
that moment of farewell, the very last:
then in the city where hooting motors thicken
they lost each other's traces, one by one,
each other's hearts, and anguish veiled the sun
and turned the moon to stone, yet was not fear;
for old men's wisdom, shining silver-clear,
illumined them until their anguish grew
into the richest dower that they knew.
Was it not anguish drew them first of all
together, like tired leaves upon the way?
And their love's anguish, was it not a ray
from Heaven's own anguish, beneath whose purple pall
His glances in their silvery radiance play?
The shy dove spreads its wings and flies abroad
across the rolling billows of the sullen flood,
bringing the covenant o'er the waters grey:
in anguish God is throned, is throned in desolation,
in Him love turns to anguish, and anguish is love's motion,
a covenant between Time and Time in earth's duress,
a covenant between loneliness and loneliness—
the anguish God sent down with deepest love was fraught,
and God's own anguish changed His being into Thought.

CHAPTER LXXXIV

The Bible readings were now badly attended. The urgency of external events drew men's attention away from what was happening in their own souls, and that applied especially to strangers, who lent a ready ear to every rumour that conveyed the possibility of their imminent return home. The townsmen were more constant; the Bible class had already become for them a part of the established order which they wished to preserve independently of war or peace, and in some corner of himself each of them was secretly disturbed rather than pleased by the rumours of peace.

Fendrich and Samwald were natives of the town and were amongst the most faithful. Huguenau, indeed, asserted that Fendrich only came because Frau Esch had always milk in the house; he even went so far as to complain that he was skimped of his breakfast coffee because Frau Esch wanted to save the milk for the pious Fendrich. And he said this not only behind her back; but Frau Esch laughed at him: " Fancy being so jealous as that, Herr Huguenau," and Huguenau retorted: " You just look out, Mother Esch, or your husband's canting crew will eat you out of house and home." Huguenau's reproaches, however, were unjust; Fendrich would have come even without the milk-coffee.

In any case there they were again in the kitchen, both Samwald and Fendrich. Huguenau, who had just made ready to go out, stuck his nose in at the door: " Having a good guzzle? " Frau Esch answered for them: " Oh, I haven't a thing in the house." Huguenau eyed them both to see if they were chewing, and glanced at the table, but on assuring himself that there was no food set out he was quite satisfied. " Then I can leave you with a good conscience," he said, " you're in the best of company, Mother Esch." Yet he did not go; he was anxious to find out what she was saying to them. But they were all silent, so he began to talk himself: " Where's your friend to-day, Herr Samwald? the one with the sticks? " Samwald indicated the window which was rattling in the wind: " When the weather's bad he has aches and pains . . . he feels it beforehand." " Oh, la la," said Huguenau, " rheumatism; yes, that's a trial." Samwald shook his head: " No, he feels changes beforehand . . . he knows lots of things beforehand." Huguenau was only half listening: " Of course, it might be gout." Fendrich shivered a little: " I can feel it too

in all my bones . . . in our factory there are more than twenty down with
'flu . . . old Petri's daughter died yesterday . . . there have been some
deaths in the hospital, too. Esch say it's the plague . . . the lung plague."
Huguenau was disgusted: " He should be more careful with his defeatist
arguments. . . . Plague! That would be a fine thing, indeed." Samwald
said: " As for Gödicke, even the plague couldn't touch him . . . he has
been raised from the dead." Fendrich had still more to add on the subject:
" According to the Bible all the plagues of the Apocalypse are bound to
come now . . . the Major prophesied that too . . . so did Esch." " Merde,
I've had enough of this," said Huguenau, " I wish you a very merry
meeting. Salut."

On the stairway he met Esch: " Two of your jolly companions are
sitting waiting for you up there . . . if the whole town starts babbling of
the plague it'll be your fault . . . you and your canting crew will send the
whole world crazy, you're just making people besotted." Esch showed
his strong teeth and waved his hand airily, which provoked Huguenau:
" There's nothing to grin at, Sir Reverend." To his surprise Esch became
serious at once: " You're right, this is no time for laughing . . . the two
up there are quite right." Huguenau felt uncomfortable: " How are they
right? . . . about the plague, for instance? " Esch said quietly: " Yes, and
it would be better for you, yes, for you, my dear sir, if you were to realize
at last that we're in the midst of fear and tribulation. . . ." " I'd like to
know what good that could do me," said Huguenau, and began to continue his way downstairs. Esch had his schoolmastering voice: " I could
soon enlighten you on that, but you don't want to find out . . . you're
afraid to find out. . . ." Huguenau turned round. Esch was standing two
steps above him and looked hugely powerful; it was annoying to have to
look up at him like that, and Huguenau hopped up a step again. Suspicion
was awakening in him again. What was it that Esch was keeping to himself? What could he know? But when Esch went on: " Only he who is
in tribulation will partake of grace . . ." Huguenau stopped him: " Here,
I want to listen to no more of that. . . ." Again Esch displayed his abominable sarcastic grin: " Didn't I tell you? it doesn't suit your new change
of front . . . in fact, it has never suited you."

And he turned to continue his ascent.

There was a lightning flash behind Huguenau's eyeglasses:

" One moment, Herr Esch. . . ."

Esch paused.

" Yes, Herr Esch, I've something to say to you . . . of course that drivel doesn't suit me . . . grin if you like, it never has suited me. . . . I've always been a Freethinker and never made any secret of it. . . . I've never interfered with your canting piety, so you'll kindly leave me to find happiness in my own fashion . . . you can call it a new change of front for all I care, and you can come nosing behind me too if you like, as you've evidently been doing, and I'm no demagogue either like you, and I don't make people into besotted fools as you do, I'm not ambitious, but when I hear what's being said, not by your hypocrites upstairs, of course not, but by other people, then I think it's likely that things will take a very different turn from what you expect, Herr Reverend. . . . I mean, you're going to see strange things, and you'll see some people strung up on lamp-posts too . . . if the Major hadn't taken it into his head to be angry with me I would give him a friendly warning, I'm a decent chap, I am . . . he's got his back up against you, too, the doddering old fool, but all the same I'm giving you the chance of passing on the warning. You see, I play with all my cards on the table: I don't stab people in the back like some others I know."

And with that he turned at last to go and tramped whistling down the stairs. Afterwards he was annoyed with himself for having been so good-natured—there was no reason why he should feel that he owed anything to the Herren Pasenow and Esch—why on earth had he warned them, and of what?

Esch stood still for a moment. He felt for some reason struck to the heart. Then he said to himself: " A man who sacrifices himself must be a decent chap." And although one couldn't put it past Huguenau to commit any abomination, yet so long as he blustered so much it was all right: dogs that bark don't bite. Let him jaw in the public-houses as much as he liked, it wouldn't hurt anybody, least of all the Major. Esch smiled, he stood firm and strong on his feet, and then he stretched his arms like one who awakes from sleep or is nailed on a cross. He felt strong, firm and robust, and as if it were an entry settling the world's account he repeated: "A man who sacrifices himself must be a decent chap," then he pushed open the door of the kitchen.

CHAPTER LXXXV
" No one can see another in the darkness."

Events of 3rd, 4th and 5th November 1918.

What Huguenau had prophesied actually came to pass: one did see strange things, and these strange things took place on the 3rd and 4th of November.

On the morning of the 2nd of November a small demonstration was made by the workers from the paper factory. It proceeded, as such processions always do, towards the Town Hall, but this time, really for no particular reason, the windows were smashed in. The Major called out the half-company which still remained at his disposal, and the demonstrators dispersed. Nevertheless the ensuing calm was only on the surface. The town was filled with rumours; the collapse of the German front was known, but nobody could ascertain if there were any negotiations for an armistice, and terrible things hung in the air.

So the day passed. In the evening a red glare could be seen in the west and it was said that all Trier was in flames. Huguenau, who regretted now that he had not long since sold the paper to the communists, resolved to run off a special edition, but his two workers were nowhere to be found. During the night there was firing in the neighbourhood of the prison. The rumour went that it had been a signal inciting the prisoners to a revolt. Later the information was divulged that a prison warder had let off several alarm shots on account of a misunderstanding; but nobody believed it.

Meantime morning had come, cold, foggy and winter-like. Already by seven the town council had assembled in the unheated, faintly lit, panelled council-chamber; the arming of respectable citizens was universally demanded—but on the objection, which became stronger and stronger, that this might be interpreted as a provocative step against the workers, the formation of a Civil Guard which should include workers and middle class alike was decided upon. There arose certain difficulties with the Town Commandant regarding the giving out of rifles from the stock in the munition stores, but finally—almost over the Major's head—the arms were requisitioned. Naturally there was no time left for a systematic levy, and so a committee under the chairmanship of the Burgomaster was chosen, which was to be responsible for the distribution of arms. That morning rifles were already being given out to all those who could prove that they were citizens of the town and could use a gun, and as things had reached that stage the Town Commandant could no longer refuse the collaboration of the military with the Civil Guard; the allocation of posts was already being made from the Commandant's office.

Esch and Huguenau had reported as a matter of course. Esch, resolved above all to remain near the Major, asked urgently to be employed within the town. He was put on night service, while Huguenau had to stand guard on the bridge during the afternoon.

Huguenau sat on the stone parapet of the bridge and shivered in the November fog. His rifle with its bayonet fixed leant beside him. Grass grew between the stone blocks of the parapet, and Huguenau occupied himself in plucking it out. One could also unloosen ancient pieces of mortar from between the stones and then let them drop into the water. He was intensely bored and found the whole affair stupid. The upturned collar of his recently purchased overcoat chafed roughly against his neck and chin and gave no warmth. Out of pure boredom he satisfied the calls of nature, but that also was presently over, and he merely sat there again. It was stupid to sit there with the silly green band on one's sleeve, and cold besides. And he considered whether he should not step over to the brothel—for the Major's order closing it had not had the slightest effect; it now ran a secret trade.

He was just picturing to himself that the old dame in the brothel must have put on the fires by this time and that it would be beautifully warm in there, when Marguerite appeared before him. Huguenau was glad to see her:

"Tiens," he said, "what are you doing here. . . . I thought you had run away . . . what have you done with the mark I gave you?"

Marguerite did not reply.

Huguenau felt he would be happier in the brothel:

"You're no use to me . . . you're not fourteen yet . . . see that you get safely home."

Nevertheless he took her on his knee; it was warmer. After a while he asked: "Have you got on your warm knickers?" When she said yes he felt reassured. They snuggled closely to each other. The Town Hall clock rang through the fog; five o'clock, and how dark it was already.

" Short days," said Huguenau, " another year going past already."

A second clock followed with four and then five strokes. Huguenau grew more and more melancholy. What was the use of all this? what was he doing here? over there across the fields lay Esch's place, and Huguenau spat in a wide arc in its direction. But then a sudden fear clutched him; he had left the door of the printing-shed wide open, and if there should be any looting that day they would smash his machine to pieces.

" Get down," he said roughly to Marguerite, and when she hesitated he boxed her ears. Hastily he searched his pockets for the printing-shed key. Should he himself return or should he send Marguerite with the key to Frau Esch?

He was almost on the point of deserting his post and betaking himself home when he shrank back, for now there came a real terror that pierced him to the marrow; on the edge of the forest there was a dazzling flash, followed the next moment by a frightful detonation. He was just able to realize that it came from the barracks of the trench mortar company where some fool must have exploded what remained of the ammunition, but he at once instinctively flung himself down and was wise enough to remain lying on the ground to await further explosions. Right enough, two more violent detonations followed at short intervals and then the din subsided into a sporadic crackle.

Huguenau peered cautiously over the stone parapet and saw the walls of the munition-sheds red and smouldering with the fire inside, and the roof of the barracks burning. " So it's begun," he told himself, stood up, and removed the dirt from his new winter overcoat. Then he looked round for Marguerite and whistled for her several times, but she had run away—home, he hoped. He had little time to deliberate, for already a crowd of men were coming running down towards him from the barracks with sticks, stones and some even with rifles in their hands. And to Huguenau's astonishment Marguerite was running along beside them.

Their objective was the jail, that was clear. Huguenau grasped that in an instant, and he felt like a chief of staff whose commands were being exactly carried out to the minute. " Fine fellows," said something within him, and he found it the most natural thing in the world that he should join them.

They reached the prison at the double, shouting and yelling. The gate was shut. A hail of stones rattled against it and then a direct attack was attempted. With the butt end of his rifle Huguenau crashed the first blow against the oaken panels. Someone had got hold of a crowbar, they had not to employ it very long, a breach was soon made, the door sprang open and the crowd surged into the courtyard. It was deserted, the staff had hidden themselves somewhere; well, they would soon be smoked out, these fellows—but from the cells rang a wild chorus: " Hurrah for freedom! Hurrah for freedom! Hip, hip, hooray! "

When the first detonation came Esch was sitting in the kitchen. With one bound he was at the window, but started back when at the second explosion the loosened window together with the window frame flew at his head. Was it an air raid? His wife crouched on her knees among the splintered glass and babbled a Paternoster. For one second he gaped at her in open-mouthed amazement; all her life she had not prayed! then he jerked her to her feet. " Into the cellar, air raid." Meanwhile from the top of the stairs he saw the munition store in flames, and heard the crackle of explosions coming from it. So it had begun. And his next thought was: " The Major! " To push his whimpering wife back into the room—her lamenting voice imploring him not to leave her still rang in his ears—to seize his rifle and rush downstairs was the work of a moment. The street was full of yelling people. From the market-place came a trumpet call. Esch panted up the street. Behind him a pair of harnessed horses were being led forward at a trot; he knew that they were intended for the fire brigade and it did him good to think that a remnant of order still remained intact. The fire-engine was already standing in the market-place, it had been drawn out, but the crew had not yet arrived in full force. The bugler climbed on to the driver's seat and blew the summons again and again, but as yet only six men had turned up. From the other side of the market-place a troop of soldiers came running and the captain was sensible enough to put them at the disposal of the fire brigade; the fire-engine rolled away with a full complement.

In the Town Hall all the doors were open. Nobody to be found : the Commandant's headquarters empty. That was a relief to Esch; for at least they would not find the old man here if they came. But where was he? When Esch came out again he at last caught sight of a soldier and shouted at him asking whether he had seen the Commandant. Yes, the Commandant had called out the Civil Guard and was either at the barracks or the prison . . . which apparently had been stormed.

To the prison, then! Esch broke into an awkward, heavy trot.

While the crowd pushed their way into the prison buildings Huguenau had remained standing in the courtyard. It had been a success, without doubt it was a success—Huguenau made the sarcastic grimace that he could now manage quite well. The Major would get a nice surprise if he were to see him here, and Esch ditto. No doubt about it, it was a brilliantly triumphal success! nevertheless Huguenau felt uncomfortable—what next? he regarded the courtyard, the burning barracks gave a splendid light, but it was nothing so extraordinary after all, the courtyard looked just as he had always expected it to look. And he had had enough of this crowd too.

Suddenly he heard piercing screams. They had hunted out a warder and were dragging him out into the courtyard. When Huguenau came up the man was lying as though crucified on the ground, except that one rigid leg jerked convulsively and rhythmically in the air. Two women had thrown themselves upon him, and the man with the crowbar was standing with hobnailed boots on one of the poor wretch's hands and bringing the iron bar down with a thud on his tortured limbs. Huguenau felt that he was about to vomit. With panic in his belly and heart he shouldered his rifle and ran back to the town.

The town lay sharply outlined with its pointed gables in the glare of the burning barracks, the black contours of the houses surmounted by the towers of the Town Hall and the churches. From these the clocks struck the half-hour serenely, as though a still deeper peace hovered over this human community. And the familiar strokes of the bells, the familiar sight of the houses, all the peace that was still there while round about everything was burning, turned Huguenau's choking fear into a wild longing for human proximity. He ran straight across the fields, sometimes stopping to recover his breath. Then he caught a smell of cooked meat and once more the thought transfixed him that the door of the printing-shed was not locked, that the burglars and housebreakers would be streaming out of the prison now, and with redoubled fear, with redoubled resolution, he struggled on towards home.

Hanna Wendling was lying in bed with a high fever. At first Dr Kessel had tried to lay the blame for it on her keeping her bedroom window open every night; but later he had had to admit that it was Spanish influenza.

When the explosion took place and the window panes came crashing into the room Hanna was not in the least surprised: it was not she who was responsible for the closing of the windows, it had been forced upon her, and as Heinrich had neglected to have bars put on them, of course the burglars would climb in now. Almost with satisfaction she mentally noted: " The invasion from below," and waited for what would follow next. But when a more deafening crash ensued she came to her senses and jumped out of bed with the sudden knowledge that she must go to her son.

She held fast to the bed-post and tried to marshal her thoughts; the boy was in the kitchen, yes, now she remembered that she had sent him downstairs to be out of the reach of infection. She must go down to him.

A strong draught blew through the room, blew through the whole house. All the windows and doors were driven out of their frames and on the first floor the panes of the whole glass frontage had been burst in, for at this high-lying part of the valley the air-pressure was particularly violent. The next detonation swept half of the tiled roof off with a great clatter. If the house had not been centrally heated a conflagration would have been unavoidable. Hanna, however, did not feel the cold, she scarcely noticed even the clattering din, she did not understand what had happened, nor did she try in the least to understand: passing the screaming housemaid, whom she met in the dressing-room, she hastened to the kitchen.

In the kitchen it struck her that she must have been cold before, for here it was cosy. The windows down here had not suffered. The cook was crouching in a corner with the sobbing trembling child on her lap. The cat was lying peacefully in front of the stove. Also the curious smell of burning fireworks had vanished; this place smelt clean and warm. One had the feeling of having been rescued. Then she discovered that with incomprehensible presence of mind she had brought her bed-quilt with her. She wrapped herself in the quilt and sat down in the corner farthest from her son; she must take care that he did not catch the influenza from her, and she waved him away when he made to go over to her. The housemaid had followed her, and now the gardener and his wife arrived too: " The barracks are on fire ... look there." The gardener pointed towards the window, but the women did not dare to go across to it, but remained sitting where they were. Hanna felt perfectly clear in the head. She said: " We must wait for it to end," and wrapped herself more firmly in her quilt. Suddenly for some reason the electric light went out. The housemaid screamed again, Hanna repeated in the darkness: " We must wait for it to end, ' and then she fell again into a vague doze. The boy had fallen asleep in the cook's arms. The housemaid and the gardener's wife sat on the coal bunker, the gardener leaned against the fireplace. The windows still rattled, and from time to time another row of tiles fell from the roof. They sat in darkness, they all gazed at the lighted windows, they gazed without moving, and they grew more and more motionless

Esch hastened along the road that led downwards to the prison—his rifle had slid down from his shoulder, and he held it in his hands like a charging soldier. About half-way to the prison he heard the shouting of an approaching crowd. He flung himself into the bushes until they should have gone past. There were some two hundred men, a very mixed rabble, convicts among them, recognizable by their grey uniforms. Some of them were trying to sing the *Marseillaise*, others the *Internationale*. A man with a sergeant's voice kept shouting perpetually: " Form fours," but nobody paid any attention. At the head of the procession, above the heads of the marchers, swayed a puppet; it was the stuffed uniform of a prison warder hung from a cross-bar, from a sort of gallows—apparently they had stripped someone naked for this purpose; to the puppet's chest a white placard was fastened, and in the flickering light of the burning depot Esch could make out the words " Town Commandant." They actually had a child with them, perched on one of the men's shoulders, a little girl who reminded one somewhat of Marguerite, but Esch had no time to think of such things; he waited until the procession passed and then, to avoid any stragglers, he kept to the fields adjoining the road and ran on.

The lights of a motor-car suddenly appeared in front of him. Esch's blood ran cold—it could only be the Major! the Major, blindly rushing into the arms of the rebels. He must be stopped! stopped at any cost! Esch slithered down the bank and stationed himself in the middle of the road, waving his arms and shouting at the top of his voice. But the occupants of the car did not notice him or did not want to notice him, and if he had not leapt to the side he would have been run over. He had just time to make sure that it was actually the Major's car, and that besides the Major three soldiers were in it, one of them standing on the footboard. He stared helplessly after the car, then he ran for all he was worth behind it, he ran in terrible fear, expecting every moment to see something dreadful happening. And already in front of him there were several reports; they were followed by a crashing blow somewhat like an explosion, then came shouts and a general hubbub. Esch rushed up the bank again.

The crowd was standing beside the first houses of the town; the neighbourhood was still lighted up by the fire. Taking cover behind the bushes Esch reached the first garden fence and creeping behind it could now draw near. The car had fallen on its side and lay burning on the opposite bank of the road. From all appearances the driver had lost control over the car and run into the bank when he saw the crowd, or he may have been hit by a stone. Half-doubled up in front of a tree on which he had split his skull, he was still groaning, while one of the soldiers lay outstretched on the road. Another, a sergeant, who appeared to have escaped with a whole skin, was surrounded by the raving mob. Under the fists and cudgels of the rioters he was making feeble and imploring gestures, saying something which could not be heard amid the noise: then he too sank down. Esch considered whether he should open fire on the crowd, but at that moment a blue flame burst from the bonnet of the car and someone shouted: " The car is exploding! " The crowd retreated, became silent and waited for the explosion. But when nothing happened, and the car merely went on quietly burning, cries arose of " To the Commandant's quarters! " " To the Town Hall," and the mob rolled on again towards the town.

But where was the Major? Suddenly Esch knew; he was beneath the car and in danger of being burned alive. Goaded by fear Esch clambered over the wooden fence, rushed up to the car, and tugged at the wreckage; a dry sobbing overcame him when he saw clearly that he would not be able to lift it by himself. He stood in despair in front of the burning car, and burned his helpless hands with fresh attempts. Then a man came up. It was the third soldier and he was unhurt, for he had been flung right over the road bank and fallen in a field. Together they managed to raise one side of the car. Esch crawled underneath, supporting the body of the car on his back, and the soldier pulled out the Major. Thank God! But still they were not out of the wood, they must get out of reach of the perilously burning car as quickly as possible, and so they carried the

unconscious Major up the bank and laid him down behind a few bushes
on the grass.

Esch knelt down beside the Major and gazed into his face; it was a
peaceful face, and his breathing was regular, though feeble. His heart
also was beating quietly and rhythmically—Esch had torn open the
Major's overcoat and tunic—and with the exception of a few burns and
abrasions no external wound was to be found. The soldier stood by:
"There's the others too. . . ." Esch straightened himself with difficulty.
All at once he felt that he could hardly drag even himself along, nevertheless he pulled himself together once more, and they carried the wounded
sergeant also to safety. The bodies of the dead soldier and the dead
chauffeur they laid at the side of the road.

When it was finished Esch flung himself down on the grass beside the
Major: "Must take a breath for a minute. . . . I'm done in." He was so
exhausted that when flames suddenly flared over the roofs of the town
and the soldier shouted: "The fools have set fire to the Town Hall!" he
scarcely paid any attention.

In the hospital there had been chaos and confusion.

At first everybody had rushed into the garden without regard
to the patients who were unable to move; nobody listened to their
lamentations.

Kühlenbeck had had to exert all his authority to restore order again.
He had single-handed shifted the gravest cases to the basement; he
carried the patients like children in his arms, his voice boomed through
the corridors, and he cursed at everybody like a bargee, including even
Flurschütz and Sister Mathilde, if his commands were not executed on
the spot. Sister Carla had disappeared and could not be found.

Finally things began to look ship-shape again. The beds were carried
down from the devastated upper floor, and by twos and threes the
patients reappeared. Some were missing. They were in the garden,
or perhaps had strayed still farther, into the woods or somewhere.

Flurschütz and an attendant set out to look for them. One of the
first that they discovered outside the garden was Gödicke; he had not got
very far and was standing on the hillside, which he had chosen as a coign
of vantage, his two sticks uplifted towards the heavens.

One would have thought that he was exulting.

And in fact when they came nearer they heard him laughing with that barking, animal laughter for which all the inmates had been waiting for months.

He paid no attention to the two of them when they shouted to him, and when they came nearer and made as though to lead him back he shook his sticks threateningly.

Flurschütz felt somewhat at a loss:

" But, Gödicke, do come along. . . ."

Gödicke pointed with his sticks at the flames and bawled in delight:

" The Judgment Day . . . arisen from the dead . . . arisen from the dead . . . you must go to hell if you don't rise from the dead . . . the devil will get you all . . . he'll get you all now. . . ."

What was to be done with the man! But after they had stared at him for a while the attendant found the right words:

" Ludwig, it's the dinner-hour, come down from the scaffolding."

Gödicke fell silent; he gazed suspiciously at them out of his bearded face, but finally he hobbled after them.

Breathless and trembling Huguenau crossed the garden and reached the printing-shed. For a moment he did not know what had led him there. Then he remembered. The printing-press!

He entered. The dark room was fitfully illumined from outside and lay in Sabbath-like order and neatness. Huguenau, his rifle between his knees, sat down in front of the press. He felt disappointed; the machine did not repay his exertions; cold and impassive it stood there and merely threw restless shadows which made him feel uncomfortable. If the convict rabble came it would serve the bloody machine jolly well right if they smashed it to pieces. Although it was a beautiful little machine . . . he laid his hands on it and was angry because the iron felt so cold. Merde, why should he get angry about that? Huguenau shrugged his shoulders, gazed out into the courtyard, across at the barn where the Sunday meetings were held. Would Esch be preaching there again next Sunday? Haïssez les ennemis de la sainte religion. Pious hypocrites. An empty barn, that was all their stock in trade . . . what had a man like that to lose! A man like that should have his bones broken for him. He had no worries . . . preached on Sunday, and now he was sitting upstairs with his wife and they were comforting each other, while a fellow had to sit down here beside this bloody machine.

Once more he forgot why he had come. He leant his rifle against the printing-press. Standing in the courtyard he sniffed: again a smell of meat cooking was wafted to him. To-night of course there would be no supper, but upstairs they would be having something all right—she would see that Esch didn't want.

When he reached the landing above he started back, for the door of his room was lifted out of its hinges. That wasn't as it should be. The door was jammed too, only with a great effort was he able to push it open, and inside in his room things looked still more desolate: the mirror no longer hung above the washing-table, but lay on the top of the broken crockery. A wilderness. Incomprehensible and disturbing, it reminded one of splintered bones. Huguenau sat down on the sofa, he wanted to realize what had happened but he did not want to think . . . someone should come to explain it all to him and comfort him . . . stroke his hair.

Then it occurred to him that he must summon Frau Esch in any case to show her the damage . . . otherwise she would finish by holding him responsible for it . . . he had no intention of paying for damage that he had not caused. But just as he was about to call to her she rushed into his room, having heard his footsteps: "Where is my man?"

A spacious, blissful and deeply moving sense of comfort descended on Huguenau at the sight of a familiar face. He smiled to her frankly and cordially: "Mother Esch . . ." he literally beamed upon her . . . now all will be well, she'll put me to bed. . . . Meanwhile she did not seem even to see him: "Where is my man?" The stupid question disturbed him—what did the woman want Esch for now? if he wasn't there, it was surely all the better . . . he replied roughly: "How should I know where he's loafing about? He'll come back for his supper all right."

Perhaps she had not even listened, for she stepped up to him, seized him by the shoulders, and almost screamed at him:

"He's gone, he's gone with his rifle. . . . I've heard firing."

A hope rose in Huguenau: Esch was shot! but why in that case did the woman have such a lamenting voice? why did she have the wrong reaction? He wanted her to comfort him, and instead of that he must keep her here and comfort her, and all on account of Esch too! She was still beseeching him: "Where is he?" and she was still clutching him by the shoulder. Both embarrassed and furious he stroked her thick arm as if she were a weeping child, he would even have gladly shown her some kindness, he ran his hand up and down her arm, but his mouth spoke unkind words: " What are you snivelling about Esch for? haven't we all had enough of the schoolmaster? . . . after all, you've got me . . ." and only while he was saying this did he himself become aware that he was making a more brutal demand on her . . . as a sort of substitute for what she had failed to give him. Now she too guessed what he was after: " Herr Huguenau, for God's sake, Herr Huguenau. . . ." And already almost bereft of will-power, she made scarcely any further resistance to his panting urgency. Like a criminal trying to save the hangman trouble she undid her underclothes, and without even a kiss he fell with her on the sofa.

Afterwards her first words were: " Save my man! " Huguenau felt indifferent about that; Esch could live now as long as he liked. But the next moment she broke out into shrill screams: the window was suddenly illumined a blood red, orange-yellow flames shot up, the Town Hall was burning. She sank to the floor, a shapeless lump . . . she, she was to blame for everything: " Jesus Maria, what have I done, what have I done . . ." she crept over to him, " . . . save him, save him. . . ." Huguenau had stepped to the window. He felt annoyed; now trouble was beginning here too. He had had enough of it out there already, more than enough. And what did this woman want from him? it was Esch that was finally responsible . . . he could burn out there with the Major if he liked, holy men had always been burned. And now there would be looting on the top of everything else . . . and he had forgotten again to lock up the printing-shed . . . he took the opportunity of escaping with credit: " I'll look after him." If he should meet Esch now, he reflected as he went out, he would fling him down the stairs.

But in the printing-shed everything was neat and orderly as before. His rifle leant there and the machine threw its restless shadows. Red, black, yellow and orange-coloured, the sheaves of fire from the Town Hall shot up into the sky, while the barracks and the munition depot on the other side were still smouldering, a dirty brown. The bare branches of the fruit-trees were stiffly outlined. Huguenau contemplated the spectacle and found all at once that it was as it should be . . . everything was as it should be, and the printing-machine too pleased him once more . . . everything was as it should be, everything had been put right, he had been given back his customary nature and his clear common sense . . . now all that was needed was to put the final touch to the business and all would be well!

He softly climbed the stairs again, peeped cautiously into the devastated kitchen, stole over to the bread cupboard and cut himself a good slice, and as he could find nothing more returned to the printing-shed, settled himself comfortably, took the rifle between his outstretched legs, and began slowly to eat . . . one would manage somehow or other to settle the looters too.

Esch and the soldier knelt beside the Major. They were trying to bring him back to consciousness and rubbing his chest and hands with the damp grass. When at last he opened his eyes, they moved his arms and legs up and down, and it proved that nothing was broken. But he responded to none of their appeals, he remained lying outstretched on his back, and only his hands had grown restless, clutching at the damp earth, burrowing in the earth, seeking for clods and crumbling them to pieces.

It was clear that they must get him away as quickly as possible. To summon help from the town was out of the question; so they would have to manage by themselves. The wounded sergeant had meantime gathered his strength sufficiently to sit up—one could therefore leave him by himself for a little, and they decided first of all to carry the Major across the fields to Esch's house; it would have been too risky to take him by the main road.

As they were debating over the best way to set about it, the Major made signs as though he wished to speak: clutching a fragment of earth in his fingers he raised his hand, and his lips opened and pushed themselves forward, but his hand fell again and again to the ground and no sound could be caught. Esch put his ear quite close to the Major's mouth and waited: at last he made out the words: " Fell with my horse . . . an easy obstacle, fell all the same . . . the right foreleg broken. . . . I'll shoot him myself . . . wipe out dishonour with a bullet . . ." and then more distinctly and as though he were seeking for assent: " . . . with a bullet, not with unchivalrous weapons. . . ." " What did he say ? " asked the soldier. Esch replied softly: " He thinks that he's fallen from his horse . . . but now we must go . . . if only it wasn't so damned light . . . we'll better take our rifles with us in any case."

The Major had closed his eyes again. They raised him cautiously, and every now and then resting and exchanging places, they carried him across the sodden rain-soaked fields, whose miry soil clung persistently and heavily to their shoes. The Major opened his eyes once, saw the conflagration in the town, and looking straight at Esch, commanded: " Gas bombs . . . go and put them out." Then he sank back again into somnolence.

Arrived in his courtyard Esch dismissed the soldier; he was to go back at once to his comrades—Esch himself would follow later, he would easily find someone in the house to help him to carry the Major upstairs. So for the time being they laid him on the bench in front of the garden. But when the soldier was gone Esch went quietly into the house, leant his rifle against the wall and opened the trap-door to the cellar. Then he took the Major on his back and carried him in, cautiously feeling his way down the steps leading into the cellar, and when he reached the bottom laid him on a heap of potatoes, which he first carefully covered with a woollen rug. Then he lighted the paraffin lamp fastened to the dingy wall and stopped up the chinks in the cellar with boards and rags, so that no ray of light might pierce through and be seen from outside. Finally he scribbled a note which he stuck into the Major's clasped hands: " Herr Major, you were knocked unconscious in an accident to the motor-car. I shall come back soon. Yours faithfully Esch." He examined the lamp once more to see whether there was enough oil in it; perhaps he would not be able to return for a long time. The ladder leading up to the cellar door had only three steps: before Esch opened it he turned round for a last time, regarded almost with misgiving the low-vaulted roof and the man lying motionlessly outstretched: but for the smell of paraffin one might have taken it for a tomb.

Slowly he climbed out. At the foot of the house stairs he listened for a little for any sound from above. Nothing moved—well, his wife would have calmed down by now . . . the wounded man outside the town was more important at present. He shouldered his rifle and stepped out into the street.

But his thoughts were with the man who lay in the cellar, the paraffin lamp at his head. When the light expires the Redeemer is near. The light must expire so that the debt of time might be paid.

Huguenau had just finished his slice of bread and was considering how he could get hold of further nourishment, when in the sharp light outside he caught sight of a figure in the garden. He seized his rifle, but recognized at the same moment that it was Esch himself, carrying a sort of sack on his shoulders. So the Herr Reverend had actually joined the looters! of course that wasn't surprising; well, he would soon make sure, and he waited curiously for Esch to come nearer with his burden. Esch's footsteps approached slowly and heavily through the courtyard; it was quite a long time before he was visible through the window. But then Huguenau became almost breathless with astonishment—Esch was carrying a man! Esch was carrying the Major out there! there was no possible mistake about it, it was the Major that Esch was carrying. Huguenau stole on tiptoe to the door and stuck out his head through the opening—no doubt about it, it was the Major—and he saw Esch disappearing with his burden through the cellar door.

Huguenau was intensely excited while he waited to see how things would develop further. And when Esch once more appeared and stepped out into the street, Huguenau too shouldered his rifle and followed at a safe distance.

The streets running in the direction of the Town Hall were fully illumined by the glare, but in the side-streets the houses threw sharp flickering shadows. Not a human being was to be seen. Everybody had rushed to the market-place, from which came a vague sound of tumult. Huguenau could not help thinking that in these deserted streets anyone could loot to his heart's delight; and if he himself were to force his way into some house now and carry out whatever he liked, no one would seek to prevent him—though of course what was there of any value that one could lift from such hovels, and the phrase " better game " came into his mind. Esch turned round the next corner; so he wasn't going to the Town Hall, the sanctimonious villain. Two youths ran past; Huguenau clutched his rifle in his hands, ready to strike. From a side-street a man leading a bicycle reeled towards him; he held the handle-bar convulsively with his left hand, the right arm dangled by his side as though broken; Huguenau gazed with horror into a smashed and battered face, from which one of the eyes still stared unseeingly into vacancy. Caring for nothing save to keep hold of his bicycle, as though he were resolved to take it with him into the next world, the stricken man reeled past. Face bashed in with a rifle butt, Huguenau told himself, and he clutched his rifle more firmly. A dog detached itself from a house door, ran sniffing behind the wounded man and licked the drops of blood as they fell. Esch was no longer to be seen. Huguenau quickened his steps. At the next street-crossing he caught again the glint of Esch's fixed bayonet. He followed more quickly.

Esch marched straight on, looking neither to the right nor the left; even the burning Town Hall did not seem to arouse his interest. Now his footsteps echoed no longer on the uneven pavement, for it came to a stop out here, and presently he turned into a narrow lane which ran along the town walls. Huguenau began to walk fast; he was now some twenty paces behind Esch, who calmly continued on his way: should he knock him over the head with the rifle butt? no, that would only be silly, what was needed was something that would end the business for good. And then it overwhelmed him like an illumination—he lowered his rifle, reached Esch with a few feline tango-like leaps, and ran the bayonet into his angular back. To the murderer's great astonishment Esch went on calmly for a few steps more, then he fell forward on his face without a sound.

Huguenau stood beside the fallen man. His foot touched Esch's hand, which lay across a wheel-track in the sticky mire. Should he stamp on it? no doubt about it, the man was dead. Huguenau felt grateful to him— all was well now! he crouched down and looked into the sidewards-turned face with its unshaven stubble of hair. When he failed to find in it the jeering expression that he feared he was satisfied and clapped the dead man benevolently, almost tenderly, on the shoulder.

All was well.

He exchanged the rifles, leaving his own bloodstained one with the dead man, assuredly a superfluous piece of caution on such a day, but he liked to do everything methodically and in order. And after that he set out on his return journey. The town wall was brilliantly lighted up by the burning buildings, the shadows of the trees were outlined on it, a last orange-yellow shower of sparks shot up from the roof—Huguenau could not help remembering the man in the picture in Colmar soaring up into the opening heaven, and would have liked to shake him by the uplifted right hand, so light and happy did he feel—then the Town Hall tower crashed in and the conflagration ebbed to a brownish smoky red.

"Rose Cottage," half-wrecked, still lay dark and silent in the night breeze which blew up there.

In the kitchen nothing had changed. In rigid immobility the six people still sat petrified in their places, still sat there motionless, more motionless perhaps even than before, as if bound and fettered in the stretched wires of expectation. They neither slept nor watched, nor did they know how long this state had already lasted. Only the child slept. The quilt had slipped from Hanna's shoulder, but she did not feel cold. Once she said into the silence: " We must wait for it to end," but the others probably did not even hear. And yet they listened, listened into vacancy, listened for the voices which came to them from outside. And though in Hanna's ear the words " The invasion from below " kept perpetually repeating themselves, and though she could no longer attach any meaning to them, meaningless words, meaningless sounds, yet she listened to see whether it was not these meaningless words that people were shouting outside there. The water-tap dripped monotonously. None of the six moved. Perhaps the others also heard the words she was listening to, for in spite of the wide social differences between them, in spite of their isolation and estrangement, they had all become a unified whole; a magic ring was cast round them, a chain whose links were themselves and which could not be broken through without grave injury. And in this enchantment, in this collective state of trance, it is comprehensible enough that for Hanna the cry of invasion should become more and more distinct, more distinct than she could ever have apprehended it with her physical hearing; the cry came to her as though winged by the power of their collective listening, it was borne on the current of that power, which was nevertheless a powerless power, power merely to accept and to hear, and the cry was very loud, the voice grew mightier and mightier and was like a rushing wind sweeping through the world. The dog whined in the garden and several times started barking. Then the dog too fell silent, and she heard nothing more save the voice. And at the voice's command she stood up; the others did not seem to notice it, not even when she opened the door and left the room; she went in her bare feet, but she did not know it. Her bare soles went over a stretch of concrete, that was the passage, they went up five stone steps, went over linoleum, that was the office, went over parquet-flooring and carpeting, that was the hall, went over very dry coconut-matting, over splintered tiles, over the paving of a garden-path. In such an undeviating advance as this, which may almost be called a march, only the footsoles know the way, for the eyes see only the goal—and as she stepped out of the door she saw it, she saw the goal! at the end of the endlessly stretching paved path, stretching like a long bridge, there, with one leg swung over the garden fence, was the invader, the housebreaker, there, clambering over the parapet of the bridge—a man in grey convict's clothes; like a grey block of stone he clung there. And did not move. With her hands outstretched before her she stepped on to the bridge, she let the quilt fall, her nightgown billowed in the wind, and thus she strode towards the motionless man. But whether it was that the others in the kitchen had after all noticed her leaving, or that they were drawn in a magical chain after her, the gardener appeared, followed by the housemaid, followed by the cook, followed by the gardener's wife, and, though in faint and subdued voices, they called now to their mistress.

It was no doubt the weirdness of this procession led by the white lady with the ghostly robes that made the hair bristle on the housebreaker's head and paralysed him so completely that he was scarcely capable of swinging his leg back over the fence again. And when he had done so he gaped for a while longer at the spectral apparition, and then he ran from the place and vanished in the darkness.

Meanwhile Hanna went on her way, and when she reached the fence she stuck her hand through the railings as through the bars of a window, and seemed to be waving good-bye to someone. From the town came the glare of the conflagration, but the explosions had ceased and the spell was broken. And even the wind had fallen. She sank to sleep against the bars of the fence and was carried back into the house by the gardener and the cook, where they prepared a bed for her in the storeroom next to the kitchen.

(There next day Hanna Wendling succumbed to a severe attack of influenza complicated by pneumonia.)

Huguenau marched back. Before a house a sobbing child was standing, it was certainly not more than three at most. Where could Marguerite be hiding? he wondered. He lifted up the child, pointed out to it the beautiful fireworks sending their light over from the market-place; and he imitated the crackling and hissing of the flames and the crashing of the falling beams, his-s-ss whish-sh-sh-sh bang! until he made the child laugh. Then he carried it into the house and informed the mother that she shouldn't leave a small child out in the street in times such as these without someone to look after it.

When he reached the house he leant his rifle against the wall of the entrance hall just as Esch had done, then lifted the trap-door and climbed down to the Major.

Since Esch left the Major had not changed his position; he was still lying on the heap of potatoes, the note between his fingers; but his blue eyes were open and staring at the flame of the cellar lamp. Nor did he turn his eyes away from it when Huguenau entered. Huguenau cleared his throat, and when the Major gave no sign he felt offended. This wasn't a time to continue keeping up a childish quarrel. He pulled in the stool which Frau Esch used when she picked the potatoes, and with a polite bow seated himself opposite the Major:

" Herr Major, I can understand of course that you have reasons for not wanting to see me, but that's ancient history by now, and besides events have ended by justifying me, and I can't keep silent about the fact that you have seen me in a quite false light; don't forget, Herr Major, that I have been the victim of a miserable intrigue, one shouldn't speak ill of the dead, but only think of the contempt that that canting parson treated me with from the very beginning, Herr Major. And never a word of thanks! Has the Herr Major ever given me a word of recognition for all the functions I've arranged in honour of the Herr Major? no, never more than ' I thank you '—but for the rest: you keep your distance and I'll keep mine. But I don't want to be unjust, once you did give me your hand quite spontaneously, that time the Iron Bismarck was unveiled: you see, Herr Major, that I've cherished in my memory every act of kindness you've shown me, but even then the Herr Major's lips had an ironical expression on them. If you only knew how I hated it when Esch put on that expression. I was always shut out, if I may be permitted to say so. And why? simply because I didn't happen to belong to the town from the beginning . . . a foreigner, so to speak, an interloper, as Esch so kindly put it. That was no reason for jeering at me and slighting me; I had always to decrease, that was another of his expressions—I had always to decrease, so that our Reverend Parson might increase and cut a great figure before the Herr Major. I saw that all right, and I can assure Herr Major that that hurts a man's feelings; and the insinuations you used to throw out about ' evil,' all pointing at me, ah yes, I understood them quite well too, just try and remember, Herr Major, for a whole evening you talked about evil, no wonder if a man who gets such things said to him should end by becoming really evil. I admit too that the facts seemed to support it, and that the Herr Major would perhaps call me a blackmailer or a murderer to-day. And yet it's only a matter of appearance, in reality it's all quite different, only one can't express it exactly, so to speak; besides, it looks as though you haven't the slightest desire to know what it really is. Yes, Herr Major, you talked a great deal about love that evening too, and Esch has been drivelling about love ever since—his drivel always made me sick, in any case, but when one is continually talking about love one might at least try to understand a fellow-creature. Oh, Herr Major, I know of course that I can't ask for that, and that a man in Herr Major's position would never condescend to have such feelings for a man like me, after all nothing better than a common deserter, though I would like to be allowed to say that Esch wasn't such a great deal better than myself. . . . I don't know whether the Herr Major quite understands what I mean, but I beg the Herr Major to have patience. . . ."

Polishing his eyeglasses he gazed at the Major, from whom there still proceeded neither movement nor sound:

" I beg the Herr Major most urgently not to imagine that I am keeping him imprisoned in this cellar for the purpose of forcing him to listen to me; frightful things are happening out there in the town, and if the Herr Major were to go out the Herr Major would be strung up to a lamp-post. The Herr Major will be able to convince himself of that to-morrow with his own eyes; for God's sake, put some trust in me for once. . . ."

So Huguenau spoke on to the living and motionless puppet, until he saw at last that the Major did not hear him. But even then he did not want to believe it:

" I beg pardon, the Herr Major is exhausted and here I am talking. I'll fetch something to eat."

He hastily rushed upstairs. Frau Esch sat humped together on one of the kitchen chairs, sobbing to herself, her body shaking convulsively. When he entered she started up:

" Where is my man? "

" He's all right, he'll be here presently. Have you anything to eat? I need it for a wounded man."

" Is my man wounded? "

" No, I told you he'll be here presently. Give me something to eat. Could you make an omelette? No, that would take too long. . . ."

He went into the living-room; a plate with a slice of sausage stood on the table. Without asking he seized it and stuck it between two slices of bread. Frau Esch had followed him and in a voice shrill with anxiety cried:

" Let that be, that belongs to my man."

Huguenau had the uncomfortable feeling that one dared take nothing belonging to the dead; perhaps too it would bring the Major ill luck if he ate the food of the dead. Besides, sausage wasn't the right sort of thing for him in any case. He reflected for a moment:

" Right, but surely you must have some milk . . . you always have milk in the house."

Yes, she had some milk. He filled a milk-jug and carried it carefully down to the cellar.

" Herr Major, here's milk, lovely rich new milk! " he cried in a brisk voice.

The Major did not move. Obviously milk wasn't the right thing either; Huguenau was annoyed at his mistake: perhaps I should have brought him wine instead? that would have roused and strengthened him . . . still he seems to be very feeble . . . well, now we'll try him with it all the same! And Huguenau bent down and lifted the old man's head, and the Major let him do it without making any resistance and even obediently opened his lips when Huguenau put the beak of the milk-jug to them. And when the Major accepted and swallowed the slowly trickling milk Huguenau felt happy. He ran upstairs to fetch a second jugful; at the door he glanced back, saw that the Major had turned his head to see where he was going, and nodding back kindly he waved a hand: " I'll be back at once." And when he descended once more the Major was still gazing at the cellar door and greeted him with a little smile, indeed it was more like a faint laugh. But he drank only a few drops more. Holding Huguenau by the finger he had fallen asleep.

With his finger in the Major's hand Huguenau sat on. He read the note which was still lying on the Major's breast and put this piece of evidence in his pocket. Of course he wouldn't need it, for if he found himself in a tight corner he would say in any case that the Major had been given into his keeping by Esch: all the same, best to make doubly sure. From time to time he tried cautiously to free his finger, but then the Major wakened, smiled vaguely and without releasing the finger fell asleep again. The stool was very hard and uncomfortable. Thus they passed the rest of the night.

Towards morning Huguenau managed to free himself. No joke to sit all night on a stool. He climbed out to the street. It was still dark.

The town seemed to be quiet. He went across to the market-place. The Town Hall, gutted to the very ground, was smouldering and smoking. The military and the fire brigade had set sentries round it. Two houses in the market-place had also caught fire, and house furniture lay piled up in confusion in front of them. Now and then the hose was again set in action to damp down some new smouldering outbreak. Huguenau was struck by the fact that men in convict uniform were also helping to work the hose and eagerly taking part in the work of clearing up the mess. He spoke to a man who like himself was wearing a green armlet, and asked what had happened since last evening, for he himself had been occupied elsewhere. The man was glad to talk: the collapse of the Town Hall, he said, had really finished the whole business. After that they had all stood round the fire looking pretty foolish, friend and foe alike, and had their work cut out to save the neighbouring houses. A few ruffians, it was true, had tried to force their way into the houses, but when their own comrades heard the women screaming they had fallen on the looters. One or two of them had got their skulls caved in, and that was all to the good, for after that nobody had thought of looting any more. Just a few minutes ago the wounded had been taken over to the hospital—it was high time too, for their shrieks and groans were almost past endurance. Of course the authorities in Trier had been rung up straight away, but there was chaos and rioting there too, naturally, and two car-loads of soldiers had only arrived a little while ago, when all was over. It was said too that the Town Commandant was missing. . . .

No need to worry about the Commandant, said Huguenau, he himself had got him in safe keeping; and the Major had been in a pretty tight corner too, really he himself deserved a medal for lifesaving, for now the old man was being well looked after, and as he said before, quite safe.

He raised his fingers to his hat in salute, turned back the way he had come, and set out at a trot for the hospital. The dawn was already breaking.

Kühlenbeck was not to be found at first, but presently he appeared, and when he caught sight of Huguenau, bawled at him: "What do you want here, you clown?" Huguenau put on his most offended expression: "Herr Doctor Kühlenbeck, I have to report to you that Herr Esch and myself had to hide the Herr Town Commandant, who is gravely wounded, in our premises all night . . . will you be so good as to give instructions for him to be removed at once." Kühlenbeck rushed to the door:

" Doctor Flurschütz," he thundered down the corridor. Flurschütz came. " Take a car—the cars have returned now, haven't they?—and drive to the newspaper place, take two attendants with you . . . you know where it is, I suppose . . . but it's all one," he barked at Huguenau, " for you're going with them." Then he seemed to soften: he actually gave Huguenau his hand and said: " Come, it was very nice of you both to look after him. . . ."

When they reached the cellar the Major was still peacefully sleeping on his heap of potatoes, and still asleep he was carried out. Meanwhile Huguenau had run across to the editorial office. There wasn't much ready cash in the place, it was true, only the petty cash and some stamps; the rest he carried upon him, except for what he had sent to Cologne and put in the bank; but it would be a pity to leave the stamps . . . one never knew what might happen . . . perhaps there might be some more looting after all! When he returned the Major was already installed in the car, a few people were standing round it asking what had happened, and Flurschütz was preparing to drive off. It was like a blow in the face to Huguenau; they were about to take the Major away without him. And suddenly he saw clearly that he himself dared not in any circumstances stay behind, he hadn't the slightest wish to be present when Esch's body was brought home.

" Wait for me, I'm coming immediately, Doctor," he cried, " immediately! "

" How? Do you want to come with us, Herr Huguenau? "

" But of course! I've got to give my report on the whole business . . . just one minute, please."

He rushed upstairs. Frau Esch was praying on her knees in the kitchen. When Huguenau appeared in the doorway she made towards him, still on her knees. He did not listen to her appeals, but dashed past her into his room, seized such of his possessions as he could lay hands on—and he did not possess much—rammed them into his fibre suitcase, sat upon it until the lock snapped to, and then flew back. " Ready," he shouted to the chauffeur, and they drove off.

At the hospital Kühlenbeck was standing in front of the door, his watch in his hand:

" Well, what's the matter with him? "

Flurschütz, who had got out first, gazed across at the Major with his somewhat inflamed eyes:

" Perhaps concussion . . . perhaps something more serious. . . ."

Kühlenbeck said:

" This place is a pure madhouse already . . . and it calls itself a hospital . . . well, we'll see. . . ."

The Major, who during the drive had begun to blink up at the pallid morning sky, was now wide awake. As he was being lifted out of the car he became excited; he flung himself about, and it was obvious that he was looking for something. Kühlenbeck stepped across and bent over him:

" Come, this is a nice way to behave, Herr Major! "

But at that the Major became quite furious. Whether it was that he recognized Kühlenbeck, or that he did not recognize him, at any rate he seized him by the beard, tugged at it fiercely, gnashing his teeth, and only with difficulty could be got under control. But he became peaceable and docile at once as soon as Huguenau stepped up to the stretcher. He took hold of Huguenau's finger again, Huguenau had to walk alongside the stretcher, and he would only submit to be examined so long as Huguenau sat by his side.

Kühlenbeck, however, broke off his examination very soon:

" It has no object," he said, " we'll give him an injection and then we'll just have to send him away . . . this place will have to be evacuated in any case . . . so get him off to Cologne as quickly as possible . . . but how? I can't spare anybody here, the order to evacuate the hospital may arrive at any moment. . . .

Huguenau stepped forward:

" Perhaps I could take the Herr Major to Cologne . . . as a voluntary ambulance attendant, if I may put it like that . . . the gentlemen can see for themselves that the Herr Major is satisfied with my attendance."

Kühlenbeck reflected:

" With the afternoon train? . . . no, that's far too uncertain now. . . ."

Flurschütz had an idea:

" But there must be a motor-van going to Cologne to-day . . . couldn't one arrange somehow or other for it to take him? "

" To-day anything can be arranged," said Kühlenbeck.

" Then may I ask you to give me a permit to proceed to Cologne? "
said Huguenau.

And so it happened that Huguenau, furnished with authentic military
documents, on his sleeve a red-cross armlet which he had extracted from
Sister Mathilde, was given official charge of the Major, and conducted
him to Cologne. They fixed up the stretcher in the van, Huguenau took
up his post beside it on his fibre case, and the Major seized his hand and
did not let it go again. After a while Huguenau too was overcome by
fatigue. He settled himself as well as he could beside the stretcher, pushed
his case under his head, and lying side by side, hand in hand, they slept
like two friends. And so they arrived at Cologne.

Huguenau delivered the Major at the hospital according to orders,
waited patiently by his bed until an injection had banished all danger of
a new outbreak, and then he was able to steal away. From the hospital
authorities he actually engineered a permit to return to his Colmar home,
whereupon he lifted from the bank the remainder of the balance credited
to the *Kur-Trier Herald*, and next day he departed. His war Odyssey,
his lovely holiday was at an end. It was the 5th of November.

CHAPTER LXXXVI

STORY OF THE SALVATION ARMY GIRL IN BERLIN (16)

Who can be more light-hearted than an invalid? there is nothing to
force him into the struggle for life, he is quite at liberty even to die if he
likes. He is not obliged to draw inductive conclusions from the events
of the day in order to orient his behaviour; he can remain wrapped in
the cocoon of his own thoughts,—wrapped in the autonomy of his own
knowledge he is free to think deductively, to think theologically. Who
can be happier than the man who is at freedom to think out his
religion!

Sometimes I go out by myself. I walk along slowly, my hands in my
pockets, and gaze into the faces of the passers-by. They are finite faces,
but often, indeed always, I can manage to discover the infinite behind
them. These are, so to speak, my inductive escapades. The fact that
during these roving expeditions, which certainly never take me very far
—only once did I get as far as Schöneberg, and that made me very tired—
I have never encountered Marie, that among all the faces hers has never

emerged, that she has so completely vanished from my ken, hardly even disappoints me, for the times are uncertain, and she was always expecting to be sent away on foreign missionary service. I am quite happy without her, as it is.

The days have grown short. And as electric current is expensive and a man wrapped in the cocoon of his own autonomy can easily dispense with light, I have long nights. Nuchem often sits with me. Sits in the darkness and says little. His thoughts no doubt are with Marie, but he has never mentioned her.

Once he said:

" The war will stop now."

" Indeed," I said.

" Then there will be a revolution," he went on.

I saw a chance of pouncing upon him:

" Then they will put an end to religion."

I heard him laughing silently in the darkness:

" Is that said in your books? "

" Hegel says: it is infinite love that makes God identify Himself with what is alien to Him so as to annihilate it. So Hegel says . . . and then the absolute religion will come."

He laughed again, a vague shadow in the darkness:

" The law remains," he said.

His obduracy was unshakable: I said:

" Yes, yes, I know, you're the eternal Jew."

He said softly:

" We'll go back to Jerusalem now."

I had talked too much in any case and let the matter drop there.

CHAPTER LXXXVII

The broad keel of the ship whose port is never found
Cleaves heavy furrows in the phantom waves
That die far off in shoreless watery graves:
O sea of sleep, whose spindrift rings our void around!
Dream heavy with blind freightage! dream of founts unsealed,
Dream seeking for Another on that swift bark,
Dread longings! far more dreadful through the stark
Law by which far from land their soundless knell is pealed:

No dream has ever found another's dream,
Lonely the night, even though Thy mighty breath
Wraps it, a deep from whence suspires our faith
That we some time transfigured and raised on high
May face each other in the radiant beam
Of grace, may face each other and yet not die.

CHAPTER LXXXVIII

DISINTEGRATION OF VALUES (10)

Epilogue.

All was well.

And Huguenau, furnished with an authentic military permit, had returned to his home in Colmar at the army's expense.

Had he committed a murder? had he done a revolutionary deed? he had no need to reflect upon it, nor did he do so. Had he done so, however, he might simply have said that his procedure had been quite reasonable and that any one of the town's prominent citizens, among whom, after all, he had a right to range himself, would have done exactly the same. For there was a firm line of demarcation between what was reasonable and what was unreasonable, between reality and unreality, and Huguenau would have conceded at most that in less warlike or less revolutionary times he would have left the deed undone, which would have been a pity. And he would probably have added judiciously: " There's a time for everything." But the opportunity did not arise, for he never gave a thought to that deed, nor was he ever to think of it again.

Huguenau did not think of what he had done, and still less did he recognize the irrationality that had pervaded his actions, pervaded them indeed to such an extent that one could have said the irrational had burst its bounds; a man never knows anything about the irrationality that informs his wordless actions; he knows nothing of " the invasion from below " to which he is subject, he cannot know anything about it, since at every moment he is ruled by some system of values that has no other aim but to conceal and control all the irrationality on which his earth-bound empirical life is based. The irrational, as well as consciousness, is, in the Kantian sense, a vehicle that accompanies all categories—it is the absolute of Life, running parallel, with all its instincts, conations and emotions, to the other absolute of Thought: irrationality not only supports every value-system—for the spontaneous act of positing a value, on which the value-system is based, is an irrational act—but it informs the whole general feeling of every age, the feeling which assures the prevalence of the value-system, and which both in its origin and in its nature is insusceptible to rational evidence. And the powerful apparatus of cognitive interpretation which is erected around all atomic facts to make their content plausible has the same function as that other and not less powerful apparatus of ethical interpretation which makes human conduct plausible; both of them consist of bridges thrown out by reason, crossing and recrossing at different levels, for the sole purpose of leading earthly existence out of its essential irrationality, out of " evil," by way of a higher and " reasonable " meaning up to that ultimate metaphysical value which by its deductive structure helps man to assign a fitting relevance to his own actions, to all things and to the world, but at the same time enables him to find himself again so that his vision ceases to be erratic and transient. In circumstances like these it is not surprising that Huguenau knew nothing about his own irrationality.

Every system of values springs from irrational impulses, and to transform those irrational, ethically invalid contacts with the world into something absolutely rational becomes the aim of every super-personal system of values—an essential and radical task of " formation." And every system of values comes to grief in the endeavour. For the only method that the rational can follow is that of approximation, an encircling method that seeks to reach the irrational by describing smaller and smaller arcs around it, yet never in fact reaches it, whether the irrational appears as an irrationality of one's inner feelings, an unconsciousness of what is actually being lived and experienced, or as an irrationality of world conditions and of the infinitely complex nature of the universe—all that the rational can do is to atomize it. And when people say that " a man without feelings is no man at all," they say so out of some perception of the truth that no system of values can exist without an irreducible residue of the irrational which preserves the rational itself from a literally suicidal autonomy, from a " super rationality " that is, if anything, still more objectionable, still more " evil " and " sinful " from the standpoint of the value-system, than the irrational: for, in contradistinction to the plastic irrational, the pure Ratio, arising through dialectic and deduction, becomes set and incapable of further formation when it grows autonomous, and this rigidity annuls its own logicality and brings it up against its logical limit of infinity,—when reason becomes autonomous it is thus radically evil, for in annulling the logicality of the value-system it destroys the system itself; it inaugurates the system's disintegration and ultimate collapse.

There is a stage in the development of every system of values during which the mutual interpenetration of the rational and the irrational reaches its maximum, a kind of saturated condition of equilibrium in which the elements of evil on both sides become ineffective, invisible and harmless—and these are the times of culminating achievement and of perfect style! for the style of an epoch could almost be defined in terms of this interpenetration: when such a stage of culminating achievement is reached the rational may penetrate through countless pores into life, but it remains subject to life and to the central will to value; and the irrational may flow through countless veins of the value-system, but is as it were canalized, and even in its most minute ramifications subserves and assists the central will to value,—the irrational by itself has no style, the rational by itself has no style, or rather they are both liberated from style, the one in the freedom of Nature, the other in the freedom of mathematics; but when they are combined, when they mutually restrain each other, the result of this restrained and rational life of the irrational is the phenomenon that may be described as the peculiar style of a value-system.

But this condition of equilibrium is never permanent, it is only a transitional stage; the logic of facts drives the rational towards the super-rational, and drives the super-rational towards its limits; it initiates the process of disintegration, the splitting up of the whole value-system into partial systems, a process which ends in complete dissociation, with free and autonomous Reason on the one hand, and free and autonomous Life on the other. For a time, of course, the partial systems are still penetrated by reason and even led by reason to their own independent autonomy, to the limits of their own autonomous infinity; but the play of reason within a partial system is restricted to its immediate environment. So there arises a specific commercial kind of thinking, or a specific military kind of thinking, each of which strives towards ruthless and consistent absoluteness, each of which constructs a deductive *schema* of plausibility to suit itself, each of which has its " theology," or its " private theology," if one may call it so—and the degree of success attained by such a military or commercial theology in constructing a specific and diminished organon of its own is precisely determined by the proportion of irrational elements which have been retained in its partial system: for the partial systems also are reflections of the Self and of the total system, and they too pass through or strive towards a phase of equilibrium which gives them style, so that it is possible to speak of a military or a commercial style of living. The smaller the system becomes, however, the more restricted is its power of ethical expansion and its ethical will, the more hardened and indifferent does it become to evil, to the super-rational and to the irrational that is still alive within it, the smaller grows the number of forces at its disposal and the greater the number of those to which it is indifferent, relegating them to the individual as his private concern: the further the breaking-up of the total system proceeds, the more the reason in the world becomes detached, the more visible and effective does the irrational become. The total system of a religion makes the world that it dominates a rational world, and in the same way the independent sovereignty of reason must liberate all that is irrational and mute.

The final indivisible unit in the disintegration of values is the human individual. And the less that individual partakes in some authoritative system, and the more he is left to his own empiric autonomy—in that respect, too, the heir of the Renaissance and of the individualism that it heralded—the narrower and more modest does his " private theology " become, the more incapable is it of comprehending any values beyond its immediate and most personal environment: whatever comes from beyond the limits of its narrow circle can be accepted only in a crude and undigested state, in other words accepted as dogma—and so arises that empty and dogmatic play of conventions, that is to say of super-rationalities reduced to the smallest dimensions, which is typical of the average Philistine (a term which undeniably fits Huguenau), a play of unconflicting interaction between a living vitality sunk in the irrational and the empty form of a super-rationality that functions in a vacuum and subserves nothing but the irrational; both of them unrestrained and without style, associated in an incongruity that is incapable of creating any further value. The man who is thus outside the confines of every value-combination, and has become the exclusive representative of an individual value, is metaphysically an outcast, for his autonomy presupposes the resolution and disintegration of all system into its individual elements; such a man is liberated from values and from style, and can be influenced only by the irrational.

Huguenau, a man liberated from values, was nevertheless still a member of the commercial system; he was a man who had a good reputation in provincial business circles; he was a conscientious and prudent agent, and he had always fulfilled his commercial duties wholly and completely, even with radical thoroughness. His murder of Esch, moreover, while it hardly came within the province of his duty as a business man, was not an infringement of the business code. It had been a kind of holiday deed, committed at a time when even the commercial system of values was temporarily suspended and only individual motives remained. On the other hand it was quite in accordance with business ethics, to which Huguenau had now reverted, when in consideration of the depreciation of the mark after the conclusion of peace he addressed the following letter to Frau Gertrud Esch:

DEAR MADAM,

Hoping that this finds you well as it leaves me at present, I take the opportunity of reminding you that according to our contract of 14.5.1918 I am in control of 90 per cent. of the shares of the " Kur-Trier Herald," including, to be correct, 30 per cent. belonging to various gentlemen of that town, whose representative however I have the honour to be, so that without my knowledge and consent the business cannot be carried on nor any fresh commitments undertaken, and I must hold you and these gentlemen wholly and completely responsible for all possible losses arising out of any such infringement of my rights. Should you and these gentlemen, however, be continuing to issue the paper, I must beg you to remit immediately a statement of accounts and the profits accruing to my group of shareholders, amounting to 60 per cent. of the whole (see contract § 3), and courteously reserve to myself the right of taking further action.

On the other hand, with my customary loyalty, of which you are already aware, I admit frankly that the force majeure of the war collapse has prevented me from remitting at the proper time the two remaining instalments due from me on behalf of my group, amounting in all to 13.400 marks, of which 8000 marks fall to you as heir of the late Herr August Esch. With the same frankness, however, I must point out that you, as you must admit, have neglected to send to me, as business manager of the paper, a demand note properly registered claiming the payment of these instalments before a duly fixed date, so that now, should you present the said demand note, I am merely bound to pay you that sum of money plus deferred interest in order to settle all legal claims between us.

But since I am anxious to avoid having any dispute in a law-court with the amiable wife of my late respected friend Herr August Esch, even although the property in question lies in occupied territory and my French nationality would give me the greatest advantage in any such dispute, and since moreover I prefer to have things settled out of hand, I beg to propose that we should compound our affair by mutual agreement, which would be all to your advantage, considering the legal position.

The simplest way of doing this would be for you to buy back from me, acting on behalf of my group, our 60 per cent. of shares in the business, and I am ready to sell them on the most favourable conditions; and without prejudice, unless I can dispose of them meanwhile on better terms, I offer them to you for the half of the original price, reckoned in francs at par. The total price was 13.400 marks—at par about 16,000 francs—so that I am giving you exceptionally favourable terms if I offer them at 8000 francs (eight thousand French francs), with the reminder that I have not taken into consideration at all either the sums of money I expended privately on the business, or my current expenses, or the time and labour I sacrificed on its behalf, although these alone have increased the value of the business to considerably more than when I took it over. And in adopting this generous attitude and offering you such exceptionally favourable terms, my only motive is to make things easy for you and bring about a convenient settlement, all the more as you can easily raise the money by a mortgage on your freehold, if you do not have it at hand.

Finally I take the liberty of pointing out that with my group's 60 per cent. of shares in addition to your own existing 10 per cent. you will have an overwhelming majority of 70 per cent. under your control, with which you can easily squeeze out the other minority group, and I am convinced that you will shortly find yourself sole proprietor of a flourishing business, and in this connection I cannot refrain from adding that the advertising department, after the way in which I flatter myself that I organized it, is a gold mine in itself, and that I put myself gladly at your disposal to assist you further with it by word and deed.

Under these circumstances you can quite well see that I am sacrificing my own interests in making you this offer, merely because it would be difficult for me to manage the paper from here, but I am convinced that I could get a

considerably better offer from other clients, which would not redound to your
advantage, and so I beg you to send me an affirmative answer within 14 days,
in default of which I shall put the matter in the hands of my lawyers.

In the pleasant conviction that you will appreciate my friendly and generous
proposal, so that we shall come to a complete and final settlement, I take the
liberty of informing you that business in our district is extremely satisfactory
and that I am doing very well, and remain

Yours respectfully

WILH. HUGUENAU.

Registered.   *(André Huguenau and Co.)*

That was an ugly and oppressive proceeding, but it did not appear in
that light to Huguenau; it violated neither his private theology nor that
of the commercial value-system; indeed, not one of Huguenau's fellow-
citizens would have found it objectionable; for no exception could have
been taken to the letter on legal or commercial grounds, and even Frau
Esch accepted its legality as a fate to which she could submit with a better
grace than to a confiscation by communists, for instance. Huguenau
himself regretted afterwards that he had been so unnecessarily modest
in his demands—the half of what it had cost him!—only one must never
put on the screw too much, and the 8000 francs, when they actually
arrived, made a welcome contribution to the firm in Colmar, and more
than that: they were the final liquidation of his war adventures, the final
seal set upon his return home, and perhaps, although only perhaps, that
gave him a twinge of sorrow. For now his holiday was definitely at an
end. And in so far as human life, running its insignificant course, can be
said to contain anything worthy of comment, nothing of the kind occurred
during the rest of Huguenau's life. He had taken over his father's business,
and he carried it on in the spirit of his forefathers, solidly and with an
eye to profit. And since a bachelor's life is no life for a prosperous business
man, and the tradition of his family, that had determined his own
existence, required him to marry some worthy woman, both for the sake
of having children and because her dowry could be used in consolidating
the family business, he set about taking the necessary steps to that end.
And since the franc meanwhile had begun to depreciate, while the
Germans had established a gold currency, it was only natural and not
worth commenting on that he should look for his bride on the right bank
of the Rhine. And since it was in Nassau that he eventually found a girl

with a suitable dowry, and Nassau is a Protestant district, it was not surprising that love and financial advantage combined should persuade a Freethinker to change his religion. And since the bride and her family were stupid enough to attach some weight to the question, he did adopt the evangelical creed to please them. And when one or another of his fellow-citizens shook a disapproving head over such a step, Huguenau the Freethinker pointed out that it was a meaningless formality, and as if to emphasize the fact voted, in spite of his Protestantism, for the Catholic Party when it formed a political alliance in the year 1926 with the communists. And since the Alsatians, like most of the Alemanni, are often whimsical people and many of them have a slate loose somewhere, they did not wonder for very long over Huguenau's eccentricities, which were really not eccentricities at all, for Huguenau's life flowed peacefully on between sacks of coffee and bales of cloth, between sleeping and eating, between business deals and games of cards. He became the father of a family, his elastic plumpness grew rounder and in time became a little flabby; his upright walk, too, visibly degenerated into a waddle; he was courteous to his customers, and to his subordinates a strict master and a model of industry; he was out and about early every morning, he indulged in no holidays, his pleasures were few and his æsthetic enjoyments either non-existent or dismissed with contempt; his obligations left him barely time even to go for a walk on Sundays with his wife and children, so how could he visit the Museum?—he didn't care for pictures anyhow. He rose to municipal honours, his feet were again on the path of duty. His life was the same life that his physical forbears had led for two hundred years, and his face was their face. They all resembled each other strongly, the Huguenaus, fat and complacent and serious in their folds of solid flesh, and it was hardly to be suspected that one of them should develop an ironically sarcastic expression. But whether this peculiarity was the result of mixed blood, or was merely a freak of nature, or marked a certain maturity in this descendant of the Huguenaus, a maturity that detached him from the family tree, it is difficult to determine, and in any case it was not considered important by anybody, least of all by Huguenau. For many things had become indifferent to Huguenau, and whenever his war adventures came into his mind they shrank into smaller and smaller compass, until at last all that remained was a single entry of 8000 francs in which they were symbolized and which was their final balance; and all that he had experienced at that time faded into a mere silhouette, into the delicate half-tones of the French banknotes that Huguenau the business man had been handling ever since. The soft grey shadow of dream-like and silvery sleep drew a veil over all that had happened; it grew more and more vague, more and more shadowy, as if a darkened glass had been set before it, and in the end he could not tell whether he had lived that life or whether it was a tale someone had told him.

It could perhaps be argued that all this fading away and forgetting was merely symptomatic of a state of resignation induced by the fact that the bourgeois system of values had been set up again in Alsace, including Colmar, of course, with the help of the victorious French bayonets, although the land itself, thanks to the wrongs it had had to suffer for centuries from right and left alike, was still as full of revolutionary spirit as any other frontier region, and even in Huguenau rebellion was still raising its head. It could be argued in any case that irrational forces once liberated are unwilling to submit themselves again to any old system of values, and that if they are compelled to submission they must necessarily diffuse a blight of deadness over the community and the individual alike. And out of that arises the problem of what happens to the irrational forces liberated by the disintegration of values: are they really nothing but fighting forces in the struggle between the several value-systems? are they really nothing but means for mutual destruction? are they really nothing but murder? and when the disintegration of values has gone as far as it can go in a reduction to the final indivisible units, to a struggle between one individual and another, must these guerrilla forces inevitably provoke a general dissension, a struggle of all against all? Or, to confine the question to Huguenau's particular case: can a partial value-system, such as the commercial one to which Huguenau reverted, possess a sufficient power of cohesion without external help from bayonets or police truncheons to combine the dissociated irrational impulses into a new organon, and to provide a new focus for the equally dissociated will-to-value?

Epistemologically, of course, these questions are inadmissible, since they make assumptions regarding the nature of the irrational. By the mere use of the word " forces " they assume a mechanistic theory and an anthropomorphic and voluntarist metaphysic; in short, they give a meaning to the irrational, and the irrational invalidates any meaning attached to it. In its original and undifferentiated condition the irrational

admits of no theorizing and no interpretation beyond the simple affirmation of its anonymous existence, even although its living inarticulateness
provides all the material for rational value-formations. This recalcitrance
of the irrational is fully recognized by the total system superimposed
upon it, that is to say by the religious system, the system of the Church.
The Church recognizes only one value-system, her own, because her
Platonic origin compels her to acknowledge only one Truth, only one
Logos: her wholly rational alignment rules out any tolerance of the
illogical, and compels her *a priori* to deny to the irrational and its hypothetical " attributes " any epistemological or even ethical significance.
For the Church the irrational is simply the bestial, and all that can be
said about it is that it is there and must be subsumed in the category of
evil. From this point of view the irrational presents no problem for consideration, except in relation to the question of how evil can possibly exist
within a world created by God; and the alleged capacity of the irrational
to construct systems is not even considered except in reference to the
possible ways in which evil can become manifest. True, these are questions
which the Church has never ignored nor ever can ignore; the existence
of evil is a necessary presupposition for the *ecclesia militans*, and since the
progressive disintegration of values releases continuous manifestations of
evil, the Church is constantly forced to stigmatize as evil whatever causes
the disintegration; in other words, the Church has to discard the super-
rational and relegate it to the category of evil along with the irrational.
But since the Church on the one hand knows as well as any private person
that every manifestation is the " product of a product," knowing perhaps
even more clearly than any private person that the condition of possible
experience for all manifestations is determined by some " value," and
since on the other hand she must regard her own value-structure as the
only admissible one, she is bound to maintain that irrational evil, while
incapable of constructing a system, is yet capable of aping the form of
an existent system in order to manifest itself, and whatever its manifestations, she will regard them merely as imitations of her own structure;
she is bound to maintain that evil, while it cannot think rationally, is yet
capable of an empty aping of thought, a thought without true content
(evil as the *privatio* of good), an empty, super-rational and dogmatic play
of conventions, a kind of sophistry led astray by the irrational, subserving
only the irrational, perverting the ethical will into an empty echo of moral
maxims; but a sophistry that ultimately swells to the dimensions of a total

system and raises evil from the Philistine level to the dignity of an Anti-christ. For the Church the more completely evil establishes itself in the world, the more completely is Christ menaced by the mock Antichrist, the more menacing becomes the value-system of the Antichrist, which has to be a total system simply because the system of the Church is already a total system; so the Church sees evil spreading itself and becoming indivisible and homogeneous like the opposing truth which it imitates. Such a total system of evil as conceived by the Church throws into the shade all partial systems, and the most outstanding expression of the disintegration of values, the Protestant idea, acquires in the eyes of Catholicism a preponderant significance among the phenomena of dis-integration, being regarded as the main idea, the *leit-motif*, in that fateful and irrational process, although Protestantism and all other partial systems are looked upon as merely distorted reflections of the true value, prelimin-ary stages for the menacing total system of Antichrist which is to come. This estimate of Protestantism not only accords with the Church's special point of view, but has some foundation in objective fact, in the fact, for instance, that Protestantism displays a remarkable affinity with every other partial system of whatever kind: let it be capitalist or nationalist or what you will, every partial system can be brought under the same " revolutionary " anti-Catholic denominator as Protestantism; from the Church's point of view, that is to say, they all belong to the criminal category in which the irrational value-destroying forces of heresy are manifest. And although the Church often makes external concessions and, preferring the lesser evil to the greater, appears to tolerate this or the other separatist movement, such as a nationalist movement, as a nucleus of conservation against the more radical and purely revolutionary sects, yet she will never abandon the severity of her attitude towards the fundamental problem of how to align the irrational forces: for her it means either Christ or Antichrist, either a return into the bosom of the Church or the downfall of the world in the complete disintegration of values caused by the internecine struggle.

Every partial system, considered as a value-system, must imitate the structure of the total system, whether it be a simple reflection of that or its distorted perversion, and in so far as the tenets of the original system are based on formal principles, they must be reproduced and confirmed in the smaller sect; substantive differences, however, in the interpretation of these tenets, differences which are inevitable because no system can admit that it is " evil," must arise from a different orientation towards the irrational. The logical genesis, the logical basis of every partial system compels it to be revolutionary: a nationalist movement, for instance, following its logical development towards an absolute, sets up an organon in which the National State takes the central place of God, and in thus relating all values to the idea of the State, in thus subordinating the individual and his spiritual freedom to the power of the State, it not only finds itself in a revolutionary anti-capitalist position, but is even more stringently propelled in an anti-religious, anti-ecclesiastical direction which leads by a plain, undeviating path to the absolute revolutionary disintegration of values, and so, of course, to the ultimate supersession of the partial system itself. If a partial system, therefore, is to secure its continued existence in this process of disintegration, if it is to be able to bridle its own Ratio which hurries it towards ultimate extinction, it must take refuge in an alliance with the irrational. Thus arises that remarkable ambiguity characterizing every partial system, an ambiguity which amounts to dishonesty, epistemologically speaking: on the one hand the partial system adopts the attitude of a total system towards the process of advancing disintegration and stigmatizes the irrational as rebellious and criminal, while on the other hand it is compelled to distinguish among the homogeneous mass of irrationality and anonymous wickedness a group of " good " irrational forces which are needed to help it in checking further disintegration and in establishing its own claim to survival. Every half-way revolution, and in this sense all partial systems are half-way revolutions, bases its case on irrational assumptions, on mass feeling, on the dignity of an " irrational inspiration " that is exploited to discredit the radical logic of complete revolution; every partial system must expressly acknowledge a residue of " unformed " irrationality, which it maintains, so to speak, as a private preserve exempt from reason, in order to keep itself stable in the flux of disintegration.

For revolutions are insurrections of evil against evil, insurrections of the irrational against the rational, insurrections of the irrational masquerading as extreme logical reasoning against rational institutions complacently defending themselves by an appeal to irrational sentiment: revolutions are struggles between unreality and unreality, between tyranny and tyranny, and they are inevitable once the release of the super-rational has drawn in its train the release of the irrational, once the disintegration of values has advanced to its last integral unit, the individual;

for the individual, isolated and autonomous, stripped of all prejudice, is defenceless before the invasion of the irrational. Revolution is the breaking through of the irrational, the breaking through of the autonomous, the breaking through of life, and the isolated human being, stripped of values, is its instrument; and since the human outcast is the first to suffer the extremes of human misery and loneliness, the proletarian, for instance, victimized by hunger, or the soldier in the trenches victimized by intensive artillery fire, and since these literal outcasts must be the first to achieve freedom from values, they must also be the first to hear the voice of murder that drowns the muteness of the irrational with its clangour as of iron ringing upon iron. And it is always the adherent of the smaller value-system who slays the adherent of the larger system that is breaking up; it is always he, unfortunate wretch, who assumes the rôle of executioner in the process of value-disintegration, and on the day when the trumpets of judgment sound it is the man released from all values who becomes the executioner of a world that has pronounced its own sentence.

Huguenau had committed a murder. He forgot it afterwards; it never came into his mind again, while every single business *coup* that he had successfully brought off (his letter to Frau Esch!) remained accurately imprinted on his memory. And that was only natural: for none of our actions remains alive except those that consort with our reigning system of values, and Huguenau had reverted once more to the commercial system. And in exactly the same way, had circumstances been more favourable, he could have become as staunch a supporter of revolution as he was now of commerce, even although he was heir to a flourishing family business. For the proletarian who supports a revolution is not essentially the " revolutionist " he thinks himself; there is no difference, for instance, between the crowd that exulted in the quartering of Damien, the man who attempted a King's assassination, and the crowd that thronged thirty-five years later around the guillotine of a King, Louis XVI. —the revolutionist as an independent figure does not exist, he is merely the exponent of something greater than himself, the exponent in this case of the European spirit. The individual man may be sunk in a Philistine life, he may even be set in the mould of an old partial system; like Huguenau he may land in the commercial system; or he may attach himself to a preliminary revolutionary movement or to the definitive revolution; but none the less the spirit of positivistic disintegration is spread over all the Occidental world, nor is its visible expression restricted to the materialism of the Russian proletariat, which is merely one variation of the positivism into which the whole of Western philosophy, in so far as it can still be called philosophy, has resolved itself. Compared with this greater unity dissensions about the distribution of wealth sink into the background, although even there the distinction between Americanized methods of organization and communist methods is becoming less and less noticeable: our thought-patterns are moving with increasing urgency towards a common conclusion, a conclusion that makes it irrelevant whether the stamp of this or the other political party is affixed to it, since its whole significance, fundamentally speaking, lies solely in the fact that it is capable of becoming a total system and of once more combining the insurgent forces of the irrational. That is why a preliminary revolution based on the irrational does not matter in the long run, whether it is abortive or not; for it cannot prevent the definitive rational revolution into which it must inevitably be drawn, although as a temporary phenomenon it may be useful in revealing what a more complete system cannot reveal: that there are irrational forces, that they are effective, and that their very nature impels them to attach themselves to a new organon of values, to a total system which in the eyes of the Church can be no other than that of Antichrist. This judgment of the Church is not based on the appearance of such subordinate symptoms as the fanatical anti-Platonism of the communists, or the rationalist propaganda of Marxist or bourgeois Freethinkers; that kind of atheism, sinful as it may be, is too insignificant, indeed too pathetic, in the eyes of the Church, to be named in the same breath as the evil of Antichrist: what concerns the Church is the whole spirit of Europe, the " heretical " spirit of immediacy, of positivism, in face of which it does not really matter whether Protestantism is the progenitor of revolutionary nationalism by way of Fichte or, more obviously, of Marxian communism by way of Hegel; and although the Church, with the unfailing intuition of hatred, the hatred of heresy, can identify Protestantism in its remotest offshoots, and for that very reason denounces communism with an intransigence otherwise inexplicable, since she could quite well accept the primitive Christian conceptions underlying it, yet for all that the concrete phenomenon of communism is not yet the final formal elaboration of Antichrist, but merely a preliminary phase. It is not yet a total system in itself, even although it displays a regular Marxist theology derived from the Protestant theology of Kantianism, and a strictly expounded doctrine with a fixed ontology and an unassailable ethic; even although, indeed, it is provided with all the concomitants of a regular theology organized into what looks like a visible church, and although that church is deliberately setting itself up as an anti-church with machines as the apparatus of its cult and engineers and demagogues as its priesthood; it is not yet a total system as such, it is not yet Antichrist, but a preliminary phase, an indication of the approaching disintegration of the Christian-Platonic world. And in this dogmatic structure, in this uprearing of a Marxist anti-church with an ascetic and severe conception of the State, it is already possible clearly to discern— and no one discerns it more clearly than the Catholic Church—the gigantic contour of a spirit that rises far beyond Marxism, far beyond the apotheosis of the State, a spirit that is so far ahead of revolutionary doctrine of any kind that it makes even Marxism look like a circuitous advance: it is the contour of a churchless " Church in itself," the ontology of an abstract natural science without substance, an abstract ethic without dogma; in short, an organon of that severe and logical ultimate abstraction which is attained when the point of plausibility has receded into the infinite, and in which all the radicality of Protestantism is evident. It is the positivism that characterized Luther and the whole Renaissance, the same double affirmation of the given world and of the need for ascetic severity, a doctrine that is now fulfilling its essential implications and tending towards a new unity of Thought and Being, towards a new unity of ethical and material infinity. It is the unity which informs every system of theology and which must endure even if the attempt is made to deny the reality of Thought, but which takes on a new lease of life when the scientific point at which things are assumed as true coincides with the point at which things are believed to be true, so that the double truth once more becomes single and unambiguous. For at the end of the infinite line of inquiry which leads to this point there stands the pure deed-in-itself, the idea of a pure organon of abstract duty, the idea of a rational belief without a God; there stands the unyielding Law of an abstract religion devoid of content, perhaps even the rational immediacy of an abstract mysticism whose wordless asceticism and unornamented religiosity, governed by austerity and by austerity alone, points the way to the last goal of this completely Protestant revolution: the unaccented vacuum of a ruthless absoluteness in which is throned the abstract Spirit of God, God's Spirit, not Himself and yet Himself, reigning in sorrow amid the terror of dreamless, unbroken silence that constitutes the pure Logos.

In this predicament of the European spirit Huguenau was scarcely involved at all, but he was involved in the prevailing uncertainty. For the irrational in man has an affinity with the irrational in the world; and although the uncertainty in the world is, so to speak, a rational uncertainty, often, indeed, merely an economic uncertainty, yet it springs from the irrationality of the super-rational, from an independent reason that strives towards infinity in every province of human activity, and so, reaching the super-rational limits of its infinity, overthrows itself and becomes irrational, passing beyond comprehension. Currency hitherto accepted becomes incalculable, standards fluctuate, and, in spite of all the explanations that can be adduced to account for the irrational, what is finite fails to keep pace with the infinite and no reasonable means avail to reduce the irrational uncertainty of the infinite to sense and reason again. It is as though the infinite awakens to a concrete and independent life of its own, informed and drawn out by the Absolute that glimmers on the farthest horizon in this hour between downfall and uprising, in this magical hour of death and birth. And Huguenau, although he might avert his eyes from that distant dawn and refuse to acknowledge anything of the kind, could not but feel the icy breath sweeping over the world, freezing it to rigidity and withering all meaning out of the things of the world. And when Huguenau followed each morning the chronicle of events in his newspaper he did so with the uneasiness of all newspaper readers who greedily clutch at the facts presented to them, especially those facts that are supplemented by illustrations, in the daily and renewed hope that the mass of facts may fill the emptiness of a world that has fallen silent, the emptiness of a soul that has fallen silent. They read their newspapers and in their hearts is the terror that comes from awakening every morning to loneliness, for the speech of the old community life has failed them and that of the new is too faint for them to hear. They sustain, indeed, a pose of understanding and clear-sightedness by sharply criticizing the political and social situation or the working of the legal system, and they even exchange opinions on these subjects during the course of the day; but in reality they are without a language, standing mutely between what has been and what is not yet; they give no credence to words and require them to be confirmed by pictures, they have even ceased to believe in the adequacy of their own utterances, and thus caught

between an end and a beginning they know only that the logic of facts is
ruthless and that the Law remains unassailable: there is no soul, however
degenerate, however base, however Philistine and devoted to the tritest
dogmas, that can avoid this knowledge and this terror,—like a child surprised and overwhelmed by loneliness, a prey to the terror of the creature
that has begun to die, man must go seeking the fordable passage that
shall at last assure his life and his safety. Nowhere does he find help. And
it is in vain that he strives continuously to find a haven in some partial
system; in vain he may expect to be sheltered from uncertainty in old
romantic structures, or hope that in a partial revolution all that is known
and familiar to him will yield only with the utmost slowness, in a kind
of painless transition, to what is inexorably alien,—he can get no help,
for he finds himself cozened by the false glamour of a sham communal
life, and the deeper, more secret relationship he is groping for flutters
from the hand that thought to grasp it; and even if in his disappointment
he takes refuge in the monetary-commercial system still he cannot escape
disappointment: even that most characteristic mode of the bourgeois
existence, that partial system which is hardier than all others because it
promises an unshakable unity in the world, the unity that man needs to
reassure his uncertainty—two marks are always more than one mark and
a sum of eight thousand francs is made up of many francs and yet is a
whole, a rational organon in terms of which the world can be reckoned
up—even that hardy and enduring growth, in which the bourgeois desires
so strongly to believe even while all currencies are tottering, is beginning
to wither away; the irrational cannot be kept out at any point, and no
vision of the world can any longer be reduced to a sum in rational addition.
And even Wilhelm Huguenau, now a prosperous business man risen to
municipal honours, a man whose first inquiry about everything in life
usually concerned its price and the profit it might yield, even Wilhelm
Huguenau, although he thought it quite rational in such times of financial
insecurity to show a more suspicious face to the world, even he found
himself at times ironically shrugging off something, or with a sweeping
gesture trying to brush away something that, strangely enough, he could
not account for at all; and then in sudden perplexity he would ask " What
is money ? " and sometimes even refuse credit to a customer, after mustering him with a sharp, suspicious look, simply because he took a dislike
to the man or objected to something in his expression, a sarcastic twitch
of the lips, perhaps—and whether this capriciousness served him well or

ill, whether it drove a potentially good customer into the arms of a rival
or got rid of a bad customer at the right moment, quite apart from all
practical considerations it was an abrupt method, though, perhaps, a
lucid one, that resulted from a kind of short-circuiting; it was in any case
unusual in business dealings, undoubtedly irrational, and probably largely
responsible for the gulf that imperceptibly began to widen between
Huguenau and his fellow-citizens as if he were isolated in a dead zone of
silence. Huguenau had but the vaguest inkling of its existence, yet its
outlines became less vague and almost palpable as soon as he found himself in any social gathering, in a cinema, or in a beer-hall where young
people were dancing, or at banquets celebrating the anniversary of the
French triumph: on such occasions Huguenau, himself a probable future
Burgomaster, would sit among the other notables at the flower-decked
table and watch the dancers with a serious, vacant, boyish gaze behind
his thick eyeglasses, and although he was by no means of an age to renounce dancing, yet he could hardly believe it himself when he whispered
to his neighbour (as he never omitted to do) that at one time he had been
a good enough dancer. For whether he was sitting in such a patriotic
assembly or strolling on Sundays with his eldest boy along the Strass-
burger Allee to watch the bicycle races, he found himself falling irresistibly
into a strange state of uneasiness, so that he even began to attend social
gatherings merely to put himself to the test; it was an uneasiness in which
things imperceptibly moved out of their places and in which every social
gathering, although it ought to have presented an integral aspect, began
to disintegrate into something that was disconcertingly multifarious,
something that somebody or other, by means of decorations, garlands and
banners, had combined into an artificial unity, against his own better
judgment. And if Huguenau had not shied off from such out-of-the-way
thoughts he would undoubtedly have discovered that there is not a single
idea, not a single name, that has a corresponding concrete unity underlying it; he would certainly have discovered that the unity of any event
and the integrity of the world are guaranteed merely by enigmatic,
although visible, symbols, which are necessary because without them the
visible world would fall asunder into unnameable, bodiless, dry layers of
cold and transparent ash—and so Huguenau would have perceived the
curse of the casual, of the fortuitous, that spreads itself over things and
their relations to each other, making it impossible to think of any arrangement that would not be equally arbitrary and fortuitous: would not the

racing bicyclists have to scatter to the four winds if they were no longer combined by a common uniform and a common club badge? Huguenau did not ask such a question, for it exceeded the grasp of what might be called, not without reason, his private theology; yet the unasked question irritated him no less than the elusiveness of the experiences that worried him, and his irritation might, for instance, discharge itself in boxing his child on the ear for no reason at all on the way home. Having relieved his feelings in this manner, however, he found it easy to come back to sober reality, thus confirming Hegel's maxim: " Real freedom of will is a harmony between the theoretical and the practical spirit." In the best of tempers he would march back into the town, past the various churches out of which the congregations were just emerging, humming merrily to himself as he went and beating time with his stick, and whenever he met an acquaintance he would greet him and say " Salut."

For everything ultimately depends on one's relation to freedom, and even the pettiest and narrowest theology that extends merely far enough to make plausible the meanest actions of an empirical ego, in other words even the private theology of a Huguenau, is enlisted in the service of freedom, and regards freedom as the real centre of its deductions, its real mystic centre (and that was true for Huguenau at least from the day on which he deserted his trench in the grey dawn, thus following out an apparently irrational but none the less highly rational course of action in the service of freedom, so that everything he had striven towards since that day and everything he was yet to strive for in his life could be taken as a repetition of his actions in that first high-day and holiday mood): indeed it is almost as if freedom were in a lofty category by itself, soaring high above all that is rational and irrational, like an end and a beginning, resembling the Absolute with which its light is blended and yet which it surpasses, as if it were an ultimate, serene ray shining beyond the fiery caverns of the opening heavens. The irrational could never attach itself to the rational, nor the rational diffuse itself in the harmony of living feeling, were they not both partakers in an overarching and majestic Being which is at once the highest reality and the profoundest unreality: it is only in this conjunction of reality and unreality that the wholeness of the world and its form can be apprehended; it is the idea of freedom that justifies the continued rebirth of humanity, for it can never be realized on earth and the road that leads to it must ever be trodden anew. Oh, agonizing compulsion towards freedom! terrible and ever-renewed revolution of knowledge! which justifies the insurrection of Absolute against Absolute, the insurrection of life against reason—justifying reason when, apparently at variance with itself, it unleashes the absolute of the irrational against the absolute of the rational, justifying it by providing the final assurance that the unleashed irrational forces will once more combine into a value-system. There is no value-system that does not subordinate itself to freedom; even the most reduced system is groping towards freedom, even the outcast victim of all earthly loneliness and detachment, the man who achieves no more than the freedom to commit a murder, the freedom to enter prison, or at most the freedom of a deserter, even he, the man stripped of all values, on whom all earthly compulsions press—there is no man exposed to the breath of the Eternal who does not once see the star of freedom rising in the night of his isolation: each man must fulfil his dream, unhallowed or holy, and he does so to have his share of freedom in the darkness and dullness of his life. And so Huguenau often had the feeling that he was sitting in some pit or dark cavern looking out over a cold zone that lay like a girdle of loneliness around his station, while life streamed in distant pictures over the dusky firmament, and then he had a great yearning to creep out of his pen and share in the freedom and loneliness outside, the existence of which he vaguely guessed at as if it were a vision blown in from somewhere or other upon him alone; it was like a knowledge of the deepest community of the spirit into which that most profound loneliness must inevitably change, but it never got beyond the dull conviction that out there it would be somehow or other possible to compel people to be warm and friendly, to compel them by threats of murder or violence, or at least by a box on the ear, to accept him and to listen to his truth, which he was yet incapable of articulating. For even although he was scarcely distinguishable from others in his actions and his mode of life, even although he ran more and more surely on the lines that had been laid down for him in youth, and that he never thought of leaving again, even although it was an utterly carnal, yes, a solid life that was advancing in him towards death, yet in a certain sense it grew more lofty and airy as he felt himself daily more cut off and isolated while ceasing to suffer from the isolation: cut off from the world and yet in it, he saw men receding from him into regions ever more remote and more longed-for, but he made no attempt to explore that far country; and in thus resigning himself he again showed his complete likeness to all other mortals. For every man knows that human life does not stretch far enough for a journey to the end of the path that mounts like a spiral road to higher and higher reaches, the path on which all that has vanished behind one's back rises again in front on a loftier level, only to fade into the distant haze with every fresh step one takes: that endless course of the closed circle and of fulfilment, that lucid reality in which things fall asunder and recede to the poles, to the uttermost limits of the world where all that has been sundered is again joined into one, where distance is again annulled and the irrational takes on its visible shape, where fear no more becomes longing and longing no more turns into fear, where the freedom of the self is received again into the Platonic freedom of God; that endless course of the closed circle and of fulfilment that can be trodden only by him who has fulfilled his nature—unattainable for any man.

Unattainable for any man! And even if Huguenau had landed in a revolutionary instead of in a commercial system he would still have been barred from entering on the path of fulfilment. For murder remains murder, evil remains evil, and the Philistinism of a value-system whose field is restricted to the individual and his irrational impulses, that last product of every disintegration of values, remains the point of absolute degeneracy; the point, so to speak, of an invariant absolute zero that is common to all scales of value and all value-systems without reference to their mutual relativity, and that must be common to all of them since no value-system can be conceived unless in its idea and logical nature it observes the " condition of possible experience," the empirical draft of a logical structure common to all systems and of an *a priori* immutability that is bound up with the Logos. And it almost seems like an outcrop of the same logical necessity that the transition from any value-system to a new one must pass through that zero-point of atomic dissolution, must take its way through a generation destitute of any connection with either the old or the new system, a generation whose very detachment, whose almost insane indifference to the suffering of others, whose stark denudation of values provides an ethical and so an historical justification for the ruthless rejection in times of revolution of all that is humane. And perhaps it must be so, since only such a silent and self-contained generation is able to endure the sight of the Absolute and the rising glare of freedom, the light that flares out over the deepest darkness, and only over the deepest darkness: the earthly reflection of the Absolute is like an image in a dark pool, and the earthly echo of its silence is the iron clangour of murder, which yet sends mute vibrations rolling like an impenetrable wall of deafening silence between man and man, so that no voice can rise beyond it or through it, and man must tremble. Dread reflection, dread echo of the Ratio bursting its way through to the Absolute! its ruthlessness finds an earthly counterpart in violence and mute force, and the rational immediacy of its divine end becomes on earth the immediacy of the irrational that forces men to reluctant yet dumb obedience; its endless chain of inquiry is reduced on earth to the single link of the irrational that asks no more questions but merely acts, setting out to destroy a community of life that has ceased to justify its existence, a so-called community devoid of force but filled with evil will, a community that drowns itself in blood and chokes in its own poison-gases. What a lonely death is the earthly counterpart of divine isolation! Man, exposed to the horror of unrestrained reason, bidden to serve it without comprehending it, caught in the toils of a process that develops far over his head, caught in the toils of his own irrationality, man is like the savage who is bewitched by black magic and cannot see the connection between means and effect, he is like the madman who cannot find his way out of the tangle of his Irrational and Super-rational, he is like the criminal who cannot find his way into the value-realities of the community he desires to enter. Irrevocably the past escapes him, irrevocably the future flees from him, and the droning of machines gives him no indication of the path to his goal that rises unattainable and formless in the haze of the infinite, bearing aloft the black torch of the Absolute. Dread hour of death and of birth, dread hour of the Absolute sustained by a generation that has extinguished itself, a generation that knows nothing about the infinite into which it is driven by its own logic—inexperienced, helpless, and insensate, the men of this generation are delivered to the icy hurricane, they must forget in order to live and they do not know why they die. Their path is the path of Ahasuerus, their duty is his duty, their freedom is the freedom of the hunted creature and their aim is forgetfulness. Lost generation! as non-existent as Evil itself, featureless and traditionless in the morass of the indiscriminate, doomed to lose itself temporally, to have no tradition in an age that is making absolute history! Whatever the individual man's attitude to the course of the revolution, whether he turns reactionary and clings to outworn forms, mistaking the æsthetic for the ethical as all conservatives do, or whether he holds aloof in the passivity of egoistic knowledge, or whether he gives himself up to

his irrational impulses and applies himself to the destructive work of
the revolution:

he remains unethical in his destiny, an outcast from his epoch, an
outcast from Time,

yet nowhere and never is the spirit of the epoch so strong, so truly
ethical and historical as in that last and first flare-up which is revolution,
that act of self-elimination and self-renewal, the last and greatest ethical
achievement of the old disintegrating system and the first achievement
of the new, the moment when time is annulled and history radically
formed in the pathos of the absolute zero!

Great is the anguish of the man who becomes aware of his isolation
and seeks to escape from his own memory; he is obsessed and outcast,
flung back into the deepest animal anguish, into the anguish of the creature
that suffers violence and inflicts violence, flung back into an overwhelming
loneliness in which his flight and his despair and his stupor may become
so great that he cannot help thinking of inflicting violence on himself
so as to escape the immutable law of events. And in his fear of the voice
of judgment that threatens to issue from the darkness, there awakens
within him a doubly strong yearning for a Leader to take him tenderly
and lightly by the hand, to set things in order and show him the way; a
Leader who is nobody's follower and who will precede him on the un-
trodden path of the closed circle and lead him on to ever-higher reaches,
to an ever-brighter revelation; the Leader who will build the house anew
that the dead may come to life again, and who himself has risen again
from the multitude of the dead; the Healer who by his own actions will
give a meaning to the incomprehensible events of the age, so that Time
can begin anew. That is his yearning. Yet even if the Leader were to come
the hoped-for miracle would not happen; his life would be an ordinary
life on earth; and just as belief has taken on the disguise of provisional
assumption, and assumption that of belief in rational religion, so the
healer walks in the most unlikely guise and may even be the casual passer-
by now crossing the street—for wherever he walks, whether in the turmoil
of city streets or in the light of evening fields, his road is the road to Zion
and yet the road we must all take; his journey is a search for the fordable
passage between the evil of the irrational and the evil of the super-rational,
and his freedom is the anguished freedom of duty, is sacrifice and expiation for the past; even for him the way is the way of trial, determined by
austerity, and his isolation is that of a lost child, is that of the lost son

whose bourne fades into the unattainable since he has been abandoned by his father. And despite all that: the mere hope of wisdom from a Leader is wisdom for us, the mere divination of grace is grace, and unavailing as may be our hope that in a Leader's visible life the Absolute will one day fulfil itself on earth, yet our goal remains accessible, our hope that a Messiah will lead us to it remains imperishable, and the renascence of values is fated to recur. And hemmed in as we may be by the increasing muteness of the abstract, each man a victim of the iciest necessity, flung into nothingness, his ego flung to the winds—it is the breath of the Absolute that sweeps across the world, and from our dim inklings and gropings for truth there will spring up the high-day and holiday assurance with which we shall know that every man has the divine spark in his soul and that our oneness cannot be forfeited; unforfeitable the brotherhood of humble human creatures, from whose deepest anguish there shines unforfeitable and unforfeited the anguish of a divine grace, the oneness of all men, gleaming in all things, beyond all Space and all Time; the oneness in which all light has its source and from which springs the healing of all living things—symbol of a symbol, image of an image, emerging from the destiny that is sinking in darkness, welling up out of madness and dreamlessness like the gift of maternal life wrested from the unknown and rewon as a heritage, the prototype of all imagery rising in the insurrection of the irrational, blotting out the self and transcending its confines, annulling time and distance; in the icy hurricane, in the tempest of collapse all the doors spring open, the foundations of our prison are troubled, and from the profoundest darkness of the world, from our bitterest and profoundest darkness the cry of succour comes to the helpless, there sounds the voice that binds all that has been to all that is to come, that binds our loneliness to all other lonelinesses, and it is not the voice of dread and doom; it falters in the silence of the Logos and yet is borne on by it, raised high over the clamour of the non-existent; it is the voice of man and of the tribes of men, the voice of comfort and hope and immediate love: " Do thyself no harm! for we are all here ! "

Vienna, 1928–31.

ABOUT THE AUTHOR

HERMANN BROCH (1886–1951) was born in Vienna, where he trained as an engineer and for a time directed his family's textile firm. He gradually increased his involvement in the intellectual life of Vienna, becoming acquainted with Ludwig Wittgenstein, Sigmund Freud, and Robert Musil, among others, and in 1928 he sold the textile business and devoted himself to literary activities. *The Sleepwalkers* (1930–32) was his first major work. In 1938, he was imprisoned as a subversive by the Nazis, but was freed and fled to the United States. In the years before his death, he was researching mass psychology at Yale University. *The Death of Virgil* and *The Guiltless*, his other major novels, were published in 1945 and 1950.